THE COMPLETE ADVENTURES OF BLUE SHAEFER

Collecting Haunting Blue, Virtual Blue, and Blue Christmas

R. J. SULLIVAN

Dedicated to Dorothy Sullivan, AKA Mom. Her belief that I can do anything I want to do, even if what I want to do is write these sci-fi and monster books, remains unwavering, and means everything to me.

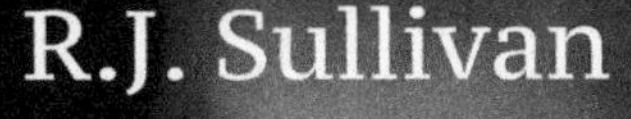

R.J. Sullivan
HAUNTING BLUE
REVISED EDITION
"She discovered the town's biggest secret... now there's hell to pay."
"...a fast-paced story, with plenty of excitement and intrigue, and I enjoyed every word."
5 out of 5. Bitten by Books

Copyright © 2010 by R.J. Sullivan. Published by DarkWhimsy Books.

All rights reserved. No portion of this book may be copied or transmitted in any form, electronic or otherwise, without express written consent of the publisher or author.

Photo: Heather Stokes, Oh SNAP! Photography

Interior Layout: Bryan Donihue, Section 28 Publishing

Haunting Blue is a work of fiction. All names, characters, and places are a product of the author's imagination or used in a fictitious manner. Any resemblance to actual persons, places, locales, events, and etc. are purely coincidental.

Third Edition

DEDICATION

To Linda, who never doubted this would happen.

ORIGINAL 2010 ACKNOWLEDGEMENTS

What a long, strange trip it's been! I have many friends, editors, and peer writers to thank: Debra Holland, Ash Roland, Kelly Mortimer, Charles Cafrelli, Mary Kay Woolsey, Cory Emberson and Mom and Dad. Their suggestions and input all helped to make this story stronger. Anything that still doesn't work at this point is strictly my fault.

2014 NOTES AND ACKNOWLEDGMENTS

This book is a re-release of my first novel, originally published in 2010. I did some tweaking throughout and corrected a mistake in the timeline I'd overlooked the first time. Because I liked it, I added a short poem by Nicole Rinaldi and slipped it into chapter one. In the original release, the main story chapters read "Present Day." Because I have since written *Virtual Blue*, a sequel set in 2013, those chapters now read "2010". This not only locks the story in time, but I won't have to adjust the pop culture, computer technology, and music references. So there.

2014 THANKS

John F. Allen, Rodney Carlstrom, E. Chris Garrison, Monica Kelver-Kellogg, Nicole Rinaldi, Michael West, Amanda DeBord, Bonnie Wasson, and Stephen Zimmer.

2020 THANKS

Bryan Donihue for helping me through the republishing nightmare...er... process.

CHAPTER ONE

These are the longest three hours of my life.

I knew this would happen, and, sure enough, here I was, stuck in the car with Mom giving me the evil eye. Mother and daughter trapped together in our Range Rover for 180 intolerable minutes.

In all fairness, it didn't start out that way. While Mom made her client calls on the cell phone, I created a zone of rock music around myself while scribbling out a poem to vent off steam. Just me, the iPod, the earbuds, and the cooler-than-Aragorn lead singer taking me away, freeing my mind and spirit. I folded my knees against my body, crouching so no one driving past could see me.

At seventeen, already a high school junior, I still waited for the growth and boob fairies to visit me the way they had my classmates years ago.

Most of the time, I hated being so small, but today, I could shrink down into the seat and close my eyes, bobbing and rocking to the rhythm of the tunes.

So I jotted this rant poem about not being ignored by Mom while Mom ignored me. Your daily dose of irony.

Mombot

An empty space on the couch,
A droning in my ear;
You provide for me,
But you're never here.

You don't see me.
You don't hear me.
I can't be me.

You want your own robot,
A perfect, genial girlbot.

No blue hair,
No need to care,
An empty space on the couch.

Antsy punk teen pens a mother poem. That's me. What can I say? The cliché exists for a reason. I'm the 2010 model, the latest of an endless string.

Not that all of my poetry is like this. No one's going to read this one; it's just to keep me sane during the drive. I have a professional standard, after all. Better to stab the paper than stab other things, right?

Mom punctured my "zone" with what she considered the height of mother-daughter diplomacy. "What *is* that crap you're listening to?"

I braced myself for the argument but tried to answer the question. "It's Linkin Park, Mom."

"Like Abraham Lincoln?"

I fought back the smirk that threatened to cross my face. "No,

Linkin like...um...L-i-n-k-i-n." I spelled the name, trying not to roll my eyes. *God, my mom is so out of touch.*

"Well, they're louder than hell, Fiona. I can hear them right through your headphones."

I wanted to reply that I could hear her right through the earbuds, too, but I had promised myself I'd be on good behavior today.

"Where's the Britney disc I got you for your birthday?"

My birthday? You mean my tenth birthday? Melted into a silver puddle in the trunk if I'm lucky. "It's packed away. I just felt like a change of sound, Mommy Dearest." *Oops, better watch it. That came close to pushing her buttons.*

Too late. I could tell I'd already gotten to her.

She took a deep breath, brushing the dark bangs from her eyes before continuing. Mom had let her normal business-friendly short haircut grow long the last few weeks in favor of attending to the more important chores associated with moving the office.

When she got angry, like now, the wrinkles around her mouth became more pronounced, and her dark blue eyes flashed; a predator-like warning I'd learned to recognize over the years.

She spoke through gritted teeth. "I thought you *liked* Britney Spears."

"Well, yeah, when I was a kid." Of course, Linkin Park also went back a few years, but the difference in quality made it unfair to compare.

"When did you get into this loud crap? What happened to those nice singing bands like Boyz II Men and INXS?"

I stifled a chuckle. She didn't mean INXS. But it wasn't worth correcting her. We had enough to fight about.

But Mom didn't want to argue about music. She'd just set me up to blindside me. "This is Joey's influence, isn't it?"

Actually, over half the tunes I'd ripped into my iPod had come from Joey. U2, Tori Amos, The Doors; a whole world of music I'd never experienced until him. "It's not just Joey. This is what everyone listens to in Broad Ripple." True enough. In Broad Ripple, everyone hung out at the coffeehouses, and most were college students. What did she *think* was gonna happen to my impressionable young mind?

Mom's nostrils flared. At times like this, the stress caused from years of balancing single motherhood with her skyrocketing career would shine right through the caked on makeup. I could almost feel sorry for her, but then she would blow it all by saying something obvious and dumb.

No exception today. "Your friends from the Café Expresso were too mature for you."

"Well, stop the presses and rewrite page one!" I rolled my eyes at the familiar complaint. Next would come a comment about my blue hair. I decided to forestall it. "*You* moved us to Broad Ripple, remember? *You* took me to the biggest college hangout in Indy, and I ended up making friends with the college students. And now you finally stop playing super-lawyer long enough to notice? Here's a clue, when I take up bingo and shuffleboard, you can safely assume I'm hanging out with an even older crowd."

I reached into my pocket where normally I kept my trusty cell, intent on escaping into my own conversation or at least say hi to Joey. My fist clasped on the hollow cloth pocket and I couldn't hide the disappointment from my face.

Mom didn't miss any of it. She saw the look, read my hurt, and attacked. "Oh, no, no cell phone calls. Your cell stays with me until I get every penny back from the overcharges last month. Four hundred dollars! Spent to text a boy just down the road! Don't you have any sense of responsibility?"

I folded my arms, feeling my face burn, and tried to shrink down into the seat. "Well, since I just quit my job, you might have to keep that phone for a while."

"I'm sure they have fast food restaurants in Perionne. You'll figure something out."

We sped along I-69, stewing in an uncomfortable silence. I averted my eyes and looked out the window, watching the endless flat farmland whisk by. The moving van followed.

Mom started again, her forced, even tone revealing the hot temper percolating beneath the surface. "Those hours I put in paid off. As the senior partner of *Shaefer and Gerrold*, I helped build the firm, and I've kept us living pretty damn good while I did it."

Now, the whining started. I'd heard it all before, and I could easily tune it out. She rambled on anyway. "The property opportunities are so much greater in Perionne than in Broad Ripple. More land, larger houses, older families. Clients from there have requested me specifically." She nodded once, convinced she'd made her point.

My mother, the lawyer. Sounds like a bad TV sitcom. She handled acquisitions, bankruptcies, and property distribution. She practiced her courtroom delivery all the time, though I'm sure any conversations she'd had with judges took place over email or a minute or two in their office long enough to get a signature.

"Opportunities like this keep a nice roof over your head. They also keep you in the best schools in town." She stopped defending herself and attacked. Sharpness entered her tone. "Even when you can't keep up the grades."

So much for being on my best behavior. She wants the "Mom of the Year" award? I'll pop this little bubble right now. "Mom, what time did I come home last night?"

Her face flared red beneath her makeup, and the car swerved. The silence that followed spoke volumes. She knew as well as I she couldn't answer. Not last night, not any night, six months back.

I reached for my iPod, thinking we'd finished the conversation. But Mom collected her composure and started in again. "I understand they have an amusement park in Perionne."

Apparently, the question about my comings and goings was too hot for her. She continued on like the previous five minutes had never happened. "You'll probably have an easy time finding kids your own age there. I'll admit I didn't know that much about your 'friend' Joey, but I could see enough. Look at how much you've changed, just in the last month."

"That had nothing to do with Joey." Now, it was my turn to

flush. Every time she said the word "Joey," heat would creep into my face.

Mom didn't approve of the denim jacket, the earrings, the bracelets, the half-tees, or anything else I chose for myself. She'd hit the roof when she saw the dye job. I didn't explain the blue hair. Everyone in the Café Expresso wore some form of colored hair, streaks, spikes, highlights, especially the poets and writers I hung out with. They were comfortable expressing their individuality, and that's how I wanted to be.

Instead, I'm sitting here, trapped and squirming. That'll teach me.

I ruffled the pages of my paperback, *To Kill a Mockingbird*, wondering if I would have a chance to read any more of it. The novel sure had me pumped up for small town hospitality, yessirree.

We continued north to a road laughably labeled *Highway 20*. We passed a sign informing us that Perionne lay ten miles east of La Grange. Helpful, I suppose, if you knew where or what La Grange is. We took the exit, and the road deteriorated into large chuck-holes, sudden dips, and narrow shoulders, which made the car rock maddeningly for those of us trying to read in the passenger seat. The signs insisted you could still travel fifty-five miles an hour. Through the trees, I could see a billboard advertisement of Perionne Park. The aerial photo looked like a traveling carnival with rickety spin-and-barf fair rides.

"This will be good for you," Mom said. "Maybe you'll realize how ridiculous you look, and you'll dye your hair a more respectable color."

I knew she'd get around to the hair. "Thanks for the support, Mother."

"Oh, you think I'm being mean?" The lawyer façade dropped, and she scowled at me. "I should have made you cut it off. Shave it off and go to school bald."

"That's child abuse, Mother."

"Are you telling me about the law, young lady?"

Whoops. Wrong approach. "My friends liked me this way."

"You mean Joey liked it. Were you going to get a nose ring like his, too? That would look really attractive. Jesus, Fiona, I thought you had more brains than that."

I slipped lower into my seat, wishing I could somehow float up through the roof and out of the car.

"You're better off never seeing him again. One thing I've learned in life is that you have to make your own mistakes, so go to school looking however you want."

I shrugged. Soon, Mom would settle into her new office, and I'd be left alone. I just had to endure another few days. But she'd brought up Joey, the one person I'd been trying desperately to forget. Those thoughts only dredged up the hurt, and I didn't want to face the pain right now. It was too fresh. We'd only said goodbye last night.

Sweet, crazy Joey. I'd let him pick the color of my hair. He had loved to run his fingers through the strands. We'd had a rocky relationship, but my heart hurt when I thought about breaking up with him. Every time I'd tried, I would feel a cold hollowness in my chest. Then, I'd put it off another day and the pain left.

Over time, I realized Joey was no good. The drinking, the smoking, the fits of self-abuse. He said nice things to me, he truly had a talent for poetry, and he was great in bed. *Oh, yes.* The first man I'd been devoted to. My head spun from the previous six months of passion. I wanted to be with him forever. It killed me when I found out I couldn't control the monster side of him.

Especially after the incident last month.

Then, Mom laid the news about the move on me, and the point was moot. In her own way, Mom had done me a favor. Not that she needed to know. Any of it.

The pain returned. And this time, nothing I did would make it go away.

I grabbed at my abandoned earbuds. My silver bracelets rattled. Between my earrings, the chains, and the buttons strewn across my denim jacket, I served as a walking advertisement for Claire's. I liked the look. Still did. But if I really wanted to, I could've ditched the buttons. Heck, I could've dyed my hair brown and been done with the whole thing. Let Mom think she'd won.

No way.

I'd keep the hair. And if I was going to glow in the dark, I might as well jingle. Better to be damned for who I am. Either that, or shave my head and go dyke.

I looked out across the expanse of highway and over the tops of the trees to a cluster of rust-colored track supported by a wooden framework. The roller coaster of Perionne Park appeared as a series of arcs dropping off and disappearing through a gathering of high-rising branches.

Having nothing better to do, I stared at the towering structure, then had an uneasy feeling the coaster stared back; the arched structure bearing a closer resemblance to a lumpy sea creature than wood and steel. We approached, the highway leading us past the park, and a cold, chilling jolt of fear coursed down my spine.

Panic overcame me, along with an urge to throw open the door, jump for it, and run like hell. My body tensed from the anxiety. Something wasn't right about that place. What, I couldn't tell.

Even though I didn't want to do anything that might get her attention, I risked a quick glance at my mother. She projected her usual stylish confidence, showing no symptoms of the uneasiness overwhelming me.

Uneasiness? More like sheer terror. I swiped a hand across my forehead and stared, dumbfounded, at the cold wetness reflected on it. I craned my neck in the direction we'd come. I could still see the coaster, slipping away over the horizon. I took a deep breath.

With a clear head, the ride looked neither impressive nor scary. Instead, I saw a dilapidated old relic; outdated, rickety, and pathetic. A few hundred yards from the coaster, the top half of a Ferris wheel rotated above the trees, seats sun-bleached in pasty yellow and pink. That was the only other object visible from the highway, completing the depressing picture. Cheap, small fun for cheap, small minds.

Abandon hope all ye who enter here.

Perionne, Indiana, a sign read, *Population: 6500. Soon, 6502.* Up ahead, I saw a small cluster of suburbia surrounding a town hall and school building. *Must be a ninety-minute drive to anything remotely resembling decent shopping.* Even Walmart had passed through without stopping. I swallowed back cold fear, telling myself it could all turn out okay if I stayed on my best behavior.

For all the good it'd done me so far.

$$\text{---}$$

CHAPTER TWO

$$\text{---}$$

My first day at Perionne High School was a disaster.

The beginning of the end started in American Folklore, taught by a Mr. Haplin. Well, my schedule listed him as "Haplin," but everyone called him "Hap." Fine with me, I'm sure he imagined it endeared him to us and made him cool. He couldn't have been further from the truth.

I wanted to grab a seat in the last row, but a fat guy with dark hair and greasy corkscrew curls already occupied the back. Like Jabba the Hut surrounded by three toadies, he lorded over his domain. The guy wore a sweat-spotted redneck T-shirt and a black denim jacket. He could barely squeeze his oppressive bulk into the chair attached to the desk. His beady dark eyes bugged out of his piggy-face when he saw me. He scratched five-day stubble on his reddened cheek, daring me to invade their space.

Hap entered the classroom, shutting the door behind him. Tall and lean, he towered over us. A huge bald spot circled his head as if he'd been freshly scalped. Perching on the edge of his desk, he looked and acted young, for a teacher, I mean, perhaps in his early thirties, and he spoke with a quiet hesitation, as though still new to the whole public-speaking thing.

"Hi, kids," he announced, sounding like Mr. Rogers. "Today, we're going to continue our discussion on Perionne legends." He glanced at a single sheet of paper before placing it behind him on his desk. "But first, I want to introduce a new student joining us from Indianapolis. You've probably already noticed this colorful girl sitting toward the front. I'm sure you'll want to introduce yourself." He grabbed a loose sheet of paper and searched for my name.

I started talking before he could announce me. My nickname bore little resemblance to my real name, so there wasn't much point in saying it. "My name's...my last name's Shaefer, but my friends back home called me Fi-Fi." I folded my arms and stared at the other students. I could see a couple of guys open their mouths to say something, but I glared at them, and they drifted into silence. I created my own aura of intimidation and shook everyone up, almost.

The large guy sitting in the back row cackled. "Now I know why she looks like a dog."

The entire room laughed, pretty much ruining my forceful first impression.

"Clinty!" the teacher snapped. "Are you looking for another suspension? You know I'll do it."

Clinty shut up, and the rest of the class clamped down on their own laughter.

Mr. Haplin turned to me. "Sorry. Tell us about your look. It's quite different. Is blue hair the thing in Indianapolis?"

"Not quite. Maybe downtown. You see more of this look in Broad Ripple. It's by Butler University, so it's an older Indy suburb, but also a college town. A lot of people dress like this, though nowadays, you see more vampire children than anything else."

Mr. Haplin nodded and smiled, but kept any conclusions to himself.

"Well, class, take the time to welcome...Fi... Ms. Shaefer...on your own time. I'm sure you'll have a lot to learn from each other."

Hap grabbed a large spiral-bound booklet from his desk and held it out to me. "This is our material for local legends. We're reaching the end of it and then going on to worldwide folklore, but I suggest you study it on your own, as the material will be on the first test at the end of September. So you only have a week. I've also attached a schedule. After that, we'll begin on the textbook."

I took the offered papers.

He turned, approached his desk, and sat on the edge of it.

"Now...Fi-Fi...this provides the rest of us with a unique opportunity. Turn to page twenty and tell me what you know about Gunther Stalt."

I flipped through the handout as I replied, "Gunther who?"

"Oh, come on," a student whispered.

I opened the handout to a newspaper clipping. A head-and-shoulders photograph of a middle-aged man stared back at me, his gaze glaring off the page. His hair, which hung down to his broad shoulders, appeared to be graying, though it was hard to tell from the Xerox. The headline to the article read, ***PERIONNE LOCAL ROBS BANK***. A second clipping screamed the headline, ***STALT STILL AT LARGE***.

"You just handed it to me. How am I supposed to answer the question?"

"Puh-lease." This time, I could tell the comment came from Clinty.

"I see," Mr. Haplin said. "So, living in Indianapolis, you've never heard of Gunther Stalt?"

"No. Not a word. But I guess he robbed a bank."

Disbelieving laughter filled the room.

Hap turned toward the group. "Class! Now, Fi-Fi, what would you say if I told you Gunther Stalt is as famous here in Perionne as, oh, say, Kelly Clarkson or Steve Jobs are around the world?"

"I guess I'd have to take your word for it."

On the next page, another headline caught my eye. Dated November of 1992, it read, ***GHOST OF GUNTHER STALKS FORMER GIRLFRIEND***. A sketch of a scarecrow-like apparition accompanied the article. The apparition extended its left arm, with a hook for a hand, foreshortened and out-of-proportion, as if the character was reaching off the page toward the reader. I couldn't help but smile at the melodrama.

"This proves an important point." Hap strode to the dry-wipe board and started scribbling with a bright green marker. "A lot of folklore is <u>regional</u>." He underlined the word. "In fact, most folklore is known only in a specific area. The Robin Hoods and Johnny Appleseeds are few and far between." He turned toward the class and smiled at me.

I couldn't help squirming. *Oh, shit, I'm starting to become the teacher's pet. This isn't happening.*

"Now. Who can tell Fi-Fi about Gunther?" He looked at the front row. "Steve?"

A clean-cut, average guy in a gray Nike polo shirt answered. He looked at his desk as he spoke. I had a better view of his swoosh on the left pocket than I did of his face. "Gunther robbed the Perionne National Bank in 1990. He disappeared that night, taking the money with him, and has never been seen again," he lowered his voice, "Unless you count the ghost."

The class tittered.

Hap chose to ignore the comment. "Right. Now, does anyone know why this was such a big deal?"

I certainly didn't. Judging from the silence that followed, no one else did, either.

"Ah," the teacher declared, his tone chastising the class as a whole. "You all thought you could fake your way through the discussion without reading the material, didn't you? Thought you knew everything about Gunther? Chuck, why is he such a big deal?"

Chuck shrugged, but offered up, "I guess because people started seeing his ghost afterwards."

"Well, that's true. The Ghost of Gunther."

A quiet murmur buzzed around the room.

Hap waited for the class to settle down. "In general, folklore has a habit of tying back to the supernatural or fantastic, and Perionne folklore is no exception. The facts behind the folklore relate to someone who died under mysterious circumstances. In this case,

Gunther Stalt." He waved a hand in the air to dismiss the topic. "We'll get to that in a minute. Why did people start seeing Gunther, though? What created the excitement?"

Nobody answered.

"Think, kids. How many bank robberies have occurred in Perionne?"

Not too damn many, I would guess, but nobody raised their hand.

A hint of frustration leaked into Hap's easygoing façade. "You kids remember Hank Simone last year? They picked him up the next day in Michigan. And remember Fred Lionel? What happened to him?"

One student called out, "His girlfriend found the money crammed in his mattress."

A few people chuckled.

"Correct. What happened to Gunther?"

Steve raised his hand. "Nothing. He never got caught."

"That's right, Steve. An unprecedented situation. It had never happened before, and, in fact, hasn't happened since. Now, here's what you would have found out, had you read your articles."

I had scanned the article while Hap talked and found the answer a few seconds before he asked, but thought it might compound my popularity problem to volunteer a correct answer.

"Gunther's bank heist is the only unsolved robbery in Perionne." Hap paused a moment to let the fact sink in. "Think about where you live. We're a fairly closed community. Everybody knows everybody. What do we know about each other? Clinty smokes marijuana in his dad's tool shed. It's not something I normally bring up in class, but Michelle McKinley and George Lewis were discovered messing around behind the large pine tree near Baptism Lake last month." Haps raised his hands, wiggling his fingers into a pair of quote marks while saying "messing around."

I cringed, wondering if Michelle and George attended the school and would have appreciated being used as scandalous examples. *American Folklore Lesson Number One: Better be careful, or I could wind up as an example in next year's class.*

"Gunther robbed the bank wearing a white mask. There was no clearly identifiable picture taken of him by the security camera, but all the eyewitnesses positively identified him. Why? Because they knew him. They recognized his jacket. They knew he had his hand in his pocket to hide the prosthetic arm and hook. They knew his walk. They knew his voice."

Silence settled into the room. At last, Hap had everyone's attention.

As if he sensed enlightenment dawning upon his class, Hap's voice grew more animated.

"In theory, it's nearly impossible for a local citizen to commit a felony in Perionne. Quite simply, you're going to get found out. From a parent's perspective, it's one of the great attractions of living in a small town. I'm not saying that to scare you, it's just a fact. And yet...the article tells us Gunther escaped authorities. It was many hours before the police found the body of Jeff Crimley, Gunther's accomplice, dead in the hospital parking lot."

Hap scrawled a second phrase on the board, <u>*unresolved mystery*</u>.

"Okay, class. What mystery are we talking about?"

Hands shot up around the room. I listened while scanning an article about a middle-aged lady who'd seen Gunther's Ghost staring at her on numerous occasions. The article featured an accompanying photo of Gunther Stalt and a young woman, petite with dark hair and a wide smile. The year under the photo read, *1983*; the article's dateline read, *1995*. The article identified the woman as Mary Steeber, Gunther's high school sweetheart, and further claimed Gunther's Ghost stalked her almost every night. Apparently, the ghost got its kicks torturing the exes.

The smiling image of Gunther held me for several seconds before I turned the page. Even in the old photograph, his aggressive, mesmerizing personality shone through.

"They never found the money," one student said. "My dad says Gunther still has the money, and it's cursed."

"There was no body," a second, feminine voice called out. "Gunther is still alive and pretending to haunt people. He's living in another town and coming through Perionne every now and again to scare people. That's what *I* think."

Hap paused. "Ah...right. You're all correct, in one way or another. There's no money, no body, and not one policeman found any clues, except the getaway car. Gunther eluded authorities until the trail ran cold, which brings us to our next topic. What happened? Jen has touched upon one of the more colorful ideas going around. Although I admit, it's more plausible than the ghost sightings we're always hearing about."

"Hey," Clinty called out. "My pa told me he saw Gunther. My pa was driving north on Summit Street, and he looked out the window and saw this guy hitchhiking; only the guy was holding out a hook. Pa got so freaked, he skidded his car onto the shoulder of the road and went right through the body."

"Yes, Clinty. Fantastic stories like your father's keep everyone talking about—"

"Are you calling my pa a liar?" Clinty's beefy fist pounded the tabletop.

I cringed, fully expecting foam to spew from Clinty's mouth. A laugh, sharp and purely involuntary, escaped my lips. The rest of the class had kept their responses to a quiet murmur, so my outburst proved loud and cutting, unfortunate for me.

Clinty turned in my direction. His look said it all, *You're dead meat.*

Great. Just what I need. Clinty as an enemy.

Hap, oblivious to the drama playing out in the form of exchanged glares, pressed his argument. "I'm not calling your father a liar, Clinty. But the situation has created the proper conditions for people to think they're seeing a ghost because that's what they want to see. Like the Loch Ness monster that is really a floating log."

"Pa didn't drive through a floating log, Hap," Clinty said. "You can't drive through anything but ghosts. Gunther is dead, all right, but he has a score to settle. We just don't know what it is yet.

That's what my pa told me." A hint of intelligence lit the blustering bully's eyes. But only for a moment, and then it flickered out.

No one spoke. Nobody else wanted to contradict the volatile redneck. They didn't care to be next on Clinty's shit list, right beneath me.

"Well," Hap said, "this has certainly stimulated passionate conversation. Let me ask you kids, how many of you believe in the Ghost of Gunther?"

Clinty's hand shot up, along with the rest of the back two rows. Certainly not an accurate poll, but five others, over half of the rest of the class, raised their hands as well.

I listened without comment, even as the opening notes to *The Twilight Zone* theme played in my head.

———

I OPENED my locker and stashed the Xeroxed handout on the shelf. When I reached for my English book, two pairs of hands grabbed me from behind and pinned my wrists against either side of the locker frame.

The old locker ambush. Clinty couldn't wait until lunch or after school. He wanted to get into it right here. Stupid me had expected something clever, or at least subtle, from him. I wouldn't make that mistake again.

Between the two of them, Clinty's eager helpers subdued me with ease, whipping me around to confront him face-to-face. I didn't fight. The pair of large brutes could easily manhandle my tiny frame, even if I *did* struggle.

Panicking wouldn't help me, so why bother? Besides, the anger flaring in Clinty's eyes at my decided *lack* of cowering made it all worthwhile.

The two thugs made quite a show of jerking me from my locker while keeping my arms pinned to my sides, pulling me into the middle of the hall for everyone to see. I cursed my own stupidity and Clinty's lack of forethought at this attack. But I knew my moment would come. I just had to wait him out.

They didn't realize where I'd come from, or what I could do. On my old turf, I had to fend off the drunks and the drug addicts looking for an easy mug-and-grab, looking to steal something they could trade for another fix. Then, there were the college linebackers. After a couple drinks, they all thought they were God's gift. All I needed was a little persuading.

These pricks would be simple in comparison.

The two laughing buffoons, mistaking my submission for defeat, had already loosened their grips on my arms. The thug on my right even released one hand to scratch his head. I restrained a reaction, even when Clinty circled behind me. I could feel his eyes checking me out. I wasn't at all surprised when a large hand prodded against my shirt and groped one of my boobs.

Still, I yelped, and my face flushed.

Clinty sauntered in front of me. "Laugh at me, will ya? Think you're so smart, do ya?"

A crowd gathered to see if they could get their sensibilities assaulted.

The two henchmen pinned my arms around my back then shoved me toward a grinning, drooling Clinty.

"Three against one. Pretty brave, assholes."

Clinty reached out and gripped a handful of hair, pulling 'til my eyes watered. "Wha's this? It's a blue-haired bitch in heat!" He snorted a whistling laugh. "Hey," he said, thrusting his chubby face so close to mine I could smell rancid chewing tobacco on his breath. "Is this all the blue hair you got? I'm curious."

One thing I'd learned in Broad Ripple; when a stranger underestimates you, play the game. But make it count, because surprise only works once.

I made it count.

I kicked out. The toe of my combat boot connected with his shin. It cut through his jeans, and he yelped in pain. His grip slackened on my hair.

Throwing out my elbows, I dropped toward the floor and slid through the hold his cronies had on me.

I thrust my hand into my jacket pocket, where I kept a studded leather strap for situations like this. The looped leather eased over my knuckles. I pulled my fist out of my pocket, drew back, and smacked Clinty in the face with everything I had.

All three hundred pounds of redneck staggered, his head whipping sideways from the impact.

My other assailants turned and bolted.

Clinty shifted his head back into place. A look of stunned stupidity slipped across his features. Blood poured from his nose. It seemed to dawn on him that his friends had disappeared. His panicked gaze darted around the growing crowd, realizing that whatever the outcome, this fight had become public.

People started yelling. Whether they cheered against him or for me made no difference to me.

He screamed and charged, but I had already moved away from the lockers, punching at his chest while I backpedaled down the hall. I waited a few beats, sidestepped his attack, and set my legs. I drew both arms back, hands wrapped around the studded leather. I waited until he charged me, then slammed my fists into his ribcage.

The blow made a popping sound that brought a hush to the crowd.

Clinty teetered and veered toward the wall, losing control of his knees. He went down with a crashing thud right into the row of closed lockers, more closely resembling a falling oak tree than a human being.

Something snapped inside me, and I lost control. "Small town shit! I'll kill you!"

The crowd burst into an enormous cheer, not that I paid much attention.

All the frustrations from the last few days gathered in my dinky, lightweight body, and then erupted. I pounded Clinty's face, chest, and stomach. I kicked and punched and clawed and screamed until two teachers and a group of students managed to pull me away.

The vice principal wasn't amused. Neither was Mom. She pulled up right behind the ambulance.

Both Clinty and I got suspended. The vice principal told me to go home. Clinty would be taken to the hospital. The school nurse said Clinty had a broken nose, needed stitches, and probably had several cracked or broken ribs. I seriously doubted the part about the ribs, but that didn't keep the school nurse from saying it loudly and often to any teacher or faculty member within hearing range.

I walked the gauntlet to Mom's SUV, overhearing the awed whispers of my classmates.

I stood near a small group in various branded shorts, T-shirts, and running shoes. Apparently, gym class had stopped so that everyone could gather to watch the paramedics wheel a moaning Clinty toward his ride.

His gaze found me, and his body jerked like a wild animal. "I'll get you for this, you bitch!"

I grinned back at him and waved, knowing I'd infuriate him even more. Lying on the gurney, beaten and bruised, his threats fell flat.

The crowd turned as one, taking a step back to give me room or make sure they weren't next. I thought I saw stares of respect, or fear.

————

MOM DID NOT TAKE the news of my suspension well. She hadn't said a word the entire trip home.

With a distant feeling of dread, I sat in the living room, sinking into the darkened leather couch. No sense trying to avoid the inevitable. Part of my mind admired how the matching leather chair and glass tables fit so much better in this new house than the old one. After years of wondering about my mother's taste for big, expensive furniture, I realized she'd finally found the big, expensive house to match.

Today, before she left for the new office, Mom had absorbed

herself into her Cool Professional character — that's *Miz* Leona Shaefer to you. I knew she planned overseeing the reloading of the Shaefer and Gerrold client database at the new offices. Now she'd had to leave her "important" work early and come to the school, then home to reason with the problem child.

Mom's face was red from the heat of anger. She didn't bother to ask me if I'd been hurt. She went straight for the lecture. "What the hell is this, Fiona? You think I don't have enough troubles? Do you know what it's like to completely remodel an office? Do you have any concept of what I've been going through today?"

The irony triggered my own anger, and the sarcastic reply spit from my mouth before I could contain it. "No, Mom. Do you have any idea what it's like to have a group of boys try to gang-bang you in the hallway? During school hours, I mean."

Her hand jerked to hit me, but she held back. The anger my jibe caused disappeared in a flash, and her face transformed from red-hot anger to a barely contained patience. "Fiona, I know this transition is rough, but try to give it a few weeks. You have to learn to like it." She sighed in resignation. "But you might try wearing a hat for a while until your natural hair color grows back in. Or how about we go ahead and dye it to something less outrageous? I'll spring for the bottle."

"Jesus, Mom! I get jumped in the halls, so it must be my fault. That's your idea of supportive? I happen to be in the right here, just in case you were wondering."

"Fiona, they confiscated a weapon from you."

"And a good thing I had it, too, or else we'd be having this conversation in the hospital."

"Then you'd better adapt to the situation! You don't have a choice. Besides, what were you thinking, getting into a fight? This is all because of that Joey..."

Great. Only two days after the move, and she was already repeating herself. I sighed and waited out the tirade. I knew, from past experience, she had nothing more important to say.

CHAPTER THREE

"WAKE ME UP INSIDE! WAKE ME UP INSIDE!" I snapped my eyes open to the siren vocals of Evanescence's Amy Lee exploding from my iPod alarm clock at a volume set to rattle teeth. "SAVE ME FROM THE NOTHING I'VE BECOME!" I slapped the off button, muttering a quiet "Amen."

I sat up, momentarily shocked I hadn't awakened from the bright sunlight showing through the sheets I'd hung over the windows. Mom said we'd have to shop for "window treatments" as soon as she had time. I knew, unless I'd made a prior appointment, I was out of luck for several months.

The alarm could mean only one thing. School. My uneventful suspension was over. Uneventful? Okay, maybe boring would be the better word describing my last few days. I even broke down and read a science fiction novel, even though sci-fi didn't interest me much. That was more Joey's thing. And *Stranger in a Strange Land* had a rep as something special. According to Wikipedia, it had cultivated some sort of cult following back in the sixties, similar to the very awesome *The Lord of the Rings*. A guy raised on Mars is taken to Earth and is perplexed by what passes for "normal" here. I could *grok* it.

I listened for sounds of Mom. *Total silence. She must have an early meeting.*

I slogged through the morning bathroom ritual, dressed for the day, and then grabbed my backpack off my rumpled *Lord of the Rings* quilt. I almost made it to the door when I thought better of it. I returned to my room, making a beeline for the wooden closet door.

The Box, an old cigar box held closed by rubber bands, lay at the bottom of the closet toward the back, already buried by fallen clothes. I rifled through the contents until I found my switchblade. I reverently picked it up, gripping the cool, heavy handle; the blade still shone from the recent polish I'd given it right before I'd stashed it for moving day. *If Clinty wants a rematch, I'll be ready.*

I stepped out the front door, overcome with a sudden uneasiness.

The previous owners had kept our lawn lush and trimmed. They'd also added a stepping stone path that cut through the grass to the driveway. I stepped off the porch and onto the path, sensing someone watching me.

I looked at the house next door. An old woman, no, an *ancient* woman perched in a rocker on her covered porch. She stared at me. Her gaze took me in. I slowed my steps to a meek walk, and then I stopped. My feet didn't want to move, so I stood where I was.

A faded, off-white cloth-like *something* lay over her knees like a pile of cobwebs, a pair of knitting needles entangled within. Her lips pulled upward into a crinkled smile.

I turned away and walked toward the sidewalk.

"Young woman," the crackling voice called.

Damn. Just a few seconds from a clean getaway. This I *did not* need.

I replied with my most respectful voice. "Yes, ma'am?"

"You're the new neighbor," she proclaimed with deliberate slowness, as if we didn't exist until she'd spoken it. "It's good to have young people around. There aren't enough in this town. Just a bunch of us old ghosts haunting the streets." Her eyes glazed over. She seemed to drift away for a moment.

Who was I to pick a fight with a senile bag? "Yes, ma'am."

The woman squinted at me, staring. An uncomfortable chill ran through my body at the close scrutiny.

"My eyes ain't what they used to be, girlie. Come closer. I swear, your hair looks blue! Come, girlie." She motioned with one gnarled hand. "Closer. I won't bite you."

I stepped across the yard and waited for her to realize my hair color was not a trick of the light.

"My name's Sylvia, and I'm pleased to make your acquaintance." Her eyes widened. "My goodness, girlie, I thought *my* hair looked bad after my last trip to the beauty parlor. I hope they gave you a refund." She attempted a laugh that came out a shrill cackle.

"Actually, I did it myself. On purpose."

Even *I* couldn't help but smile. She broke into a cough and had to catch her breath.

She leaned forward in her chair. "So, you're Fiona Felicity, the Shaefer daughter. Fine mother you got there. Bringing a lot to our community."

I shuffled in the tall grass, crackling the brown leaves, wondering if I should take credit for something I had no control over. I decided to keep it neutral. I focused on the oak tree in her yard, something we didn't have.

This was one of those "mixed" neighborhoods. The older home-owners had cute little houses with wraparound porches. Then, there were the newbies, like us. The previous owners had taken the small lot and built a house covering nearly every inch of land. We still had a front yard, but no back. I wondered how long it would be before all the houses were like ours, large and grand, but missing the charm and warmth of the smaller places. Still, I had to admit, Sylvia hadn't been diligent with the upkeep. Her place could use a coat of paint and a gardener with a troop of helpers.

"Yes, ma'am. Please, call me Fi-Fi, though, ma'am."

"Fi-Fi. I already heard stories about you." She cackled and sputtered like a dying car engine. "Great, wonderful stories."

"Stories?"

"Inquisitive. Destined for trouble. But a great spirit. I'll be watching you. Each spirit offers its own unique shape to the community. Yours could shape the rest of us, if you put in the effort."

I rolled my eyes. "That...trouble...was just a misunderstanding. Someone at school was looking for a fight, so I gave him one. But I don't plan to stay in this town long enough for anyone to have to worry about me being a problem. Soon as I graduate, I'm gone."

The old woman sighed. "Perhaps. But if you're always looking over the next hill, you can never enjoy the valley."

"I didn't ask to be here. And yeah," I shrugged. What did it matter what I admitted? "I don't like it here."

"Well, perhaps we can change your mind if you give us a chance. Then again, perhaps not."

She continued to stare at me, and my legs weakened.

I took a step. "I need to get to school." I struggled for an appropriate exit line. "Nice to meet you, Sylvia."

"Wait just a minute, girlie."

I stopped. *What more does she want from me? Last thing I need is to be late my first day back.*

"You got sumthin' in that pack of yours you need to be leavin' at home." She pursed her lips and raised an eyebrow.

My thoughts went straight to the knife safely nestled among my books and papers. "I don't know what you mean."

"Nothin' but trouble in there, trouble you don't be needin', girlie."

The look of confusion I gave was real. I remained silent. *There is no way she could possibly know...*

"The knife, girlie. Get caught with that, and you'll never be goin' back to that-there school, and young ladies need to learn."

My mouth opened and my jaw dropped about five inches. "How did you—"

"Doesn't matter. You turn right around and put that thing away."

I wanted to leave, but my feet felt like they were encased in cement.

"Go on, git!"

My feet decided to oblige. I turned and took two steps but then chanced a glance over my shoulder.

The old woman was gone. The rocker moved at a steady pace, even though there wasn't a lick of wind. *How did she possibly get up and go into the house in the span of two seconds? I don't want to know.*

I turned and stumbled toward the door of my house, grateful to shut out the old woman and the old rocker. She gave me the creeps.

I returned the switchblade to The Box. She was right about one thing, that sort of mischief had caused me enough problems. I hoped I could stay out of trouble long enough to graduate.

———

I MADE it to school on time and decided to ignore my classmates, absorbing myself in my classes. Back in Ripple, in spite of what my teachers liked to call my "personality conflicts," I'd made it a point to maintain an "A" average. That is, until last year when Joey made my head spin and my brain work backwards, as well as my grades. If nothing else, I came into town with a clean slate and no distractions.

I'd made it through third period without an incident. Clinty had yet to return to school, and I took some satisfaction in the thought that his injuries had left him in so much pain (but only *bruised* ribs, thank you very much) he might be out another few days. More likely, he'd skipped class to light up with his cronies, but hey, I can dream, can't I?

My new English teacher, Mr. Robbins, a humorless man with thinning dark hair, stood before the class like the executioner waiting for the condemned. To me, however, his assignment offered a ray of hope and an easy "A."

He wanted us to write a free-verse poem on any subject. Most of the students groaned, asking the usual delaying questions, "How many pages?" "What's the minimum number of lines?" "How many words per line?" Et cetera, et cetera, et cetera, as the king of Siam might say. Meanwhile, I penned a rough draft into my notebook before the hour ended.

I scribbled, biting my lip, unable to contain my excitement. A creative assignment, right up my alley, just what I needed to boost my average while I tried to catch up on all the days I'd missed.

I read through the lines of my draft:

American Idol Finalist
The camera eye
the single I
Ole One-Eye
Pans
down her shirt
and up her skirt

She'll be singing
something
about teen suicide
I think

I left class in a terrific mood, letting the current of the crowd carry me to the cafeteria. Most people ignored me, and I ignored them. Fine with me. It would change or it wouldn't. Today, I floated on a cloud of optimism. Even the pizza-shaped grease couldn't wreck my spirits. I methodically chewed my food, holding pizza-stuff in one hand and my copy of *The Bell Jar* close to my nose.

A thumping noise shook the table. I glanced over the book. A small, wiry guy had taken the seat across from me. Most guys I knew were putting on weight, but he hadn't started yet. His short brown hair was rumpled in spite of his severe military cut.

I stared at the source of the impressive thud that had ruined my concentration. A stack of paper filled with some sort of programming code lay between us. I saw enough programming nerds in the halls to know programming code on sight. What that code *meant*, however, was another story.

I couldn't concentrate on the book. The amazing thing was he'd buried his face between two pages, and he hadn't looked up yet. He must have found the table by some sort of sixth sense, which now helped him find the food on his tray while he flipped through the pages.

The nerve *of this geek; sitting at* my *table, taking me out of* my *novel, and ruining* my *concentration. And not even bothering to notice* me.

I studied his face. He'd been trying to create a goatee, but so far had succeeded in growing dirt-colored peach fuzz under his chin. He wore a jacket of slick brown leather that looked too nice and fit too well, and thus blew his façade.

It was the sort of lame-ass camouflage a computer geek would use to keep punks like me off him, ironically guaranteeing we'd whale on his ass the moment we had a chance.

Still, that was then. I no longer condoned the hassling business. Besides, I thought I noticed Aragorn-blue eyes. If I could get his attention, I could confirm it.

Numbered lines filled the pages he held. Computer-garble. Several years ago, my second-grade teacher taught us some commands in BASIC to help us understand how a computer "thought." I could probably make "Fi-Fi Shaefer is a Beauty Queen" scroll up the screen forever until you stopped the program, but nothing more. If you could find a computer that accepted BASIC. I used spreadsheet and word processing software, and, like everyone else, lived part-time on the Web, though I hadn't found the time to check my Facebook page since we'd moved. But I knew nothing about programming, on account of my allergy to math.

I had to clear my throat about three times before he glanced my way, a startled expression cracking his zombie-bland face.

"Oh, hello." His voice was normal enough, not hesitant or quiet; a little apologetic, perhaps.

And I was right about the piercing blues. Lucky me.

I indicated the stack of papers with the grease-covered dough in my hand. "School project?"

"Oh, no. Just a program I wrote. It's sort of a number random-izer, for a role-playing game. You know, *Dungeons & Dragons*?"

"Oh, yeah," I nodded. D&D, in spite of its reputation for being a geek-fest, permeated several cliques in the college crowds to different extents; though, of course, the Goths in Ripple preferred a live action vampire version. "I know some people who played, back in Ripple. I figured there'd be some sort of law against D&D around here."

He laughed. "Well, there was, but my friends and I erased it from the town's computer files a few months ago." An embarrassing, seal-like laugh erupted from his throat. He cut it off a few seconds later when he realized I hadn't joined him. He moved right into his next thought without skipping a beat. "That hasn't kept a group of us from getting together."

He extended a thin-fingered hand. "I'm Chip. Chip Farren. And you're Fi-Fi Shaefer, the girl who beat the shit out of Clinty Buckner."

I couldn't help it. I giggled and grinned. "My reputation precedes me."

"I know a lot of guys who are glad you did that, including me. He's been tripping me all semester. Real pain in the ass, but I couldn't...." He seemed to internally switch gears and then restarted. "Well, hey, I guess you want to be left alone. I'll just sit somewhere else."

"No. Wait, Chip Farren. You're the first person who's approached me since I've come to this town, even if you didn't see me for the first five minutes."

Chip grinned. "How do you know? Maybe that's just what I *wanted* you to think."

I laughed. "Nice recovery." That's when I noticed the *Starship Troopers* paperback sticking out of his backpack.

I pointed. "I just read a Robert Heinlein."

Chip's eyes followed the direction of my finger. "Yeah? Which one?"

"*Stranger in a Strange Land.*"

Chip grinned, and his eyes lit up. I imagine I looked the same way. "That is a great one, if you can get past the two-by-four messianic symbolism at the end."

I nodded. "I wish they'd make *Stranger* into a movie instead of the one you're reading. *Starship Troopers* the movie was a steaming pile. But my..." I stopped myself short of saying "my boyfriend". "A *friend of mine* owned the DVD. Watched it all the time. I think he just loved the co-ed shower scene."

Chip rolled his eyes and plucked the paperback out of his pack. "Here. If you already thought the movie was bad, you'll really hate it after reading the book."

I gripped the paperback, marveling at the crinkled, ruffled pages, noting the bookmark partway in. "Don't you want to finish it? This looks pretty old."

Chip waved a dismissive hand. "I'm on my third time through it. It's my dad's. We won't miss it for a few days."

I held the book between my fingers for a few moments. Accepting his offer meant committing to something. At the very least, we'd have to talk again.

I decided that would be a good thing, and placed the book in my own pack. "Thanks, Chip." I returned his grin, happy I had made my first friend.

CHAPTER FOUR

PERIONNE – NOVEMBER 1990

"I got laid off today." In the living room of the clean but small house he shared with his mother and pregnant girlfriend, Gunther Stalt broke the bad news.

"What?" Lily Mills didn't give him a chance to say more. Her long dark hair bobbed in emphasis to her screaming tirade. "How in the hell could you lose your job? All you were doing was pushing a broom through an amusement park!"

Gunther dropped onto the worn leather couch, once an attractive tan, years later faded to the color of old paper grocery bags, and hung his head. He let a deep sigh escape. *Just what I need, Lily all pissed off and making me feel more like a failure.*

"What the hell good are you?" Dropping her arms to her sides, Lily paced and yelled. "We're living in your mother's house. We have a baby coming. You promised we'd get our own place. All you had to do was keep your job."

"It wasn't like that." Gunther hated the whine he heard in his own voice, hated being in this position. "I'd already told you once the season was over..."

Lily cut in. "And you're drunk, too! Don't try to deny it."

So he'd had a few beers. His supervisor had lowered the boom right before lunch. He knew better than to come straight home, so he'd spent the rest of the day at the Cat's Cradle, tossing down a few and steeling up his courage.

The boss's poor timing infuriated him. He and Crimley had just locked their plan in place. A couple more days would've made all the difference. Now, he had to take shit from Lily, and he couldn't say anything about the plan. All Lily could see was his failure, and that angered him most of all.

His prosthetic arm hung limp against the side of the couch. By old habit, he turned the hook so the dull curve could beat a rhythm against the leather without puncturing it. "Mama said we could stay. It ain't so bad here. At least she keeps the place clean."

Arms akimbo, Lily looked ready to spit fire at him. Lit from behind, her shadow cast into the room. The darkness caused by her overlarge belly threatened to devour him.

Gunther avoided her gaze. "I'll take care of it. I know this is screwed up. I know. Look, the park is closing for the season. They had to make some cuts."

"The park's not closed yet," Lily huffed. "And of course, you're the first man they got rid of."

Gunther clenched his teeth against his seething anger, trying to respond in a calm voice. "They don't keep the park running in the winter, and it's almost winter. I can try to get back on next spring. It's not my fault."

Lily's dark eyes bulged in self-righteous anger. "It's never your fault, Gunther." She winced and placed a hand against her lower back, while her other arm gripped the back of a chair. "It's not your fault you lost your arm. It's not your fault you lost your job. I suppose it's not your fault that I'm pregnant, either. Well, guess what? You're at least half to blame for that, and you can't weasel out of your responsibility."

Gunther struggled to keep from rolling his eyes at Lily's tirade. He hated to grovel. "I'm not gonna run away. I told you I'm gonna take care of this." He lifted his head and met Lily's gaze. "I promise."

"Shit!" Lily yelled. "How're you going to take care of anything?"

"That's enough. Shut your mouth." Gunther couldn't take much more of this.

Lily stomped closer. "I can't keep waitin' tables. And I'm not gonna support your lazy ass *and* a baby."

Gunther stared ahead at the maple coffee table before him, decorated with an oversized tacky green candle. He hated that candle. Lilly had bought it three months ago to "add a little color to the house." Everything about it screamed "bought by white trash from the clearance shelf." It hurt his head just looking at it.

Tears welled in Lily's eyes.

She shook her head, wiping at the wetness on her face. "Look at you. You think 'cause you lost your arm the world owes you a living? It's been three years. Get over it. Find a real job so we can move out."

"I said that's enough, woman." His good hand reached out and wrapped around the broad base of the candle. His knuckles whitened from the grip he held on it. *I need to get control again. I need control over something in my life.*

"Lord A'mighty, you think your dick been cut off 'stead of your hand, the way you go on, I swear..."

With a growl and a flip of his wrist, Gunther sent the bulky candle sailing across the room, slamming Lily in the chest. She toppled backward against the wall, stunned.

Gunther rose from the couch, storming toward her, holding the hook out like a weapon.

Lily blinked, her eyes staring through him, unfocused.

He towered over her, gloating at her helplessness.

She held one hand up as if to ward him off, the other arm cradled around her protruding belly. "Gunther! Gunther, wait!"

He drew the hook back and swept it forward.

She screamed and rolled away from him. The hook punched a

hole in the wall just above Lily's head. *I'll shut her whining mouth and get rid of the brat she's carrying, too!*

"God! Gunther, stop! I'm sorry, baby." She shrank away from him.

"Oh, you're sorry now, huh? Ya little bitch." He grinned down at her. He had control now. For these few seconds, he held her life in his hands, and he liked the way it felt. "I gonna slice ya for what you said."

The front door swung open and an elderly woman stood in the doorway, a scowl smeared across her wrinkled features. "Gunther Luke Stalt, what the hell do you think you're doing?"

"Mama?" As if he'd uncovered a nest of hornets, Gunther jumped back several feet.

The woman stepped forward, standing straight and tall, wedging herself between her son and the frightened girl. Her voice carried the confidence of final authority. "You just shamed me. You've shamed the family, bullying the woman who's carrying your child."

Gunther crossed his arms. "Mama, she said terrible things. She didn't show me any respect." He could hear the pouting tone of his own voice, and his face warmed at the realization.

"You'll get no respect here. Haven't earned any. Go on, Son," the old woman spoke.

Gunther stomped toward the refrigerator and snatched a bottle of beer. The room closed in around him.

His own mama ordering him to leave the house! It might be small, and not too fancy, but his mama had raised him here. "So be it, then. I don't need either of you. I can do fine on my own." He'd show them.

He'd show everyone.

———

A RELENTLESS EARLY November sun beat down on the tiny hotel room. Gunther looked around his pitiful surroundings; a beat-up recliner that looked like it'd been left at the side of the road leaned against the wall. Across from the flea-infested excuse of a bed sat a twelve-inch black and white TV perched on a rusty metal stand. He'd tried to watch it earlier, but could only get one station to come in. In the corner, a small square of linoleum with a stopped-up toilet served as the bathroom.

He grabbed a bottle of beer and tried to get comfortable on the chair, but a spring bulged out right where the center of his back should rest.

Gunther leaned forward. The cool beer sliding down his throat eased the tight knot in his belly. He took a shaky breath, frustrated at his mama for taking Lily's side.

What about *him?* What about *his* pain? *He* was the one who lost his arm.

He closed his eyes at the memory. Every night, he tried to put the memory behind him, and every night it haunted him. In his mind's eye, he still saw the meat plant where he'd made a good living before the grinder accident. He felt the grinder lock onto his hand, and that damned machine pulling him forward as it chewed his bones and muscles. Did Mama and Lily have any idea what kind of torture that was? And now, he couldn't even keep a job as a janitor because the damn broom kept slipping off his hook.

How could he begin to explain his anger? Like a dam ready to burst from the strain, he wanted to scream that what happened to him wasn't fair. That he shouldn't have to spend his life barely able to clean up after other people, to work like a dog for peanuts.

Gunther threw his head back and swallowed the final gulp of beer. On impulse, he hurled the bottle across the room. The satisfying shatter of glass impacting the worthless TV screen calmed his nerves in an instant.

He took a deep breath and thought about the plan then spoke into the still-warm air. "I've got to do something. Might as well get started."

Gunther rose, walking out of the stuffy room and into the dark night.

CHAPTER FIVE

I got my poem back with a screaming red *F* slashed in thin lines across the top half of the page.

I stared down at the paper in disbelief. The bell rang for dismissal, but I stuck around, furious and shaking, while the rest of the class filed toward the door.

Mr. Robbins stood in front of his desk, arms folded across his chest, watching my consternation with a bland expression of indifference.

I started right in as soon as the last student disappeared around the corner. "What the hell is this all about, Mr. Robbins?"

He spoke with the calm, forthright sort of baritone he used when lecturing. "I'm not sure I know what you're talking about, Miss Shaefer."

"The hell you don't." I slapped the crinkled paper on his desk. "Why'd you give me an F on this?"

"The meaning is you failed the assignment, Miss Shaefer." Unruffled, Mr. Robbins answered without a hint of sarcasm in his voice. "I found your poem tasteless and without merit. Try to do better next time."

"What?" My brain tried to sort out his response.

He waited, stone-faced.

It didn't make any sense. I tried again. "Excuse me, but you gave a B minus to Frankie Jones for writing about hooking a worm onto his fishing pole. Is that what you consider deeper merit?"

"Franklin's poem was finely crafted with excellent meter. You could learn by its example."

I couldn't believe what I was hearing. "Meter, my ass! It was a free-verse poetry assignment. I turn in a piece about the exploitation of women, and you say it's without merit? Do I really have to explain the poem to you, or should we skip all that and go straight to the principal?"

"I think you'd better watch your language, Miss Shaefer." He walked toward the classroom door, looking a touch ruffled.

Fine. I was more than ruffled, and on a roll.

"Where do you think you're going? I deserve an explanation for this. My poem was better than ninety-nine percent of the crap you received."

That wasn't ego talking. I'd dated a college-leveled poetry major for over six months. I sat in on readings with his friends. They became *my* friends. I'd had my own poems critiqued by people who ate and drank the craft and passion of poetry. I knew good poetry from bad poetry and could define both in ways the teacher had yet to hint at in his basic-level lectures. This was an easy A, plain and simple, and it was ridiculous I even had to discuss it.

"That's really for me to judge, Miss Shaefer." He pushed the door to close it. "I wanted to keep the entire school from hearing our conversation, that's all."

Once the door shut, Mr. Robbins turned toward me. A pencil-thin smile formed on his face, a cocky, self-assured grin of confidence betraying his indifferent tone.

"I think it's safe to say that you're on your way to failing this class, Miss Shaefer. In fact, I'm sure of it."

A chill ran through me. I blinked at him, thrown off-guard.

"Are you threatening me, Mr. Robbins?"

He seemed amused at the idea. "Threatening you? I'd get in a lot of trouble for doing something like that, Miss Shaefer. English is a subjective class, and I'm allowed to give subjective grades, based on my own subjective standards. And I'm afraid, right now, based on those standards, you're just not going to cut it." He shrugged, indicating that nothing could be done.

I kept my mouth shut, my mind circling around his words like a lost airplane. He'd called my bluff and had thrown out a promise of his own. In my mind, I could hear myself whine and beg. I could break down and cry, tell him I'd be good, or throw a hissy fit.

Not in a million years.

"You have only yourself to blame, you know," he continued. "Picking fights with the other students on day one. That trashy costume you call clothing. You're a real discipline problem. I moved from Chicago many years ago to get away from teaching people like you. I have no interest in trying to teach smart-aleck punks who have no interest in learning."

I glared back at him in hopeless defiance. I hoped he'd finish soon, before the desire to throttle him overwhelmed me. Of course, that would only make matters worse.

He stepped behind his desk, his head low, tone solemn, like he was delivering a eulogy. "You think you can smart off and start fights and do whatever you want, and then somehow your teachers will just let you slide by. Unfortunately for you, I'm the only one teaching senior English, and that's not going to happen." He stopped and leaned forward, his calm manner of speech cracking.

I took a step back, reeling at the intensity of his fury.

His face turned red, and he stopped himself to catch his breath. "If you drop out, you'll have to commute to La Grange over the summer to graduate. That's a forty-mile drive, one way. Not a lot of fun, but acceptable. If you stay, your GPA will suffer, and you'll still have to commute. The point is, it would be best for both of us if you quit my class now."

Somehow, I got my head back on straight while he rambled. Hatred I could deal with, at least I knew where I stood.

I put on my bravado and charged ahead. "You're being absurd. I'll just take this to the school board."

He chuckled at my threat. "What are you going to tell them, Miss Shaefer? That the senior English teacher won't give your incredibly clever work a passing grade? That I can't recognize sheer genius when I see it?"

He removed his glasses and wiped the lenses with a white handkerchief he'd pulled from his breast pocket. "You don't know much about our school, or our town, if you think that will work."

All pretenses at humor stopped, and he leaned forward, setting aside the glasses and placing both hands flat on his desktop.

"I'll tell you what will happen," he spoke between clenched teeth. "They'll open your file. They'll see your suspension for fighting. They'll look at how you're dressed. Then they'll laugh you right out of the room. And if they bother to call me in to explain myself, I'll find a reason, and I'll make it stick. They'll accept it."

He stood and straightened, placing his glasses back on his face and straightening his lapels as if recovering from a minor scuffle not worth his time. "They'll believe me because they don't want little punks like you in this school any more than I do. So tell the school board. That would be the best thing to happen to me all year."

I couldn't think anymore. I just stood, sinking into oblivion while he finished. I continued to lock eyes with him, head up, but it didn't matter. He knew he'd won in every way that mattered.

Mr. Robbins pulled the chair out from his desk. "I don't think there's anything more you need to say, Miss Shaefer. When you're ready to admit that you can't handle my class, I'll sign your dropout slip. Good day." He sat and returned to his work.

I'd been dismissed.

———

SOMEHOW, I stumbled to the cafeteria and stepped through the line in a zombie-like state before the despair welling up within me burst forward full force. I stared dumbly at my food, wondering what I could possibly do to stop the inevitable. But I already knew I had no chance. I had as much choice as a fish in an aquarium. No options. Fi-Fi Shaefer blows chance at a college English degree due to failing the class in high school. *The end.*

I could commute, but I would need parental approval to do so. And convincing my mother would be impossible. She wouldn't believe me, anyway. This stank of exactly the type of story I'd tell to get transferred out of the school or to force her to move. Just the sort of thing I'd do to get back at her.

And Mom would gamble with my grades. I knew that. I could already hear her accusing me of failing on purpose, just to prove my story.

I sank deeper, trembling. The room lost its edges. My lunch smeared out of focus from the buildup of tears.

A drop splattered on my tray. My hand shook as I touched the wetness, realizing it was a tear from my own face. The tremor built up my hand and through my body.

"Oh, shit." Tears flowed. I covered my face with both hands while I wept like a little baby. And I couldn't stop.

Worse, I heard a voice at the table.

"Fi-Fi? What's wrong?" Chip had sat down across from me. I wanted to crawl away and die.

"Go away!"

I wiped a denim sleeve across my face. I couldn't see very well, but he wasn't listening to me, anyway. He just continued to stare.

One kid at the table next to us glared hard at his tray. The girl next to him shifted her eyes in my direction and grinned.

"Great. I'm the afternoon entertainment." I grabbed a napkin and wiped tears away. Chip watched me in open shock. I glared back. "Enjoying the view? Get the hell away from me!"

I could hear a couple of snickers from somewhere around me. Chip looked hurt. "Hey, I just wanted to know. Maybe I can help."

"Yeah? Great. I'm fucked, and you can't help. Happy?"

I stood, pushed aside my untouched tray, and stormed away from Chip. I stepped through the foyer and out the double-door entrance. Nobody stopped me. Because of the beautiful late September weather, we could go outside as long as we remained on the school grounds.

Sure enough, the sun shone brightly. *Good for the sun.* I stepped across the grass, the light stinging my eyes. My jewelry jangled. A couple of students played Frisbee nearby. Clinty and his followers huddled across the lot using each other's bodies to hide the joint they passed. He glared at me and snarled then returned to the important business of getting stoned.

The cool breeze chilled me, and my teeth chattered. I reached an open area of lawn and sank down with a tired sigh. I considered ditching the rest of the day. It wouldn't hurt my other classes much, provided Mr. Robbins hadn't started some sort of club in the teacher's lounge with everyone out to get me. Of course, I could wind up getting suspended again. Kick me out of class for skipping class; leave it to the Board of Education. No wonder failure seemed inevitable.

A pair of Payless tennies approached me. I looked up the jean-clad leg.

"Oh, shit, Chip. Go away." I sighed. I didn't have the strength to chase him off or run.

He plopped down next to me while I rubbed my tired, wet eyes.

One thing I'd already learned about Chip, he'd get an idea into his head and couldn't be deterred, no matter how hard you applied the sledgehammer.

Right in character, he said, "I'm not going anywhere until you tell me what happened."

I sighed. "You know, you're real sweet. But in case you haven't figured it out, you're getting yourself in trouble just by hanging around me. Do yourself a favor and get lost." My stomach fluttered, and I feared I'd lose my temper again. I clenched my fists and couldn't talk for a long time.

"Look." Chip's matter-of-fact tone jarred me from my self-loathing. "It must make you feel unique to think you're the only unpopular kid in school. If you think I have a reputation to blow, believe me, hanging out with you has gotten me more recognition in the last two weeks than I've had my entire life. You think it's bad to be the center of attention, try being invisible for a while."

I sat for a few moments, absorbing what he'd said. Then, I repeated, "Why are you doing this?"

"Because whatever the problem is, you don't deserve it. And because you kicked the shit out of Clinty, so maybe I admire you for that, because I never could."

He hunched down in the grass, placing all his weight on his feet, his knees folded up near his shoulders. "You know, I watched the fight. I just stood and watched while they pinned you against the locker, knowing that Clinty was about to take it to somebody else. Some other nobody at the wrong place at the wrong time. No matter what happened, I was going to stand and watch. When you did what you did, I guess I felt pretty bad."

I sighed, and, when I spoke, my voice dripped venom. "Don't go around wearing your heart on your sleeve, Chip. Somebody will tear it off and squash it."

"Well, maybe so, but I'm not going away until you tell me what happened. So if you really want me to get lost, there's only one way to accomplish that."

I glared at him, fighting the desire to scream.

He looked back in utter calm, maybe even a little amused at my behavior.

Even in my current state, I couldn't take my anger out on him. In no way did he deserve it, and I knew he only wanted to help. So I put my head into my curved arm, taking a deep breath and putting a lid on my frustration.

I sat up in the grass and started talking. He listened. He didn't comment or judge; he just let me pour out my rage, without interruption. Because of that, I told the entire story in a drained monotone.

His enthusiastic face slowly bleached white.

I finished, "...So, if you want to go over there and kick the shit out of Mr. Robbins, I'll be happy to watch, and we'll be even."

Chip's blue eyes flared icy anger. "Don't patronize me. I'm holding my hand out, and you're chewing it off."

"I warned you!" I took a deep breath. "I'm sorry. You really are sweet, Chip. You're the only one in this town who even gives a shit about me. And I'm grateful. But you can't do any good."

"There has to be something you can do. Do you think the school board would really back his play?"

I shrugged. "How should I know? You think I've ever actually had to report anyone before? You live in this town. Does it *sound* like something that could happen?"

Chip shrugged. "I'd like to think common sense would prevail, but..." He shrugged and shook his head.

"Well, okay, then. I can't risk getting kicked out of school on an answer like that. So I guess I have to write off the school board idea."

We sat and stewed. I'd gotten past the anger and frustration. Failure still loomed over my head, but at least I could get through the rest of the day.

Chip, however, appeared to be thinking. His face held a look of such intense concentration, I could almost see smoke coming out his ears.

After a while, he shook his head and seemed to dismiss his train of thought. "C'mon, Blue, we'd better go back inside. Try not to worry about it. Things could turn out all right after all."

Blue? Where'd that come from?

But exhaustion bore down on me, and I let the matter go for now. "If you don't mind, I want to stay outside for a couple more minutes."

Chip gave me one last look. "Okay, see ya."

I curled up in the grass, letting the breeze and the sun comfort me because I could find comfort nowhere else.

CHAPTER SIX

Jeff Crimley watched Perionne Park's roller coaster chug through the darkness, then return to the launch shelter. The piston burst of hissing brakes cut through the silence. No passengers exited. No expectant crowd waited to board.

The train chugged over the track; Jeff turned his head to watch. First, a near-vertical ascent, drawn out to maddening slowness, then a suicidal dive straight to the ground.

No one screamed. No one laughed.

In his mind's eye, Crimley saw the kids and teens who should be riding, getting tossed about and shaken as the coaster plummeted through the corkscrew to the finish of the ride. Happy screams.

Crimley shook off a chill, watching the train charge forward for yet another solitary run.

One last adjustment before packing away for the winter; one last chance to catch the small problems before they turned into big ones.

Crimley perched on the edge of the stool, seated in the control booth overlooking the boarding platform of The Whirlwind. The brakes were turned on full, set to jerk the coaster to a jolting slow-down at every turn. So far, the coaster performed with its usual shakiness. Someday, he'd figure a way to smooth it out, but not in the dead of night, not right before winter.

Flipping a switch, Crimley released the brakes and launched the cars again.

The coaster charged forward like a fighter in training, ready to go one more round.

The little hairs on the back of Crimley's neck stood at attention. The only bad thing about working in the dark was the eeriness. Except for him, there wasn't a soul—

"Gotcha, Crimley!" Hard metal pushed against Crimley's shoulder. He yelped, jumping out of his seat and spinning around. He caught the metal object in his hand, his fist drawn back to attack the assailant. As recognition sank in, he stopped his action short.

"Gunther. You sunuvabitch! I oughta pound ya for that."

Gunther grinned, his white teeth gleaming in the dark. A hint of malice behind Gunther's blue eyes made Crimley pause.

Gunther's cackle sounded genuine enough, though. "You shouldn't make it so damn easy. Ya get working on this train and ya go into another world. I've never seen anyone get off on a kiddy ride like you do."

Crimley smiled, unable to deny it. He shook off a chill as Gunther folded his arms over the control booth railing and leaned forward. Something in Gunther's obsessed stare bothered him. Neither man could claim to be on the up-and-up, but Crimley had never sensed any instability in Gunther.

Before tonight.

Crimley wanted to explain away the bad vibes he felt as simple nerves. But now he wondered if he wouldn't regret agreeing to this nasty business.

As co-workers, Gunther and Crimley became fast friends. Gunther swept the coaster deck every hour or so. Last week, he visited the control booth, where they sat and sipped a couple of Cokes together.

That's when Gunther let Crimley in on his scheme. Crimley was willing enough to join, provided Gunther agreed to his one stipulation, a stipulation he'd maintained his entire life; no one got hurt, and, certainly, no one died. If Gunther wanted him along, Crimley'd be no part of any nastiness.

Now, looking into Gunther's predatory gaze, Crimley tried to shake off the feeling he'd made a huge mistake. One he might have to take care of.

Gunther let out a shuddering sigh. "I'm tired of Perionne. We're goin' forward with the plan. We pull this off, neither of us will have any more worries."

Crimley shrugged. "We just better not get caught."

Gunther cackled, a hard gleam returning to his eyes. "Who's gonna catch us? The Perionne P.D.? They're barely equipped to handle jaywalkers, let alone bank robbers."

"Guess you're right."

Gunther's eyes narrowed. "You still in?"

"'Course I'm in. I told ya I was, didn't I?"

"Then you got the car?"

Crimley produced a set of keys, dangling them from his fingers. "Just like I said."

"What is it?"

"A '76 Thunderbird. Four doors, just like ya asked."

Gunther snagged the keys. "'76? That's a fourteen-year-old car. You sure it runs well?"

Crimly nodded. "V-8. Clean interior. Purrs like a kitten. And it's plenty fast enough to blow us right through this town."

"Color?"

"Yella."

Gunther paused, unable to contain a worried expression. "We're going to rob a bank with a *hot* yellow ancient T-Bird? You couldn't find anything else?"

Crimley suppressed his own apprehension. "Hell, no. Look, you wanna tour the town, I got a great station wagon. You wanna blow through town like a bat outta hell, the T-Bird's gonna do it. You've got my guarantee."

The coaster skidded to a halt before them. Crimley wanted to run it again. Instead, he turned his attention back to Gunther. Crimley explained, "The car's parked on I-69 north of the first Michigan rest stop, 'bout ten miles up. Just like we agreed. Jim still going to drive?"

"I think I can guarantee his cooperation."

"He ain't gonna fuck around, is he?"

Crimley didn't like the calm, maniacal grin dominating Gunther's face. "Don't worry about Jim. I'll see to it that he don't. I gotta go. See ya."

As Gunther vanished into the night, Crimley shivered, but not from the cooling night air.

———

MOST PEOPLE WOULD THINK TWICE ABOUT PAYING a visit to a household at 11 p.m., particularly unannounced. But tonight, Gunther's obsession propelled him up the well-tended pathway to the roomy porch.

The modest single-story house shone with a coat of new white paint, even in the moonlight. As he strolled past the front wooden gate, Gunther could make out the dug-out strips of a new garden bordering the lawn, and jealousy raged within him.

The domestic tranquility galled Gunther. His old "buddy," Jim, with no more skill or talent than Gunther, enjoyed a home all to himself. Jim had married Jessie Beauchamp, quiet and beautiful. Not because of an unwanted pregnancy or desperation, but after careful planning and considerable success. So knocking on Jim's door late at night to bring a little chaos into Jim's life brought a secret glee to Gunther's soul.

The porch light snapped on, and the door opened. Gunther smiled down on the petite blonde framed in the doorway. "'Evening, Jessie. Jim here?"

Jessie stared back with wide, frightened brown eyes. "Just a sec, Gunther. I'll get 'im. You wanna come in?"

"Nah. I'll just wait here on the porch." Jim had a front porch swing, and he owned his house.

Gunther helped himself to a corner seat and flopped down. The breeze had picked up with the settling of evening.

Jessie still eyed Gunther. "Care for something to drink?" Her words held a nervous edge. The scowl on her face undermined the polite gesture, but Gunther didn't care.

"I'll take a beer, thanks." Gunther showed his teeth to her, an over-large, toothy grin he knew made people uncomfortable.

Jessie's scowl vanished, replaced with a robotic smile. She disappeared into the house.

He could hear Jim's voice from inside. Gunther sat back and enjoyed the night air. His steel arm clanged against the metal bench beneath him. *Tomorrow, I'll get what's due me.*

But first, he needed Jim's cooperation.

"Gunther, what the hell you doin' here?"

"'Evenin', Jim." He looked up at the broad, youthful man standing before him. An imposing figure normally, Jim rose to his broad-shouldered six feet-four inches in response to Gunther's presence. Jim wore a full beard and mustache that, in general, would be parted in a kind smile. Jim offered no such smile to Gunther tonight.

Jim shifted his weight from foot to foot. "You dare to come around here in the dead of night, scaring my wife?" He spoke in a lowered voice, though his tone indicated intense anger. "I already told you, I don't want nothin' to do with your crazy schemes. I'm not doing it, so just get out of here."

Gunther grinned back at Jim. His gaze roamed over the property. "Been working hard on the lawn, I see. Even in the dark, it looks thick and lush."

"You're not here to talk about my lawn. And I'm not playing this game with you."

The front door swung open.

Gunther smirked at Jessie, who stepped onto the porch, carrying two beer bottles. "Hello again, Jessie. I was just telling Jim here you and he's fixing the place up real nice."

Jessie looked down at the porch, her lashes obscuring her piercing green eyes. She extended the bottle toward Gunther.

Jim took the other bottle, refusing to make eye contact with his wife. "You just enjoy. I'll be back in the kitchen if you need anything."

Jessie paused. When neither man said anything further, she vanished through the front door.

Gunther chuckled, enjoying the tension. "Yessir. House is looking real good, Jim. Must be getting ready to start a family. Ain't that right? Seems like I heard that."

"Gunther, I don't care what you heard. There ain't no amount of money that will make me be a part of this. I don't need it. We're doing just fine."

Gunther shook his head. He intended to rub Jim's nose in as much shit as possible. "Five glorious years of marriage, right? Got the good job, the good house, oh, and a Buick Regal in the driveway, I see. Gave up the stock car driving. Well, that was just a craze in your youth, right? Still, you were a hell of a driver. I remember watchin' you."

"Stop it, Gunther. I already gave you my answer."

Gunther nodded his head in mock acknowledgment. "And please allow me to respond, Jim. Y'see, it ain't that easy."

Jim stepped forward, engulfing Gunther in his shadow. "It *is* that easy. Now, get the hell off my property, or I'll call the cops."

But Gunther refused to be intimidated. "You either hear it from me, or I tell Jessie all about it."

Jim rolled his eyes, the beginnings of a smile, not a friendly one, forming on his lips. "What are you talking about? You can't threaten me."

Gunther took a swig of beer before continuing in a mocking conversational manner. "Oh, I'm not here to threaten you about helping me, Jim. Just warn you, man to man. Keep your damn hands off Lily."

The look of shock on Jim's face erased Gunther's earlier humiliations of the day.

"Are you crazy? I've never touched Lily Mills."

Gunther let his eyebrows rise with a mock indignant look. "Hey, whoa now, buddy. That's not how Lily told it. You remember. About a year ago, shortly before I met her?"

Jim placed a hand on his waist and puffed out his chest. "What kind of bullshit is this?"

Gunther shrugged. "Now, why you gotta be that way? Lily told me all about it. She ran into you at the Cat's Cradle. You two snuck off to the back room and started playing pool. No one else was back there, so you locked the door and ended up on the pool table."

An angry scowl disfigured Jim's face, and Gunther slapped Jim's arm, then chuckled. "I tell ya, it's amazing some of the things a woman will tell her man, whether he wants to hear them or not. Really, Jim, taking advantage of a drunken woman."

"It wasn't like that. Jessie and I'd had a fight." Jim spoke with great care, spacing out his words. "Lily and I played a few rounds of pool. Drank a few beers. She kissed me once. But we stopped and that's it." Panic overcame his stone-like features. "What did she tell you?"

"She didn't tell me nothin', Jim. And she won't tell Jessie nothin', either. If you cooperate." Gunther waited for his words to sink in.

Jim grabbed Gunther by his shirtfront and pulled him close. "You're bluffing. You can't possibly think you can hold something that petty over me."

Gunther turned his head and took a swig of his beer, ignoring the grip on his shirt. He fought back the urge to swing his bottle and smash Jim's face. The power Gunther now held over Jim, the mental anguish he'd brought to the bigger man, counted for more than the momentary satisfaction any physical blow would bring.

Gunther flashed another humorless smile. "I'll tell you what I do know, Jim. My girl is pregnant. And she'll say or do just about anything if it will help her child. She's certainly willing to take nothing and make it sound like something." He reached down, pried open Jim's unresisting fingers, and straightened the rumpled shirt with exaggerated gentleness. "And I'll do anything, too. With or without your help."

Jim's shoulders slumped, and he sank onto the swing.

Gunther resumed his original seat on the opposite end. "Now then, would you care to reconsider my offer?"

The words came out of Jim as little more than a whisper. "What time?"

"Tomorrow. Two o'clock. Don't be late." Gunther fished into his pocket and pulled out a pair of keys. He handed them to Jim, who held them loosely in his fingers.

The front door swung open.

Jim's hand snapped shut around the keys. He spun around on his wife.

"Is everything al—"

"Jessie, get in the house!" Jim ordered.

Jessie jumped back.

Jim spoke in a softened voice. "Get in the house, honey, please. I won't be much longer."

Jim watched his wife turn and retreat through the door. Gunther sensed an aching agony burning through the man. "Damn you, Gunther. What do I have to do?"

"Well, that's the kind of fire we need."

Gunther leaned forward, closing the space between them. "Take your car to Darby's Drag Racing Arena."

Gunther relished watching the shocked scowl cross Jim's face. He nodded. "That's right. The old track where you used to drive every Wednesday night. Just like the glory days. Go to the east parking lot. It'll be deserted, but you'll find a yellow '76 Thunderbird with a souped-up engine. Park your car in the lot, but don't park it next to the T-bird. Put it five or six spaces away, any direction. Leave your car, take the Thunderbird. Got that?" Jim nodded.

"Pick up Crimley and me at his house. From there, we go

straight to the bank. You wait in the car while Crimley and I take care of business. If you play it cool, we'll get away without a hitch. Then, drive us back to the racetrack and we hop back into your car. From there, we catch the exit to I-65 and drive easy as you please ten minutes north to Michigan. You drop us off the first exit past the state line."

"Then what?"

Gunther shrugged. "That's our problem. Ya drive back home, kiss the wife, make up some bullshit story about a late meeting, I don't care. That's the deal. That's the plan. Agreed?"

Jim nodded. "Agreed, you bastard. But in the meantime, I don't need you hanging around bothering me or my wife. So get the hell out of here."

Gunther stood. "Not very neighborly of you, Jimbo. But under the circumstances, I guess I can live with it. I can live with a lot of things. I hope you can, too."

Gunther was satisfied all would go according to plan. He threw his head back and finished the last swallow of beer then stepped into the darkness, leaving Jim sitting on the porch, head still bowed, stewing in helpless anger.

Gunther'd already gotten some of his power back.

CHAPTER SEVEN

Later that week, Chip asked if I wanted to sit in on a *Dungeons & Dragons* game with his buddies. He had plans for a big Saturday night session. I'd known people in Broad Ripple who were into roleplaying games, but I'd never played one. I'd seen D&D mocked on *Buffy the Vampire Slayer* reruns. It involved lots of maps, papers, and oddly shaped dice.

I checked my calendar, twice. Both times, I had nothing else going on, so by the end of the week, I'd agreed to show up.

I hoofed the several blocks to his house, feeling safe enough in the late afternoon. Chip's house evoked the family-centric quality of the town; two stories, constructed of solid red brick with white panel highlights, a design that could have been from the 1930s, the 1990s, or any era in between.

The white picket fence surrounding the home (actually painted white and made of pickets, the cliché comes from *somewhere*) had seen better days. Even in the coming darkness, I could make out many spots where the worn wood shone through the pale coating.

The wooden planks surrounded a lush green lawn and a cobblestone walkway that seemed mandatory in this town, even in our own yard.

I stepped onto the roomy, bare porch, once painted a dark green but now faded and sun-bleached, and knocked on the door.

Chip answered, a wide grin appearing on his face the moment he saw me.

I returned the smile.

"You're here!" he exclaimed.

"Uh, yeah, I sort of promised I would be."

We stood looking at each other in comical silence until he snapped out of his daze to step away from the door. "Sorry. Please, come in."

A tiny foyer led directly to a coat closet. Beyond, carpeted stairs rose up to a loft. From my vantage, I could make out a desk and computer system set up to look out over the railing. A large oak bookcase dominated the far wall.

Beyond the stairs, we stepped into the unimpressive glory of the living room. All the essential ingredients; couch, chair, and coffee table, with off-white floors and walls tastefully, if not remarkably, decorated in the modern standards of blasé suburbia.

I lingered in the room, taking longer than necessary to check out the minimal surroundings. Something bothered me, something just on the wrong side of obvious, but I couldn't put my finger on it.

A handful of photos hung on the wall over the couch.

A larger portrait showed Chip at age ten or so. A blonde woman in her mid-thirties embraced him. Her glistening brown eyes matched the contented smile on her clear face. Behind them stood a large, hulking monster of a man wearing a blue suit. He grinned into the camera. Large dark curls topped his head, and he draped beefy hands across the both of them. The flash of the bulb added a shine to his clean-cut features and reflected the only hint of light in his dark eyes.

I shuddered and turned away from the photo, repressing sudden anxiety.

A small group sat in the connecting dining room. A group of fellow Perionne High School peers. Colleagues.

All wearing glasses, staring at me in hushed expectation.

Six guys.

Six geeks. And me.

Had Joey seen me, he would have kicked my ass on the spot.

One overweight, jolly guy, introducing himself as Phil Jenson, stood up from the head of the table and extended a beefy hand. He pumped my hand vigorously, making my entire body shake.

"You're the girl who kicked the shit out of Clinty! I don't know whether to shake your hand or bow down and worship you."

"Apparently, you're shaking my hand, but feel free to bow down later," I quipped.

A number of nervous chortles erupted all around the table.

I grinned and felt myself flush. How could I not feel honored at such adoration?

Another guy, this one much skinnier and with a more confident air toward the opposite sex, stepped forward and pulled an empty chair out, motioning me to sit.

I dropped down into the proffered seat, grinning at everyone watching me.

Chip presented me with a piece of paper, my "character sheet." He'd created the character for me that afternoon, a "pretty basic" one since I'd never played the game before. I looked the sheet over. Columns of numbers and strange abbreviations.

Chip explained the character was a "tenth level barbarian woman with a big sword and no magical powers." My job: use the big sword on the bad guys, strictly in the realm of the imagination, of course. Sounded easy enough.

Most of the group played magic users, characters requiring a more intricate understanding of the game, so my job was to make up the balance in combat situations.

Though I often floundered, someone would always volunteer information, explain a statistic, hand me an odd-shaped die to roll. As a unit, the group embraced me, eager to make me one of their own. Quite a difference from how I'd been treated since I'd arrived in town.

Before long, I absorbed myself in the *Lord of the Rings*-type aspect of the adventure.

An hour into the game, I laid eyes on Dad Farren in the flesh. Chip's dad would have intimidated me with the sheer massiveness of his bulk, even if I *hadn't* been sitting when he entered the room. Dressed in a red plaid button-down shirt, his face now covered in graying dark whiskers, he towered over everyone.

In all fairness, he spoke with refined quietness and gripped my tiny hand in his massive one with practiced gentleness. In spite of this, a shiver ran through my spine. I expected him to growl any moment, and clear the table of books and maps with one swoop of his massive arm. He kept calling his son "Eugene" but, with a name like "Fiona", I wasn't about to comment. He checked on us occasionally, bringing sodas and snacks, but otherwise leaving us alone as he *thump-thump-thumped* up the stairs, presumably to work at his desk up in the loft.

He chatted with us briefly during one break. I learned he provided tech support for a fairly large accounting firm, and that his firm had discussed taking on Shaefer and Gerrold. My mom's office wanted someone local to handle their payroll, provide accounting software, and oversee their mainframe. Mr. Farren commented on Mom's professionalism.

I swallowed a response, not inclined to engage a man who, for whatever reason, made my "Spidey-Sense" tingle.

As we joked and played, hours disappeared. Chip "dungeon mastered," narrating the action and refereeing battles. Working as a team, we tried to solve Chip's puzzles and "win" the adventures, but, as the night wore on, we grew progressively slap-happy. My boundaries dropped, and I turned flirtatious, character-to-character, with Phil.

I, Daria, the barbarian warrior from Corinthos, stumbled upon a magic crystal embedded in one of the dungeon walls. Being the only person strong enough to pry it from the wall, I claimed ownership of the crystal. So I carried around a magical charm, dangling on a chain between ample bosoms that bore no resemblance to the real me. I carried in my possession a mysterious object that did "gods-knew-what," a problematic situation inviting trouble.

Phil played a powerful sorcerer who could identify the crystal for me. I asked for his help, putting an intimidating inflection to Daria's words.

Phil huffed in a deep character voice. "Why should I, Magtog the Great, help a barbarian wench the likes of you?" He waved his arms with theatrical flair. "I, Magtog, who can turn sand into diamonds, bring forth cleansed water from the tar pits, and heal all my wounds with but a single touch. What have you to barter with that is of any interest to my greatness?"

My eyes locked on his and I responded with utter seriousness. "Tell me the secrets of the crystal, and I'll be your sex slave for the night."

The entire room erupted in laughter.

Phil flushed red from forehead to neck, broke eye contact, and let his head drop toward the table into his forearm. But he laughed the whole time.

I cracked up myself, and, soon, we were all wiping tears from our eyes.

Chip stared at me, mouth hanging open, aghast.

I winked at Chip, then watched Phil struggle to return to character as the high and mighty Magtog.

"Uh...I, Magtog the Great, will consider your offer." A moment later, he said, "It's a deal."

Chip shrugged. "Great." Then a twinkle in his eye hinted that an amusing idea occurred to him.

"Magtog" recovered some of his previous bluster. "But I'll only tell you what you want to know if I've had a good time."

I quickly referenced my character sheet. "Listen here, wizard. I have a dexterity of sixty-five and a strength of seventy-three. I think you'll find me adequate. The only real question is, can your wand measure up?"

A frown fell over Phil's puffy features. "Well, my dexterity is low, because, you see, when you're a wizard, you generally don't need—"

Chip interrupted. "Magtog, roll your dexterity."

Phil threw the odd-sided dice across the map, squinting at the result. "Uh, I failed."

"Okay," Chip said. He turned and addressed me, a sheepish grin spread across his face. "Daria, at about three in the morning, Magtog is asleep, snoring, and uh, finished, passed out on this sleeping gear. No matter what you do, you can't revive him."

"Ah. So, uh, how am I?"

Chip blushed but kept a straight face. "How bad was your roll, Phil?"

Phil shook his head. "Pretty bad."

I sighed. "'Magtog the Great,' indeed!"

The group broke out into hysterics.

Chip pointed at Phil. "Magtog, for the next twenty-four hours, you're unable to cast a spell over level three."

"Level three? But I'm a tenth level..." He stopped, shrugged, and grinned. "Oh, hell. It was worth it. Let's find something I *can* do right and identify that crystal." Phil rolled the dice again.

I reached for a potato chip. "Daria stands up and yells, 'This one's done. Bring me another!'" I batted my eyelashes, yes, batted my eyelashes, at the guys staring back at me.

I sighed and grinned. Boys!

The game broke up late in the evening. With the bad guys slain and the good guys counting the leftover treasures, we moved as a group into Chip's living room. He took a moment to say goodbye to a couple members of the gang.

I still had troubles with names, opting to wave and offer a "see you later" to their retreating forms. To my surprise, I'd had a lot of fun and didn't want it to end.

Phil had driven his own car and intended to hang out for a bit. He offered to drive me home if I wanted to stay later, and I happily accepted.

The rest of us followed Chip up the wooden stairs, *clomp-clomp-clomp*-ing the entire time, through the roomy loft. As we passed, Mr. Farren grunted, his face magnetized to the monitor.

Like father, like son.

Chip led us down the hall and into his tiny bedroom. Somehow, the four of us who remained all packed onto his double bed, hip to hip to hip to hip. Chip introduced me to his pride and joy, "My own hand-built dual-core, dual processor system with two gigs of memory, one terabyte of hard drive space in a raid configuration, a PCIe video card, one physics card and a sweet twenty-four-inch

LCD widescreen flat panel monitor." I took that to mean state-of-the-art. I nodded, hoping I looked appropriately impressed.

This prompted him to continue. "I compile my own Linux kernel, too, but run Windows for the games." I still had no idea what he was talking about, but he sure *meant* it.

The computer came to life with the shift of his mouse. He started off showing a couple of sci-fi movie trailers to Phil and couple of others who hadn't seen them yet. While the trailer ran, he opened a second window, fiddling with a DOS screen, and explaining to me how he and Phil had made it a practice to hack into local company databases for kicks. Not actually monkeying with the data, just getting in and out. I shrugged. Everyone needed to rebel.

Don't I know it?

Chip had just conquered a watershed goal, hacking into the First Bank of Perionne, and accessing the current balances of several friends and relatives.

Cool. Now we're talking. "So," I teased, "why's a nice kid like you busting into bank records?"

He shrugged, but red crept into his cheeks. "I wanted the challenge."

I watched over his shoulder as he called up a sci-fi blog and posted a message about some supposed nonsensical moments in the *Battlestar Galactica* finale, a thread of perplexed emails apparently extending back more than a year. I shuddered. As the nerdiness ramped up, I knew I'd have to excuse myself.

Phil, by no means a tiny guy, also had no sense of personal space. Neither did the red-haired geek on the other side of me. Arms and shoulders brushed innocuously against my chest. The bed provided convenient close quarters for hard-up guys copping an incidental grope. I gave Phil, at least, the benefit of the doubt. I liked the guy. He, at least, couldn't help his considerable bulk.

Chip worked, poised over his keyboard, I saw a glint in his eyes. I sensed he occupied a time and space where he truly belonged.

"And now," he said, "let me show you my webpage." The

browser window dissolved to his personal page. He rose and waved a hand for me to sit.

"I don't want to." I'd dabbled with creating my own page a couple of years ago. Low-res photo, bio paragraph. A webpage struck me as too much effort for too little result, and mine suffered the same case of terminal boredom as most of the others. Besides, Facebook was much easier.

"It's easy," he insisted. "You know how to web browse, right?"

I stepped forward and yanked the mouse from his hand.

"Let me drive, smart ass." I squatted into the chair.

The home page declared,

The Ghost of Gunther Webpage

Beneath the text was a highly detailed rendering of a wraithlike figure waving a bloody hook for one hand. I noted a scanned photograph of Gunther Stalt, identical to the one in my Xeroxed article. The text read:

———

Webpage created by Chip Farren. <u>Click Here</u> to leave me an email!
*** <u>Click Here</u> to Join the Ghost of Gunther Discussion Group!*
*** <u>Click Here</u> to View the Article Archive!*

———

On the one hand, Chip's research could prove handy for the big test in Hap's class next week. On the other…"Damn, man," I said. "You really *are* obsessed."

Chip answered, "Actually, Blue, you'd be surprised. I have thirteen hundred people participating in the discussion group."

In a town of six thousand. Clearly, a significant demographic shared this insanity.

Phil chuckled. "Boy, *is* he obsessed. That's the word for it." He leaned forward, a bed spring squeaking in protest. "He had me up 'til three in the morning last month configuring the chat site."

The conversation quickly digressed into computer hard drives and blips per second and the latest micro processing speed-zoids, or something. The four geeks lost me pretty quick, and the warmth of the combined bodies became oppressive. Rude or not, I had to get out. Besides, the little geeks had gotten lost in the world of *Dr. Who* and technology. It would be some time before they even noticed I'd slipped away.

————

LEANING against the stair railing overlooking the living room, I stood in somber thought, enjoying the solitude. Ambient light from the small kitchen lit the ground floor.

The solidity of the real-wood floors made for a comfortable place. Still, something didn't set right with me. I remembered puzzling over it earlier. The walls lacked significant décor, save a couple of small family pictures. The furniture in the living room consisted of a piecemeal arrangement. Up in the loft, a computer on a fancy redwood desk near a large bookcase of mismatched oak.

A large shadow crossed through the open doorway to the pantry. A silhouette blocked most of the light from the kitchen, and I found myself standing in almost complete darkness.

I heard a creak.

A chill ran up my spine, and I knew without looking that Chip's father had stepped through swinging doors and into the living room. I suppressed the shiver.

His smile was friendly enough, and he waved his thick, beefy hand my direction before retreating back to the kitchen.

I swallowed, trying to shake off my trepidation. Chip's dad couldn't help his imposing presence. Naturally, his bulk intimidated me, but I needed to get past this issue. I gathered my courage. They say the best way to conquer a fear was to face it. At least, that's what I told myself as I clomped down the wooden stairs.

Walking through swinging doors, I saw Chip's father sitting at the breakfast bar, pouring a fresh Sprite for me. I thanked the courtesy gods that he didn't pour yet another Mountain Dew. Like I wouldn't be bouncing off the walls enough. I'd vowed hours ago to swear off that green piss for another month, at least.

He motioned to the barstool near him. "I kinda suspected you were going to take a break from all that."

"Uh...yeah, I suppose." I hadn't considered a conversation with Chip's dad a preferred choice, but, until Phil remembered he'd promised to take me home, I pretty much had nothing better to do.

I took a deep breath and made eye contact, determined to break down the barriers for Chip's sake, if not my own.

Mr. Farren looked to be in his late forties. The dark hair atop his head showed some gray at the temples and maintained the same tight curls I'd seen in the earlier portrait.

He folded his arms across the table. "My son gets to talking about computers, and, to me, it's another language. And I'm no dummy when it comes to computers, either." He grinned, showing large, white, even teeth.

I nodded, unable to think of a reply in the deadening silence. I shifted on the stool, trying to ignore his open scrutiny. That's when I noticed the annoying, rhythmic thump from my own fingers drumming against the tabletop. "Sorry." I halted the drumbeat and resorted to watching bubbles float through the ice of my Sprite glass.

As if picking up the thread of an old topic, Mr. Farren said, "You know, your hair is quite something."

I shrugged. "Actually, it's considered retro in Indy. Very eighties. Not a bad thing, just not exactly edgy, either. It's all black leather and piercing these days. But I prefer the color."

He grunted and sipped from his own Sprite. "I bet you have to take a lot of shit for it, don't you? Take my wife, God rest her soul." His eyes traveled upward for a brief moment.

"If you were her daughter, she wouldn't allow it. You know how it is. She was born and raised here in this town. Everyone cut from the same cookie-cutter mold." Mr. Farren shook his head. "You're lucky your mother allows you to find your own way."

Keeping my voice neutral, I answered, "I appreciate what you're saying." He knew nothing about me, *or* my situation, but, in his own way, I sensed he was trying to reach out.

Then the missing piece slipped into place. In my head, I could practically hear a "clicking" sound. Mrs. Farren had died. She wasn't at a friend's, or staying with family, and they weren't separated. She no longer inhabited the house.

The barrenness, the haphazard furniture layout, the pure functionality, suddenly made sense. No plants, no floral patterns, no candles, no *softness*; no trace of a woman's touch. All her decorative touches had probably turned worn and tattered over time, or broken, or stored away. Piece by piece, Chip and his father had removed almost all memory of what she'd brought to the home, except a single picture hung in memoriam. What remained were the awkward traces of a single Dad, clueless to decorum, doing his best to provide a home for his only son.

A profound sadness fell over me.

Mr. Farren spoke in a solemn tone. "Years ago, I guess it's been almost eight years now, Chip wanted his own computer. Of course, he had no way to afford one, and using mine didn't give him the hours he wanted to explore programming to the extent he needed to, even then."

Mr. Farren shrugged. "What could he do? He was only ten, but he pleaded and begged. He collected aluminum cans, glass, he mowed yards, raked leaves, anything to raise the money. After three months, he presented me with $150 in change." He chuckled at the memory and shrugged his shoulders.

"He knew what he wanted, even when he had no way of reaching his goal. So I bought it for him. What else could I do?"

When I didn't volunteer a response, he shoved on. "I suppose I could've refused him. He'd be just like most of the people in this town, but instead I think he's unique. Know what I mean?"

I grinned back. "I suppose I do."

"See, my son, he admires you very much. For the most part, he just lets people pass by. But you caught his attention right away. He could sense something different. So much so he told me about it. He's also told me a few things about what happened to you at school. With the teacher and the fight and all. For what it's worth, I think it's a bunch of shit."

I kept my stone-neutral expression, but, inside, my head spun. After the grief from my mother, the outrageous hatred from Mr. Robbins, I didn't know how to respond to an adult, a *parent*, jumping to my defense.

He continued, "It's a sad fact, though, that in this town, you're going to get that sort of treatment all the time." He sighed and shook his head. His voice welled with emotion. "A lot of people here, they'll keep at you and try to knock you down until you get *proper*; 'til you cut your hair, put on a decent skirt and show up to the church pitch-in with your side dish."

He took another gulp from his drink. I sensed I'd better not interrupt. "This town doesn't change for nothin'. They keep at you and at you, so that even five years from now you'll still be getting an earful."

I wanted to comment about the earful I was getting now but instead said, "I have no intention of being around here in five years."

Mr. Farren grinned, as if we'd made some sort of connection. "When Chip graduates, he's getting out of here. I'll send him away to college. Doesn't really matter which one. There's plenty of great engineering schools to choose from in Indiana. I just want him get clear of this place and not look back."

I shifted in my chair while he rambled on. "I don't want to see somebody who thinks a little differently change just to please the town. You do that, you've been beaten in any way that counts."

Yes! I wanted to shout, dance, and high-five the old guy.

I did none of those things. The whole thing still creeped me out. I couldn't decide if my feelings originated from Mr. Farren himself, or just the idea of talking to a *grown-up* who understood my problem.

But then again, what did I know about how *caring* parents might feel? Especially a dad?

The now-empty glass slipped from my hand, tipping onto the table. Ice cubes slid across the surface. I fumbled with the cubes and dropped them back into the glass. I stood and wiped my hands on my blue jeans. I never returned his gaze, which I felt penetrating into me. "I've gotta check on the guys upstairs."

"Sure, go on."

I walked through the doors into the darkness.

I sat on the couch in the living room by myself. Mr. Farren must have sensed that I wanted to be alone because he didn't follow me. I heard him puttering around for several minutes until a door opened upstairs, and Chip's friends descended to the foyer.

Strange, for the first time, my blue hair and jewelry struck me as stupid and shallow because an adult expressed approval. Baffling.

CHAPTER NINE

But not nearly as baffling as when I arrived at school Monday morning.

I stepped into a room full of chatter, the class buzzing with the conspiratorial pitch of fresh gossip. The entire class stood or sat around one student.

Clinty.

My apprehension kicked to high. Clinty no longer commanded just through the power of intimidation. This time, for once and truly, he held the people around him captivated with his every word. The look of joy on his face spoke volumes.

I took my usual seat in the front row, pretending indifference, but my ears all but jumped off my head to catch every word.

"The cops paid a visit to Goody-two-shoes Robbins over the weekend," Clinty gloated. "Seems he won't be teaching the rest of the semester, at least."

I turned in my chair to face him. As much as I hated to address Clinty directly, this was too important. "What did he do?"

Clinty glared, but answered, anyway. He, too, must have decided the news of a faculty member's downfall warranted a temporary cease of hostilities. "Looks like Mr. Robbins fled Cincinnati five years ago to dodge multiple DUI charges. Took this long, but some-body finally recognized him. Now, he's suspended."

I sighed. "Suspended. Why are they keeping him at all?"

A small girl, seated toward the front but on the other end of the room, piped up. She wore her blond hair in a pair of short-cropped pigtails that bobbed when she spoke. "The school can't fire him. At least not yet. Not until after a trial." Her pigtails wiggled with the nodding of her head. "Mr. Robbins is saying he's innocent. So they can't fire him until he's found guilty. But from what I hear, the description in the police report is an exact match. They say he ran over a little kid."

After dropping this bomb, she looked down at her desk, looking properly mortified.

"That's not what I heard," Clinty chimed back in. "I heard he drove over his grandmama. Ran her over dead."

One of Clinty's toadies added to the confusion. "I thought he just skipped town. That's why they can't fire him yet."

"Doesn't matter," the pigtailed girl insisted. "The suspension's just the beginning. He's through here. And good riddance."

At this point, Hap called us to attention.

My head spun at the news.

Mr. Robbins; arrested, suspended from teaching. Had my hope-less predicament taken a sudden turn for the better? Had I somehow managed to dodge a bullet fired straight at my head?

And the story made so much sense. Given all the unjustified anger he'd displayed toward me, it only figured he'd have other skeletons in his closet.

———

I SAUNTERED into my late morning senior English class to see a tall, balding man occupying Mr. Robbins' chair. Probably in his late forties, his large Coke-bottle glasses made him appear older.

The bell rang, and he scowled at us. "When the bell rings, class, we open our books and close our mouths."

The new teacher's voice droned loudly over the classroom, in sharp contrast to his nerdy, studious appearance. The buzz in the room quieted.

The teacher rose to his full height, a thin, but authoritative, presence.

"As many of you who have taken my class before may know, I'm Mr. Tyers from senior composition. I've been asked to fill in for Mr. Robbins, who has chosen to take a sudden leave of absence for the rest of the semester."

I chuckled and then choked as multiple sets of eyes glared at me. Embarrassed, I stared down at my desk.

For a moment, I wondered if I'd do any better with Mr. Tyers than the first time around with Mr. Robbins.

As class continued, I decided I at least had a shot. Mr. Tyers balanced a stern disposition with clear instructions on his expectations. He wanted homework turned in on time with no excuses. Book chapters read with no excuses. Tests passed with no excuses. Writing assignments turned in following the proper format, as shown in our textbooks. Did I mention no excuses?

By the end of class, I decided I had nothing to lose by approaching him. I stayed behind after the last student shuffled out the door.

Sitting behind Mr. Robbins' desk, he eyed me with practiced patience, folding his hands and placing them on the paper-strewn surface.

"Can I help you with something, miss?"

"Shaefer," I started. I held out the stack of my crumpled assignments I'd been carrying around in my backpack. "Fiona Shaefer."

"Ah, yes, Miss Shaefer. I noticed your name in the grade book. I'm afraid it's the standout of the bunch."

"Yeah. Well, I'm sure it is. Look, Mr. Tyers. Can I be direct?"

"Please."

"I know this is an unusual request, but Mr. Robbins' situation is an unusual one as well."

"You shouldn't believe everything you hear, Miss Shaefer," Tyers interrupted.

I paused while he returned an unreadable stare.

I took a deep breath and tried again. "Fair enough. But the rumors I've heard sort of confirm my suspicions."

I placed the papers on the desktop before him. "I'm not demanding that you change my grades. But here're my assignments. Just look them over again. I think Robbins may have had a personal issue. With me."

He raised his eyebrows.

I hurried on. "I don't believe my work is as bad as the grades would make you think."

He lifted the first page, "'American Idol Finalist,'" grunted, shook his head, and then placed the paper down.

I thought I detected a crack in his stone-like façade, perhaps the slightest hint of a smile.

Or I could have imagined it.

He lifted the entire stack of papers in one hand and opened a side desk drawer with the other then dropped my work down into it.

He refolded his hands across the top of the desk while meeting my gaze with studied indifference. "I think, given the circumstances of Mr. Robbins' sudden departure, it might be worth giving your work a second reading for a fresh perspective."

"Thank you, sir." I used my most respectful voice. I knew my only chance of winning him over was to play the innocent victim angle to the hilt.

And why not? I am *an innocent victim.*

I stepped toward the door.

"One thing, Miss Shaefer." I paused in mid-step, turning my head toward him, trying not to look too hopeful.

He continued, "I want you to know that, if I do find Mr. Robbins graded your material with clear prejudice, I will not hesitate to bring this matter to the attention of the school board. I'll probably only end up speeding up a process that is already underway."

Keeping my face as neutral as I could, I nodded and left the room.

The moment the door shut behind me, I let out a whoop of triumph probably heard the full length of the corridor. Heads turned, but I didn't care.

I tossed my backpack over my shoulder and raced down the hall, dodging anyone in my way.

Wait until I tell Chip.

————

MUMBLING AROUND CHEWED CRUST, I exclaimed, "It's chust too goo to be twue!" I paused to swallow my bite and washed it down with more milk.

Chip listened in patient nonchalance as I talked between mouthfuls, relaying all my lucky breaks since the day began.

Pizza practically flew into my mouth. For the last several days, I'd eaten almost nothing, my stomach too upset to really deal with food. Today, I'd hopped into the cafeteria line and ordered doubles of everything. Even before Chip approached what had become "our" table, I'd been wolfing down the largest bites I could handle.

I paused to wipe my face with a napkin and take a deep breath. I was all smiles. "I can't believe Mr. Robbins could be so holier-than-thou when he was dodging the cops. Incredible."

Chip studied his nails as he answered. "You're right about one thing. It *is* too good to be true."

Alarm flushed through me, and I dropped the fry I'd been holding into its little divider. "What do you mean? What have you heard?"

No longer able to keep his poker face, Chip grinned. "Let's just say a certain report was faxed to the Perionne Police Station over the weekend. And, although it was electronically dated and time-stamped Cincinnati, it didn't technically come from there. And for the record, it was about a man who ran out on his parole for multiple DUIs. That's all. No hit-and-run, no one killed at any accident scene."

He rolled his eyes. "Just some shmoe fleeing house arrest. The man they're really looking for is about a foot shorter than Mr. Robbins, and the hair color is all wrong." Chip frowned, staring into space at an imaginary document floating before his eyes. "Otherwise, the description's pretty close."

Is he saying what I think he's saying? I dropped the pizza and wiped my hands, though my eyes locked with his. "What are you talking about? Stop being so coy and explain."

Chip shrugged, though he squirmed a bit under my command. "I predict Mr. Robbins will fight this. He'll hire an attorney, who will trace the fax back to the original file. They'll find these discrepancies, sooner or later. Probably sooner. But not before the gossip has ruined him."

His story picked up steam, and he leaned forward.

"Meanwhile, the police will wonder who mistyped the information. They'll want to make an example of somebody, so they'll check the original send file and see the information was entered accurately, and arrived correctly, everywhere else."

Chip took a casual sip of milk before continuing. "What they won't know is that someone intercepted the police fax before it printed off at the Perionne precinct. In fact, someone intercepted *all* the reports last week and read over them, waiting for something to come through that could be used. Once the DUI was found, that same someone changed certain details and facts, and then sent the revised report on to the Perionne Police Station."

He stabbed a fork at his own pizza, his face calm, except for the trace of a smirk in the corner of his mouth.

I couldn't speak. It all made sense. At no time did I doubt the truth of what he said. I'd been too lucky for this to be dumb coincidence. While I believed in poetic justice, did it ever really arrive so perfectly positioned, and so timely, without a little outside prodding?

Chip had changed a police report to get back at Robbins.

My mind reeled as Chip continued his narrative. "Those details are moot, though. Robbins'll never come back to Perionne High School. Or if he does, Tyers will be after him for what he did to your English papers."

I should have known. I should have guessed.

"Shit!" The curse hiccupped out of me, both a whisper and a scream. "Did you...Chip, you hacked into the police station?"

As if giving a lecture, Chip's voice took on a droning quality. "It's simple enough. I just had to find the backdoor program and key it to—"

"I don't give a shit about that. You didn't think this out. What do you think will happen if the police find out about you?" For the first time, it hit me that I shouldn't be speaking these things aloud.

I drew close to him, hissing between my teeth. "Do you know what they do to people who hack government institutions? Ever since 9-1-1, the feds take a *particularly* dim view of this sort of thing."

"You didn't seem so concerned when I took an unauthorized tour of the bank files."

"That's different. You didn't *do* anything to those files."

Chip shrugged. "Doesn't matter. No one will ever know."

I clenched my fists to keep my hands from shaking. "Famous last words, Dillinger! You think Mr. Robbins can't figure out who could have done this? You think half the school hasn't noticed you, and Phil, and me, all hanging out together? You want to do me a favor? Don't be a criminal. You don't think like one."

His face betrayed hurt. "No, really, Blue, it was nothing. Just your entire future."

The momentum dropped out of my lecture, as if I'd driven over an ice patch in the middle of July. I flushed at the realization that my friend, my dear, dear friend, knew the stakes, but proceeded, anyway. To save my ass. To him, that victory made it worth the risk.

Chip leaned close, eyes flashing, his voice barely a whisper. "First of all, I don't *care* if he knows or not. His word won't be worth shit in a couple of days. He could tell the police the honest truth, if he's able to figure it out, and the locals won't give him the time of day. Don't give people too much credit, Blue. They're lazy, and they accept the obvious explanation." Chip's voice cracked with passion.

"Why?" I had to know. "You don't do this all the time...for other people?"

Again, he looked stung. "Because I can't stand the thought of anyone getting away with an attitude like his. It's wrong, whether it happens to you, or Clinty, or anyone. I had a chance to stop him, so I did."

I could hardly talk. "You could get in a whole lot of trouble if you get caught."

He shrugged. "I won't get caught. Besides, I couldn't let you down again."

"Thank you." Overwhelmed, I stared down at my tray full of cold lunch, trying to collect myself.

I picked up a cold fry and tossed it in my mouth, rolling my eyes and shaking my head. "Listen to me. Preaching to you about breaking the law. I've already been in this town too long."

CHAPTER TEN

Jim wiped the sweat from his brow with the back of his hand. How had he gotten into this? Their yellow Thunderbird crept along Main Street. He pulled the car next to the curb in front of the First National Bank of Perionne. He almost kept driving.

The bank stood in sharp contrast to the archaic structures on each side, a brick frame with modern curved corners. Jim looked around. The street shone with unseasonal sunny sharpness, bringing glorious warmth to the pedestrians bustling about their mid-morning activities, making the idea of stealth pretty much moot.

Gunther and Crimley looked ready to go, hooded and gloved, prepared to spring into action.

Jim tensed behind the steering wheel, trying to ignore the lump in his throat. His entire future depended on whether or not these maniacs were clever enough to pull this heist off without getting caught. He didn't like the odds.

He craned his neck to take in Gunther's panting form in the back seat before settling his gaze upon Crimley, who sat up front. "Don't screw anything up," he growled before pulling the blue knitted ski mask over his face. "If the cops come chasing me, I'm pulling over. I'm not dying in a car wreck."

Gunther grunted, shoving a pistol handle-first over the passenger seat to Crimley. Gunther's breath sounded sharp and fast in the confinement of the car. "Dammit. Can't load this. Put the cartridge in for me."

Crimley's eyes, the only part of his face peering out through the slot of the mask, rolled in exasperation. He cocked his shotgun and flipped the safety on before laying it across his lap.

"Hey. That thing's pointed at me!" Jim said.

"Safety's on. Hold your horses while I take care of Gimpy's pistol. Ain't nothin' gonna happen for five seconds." Working around the confines of his gloves, Crimley grabbed a loaded cartridge from the glove box and snapped it into the pistol.

Jim shut his mouth, but kept a wary eye on the gun.

Crimley reached back and shoved the pistol into Gunther's eager hand. "There ya go. The one-handed special. Just point and shoot."

Gunther slid the pistol into the right pocket of his tattered jean jacket. "You ready, Crimley?"

"All set. Let's do it. Remember, no one gets killed."

In unison, Crimley and Gunther popped open the car doors and sprinted toward the bank's glass double doors.

Jim lowered his forehead to the steering wheel, fighting back stark terror. He could do nothing now, but wait.

———

CRIMLEY AND GUNTHER burst into the lobby before the small group of people had a chance to react.

Crimley ran a beeline for the front counter.

Gunther held back, waving his pistol at six customers cordoned in the roped-off queue. "Everyone on the ground! Now!"

The women screamed, dropping paperwork, and men stared with their mouths hanging open.

As Gunther danced around them like a tribal wild man, the customers fell over themselves to drop prone on the floor.

Crimley sprinted through the swinging side door partition that led back to the teller's area. He barely had a moment to recognize the blue of a uniformed guard across the lobby before the figure blurred into motion. With practiced ease, Crimley locked in a critical shot and then dropped his aim low.

He fired; the air crackled.

Red flesh tore from the guard's thigh. He stumbled, teetering off balance and falling face-first on the floor, the gun flying from his hand and skittering across the marble tile.

A scream erupted from one of the women lying on the floor.

Crimley kept the shotgun trained on the bleeding man standing between him and the row of tellers.

From under the wounded man, a puddle of blood spread, slowly creeping across the marble floor.

Gunther's yell cut through the room, trying to overpower the shrill screams of the hysterical customers. "Don't anyone fuckin' move! No heroes. You hear me? I said don't move. Lady, shut up!"

Crimley ignored his partner, now pointing his gun at the first teller. "You. Open your drawer. Quickly. Move it."

Crimley watched, eagle-eyed, as the teller's shaking hands struggled with a ring of keys. His gaze fell upon an empty money sack in the storage space beneath her station. "Stop. Reach down. Grab that sack. Not too fast."

Behind him, Crimley heard Gunther's screaming voice. "Dammit, lady, I told you to shut up!"

Crimley risked a glance toward the lobby. He saw Gunther bent over the queue, waving his gun at the tearful older woman.

He glimpsed the combat-crazed gleam in Gunther's eyes and saw a man who had been pushed too far, like a predator animal. Crimley sensed fear and imminent death in the air. He needed to take control of the situation.

Crimley almost yelled Gunther's name but caught himself. "Hey! Calm down. Just watch them. We've got it under control."

"She'd better shut up, or she gets it." Gunther stepped over the rope and stood over the sprawled woman, who still whimpered.

Crimley heard a sudden thump that brought his attention to the teller next to him. In a shaking panic, she'd dropped the bag, and now stood watching him, wringing her hands.

"Hey! Pick up the sack."

The teller leaned over and gripped the satchel.

"Open it up. Let's see the inside. Looks good. Now, open your drawer and put the money in. Quickly!" He shouted. "Hurry the hell up!"

The teller yanked her drawer open.

"Just the loose money. No bound cash. I'm not stupid. I know about marked money. So don't dig too deep."

The teller shoved loose cash into the bag by the handful.

"That's good. Now, walk to the next one."

The woman gripped the satchel with both hands, trying to control her shaking fingers. She crab-shuffled to the next station.

"Open it."

"I...I can't. I don't have the keys." Her eyes closed, and her voice took on a high, whining beg. "Please don't shoot me."

Crimley didn't like her answer. "Don't fuck with me. Who can open it?"

An older blonde woman with graying streaks in her hair stepped forward from the gathered group of tellers in the middle of the room, approaching slowly, arms raised over her head, a ring of keys hooked over her index finger.

Crimley trained the gun on the approaching woman.

Her blue-eyed gaze remained steady. "I'm the manager." She spoke in an even tone. "I'm holding the keys to all the drawers. I'll get the money for you." Her voice continued in calm conviction as she approached the swinging door, even though Crimley's gun, pointed straight at her head, never wavered.

Crimley gathered this was not her first experience with a bank robbery. *Even better. The last thing I need is some teenage moron freaking out on me.* He prodded the young girl next to him with the end of his shotgun. "Give your boss the money bag, then get on the floor. Quickly!"

"Are they fucking with you?" Gunther called.

The manager reached out to unlock the drawer, but her hands shook, and the key ring fell.

"Pick it up!" Crimley's voice echoed through the bank.

"I knew it!" Gunther called. "We need to show these fuckers we mean business."

A shot shattered the air; a woman's hysteria cut off in mid-cry.

Crimley's blood turned to ice.

He whirled to face the lobby, no longer concerned about the money bag. He saw a woman pinned under Gunther's feet, a pool of blood forming under her body. "Damn you, Gunther! You killed her."

"Goddam right." Grinning madly, Gunther pointed his gun at a young man in a three-piece business suit. The man lay face down, eyes squeezed shut, mumbling to himself.

Gunther called out, "They fuck with you anymore, this one gets it next."

Crimley gawked at the mad scene before him, unable to move for several precious seconds. He stared at the pool of the woman's blood flowing across the marble floor.

My fault, puttin' my lot in with that psychopath. Damn it all.

Then, clarity returned, and Crimley leveled the shotgun at the manager with renewed purpose. Now wasn't the time to dwell on what couldn't be undone.

"Pick up the keys! Now!"

The manager grabbed the keys, but her hands trembled too much to work them.

"Give 'em to me!" He snatched the key ring from her and motioned her aside.

Gunther continued to scream at the prone, terrified young man on the floor. "Goddamn right I shot her! I'll shoot all of you if you don't shut up!"

Crimley unlocked the drawer and pulled up a large stack of loose money. He called out into the lobby. "Be cool! I've got it!"

While Crimley worked, Gunther's voice continued to reach him.

"You wanna' fuck with somebody? How about this?" A second shot rang out.

Crimley swore, realizing too late the unforgivable part he'd played in setting a crazed maniac loose on innocent victims, but his hands never stopped manipulating a third drawer. He shoved a large pile of money into the bag.

Gunther's voice reached Crimley as he sealed up the bag. "Guy kept mumbling and praying, like God could stop a bullet or something. I guess it didn't work." Gunther's evil cackle resonated through the building.

All Crimley could think about was getting Gunther out as fast as possible.

Gunther continued to taunt. "Anyone else wanna start something?"

The bag bulged. Crimley had planned to empty all of the drawers and the vault. No way to do that now. "We're getting the hell out of here."

"What? Why? We're not done."

"Yes, we are. We've got plenty." Crimley jogged through the swinging partition. "Let's move! Go! Now!"

They bolted through the doors, across the short cement path, and into the waiting car. The Thunderbird's tires squealed, and the car sped down the road.

———

JIM STEERED with one hand and pulled his mask off with the other. He took a sharp turn on Main Street while releasing a hissing breath. They had to go another half a mile to the town limits, where they could access the dirt roads.

Crimley tore off his mask and twisted his body to scream at the man behind him. "Goddamn it, Gunther! You shot two people! You killed them!"

"Hold on! Red light!" Jim gunned the car across the yellow line, blowing past the waiting cars and through the intersection, narrowly avoiding a collision with a pickup truck. Then, Crimley's words sank in.

"What?" Jim shouted. *Please tell me I didn't hear them right.*

"So what?" Gunther said. "You shot the guard."

The inside of the car exploded in screaming chaos, but only one fact sunk into Jim's shell-shocked mind. *People died today because of me.* Somehow, his body responded automatically to the task of manipulating the car through traffic and keeping them alive. Unable to take the noise of the other two, Jim bellowed his own warning. "Shut up and hold on!"

The car roared up the street; Jim jerked the wheel to the right, steering the car onto the dirt road. "Here we go!" Jim floored the car, opening all eight cylinders of the T-Bird's power.

The car shot forward like a rocket, pushing Jim back into the seat with familiar velocity. So far, no one chased them.

"Perfect!" Gunther cackled. "By the time Perionne's finest gets organized, we'll be in another car and out of town."

"Gunther," Jim yelled, "did you kill someone, you son of a bitch?"

Crimley answered with a voice of shocked mourning. "Two people. Shot 'em in cold blood."

Gunther slammed his arm against the back of the seat with a leathery thump. "Fuck you, Crimley! You shot the guard."

"Oh, God." Jim groaned.

"I shot him in the leg, you dumb asshole! He's still alive."

Jim jabbed an accusing finger at Gunther. "You got me involved with murder, you sonofabitch!"

The seats shook. The car had drifted off the road, and a thousand pounds of speeding bulk tore through dirt and side-brush. Crimley gripped the wheel and eased the roaring beast of a car back on the road. "Careful. The way you're driving, we'll be pulled over for speeding before they even know who they're chasing."

"They won't chase us. A cop starts after us, I'm pulling over."

"You are not!" screamed Gunther. "I'll blow your brains out right here if—"

"That's enough from you," yelled Crimley.

Jim needed to pay attention. The dirt road they followed ran parallel to the paved road leading to the highway overpass. Flashing red sirens caught and held Jim's attention.

"Crimley, Gunther, duck!"

Jim cut the wheel hard left, turning off into loose dirt and brush. The car veered away from the blockade of cars and officers stationed at the on-ramp; the robbers focused their attention on the oncoming traffic moving from the other direction.

The ride grew bumpy, but Jim controlled the car's path, testing old reflexes he thought had left him years ago. For the next three miles, Jim guided the T-Bird as it tore across the countryside, keeping a true course across the dusty land. He waited for the squealing of sirens that never came. They'd escaped the police, at least for now.

Crimley spoke first, unable to hide the awe in his voice. "Who'da thought they'd get a roadblock up so fast? Looks like the Perionne Police Force doesn't take kindly to a couple of their citizens getting murdered. Just the fire up their ass they needed to get those roadblocks in place, pronto." He directed his next words at Jim. "You saved us back there. Thanks."

Jim ignored the gratitude. "Here's the turnoff. Everyone hold on."

Jim skidded the Thunderbird off the dirt road and across the parking lot of the derby arena. He pulled the car into a spot near his own. The doors popped open, and the three men jumped out.

Crimley and Gunther ran up to Jim's car and waited expectantly.

Jim looked from one to the other. "No way, deal's off. I can't even get you onto the highway. You might as well turn yourselves in. I'm done."

"Jim," Gunther shouted, and pointed his handgun at Jim's head. "You're done when we say you're done."

"Shit!" Crimley swatted the shotgun handle down on Gunther's good hand.

Gunther yelped, and the pistol dropped to the ground.

Crimley brought the shotgun up and rammed the stock into Gunther's chest.

Gunther fell back against the car, pinned for the moment.

Crimley held the gun between them. "That's enough!" In a flash of motion, he pressed the edge of a knife against Gunther's throat.

Jim could only watch, mouth hanging open.

Gunther tensed and froze.

"I said, '*that's enough*,' little man. Think you're tough, 'cause you shot a couple of defenseless people? Well, I'll slit you from ear to ear, and leave yer body for the crows."

Gunther glared but held back. He took a deep breath and answered in a slower tone. "Okay, Crimley. You win."

There was a long, tense pause between the three men. Jim watched, wide-eyed, while Crimley glared at the now-cowering Gunther.

"All right," said Crimley. "For starters, no more pistols for you. Second, we're burying the guns and the money."

"Why the hell we doing that?" asked Gunther.

"Because I win, and we're doing what I say." Crimley lowered his knife and offered Gunther a contrite smile.

He pounded Gunther on the shoulder. "We can't get out of town now. We have to ditch the money and come back for it later. Relax, Gunther, I have an idea. Jim, pop the trunk, then get in the car, both of you."

Responding to Crimley's authority, Gunther and Jim ran to the Buick.

Crimley loaded the weapons and the money bag into the trunk and slammed it. He then hopped in the back.

Jim pulled out of the parking lot and onto the main road, this time in his own car, with two unwanted passengers crouched on the floor of the back seat.

"Okay," Crimley said, "drive back to town. Nice and easy. We'll need to stop and pick up supplies for tonight."

Jim drove without comment, trying to bury his fear and concentrate on the task at hand as if his very survival depended on it.

Because it did.

CHAPTER ELEVEN

SOMEONE CALL THE DOCTOR! GOT A CASE OF LOVE BI-POLAR! My eyes snapped open to the awesomeness that is Katy Perry screeching from my iPod alarm clock. STUCK ON A ROLLER COASTER! CAN'T GET OFF THIS RIDE!

I groaned, realizing, belatedly, that today was a Saturday and I'd forgotten to turn off my alarm. Katy went on a few more seconds about her boyfriend being hot and cold, yes then no, in and out, wrong when it's right.

Bitch, then moan, I added in my head as I hit the off button.

Well, I was up now, even if I wouldn't define my current state as "awake."

I flung aside the covers and wandered into the living room, still wearing my oversized T-shirt, stifling a yawn and trying to blink the sleep away.

I wonder if Mom would notice one less cup of coffee?

The smell of fresh-brewed coffee had drifted over from the kitchen. Mom had set the timer to auto-brew at six every morning, but with today being a Saturday and ninety minutes past brew time, the life-giving broth might stew another half hour or more before Her Majesty stumbled out of bed.

I considered the pros and cons and instead poured myself a glass of orange juice. In Mom's head, coffee might stunt my growth, even at age seventeen. I didn't even like coffee, just loved the smell. Plus, I wanted to deny some of it to Mizz High and Mighty snoozing down the hall.

And yet, I didn't.

Screw the school routine, anyway, or I'd also still be sleeping. And because I was a good girl last night, I actually made it home at a reasonable hour.

Well...11:30 was a reasonable hour, compared to how I used to prowl around until well after midnight.

My thoughts fell to the other prowlers who still stalked the streets of Broad Ripple without me. With an ache in my chest, I wondered what Joey was doing. And if he missed me as much as I missed him.

I spied the desk in the corner of the living room, with Mom's computer on top. Technically, the computer was for both of us, but she used it ninety-nine percent of the time. I usually checked my Facebook and email on my cell phone or at the computer lab at school.

Since I was grounded from my phone through the weekend, and no one was awake to kick me off, I stabbed the power button and filled the room with the humming of the cooling fan.

The 'puter was about three years old, and it never booted Vista up particularly fast, but it ran well enough once it ground through the almost-five-minute startup. I made good use of this time by wolfing down a bowl of Frosted Flakes, and I settled in front of the screen just as the machine relinquished control over to me.

I brought up Facebook and typed in my account. I hadn't been on in almost two weeks. I was greeted to the usual plethora of notifications sorted by subcategories, but my attention riveted on my friend count, which had dropped by one.

I knew it would eventually happen. We were no longer together, and promises made in the past meant nothing in the temptations of today. *But so soon?* I brought up Joey's home page, and the Add Friend button stared back at me, telling me I'd been removed.

I scanned five new messages in my inbox. Surely, he had the courtesy to send me a Dear Jane before cutting me off at the knees. Surely, even a *self-obsessed little shit* like Joey, poet extraordinaire, would take five minutes to lessen the pain and leave some sort of final thought. Something even as trite as "we were great together but it just wasn't meant to be" would have been preferable to a "no comment."

One of the five messages in my box, from my friend Zadora, who hung out with us at the café, caught my attention with the header "RE: Joey." I took a deep breath, bracing myself as I clicked the message.

Hi, Feef!

Sure miss you on reading night! As you know by now, Joey decided to make a clean break. He told us last night not to say anything to you. Screw him, right? Ay, Caramba, gotta hurt bad, Chica! I'm sorry. He's in a bad way, but we'll keep him out of trouble — we owe you that much.

I always liked you, Chica, but you two were poison. Best thing for you was to get the hell out of here. I know you don't see it that way, but take it from this senorita (at the ripe old age of 22 lol) forget about him and move on. You have a special heart, Chica, find someone worthy of you. You deserve it.

Zadora

I sat for, well, I don't know how long, staring at the words on the screen, delivered like a long-distance, glowing electronic punch. I waited for the shock to wear off and wondered if I would cry once it did. *The cowardly shit couldn't even write me himself; I had to receive a pity note from someone else.* Because that's all Zadora could do now was feel sorry for me, the poor Chiquita high school kid dumped by her stoner boyfriend. And because she knew Joey for the shit that he was, she tried to provide the closure she knew he wouldn't.

Soon, the words blurred away in predicable tears, but what surprised me was the lack of resonance down in my gut. I'd known this was coming and had been bracing myself. Now here it was, and in reality...maybe it wasn't so bad.

Today marked a new beginning, a fresh start. Except for one thing, *I hate it here.*

Classmates out to kill me, teachers out to flunk me. But on the bright side, all the computer geeks want to be my friend.

The first real sniffle came, just audible enough to catch *someone's* attention, the just-rising Queen of the Abode herself. "Fiona? Are you okay?"

I clicked the window shut with one hand as I wiped a sleeve across my face with the other. If the first sniffle was audible, the second one echoed through the house. *Dammit. Last thing I need to hear right now is 'I told you he was no good for you' from the Prophetess.*

"I'm okay, just...saw something sad on YouTube." I heard the distinct gurgle of coffee being poured. Mom wouldn't venture far from the kitchen without a full mug, loaded with sugar and creamer. Her addiction to caffeine bought me almost two minutes to dab at my face and dry my tears.

She wandered in, dressed in her white silk robe and vanilla slippers, which happened to match the shag carpet. Though still bleary-eyed, her suspicious gaze fell upon me. She sank into the black leather couch near the computer. "Are you sure you're okay?"

I mustered up a smile. "Couldn't be better. Just a little tired."

"It's not Joey?"

Somehow, I froze the smile on my face. "No idea, Mom. Haven't checked in with him since we got here."

"It's Joey." This time, no question. She took a deep breath of self-righteousness, which I cut off.

"Mom, *please*...can we not do this? It's over, I won't be

contacting him again. You can take that away as a victory, and we'll just skip the part where you rub my nose in it. Just this once."

I waited, bracing, and could almost see the mental switching of gears in her head as she took pity on me and changed topics. "Actually, I have good news. And because you didn't have your cell phone, I couldn't tell you last night. Joke's on me, I guess."

I bit back my comment. If she could be nice, so could I. She extended my silver flip-top phone at me. I let it drop into my open palm and wrapped my fingers around it. "Thanks for that, but I gather that's not the good news?"

"No, hon. I found a job for you. In fact, you start today."

Uh-oh! "A job? Today? Doing what?" I'd spent a couple days during my week of suspension looking for a job to earn a few bucks, but, with school already in session, most places had filled their quota of weekend and evening help. I'd tried the video store, some retail clothing places, even an ice cream store.

"One of my new clients, Ted Adams, he bought the Southern Chick'n Stop fast food place down the road." I had, in fact, tried the Chick'n Stop a couple of weeks ago, but the impatient, fat manager with the rattling keychain attached to her side made it clear in no uncertain terms they had no open spots.

I repeated this to Mom, as if I had to justify that I might have missed this golden opportunity. She nodded and waved her hand to brush it aside. "Well, since then, he had to let a few people go, and now he needs help. He said you can come in later this morning to fill out the paperwork and watch some videos."

Actually, I was hoping to avoid fast food. I'd worked both at a deli and a secondhand clothing store in 'Ripple, and there was no comparing the two.

Okay, well, as far as fast food goes, the Southern Chick'n Stop could be pretty tasty. Maybe I can land a spot behind the counter instead of back in the grill.

A twinge of something akin to gratitude tugged at me, but I shook it off before it could stick. I reminded myself that Mom just wanted my commitment to someplace I could be while she worked overtime at her office. The job amounted, in her head, to a glorified daycare where they paid me instead of the other way around.

Still, that glorified daycare meant extra spending money, something Ms. Stingy usually divvied out sparingly and only after much pleading on my part. So this job thing definitely had an upside.

I nodded and rubbed the last of the sleep from my eyes. "I guess I'd better get dressed and head over. Thanks, Mom."

And I meant it.

———

WALKING the few blocks to the Chick'n Stop took about half an hour, just like anyplace else in this town. Mom offered to give me a lift, but, as it was warming up into another hot day, and I wanted to enjoy the sunshine while we still had it; I decided to hoof it.

Besides, I wasn't *that* anxious to get started.

Dressed and showered, I grabbed a slip of paper on my way out the door where I'd jotted Chip's cell phone number. I'd guessed, correctly, that I'd be able to add it to my phonebook soon. Skipping along the sidewalk, I fired off a quick text message to him.

```
C got a job Chikstop start 2day ttyl B.
```

I hit SEND, set the ringer for vibrate, dropped the fliptop into my denim jacket, and then forgot about it. I waved at Sylvia, still rockin' and knittin', bless her pointy old head, and broke into a light jog.

I arrived twenty minutes later, a bit after 10:00, still feeling good but glad to step into the AC for a while.

I approached the front counter, in the corner, away from the small group of customers and three open registers. The two dudes and one girl behind the counter all looked about my age, or close. One gave me a quick, impatient glance before turning his attention back to the customer rattling off his order.

Standing behind them, a puffy-faced fat girl turned my way. She blinked dark, beady eyes at me, and I realized this was the same manager I'd spoken two a couple weeks ago, the one who'd told me they had no positions open.

She came nearer, taking off her headset. By way of greeting, she said, "I told you last time we don't have no open spots."

Ugh, she remembered me. But then again, my bright blue hair beacon *and* sparkling personality rendered me virtually unforgettable. "Actually, I'm already hired. I'm supposed to watch videos today."

The glare she gave me made it quite clear how little she thought of being kept in the dark about new hires, particularly those she'd already shooed away. "You're the fresh meat? Fona something?"

"Fiona," I corrected. "Shaefer."

"Okay, come back this way. We'll get you set up on the videos." She indicated the swinging door set into the counter. The manager passed the headset off to a tall, skinny dude back by the deep fryers and grabbed a clipboard up from behind the counter. She held the clipboard up with the self-importance of a health inspector paying a surprise visit. "Birthdate and soc'?"

I rattled off my birthdate and social security number.

She tapped on the touch screen of the closest register on the counter.

I waited patiently, then impatiently, as the seconds dragged on. I could see various windows opening and closing but had no idea what was going on.

Finally satisfied, perhaps two minutes later, she scribbled a note on her clipboard.

"Everyone clocks in on this register," she said. "You enter your birthdate and soc' to clock in; enter it again to clock out. Simple." She waved a beefy arm at the swinging door leading to the back of the store. "Follow me, fresh meat."

We walked up a narrow path past the grill. The aroma of just-cooked southern fried chicken patty, so pleasant from the counter, transitioned into old grease and caked-on raw poultry juice. My nose twitched. I wondered if I'd ever want to eat here after this, or if I'd get used to the smell.

I followed her back to a tiny rectangle of a break room, dominated by a small table and restaurant chairs scattered in disarray. A ten-inch TV with a built-in DVD player sat on a high shelf facing the table. I noted the manager's office against the far wall, recognizable by the heavy steel door with the inset horizontal slot-shaped window.

"Have a seat, fresh meat. My name's Kim, by the way."

I flashed my most disarming smile. "My name's Fiona, by the way." I'd considered adding that everyone called me Fi-Fi but didn't have the energy. Fiona, for today, at least, would be preferable to fresh meat.

To my surprise, Kim laughed. "Spunky. I like that. Don't worry, fresh meat. You'll lose the title in a couple days." She reached out and clapped me on the back, not hard, but I flinched, anyway. Kim creeped me out, and I couldn't help but cringe at the thought of working with her. She took her job and the power it brought her *waaaay* too seriously, which meant she didn't have much else going for her.

I waited while Kim disappeared into the office.

She reappeared moments later with some DVD cases. Behind her, a short, older man, maybe thirty, balding and graying at the temples and well into inflating the spare tire around his middle, also emerged from the office. He smiled at me and extended his hand. "Hello, Fiona, my name's Teddy. I'm the owner-operator of the Perionne Southern Chick'n' Stop."

I met his hand with a firm squeeze. "Hello, sir."

"Your mother told me about your job search just in time. We lost a lot of kids when school started, and we really need the help. Welcome aboard." I smiled at the warm welcome, noting that Kim would do well to follow his example.

"Thank you, sir. I'm anxious to start."

I stood there a few moments while Teddy's gaze traveled over my form, top to bottom.

"Well, I can't say I'm thrilled about the hair, but, if you work the counter, you'll have a hat on, anyway. No nail polish, rings, or any other jewelry when you're on duty. We can't have anyone losing something while handling the food.

"Cell phones stay in your locker when you're on the clock. I won't tolerate texting or phone calls when you're supposed to be working. I expect you to take ownership of whatever task we give you, even if that's scrubbing the urinals. You are always polite and courteous to our customers, no matter how rude they might get. And absolutely no profanity anywhere on the property, whether you're on duty or off."

I nodded. So far it all seemed reasonable, even though I'd have to take extra precautions to watch my damn mouth.

Teddy extended a clipboard at me. I glanced down at the W-2 and various forms and rules. "The training videos will go into a lot of procedures, but those are my rules of the road. Any problems so far?"

"No problems, sir."

Teddy nodded. "You can fill those out while you're watching the videos. Better settle in, it can take three hours or so. Oh, you have unlimited drink refills throughout the day."

I grinned at that. "Even the sweet tea?"

"Of course. Ready to get started?"

I grabbed a cup and turned in the direction of the counter. "Just give me a minute to fill up, and I'll be ready."

I worked my way back to the drink station, dodging metal fry baskets and cardboard boxes cluttering the aisle. *Maybe this won't be so bad after all.*

I was *so* wrong.

CHAPTER TWELVE

Twenty minutes later, I was taking notes about FILO, the first-in, last-out rule of storing food in a walk-in freezer. I'd already been interrupted five times by other workers cutting through on their way from here to there and wanting to say hi to the "fresh meat," so I was only about ten minutes into the video, such as it was.

As I stared at a badly acted scenario demonstrating the various ways to pollute your food with salmonella, Manager Kim waddled through, past the office and into an area I hadn't entered. She returned moments later, dragging behind her a large, oversized duffel bag. She placed it before her like Indiana Jones returning with the buried treasure. "Kill the video, fresh meat. Duty calls."

"What's up?" I asked, stabbing the stop button on the remote.

"We had two people call in sick today, so we're short." As she spoke, she unzipped the top of the duffel, exposing a bulbous, golden polyester chicken head with an open, bright orange beak. The gold polyester cut off at the neck, extending out to shoulder pads of white foam.

I stared at the smiling chicken head, my mind screaming out a three-alarmer. "You *can't* be serious."

Kim returned my appalled gawk with a sadistic grin. "As a heart attack, fresh meat. We're offering free samples of our new Mocha Shakes with each combo meal during lunch today."

"And this concerns me, how?" The sarcasm bubbled up in spite of my best intentions.

Manager Kim reached into the bag and pulled out a sign, a homemade sign consisting of a two-foot-long stir stick intended for mixing exterior paint glued to a rectangular piece of plastic. Across the face, I could read letters stenciled from a kit at an office supply store,

**Try NEW! Chicka-Delicious
Mocha Shakes 11-2!**

I stared, aghast, at the chicka-retarded sign. As words continued to fail me, Kim offered, "I made the sign myself."

"Nice," I croaked then grabbed my sweet tea, sucking deep from the cool, comforting brew.

"Lunch rush is hitting, and we need Chicka-D outside by the road waving the sign. And you've just been volunteered."

"Okay, I get it." Her tone and evil grin told me she'd entertain no argument. At least, from the looks of it, no one would recognize me inside the costume.

I waited for the blindfold and cigarette. "What do we do first?"

"Lose the shoes. Socks only." As I kicked off my tennies, Manager Kim hefted the foam chicken head between her hands and held it above my head. A weight of snug foam dropped on my shoulders. The light dimmed, and sound closed in around me.

I could hear my own breathing, panting in the confines of the foam. Luckily, I wasn't claustrophobic, or I would have been in trouble before we began.

It took a few moments for the light to find me through the mesh portal that, I was pretty sure, filled the gap of blackness in the mascot's open beak. I could see fairly well, at least directly in front of me, through a porous round portal about eight inches in diameter.

Still grinning, Manager Kim held the chicken body suit to my eye level, looking like a pair of warm golden footie pajamas with orange leggings, from which dangled a pair of oversized three-pronged claws for the footies. And these PJs zipped up the back.

"Okay." I heard Kim's voice through the layer of foam. "Take a big step forward into the leg."

I did, and my left foot sank into a thick wrapping of polyester.

She helped guide me into the costume with practiced ease, her voice rattling off the "rules" of the mascot secret society which I must obey or risk the terrible consequences. No talking in public under any circumstances. No bending at the waist; I couldn't see if my head might hit someone. Bend only at the knees. No chasing children, no hugging them. Let them come to you and hug you.

She rattled off a bunch of other things that had nothing to do with standing on the side of the road waving a sign. After she wound down, I asked the one question on my mind, "How long?"

"You can't be out there longer than forty-five minutes. I won't lie to you. It's in the high eighties now, and that thing is going to heat up to a light simmer, about forty degrees higher than wherever you are." She briskly turned me in place so she could zip me up. "So it'll get uncomfortable." She pulled the costume closed with one fast yank. I lost half my light, again, and the foam closed tight with even greater stifling urgency. "Be grateful you're the first today."

"Why?"

"Because the costume's dry now. Someone else will put it on right after you to finish lunch rush. After you've soaked the inside with sweat."

"Yuck!" I tried not to think about it. Nausea at this point would be a *very* bad thing.

Manager Kim walked down the cluttered aisle.

I started to follow, but one oversized claw stepped on the other, and I stumbled. I reached out and braced myself against the side of the walk-in freezer then continued after her, consciously taking larger-than-normal steps. That seemed to work okay.

I chugged through the grill area, exaggerating my movements as the manager had instructed me, shadowboxing into the air. *Hey, I'm stuck with it; I might as well have some fun.* Through my portal to the outside world, I saw the fry cook nod, raising his spatula in a mock salute.

Kim held the door open as I stepped through to the counter. "Duck, Chicka-D. Low door." She warned me just in time.

I emerged from the counter area to the combined squeals and yells of every kid in the place. "Mom! Look! Chickie!" "I'm gonna give him a hug!"

I barely made it onto the dining floor before I felt several small collisions about my abdomen. I had to crane my head uncomfortably down to see the small girls grappling my waist and legs in various death-hugs.

I reached down and patted each child on the back, waiting patiently as, one by one, they released their grip and ran back to their parents. One ten-year-old boy, clearly too old for that hugging nonsense, followed after, holding up his hand. "High-five, Chick!" I swatted at it, and he nodded and walked away, apparently satisfied. "Stay cool!"

"This way, Chicka-D," cued Manager Kim, heading toward the entrance. I relaxed my neck, now able to center her in my portal of vision, and followed.

I spotted someone familiar out of the corner of what I could laughably call my peripheral vision. Actually, he sat in the booth closest to the door, or I wouldn't have noticed.

Chip held a cup under his chin, sucking through a straw on one of the coveted new Mocha Milkshakes. I detoured, stepping toward him, and pumped fists in his direction.

This caught his attention, and he gazed in apparent confusion. I *so* wanted to laugh or say something, but I caught myself. I waved a frantic hand, or (wing?) toward him.

He stared at his own hand, as though an alien thing, then

extended it, palm facing me, swaying his arm back and forth a couple of times in a feeble return of my greeting.

I turned back toward the door.

Kim stood in the doorway, gripping the paint stick attached to the sign face, which rested against her bulging polyester pants. "This way, Chicka-D, time to go play in traffic." She chuckled at her own joke.

Ducking slightly, I stepped out into the blazing noon sun. The portal-shaped window to the outside in my headpiece radiated a disc of intensified light. The individual holes in the mesh took on greater definition, and, more importantly, I could see the sidewalk, parking lot, and grass leading to the edge of the road.

And, more disconcerting, I felt the air within the tight space warming up.

As we approached the sidewalk, Manager Kim's hand gripped my shoulder. "Step," she cued, warning me of the downward drop to the blacktop. "Big step," she said, helping me cross the drainage ditch in the grass. I took three tough shuffles uphill to get to the sidewalk running parallel to the main street.

Near the side of the street, traffic noises from the steady stream of passing cars crescendoed. A car cruised by and honked, making me jump. A second car, driving the opposite direction, also emitted a friendly beep. I suspected I'd get used to it pretty fast.

Kim leaned in close and had to yell to be heard. "We'll get you in forty-five minutes! Here's the sign! Just walk back and forth and try to have fun!"

Have fun, yeah, right! I grabbed the sign in my mittened hand, not easy. As the next car raced past, the sign, like an aerial flap pointed the wrong direction, caught the windfall, and tried to jump from my hand.

I gripped that sucker two-handed to keep it from flying off. I turned to tell Kim the wind might be a problem, only to see her stomping away.

Resigned, I paced back and forth, waving the sign up and down over my head. A car flew past and honked. A second one honked. I realized they would *all* honk. *Just not much going for entertainment in this town.*

Occasionally, a car in the lane closest to me would honk, then slow, turn, and pull into the store. Other times, a car in the lane across traffic would slow as they honked then skid-brake into the turn lane and pull into the parking lot.

Those are my *customers! Holy crap, this works!*

As cars pulled into the parking lot, I did a quick release of one hand from the sign to flash a quick thumbs-up. The passenger would usually reward me with a second friendly toot.

I started hop-walking back and forth, in a long, pacing trail along the sidewalk. Instead of simply turning, I'd jump in the air and spin in place, shaking my "tailfeathers" as I landed. This almost always resulted in a passing car honking. *Not a bad workout.*

And, for a while, I had fun.

After another while, I stopped hop-walking and slowed to a standard walk.

And after a long while after that, I started noticing how much I was panting and how *damn* hot it was in this stupid thing.

That's when the thought hit me that I had no idea how long I'd been pacing out here. I knew that time had a tricky way of being relative when paired with hard work, and it could have been anywhere from five minutes to over half an hour. All I knew for sure was that the sweat had built up around my neck and dribbled down the back of my collar and into my blouse. Moisture soaked my bra. The foamy polyester basking in the sun roasted the denim of my jeans and burned my legs.

The panting in my ears took on a more urgent intensity.

A Mitsubishi Spider honked, then slowed, pulling up near the curb. I woke up, realizing I'd been daydreaming. Some buffed guy behind the wheel turned in the seat where he'd pulled up the sports car. "Look alive, chicken!" His Barbie doll girlfriend giggled nonstop.

I raised the sign and ran after him. As the tires squealed, I swatted the sign through the air in an indignant pantomime.

A couple cars driving the opposite direction honked in apparent appreciation.

I continued my patrol with renewed enthusiasm. *I can do this. Forty-five minutes isn't* that *long. I must be just about finished by now.*

Right?

Except...

I turned and looked back at the restaurant, blinking sweat from my eyes as I peered through the portal. The cars in the drive-thru wrapped around the building, a segmented serpent of hungry customers. The parking lot, practically full, continued to receive a steady stream of cars from both the road where I patrolled and the strip mall beyond our parking lot.

But the rules were clear. I couldn't be out here more than forty-five minutes. *Surely they wouldn't forget about me. That would just be...wrong!*

Right?

I swallowed back my fear with a throat that suddenly hurt. I slid a dry tongue around in a dry mouth.

How long had I been out here? I had no idea. My prideful inner self started giving me hell. *They're keeping track inside. So don't be a wuss, and do your job.*

I raised my hand to lift the sign. *When had I dropped it to my side?*

I couldn't lift the sign.

The sidewalk in front of me blurred. I blinked rapidly to clear sweat from my eyes. I realized I wasn't feeling the sting of sweat, and, no matter how much I blinked, the sidewalk wouldn't snap back into focus.

I turned toward the grass decline. I took a couple of wobbly steps toward the building, felt the stupid sign drop from my hands, my feet get tangled up, and my body pitch forward like some bright golden Humpty-Dumpty.

Padded and cushioned, I don't remember the fall hurting much. Then, everything went black.

CHAPTER THIRTEEN

The world returned some time later. I could feel myself splayed face down in the drainage ditch, my clothes soaking, in total darkness. The timeout gave me a burst of energy, or so I thought, and I fought to stand up.

I shoved against the ground with both hands, feeling the costume rise into a push-up position. Warm water poured from the back of my head into my face. Light streamed through the portal, but my strength gave out in one arm, and I toppled sideways.

Grunting, I kicked at the ground, and succeeded in rolling over.

I flopped onto my back. On the positive side, light shone through the grill again. But I couldn't get up.

I heard a distinct change in the normal sounds of the passing vehicles. One, I could sense, pulled close, then skidded to a stop nearby. *Help is on the way!*

I heard the laughter of an approaching man, and a second person calling, maybe from the car.

"Greg, what the hell are you doing? Let's go, man, we're going to be late!"

"Hold on, this is priceless."

The silhouette of a head and shoulders blocked part of the light.

I opened my mouth to speak, but I had no voice, no words of pleading would come out of my mouth.

I waited. He waited. I could see arms reach up, holding a device in front of his face.

No, he isn't!

I heard the click of a camera shutter.

Laughter, then someone shouted at me. "What a loser! You should be in a turtle costume!"

I heard a more distant shout, vaguely familiar from a million miles away. The shithead hovering over me cut off his laugh and looked toward the restaurant, at least, I think it was the restaurant. I heard footsteps run off, followed by more laughter, the squeal of tires, and the acceleration of a car driving away.

More cars honked, passing by, but I also heard distant footfalls running toward me from the restaurant.

"Blue! Oh, my God, it *is* you, isn't it?"

Chip? I must be hallucinating...

Except there he was, moments later, recognizable, even though his face leaned in close and cut off most of the light. "Hold on, I'm going to get you out of this..."

A woman bellowed from a distance, accentuated by the thumping stomps of Manager Kim approaching. "Sir? You can't open the costume here, sir!"

"She may be dying in there!"

"We'll get her inside right now, sir, if you'll help me, but we can't unzip her out here."

"Blue, can you hear me?"

I couldn't answer, but I waved my hand, and, a moment later, he gripped it in return.

His other hand traveled up my arm and positioned itself under my shoulder.

I pulled myself into a sitting position.

My face burned as if on fire, and I felt old sweat dripping down the crevices and contours of my body. A wave of nausea passed through me, and I closed my eyes. *If there is a God, He will* not *let me puke inside this costume!*

"Sir, I can get her, thank you."

"You need my help. I don't think she can walk on her own."

A second pair of hands grabbed a hold of my other arm. "Fiona, if you can hear me, squeeze my hand." Through the layers of material, I gave her fingers a tentative squeeze. "Okay, count of three, we're going to lift you to your feet."

She counted, and I rose, through no action of my own. "Okay, just step as we go, and we'll guide you."

Somehow, walking mechanically, gripping Chip's hand for dear life the entire time, I was guided and prodded back across the grass and over the cement. I ignored the honks and callings, though they sounded more urgent and mocking than ever. I closed my eyes, waiting for the burning on my head to stop, realizing I had no fresh sweat beading on my forehead or in my eyes. I knew, distantly, that wasn't good.

Somehow, I ended up back in the restaurant. The raised voices of Kim and Chip roused me from a stupor. Chip wanted to stay at my side, and Kim was reading him the riot act for trying to step behind the counter. Kim called out a name, and Chip pried his hand loose from my death grip.

A second body slid under my arm, and they dragged me back into the break area.

"Hold her up," Kim ordered, and she slipped behind me while some other body stood in front and gripped each of my upper arms. I heard a fast *zip*, and a blast of cold air attacked my back. The sopping-wet polyester dropped from my chest and gathered along my arms. The hot air escaping made an audible hissing sound, replaced almost instantly by a sharp cold chill.

"Oh, my God!" the guy in front of me gripping my shoulders exclaimed.

Another pair of hands grabbed the costume head on either side, and pulled. Again, a vague sucking sensation, and harsh, brilliant light hit my face at the same time a blast of cold air attacked my head and shoulders.

I saw, not just one person standing nearby, but two dudes, and the girl I recognized from the front counter area. I'd officially made a scene. And I didn't much care.

And then my legs gave out, and bodies rushed forward to hold me up, and then lower me into a chair. "Jesus, look how red she is!"

I closed my eyes, waiting for the room to stop spinning. Someone held a straw under my mouth.

A timid woman's voice spoke near my ear. "Here, drink this, but slow..."

I sucked a huge gulp. The liquid hit my mouth like tiny paper cuts, and I immediately coughed it up.

Everything dropped away for a while.

I woke up to swaths of ice cold against my face and shoulders, opening my eyes against a white cloth. The chilling weight of an ice pack lay awkwardly across the front of my chest.

"What the hell's going on here? Back to your stations! Stacy, you stay. Kim, you, too!" I recognized the voice of owner Teddy, though the severe tone was something new. People were shuffling and leaving in a turmoil.

I reached a hand up toward my face.

Still in the seated position, I pulled the cold towel down and looked up into the girl's kind stare, her blonde hair pulled back and framing a pretty face. Her large blue eyes reflected clear concern as she observed me.

She smiled and extended the large cup of ice water. "Here, try again." Though she spoke softly, her voice reached me. "Slowly, this time. You need to replace all that liquid you lost."

I sipped, and, even though my mouth still hurt, I could swallow. And after a couple swallows, I could breathe deeply again.

"How long?" I heard Teddy snap.

"I'm not sure," Manager Kim admitted. "We were so busy. Did you see the numbers? The customer count was off the chart, so—"

"How long?"

"Maybe an hour, seventy minutes at the most, but we were too busy to—"

"Are you crazy!" The bellowing response cut off any further

protests from Kim. "Seventy minutes in this heat! She might have died, and that would have ended our great lunch in a *very* bad way, wouldn't it?"

"I'm sorry sir, I just thought—"

"Obviously, you weren't thinking! I ought to put *your* ass in that costume and send *you* out for an hour, except we both know you couldn't fit in it!"

"I'm sorry, Ted."

"Clock out and go home! I'll call you later and tell you whether you're coming in tomorrow to work your shift or to just turn in your keys. Get out of my sight!"

I patted my face with one of the no-longer-cold cloths. I winced. My whole face felt sunburned wherever the towels touched.

I craned my head to see Kim walk out of the room, but she refused to look at me as she mumbled under her breath.

I coughed, and my mouth filled with snot, an improvement over the dryness of minutes earlier. I swallowed the phlegm down with another mouthful of water.

I reached for my sweet tea, still on the table from when I'd watched the videos. I found I actually had the strength to hold my own cup and sucked on that. The sugar-brewed liquid tasted *so* good.

The room stopped spinning, and I looked over at Teddy, seated in a chair across from me, arms folded across his chest defensively, watching me.

Worker Stacy had vanished, and I realized I must have zoned out again. He looked upon me with what appeared to be genuine concern. "How are you feeling?"

"I think...a whole lot better." I'd found my voice, so I guess that proved the truth of what I said. I pulled my hands out of the yellow feathered sleeves and struggled out of the body suit. Even through the denim, I felt the frosty air hit my sticky-wet legs as I pulled them free of the chicken legs. The costume fell in a yellow heap next to the staring, lifeless head, looking in many ways like some sort of bizarre mafia murder.

"Just leave it," Teddy said, even though I had no intention of cleaning it up.

Bracing my hand on the chair behind me, I rose onto shaking, wobbly legs and waited for balance to return.

Teddy rose, watching me closely as I popped open the locker where I'd stashed my denim jacket. "I don't even know what to say."

I nodded. "Just imagine how *I* feel."

"How *do* you feel? There's a Med-check down the road if you want me to drive you there."

I shook my head. I just wanted to get the hell out of there. I took a couple of steps. My legs shook, but I wasn't in danger of falling, and the second step was easier than the first.

I turned the corner and spied a hand-washing sink, complete with a small shaving mirror. I gasped at the red-faced horror that stared back at me. I looked as if someone had fired a blowtorch a couple inches away from my face; my entire complexion shone a dull pink with highlights of red around the eyes and lips. I turned on the cold water and splashed my face over and over, trying to placate the screaming nerve endings of my tender skin.

I grabbed a paper towel and dabbed it over my face, which only scratched and irritated my skin. I stared at the shocked, sick face reflected back at me.

"You're welcome to come back Monday after school and finish those videos if you want."

I glared at the humbled owner standing nearby. "I like you all right, Teddy. But I wouldn't hold my breath on that happening if I were you."

"Take a day to think about it."

I nodded and turned my back on him, walking up the aisle. If I said anything more, things might get ugly.

He called after me. "Don't worry about clocking out! I'll take care of it."

Furthest thing from my mind, but I didn't say *that*, either.

"Can I give you a ride ba—"

"Goodbye!"

I paused long enough to top off my super-sized sweet tea, the very least they owed me, and made a beeline for the door.

I stumbled across the blacktop and into the grass when I heard someone calling after me.

"Blue! Wait up!"

Chip? I turned and saw him coming up the grass toward me. "Oh, my God!" I reached out. "Thank you *so much!*" As he stepped forward, I wrapped my arms around his waist and held on tight.

His arms draped and clasped behind my back, and his chin nuzzled the top of my head.

"You really saved my ass. I guess that's two I owe you," I said into his shirt.

He planted an affectionate kiss on top of my head. "It wasn't just your ass I was trying to save. I prefer you all in one piece."

Ewww, my hair is still pretty sweaty. For that matter, I was a walking, talking damp rag. But he continued to hold me. *And scoring points every moment.*

A couple of passing cars honked. I giggled as he flinched. "Oh, let them honk, I'm used to it."

We separated moments later, continuing to walk in the direction of home.

I pressed the cool side of the sweet tea cup to my forehead. My scalp started to itch. My other hand was enfolded in his. "What were you doing there? I mean, I'm glad you were, but did you really hang out for over two hours?"

"Well, *yeah*," he said, as if stating the obvious. "I got your text message and wanted to come see you, wish you luck, that sort of thing. I hung out for a while and ate lunch. Just when I was getting ready to give up, you came out in the chicken outfit, or I was pretty sure it was you once you waved at me."

"Good to know you received my telepathic message."

He chuckled. "Something like that. Anyway, I figured I'd better hang out, and I'm glad I did. I kept looking out the window to see how you were doing. After about an hour, I told the manager you probably needed to come in, but she said they couldn't spare anyone while they were so busy."

Chip shook his head and released an exasperated sigh. "Stupid bitch."

I flinched. An expletive from the Chipster was a fairly singular event.

"And somewhere between one glance and the next, that's when you fell. I told the manager I was going to get you, and, of course, she chased after me, suddenly all concerned."

The sidewalk dipped sideways and blurred out of focus. I stopped, waiting for the dizzy spell to pass. Chip's hand squeezed tight, and I pressed down to keep my balance.

"Take it easy. We'll take it slow. I'll make sure you get home okay."

I nodded, glad for his support.

We sorta forgot to release our hands the entire walk home.

I'D NEVER SEEN Mom dote before, but she was hovering around me the moment I cracked open the door, guiding me by the shoulders to the recliner. "Oh, my poor baby, I'm so sorry!"

Okay, who are you and what did you do with my real mom? But I let her seat me then pull the handle so my legs dangled above my head. I flinched at the sight of a white washcloth lowering toward my face then closed my eyes as the cold cloth soothed my still-tender face. *Aaah, now just leave me alone for the next ten years.*

Her hand stroked my head in the lingering silence. I had neither the energy nor the desire to ponder my strange day. I'd practically drifted off to sleep when she spoke. "Ted called and told me what happened."

I tugged the ends of the washcloth and let it drop across my chest. "I've thought about it, and I don't want to pursue legal action. I'd rather just let it alone."

Mom moved to the couch and turned to face me. "Legal action? Why would you want to do that?"

I shrugged, assuming a mock tone of deep thought. "Oh, gee, I don't know. Negligence, endangerment, at the very least they broke one of the super-secret mascot covenants, if not a few laws regarding the safety of a minor. Something there must be actionable, but you'd know better than me."

Mom threw her hands in the air. "I told him I was reluctant to have you go back, but he told me he fired the manager responsible for your incident. He's willing to throw in a twenty-five-cent-per-hour raise if you'll come back and just forget about it."

I shrugged. "A twenty-five-cent raise doesn't mean anything. Nobody had time to tell me what I was making before sending me out to get slow-roasted."

"But he's trying to make it right. He assured me it would never happen again."

"Teddy trained the manager on duty, and, best I can tell, he sat hiding away in the office through the entire lunch rush. *He's* ultimately responsible for what happened to me."

Mom drummed her fingers on the arm of the couch, the *thump-thump-thump* emphasizing the level of her impatience. "Jobs are *so* hard to come by now. I want you to reconsider."

"Mom, do you think what happened to me was some sort of fluke? That they never get crowds at lunch time? That some other kid's never been stranded out there? Now that I think about it, those other workers seemed to know *exactly* what to do to take care of me."

Mom released a slow, hissing breath as she considered my words. "So this is the thanks I get when I try to help you?"

"Mom, I can't go work at a place that treats their employees like that. Please, I need you to support me on this. I'll find another job."

But I could tell my words had no effect. She'd already made up her mind. Even as she stewed, she was going over the old rant in her head, which I could hear as plain as day. *Good for nothing, ungrateful daughter, after all the sacrifices, yadda-yadda-yadda.*

But she said none of those things. Instead, she slapped the arm of the couch and stood. "Fine. Quit. I give up!" With that, she stormed out of the room.

I sighed and pulled the cloth, no longer cold, across my face.

That makes two of us.

CHAPTER FOURTEEN

Jim watched Jeff Crimley run from the shelter of the car toward the locked gate of Perionne Amusement Park, using the illumination from the headlights to see through the heavy rain.

Crimley fiddled with his maintenance keys until the gate swung open.

Jim eased the car forward.

The car door opened, and Crimley settled into the back seat behind Jim. Glancing into the rearview mirror, he saw Crimley wiping his hands across his wet face, trying to clear his vision. "Damn. Just our luck."

Jim finally asked the one question he'd dreaded voicing all day. "What are we doing?"

Crimley and Gunther had kept Jim cruising the back roads of town all day. They spent several hours driving randomly and getting nowhere, though they did stop long enough for Gunther and Crimley to break into someone's tool shed and run off with a couple of shovels. Now, as it crept up on 10:00, they directed him to the amusement park. Jim knew he couldn't deflect Jessie's suspicions once he returned home. With a tightening in his gut, he wondered about his chances of getting home at all.

He drove slowly along the walking path. Except for the twin beams of light in front of him, the park remained shrouded in total darkness.

Jim knew from previous visits that the roller coaster stretched dead ahead. He squinted through the windshield, peering at the blacktop, which now split off in two directions, straight ahead and to the right. He barely managed to keep the car on the footpath.

"Take the right split," Crimley ordered.

He did as instructed.

Eventually, his headlights revealed a large domed cement structure. He recognized it as the rear wall of the Pirates of Perionne boat ride.

"There." Crimley pointed to a back doorway. "I can get us in there."

Jim turned the car into the mud, centering the headlights on the plain metal door.

Jim fought a growing panic. The memory of all the gangster films he'd seen flooded his brain, movies in which the criminal masterminds inevitably decide the hired flunky has outlived his usefulness and must now "disappear."

"Okay," said Gunther, "It's your plan, Crimley. What's up?"

Crimley shifted in his seat. "Relax, Gunther. We can't be seen with all this money right now. But we gotta make sure no one else finds it."

Gunther cackled. "So we're going to bury it inside the ride?"

"I knew you'd appreciate the joke," Crimley said. "The buried treasure under the buried treasure. No one would ever think to look for it in a place like this. We'll take enough cash to lay low in Michigan for a few weeks. Then when the heat cools down and they think we're long gone, we just sneak back into town and pick it up." Crimley directed his next words to Jim. "You won't have to worry about a thing."

Because I won't be around to worry? Otherwise, why tell me? They know I can steal the money. The moment the thought came, Jim knew himself for a coward. He'd never return here, no matter what. But would Gunther and Crimley take that chance?

Jim drew a deep breath and put on his bravado. "Go on, then. Get your burying done and over with."

Gunther reached across his lap for the door handle.

"Why don't you come with us, Jim? It'll go a lot quicker with three people digging."

"Hell, no, Gunther. I'm not going to have any part of this. You already got me in deeper than I wanted to be."

The fury he'd fought to keep buried pushed forward. Jim twisted in the seat and stared Gunther in the face. "Now you get your ass in there and hurry it up. Then, I'm dropping you off, and I don't expect to ever see you again. Got me?"

During this exchange, Jim peripherally registered that Crimley had already opened the car door and ran to the building. Now, he struggled with the keys and the maintenance lock to the back door of the ride.

Gunther shrugged, returning Jim's glare with a deadly calm of his own. "Suit yourself. I need the keys to get in the trunk. Then you sit tight. Don't even think of moving 'til we get back. You got me?"

Gunther shifted forward, and Jim could see a glint of madness reflected in his eyes. "If you take off and we get caught, we'll tell the cops all about your part in it."

Jim let out a shaky breath. "The one thing on my mind is getting you two out of my life." He turned the ignition off and handed the keys behind to Crimley.

The rear door opened then slammed shut. Gunther's silhouette moved away from the car. Jim closed his eyes, focusing on the gentle patter of the rain on the roof. *Here it comes. One shot through the windshield, and I'm done.*

For the next couple of minutes, Jim calmed his breathing and listened to the rain.

A flash of red lit the back of his retina, followed by the percussive boom of thunder. Jim's eyes snapped open, and he shrieked. *I don't want to die. I don't want this to be my burial ground.*

The car shifted. Gunther had opened the trunk.

A few seconds later, the car rocked from the sharp slam. There was a knock on the window near his ear. Jim jumped and bit back another whimper.

Gunther's angry voice reached him from the outside. "Open the goddamn window!"

Jim rolled the window down and blinked into the spitting rain.

"Here!" Gunther dropped the ring of keys in Jim's lap. "Listen to the radio or something. But stay put!"

Gunther ran toward the building. He probably knew Jim for the coward he was, knew him with such confidence, he'd let Jim keep the keys to his freedom, positive he'd be too terrified to leave. Perhaps he'd live after all.

———

GUNTHER STEPPED through the back door of the ride carrying the two shovels in his hand. He brushed a sopping forearm across his face, redistributing the wetness just enough to clear his vision.

He heard a series of loud *click-clacks* overhead, and then the room lit up, showing the small pirate island before him. He stood on a sandy islet surrounded on three sides by the now-silent moat-track leading to a set of double doors.

A wicked-looking pirate mannequin wearing an eye patch loomed close, ready to pivot toward the next boat full of riders. Nearby, a black cauldron sat upon a small rectangular wood porch in the center of the islet. The rain pounded on the roof of the chamber, creating loud and oppressive echoes within.

The side door in the back wall opened. Crimley stepped through, juggling his ring of keys. "That should give us the light we need." Gunther could make out a control room about the size of a broom closet over Crimley's shoulder.

Crimley looked grim-faced. "We got some work ahead of us. Best get started."

Gunther dropped both shovels in the sand. "Here. Help me lift this."

Together, they moved the black cauldron and the framework to one side.

Gunther extended his hook, pointing. "If we bury it right here, and put the black pot back on top of it, we'll have a perfect marker for when we come back."

Crimley nodded. He picked up a shovel and pushed it into the ground. "We should dig down about four feet or so to make sure the money's good 'n buried."

Gunther grabbed the second shovel. He latched his prosthetic hook to the lower part of the wooden handle and pressed the business end of the shovel into the ground using the strength of his good arm. "I'll keep up well enough. Don't worry about me."

They dug together in silence for several minutes until they created a pit large enough for the both of them to stand side by side, burrowing about half a foot.

Gunther continued digging, even when he saw Crimley stop, sweaty and tired. A surge of minor triumph coursed through him. *Another endurance victory for the handicapped man.*

He could sense Crimley's puzzlement. "Gunther, are you sure draggin' Jim into this was a good idea? He doesn't seem up to it. He may be long gone for all we know."

Gunther chuckled. "Just leave ole' Jim to me. I've got him under control."

Crimley sighed. "You're some piece of work."

Gunther stood to his full height, gripping the shovel in his good hand. "What do you care? I got you the driver, just like we agreed."

Crimley stared him down, clearly not intimidated. "Oh, you did a *lot* of things that had nothing to do with our agreement."

"What are you talkin' about?"

Crimley pointed an accusing finger. "You've made us both accessories to murder. That, *partner,* was not a part of the original deal."

Oh, that. He'd forgotten about the killings, and he shrugged off the accusation. "You think I ever robbed a bank before? I just...went nuts when I had the gun in my hand. It's over now. We were leaving town, anyway; now we'll have to leave the country. What difference does it make?"

Gunther waited, wondering how far Crimley would dare to elevate this. Instead, Crimley sighed and said nothing, apparently choosing to keep his thoughts to himself.

———

AFTER ANOTHER HOUR OF HARD, sweaty work, both men were up to their waists in the hole. They'd removed their jackets long ago. Plenty of time for Crimley to fume over the danger Gunther had put him in.

Crimley finally tossed aside the shovel, bracing himself to finish the unpleasant work ahead. "Okay. This should be more than plenty."

He watched Gunther drop his shovel. "Yeah. I still don't get why it had to be so deep. I mean, there's no way anyone is going to find the money."

Crimley reached his hand into his pocket. "You can never be too sure."

Gunther turned his back to climb out. Quiet as a cat.

Crimley pulled out his pocketknife, unfolding the silver blade.

Gunther shook his head. "Yeah, well, this should be deep enough to discourage any—"

Crimley pressed in close, slamming Gunther against the side of the hole and thrusting the knife between his ex-partner's ribs.

"I needed a big enough hole to bury *you,* you crazy bastard."

Gunther sagged against the hard-packed earth.

Crimley pulled the knife up and out, then took a half-step back. *I need to get out of here.* He realized his mistake too late.

Gunther growled, apparently still having some fight in him. He made a sweeping motion with his arm, catching Crimley off guard.

A distant stab of pain penetrated the red fury of Crimley's anger as Gunther's prosthetic hook sunk in his chest, but he aimed his knife at Gunther's gut, jabbing with all his strength.

"Traitor!" Gunther moaned. "I'll kill you for this."

Crimley pulled the knife out and thrust again, not caring where he hit, as long as the blade penetrated.

Gunther's fingers locked around Crimley's throat in a death grip. The hook twisted in his chest. Crimley pulled up in an automatic reflex, ripping a huge hole in Gunther's exposed belly as they fell.

Before they hit the ground, darkness overcame him.

CHAPTER FIFTEEN

A huge boom of thunder woke Jim from his doze. He twisted the knob to light up the overhead dash and look at his watch. *It's quarter 'ta one, for Chris' sakes.* He'd sat with the engine running and the radio on for three hours, and the rain kept on pouring. He turned the high-beams on, illuminating the metal door in yellow light. *This is crazy.*

The only thing left to do was the last thing he wanted to do.

Mustering his courage, he got out of the car and bolted for the entrance. The door to the ride swung inward, and he scanned the brightly lit treasure scene.

They had moved the cauldron. His eyes focused on the hole in the midst of the island for several seconds before his brain realized its existence.

The hole spread out deep and wide, but from his vantage point, Jim could easily make out the two unmoving figures lying inside, smeared in liquid red.

"Oh, hell!" Jim rushed forward and crouched down, then hopped in.

He stared at Gunther's back for a moment before he latched

onto Gunther's shoulders and pulled him up. Gunther fell over, unresisting, into a reclined position.

The crazed eyes continued to stare ahead.

Jim gripped Gunther by the hair and placed two fingers at his neck to feel for a pulse. *Nothing. Damn it!*

A rush of lightheadedness froze him, and his mind locked. *How could things have gone so horribly wrong?*

A groan of misery reached his ears as if from a great distance. He turned his head to stare at Crimley, who struggled to sit up.

Crimley's eyes blinked open, and cleared in recognition. "Help me. Hurry." The weakness of Crimley's voice shook Jim from his stupor.

Jim abandoned the staring corpse and crawled to get closer to Crimley. "How did this happen?"

"Help me, Jim. I'm dyin'."

Jim rose to his feet, staring down at the torn and bleeding man. The gaping wound in Crimley's chest bled freely, soaking the front of Crimley's T-shirt.

Jim took off his denim jacket and wadded it into a ball. He shoved it against Crimley's chest. "Here. Hold this, and press down hard, you hear me?"

Crimley nodded.

Jim gripped him by the shoulders, then pulled him up and propped him against the edge of the hole.

"Stay right here." He muttered a string of curses. *That's a dumb thing to say. As if Crimley can move.* He grabbed Crimley's shovel and tossed it up, then pulled himself out of the hole.

He stared at the moneybag lying on the ground near the edge. The thought of touching the bag revolted him. With a swift kick of his boot, he sent the moneybag flying, landing atop Gunther's corpse. "There ya' go, ya' son of a bitch. I hope it was worth it."

Jim grunted and cursed, but, with quiet efficiency, he buried Gunther's body and the moneybag in the dirt.

During the process, Crimley kept fading in and out of

consciousness, but the man didn't complain. Jim knew Crimley would not live through the night without help.

He lifted Crimley out of his corner of the hole and carried him out to the car.

"Here," Crimley said, reaching out and handing Jim the keys. "Turn out the lights in the control booth. But make sure the room looks the same."

Jim nodded and ran back.

In less than half an hour, he finished the burial. He glanced at the platform underneath the cauldron that hid the freshly turned dirt beneath. Jim scattered the decorative doubloon coins around as best he could. On a boat ride in the dark, it would look good enough.

He found three small dots of blood near the door, still wet, which he wiped clean with a handkerchief.

Jim threw the shovel in the trunk and got into the car, driving back toward town, uncertain what to do.

Crimley stirred next to him and called out. "Jim! I need to get to the hospital. Please, hurry. I'm gonna die."

Jim gunned the engine. He could reach the emergency room in three minutes.

"Jim, come on, I'm..." Crimley passed out again.

Fighting back a growing dread, Jim pulled over and checked for a pulse. He could barely find it. "Crimley? Crimley! Oh, no."

Jim buried his face in his hand. The rain continued to pour. *I can't go to the hospital. I can't keep Crimley. I can't stay here with a body in my car.*

He strained to come up with options. *Crimley's as good as dead; why should all our lives be ruined?*

The answer came to him in sudden clarity, along with a cold determination to see it through.

He got out of the car, walked to the passenger side, and yanked at Crimley's shirt.

Crimley slumped sideways, fell to the shoulder, and landed with a thud. A grunt escaped his lips. "Jim, don't do this..."

As Jim tried to stand, Crimley reached up, pulling at Jim in desperation.

Jim cursed and pulled his jacket out of from the clawing grip of the dying man. He popped the trunk and threw the jacket inside.

"Jim!" The voice calling out in the rain seemed to find new strength. "Don't leave me!"

A flicker of compassion lit up deep inside. "I'm sorry, Crimley. I truly am. But you did this to yourself. I won't pay for it the rest of my life."

Jim climbed back into the car. He took a deep breath, mentally shutting out the quiet voice of his conscience begging him to turn around before it was too late. Instead, he hit the accelerator and drove off into the rainy night.

CHAPTER SIXTEEN

Without Joey-like distractions, I absorbed myself in schoolwork. For pleasure, I read my books and fiddled with my poetry, basking in the theoretical freedom to smoke, drink, and party at will. At the same time, I patted myself on the back for not doing any of those things. I chalked it up to my newfound self-discipline.

Miz Leona Shaefer, Super-Attorney, drummed up enough business to keep her in the office after-hours an average of four nights a week. But not tonight. "I'm taking a short trip. I need to wrap a few things up in Indy this weekend."

Seated at the dinner table, I tried to keep my voice casual. "Can I go with you?"

She shook her head. "I'm checking into a hotel room and eating out. I'm spending the rest of my time at the old office building. It's not a vacation, Fiona."

Before I could argue, she pointed at my plate. "Eat your vegetables."

I stabbed a fork into an unnaturally hard carrot. "Yes, Mommy

Dearest. It's the least I can do after all the minutes you spent defrosting this delicacy in a pot of boiling water."

She opened her mouth to fire off what was sure to be a scathing retort when the phone rang. I rose from my chair before she could move. "I'll get that."

The wireless headset laid free of its cradle on the edge of the counter I stabbed the "Call" button. "Hello?"

"Hi, Blue."

"Chip! Great timing. I just finished eating." I waved at Mom, who shook her head in disgust and picked up our dishes.

As I made small talk, I watched Mom dart around the house to set up shop in the living room. She barely glanced at me as she strolled by to turn on the TV and then grabbed a stack of paperwork.

I hurried into my room with the cordless to keep the conversation private.

I curled up on the bed and made myself comfortable, determined to put off my algebra homework as long as possible.

Chip chattered in my ear. "So how long do you think before Perionne Park closes?" His voice filled with a casual curiosity, as if he presumed I had some stake in the question.

It took me a while to recall the dilapidated old amusement park I'd seen on my way into town, and I hadn't given the wannabe-Disneyland another thought.

"Why? Is the Board of Safety looking to shut it down?" I rolled over and got comfortable.

"No, Blue. The park closes every year when it gets too cold to support business. Last year, they'd already ended the season by this time."

"From the road, it looks deserted."

"Oh, no, not at all!"

I held the phone away from my ear to save my eardrum from his enthusiasm.

"Perionne Park's been doing great business since it opened."

As much as I wanted to give Chip one hundred percent of my

attention, just about anything else was more interesting than Peri-onne Park.

Chip droned on. "It'll probably be around long after you and I have left here."

That deserved a response. "Well, it will certainly outlast *me*, since I graduate next May, and am fully prepared to do a disappearing act immediately afterward."

Somehow Chip sounded put off by my lack of excitement. "Clearly you mock what you don't understand. We're pretty proud of the park around here."

When I added nothing to the conversation, he continued. "Every year, we try to guess how many more weeks we have before it closes."

"Mmm-hmm. That's very interesting. No, wait, I'm wrong. It's not interesting at all." I grinned at the mouthpiece, expecting a big laugh at my amazing wit.

Instead, Chip ran right over my sarcasm. "The Pirates of Peri-onne is one of the best rides of its kind. It's a pirate boat ride. Kinda slow, but it has outstanding mannequin effects. I've been hoping to one day use some of the imagery in a video game."

I grinned again. His dorky excitement had a certain charm that made it hard for me to make fun of him. But I still tried.

"We-ell," I said. "Let me check my busy social calendar. Hmm. You know what? I think the idea of us, you and I, together at the town park would be mind-blowing, just to see the looks on everyone else's faces. Okay, it's a date. *If* you think you can handle it. Tell ya what. I'll spike the hair extra high and break out my leather miniskirt and high-heeled boots. I'll put on my prowler girl costume just for you, Chip. They'll think you won a contest at the local strip club."

"Ah..." Chip floundered.

I showed no mercy. "You *do* have a strip club around here, or do I presume too much?"

Chip ignored the question. "Maybe you should just put on what you normally wear."

"Ha! Chicken shit. As if *that* will save you." I propped myself on an elbow. "Listen. Mom's going back to Indy for the weekend. Let's head straight to the park after school, and we'll make an evening of it. Maybe Saturday we can catch a movie."

"Sounds good. I guess it's a date."

———

WALKING home from school the next evening, shuffling across the sidewalk to the house, I saw the old woman. Sylvia slowly rocked and stared out at the street.

As I passed the house, her head craned to follow me. She squinted in open scrutiny. I walked along the stone bricks cutting though my lawn, trying to pretend her attention didn't give me goosebumps.

Her hands wove her knitting needles in an automatic motion through the off-white something spread upon her lap, the same something she'd been working on the day we'd met. The intensity of her gaze sent a chill through me.

She spoke in a rasping whisper that didn't quite carry across the yard.

I fished in my pocket, looking for my keys, debating whether or not I should pretend I didn't hear her.

Like they had a mind of their own, the keys slipped from my hands and bounced across the cement and into the lawn.

"Young girl, come here, I say!" She must have known her voice reached my ears this time; no sense in denying it.

I stepped onto the grass, retrieved my mutinous key chain, and trudged across my lawn to trade words with my creepy neighbor.

Her cloudy eyes reminded me of nonfat milk. Kinda opaque white with a bluish tint surrounding them.

Hands in pockets, I stared at her, waiting.

She rocked back and forth, a half-smile curling her thin lips.

"I hear you are beginning to settle into our town." Her voice grated on me like crinkled sandpaper, and my legs itched from the contact with the dried stalks of what used to be a lawn.

"Oh. I didn't know we had any mutual friends."

"I hear things."

I waited, but she didn't elaborate.

I was not in the mood to play "cryptic comments" with her. "Look. Not that it's any of your business, but I'm only committed to this nut house until graduation." I fidgeted where I stood. Being around this old woman made me want to have a cigarette, a habit I'd hoped I'd given up when I gave up Joey.

Sylvia settled back into her knitting, her gaze dropping down, away from me. "Where would you say, then, that you belong, young lady?" Her hands moved, continuing in their mundane repetition. Her rocking remained constant.

I shrugged. "Chicago, Los Angeles, New York. Any big city. Even Indy will do. Someplace with good music and lots of people. Someplace relevant."

"Strange to want to leave. When I was a girl, growin' up in Perionne, I didn't want to ever move away."

For a wicked moment, I entertained asking if she grew up with a car or if she rode to school on horseback. I resisted the urge. Instead, I reached down and plucked a piece of dead grass. "Times have changed."

She nodded and continued her knitting. "Kids leave for the city while the city folk, why, they turn around and hightail it out to us. Everyone's restless for something different. Nobody's satisfied. Hmmm."

Just when I thought she must have lost her train of thought, she started up again. "My boy wasn't ever satisfied." She looked up, shaking a bony finger at me like I'd been personally responsible for her "boy's" selfishness. "Always restless. Always wanting more."

"Boy?" How old might Sylvia's son be now? Quite possibly a grandfather himself.

I couldn't figure out how Sylvia's legs didn't give out from all the rocking she did. The woman must be in her early nineties, yet her hands were as nimble as her feet.

Sylvia took a deep, shaky breath. "Thing is, my boy never left the town, either. Been restless his whole life, but he's never seen more than the twenty miles of Perionne. I told him one time he should git'. But he never did." She stopped knitting and looked me straight in the eye. "Paid for it, too."

Okay, now I want to run home and slam the door.

Sylvia shook her frail head. "Nope, he never left. Shoulda tried harder to kick him out. He mighta thanked me in the end."

"Where is he now?"

She continued rocking. "He's around. Here and there." I contemplated the latest cryptic comment. A strong breeze blew across the yard, rustling my jacket and causing a bunch of leaves to flurry over the cracked pavement. "He's around," she repeated, her words almost lost to the wind blowing across my ears.

The chill from the resulting gust cut through my denim jacket. Now I was *cold*. "Look, Sylvia, I'd better get going. I have a test to study for."

Sylvia perked up. "Test, you say?"

"Yes. The midterm for American Folklore's going to have a lot on that Gunther guy everyone gets so worked up about."

"You're studying Gunther," she said, her eyes reflecting intense interest. "Learning about the ghost, are ya?"

"Sort of. The teacher doesn't believe the stories, but we're learning them, anyway."

Her eyes flashed anger. "Thomas Haplin is a young fool. You take heed in what you hear about the ghost. The ghost of Gunther is real, girlie. Seen him myself several times. Never sneer at things you don't understand." She waved a tangled knitting needle at me. "You remember that, an' you'll live to be older than me." She cackled in that freaky way again.

Oh, Lord, I hope not! "Yes, ma'am," I answered, backing away.

She nodded and dropped her gaze back toward her knitting, apparently satisfied she'd confused me enough for one day.

I stepped across the crunching leaves and angled toward the door of the house, my sanctuary. Only after shutting the door behind me did I breathe a sigh of relief. I wiped cold sweat from my brow, even as I told myself not to get worked up about the delusions of an old woman.

———

THAT NIGHT, I curled up on Mom's leather chair in the darkened living room, the single spotlight lamp behind my shoulder illuminating the stack of papers on the coffee table before me. Mom had crashed early, a little after eight, to be fresh for her weekend trip.

Outside, the wind howled, rattling the windows and shaking the blinds with unusual ferocity. I unfolded the handout, trying to read the first article regarding the legend of Gunther Stalt. I'd barely glanced at the material since the first day of school.

This afternoon, Chip had tried to assure me that the test would probably not focus on Gunther all that much. After all, Gunther remained the homegrown legend, discussed over and over, year after year. An easy "A" for the rest of the class.

The first blurry Xeroxed article, dated July 15th, 1991, offered an overview of the November 10th incident of the previous year, encapsulating the events of the daring daylight robbery at Perionne National Bank. Since the money was never recovered, it remains the only unsolved bank robbery in the town's one hundred and thirty year history. Remembering that Hap had said something to the same effect, I ran a highlighter across this sentence and turned the page.

The next article showed a copy of the front page of the *Perionne Gazette* the day after the actual robbery. The headline read, ***TWO DEAD IN DARING BANK HEIST***.

I read the story, trying to absorb the facts. All in all, the crime was pretty cut and dry. They botched it. Crimley calling out Gunther's name, for instance, struck me as tragic and comical at the same time. How did Gunther manage to disappear without a trace?

I turned the page and found myself staring at an article dated a week later, providing a bullet-point overview of the robbery and its after-effects, while reminding the community about a theoretical getaway driver.

So the questions remained. Had Gunther died? Where had the stolen money disappeared to? Did Gunther manage to get past the roadblocks and take it across state lines, or was the money still somewhere in town?

I rubbed my eyes, checking over my outline, certain I'd snagged all the facts regarding the legend.

I sighed, turning the handout pages to Section Two. These articles involved the various, and numerous, sightings of the "ghost of Gunther Stalt." I held between my fingers a stack of thirty pages. No longer fit for the front page, the *Gazette* buried these bits of gossip on the middle or back pages. Based on Hap's assessment of the ghost sightings, I treated the stories the same way.

Since the robbery, witnesses claimed to see an apparition with a hook for a hand in various cornfields and alleyways around the town, often witnesses of questionable sobriety or mental capacity. I stared again at the Gothic sketch of a wraith-like comic-book ghost reaching off the page.

I flipped to the next article, a three-part series of interviews with Gunther's mother, in which she admitted to hearing her son's voice from the Netherworld. He apparently whispered in his mother's ear, telling the deep, dark secrets of Perionne society. Strange and bizarre stuff; the reporter assured us much of it was unsubstantiated gossip that could not be printed in the article.

But the accompanying photograph of Gunther's mother, with her familiar features, made my head spin. I stared at the image of Sylvia Stalt, already ancient back in 1991. Her listed address, even at the time? *Right fucking next door, thank you very much.*

The door rattled from a sudden gust of wind, making me jump

and emit a squeaky gasp. *Good going, tough girl.* I walked through the darkness to shut the blinds and block out the moonlight.

Through the slits, I could see the empty rocking chair on the porch next door, swaying back and forth. I shut the blinds on the eerie scene, trying to shake off a chill that wouldn't leave me.

I spent the rest of the week anticipating my date with Chip. I surprised myself at how much I looked forward to it. As I slogged through my classes, Friday evening lingered on my mind. I counted the hours 'til I could put the schoolwork away and spend quality time with my buddy outside of a school setting. Even the backdrop of a broken-down amusement park beat the hell out of the cafeteria.

Friday finally blew in on a not-too-bitter early October breeze, carrying a billow of dark clouds that overcast the sun. I'd wrapped my leather jacket over a bundle of clothes, stashed them in my locker, and, after school, changed in the restroom.

The jacket fit snugly across my chest and cropped across my ribcage. I wore a tie-dye T-shirt that extended a bit farther down than the jacket. A rim of skin showed around my waist, revealing the top of my hip-hugging blue jeans. The high-heeled black stripper boots and a pair of cheap sunglasses, hiked up over my forehead, and my super-spiked blue hair completed the scandalous image.

I sauntered down the hallway, where Chip waited for me, his

back against a row of battered lockers. He straightened when he saw me, and I couldn't help but enjoy his bug-eyed gawk.

Chip took my hand, and we gabbed about nothing much while we hoofed it to the park.

Once there, Chip sprang the eight bucks for a pair of enter-all passes, little bracelets of plastic clipped around our wrists.

I held out my wrist and grinned at the shocked expression of the woman in the ticket booth. I guess she didn't appreciate the latest in skanky 'ho fashion.

Chip and I strolled along the main paved walkway. The groups and couples shuffling back and forth gave us a wide berth. Chip pretended he didn't see the stares and gawks, and I ignored them. In my peripheral vision, I spied Clinty and a couple of his gang draped over a park bench like damp laundry. As we walked past, they turned to glare at us.

I couldn't help it; feeling their eyes upon me, I strutted, putting an extra swing to my hips. I recognized several of the gawking faces, boys I'd seen in the halls, or doing chores in the yard.

The walkway appeared to loop in a gradual curve, circling the park. Chip leaned close. "What first?"

I'd already spotted five variations of the "spin-and-barf." We hadn't eaten yet, but I wasn't ready to shake up my intestines. Spotlights brightened the roller coaster framework. Craning my neck to take in the coaster, immodestly called the Whirlwind, I could only see a portion of the first drop, which rose high above us. The train reached the top of the hill, and we could hear the sudden acceleration of the wooden cart. The *click-clack* of the rails increased, and the car dropped over the abyss. Loud, distant screams echoed with the plunge.

I dipped my head toward the Whirlwind. "Oh, come on, Chip, I'm a big coaster fan. I hit King's Island and Holiday World at least twice a year. This is *bound* to be a disappointment."

The walkway forked toward the coaster line. Chip shrugged. "I've ridden those coasters, too, and I actually prefer the Whirlwind. It's older and in disrepair, which actually gives it an advantage in offering thrills."

I squeezed his hand. "Popcorn, ice cream, and a threat to life and limb. What more can a girl ask for? Oh, wait, I guess I shouldn't ask until I get the popcorn and ice cream." I grinned.

His fingers tightened on mine. A flush ran up my body, and I felt oddly like Prom Girl Barbie on her date with Quarterback Ken. *Strange.*

We reached the back of the line, and a few hostile faces turned toward us. No comments, but some of the twenty-something guys leered openly, and I saw someone's girlfriend elbow her companion for gazing too long. I untangled Chip's fingers from mine, and slipped my hand around his upper arm, gripping affectionately.

Up ahead, I recognized the friendly face and dumpy profile of Phil, Chip's D&D friend. Phil held hands with a petite redhead I didn't recognize. They leaned against the metal bar partition in the long line for the first car.

Phil waved at us from across the line, and I waved back.

The redhead, taken aback, gave Phil a perplexed look.

He whispered a few words to her, and then she smiled at me. The cars loaded up, and we eased forward.

We shuffled our way around the partition and caught up with Phil and his date.

"Hiya, Fi-Fi!" Phil reached out and gripped my arm. "I want you to meet Mary Rowan. Mary, this is Fi-Fi Shaefer, the new girl I told you about the other day."

"Ah..." Mary glanced around. I tried to ignore the turning faces, the watching eyes, the barely heard whispers all around us.

Mary waved in my direction and I waved back. Her bright red hair and pretty face worked to her advantage. She carried her stocky, compact body with exactly that sort of demeanor that screamed "loving and loyal, serious relationships only."

I tried not to instantly hate her. To her credit, when she spoke in her hard Indiana drawl, her voice sounded genuine and unchallenging. "Hi...Fi-Fi. Yer every bit as flamboyant as I've heard. And Phil told me 'bout your run-in with Clinty."

I raised my eyebrows.

Mary hurried on. "I'm real sorry about that. Must not 'a given a good impression of our town." She spoke with a sincerity that made me blush.

"I don't hold the town responsible for the actions of one bully."

We stood in an awkward silence, which she eventually broke. "Perionne ain't bad. We just take a while getting used to some types."

I nodded.

"I won't jump to conclusions if you won't." Though I remembered all-too-well the attitude I wore the first day of school. Not *whether* there'd be trouble, but rather who would it come from, and how soon.

Rather than jumping at my challenge, Mary continued in her apologetic tone. "We're not exactly throwing Clinty a ticker-tape parade. In fact, that fight earned you a little fan club."

I shook my head. I didn't want to argue, partly because she was Phil's friend, and I liked Phil. "Forget it."

Phil interrupted, clearly anxious to change the subject. "So has Chip taken you on The Pirates of Perionne boat ride yet?" I saw a mischievous gleam in his eyes.

"Ah, no; why?"

"We're doing that next," Chip said. I could feel his entire body bristle through my hand on his forearm.

Phil chuckled and moved closer to me. "Be careful with him on that. It's, like, his personal obsession. In an unhealthy kind of way. I don't even think he realizes the ride's just an excuse to make out."

I smirked. "Oh, well, maybe I can enlighten him."

Chip pulled me forward, away from the couple. "Come on, Blue, the line's moving."

Playing up the moment, Phil cupped his hands to his mouth, calling out. "He's weird. He thinks that pirate ride is the greatest thing ever created. Check out his notebook. Sketches, notes, diagrams. Weird, I tell you. I mean, I thought *Catwoman* was a pretty good movie, but...okay, maybe that makes me weird."

I raised my eyebrows. "Maybe?"

Phil grinned. "But this is a whole other level."

"But, Phil," I said, "I'm told it's one of the best rides of its kind."

"Blue!" Chip sounded betrayed.

On a roll, I barely noticed. "And the mannequin effects are truly outstanding."

Phil laughed. "Did you believe him?"

I shrugged. "I just figured it was a pickup line."

Chip hunched his shoulders. "It wasn't!"

I turned to look at him. "Relax, dear. It's *okay* that it was a pickup line."

Phil made a twirling motion with his index finger pointed to his head. "He even tried to hack the blueprints. Threw a hissy when we found the blueprints were pre-Internet."

Mary's quiet voice interrupted us. "That's enough."

I tugged at Chip's arm, pulling him against me and speaking with a seductive purr. "Golly, Mister Farren, is the ride as good as all that? I'm always up to trying a new good ride! *Meow!*"

Mary called. "Phil, the line's moving."

Chip waved at the departing couple. "Sorry to see you go."

I wiggled my fingers at Phil and Mary. They pushed forward with the crowd, and we walked the opposite direction.

I strolled after Chip, who stomped ahead, pulling away from me.

I caught up to him and grabbed his hand. "So, Chip, how come I keep hearing your name associated with the word 'hacker?'"

"Oh, lay off already!" He yanked his hand away. The bitter undertone in his comment took me out of teasing mode.

"Hey, come on, we were only kidding." The way he'd withdrawn from me stung more than I'd expected.

"He was being an asshole," Chip said. "And you were egging him on."

I stepped in front of him, forcing him to stop. I couldn't believe the pout hanging on his face. "We were *kidding.* Come on, will you lighten up? You're *supposed* to be silly."

Just when I thought I'd be stuck with a sullen date, Chip's mood changed, like he flipped an internal switch. He reached out and put his hand over mine. "You're right, Blue. Let's forget about it."

Satisfied that my irresistible charm had won him over, I practically skipped alongside him while we closed the gap in the line.

He grinned in my direction. "Did you see the folks watching you talk with Mary Rowan? If that keeps up, you'll be getting invitations to the sleepovers in no time."

"Now who's teasing?"

We entered the gate for the second car, and I saw the loading and unloading process for the first time. I found something oddly disturbing about the cars.

"Where are the bars? I only see a leather strap."

"Bars?" Chip's eyes squinted.

I watched while the couple in front of us pulled the single belt across their laps and clamped the end into a metal hook attached to the side of the care. "Oh, you mean the restraint? This coaster doesn't have one. The safety commissioner was supposed to oversee the installation of modern harnesses three years ago."

"And?"

"Perionne hasn't had a safety commissioner in office for five years."

"You're not serious!" But nothing in his tone suggested amusement. I turned toward him in indignation. "I'm going to go sliding all over that seat. There's room for three of me in there."

"That's because you have no butt to speak of." His inflection never changed, but I could see a twinkle of humor in his eyes.

I swatted his arm, but without anger. "That's for peeking. Is that any way to talk to a lady?"

Chip chose to ignore that opening. "Relax, Blue. I'm here to protect you."

"Yeah? So why am I not filled with confidence?"

The train pulled forward. I could see the couple, still laughing, their faces flushed, struggling to remove themselves from the car.

I tried to be a good sport but, in spite of myself, I cringed when the coaster pulled forward, and I saw the wide seat I had to step into. Chip, not exactly a bulky guy, dropped down into the rickety wood car and slid onto the ripped red upholstery seat.

Biting the bullet, I dropped down next to him. His arm slipped across the back of my shoulders. Our clones could have fit on either side of us, and the four of us would have been quite comfortable.

Chip reached over with the leather strap, pulling it across our laps and tucking the eye over the metal hook attached to the train just outside the seating compartment, giving the belt a hard, meaningful tug.

"Oh. Oh, *hell*, no!" I tugged at the strap, examining the slack...the *gaping* slack...across my lap. "Chip, I'm serious. This won't hold me."

"Blue, relax. After all, you've ridden the *big* coasters at King's Island and Holiday World. This is bound to be a disappointment."

"Oh, you! Fine, I promise I'll never use your words against you again. Let's just—"

The car jerked forward, and I fell back. A gust of wind flew into my face, and the rest of my complaint vanished down the back of my throat as the coaster chugged away into the darkness.

The car shook when the train tipped up the incline, and I dropped back against the seat, my feet flailing in open space, just out of reach of the floor. I heard more preliminary screaming and the monotonous *click-clack* as the coaster started the ascent.

I had no leverage.

Sheer terror jolted through me.

My left hand gripped for dear life against the side of the car. The other hand found a wad of Chip's shirt. "Shit!"

I turned to see a wide grin on Chip's face.

"You're enjoying this, you pig!" But I grinned back, elated and terrified all at once.

Chip squeezed my shoulder, and I could feel his legs press

toward the floorboards. "Hold on." He kicked down and secured his feet. I pulled against him to wiggle firmly into the seat just as the car's *click-clack* slowed, indicating the coaster had reached the top of the hill and righted momentarily. I pressed my legs against the interior. The rest of my body braced for the inevitable plummet.

I caught an aerial view of the town, splayed out across the distant horizon, a tiny spot of suburbia dotted along a stretch of highway and farmland. Under different circumstances, I might have enjoyed the sight.

The bottom dropped out beneath me, and wind whipped into a vortex across my face.

I heard a whisper blow over the air.

Bluuuue...

Icy terror caught in my throat. My breath seized up.

The train dropped into a violent descent.

Fierce velocity pressed against me. *Click-clack* sped into a deafening *clatter*.

The strap dug into my abdomen, burning. Flutter winds darted up my legs.

I could no longer feel the seat under me. I flew through the darkness, my screams mingling with the euphoric terror of the other passengers.

My sunglasses, forgotten until that moment, spun off my head, never to be seen again.

The coaster dipped out of its first decline and charged uphill. I slammed into the seat, the pressure forcing tears from my eyes. They streaked across my face, and I didn't dare let go to wipe them away.

Up and down, and up, the coaster threw me around, rendering me bruised and breathless.

I hated it.

I loved it.

Then, we hit a corkscrew, plummeting into total darkness.

The world twisted, turned inside out, and then righted itself.

The coaster fell like a tornado, a constant, spiraling decline.

We spun into the forest, and the wind called me again, stinging my face.

Bluuuuuuuue...

I raised my arms and screamed through the final dizzying moments.

Brakes screeched, jarring us to jolting halt. Spent, I squeezed my eyes shut, feeling the car chug along the last few feet of track at a more conventional speed.

My throat hurt, and I couldn't find my voice.

The next thing I knew, Chip scrambled out to stand on the wooden platform, reaching down toward me. I placed my chilled hands in his.

He pulled me up and out of the coaster.

I leaned against him, dazed and giggling like a madwoman. I could feel solid planked floor beneath my shaking legs, and I clung to Chip.

He put his arm over my shoulder, although he was none-too-steady himself, and we stumbled to the exit.

I finally found my voice. "Wow. I mean...fucking wow!"

Chip panted his response. "It's only great because it's a safety hazard."

If Chip wanted to prep me for a slow ride, I could not have been more ready. I still had trouble willing my trembling legs to hold my weight. And so, with a hand grasped on either shoulder, Chip led me, unresisting, down the sidewalk path to the Pirates of Perionne.

No more than five people stood in line waiting to get onto the boat ride. Chip took me off the path to a set of wooden stairs. A wood-carved handrail split the middle of the stairs to create separate enter/exit lanes. We descended down the "enter" side, which led us to a circular cement platform in the midst of a small manmade lake. Surrounding the cement base, a motorized, rotating, circular wood porch guided the tiny boats in and out of the enclosed track.

Two attendants scrambled across the rotating platform, one helping couples and families exit out of the floating capsules, the other running a squeegee over the plastic interior and guiding the entering groups to their ride.

We stepped onto the rotating platform. In spite of my shaky legs, it only took a moment to adjust. As we walked across the platform, Chip took my hand.

Our shoes made loud clomping noises on the wood.

Chip stopped at the edge of the dock and handed me into the slippery plastic of the boat interior. I squatted down, and he dropped directly behind me.

Nice!

I generally enjoyed this sort of Tunnel of Love thing as a lark. As Phil had indicated, mannequin boat rides provided the perfect backdrop for a little snuggling, and I needed some snuggling in the absolute worst way.

I leaned back, placing my head on Chip's shoulder.

His arms enclosed either side of me, fingers brushing across my stomach. I reached down and enfolded my hands in his.

A shiver ran up my spine, partly from a chill and partly from something else. His body shifted, and he pulled me against him into a more secure embrace. His hands trembled in mine.

Chip's warm breath brushed against my ear. "Better?"

"Much, thank you, sir." If I were a kitten, I would have purred.

I saw a sheepish grin on his face. I grinned back, and then settled against him, caressing his warm hands. Now that the adrenaline rush had run its course, I'd become tired and droopy-eyed.

The boat disengaged from the rotating porch and propelled forward toward a double-door entry. The image of a pirate, black patch covering one eye, grinned at us before the nose of the boat forced the doors open, splitting him down the middle. The doors closed behind us, and the boat drifted into total darkness.

The sound of rippling water soothed my me, though my nose wrinkled in an involuntary response to a moldy odor riding upon the too-humid air.

I heard a click, and spotlights from overhead snapped up to reveal a huge mock pirate ship before us. The room erupted in the sound of cackles and screams and a hearty pirate "Yo-Ho-Ho" song echoing through the chamber. A large crew of stuffed pirate mannequins took turns attacking our boat as it floated past.

I smiled, amused to hear the warped musical tones, the telltale sign of an audio tape still on active duty long past its intended use.

"Argh! Is that a gold ring yer' wearing?" a "pirate" called out, swinging a plastic sword toward the boat in an arc that passed harmlessly overhead.

Giggling, I craned my head back. "Maybe he means my belly-button ring. But I think I left it at home. Care to check?"

Chip's body tensed, but his fingers tightened around my hands. "Not right now, Blue."

Oh, well.

Another pair of doors split, and we floated into a new chamber. Hedonistic tropical music assaulted my ears while the boat encircled an island.

A pirate chased a blonde damsel across the beach, the distorted music muffling the whirr of the crane carrying them both along a track. Other pirates fended off dark-skinned natives, sword-to-spear. Arms and legs gyrated and rocked in amusing fencing action.

I drifted, content to let the scenes unfold around me. On the verge of falling asleep, I watched with a sort of detached fascination.

We floated by a sandy lagoon supporting a wooden-planked deck, covered in glittering doubloons.

A cackling pirate, standing next to an ominous black cauldron, emitted a shrieking "HAR!" at us.

The soundtrack, set to eleven, jarred me from my slumber and, startled, I pressed back against Chip.

The pirate leaned forward, pointing a short sword in my direction, still shrieking too loudly, "Git yer own gold, matey! This be all mine!"

It continued to cackle at high volume while the boat floated out of the room and into the night air.

A shiver ran over my body from the chill.

Or perhaps something else.

I sat up, now fully awake and annoyed. I adjusted my jacket and shirt, let the attendants think what they wanted, and waited patiently while Chip rose up from behind me and stepped up onto the rotating plank.

I reached up with both arms, gripping his outreaching hands.

He braced himself, allowing me to stand and rise to my feet. Then, his hands dropped to my waist. He lifted me out of the wet boat and placed me down onto the platform. I sighed, sad it was already over.

Still holding my hand, Chip led me up the stairs, oddly somber and quiet for the next several moments. "So what did you think? Wasn't it great?"

"Well, I think you owe me a hotdog."

We stepped back onto the walkway. Chip chuckled. "It's a deal."

I slowed my pace, feeling somber. "Seriously, Chip, the last date I had in Broad Ripple, my ex-boyfriend escorted me down an alleyway and tried to get me to do shots with him. As if he needed to get me drunk to do whatever he wanted." *Yikes, did I just say that out loud?* "And I'm *so* sorry, I'm talking *way* too much. Let's go get that hotdog."

Chip stared at me, blank-faced. "I'm sorry, Blue."

I shrugged. I decided at that moment to stop feeling sorry for myself. "The ride was fun. The evening's been great, Chip." I reached my arm around his back and pulled him into a half-hug. "You're a good friend. And I really need one right now."

He looked down at me and smiled, draping his own arm across my shoulders. "We losers have to stick together."

I giggled. "That's right, no one's running us out of town as long as we watch each other's back."

"You're going to be okay, Blue."

I sighed, suddenly very tired. "Besides, you mentioned a movie tomorrow. I think the new Vin Deisel just opened."

"Please. I've let my testosterone shots slip."

"Or we could just go to the theater and see what's playing. I don't really care what movie we see. As long as I'm with you."

A smile warmed my entire face. "Thanks."

———

ADVANCING TOWARD HOME, we walked in darkness along the side-walk. We held hands, occasionally chatting.

We passed beyond Sylvia's porch and stopped in my front yard. The house loomed in complete darkness before us.

Chip shrugged nervously and squeezed my shoulder. "I'll come by tomorrow around noon. I'll see you then."

I grinned. "Looking forward to it." I reached out and clasped both his hands, glancing at him in expectation. "Chip, I had a great time."

He smiled back. "Me, too. Goodnight, Blue." He paused a moment, then disengaged his hands and turned away, walking off into the darkness.

I swallowed back disappointment. His fidgeting, hesitating, awkward responses throughout the night screamed inexperience. *Patience, Fi-Fi. It's* not *lack of interest.* Still, a final goodnight kiss would have been the perfect ending.

I stepped carefully across the cement stones leading to the house. My mother had already left for her trip. Only darkened windows remained to greet me.

Like a slap, the harsh white brightness of the front porch light next door struck me in the face.

What in the—

I turned toward Sylvia's house, holding a hand out to ward off the blinding light. I blinked away spots, waiting for my vision to clear.

I called out, irritated as hell. "That was *not* nice, old lady! You'd better—"

My eyesight cleared, and the vision of Sylvia, still sitting and rocking in her chair, halted the complaint in my throat.

I stole a glance at my little Indiglo digital watch, 11:42 p.m.

I stood, paralyzed with shock and fear, watching the rocking silhouette. Her head rested at an awkward angle against the side of the chair. She continued rocking even with her eyes closed.

I called out. "Ma'am?"

She didn't move. Best I could tell, her body appeared stiffened in the chair, like a pile of dry mulch. A sudden wind gusted between us, rustling the new-fallen leaves.

I walked across the yard, closing the space between us. "Sylvia," I called again.

I stepped onto the porch, fighting a sudden urge to run. *Please, God, don't let her be dead!*

I turned away, gazing at the closed door that held the sanctity of my home, and then turned back.

A musty smell hit my nose, overpowering even the cold fresh air.

Sylvia was gone.

The chair stopped rocking with an abruptness that made me jump.

The wind blew and leaves rolled across the porch. I blinked, telling myself she'd never been there, that I had imagined seeing her. *Maybe I passed out and dreamt...*

But then, a gravelly voice whispered, "Guntherrrrrr..."

A shudder passed over me like an electrical current. I couldn't shake the dreadful feeling that I had seen her.

The wind howled, and an eerie voice floated on the breeze. "Bluuuuue..."

In spite of myself, I shrieked and backed away from the porch. *Nothing more to see here.*

I bravely walked away, trotting, *not running, dammit!*, to my house.

I shut the door on the wind and the old woman's porch.

I switched on all the lights, hurrying down the hallway and into my own room at the end of the hall. I stripped off my clothes, dropping them on the floor, and pulled a long T-shirt over my head. Settling under the covers, I waited for the shakes to pass. But it took a long time.

Staring at the reflection in the bathroom mirror, I'd just finished brushing on a thin coating of blue eyeliner when the doorbell rang. I glanced at the reflection of the clock, quarter to twelve.

Chip had arrived early, but I already looked dazzling. Hair combed, slight spike, mascara, faint color on the eyes and lips so I looked less rebel and more cutie, but in a subtle way. I applied a touch of Cinnaminx, my favorite scent, to my neck.

I gave my reflection one last cheesy smile, admiring the magic of whitening toothpaste, then stepped into the hallway. I left the eyeliner and makeup scattered over the bathroom marble top. Hey, Mom was gone; fuck it.

I opened the front door into bright sunshine and Chip's smiling face. He thrust a huge bouquet of blue carnations toward me.

Startled, I took an involuntary step back into the house.

The carnations followed after me. A hopeful glow lit Chip's expression. "Here. I want you to have these." He deposited the huge bouquet into my arms.

I cradled them in a reflex action.

The perfumed fragrance overpowered my nose, and I could only imagine the dumbstruck look on my face. I continued to stare at the flowers in my arms, still unable to find my voice.

But Chip's words reached my ears. "Do you like them?"

I backed into the room, my head spinning, but I found my voice. "Come in. Shut the door, please."

Water...you're supposed to put these in water. I turned on my heel, taking mechanical strides toward the kitchen. I could hear his footsteps following me.

I reached up, popping open a white-stained cupboard, looking for a vase I knew I wouldn't find. *When was the last* year *either Mom or I had gotten a bouquet of flowers?*

I spied a wide-mouthed Taco Bell Go-Cup. I dropped it onto the counter.

I stared at the sink, not wanting to look up. I fought down the conflicting waves of pleasure and fear rising in me. I'd flirted and fished to gain his interest, but the unexpected gift of flowers had just thrown me off balance, not a place I liked to be.

I struggled against the inclination to wrap my arms around his neck, shower him with kisses, and let hormones take their course.

Exactly the way I'd surrendered to Joey.

I couldn't let that happen again, not without being sure.

I turned toward him, shaking the bundle of flowers at him like evidence to a crime. "What is this? What do you think you're doing?"

His smile vanished, replaced by a frown of confusion. "I...uh, thought you would like them. They're a gift."

"A gift?"

I deposited the flowers on the countertop next to the Go-Cup and drew a shaking breath, collecting my thoughts.

The absurdity of the situation pushed forward in my head. *Chip the suitor arrives at the door to woo his maiden fair.*

But I was anything but a fair maiden.

My feelings must have shown on my face because he tried to step away from me. I put a hand on either side of his head, locking my eyes with his and stepping close, making him look down at me. "Don't do this, Chip."

"Blue, what are you—"

"Don't try to turn me into a Mary Rowan, or some other dipshit proper Perionne girl you think you can court and win over."

I panted, and I knew he could feel my hands shaking, but the words poured out of me. "Do you have chocolates for me? Are you going to start writing me sweetheart notes? I'm not going to change for you. I'm not going to change for anyone. I'm not the good girl who gets the flowers. I'm not going to the church pitch-ins or the girl's-night-out slumber parties. I don't want the bullshit. I don't want it from Phil, or Mary, or *most* of all, you."

During my tirade, Chip's expression changed from upset to angry. "Wait, just a second. What the hell's gotten into you?"

What the hell *had* gotten into me? Well, *I* knew what I meant. I just didn't know if I could explain it.

He reached up and took my hands in his. "Look, I'm sorry the flowers upset you, Blue. I bought them because I like you, and I wanted to show you."

"Stop it."

"No, *you* stop it."

My jaw clamped shut.

"Look, I don't know who this fuckhead was from your home town, but, clearly, he messed with your mind in some horrible way, and now I'm stuck with the collateral damage. I don't expect you to change. God, I don't *want* you to change. You're unlike anyone else I've ever met, and that's *why* I like you. And if I buy you flowers today and chocolates a few days from now, it only means I want to show you that I like you. That's all."

I could feel his hot breath across my cheek, and I knew he could feel mine. His sincerity penetrated my fear. I realized that it wasn't Chip keeping me from enjoying this, but my own silly paranoia.

I took a deep breath, centering myself, and then continued more calmly. "You're right. When I first met Joey, he was so sweet, so smart, and...full of bullshit. He'd take me out to dinner, and write me poems, and buy me jewelry, and then..."

I broke off. I couldn't go there. Not yet. "No bullshit, Chip. Not from you. Joey may have been the worst, but he wasn't the only one. When someone wants something from me, they butter me up first. I get the gifts. I get the compliments. I give my heart away. Then the other shoe drops. If that happens again, I'll be *so* hurt and *so* disappointed. And I want you to leave now if that's what you're doing."

Chip took a deep, somber breath, returning my angry glare with a stone-faced stare of his own. He replied in a calm, unemotional tone. "I'm not going anywhere. And I already told you why I bought you the flowers."

I dropped my arms, letting my hands travel from the sides of his face, then reaching down and placing them back in his. "The thing is, I already trust you. You're my friend, and we've always been up-front and honest with each other."

A hint of my cinnamon scent reached my nose, a reminder that I'd been doing my part to pretty myself up and get into date mode, so who the hell was I to come down so hard on him?

The realization of my own actions hit, and I knew I needed to let him off the hook.

"So let me see if I get the hidden meaning behind your...*gift*. You want me...and you want to know what I think of that." As I spoke, my voice deepened and turned sultry on its own.

His fingers tightened around mine. I could tell he thought desperately about pulling away, but I held his gaze.

He looked so cute and off-balance. My breathing quickened, and a flush ran over my body. I realized I very much liked the idea that Chip Farren desired me.

His mouth opened, but words failed him. He shrugged and looked down at the floor.

I reached up, one hand tipping his chin to look into my eyes. "I want you, too."

I released his hands and clasped mine together, trying to still their trembling. I continued to stare, unable to speak.

The energy in the room had gotten way too intense. I glanced away, taking a deep breath until my inner shaking subsided.

Chip looked ready to bolt out the door, and I could hardly blame him.

I walked over to the flower bundle, grabbed the Go-Cup, and filled it with water.

"So, what do I do?" I called over my shoulder. "Cut the bottom of the stems?" It seemed I'd heard something about that.

"You can. The florist said it's supposed to help them take in more water."

I kept my back turned, reaching out and pulling open the drawer. I mechanically located the scissors and attended to the task of arranging the flowers in the "vase." The blue carnations created an attractive arch of beauty over the faded image of the Taco Bell logo.

Finally, I turned to see Chip sitting in the black La-Z-Boy recliner, intently watching me. Enjoying his gaze, I walked over, putting a sway into my hips. I stood next to the chair, hovering over him, and slipped my hands into his.

They trembled in mine.

I pulled, urging him to stand.

He rose, towering over me, but even as our bodies pressed together, his gaze dropped toward the floor. Again.

I reached up, clasping my hand around the back of his neck.

He let me pull him close so I could speak into his ear. "Thanks for the flowers, my dear, dear friend. But if you wanted me, all you had to do was ask."

I pressed my lips against his. A gasping exhale blew into my mouth, and I giggled against his lips. "You're not supposed to hold your breath, love. It's a lot more fun if you just relax and go with it."

This time, his lips met mine, and his arms wrapped around my shoulders. Much better.

We separated gently. "Let's go to my room."

I watched his face change from a dumbfounded stare to an awareness of my meaning. "I've never...tried to be with a woman before. I didn't know. I wasn't sure if...if you wanted–"

"Shhhh. Be sure."

He tried to speak again, but I brushed a finger against his lips. "Later. We've more important things to do now."

I smiled up at him.

His arms enfolded me. Then he lowered his face to mine.

Our lips met in mutual hunger.

My knees went limp, but he held me tight.

With a sudden burst of confidence, he scooped me off my feet, and I floated in his arms.

We continued to kiss while he held me. Passion overcame me, and I slid my tongue forward. He pulled back a moment, then welcomed the kiss.

My entire body flushed in heated response. I broke away to catch my breath.

I giggled. "So my big, strong, handsome Chip. Now that you've got me, what *are* you going to do with me?"

He grinned back a moment then cradled me against his chest, his mouth meeting mine once again.

Before long, a euphoric buzz overcame my senses. I separated from our kiss, our mutual panting filling my ears, and basking in the security of his arms. "Come on, my sweet. Carry me down the hall. My bedroom's at the end."

He paused at the doorway, and I reached out, turning the knob and opening the door.

With infinite gentleness, he lowered me to the bed. I grabbed his hand and held it to my chest, sharing the pounding of my heart.

His lips found mine again, his face pressing me back against the pillow, while his hand brushed a hesitant question against my breast.

I moaned against his mouth, enclosing my hand over his, pressing in urgent firmness.

He needed no further instruction.

The universe turned giddy with shivers and stroking and hot kisses.

Soon, my blouse lay open while his mouth left fluttering butterfly kisses along the nape of my neck. And that's when ecstasy fled before the insistent urging of responsibility.

"Wait...Chip..."

Even while I pressed my hands against his shoulders, the edges of the room blurred in yet another wave of pleasure.

"We need to...cool off a second." Chip's look of confusion snapped into focus six inches from my own.

"I don't understand." His confusion turned to hurt. "Oh, Blue, I'm sorry; I thought this was what you wanted. We don't have to—"

I laughed. I couldn't help it. "Stop, stop, stop. No, silly. That's not it. This *is* what I want. And don't even *think* about backing out *now*, mister. But we need to be smart about it."

I waited for my sentence to penetrate his fog of confusion.

Finally, he shook his head, a vague look of guilt on his face. "I guess I wasn't thinking we'd end up—"

"Well, we're ending up. Now, when I packed to move, I had to hide my box of condoms from Mom. I think I know where they are, but we may have to search through several boxes in my closet to find them."

I underestimated how focused Chip could get when given the proper motivation.

Three minutes later, he placed the small wooden trinket box in my hands.

Shortly after, we picked up where we'd left off.

———

LATE SATURDAY NIGHT, Chip figured out my body. My world dissolved into blind screaming energy and then limp darkness. I buzzed and floated, basking in the end result of a full day's work, incredible, fun, exhausting work. After my release, spent and deliriously happy, I slept. Comforting arms held me snug for the rest of the night.

I drifted into wakefulness to find his mouth caressing mine. I kissed him back, welcoming and returning his love.

Last night's euphoria lingered in the quiet of the room.

Chip settled on his side next to me. His gaze held mine, sober blue eyes that spoke their utter sincerity.

I opened my mouth to say something, but my voice had fled. I could only smile back, shaking my head and tapping my fingers against my chest in a swooning gesture.

He laughed, and then his face softened. "I love you, Blue."

Like a stab of dread, his declaration penetrated my euphoria. A flush of shame settled over me. I'd wooed and seduced this boy, and he'd fallen for me, head over heels, exactly as I'd planned. Now he waited with a hopeful look for the expected response.

The smile froze on my face. I couldn't make myself say the words. Tiny doubts and questions buzzed in my head. *Can I love him? Do I want to love him?* The time had come to give my heart, and some internal reflex wouldn't let me. *Ah, typical. Shit!*

The moment lingered, and my voice returned to me. "I'm trouble to you, Chip."

He shook his head, gripping my hand and kissing my fingers. "You're wonderful." He lay his head on my shoulder.

Even now, my body responded with a shivering tingle. "You think so now. But you don't know everything about me." I massaged his head.

"No. You are." He reached up and stroked my tangled hair with infinite gentleness. He rolled a blue strand between his fingers, and dangled the end between us. "Don't ever change. No matter what."

My eyes stung, and I pulled him close. *What have I done to us?*

CHAPTER TWENTY

I drifted in nothingness.

"Blue."

From a distance, someone whispered my name.

No, not just someone. And not just any name. "Blue," my love teased again, his voice a gentle tickle across my ear. The word, more accurate than a fingerprint, assured me that Chip lay as close as a whisper in my ear.

I'd settled like a limp rag on the bed. I eased into a slow, numb wakefulness; my mind and body synched to a world of total safety and security. A feeling I'd not had in a long time.

Scratch that. A feeling I'd never had in my life.

Savoring the moment, I took my own sweet time waking up.

I gripped the pillow, pressing it tightly against the side of my face, wanting to hide in its darkness. I could feel the warmth of Chip's body, spooned against me, his mouth hovering close to my ear.

His hand caressed my bare shoulder, causing an answering shiver to travel across my skin.

I sighed in pleasure. "What is it, Chip?"

"How did you get the name Fi-Fi?"

I opened my eyes, becoming fully awake. "It's just a name, Chip."

His chuckle reached me in the darkness. I imagined him shaking his head. "Janet is just a name, Blue. Fi-Fi is a name for a poodle."

I took in a deep breath and turned to face him. I could make out his silhouette in the dim light. He laid propped up on one elbow, just watching me from his side of the double bed.

From the intensity of his gaze, I'd wondered if he'd been watching me for hours. The idea sent shivers of loving warmth through me.

But what if I snored or kept him awake for some other embarrassing reason? God, how do I even ask? The loving warmth vanished, and I shivered against him. My traitorous mind had determined to sabotage all the positives from this moment.

I blinked sleep from my eyes, then reached out and entwined his fingers with mine. "Fi-Fi was a nickname I sort of adopted for myself. It was...originally used as a term of affection by somebody who was very close to me."

"So does that mean you'll want everyone to call you 'Blue' now?"

I giggled. "No, sweet Chip. You can call me that, but no one else." I squeezed his hand. "Just now, when I was waking, I heard you say it, and I knew it was you. I felt very safe and loved."

His arms pulled me close, and his face nuzzled into my neck. I reached up and scratched his soft, matted hair. "When I hear it, I want to know it's you every time."

His breath brushed against my arm. "I can live with that."

He planted light kisses along my shoulder, and then I picked up the discussion. "So this very special man was a sort of mentor to me when I was a child. He was very kind to me. I think he was my father."

I could feel Chip pause in mid-kiss. I waited while he pulled his face back to speak. "I don't understand."

Oh, Chip. Maybe I don't want *you to understand.*

Yet here I was, telling him. "Well, it's not exactly casual conversation, not even between Mom and me. But I've never met my father. Or maybe it's better to say, we've never been introduced."

"So who was he?"

I shrugged. "Your guess is as good as mine. I've never been told."

From nowhere, a deep well of emotion swirled within me.

Where is this coming from?

I covered my face in my hands, fighting back tears. "I just don't know, and she won't tell me. I've asked several times. And the last time, she screamed at me never to bring it up again."

"That's terrible." No longer whispering, Chip sounded angry.

"I suppose Mom decided to get herself pregnant and have a child. So she did. And that's all she thinks I need to know."

"You don't talk about your mother much."

I fidgeted against him. When Mom came up in conversation, I'd get riled. Only this time someone asked what no one had before, and I struggled to control the shaking in my body.

A tear escaped, slipping down my cheek. How he saw it, I don't know, but his hand brushed across my face.

I sniffled. "Y'know, it's not like any man could ever deal with her, so why she decided to have a child is beyond me. She's an enormously successful businesswoman. She led her law firm to a prosperous town. She can demand prime dollar for her time and professional advice. There's no way she'd let a man get in her way."

Words kept flying out of my mouth, out of my control. "Somehow, she got some man to cooperate. She banged somebody and got them out of the way, and, nine months later, I was born. Me. Fi-Fi, the pet daughter."

He stroked my back. "Don't talk about yourself that way."

As the words poured out of me, heat burned my face. "It's like that Heart song they played on the radio when I was a kid. Pick up a hitchhiker, quick bang in a hotel, and send him on his way. 'All I Want to do is Make Love to You.' Convenient for everyone involved. Everyone except me."

In the dark, I could hear my panting breath. I wiped my eyes and sniffled. So many times in the past, people would ask, and I rattled off bullshit without batting an eye. Now *Chip* asked, and I babbled away like a fool.

I slammed my head into the pillow. "Sorry."

"It's okay, Blue." His hand stroked my back. "It's okay."

I closed my eyes. My breathing calmed, and my tears stopped.

A few moments passed. "Can I know about this man?" Chip whispered.

I reached up and placed my hand over his, trying to control my tone and emotion. "His name is Paul Willis. He was one of the senior partners in Mom's firm. Paul and Mom dated on and off until I was about eight years old."

I took a deep, shaking breath. "Before they broke up for good, he would come over all the time. He was very affectionate and playful with me, but not in a gross stepdad kind of way. And there was one thing we agreed on. He hated my real name."

Chip spoke the dreaded syllables. "Fiona Felicity?"

"Have you ever heard anything so stuck up? When they'd fight, my name would often come up. He'd say she may as well have called me 'Fi-Fi' because it was just as attractive and didn't sound as snotty."

"They had fights about your name, and you're wondering if he's your father?"

"Do you think he is? Really?" I couldn't hide the hopeful tone in my voice.

"Well, based on that alone, I'd say the chances are pretty good."

I turned in the bed to face him, ticking off the facts that had rattled around in my head for years, facts I'd shared with no one. "He was the only man my mother let me go places with. We took special all-day trips, like, to the zoo, or I'd stay at his apartment on weekends when Mom was carrying a big case load. He must've been my father; I'm sure of it."

I stopped, biting my lip, but unable to prevent the next words. "But Mom drove him away, then refused to tell me one way or the other, no matter how often I'd beg her to. It's just one more thing I hate her for."

"Don't say that. You don't really mean that you hate your mother."

"You have *no fucking idea* how much I hate my mother!"

Chip almost jumped out of the bed at my eruption.

Still angry but exhausted, I started crying again, covering my face and wanting to crawl into a hole.

We wallowed in silence for a long time before his voice reached me again. "It's so...beyond my experience."

"Chip...there's more. I ran around with the Broad Ripple college punks since I was thirteen years old. And don't get me wrong. They're great people, most of the time. Except late at night when some of them got drunk. I had to learn how to protect myself, because, sometimes, I didn't get back home as early as I'd planned. Most of my friends were very protective of me. But the others..."

Apparently, Chip decided it was safe to scoot close because his arm gently wrapped around my waist.

"Chip, I hung out with a twenty-year-old wasteoid last year. He was so neat at first. So nice and so attentive. He told me how beautiful I was, how mature I was for my age. I bought all that bullshit. But then one night I came over, he decided it would be a kick to break into one of the bars."

I blinked away tears and could see Chip's eyes widen at my words. There it was. I'd said it out loud straight-up and hadn't even tried to steer the conversation away.

And I kept on talking, telling the secret only Joey and I shared until tonight.

I hid my eyes while I spoke. "Well, anyway, I stayed at the door while he messed with the safe. Jackoff didn't know how to break into it, even though he swore beforehand he could.

"Then the alarm went off, and the cops were right there on top of us. We were one lucky turn down an alleyway from getting caught. I was ready to tell him to take a hike the next day, except I chickened out.

"Joey swore up and down that he was drunk, and that it wouldn't happen again if I gave him another chance. So I stayed. Like a fool, I stuck it out. But guess what my bitch-of-a-mom did?"

Chip's body jolted at my expletive.

"A couple days later, during breakfast, Mom starts reading the newspaper out loud. It's something she does sometimes. You know, when she can't bitch about me, she'll find something we can bitch about together. I guess that's her idea of mother-daughter bonding."

"Doesn't sound like a fun way to spend your mornings," Chip said wryly.

"So, she read the story of the break-in. Mom even commented that it was a good thing I had stayed over at my girlfriend's house. And I'm sitting there, about ready to pop from the guilt, and then the bitch just dropped the topic and moved on to another article."

I could hear the confusion in Chip's words. "Well, that's good, right? That she didn't suspect? Would you have rather she kept on you about it?"

"*No.* Not at the time. For the next several weeks, I went to bed every night, praying she *wouldn't* ask. But then I started thinking about it, and, damn it, she *should* have wondered. What kind of mother doesn't ask her kid questions?" Before he could answer, I rushed on. "The kind who doesn't care."

The tears forced their way out again. "She does what she can to enjoy her career, and as long as I...stay out of trouble...she's happy." *Shut up, shut up!*

I heard his breath draw in to respond, but I kept talking.

"Chip, I'd never done anything like that before, and I'll never do anything like that again. I'm not that kind of person, and I didn't want to be. So after that, I made a point to come home early and steer clear of Joey when he was high." *Why do I keep blabbering my head off?*

"Good for you."

"And my mother doesn't even notice, except to tell everyone how my grades have improved. 'Look, everyone, my pet daughter has a new trick. Come over after work...'"

My eyes stung and the tears flowed. Again. *Damn it! Why am I doing this? Why around him?*

I shrugged him away. "Leave me alone."

He pulled his hand back.

In the smoldering silence, my tears soon stopped. "Chip, if you repeat a word of this..." I stopped in mid-threat, appalled at my own reflex.

I didn't need to see him to know he was hurt. "Oh, shit. I'm sorry. For everything."

"It's okay, Blue. Everything is okay."

His fingers clasped gently around my waist. "I want to cuddle for a bit, if that's okay with you."

I trembled at his touch, needing him to hold me. And I sensed he knew it. By reaching for me, he gave me an out and let me keep my pride. It was so damn lame.

I let him do it.

The shell that had hardened around my heart since that night with Joey loosened and fell away. I turned into his arms and buried my head against his thin chest.

Like a newly hatched chick, I settled into Chip's protective wings.

But a part of me still remained uneasy. Like that chick, I now felt exposed for all the predators to find and attack. And I didn't like that feeling, not one bit.

——————————

CHAPTER TWENTY-ONE

——————————

PERIONNE 1990

Special Agent George Carson of the FBI stormed into the waiting room of the Perionne Municipal Hospital. They'd stuck him with the Perionne bank robbery case that afternoon.

He'd received the assignment and took the three-hour drive from Indy to Perionne, not counting the ten minutes it took to find the miniscule dot labeled Perionne in his road atlas. Between then and now, the perps had slipped away.

The local bumpkin cops had identified the two assailants, but locating the rednecks proved a different matter. The yellow T-bird showed up abandoned at the rest stop, but, from there, the trail went cold.

They'd tightened the screws on Lilly Mills, girlfriend of the psycho who went on the shooting spree. They'd threatened the pregnant waitress with a federal indictment. They painted a detailed picture of her serving a life sentence in a women's prison, never to see her child again. He'd traumatized her and felt like a total asshole in the process. All for nothing. Mills didn't know anything. And the psycho's mama was no help, though she cooperated easily enough.

He'd run out of leads. Crimley had no family or close friends, at least no one but Gunther, bless his mass-murdering, shooting-spree psychotic head.

Carson's afternoon in Perionne didn't change his dim view of small towns. He longed to wrap this case up and get the hell out of here as fast as he could.

He worked late into the evening before giving up. He checked into a local dive of a hotel, only taking the time to leave the number with Perionne P.D. before collapsing onto the rock-hard mattress.

The phone rang at the ungodly hour of 3:00 a.m., jarring him awake. The calm voice of the dispatcher told him a local patrolman had found one of his perps, who now lay dying in the hospital. He was damned well going to get a few answers before the guy kicked.

CARSON APPROACHED the nurse's desk, his nose burning at the nauseating smell of alcohol and stale vomit. As a Fed, Carson had spent a lot of time in hospital wings identical to this one. It used to upset him, bringing back memories of his dad slowly giving in to the cancer. The sickness and death didn't affect him so much these days. But he still hated the smell.

He opened his mouth to address the nurse but paused as he spotted a fortyish man with a thick shock of salt-and-pepper hair and wearing a white coat approach him from across the hall. The doctor extended his hand. "You must be Agent Carson. I'm Dr. Eric Lee. I received the call from the police station."

Carson nodded back, returning the doctor's firm handshake. "Dr. Lee, I understand Jeff Crimley's your patient. I need to talk to him now."

Dr. Lee grimaced. He motioned Carson to follow him. "I'm sorry, but I have a problem with that. If I wake Crimley up, I'll most likely end up zipping him up into a body bag later tonight.

The patient is suffering from hypothermia, as well as severe loss of blood from his stab wounds."

Carson fumed. *Of course, the doctor needs to give me hassles now.*

They approached the door to a private room. A Perionne police guard straightened in his chair, seeming to come to life at the sight of the federal agent.

Carson folded his arms. "Let's start at the top. Is he going to make it or isn't he?"

The doctor shrugged. "I doubt it. We'll do all we can, of course. We just didn't get to him in time."

"Well, then, what are we discussing? If you can't keep him alive, then I need him awake now. He won't do anybody any good once he's dead."

Dr. Lee puffed out his chest. "Listen to me, agent. That man has little enough chance as it is. If we rouse him at this stage, the shock alone could kill him."

George Carson bristled, frustrated to be on the verge of breaking this case and going home, only to have this man fret about the health of one of the criminals. "No, *you* listen, *doctor.* Two people were murdered in cold blood at the Perionne National Bank today. I need to tell their families something. We know who two of these monsters were, but we also know, because of the way they blew out of there so damn fast, that a third person was very likely involved. We've tried patrols, roadblocks, and house-to-house searches. Nothing. If I can identify that third person, I can't let my only opportunity go."

Dr. Lee sighed. "There may only be one person to find. When we brought Jeff Crimley in, he babbled that he'd killed Gunther Stalt in a fight. That's what you wanted to know, right? So the murderer's dead, and the co-conspirator will likely die before the end of the night."

"He said that? Gunther's dead?"

The doctor referred to a note pad. "The admitting physician heard Crimley say Gunther gave him the stab wounds, but he still managed to kill Gunther before it was over."

Carson grunted, not impressed. "I'll still need to speak with Crimley to corroborate that. Then, I'll have to tell Gunther's mother. Damn shame. She's a sweet lady. Even if her son turned out to be a bastard."

Dr. Lee shook his head and frowned. "It puts my patient in jeopardy."

Undeterred, Carson barreled on. "There may still a third man out there."

Dr. Lee squinted and rubbed his temple. "God, I hate this. Don't you have anything else to go on?"

Carson threw up his hands. "I've got nothing, doctor. We found the getaway car this afternoon. Stolen last week. They'd abandoned it at a rest stop. Not a useful print on it. They must've had a second car waiting, but we can't find a good set of tracks."

Carson fished into his jacket and drew out his badge. "Look, we can do this one of two ways. You can wake him up now and save us all a lot of time, or I can make a phone call and have a court order dropped off early this morning. And you'll still have to wake him up."

"I doubt it's quite as easy as you make it out. But, yes, I see you'd ultimately get your way. Sit tight a minute."

———

JEFF CRIMLEY FLOATED in a haze of pain, gradually rising to consciousness. A weight pressed on his chest, making each breath a great effort. He opened his eyes, his vision blurry, but he could tell he lay in a narrow bed in unfamiliar surroundings. *A hospital?*

The monotonous beeping of his vital signs recorded on some unseen machine reached his ears.

I'm dyin'.

He looked into the face of a serious-looking man in a brown rain-spotted windbreaker.

A cop.

"Crimley? I'm Agent Carson of the FBI. Can you hear me?"

"Yes." Crimley forced the word from his lips. His throat felt raw, and his voice sounded hoarse. *I need to rest.*

"Crimley, do you remember the bank robbery? I need to ask you questions about it."

Crimley nodded. It was easier than trying to speak.

"You were identified as a participant in this robbery, along with Gunther Stalt. Can you verify for me that Gunther was involved?"

Crimley nodded again.

"Where's Gunther now? If you cooperate, we'll make things easier on you."

Even in his condition, Crimley detected an uncomfortable urgency in the man's voice. The agent was trying to play him for a fool. Well, there was no need to hold back about Gunther.

Crimley took a deep, painful breath. "Dead."

"Dead? You mean Gunther's dead? Did you kill him?"

Crimley nodded, struggling to breathe. "I stabbed him. He stabbed me. He died." *God, my chest hurts! Just let this end.*

"Crimley, there was a third person involved, wasn't there? You had a getaway car driver. Isn't that correct?"

The words slowly penetrated Crimley's fogged brain. *Poor Jim. He'd never asked to be a part of this. I forgive you, if it means anything now.*

"Can you tell me who he was?"

He remembered Jim yanking him from the car, abandoning him to die at the side of the road. But he couldn't work up any anger toward the man. *We're the ones who dragged Jim into this mess. Can't ruin it for his family.*

Crimley took a deep breath. "Getaway driver blackmailed. Forget him. No danger." Even as the world darkened around the edges, Crimley drew some satisfaction at seeing the fed's face turn a bright, angry shade of red.

"So there was a getaway driver. Tell me who."

If this is dying, it's not so bad. Just slip off into the black and see what happens next. "I'm dying. Just go away. Leave me to it."

The agent's voice faded into the background. He barely heard the next words.

"Listen, Crimley, we want to help that man as much as we want to help you. But we can't do that if..."

But for Crimley, the world blurred away for the last time, and a heavy darkness settled over him. He closed his eyes and drifted.

———

AT SEVEN-FORTY THAT MORNING, Jim pulled the blue Buick Regal into his driveway.

He'd driven all night, until the panic settled, and he could finally focus again. More punch-drunk than worried, he pulled into the parking lot of a 7-Eleven and purchased a bottle of Fantastik and a rag.

He scrubbed on the many bloodstains ground into light-gray cloth of the passenger seat. When he finished, the spots left behind resembled old chocolate more than mayhem. He'd burn his jacket later.

Exhausted, he arrived home, not noticing the squad car parked at the curb until he reached his front door.

A chill of terror ran through his body. *All this work, all my worrying, and they already knew. They've been waiting for me to show up.* In an odd way, relief washed over him. *Better to come clean early, pay for my sins, and not look over my shoulder for the rest of my life.*

But how will I explain to Jesse?

He took a deep breath. *No sense fighting. I'll surrender peacefully.* He opened the door. They'd take him away from his family and lock him away in a hole, where nothing and no one could get to him. *Nothing but the sound of Crimley's voice calling out, over and over for eternity. That's one thing they won't take from me.*

He stepped through the back door, which opened directly into the kitchen and breakfast bar. The pleasant aroma of bacon and coffee wafted toward him. Had he ever smelled anything so good, so much like home? Would he again?

Standing in front of the oven, Jesse turned and smiled at him. He could hear the still-whistling tea kettle of boiling water.

"Good morning, honey," Jesse called. He detected the strain under her nonchalance.

"Hi." Jim walked past the bar, where he could see Deputy Fred Lovison seated in the dining room. Jesse must have insisted that the informal breakfast bar wasn't an appropriate place for an officer of the law to eat.

Jim had seen Lovison, with his stocky frame and thinning brown hair, create a dominating presence, mainly when trouble broke out at the Cat's Cradle. This morning, the officer beamed a toothy smile at him. "Mornin', Jim."

"Mornin', Fred. A little early for a social call, isn't it?" His voice sounded surprisingly calm.

"I'm afraid that's true. I'm here on official business. Well, at least I was."

"Oh?" Jim noticed the almost-empty plate in front of the deputy. Lovison picked up the last piece of bacon and took a bite.

Jesse waved the spatula. "Fred drew the tiny straw. He's been going door to door since late last night, trying to find out more about that bank robbery. You remember. The one we saw on TV." She turned her back on the deputy, facing Jim, the look in her eyes penetrating like a pair of pointed daggers.

It was almost too much to take. His wife, who he'd wanted to protect most of all, was lying for him.

"Right. The bank robbery. That sounded...absolutely awful, deputy." He didn't dare say anymore. He'd avoided the news reports on the radio the last few hours.

Deputy Lovison swiped at his mouth with a cloth napkin. "It was. Relax, Jim, your wife already told me you were working around the house all day and watching TV with her, just like you always do."

Jesse stepped toward an overhead cabinet, fishing out a coffee cup. "We watched *Casablanca*. It's one of Jim's favorites."

The deputy chuckled. "I saw it, too. Love old movies. Can't beat that Bogie. And Ingrid Bergman was a dish."

Jesse entered the dining room, the mug in one hand and the kettle in the other.

The deputy grinned at her, then at Jim. "I figured since I have over half the damn town to patrol, I might as well take up Jesse's offer for breakfast. Say, what was wrong with the car?"

Already punch-drunk, Jim jumped as if he'd been slapped. "What's that?"

The deputy waved vaguely in the direction of the driveway. "Jesse told me you were having car problems."

"Oh, yeah. Spark plugs. Replaced 'em this morning with a spare set. Car's driving fine, now." A comment formed in his mind about being a former racecar driver and preparing for those emergencies, but he stopped short of saying it out loud.

How many other lies has Jesse told?

"You didn't see Gunther or Crimley recently?"

Jim shrugged and stared, maybe too long. "Uh...no. No, definitely not. That is, Gunther visited a few days ago. Hadn't heard from him in months, then he showed up at my door. He had a lot to drink, but he just blew off some steam about losing his job."

The deputy stared quizzically at Jim. "I don't suppose he told you anything useful or hinted at what he planned to do?"

"No." Jim shifted from foot to foot while the deputy waited patiently. "Well...he said he needed money because of Lilly. Hinted about a loan, but I ignored the hint. I didn't think he'd do something like rob a bank. Crazy."

Jim stood before the deputy's stern gaze, biting back the urge to scream.

The deputy took a long sip of his coffee. "Say, hear the latest?"

Jim shrugged. "I'm not sure."

"They found Jeff Crimley and took him to the hospital. Someone stabbed the poor bastard nearly to death. He'd been tossed out on the road. He died early this morning."

Jim's mind raced. "That's horrible. Did he say anything...useful?" To his amazement, his voice sounded calm.

"Crimley said he killed Gunther. He also confirmed that

someone else drove the getaway car. But Crimley refused to name him. Said it didn't matter, and that we should let it alone. You believe that? Now that's loyalty."

Jim stood on wobbly legs, blindsided by the memory of dumping Crimley on the side of the highway, and humbled that, in the end, Crimley had shown him mercy.

Jesse hollered from the kitchen. "Would you like some coffee, dear? I got a fresh pot ready."

Jim mumbled, "Yes."

The deputy nodded. "You do look mighty tired. Probably got up a lot earlier than you wanted to, eh?"

He nodded and said nothing, still trying to absorb what the deputy had told him. "So now what are you going to do?"

The deputy shook his head. "Keep going door to door like a damn vacuum cleaner salesman. My hunch is this other guy doesn't even live around here. They probably hired some professional. They say Crimley had some pretty shady connections." He took a sip of his coffee. "But, the FBI says 'do it,' so that's what I gotta do. After all, I'm just a bumpkin small town cop, what do I know?"

The sizzling of frying eggs reached Jim's ears from the kitchen.

Jesse called out. "Would you like some breakfast?"

"Okay. That sounds good."

The deputy held the coffee cup up and made an appreciative noise. "Good stuff! I'm sorry I have to bust in on you good people and bother you so early in the morning."

"It's no bother," Jesse said.

"That's right," Jim added. "You've got a thankless job ahead of you. We appreciate all you're doing."

The deputy moved on with casual questions about the neighbors. Jim answered as best he could, his mind still contemplating the tragic news about Crimley.

Finally, the deputy finished his plate and rose. He extended his hand, offered his thanks, and let Jesse lead him to the door.

Jim tottered out of the dining room and into the connecting living room, collapsing onto the leather chair. He listened to Jesse say goodbye, his head still spinning. At the welcome sound of the door closing, he placed his hands over his eyes to hide his relief.

Jesse came into the room, letting the silence linger before she finally spoke. "I don't want to know."

Ashamed, Jim looked down as her bitter, disappointed voice penetrated his soul.

"I just want you to answer about a few points, and we'll never speak of it again."

He nodded.

"Did you kill anyone? Did you shoot anyone? Did you stab Gunther? Crimley? Did you do anything else but drive the car? And I want the truth."

He swallowed down shame. Tears filled his eyes. "I didn't. I swear. I couldn't. I didn't want anything to do with—"

"Shut up!" Her shriek stunned him to silence. She took a deep, shuddering breath, holding back tears. "I just want to know that you didn't hurt or kill anybody. Nobody saw you in the bank. Nobody knows what happened after. And I don't want to know, either. Just tell me you didn't kill anyone."

"I didn't."

Jesse sobbed.

Jim sat, listening to his wife's weeping. Along with his other crimes, he'd broken Jesse's heart.

He clenched his fists and made a vow.

I'll spend the rest of my life making this up to her.

CHAPTER TWENTY-TWO

I knew being Chip's "first" would change our relationship, perhaps taking us somewhere intense and unpredictable.

For him, it was simple. He loved me. He had eyes for no one but me. I told myself it's what I wanted. I hoped I was right.

Chip and I took to texting each other during class. I certainly had enough boring classes where I could send back a few random thoughts, along with some references to our previous weekend, just to make sure he missed me.

Somewhere in one of his mid-week texts, Chip wrote that he needed to meet me in the woods for a "supr secr8" meeting. He carefully described the forested area next to the school where a road ended abruptly, blocked by a large pile of dirt. Beyond that, a recently harvested cornfield spread out over the next several acres.

According to his text, our rendezvous would take place behind the dirt pile after school on Friday. We needed privacy for this "supr secr8" discussion, his text said. I rolled my eyes. Chip and I had not followed up after our first encounter, and I figured this must be at least part of what he had in mind.

Not that I had a problem with that.

———

I ARRIVED FIRST. The dozen or so trees that made up the "forest" looked invitingly private for snuggling later on, but not private enough for anything *too* intense. Darn it all.

For all my doubts and concerns about my long-term feelings, I jumped up when I saw him approach, his arms filled with a large scrapbook. I abandoned my own backpack and rushed up to him. I needed to show how much I'd missed him since last seeing him, lunch break three hours ago.

He gratefully welcomed my insistent kiss, even while clutching the scrapbook to his chest.

My mind still wrestled with this relationship, but my body had given in days ago.

Chip put his arm over my shoulder and walked me back to the dirt path. "Thanks for coming, Blue. I want to show you something."

I cooed in my best Marilyn imitation, "I haven't come yet, Mr. President, but maybe *after* you show me."

He laughed. "Down, girl. I'm serious."

I rolled my eyes. "Oh, yes, I know. I can always tell when Chip has his serious face on. You get such a stern crinkle between your eyebrows."

He motioned to a patch of ground behind the mound. "Here, let's talk a minute."

I dropped down and folded my legs in front of me.

He deposited his five-pound scrapbook on my lap, (as well as his trademarked stack of computer paper) and talked some craziness about breaking into the Pirates of Perionne boat ride to find hidden treasure.

"I found it!" He pointed at Gunther's picture. "All we have to do is dig it up. Once we find the money, we'll be famous beyond our wildest dreams. We'll be heroes." His eyes lit up with a sort of spooky gleam that scared me.

What is he babbling about? What have I gotten myself into?

My knees started cramping from the heavy book opened up on my lap.

I looked down at the newspaper articles, trying to buy myself time. I'd aced my folklore midterm earlier in the week and thought that made me an official Gunther Stalt expert. But I'd never seen some of these articles.

Chip sat across from me, his knees pulled against his chest, dark hair rumpled. I'd seen it that way before whenever he'd been working on a computer project all night. I was getting to know this look all too well, obsessed programmer tracking down a lost equation. But this time I was only partly right.

I ran my hands through my hair, breathing in the cool October air, wondering what I should say. Nothing came to mind. Chip reached out and put a hand on my shoulder. "Listen, Blue. Nobody knows what happened to Gunther's money. Except me. And with your help, I can get it. Surely you can't tell me that you're not just a teensy bit interested."

I glared at him.

He dropped his hand from my shoulder.

"Chip, I know you're obsessed with this Gunther thing, but, to me, that was just test material; and as far as I'm concerned, I'm done with it." I shrugged. "I really don't care about some hick psychopath robbing the local bank. What bothers me more is how—"

"You're not hearing me!"

The passion of his cry took me aback and silenced me.

Chip scowled. "I know where the money is, Blue. The biggest damn secret in the town, and I know it." He folded his arms across his scrawny chest, appearing as little more than a bunch of folded angles.

I sighed, reaching out and grabbing his wrists. "Chip, get out of the clouds. Listen to me." When I saw him look into my eyes, I continued. "You're talking about breaking and entering. You could get into serious trouble."

That seemed to rouse him. He composed himself, losing a lot of that idiot look. "I know that."

"Then why take the risk?"

"So that we'll know."

That sounded consistent, and yet I still had my doubts. Maybe Chip wasn't interested in the money or even the glory of having solved *the* mystery of the town. But to tell me he wanted the satisfaction of knowing, it didn't sound right to me.

So what's really going on?

Then, he proceeded to expand on his scheme. And the scariest part was I could tell from his voice that he was going through with this, with or without me. Even though he was certain it wouldn't work without my help. *Of course. Let's fuck up two lives, why just one?*

But I had some kind of responsibility to him, as his friend, and as his lover, too, but as his friend first. For now, I had to put aside all the chills, tingles, and the emotional baggage within me caused from last weekend. I had to help him because he'd helped me in so many ways. I couldn't let him do this alone.

I reached out and took his hands in mine. "Okay, start over. Let me hear what you have in mind."

He opened the scrapbook filled with Xeroxes of old news clippings and reports all related to Gunther and the robbery. I shuffled around to get a good look. He leaned close, and I snuggled against him, and that was pretty nice, too.

He settled on a fuzzy blueprint scanned from a computer graphics file. It was the blueprint Phil had haplessly helped Chip recreate from his notes, a blueprint of *The Pirates of Perionne* ride.

I studied it while I talked. "Okay. What have you got?"

Chip sat up straight, forcing me to do the same. I watched, amused, as he glanced past trees and the road that ran beyond it. He looked straight out of a bad gangster movie.

I had to grin. "There's nobody here, Chip."

"I know there was a getaway driver, and I know who he is." He'd lowered his voice to a whisper.

"Oh," I whispered back.

He waited for me to ask, but, certain the name would mean nothing to me, I didn't.

He continued. "Look, Blue. This is going to sound crazy, but a couple of months ago my father came home with one of his old bowling buddies, and I overheard the guy telling my dad all about it."

I shrugged. "So this guy drove the getaway car? I suppose you have something to back this up with."

"You need to take me seriously. We need to be very careful about this. What he told my dad was in confidence. I just happened to be going across the loft to get a book at the time."

I could envision the length of hall in question. It stretched about twelve feet. "And how long did this trip across the loft take?"

Chip's face flushed red. "Well, hell, Blue. He mentioned Gunther at just the moment I was stepping out. What did you think I was going to do?" He turned his face away from me.

"Oh, C'mon, Chip, I was just razzing you. I would have done the same thing, if the conversation had meant anything to me." Which should not have consoled him much, but for some reason it did. "So tell me what you heard."

Chip shrugged. "Well...since it's their bowling night, and the guy's speech was kind of slurred, he must've had a few too many beers that night. My Dad kept trying to shut him up, but...he kept talking on and on like he had to get it out."

"That would fit the mold."

"So then he told my dad the whole story."

And at this point, Chip proceeded to do the same. I listened, trying to keep a skeptical view, but as the tale unfolded, all the facts fell into perfect place.

By the end, I was as convinced as Chip that he'd stumbled onto the biggest secret in the town.

"...Who could blame him for not going back all of these years?"

Chip finished. "He's probably just some family man wanting to stay as far away from the situation as possible. And to this day he has to hear the stories and the theories, hoping that no one ever closes in on him."

He reached out and took my hands.

I looked into his blue eyes, alight with fervor. "It doesn't matter who the driver was. I might know, but you don't need to, and no one else does, either. What matters is, we can solve this and return the money. And the poor guy who's been living with this guilt all these years can finally let it go. And no one need ever know who this guy is but me."

I gave his hand a gentle squeeze. "And your dad."

"Right. And my dad. C'mon, Blue. I've been working on it for months. You and I could sneak into the park and dig up the money. With your skills and my brains, we can do this easily."

I stared at him, appalled. The eagerness with which he told the tale, the scary gleam in his eye as he rattled off the details, staggered me. "Tonight? You want to break into Perionne Park tonight after closing?"

"Not exactly. But close enough. I'm more concerned about whether they lock up the pirate building itself than the gate to the park, but you said that you knew something about breaking and entering, so—"

"That's not exactly what I said. I can pick a lock or two, but—" And then the connection hit, like a two-by-four to the back of the head. A nasty piece of the puzzle slipped into place.

Fury erupted from me. "You bastard!"

I jumped to my feet, sending the scrapbook tumbling into the dirt. "You've been working on this for months? *Months!* Let me guess, looking for the perfect little girlfriend accomplice with some lock-picking skills?"

Chip stood next to me, jaw dropped, arms spread apart. He had the decency to look appalled at the accusation. "Blue, no. C'mon, you know that's not true."

I swatted him on the chest, forcing him to step backwards.

"What, Chip? What do I know? I know what you're *capable* of when you want to get your way. I know that I'm a pretty damn *convenient* piece to your *pet* project. I also know you did some pretty wonderful favors to get my attention."

I took a step back, lowering my hand. Sure, I could beat up on him, but what would be the point? *How stupid I'd been. And here I'd been feeling sorry for him!*

Chip glared back at me, looking equally hurt. His hand came up to his chest where I'd struck him. "Oh, yeah, right. How clairvoyant of me to know all about your criminal past weeks before you told me about it. And don't forget how I seduced you. Wasn't that just brilliant of me? I came at you like James Bond last weekend. I had you eating out of my hand."

I bit back an acerbic reply. He was right about the last part, and he didn't even know it. Last weekend, he'd left me one moment sighing in bliss and the next twisted in knots.

Exactly how I feel now.

I couldn't strike out at him, so I scraped at the ground with the toe of my boot. "Damn you, Chip!"

I kicked the dirt and stomped a few feet, causing a cloud of dust to rise up around me; I growled in anger to keep from shouting at the top of my lungs. "Well, fuck you, then! I'm ruining your plan, do you hear me? I'm not going along with it."

I stopped, gasping to catch my breath.

Chip sighed, and his shoulders slumped. "I...guess I can't force you to go. I told you because of how I feel about you, and because this is important to me. That's the truth. Somewhere last weekend, you really opened up to me, and I wanted to do the same. I thought you would want to help."

I shook my head. "I can't." I grabbed his arm. "Chip, damn it, listen to me. *You* can't. It's too dangerous."

He gathered up his papers, brushing dust from the scrapbook. "Well, then. I guess you'll just have to wish me luck. You know where you can catch up with me if you change your mind."

I clenched my fists in exasperation. "Chip, use that logical brain you rely on so much. You don't have a chance. I bet you'll get caught straddling the gate, and you'll go to jail. And who knows how bad it can get? You won't be a minor much longer."

Chip hung his head in resignation. "Blue, I have to know. Finding this treasure has been my only goal for years. Except for pleasing you. Hell, it would be worth it just to pull this off and you'd see what I'm capable of. Then you'd see that I'm not as incompetent as you think."

And damn if my heart didn't melt, even as I bit back a laugh. "Will you *stop* it!"

He remained hunched over, holding the scrapbook in his lap.

I stepped up to him and sat down, reaching out to touch his face. He wouldn't look at me at first, and then he did.

His eyes were wet.

And my heart broke all over again.

I pulled his notebooks from him, easing them to the ground. Then, I wrapped my arms around him.

His arms tightened around me.

I held him close. "Just stop. You're not going in there alone, damn it. If you're going to do your damnedest to fall, then I have to try to catch you."

He snuffled against my chest. "What do you mean?"

"It means, shut up and kiss me."

And he did.

———

I DON'T REMEMBER MUCH about the walk home, except the world glowed with brightness. I skipped and hummed a tune to release my cheer to the world. "When you're a Jet, you're a Jet to the end..."

I skipped past Sylvia's house, hopping onto the stepping stones and up to my porch. I risked a glance across the yard.

What I saw froze me in place.

A *FOR SALE* sign in Sylvia's yard that had never been there before today.

And yet, from the weather spots, the area of dead grass surrounding the sign, and the rust on the framework, the sign had clearly been in the yard for months.

I walked to the front of the house, taking in the familiar porch with the rocking chair, but the chair sat unused, covered in layers of matted webs across the seat and down the sides. And while it bore a striking resemblance to the off-white cloth Sylvia had been knitting, these were clearly spider-webs, several of them still inhabited. No living body had rested in the chair last week, probably not even last year.

But where's Sylvia? On reflex, I looked at the front door with the two small windows inset toward the top, like a pair of eyes. Windows I remembered a couple of days ago. Now, twin boards ran across both in an X-shape.

My gaze traveled across the front of the house, seeing for the first time the boards across the windows, set firm with nails turning brown from months of exposure to the elements.

Boards and nails I had not seen yesterday.

"Sad, isn't it?"

I jumped at the sound of the unfamiliar voice. I turned to see a woman dressed in a sharp gray business-suit, similar to the sort my mother might wear.

She held out her hand.

I extended mine automatically, letting her place a business card into my palm. I glanced at the text identifying her as, *Hariette Sanders, Certified Real Estate Agent.* The spiffy card included a full-color logo and photograph.

She stood beside me, brushed a rebellious lock of short brown hair from her eyes, and sighed. "I don't know what I'm going to do. But neither did the seven agents hired before me, so I guess I shouldn't feel bad."

My head still reeled, but I found my voice. "How long has the house been on the market?"

"Oh…the owner died over five years ago. I've been stuck with the listing for six months. Neat hair, by the way."

Five years ago? "Thanks. When you say 'the owner', you mean Sylvia?"

The real estate agent laughed pleasantly. "Oh, yes. Sylvia. *That* Sylvia. Sylvia Stalt, Gunther's mom, bless her pointy little head. They found her body on the porch, still in the rocking chair."

Hariette crossed her arms, warding off a chill. "Sylvia willed the house to Lilly Mills, Gunther's old girlfriend."

I nodded. Like a lifelong local, I knew exactly who she meant.

The agent shook her head. "Lilly split town after the robbery. She's lived in Madison, Wisconsin ever since. Raised her daughter there. Anyway, I guess Sylvia figured giving Lilly the property was the least she could do, given how Gunther treated her. Ms. Mills hired the first agent, and ordered him to sell the property any way he could. But stories had already circulated about the house being haunted. And now, I can't give the house away."

"But that's not possible. I just…" I stopped, knowing I'd sound insane if I finished the thought. Instead, I said the one thing I cared about the least. "Why is the rocking chair still on the porch?"

Hariette shook her head. "We've all dragged that piece of junk to the curb for the trash pick-up, but, every time we'd return, it was right back there on the porch, cobwebs and all. Maybe some kids playing pranks. I finally decided to leave it there. I'm not about to get my suit dirty, again."

My focus returned. I couldn't accept the obvious conclusion of my experiences. "So what do *you* think? That someone's playing a trick, or the house is haunted?"

Hariette shrugged, clearly not interested in giving the matter much thought. "Haunted or not, I was a fool to accept this challenge, and I'm stuck with it until my listing agreement runs out. One month left to go."

I stepped toward my house, biting back what I wanted to scream. *Who did I talk to? What did it mean? Am I losing my mind?* "Well, good luck."

The agent nodded, still standing in front of her cursed property. "Thanks. If you know any crazy friends who want to buy a haunted house, give me a call. I'll make them a great deal."

I approached the sanctuary of my own home, inserted my key, and opened the door.

Shaking off the chill, I walked across the living room and dropped my backpack on the couch. Someone was playing tricks, some sick old hag having fun at my expense. I could rationalize some prankster removing the sign. I could even accept that I'd been so awed by the creepy old lady, I'd never noticed the boarded-up windows. *Doesn't matter, I'll get my revenge later. I have more immediate concerns.*

Ghosts weren't real. And a good thing, too. Because tonight, I had enough to worry about dealing with the real world.

—————

CHAPTER TWENTY-THREE

—————

I burst into my bedroom, my mind already five steps ahead, focused on what I needed to bring for later tonight. I grabbed two bobby pins off my dresser and stuck them into my hair.

Pack light, Chip had said to pack light. He'd take care of the tools. I pulled open the closet door and placed my hands on The Box, still hidden away behind my shoes and winter boots.

I hadn't opened The Box since that day Sylvia, or whoever she was, made me return the switchblade. Somehow, I couldn't get rid of the items inside, no matter how much I told myself I would never need them again.

I flipped up the lid, fished past the top layer of buttons, and grabbed at the sharp metal pins. I found the three or four most useful ones from the dozen Joey had filed for me.

My fingers brushed across the carved wooden handle with the tell-tale metal switch, and a tingle ran up my arm. I scooped up the knife. It lay across my open palm, from my wrist to the second joint of my middle finger.

I closed my hand over the weapon. The silver blade *snicked* into place, doubling the length of the weapon. Light reflected on silver, and I could stare back at my own widened eyes in the edge of the blade.

Shocked eyes. Weak eyes. The look of someone who'd gone to the edge and walked away.

At the time Joey gave the illegal knife to me as a misguided birthday present, he showed me how to kill with it, all theoretical information. I'd never been in that dire of a situation. He also showed me how *not* to kill with it. Most times, the simple appearance of the blade and a couple threats got me out of almost all nasty situations in 'Ripple.

I heard the front door open and shut.

Without further thought, I retracted the blade into the sheath and slid the weapon into my pocket.

I could hear determined footsteps cross the living room and enter the hall.

I closed the box as casually as I could and placed it back into its hiding spot.

I heard the door open behind me as my hand closed around a flashlight.

I stood and turned. "Hi, Mom."

No salutations. She stood, hands folded across her chest, leaning against the doorframe. She jumped right in. "Fiona, did you have a boy over at the house while I was away?"

Oops. "Uh, just a friend, Mom. He picked me up, and we went to a movie."

Her eyes glared disappointment and fury. "You're lying to me. Your friend was Eugene Farren, and he didn't leave here all night."

"Excuse me?" I stared into her angered face. "You...spied on me?"

Undeterred, she continued with the riot act. "What could you have *possibly* been thinking? His father is a very important contact with our firm."

I still couldn't get past the first point. "*Now* you spy on me? *Now?* What did you do, pay one of our fine neighbors to watch the house for you?"

She sighed and dropped her hands to her hips. "Fiona, does it matter how I found out? If word gets out to Eugene's father, it could be a problem for the both of us. I can't believe you would jeopardize my position like this."

The train of thought only now began to sink in. "Wait...you're angry...over *who* I slept with?"

Mom's nostrils flared, and I could see her teeth grind. "I don't pretend I know how to control you. But I thought you'd be more discreet. I thought somebody should keep an eye on the house since you're never home these days. Instead, I find out that when I'm gone you never leave the bedroom."

"Well, I figured one of us should be having fun."

She opened her mouth to say more, but nothing came out. Her face contorted into a grimace I'd never seen before, and it scared me.

Then, without another word, she turned on her heel and left, slamming the door behind her.

I heard her storming through the house. I stood in the middle of my room, not daring to move. Then, she started shouting, loud enough that she knew I could hear, about how I didn't respect her and didn't know how hard she worked for me. The usual tirade.

I waited impatiently until the ranting stopped, and an uneasy quiet settled over the house.

I knew the time had come to split. I placed the flashlight into my hip pack, zipped it, and strapped the pack on.

I threw the door open and cut across the living room.

"Just one second, young lady!"

I froze in place, my hand on the doorknob.

"Look."

Like a fugitive caught by the cops, I turned, slow and easy, and relaxed my arms.

She sat on the white couch. From where I stood, with her face in profile, I could see the age lines around her eyes and mouth in clear contrast to her smooth white skin. "I suppose I should take some of the blame. I kept you on a pretty loose leash in Broad Ripple. I never could get you to behave."

I cringed at her unintentional references to my "pet daughter" analogy.

She blinked tears from her eyes. "But you're in a community now, Fiona. Everything you do has consequences in ways that they never did in Broad Ripple. I didn't try to 'spy' on you, much as it might please you to think so. Your little antics came my way quite by accident. The same way they always do."

I flinched and looked down at the rug. *She knew.*

I heard her ironic chuckle. "Oh, yes, *all* of your antics. Even the Broad Ripple break-in."

The lie started by reflex. "I don't know what—"

"Of course, you do." I heard her deep sigh, and I wanted to disappear. "Dammit, Fiona, do you really think I'm that stupid? Do you think my daughter could attempt a felony that made the news-papers, and I wouldn't figure it out?"

I glanced up, shocked.

She leaned forward on the couch. The hard, disappointed look on her face overwhelmed me with guilt and forced me to look away again. "I didn't think it was worth mentioning at the time for two reasons, one of which was how badly you botched the job, and I knew the fear of God must have hit you in a way that I never could. Anything else was redundant."

I looked down at my feet. I couldn't believe she knew, that...she'd always known.

She paused, apparently to collect her thoughts, and then took another deep breath. "It was obvious, Fiona. The way you looked away whenever it was brought up, the stiffness in your shoulders; everything you did reflected your guilt." She spoke as if giving a public testimony. "You couldn't possibly hide that from me."

My anger finally overrode my guilt, and I looked her in the face. "But I don't understand. Why didn't you say anything? Not one word the entire time."

Mom shrugged her shoulders. "Because it wouldn't have done

any good. And because you've since done more to punish yourself than any punishment I could come up with."

She knew, and she noticed. But she never said a word.

Mom brushed her hands across her face as if to wipe the new wrinkles away. "Fiona, I can't pretend that I understand you. When I was going to school, I didn't behave the way you do. You can be a real pain in the ass, but I also know, deep down, you're not a bad kid."

My breath caught in my throat at the half-compliment. Backhanded as it was, those words were the closest to praise than I'd heard since...well, since I couldn't remember.

She must have noticed. "It's true. And I know it. I could never afford to spend the time with you that children require. It just wasn't possible. And when you did something wrong, sometimes it was easier to just look past it."

She started blinking rapidly and rubbed at one eye with a palm as if trying to work out a lash. "But I also think I ignored you when you did good things, and I'm sorry about that. I just wish you didn't hate me so. But I guess most teenagers feel the same way, and sooner or later, you'll get over that, too."

Her shoulders slumped and her body seemed to more-or-less mold itself into the couch. "Somewhere down the line, you grew up, and I missed it all. When I heard what you had been doing this weekend...I thought about how much you'd slipped away from my life. If you were here to start dinner and disappear so I could rest, I was happy. But at some point, I lost touch."

Her body shook with a final sigh of defeat. "And when you turned against me, I didn't want to know you anymore."

"I never turned against you," I lied, feeling guilty because I had done exactly that.

"Oh, Fiona, of course, you did. And I reacted badly, of course. I don't know you. I've never even tried to understand you, and I don't even remember when that started happening."

I took a tentative step toward the couch where she sat, her face looking more defeated than I'd ever seen in my life. "Mom...all these years, you've been just a peripheral part of my life. I stay out of your way and I make my own space. Hell, you *taught* me how to do that. And now, all of a sudden you're concerned."

My hands balled into fists. "But you're not concerned because of me. You're more concerned about your *business* and how my latest actions might affect it." I approached the couch, gaining new strength. "But it's not about me at all. So don't pretend for one minute that it is."

She sighed, staring straight ahead with a look of resignation. After a long time, she finally spoke. "You're right." Her voice came to me in a whisper. I had to strain to hear her. "It's absolutely pathetic, but you're right."

I shook my head and matched her quiet tone. "Doesn't matter now. It's all different. As soon as we moved, it all became different."

"But...Fiona, maybe I was upset for the wrong reasons, but this afternoon I came to a decision. I want to get back in touch with my daughter. I know that we...what I mean is...just because we fight all the time, I never stopped caring about you." She swallowed. "Or loving you."

"Mom..." I couldn't recall the last time she'd said that.

I sat down next to her on the couch. She reached out to me, squeezing my limp hand and sniffling in a motherly fashion.

I'd never seen her cry. Not ever. I didn't know what to say or do.

Tears continued to run freely down her face. "Look at you. You've become a woman on me. And I've missed it."

"I've been here, Mom."

"But...you look like you're getting ready to go out, even now. Can you stay?" I heard the *please* she couldn't bring herself to say out loud.

Dammit. Now *my* eyes were stung from fresh tears. *Why is this happening tonight? It's not fair that I have to choose.*

I shook my head. "No. What I mean is, I have something I have to do tonight." I couldn't look at her. I focused on the glass coffee table in front of us.

"Will you be with Eugene?"

"Yes. Chip. He's taking me to Perionne Park." Well, that much was true.

"Oh."

We wallowed in an awkward silence. From the corner of my eye, I could see her wiping tears. "Is he...a nice boy?"

I smiled, and my composure broke. I swallowed back my own tears. "Yes. Oh, yes. Very nice. You'll like him."

"Oh, my. I've heard that tone of voice before. I sounded just like you, a long time ago." She leaned forward, trying to see my face. "Fiona, you're in love!"

I opened my mouth to state a denial, then paused. "I don't know."

I looked into her eyes and flinched, seeing genuine concern reflected back. "You sound like me, a long time ago." Then, after a moment, she added, "Be very careful."

What was she talking about? "I sound like you?"

She nodded, but didn't elaborate. A thoughtful expression covered her face. I could see, for the first time, individual gray strands standing out in her dark hair. "Listen, I'm blowing off work tomorrow to take it easy. What do you say we..." She shrugged. "...we find out what there is to do around here?"

I took a breath and prepared to tell her I couldn't. "I'd like to; I don't know."

She nodded, keeping her face emotionless, but I could read her disappointment. "Okay, well, you think about it." With that, she rose and stepped toward the kitchen.

I called out to her retreating back. "Mom?"

She stopped in mid-reach of her briefcase, which she'd earlier placed in the recliner. "Yes?"

I paused, gathering my courage, wondering if this was a good time. Then decided to plunge ahead. "What happened between you and my father?"

A pained look crossed her face, and she reached a hand up to cover her mouth. "I never told you?" Her voice trembled.

I pushed forward. "No. You refused to tell me. I always thought Paul was my father. Was he?"

Mom lifted the briefcase and placed it on the ground, seating herself. She stared into space and didn't answer for many seconds. At first, I didn't think she would. "I'm sorry, Fiona. I really messed up."

I gripped the arm of the couch, my hand digging into the arm. *Finally, I'd know.* "Will you tell me what happened?"

Mom nodded and then drew a deep, shuddering breath. "It's always been painful for me to talk about. I didn't realize that...you still remembered him." She seemed to drift off, and then return, speaking from a distant place. "You still remember your father. I think you were, what, maybe, five years old the last time you saw him?"

I pressed the question I really wanted to know. "Why did he go away, Mom? Why did he leave me? Why did he leave *us?*"

She looked away. "He was a senior partner in the firm when we started dating." Her voice took on a high, drifting quality at the memory. "Paul was a wonderful man, and, for a long time, we were *so* happy together. I would have done anything for him."

Her voice hardened with bitterness. "Then I became pregnant. And..." She shrugged, as if words failed her. "He...decided fatherhood wasn't something he really wanted."

I shook my head, not wanting to hear what she said. "But he seemed so ... he always tried really hard...to make me happy." *I had it all wrong.*

"Oh, yes. He was a great weekend dad, wasn't he? But that's all he really wanted." She shrugged. "I kept hoping some day, given enough time, he'd want to build something permanent for all three of us. But he never..." Her shoulders slumped, and she let the thought trail away. "And I got tired of waiting."

She raised her arms, then slapped them on her lap. "And then he received a job offer from New York. He's been contributing to your trust fund like clockwork, but otherwise I've never seen him. It hurts too much."

She stood, looking down at me with a sad, sober expression. "And he's never wanted to see me, either. Even at the end, if he'd offered to marry me or take us in, I would have gone. But he never offered."

She dropped down next to me on the couch. "And I didn't want you to know that your father didn't want us. And for that, I'm sorry, because you deserved better."

The world lost focus. The painful truth that my father had chosen to leave us was more than I could take. I wept, overwhelmed, aching to my soul. Unimportant tears spilled down my cheeks.

Loving arms embraced me. "Fiona, honey, I'm so sorry."

"God...I'm sorry, Mom, I didn't know..." I couldn't go on.

Like a small child, I cried against my mother's bosom. Her soft voice shushed me to a numb calmness.

I've hated her for so long...for the wrong reasons. How can I make that up?

I sniffled and took a deep breath. I reached out and gripped her arm. "I'll be here tomorrow."

"Good."

I sat up, wiping my face clean.

Her face showed visible disappointment. "But now you have to go."

"Yes. I really do. It's vitally important, or I wouldn't." On a weird impulse, I leaned over and kissed my mother's cheek. "There's something I have to do. But I'll be here tomorrow. I promise."

As the sun dipped down below the horizon, I approached the two-story brick home. The looming presence seemed to swallow me.

I reached out and knocked on the thick door made of solid redwood.

The door opened. The light from the room behind him placed me in the darkness of Mr. Farren's overwhelming shadow.

He looked down at me and grinned, folding his beefy arms across his solid lumberjack's chest, an image strengthened by the now-familiar red-striped button-down shirt and blue jeans. I couldn't shake an odd fear that he'd reach down and pat me on the head.

Did he know Chip and I were sleeping together? If he did, did he care?

"Fi-Fi. How are you?" His bearded face reflected only friendly concern. "Chip tells me you two are going to the park. Probably need a break from cracking the books, I'm sure."

Sounds pretty clueless to me, or is he being sarcastic?

I shifted my weight from foot to foot. "Yeah, Mr. Farren. I guess the park's not going to be open much longer." *Duh. No kidding, Mr. Obvious.*

But if Mr. Farren found the comment lame, he kept it to himself. "Oh, I imagine that come the first really cold weather in the next week or so, they'll decide to call it quits." He nodded vigorously, looking ready to grab his coat and join us.

Instead, he stepped aside, and I shuffled past into the small wood-paneled foyer leading to the carpeted living room. "Is Chip upstairs?"

"Yep. I imagine he'll be right down, but you can go up if you want."

"Thanks." I ascended the stairs toward the loft, my hiking boots making a loud clomping noise on the wood.

Halfway up, Mr. Farren called out. "Say, Fi-Fi, how's your mom doing? I stop in to see her sometimes, she might have told you. She looks like she has a pretty full plate."

I turned, pivoting on the step. *Have any nice chats about your son and me?*

Out loud, I said, "She's always been that way, Mr. Farren. I guess I'm used to it." *Is this still bullshit conversation, or is he fishing for something?*

Nope, I'm not paranoid.

For once, Mr. Farren had to look up at me. "I would imagine you've had to be pretty independent."

Oh, God, I just want to go upstairs. Why does he keep talking to me?

I crouched down, sitting on the stair, resigned to an extended conversation. "I get along by myself pretty well."

He nodded. "I reckon you do. But a girl your age could find herself in all kinds of trouble, left on your own." He put his hand on the railing. "It's good to be with people. That's why I stayed around after my wife died. There's always someone looking out for you, no matter what happens. Know what I mean?"

A chill ran along my back, but I gave him my best innocent grin. "I guess so. I'm just not used to it." I stuck my thumb up toward the loft. "I'm going to go upstairs now."

"Okay, sure."

I retreated up the wooden steps, feeling his gaze on my back. The thudding of my footsteps matched the pounding of my heart.

———

CHIP SAT AT HIS DESK, staring intently into the blue-lit screen. I wasn't sure he'd heard me enter until he said, without turning, "Find some room on the bed, Blue."

I stepped over to the cluttered wreck he called a bed. I moved aside a copy of *Ruby on Rails for Dummies*. I plopped down after I made enough room to wedge my butt between all his books.

After a couple minutes, I started to feel a bit like the discarded paperback, set aside until Chip was ready for me. My dear friend had tunnel-vision of the brain.

His fingers flew over the keyboard, scanning the screen for information and typing in several lines of some sort of programming code.

A few keystrokes later, he closed the window and shut down the computer with a push of a button. "That's enough for one day. Did you bring the stuff?"

I tapped my messenger bag. "Right here."

"Okay." He grinned at me then reached out and grabbed my outstretched hands. "I'm glad you're here."

I smiled back at him. "Me, too."

He led me to the door, grabbing his tan jacket off the bed. "Let's go."

———

WE WALKED THROUGH THE PARK. I curled an arm around Chip's arm, snuggling against him. In my opposite hand, I held a sugar cone, two scoops; one chocolate, the other mint chocolate chip. *Next best thing to heaven.*

The full moon glowed bright overhead, beaming white. Appropriate for mid-October, I guess.

We'd spent the last couple hours shuffling from ride to ride. Midnight approached; the crowd had thinned down to only a few of us teenagers.

As we walked along the wooded path, I glimpsed several couples hiding away in the bushes, developing a sudden and keen interest in botany, no doubt. I debated pulling Chip into the fauna to categorize a few leaves together.

The temperature had dropped rapidly. The chill failed to penetrate the warm and fuzzy energy coursing through me at the moment.

I guess Mom's right, I'm beginning to fall for this little computer geek. So be it.

I let Chip lead me along the darkened path.

He motioned toward wooden roller coaster support beams just off the path to the right. The track arched overhead. "If we cut through under the *Whirlwind*, we'll save some walking time."

I let him lead. He diverted from the main walkway into wet grass. Crisscross shadows lay across the ground where we stepped. We entered near-total darkness.

A churning rumble built up above. High-pitched screams passed overhead. Out of my peripheral vision, I spied the shadowy figures of another couple studying the track foundations, undoubtedly for a future architecture project.

As we walked arm in arm, moonbeams broken up by the track overhead created a flickering across Chip's face. I couldn't ignore the eerie, erotic sensation that drove me to act.

I stepped forward, turned in front of him, and placed a hand against his chest. The train passed overhead, causing a rumbling through the wooden planks that vibrated down my spine.

"Kiss me."

He smiled, leaning over me. The warmth of his breath traveled across my face.

I sighed and hugged him. "You drive me crazy, Chip."

A second train passed overhead, the noise building into a rumbling crescendo; a dark shadow fell over us. Playful screams overcame all sound.

A charging body slammed into us, and Chip sprawled. The blunt force caught me full in the back.

Off balance, I tumbled into a wooden support rail, hitting it with my shoulder.

Still stunned, I kicked blindly at the moss, trying to find my bearings.

A bulky pair of hands gripped my jacket at the shoulders and lifted me off the ground.

My legs kicked into the air. I locked my hands around a pair of beefy wrists, but couldn't stop myself from once again being slammed into the wooden support.

Pain shot up my back, and my vision cleared into sharp, painful focus.

I blinked, staring into the snarling face of a furious Clinty Buckner.

"Surprise, bitch!"

I kicked and twisted to no avail. His arms pulled me forward and pushed back. My back smashed into the wood.

The world exploded in pain. My legs would not respond.

Stupid, to get caught like this. Now Clinty would kick the shit out of me.

He grabbed me up, getting close to my face, showing his over-sized teeth. "I knew if I followed you, I'd get you. Now we square up for the other day. You're gonna be beggin' me. C'mon, beg!"

Fuck him. No matter what I do, he'll cream me.

I drew a deep breath of desperately needed air and snarled back. "Please...you fat shit...don't breathe on me again." I kicked my legs back against the supports, but I couldn't budge.

His eyes bugged in fury.

Someone tackled us.

Clinty staggered, releasing my jacket.

I fell back against the support.

Clinty stumbled past me.

Chip grabbed Clinty's arm.

Clinty grunted and flung his beefy hand into an arch that sent Chip sprawling.

I stared, watching, horrified, as Chip spun off and tripped over another support.

Reflex took over.

I growled, drawing my knife out of my pocket. My thumb flicked the trigger, and I charged forward.

I slashed the blade across his huge chest, cutting a thin slice through clothes and skin from his huge shoulder to prominent belly.

Clinty screamed, falling backwards.

He collapsed to his knees, his hands clasping his chest.

I stood over him, panting for air. As I watched blood trickle through his T-shirt and jacket, satisfaction welled up within me.

The overhead rumble built up around us again, drowning out all sound and light.

When I could see Clinty again, he lay sprawled on his knees, grabbing his stomach as if to keep his innards from leaking onto the grass.

His eyes darted to me. His lower lip trembled. "Oh, God, you cut me. I'm gonna die. You bitch, you cut me—"

I advanced on him, holding the blade out in front of me and trying not to wince from pain. I swiped the point toward his face. "Shut up! If I wanted to kill you, you wouldn't be talking now."

He squealed like the fat pig he resembled and scuttled away from me, his arms rising in front of him to protect himself.

The rumble built up again, and, when the cloak of darkness fell over us, I jumped around his back, leaned over, and grabbed a handful of greasy hair. I placed the point of the blade beneath his chin and pushed hard enough for him to feel it. Then, I urged him forward, forcing him onto his hands and knees.

He reached up.

I pressed the knife into the flesh under his chin. "Don't. Or you die now."

He yelped in shock and pain and then let out a pathetic sob.

I relished his helplessness.

I straddled his prone body, putting my face behind his, whispering into his ear like a lover. "You...cowardly fuck!"

"Don't kill me."

"Oh, Clinty," I whispered. "You're already begging. How disappointing. How boring." I drew the blade up as if to slash across his throat.

He screamed, his body shaking from the blow I never delivered.

And I enjoyed watching it. I enjoyed *causing* it. The arrogant bastard needed a solid dose of terror, and I aimed to deliver in spades. "Oh, but I could kill you, Clinty. Slit your throat before you could raise a hand to stop me. So fast, I wouldn't even get blood on my hands."

"*Please* don't."

"'Please don't,'" I whined a high, mocking imitation. "Don't tremble so much. It's annoying me."

But Clinty had nothing left. No threats, no pride, no bravado. He lay beneath me, begging, overwhelmed from pure terror, pleading for his life. "I'm sorry. Please, *please* don't kill me. I'll do anything you say."

I pressed the knife. "Shut up! Listen to me. You're not going to die from that scratch I gave you. I didn't even begin to cut through all that lard, but yeah, you're bleeding like a stuck pig. Big surprise."

I continued to keep one hand entwined in his hair, the other still pressing the point to his neck. "Do you understand now, who you're fucking with? But I'm giving you this one last chance. You come near me, or Chip, or Phil, or any of their friends, I'll kill you. I won't bother kicking your ass again."

My own hand, holding the knife, started to shake from the strain. I tightened my grip. I heard him wince in response. "I'll find you, and I'll cut your heart out. This is your only warning."

His head shifted in the start of a nod, unable to complete the motion from the knife pressed under his chin. He groaned something similar to a yes.

The coaster roared overhead again. I tightened my grip as he blacked out of my sight for a second.

He didn't even think about moving.

Light poured down on me again. "Now, I'm going to pull away. When I've reached Chip, you will drag your fat ass off the ground, and be careful not to dribble any blood on your way home. Otherwise I'll have to tell everybody what happened tonight. Lucky for you, I'd rather nobody knew about this."

Air blew out his nose in shaking spurts. "Okay. That's cool. You bet!"

I pulled the knife away from his neck, and, mustering my pride and strength, managed to rise to my feet and stand over him.

I walked in unsteady, stumbling steps to where Chip sat, his back against the support. In his eyes, I saw utter shock at my performance.

I watched Clinty totter to his feet.

He looked down at the slashed ruin of his T-shirt, still stupidly unaware that his injury was a simple surface wound.

His eyes met mine, reflecting sheer terror.

I crouched down next to Chip, keeping the blade out in plain view. "Get out of here."

He turned and scrambled away.

The rumbling of the coaster overhead blocked out the moonlight.

By the time the joyful screaming ended, he'd vanished, leaving in his stead a few drops of blood reflecting in the grass.

The shakes hit. My arms and legs trembled out of control.

The knife fell to the ground.

Gentle arms encircled and cradled me.

I clung to Chip, and he held me tight.

I cried into his chest, punctuating my sobs with curses. Finally, the flow stopped.

"Chip...you really came through this time. He was ready to pound me into the emergency room."

"*I* came through?" Chip's shaking voice betrayed his shock and terror. "I'd be surprised if Clinty ever shows his face in the school again after that. Jesus, Blue. Where did that *come* from?"

A bitter laugh escaped through my tears. "Oh, Chip." I whispered the same words I'd used moments earlier. "Do you understand now who you're fucking with?" I felt his body stiffen.

I looked up at the moonlight reflecting off a wooden beam. "I told you I was trouble for you. Some of what you saw, part of that's the real me. The part I had to bring out in 'Ripple, just to clear a path to an exit. And afterwards, I told myself it's just an act, but I know I'm *this* close to something dangerous and awful."

Chip held me tight. "Maybe a little dangerous. But never awful."

I laughed and wiped my face.

Chip shuffled in the grass. "We need to go. They're going to close down soon."

Loud shrieks cut through the air, and the train passed overhead. I shivered and leaned against him. "I know. Just hold me. Just for a minute."

With only a few minutes until closing, the line to the Pirates of Perionne ride no longer existed. Holding hands, Chip and I walked down the stairs, our feet clomping on the wood. We descended to the circular platform. A single bored attendant leisurely leaned on a long wooden stick marked with a red line at roughly four and a half feet high. The platform continued its endless slow rotation.

The stocky, college-aged attendant reached up, tipping his hat to reveal thick blond hair, now pressed tight around his head from too many hours of wearing the required cap. "Good evening, Sir. Milady."

His slap-happy charm made me smile.

I took a step toward the boat, but he moved forward in front of me, thumping the stick down and making a show of eyeballing the red line on the marker.

"I don't know if you're tall enough. It's going to be close."

I folded my arms. "How'd you like the stick shoved up to the red hash mark?"

Chip put a hand on my shoulder. "Blue..."

"Chuck!" An unfamiliar voice called out. "Are you flirting with the ladies again?" I peered into the darkness to see the silhouette of a second attendant, exceptionally tall and thin, with strands of dark hair peeking out from under his cap. He walked with practiced diligence along the wheel-shaped dock, using a squeegee with an extra-long handle to wipe out the boats as they emerged from the ride.

He looked over at me and tipped his own cap. "I've heard about her. She can probably do exactly what she says."

Chuck called back. "Just keep wiping the boats, Bob. Don't forget who wears the striped pants around here."

Bob grumbled. "I'm just sayin'. If she does it, I'm not pulling it back out for you."

Chuck grinned and stepped aside. "After you, Milady." He removed his hat, waving me forward.

Chip shook his head, pulling me behind him. "Must've been a long day." We walked along the dock, and he quickly outpaced me.

Bob removed his hat and waved it in the direction of the semi-dry boat. "This way, Sir. Milady." He bent over in a corny bow. "Your chariot awaits."

Chip took my hand, but I resisted, my wicked mind already foreseeing the possibilities. "You first."

Chip stepped into the boat and straddled the still-damp seat. I stepped in, but instead of settling down in front of him, I fell backwards, dropping into his lap.

He grunted *oof*, and his arms encircled around me in a tight squeeze.

Bob raised his hat and shook it above his head. "Just a friendly reminder. It's a three-minute ride." With a wink, he stepped across the dock and away from us, approaching the next couple.

My positioning on Chip's lap proved to be a happy accident. With a casual glance over his shoulder, I could confirm what we'd figured and hoped, based on what Chip had observed from past visits. The attendant had escorted the next couple to the closest ride from the entryway, leaving three empty boats between us.

Our little capsule drifted against the double-doors, which split aside. We floated through into the noisy wonderland of cackling puppets, organ music, and "Yo-Ho-Hos."

As if to ward me off, Chip pushed the flats of his hands against my lower ribs. "C'mon, Blue. We should get ready."

But my body ached from pent-up excitement. I twisted in his lap and pressed against him. "You heard the man. We have three minutes." I planted a hard, rough kiss against his mouth.

Given his agitation and nervousness, he still responded. Sort of.

As our boat drifted through the room, I sensed, more than saw, the large pirate ship.

Like palpable electricity, tension filled my body.

I separated from his unresponsive lips, and instead leaned forward into a hug, my mouth brushing against his ear. "It's going to be okay," I whispered.

Who am I trying to convince?

Breathless, I turned to confirm that the pirates were still fighting off the natives on the island and the other pirate still chased the wench on the ship.

The boat turned in its track, lining up with the double doors to the final room.

I pushed myself forward to my own seat. "Are you ready?"

"Yes."

I gripped his hand, squeezing his fingers in mine.

"Anything going on behind us?"

I craned my neck backward. "The next couple hasn't even entered this room."

The doors split open.

The boat emerged to begin a slow semi-circle around the small islet.

The large pirate with the eye patch swung his machete at us. "Get your own gold, Matey! This be all mine!"

Chip released his hand from mine. "Now!"

Chip bolted from the boat first, landing onto the sand and darting for the cardboard palm tree mockup with catlike agility.

I jumped after him.

My foot skidded off the vinyl siding, and I toppled into the sand. "Damn!"

I rolled across the ground, fighting down panic. My body slid to a stop at the edge of the pedestal, and I jumped to my feet. With one fluid motion, I stepped onto the wooden plank, gripped the sides of the plastic pot, and side-jumped into the gullet of the over-sized cauldron.

Crouching down, I could hear the thump of double-doors being driven apart. I had no way of knowing if I'd been seen. I held my breath and waited.

The pirate called out its eternal warning. "Git your own gold, Matey! This be all mine!"

Sound muted by the ancient plastic surrounding me, I strained to hear beyond the warped music tape and the gurgling water.

I released my held breath, adjusting to a squatting position, and waited for what seemed an eternity.

The unpleasant odor of mold tickled my nose. I stifled a sneeze.

If someone saw us, how long would it take before they shut the ride down and conducted a search? When would we know?

"Git your own gold, Matey! This be all mine!"

A high feminine shriek pierced the air, making me cringe. A hysterical giggle followed the shriek.

I rubbed my itching eyes, which made my nose complain further.

God, how am I going to survive?

"Git your own gold Matey! This be all mine!"

Frustrated, I banged my head against the back of the pot, and then quickly hunched down against my knees.

What if someone heard that?

How could anyone hear me? It's way too noisy in this room.

But why take the chance?

Great; now I'm arguing with myself.

Hey, stupid. You slipped and fell. How could you let that happen? This little adventure could have ended in disaster before it started. And it would have been your fault. And you harped all over Chip because you didn't think he could handle it.

"Git your own gold Matey! This be all mine!"

Ha, ha, Gunther. You're a funny guy, hiding the money in this room. Wouldn't you love to know your irony is appreciated over twenty-five years later?

How long has it been? Chip said the park could remain open for another half hour or so, depending on the crowd.

"Git your own gold—"

"Hey, fuck you, one-eye!" A deep, loud voice called out. "I got your pot of gold right here!"

I shoved a hand into my mouth, biting down to keep a loud laugh from escaping.

Is that guy passing a bottle with his buddies, or trying to impress a date? Ooooh, you're so cool, man. Now, bend over and moon it.

"Git your own gold, Matey! This be all mine!"

I wiped cold moisture from my forehead. "Screw you, Gunther. It's ours, now."

———

I HUDDLED in the confines of the plastic cauldron, biting down on my chattering teeth and waiting for the shakes to pass. Instead, they increased. The sides of the container seemed to fold over me, and I found myself holding back a scream.

I closed my eyes. *I can do this, I can do this, I can do this...*

When I thought I couldn't take another second, just when I knew I'd pop out of the cauldron like a demented life-size jack-in-the-box terrifying whichever boat riders happened to be traveling through the room at that moment, the pirate drone stopped. The loud, constant organ music also cut off. I sat engulfed in dark and silence. Only the pounding of my heart, thumping loud and fast in my own head, interrupted the otherwise total quiet of my surroundings.

I closed my eyes, hunkering down against my aching legs, but it made no difference against the sickening vertigo that insisted the room was spinning.

I panted deep breaths, a harsh hissing sound that echoed loudly off the confines of my prison walls.

My pounding heart, my gasps for breath, and a trickle of water in the distance overloaded my senses.

I forced myself to count slowly to ten; forced my hands to reach with purpose above my head. No mad jack-in-the-box antics at this point.

In my plastic-shelled confines, the rustle of denim struck me as obscenely loud.

I gripped the edge of the pot, pulling myself up. My legs stretched gratefully, the knots of pain easing.

My back, where I had taken the beating beneath the roller coaster, throbbed.

I looked over the lip of the cauldron; a blast of cool air fluttered against my face. I drew in blessed fresh air in deep, grateful gulps.

Instantly, the pounding in my head quieted and the sickening motion settled.

With intentional calm, I reached down into my messenger bag, identified the telltale thin rod via the Braille method, raised the flashlight to point in front of me, and flipped the switch.

My thin beam of light beam cut through the darkness.

I looked down, illuminating the wooden porch-like platform beneath the pot in my spot of light. Shiny plastic coins lay sprinkled on the ground around me. The platform itself was barely wide enough to hold the plastic bowl. The planks of the platform were widely spaced, showing large gaps in the pedestal. Its only purpose seemed to be to provide stability for the cauldron on the otherwise sandy island. The wood, upon careful inspection, showed varying grades and conditions, indicating several repairs through the years.

Additional twin beams lit up the night. I turned to see Chip depositing two pen-sized flashlights onto the ground. He held out his hands.

Grateful for the help, I put the penlight between my teeth. I gripped one of his hands and reached down with the other to support myself on the cauldron. With one easy hop, I cleared the edge and landed in the sand.

I took a moment to assess my surroundings. The three penlights did little to illuminate the islet. The engulfing darkness pressed in all around us.

I stared down at the wooden platform beneath the cauldron. Two people could lift and set the platform aside with ease.

I ran my hands over my face, trying to shake a surreal, dreamlike essence to my vision.

Somewhere in the room beyond the light, I heard a continuous gurgle of water, an annoying white noise further deadening my senses.

Growing annoyed, I directed my beam to the double set of doors leading to the outside. Through these doors, the boats took their exit back to reality.

I called out into the darkness. "Well. Now what?" My voice echoed several times through the domed chamber.

Chip jumped, startled. "Let's keep it down, okay?" He opened his knapsack and produced a hammer and a military-styled shovel with collapsible handle. "Umm, the thieves came through the door and onto this island, burying the money right underneath this pot."

"Chip, are you *sure* about this? If we spend the night digging up this island and we don't find anything, I'm going to stick the shovel in a *very* uncomfortable spot."

Chip looked down at the platform and shrugged. "I'm sure about this. As sure as I am about anything."

I wiped my hands across my face again, but the surreal buzzing only intensified. I'd never experienced such a level of claustrophobia before. I didn't think it affected me, but the light kept seeming to dim out and darkness kept overtaking the room. The huge, cavernous walls wanted to close in and bury me forever. "I'm sorry; I'm hot, and I'm pissed, and my back hurts. I was almost caught due to my own stupidity, and we haven't even started digging yet. And you're the only one here to take it out on."

Chip nodded. "It'll be okay, Blue." He stood on one side of the cauldron, bracing his hands along the outwardly curved lip. "Help me. It's not as light as it looks."

I gripped the other side.

Together, we lifted the cauldron to reveal the wood beneath.

"So we move the platform and dig under it? And we'll find the bag with the money in it?"

"Should be."

I smiled. "And we make the front page of the morning paper, Special Souvenir Edition? And then I don't have to hear another word about Gunther, ever again?"

Chip grinned back at me. "No fair peeking at the last page."

I extended an arm. "Okay. Hand me the hammer. And if you have any more flashlights, turn them on. It's too damn dark in here."

Chip handed me the oversized hammer with a clawed end. Gripping the handle, a surge of energy coursed through me, clearing away the surreal buzzing. Excitement filled me; excitement over finding this treasure, excitement over fulfilling Chip's long-awaited hopes.

Chip snapped on two additional flashlights. The darkness receded further, and my sense of reality returned.

The platform, though well-settled into the ground beyond the thin layer of sand, popped up with ease after I pried it with the hammer.

Together, we made short work of moving the platform, and soon he and I were standing on the flattened bare earth.

Chip grabbed a second shovel, snapped it open, and held it out to me.

With our area now exposed and well-lit, Chip raised the shovel and turned in my direction. "Ready?"

"Ready. But first..." I leaned over and kissed him quickly. "I'm sorry I got so pissed."

Chip smiled, his blue eyes glittering in the light-beams. "You're fine. Your spunk is helping me to get through this."

As if on cue, we raised our shovels together and brought them down, breaking the ground in two separate places.

CHAPTER TWENTY-SIX

I drove the clawed hammer into hardened clay dirt, the *chunk* of breaking soil creating an answering weak echo throughout the domed chamber.

Splattering sweat stung my eyes and forced me to stop.

I stepped aside, pressing the hammer into the ground and leaning on the handle, wiping my sleeve across my face. My breath came in heavy gasps, and my palms stung from developing blisters. *I'll never make a living as a manual laborer.*

During the last couple hours, we'd dug down about a foot and a half, sticking to the twelve-foot circumference, large enough for two people to stand side-by-side and dig. We deposited the growing mound of dirt beyond the circle.

I'd long pushed aside all fears of getting caught, instead focusing on the exhausted ache of simple hard work.

The light, already too dim, flickered between near darkness and back again. I looked over to spy one of Chip's flashlights pulsing in irregular repetition. Losing the light would create a handicap we really didn't need.

Outside, the harsh whistling noise of a windstorm rattled the flimsy building, adding an intense vibrating backdrop to our work and making my skin crawl.

I wondered at the ferociousness of the windstorm. Although such storms were not unusual for October in Indiana, the evening had been calm, outright pleasant, up 'til now.

Getting annoyed at our decided lack of discovery, I straightened, bringing the hammer up and over my shoulder. "Are you *sure* they buried it underneath the cauldron?"

Chip paused, glaring at me, his own shovel raised at his shoulder. "Yes, I'm sure."

I bit back my own annoyance. "Because that's what your father's bowling buddy told him? He was that specific in detail?"

Chip stood straight, letting the shovel jab into the soil. "Yes. That's what he said."

I nodded, still chewing over the facts. "Well, then. Are you sure that this pedestal hasn't been moved since then? It's been over twenty years, right? Maybe they shifted the display from one side of the island to the other."

"I...don't think so." But he couldn't hide a look of shock that told me he hadn't considered the possibility.

I raised my hammer and pounded it into the dirt. "Great."

"Well, I can't think of everything, Blue." A whine entered his voice that danced on my last nerve. "This is an old ride. It hasn't changed since it went up, at least as far back as I can remember. But I can't swear the cauldron has been here in this exact spot since before we were born."

That didn't appease my building frustration. "I don't want you to swear about anything, I just want to find something."

I slammed the hammer deep into the sand. The clawed metal impacted something. A crackling noise echoed through the chamber.

I snagged my penlight from the ground and pointed the beam toward the newly turned dirt. "Oh, shit."

Chip rushed forward. "What!"

The light reflected off small broken pieces of dull white stones.

I squatted on my haunches and picked one up. I brushed my thumb along the texture, and knew with certainty I held a small bit of bone, maybe a knuckle bone.

Chip pointed, indicating all around me. "Look. Here's more. It looks like..." His voice trailed off.

I gripped the rough digit lengthwise, holding it under the light. "Gunther?"

Chip nodded. "Has to be. They buried him here. Buried him next to his stash. This confirms it."

With a morbid fascination, I held my hand up next to the knuckle bone. The bone extended a half inch beyond my own knuckle.

The strange, buzzing nausea overtook me again. "This just seems so...wrong."

Chip stood, walked across the dug-out dirt back to his own spot, and brought his shovel down.

I passed the penlight beam across the ground. At the same time, I kept shaking my head, trying to clear it of the buzzing energy.

Exposed bone sprinkles scattered along newly exposed soil, and, at the edge, a large protrusion poked out of the dirt. Gingerly, I extended my foot, tapping away the powder and exposing a larger white bone, stuck into the ground at an angle.

An upper arm, perhaps. I couldn't be sure.

A sudden creaking noise made me jump. The billowing wind had strained the double doors.

I shifted the penlight beam to view the shaking doors, surprised at the intensity of the rippling effect across the water. The waves traveled across the surface and washed up on the islet.

A shivering dread, like insects crawling below the surface of my skin, drove me to my feet. "Christ. We could find all of him. I'm not digging anymore." I pulled myself out of the hole and stepped up to beach level.

Again, Chip paused in his work. "What? Why not? They might have buried the money underneath him."

I stared down into the hole, battling a sudden onset of nausea.

"Chip, it's a fucking grave site, and you want to know why I'm upset?"

Chip raised his shovel. "It's just a pile of bones. It can't hurt you. Look. There's no rot, there's no bugs. It's clean. It's been clean for years."

I fought back rising bile. "That's not the point."

Chip brought his shovel down.

A skewed rustling noise cut through the air, releasing a cloud of dirt that puffed around him, forcing him to step backward.

My nausea forgotten for the moment, I peered down into the hole, spying a cloth-like gray-leather pillow in the dirt. I pointed the penlight at it. "Oh, shit, Chip, that's it."

I dropped down to my hands and knees in front of the exposed cloth.

Chip joined me a moment later. His fingers clawed at the dirt. "Hold on." He broke away clay soil, exposing a large piece of gray cloth with black stenciled letters, much of it illegible, but _ionne_ and _ank_ stood out against the material.

Chip gripped the cloth and yanked, exposing a metal handle pulled loose from the dirt in a cloud. He gathered up a sizeable bank bag still securely clasped shut.

I watched Chip's face light up in euphoric relief. "Oh, God. This is it. We have it. We did it."

I laughed with delight. "Damned right we did. Never had a doubt."

He grinned. "Oh, you never had a doubt, huh?"

Seeing the look on Chip's face left me giddy with a joyous surge of happiness. "'Course not." I'd deny any statements to the contrary.

Chip fumbled with the snaps and drew the handles apart, kicking loose another cloud of dirt.

I coughed, the sound echoing through the room and joining the noise of the creaking double doors.

He peered into the open bag and then reached his hand in.

My eyes locked on the opening, anticipation filling my being like a palpable ache.

He withdrew a wad of bills, extending them to me. I took a few of them, gripping a hodgepodge of cash a couple inches thick.

I ruffled the bills. They puffed dust, and the green ink had faded to virtual nonexistence. But they still had the distinctive odor of United States currency.

My head reeled. The bag practically *bulged.*

Chip said, "You realize, you're about to become a very *famous* outsider to the town of Perionne. And probably an outsider no more."

I rubbed my itching nose. "You mean, they'll be telling stories in American Folklore fifty years from now about how the poodle with blue hair dug up the money?"

Chip laughed. "Something like that." Distracted, he turned his gaze back to the ground. "Hey, what's this?"

He aimed one of the penlights toward the ground and kicked at a small object, dislodging the item from the dirt.

I crawled around to get a better look.

Chip held a small object of reflective metal. A gray, rusty-metal handle that piqued my curiosity.

Is that what I think it is?

Even as Chip held it under the light, I reached a hand out and snatched it from him. "Hey!" I held it up to my own eager gaze. "A pocket knife." The thickened handle held at least eight various blades and contraptions.

I rubbed my hand along the handle, scraping away crusted brown corrosion, then dug my fingers into the thumb groove of the blade and pulled. It resisted.

Undaunted, I tried a second time, yanking loose a rusty, crusted blade twice the size of my palm. "An *excellent* pocket knife."

I stared, transfixed. Even after being buried all these years, I could make out intricate ornamental designs carved into the hardened wood. *With a little cleaning and some TLC, I could restore this to like-new condition.*

As I brushed crust from the blade, a realization hit me. A chill traveled across my fingertips.

"You said Crimley stabbed Gunther?"

Chip nodded. "That's what I heard."

I peered at the blade. "From your dad's bowling buddy. Well. Well, well." Somehow holding the murder weapon did not spook me the way picking through Gunther's bones did.

I looked away with an effort. "I guess I found me one hell of a souvenir."

Chip reached out. "It looks pretty crapped up, Blue. Maybe you'd better just put it in the bag."

I folded my hand around the handle and pressed it to my shoulder. "No. I want it." My tone came out whinier than I'd intended. I looked over at him, wondering at my own petulance. "I can have it, can't I?" I tried to keep my voice normal. "You keep the money and turn it over, but I want to keep this."

Chip shrugged, dropping his arm. "Sure, you can have it. Now, we've got to get this dirt back in place and get out of here."

I nodded and stood, placing the pocketknife in my jacket pocket so I wouldn't get it confused with my switchblade.

I glanced at the mounds of dirt and the huge hole, sighing. My nausea had passed for the moment, but I still dreaded the task of shoveling all that dirt back in.

CHAPTER TWENTY-SEVEN

Once we started, the shoveling took only a few minutes. Without much trouble, we adjusted the platform back to its original spot and slid the pot over it and into place.

Chip waited on his side of the cauldron as I brushed dirt from my jeans. "We need to make sure we spread the coins out like they were."

I walked over and stood across from him. "I know."

In unison, we lifted the cauldron and side-stepped together over to the platform, centering it, then setting it down.

Chip grinned at me. "Y'know, it could have been a lot worse. At least you uncovered his real hand. You might have dug up his pros-thetic hook. Think about what kind of a souvenir *that* would have been."

The thought of a curved, rusted, metal hook protruding out of the soil sent a shudder through me, bringing on another bout of nausea. I leaned over the lipped opening on the cauldron, trying to keep the contents of my stomach where it belonged. "Ugh! What's wrong with me?"

Chip's hand fell onto my shoulder. "Are you okay?"

I nodded, indicating for him not to worry. *Just nerves.* Instead, I smiled.

Our light flickered and one of the questionable flashlights suddenly died. The smile froze on my face.

It was the third one to go out in the last hour, but the first one that made a major difference. Now, we were back to the original two penlights, and the details in the chamber were much harder to see.

I looked around for a way out. I could barely see the door frame at the back of the room. "Wait a second." I rushed over to the door and reached out to turn the knob. *Surely it can't be that easy.*

I'd guessed right; it couldn't be that easy.

I tried to twist the knob, only to meet solid resistance. What's more, the keyhole faced to the outside. I had nothing to pick. "Shit. I guess we have to go with our original plan."

I had disliked the original plan. And had hoped somehow the chamber door would have a fire lock designed to allow people to exit at will. *Of course not.* Chip's casual words from several weeks ago echoed in my head. *Perionne hasn't had a safety commissioner in over five years.*

I stared across the islet into blackness. I heard the trickling water but could no longer make out the double doors.

Kneeling down, I grabbed one of the penlights and then walked along the man-made beach of gritty packaged sand.

I gave Chip's backpack one last regretful glance. "I don't suppose you brought a pair of waders with you?"

"Sorry. They'd never fit."

"Didn't think so."

I looked down at my shoes until I saw water's edge, where the moat began.

Squinting off into the distance, I could barely see the double doors, though I had no trouble hearing them strain against the windstorm.

Chip called out. "Be careful. There's a guardrail that runs underwater the entire length to guide the boats."

I nodded, stripping off my shoes and socks and handing them to Chip. Then I rolled my blue jeans up to my knees.

I stood on the shoreline, taking a deep breath and coaxing my courage.

My toes stuck into water, cold enough to make me draw in a breath. Trying to ignore that, I told myself this was the only way out. I took my first step into the moat, my bare foot sliding on the slick, algae-covered surface.

My toes pressed against a slimy metal bar, and my balance shifted forward.

My foot slipped off the metal and sank into mud. "EEEE-yyyyuck!"

I caught myself, though my foot sank mid-shin into mud and slime. I drug my other foot off the shore and into the water, and then brushed against a small vertical bar, some sort of support holding the track in place. Again, my balance shifted and I waved my arms to keep on my feet.

Chip rushed forward, his shoes already off.

I waved him back. "Nope. I'm all right."

He stood on the shore, watching me, shifting his weight from foot to foot, his arms folded.

With deliberate slowness, I inched toward the double doors, the chill water sloshing around my calves. I tried to ignore the chattering of my teeth, and the part-tingling, part numbing sensations in my feet and legs. Step by step, the waterline slowly rose, eventually covering my blue jeans until I stood in water up to my waist.

It seemed to take forever before I stood in front of the double doors.

I reached out, pressing my palm flat against the left door. I could feel the vibration of the blowing windstorm through my hand. I pushed.

The door opened a few inches then stuck.

I pressed harder. The door wouldn't give.

A flash of anger made me see red. "What...the...*hell?*"

I heard cautious splashing approach from behind me. "What is it?" Chip called.

I stepped forward, aiming the penlight beam through the small gap between the doors. "I'm not sure." I could just make out something threaded across the opening, hip-height.

Linked metal.

"Shit!" I slapped my hand against the wood, sending a tremendous boom echoing around the chamber. "It's chained."

"What?"

"The door! They wrapped a chain around the handles from the outside. I can't get to it."

Chip stood at my side, watching me with a worried expression. "You have to be able to get to it."

I sighed. "What do you expect me to do? Detach my arms and stick them through?"

"Well, how far does it open?" A hint of mild annoyance entered Chip's voice.

I shoved against the left side with both palms. The gap opened about eight inches and then caught.

Wind billowed into my face. Buffeting turbulence made both my arms vibrate from the strain. After a few seconds, I eased the pressure, and the gap closed. "That far."

He bent his head toward the gap. "Hmmm. Well, maybe we can slip under it." With that, he pressed the one side open as far as it would go, then wiggled into the gap, head-first.

As he forced his head through the opening, I grew anxious. The wood dug at his ears, and I winced. But to his credit, he shoved forward.

Only after he'd locked his head in the gap between the doors did it become apparent that his shoulders were too wide to fit through the opening. "There's no way I can do it."

I braced the door so he could pull his head back. "Here, get out of there."

I placed one hand on each of the doors and pushed against them with all my might. I estimated a total clearance of about fourteen inches, if someone forced the doors open and held them for me. "Okay...I think I can make it, but I need your help."

I linked my hands together, stirrup-style, and held them down at thigh level, demonstrating. "Do that."

Chip looked at me, then at the door, then back.

"You think you can make it over?"

I nodded. "Gotta be safer than trying to swim under. And I'll have a much easier time than you."

Chip shook his head and linked his fingers. "Famous last words."

I pinched the penlight between my teeth. "You ready?"

He bent his knees, waiting. "Okay."

Once more, I pressed against the doors, shoving them as far apart as possible. The wind created a resistance.

I braced my legs, steeling my courage.

I stepped up with my right leg, grimacing at the stiffness from my bruises, and pressed my bare foot into Chip's hands.

I jumped; he lifted.

I sailed up into the air.

Chip propelled me four feet off the ground. Gravity reasserted itself. I was above the chain, but still on the wrong side of the opening. Reflex took over, and I kicked out with my left foot, slipping it between the doors.

My foot came down onto the chain.

My own weight forced the doors together on my leg.

I flailed with my hands, grabbing the sides of the door to catch my balance, but the gap closed over my foot.

The door shifted and widened.

I realized Chip had diverted his attention to holding the doors open. I grunted approval and wrapped my fingers around the edges of the doors.

I shoved forward; my head squeezed through the opening. I willed my body to come through after it.

No luck.

After a little push and pull, I wedged my shoulder through the gap.

Brisk, chilly October wind buffeted my face, stinging my eyes. The doors tightened, like a clap, against my chest and back.

The wood pressed tight, digging into my sternum. I clawed my nails against the wood but couldn't push myself forward.

I pulled. I pulled again, to no avail.

Sweat dripped from my brow and into my face. I ached with the need to draw a deep breath.

I reached up, taking the penlight from my mouth then grunted, "shit!" Somehow, the profanity made me feel a little better.

Chip's voice reached me from within the chamber. "Blue, are you okay?"

I spat. "Fuck you."

"What was that?"

I drew a shallow breath, since it was all I could manage, ticking off in my head a mental count to three.

I pressed against the outside of the door with my arm, willing my other shoulder to come through behind me.

The door scraped against my right breast and shoulder blade. Flaring waves of hot pain burned over my chest. I kicked and pulled, trying to ignore it, shutting my eyes to the wind.

I yanked one last time, and then pushed with all my strength. My grunt turned into a growl.

My shoulder popped through the opening, with a momentum that pitched me out over the water into a backward plunge.

I flailed my arms and legs, shrieking the whole way down, making a tremendous thrashing splash into the muddy pit.

I gasped on impact. A fresh, unexpected burst of pain shot through my upper thigh. I doubled over, trying to cry out, but could only gurgle water.

I crawled up on all fours, spitting rancid water and blistering obscenities.

I struggled to my feet, knowing that if there was anyone, *anybody*, in the park, they had to have heard me.

Chip called out from behind the doors. "Blue?"

I took a first step forward, opening my mouth to reply, but stumbled over something metal and screeched.

"Blue? Are you okay?"

I cleared the distance in a single hop before my strength gave out. I collapsed against the double doors, realizing in a detached way that I'd closed the gap on Chip and shut him in. My feet, previously numb from the extreme cold, now hummed with the fresh agony.

"Blue, it's awfully dark in here. There's only one flashlight."

Panting, I braced myself against the double doors. I snarled between chattering teeth. "Chip...darling, sweetheart...will you shut the *fuck up* a minute?!"

My legs gave out, and I leaned against the door, panting heavily and listening to the sweet, blessed silence.

I brought my hand up to cover my mouth and sobbed, shaking from pain and cold. Gradually the worst of the throbbing faded, and I gulped back my tears.

I wiped my hands over my face and back over my now-slicked hair. Twenty pounds of denim hung heavily over my shoulders. I knew standing in the water would cause my bleak situation to grow even worse but struggled to clear my mind and force my abused body to move. I brought the penlight up to examine the chain.

At what point did they attach this? I recalled being in the cauldron, music blaring, water gurgling; the attendants could have attached it at any time prior to turning off the soundtrack tape, and chances are, we would not have heard it from inside.

The chain wrapped around the handles of the double doors and hung loose, a fairly standard padlock holding it in place. Standard chain, standard lock. This was not high security stuff. But then, why should it be?

The distance from shore to shore stretched across about twenty feet. Finding a good-size piece of sturdy board to straddle the moat would be a simple enough task.

From out of nowhere, a blast of cold blanketed my body.

Then, just as fast, the wind stopped.

I clamped my chattering teeth shut. Now after midnight, the temperature had probably plummeted to around forty degrees. As far as I was concerned, it was fifteen.

I wondered a moment why Chip hadn't called out from behind the doors. Then I remembered I'd frightened the hell out of him.

I reached out, gingerly tapping my knuckles against the wooden door. "Chip...darling...I'm sorry I lost it like that." My voice trembled as I forced words between my shaking lips. "I'm going to attempt to pick the padlock. I don't want you to be concerned, but, if this doesn't go smoothly, you're going to have to talk me into not leaving you here until morning."

"You wouldn't!"

"Can't talk now." I put the flashlight in my mouth.

"Blue, that's not very damn funny!"

I reached up, pulling the two bobby pins from my hair, and got to work.

A strong wind buffeted me, making my hands shake and my teeth vibrate all the more. I had to bite down on the light.

A whisper traveled on the wind. *Bluuuuuuue...*

I almost dropped the pins.

Chip called out. "Blue, it's dark. Hurry up."

I locked the first pin into place.

Return the money, Blue. You can't keep it.

That wasn't Chip. And it came from *this* side of the door.

I grabbed the penlight from my mouth and pivoted, flashing the beam over the surrounding trees and bushes.

"Who's there?" I called.

A taunting burst of wind cut through me to the bone.

I won't let you keep it...

I strained to listen but could only hear wind in the hollows of the trees.

But I'd heard words.

No, I didn't hear words, I'm creeping myself out.

Shaking my head, I bent back to my work.

This time, I heard laughter, an evil cackle that caused my hands to tremble.

I paused, fighting down nausea and panic.

Get your own, Matey! This is mine.

I shook my head. *Now I'm hearing the pirate.* I took a breath and twisted the wires.

The lock snapped open.

I pulled at the chain. No sooner had I untangled it from the handles than the doors swung open, pushed from the inside.

I stepped back. "Chip!"

He stepped forward, the backpack slung over one shoulder and holding the moneybag in his free hand. His arms wrapped around me into a hug I could barely feel through the freezing denim. "Are you all right?" His face changed to a look of alarm. "You're freezing to death."

I let him guide me out of the water and onto dry land. "I'm sorry. I'm so sorry. Everything got so out of control. And I spooked myself."

He dropped the bags, and, to my surprise, produced an over-sized towel from the backpack.

I stepped into his clasping embrace, letting him enfold and cocoon me in the billowy cotton softness.

I shivered and babbled nonsense apologies, burying my face in his chest.

"Come on," he said. "We need to get you home and into some dry clothes."

I nodded against his chest. "Yes...home."

Everything will be fine then.

CHAPTER TWENTY-EIGHT

Chip returned into the drink and reattached the lock. Throughout the entire affair, he'd stayed dry from the waist up. I just sat in the grass and pulled the towel tight.

The chills aside, scaling the fence and getting out of the park proved far easier than getting out of the ride. It wasn't as if they surrounded the park with barbed wire. We scaled a tall metal fence made of small vertical and horizontal squares. The biggest trick involved pulling ourselves over the top without getting injured on the speared points of the fence poles.

Once on the other side, no longer concerned with secrecy, we cut through a couple of yards to save time. Even wrapped in the towel, the cold drove me to move at a fast pace.

Several blocks from home, a sudden gust of wind kicked up, blowing over us. The gust penetrated my soaked clothes with a cutting-ice impact of burning intensity.

I froze in my tracks; my breath escaped out of my lungs.

In the distance, I heard a wicked cackle.

Chip's arm fell across my trembling shoulders. The shadow of a warm rush coursed through my chilled body, and I gazed at him in thankful relief. He returned my look with one of intense concern.

In his other hand, he hefted the moneybag. "We did it, Blue. All we have to do now is get somewhere safe and call the police. Then this will all be over."

I nodded, leaning against him. We stumbled together along the sidewalk, surrounded by the elegant single- and two-story houses of suburban Perionne, heading toward my house, the closest by half the distance.

Chip wanted to secure the treasure and turn it in as soon as possible. Waking Mom at one in the morning had its consequences, and I wondered if our newfound closeness could stand the disruption. But the unbearable cold forced the issue, and so we headed toward my house without any need for discussion.

I huddled against his inadequate warmth. Ominous, thick trees loomed in every yard, draping us in shadow. I kept ducking under bent branches, which seemed to reach out for us from the front lawns.

Dead leaves crunched under our feet. Reaching branches hid the moonlight, and coal-black darkness surrounded us. A sudden gust created a mini tornado of brownish leaf bits.

I bit back a squeal, and paused to cover my face, blocking the onslaught.

Then I heard the voice up ahead. *"Bring back the money, Blue. Tell him to bring it back. It belongs to me."* The voice erupted into a sinister laugh.

I called out. "Dammit, who are you?"

Chip turned to look at me, puzzled. "What?"

I gripped Chip's arm. The wind died down.

I could hear my anxious, panting breath in the stillness. I looked at Chip, growing alarmed. "I heard a voice." Thin clouds of vapor rose with my words. "I heard someone. In the park earlier, and just now up ahead. I think we're being followed."

"How could we be followed? Nobody knew what we were doing. It must be the wind."

Chip's bland response only served to set me on edge. I stared at him, frustrated. "I heard a voice. It wanted me to talk you into taking the money back." I stared at him, frustrated.

I heard a rustling in the trees up ahead.

Chip looked away. "Take the money back? No way. Besides, nobody knows about the money."

"Oh, but that's not true, Chip. And you know it." The voice spoke loud, deep, and clear directly in front of us.

A bulky figure stepped out from the bushes several yards ahead of us, standing tall and confident on the sidewalk, blocking our path. He wore a rumpled, dirty denim jacket and blue jeans. Though he stood some distance ahead and the trees continued to obscure the moonlight, I could see, with shocking clarity, the patch of thin, graying hair atop his head, and the details of the savage expression on his middle-aged face. He looked vaguely familiar, but I was certain I hadn't met him before.

Chip dug his nails into my arm, and a moan of terror escaped his lips. "Oh, Christ." His face paled with fright.

"Hey there, little boy. You know me?" The stranger stepped forward, hands in his pockets, walking with a slow, comfortable stride.

Chip took a step backward, but I stood my ground, watching in startled amazement. "Chip, come on. He won't hurt us."

Chip nodded, eyes wide. "Yes, he will."

But I'd had enough.

I took a step forward, letting the towel drop behind me. "Hey!" I wondered if the tough-gal bravado that freaked out Clinty would work on this loser. "Back off, shithead. You may have a score to settle with my friend, but now's not the time." I took another step toward him. "Maybe you saw something, maybe you didn't, but there's nothing you can do about it."

I risked a quick look behind me.

Chip stood erect, the moneybag clasped in a two-arm embrace against his chest. "Blue...it's Gunther."

"Gunther?" Unimpressed, I squinted in the dark at the scowling stranger. "Oh, yes, I see the resemblance now."

I sized up the would-be con artist. "So you're the guy wandering around pretending to be a dead man, scaring the hell out of everyone."

I glanced back at Chip. His eyes stared, riveted forward.

"Take it back, Chip. Take the money back now and bury it, and we'll forget everything."

I reached into my hip pocket and withdrew my switchblade. "All right, you sick fuck." I walked toward him, bringing the blade forward and ready. "You've got him seriously spooked now, and I don't like it. You back off, or you're going to regret it."

"How's the old man, Chip? Think he'd like a visit from me? I'll bet that'd be quite a treat."

From behind me, I heard a sickening groan.

I switched the blade to my left hand, then back to my right. "Hang in there, Chip." I closed the distance fast.

The stranger glared at me for the first time. A cruel smirk crossed his features.

I met his look with a threatening one of my own. "Last chance. Back off."

He shrugged, obviously unconcerned, and continued to approach.

The arrogance of this impostor set me off. I'd almost lost control but had enough sense to palm the knife, pointing the blade toward the ground, keeping it handy but out-of-the-way for now. Crouching low, I intended to tackle him at the knees and knock him out of the way.

The wind caught me, propelling me forward, and my body tumbled against him. I braced for an impact that never occurred. Instead, I fell through him, flailing my arms in a vain attempt to avoid spilling into the yard.

I landed hard on the grass, my accumulated bruises crying out fresh pain.

Sprawled on the ground, my mind reeled, unable to accept what had just happened.

I rolled over and scrambled to my feet, the pain from the fall registering, but distantly.

I jumped through him. Jesus, I jumped and passed right through him!
I just tried to tackle a ghost.

I stumbled back to the sidewalk in a daze.

I heard voices up the street.

"You can't have it!"

"It's mine, you little punk. It was never yours to take."

I heard a shuffling and a yelp.

Still reeling, I took a few shaky steps. "Chip?"

Then one thought overrode all my disbelief. *Chip's in trouble.*

And just like that, I assimilated the situation and broke into a run toward the struggling figures.

Ahead, too far ahead, Chip struggled as Gunther pressed him back and across another front yard. They each had one hand grasping the moneybag. Gunther's other hand squeezed Chip's throat.

With two houses between us, I pumped my legs with all my might.

Gunther pushed Chip against a large tree.

"Chip!"

I knew I'd be too late.

They twisted, and Chip fell and sprawled across the ground. Gunther's arm swung up. His hook glinted in the moonlight.

Closing in, I watched in helpless horror as the hook slashed down.

Chip's scream tore through the air.

I propelled myself, slamming full into a solid body that grunted and toppled.

I drew myself up between Gunther and Chip.

The ghost and I regained our feet at the same time.

He glared at me and then reached out for the moneybag that lay between us.

His hand passed through the satchel, and he howled in frustration.

I waited, not daring to attack again. Apparently, the ghost couldn't control his solidity.

I kept my eyes on Gunther. "Chip!"

"My leg's cut. Be careful, Blue."

A sudden burst of wind caused a blast of cold that rocked me.

The apparition grimaced, fixing me with a withering glare. *"You can't touch me, you know."*

I snarled back. "You seemed solid enough a second ago." I shifted the knife, pointing the business end at him. "I'll bet you have to make yourself solid to do anything to me, and then we'll see."

He vanished. One moment he stood in front of me; the next he faded away.

I ignored the mental hiccup. I'd always prided myself on adapting to new situations, but this took the cake.

"You're a very foolish child, Blue." I turned my head in the direction of the voice, across the street.

Gunther watched me, arms folded across his chest. Smirking, he raised the index finger on his good hand, wiggling it back and forth like a well-meaning father chastising an infant.

"This runs much deeper than you know, Blue. I will not let you turn the money over. I can't. Now, last chance, bring it back, or you'll pay in blood."

I turned to Chip. "It's your call."

Chip had pulled himself into a sitting position by the tree. I could see blood leaking across his jeans from what might have been a nasty gash.

Chip looked at me, but his voice rose toward the apparition across the street. "I can't. I won't. I've been through too much to take it back now."

"Brave words from the little man. Fine. Let what happens next be on your head."

With that, he vanished into the blowing wind.

I stared after him into the misty dark.

I turned back to Chip. He struggled to stand, a crumpled figure, looking like a long, angled bug. I grabbed his precious moneybag and walked over to him.

I extended my hand to help him up, but for the first time, I doubted my resolve. "What have you gotten us into?"

His tear-stained face looked up at me, but he didn't take my hand. "Please, Blue. Help me. It will be all right. I just need...to get this to the police. That's all."

Then I remembered. "Wait a second." One-handed, I unzipped my messenger bag and pulled out my cell phone. As I unfolded it, I noted with a growing dread the absence of backlighting or any other response.

I gave the phone a quick shake, hearing the telltale swishing of trapped water. "Shit."

I looked at Chip hopefully, but he shrugged and shook his head. "I didn't bring mine. It had a low charge."

I bit back a nasty response. "Well, that's...great."

I sighed, folding the useless device up and dropping it back into the hip-pack.

I reached down, and his hand grasped mine thankfully. I looked into his eyes as he rose up beside me. "Did you know...that this..."

The shocked look on his face spoke his sincerity. "What? God, no, Blue. How could I know? The very idea of a...spirit...it's beyond me."

I nodded. "That makes two of us, but the idea better get within our realm of understanding real damn quick. He can jump us again at any time, and I'm not sure there's much we can do about it."

"I know...but he pulled away. "I feel as if—"

"As if he's gathering strength." Even now, one of my feet tapped on the sidewalk from pent-up nervous anxiety. I stopped it with an effort. "The wind, the streets, there's a wild energy through here, like out-of-control electricity. We don't know how much time we have. So let's get going."

Chip stumbled forward and clasped my arm to keep from falling. "Ow! Dammit."

"Hold still." I bent over. The gash ran deeper than surface, but I didn't think he'd cut a vein, either. The bleeding had already slowed.

I sighed. "You'll live. C'mon, put your hand on my shoulder."

We took a couple quick steps, practicing. It proved slow going, about a quarter speed of our walk.

"Let's go. The sooner we get to my house, the better. If you want the cops, Mom will ring every alarm in the neighborhood if she has to, and do it in about three seconds."

"But—"

"Chip, don't argue with me!"

He opened his mouth and then snapped it shut, nodding instead.

"Good boy. Let's go."

While we still have time.

About twenty minutes later, we stood on the porch of my house, cloaked in total darkness. Even the moon had vanished behind the clouds. I helped Chip up onto the porch and then fished through my still-damp hip pack for the keys.

I found the key-ring, then hunted for the keyhole.

"Forget the keys, Blue." Chip said, extending a finger toward the doorbell.

"Chip, wait, it's after mid—"

I heard the faint sound of the chime ringing and laughed off a burst of nervous energy. "Nice one, Chip. That's going to make a great first impression."

We waited. I bit down against my chattering teeth. In just a few seconds the door would open, and...

"I don't see any lights coming on, Blue."

My head reeled. *He's right.*

Fresh panic sent my fingers grasping, and I dropped the keys. They tumbled into the dark and rattled across the cement.

"Hurry, Blue." He pounded on the window. "Mrs. Shaefer, open up!"

I bent down, feeling around frantically until I wrapped my hands around the icy ring.

I popped the key into the lock and pushed the door open. "Come on."

I snapped on the light. "Mom?"

I ran across the living room to the hall. "Mom! Answer me!"

In my terror, I forgot how a doorknob worked. I clawed at the closed door, then reached down and flung the door open. "Mom, wake up!" I flipped the switch.

The room lit up in bright white.

Mom lay on the bed, staring wide-eyed at the ceiling.

A flood of relief washed over me. "Mom, I need help. We—"

Then I saw the red puddle soaking through the sheets where she lay.

"Mom!" The room tilted, and my legs stopped working. I collapsed on the hardwood floor.

I crawled, pulling myself up and onto the bed. My vision blurred, spotting to red, the color of the sheets. "Mom! Mom, no."

My hands reached out, shaking her. She didn't move.

I fought back the terror. There was still a chance. I pressed a finger to her neck, probing and searching for a pulse I couldn't find.

And like that, it hit me. *My mom's dead.*

"No. Oh, *no!*"

I shook her. She was still warm, and red continued to leak, darkening the white of the sheet.

I saw the nightstand drawer pulled open. Her hand lay unmoving by her head; her fingers still curled around the tiny gun she thought would save her life from the intruder.

I slipped down the bed to my knees. Turning away, I could see the opposite wall, where three bullets had left holes in the marbled white surface. I needed to leave.

I tried to stand, but my legs wouldn't obey the command.

Then I saw a word scrawled across the white wall. In blood.

Mom's blood.

RETURN.

Reality faded along with my eyesight. Red and white phased to black.

Mom's not dead. Mom can't be dead.

Crimson drops pooled a couple feet from where I lay in a crumpled heap.

But Mom's body isn't on the bed. It can't be. Mom's not dead.

A sickening queasiness rushed through me, doubling me over as I coughed in spasms.

Distantly, I noticed Chip standing in the doorway.

Chip is here. He can fix her. He can fix everything. He'll notice what I missed, and everything will be all right. That's what he always says; everything will be all right, Blue...

Then I heard his cries, his yells of denial, and I knew he couldn't fix her.

Mom is dead. Mommmyyyy!

My face touched the cool wood of the floor. I could find no comfort here.

The puddle inched toward me, but blessed blackness overcame me first.

———

I OPENED my eyes and couldn't figure out why I was lying horizontally across the big leather recliner in my living room, wrapped in a blanket my numb body couldn't feel.

I shook myself, fighting back from the void of shock by sheer willpower.

Focus on the now. There's too much to do.

I heard Chip's voice, but he wasn't talking to me, probably on the phone. I drifted into shock like a zombie.

Mom's dead. And I did it.

The room spun, and I closed my eyes against a shudder.

Reality seeped into me. *No, Gunther did this. But I have to do something to stop him from hurting anyone else.*

In a minute. I continued to lay in black numbness, listening to Chip talking rapidly in almost incoherent phrases, pouring out the story.

There wasn't supposed to be a ghost! Maybe we'd be caught at the park and get arrested, but...I'd thought it through very carefully...had everything under control.

This wasn't supposed to happen.

Chip's words penetrated to my consciousness. "Okay. We won't move. We'll wait for the police. Be careful, Dad."

I never had a dad. Now I don't have a mom anymore, either. The fact sank in. *I don't have a mom anymore because of Chip.*

I closed my eyes against sudden nausea. I waited for it to subside and then brushed aside the blanket. Pulling myself up onto shaking legs, I stood on my own two feet. The stiff, damp denim chafed my thighs.

I need to stay focused and finish this. I owe her that much.

Nausea gave way to a burning anger.

I heard the receiver of the phone land against its cradle. Chip limped into the room from the kitchen, a white rag tied around his leg.

At the sight of me, Chip's face softened to anxious concern. He took a step toward me. "Blue, you'd better take it easy. You're still in shock and—"

My rage burst out. "Bastard!" I advanced on him.

He froze in midstep, perplexed.

"Did you see my mother? Did you see what you did?"

"Blue, I swear, I didn't know."

"You had to know. He told you. We'd pay in blood, he said. Son of a bitch! And now she's dead because of you."

I saw the moneybag, propped on the kitchen table where he must have set it. I brushed past him. *I have to get that bag, and he's not going to stop me.*

He pivoted to watch me, but did nothing. "The police are on their way, Blue. Everything will be okay in just a minute." His calm, measured voice spoke its hypnotic reason but didn't calm my anger.

Grabbing the moneybag, I snarled his words back at him. "Everything will be okay? My mother's dead and everything will be okay?"

I swung the bag in an arch with all my might, smashing it into his chest. "My mother died over this!"

Weakened by his wounded leg, Chip toppled backward without uttering a noise.

The lack of reaction fed my fury. I pounced, grabbing him by his jacket and forcing him into a sitting position against the wall. "A bag of old money, you son of a bitch!"

Hurt filled his shocked eyes, but his arms hung, unresisting, at his sides.

I screamed at him. "Damn you and your treasure hunt!"

"Blue, I'm sorry, I didn't—"

"Stop apologizing, you coward." I threw myself at him, yanking him forward by his jacket. "You think the cops can fix this? You think the police can shoot the big bad ghost?" I threw him against the wall with all my might, forcing a groan from him.

Still, he didn't fight back. *Fine with me.*

I stood, looking down at his crumpled, pathetic form. "Useless. Coward. I'm taking the money back. Now."

"Blue, you can't do that. He's beyond all control. We need to give the money to the cops." His words came out faster. "We can expose Gunther. That's what he fears most. If you reveal his secret, his legend dies. The threat to his legacy is what's feeding his power now. You can't fight him anymore."

I rattled the moneybag at him. "You don't get to call the shots anymore. Gunther's out there, getting stronger by the minute. And if this is what he really wants, then I'll find a way to use it to stop him. Or die trying."

I strode toward the front door. Chip's voice followed me, rising in pitch as I walked away from him. "He won't let you live no matter what you do."

Chip's pleading voice rose. "Blue, he'll kill you. Don't go!"

I ran out the door and into the cold night, following a distant laughter traveling on the wind from the direction of the amusement park.

CHAPTER THIRTY

I ran through the sleeping neighborhood, my boots pounding an uneven rhythm on the sidewalk. Damp denim hung over my aching shoulders, and, before long, I gasped deep breaths of frigid night air.

The wind blasted, causing dry, crumbling leaves to billow up around me. I stopped to shield my face from cutting bits. The gust penetrated my jeans and pushed against the moneybag. My hand ached from the ongoing struggle to maintain my hold on the satchel.

A sudden, vicious blast knocked me off the sidewalk, and I toppled onto someone's lawn. As I fell, I heard a distant cackling.

I hid my face until the sound passed. Sprawled on the grass, I looked up at the brick house in front of me and its immediate neighbor. I spied the narrow alley between the homes, and beyond the yards, an open field of wild grass against the horizon.

Cutting through the field would lop six blocks off the road route, plus lessen the wind.

I hopped to my feet, sprinting across the yard and between the houses.

The gust blasted again. I threw myself against the brick wall. Again, I could hear a stifled chuckle.

I yelled into the air. "Having fun, you bastard?" Gunther may have had some sort of supernatural power over the weather, but that didn't matter much between the houses. I took advantage of the respite to collect my wits.

His voice reached me, more a frustrated howling of the wind than spoken words. *"You'll pay in blood, Blue."*

"I've got the money!" I yelled. "I'm bringing it back. What more do you want?"

"You'll return the money, regardless of any deal I might offer. I know you will. You'll try to save the day and protect everyone. Better hurry, Blue. I'm getting bored. I might kill another one of your friends. How about that nice Mary Rowan or your buddy, Phil?"

"Bullshit." I called into the air. "I have what you want. No one else does. Stay with me, and we'll finish this."

I raced out the alleyway and across the unfenced backyard, heading for the field beyond. I expected constant blowing harassment, but, to my surprise, the supernatural wind stopped pursuing me. *Maybe Gunther's finally tired of that game. Small blessing.*

I swung the moneybag low into the wall of tall grass, using it as a makeshift shield to bend the blades over while I pressed forward. The dried grass rose to my chest, crackling and falling as I plowed through them.

The air erupted in evil laughter. *"I'll just go kill Phil now. It won't take but a minute. Hey, 'Kill Phil,' that's funny. I like that. Don't you, Blue?"*

"No! No more killing." I turned in a slow circle, watching the horizon for his distinct form. "I'll ditch the money in the deepest lake around here. A place you can't get to."

"So certain of yourself? I'm a god in this town, far more powerful than any bully or mugger you've fought in your miserable, pathetic existence. Not Clinty or your teachers or the Broad Ripple police. For years, my power has continued to grow. But only while the money stays lost, and the mystery remains. And you're trying to end that."

I mumbled under my breath. "Yeah, I get it." *I may be a slow learner, but I'll find out how to play his game.*

A figure stood just beyond the clearing, atop a small mound leading to a backyard. The denim-jacketed apparition grinned at me.

I stopped a couple feet away from him and stared, perplexed.

Rather than the glowing spirit I'd seen earlier, this figure looked solid, real. *"I feed off the paranoia of this town. You know something about paranoia, don't you, Blue? And now I grow stronger by the minute. The more you struggle, the stronger I become."* His head bent back as his cackle traveled on the wind.

I knew better than to jump at him. "What do you want? If you want me to hide the money somewhere else, tell me. Tell me what you want, and I'll do it."

"Poor little fool. You really were just a pawn in Chip's schemes, weren't you? Still, you know far too much. I can't possibly let you live. So if you really wish to appease me, lie down and take out your switchblade."

He stepped aside and waved his hook toward the grass. *"Once you've done that, drive the knife through your own belly and across your chest. Then we can both rest peacefully after I hide the money myself. Maybe."*

I reeled at his casual request for me to kill myself. Though I had no intention of honoring it, I reached into my jacket pocket, trying to control my shaking hands.

My hand brushed against the rusted pocketknife I'd found at the grave site. I drew the knife out of my pocket. My hand tingled, and I flicked copper-colored rust from my fingertips. *No, I don't want that one.* I withdrew my hand, reached into my jeans pocket, and drew out my switchblade.

I held the moneybag out toward him. "So...if I...offer myself, you'll leave the rest of my friends alone?"

He reached for the bag. *"You have my word."*

I pulled it away from him. "Go fuck yourself. What good is your word?"

He growled, jumping forward, and his hand gripped the moneybag.

When I felt the tug, I swiped downward, slashing the switchblade against the tendons behind his knuckles.

He howled in fury and pain, falling back.

I lunged, swiping at his arm.

I swept my arm through empty air. He'd gone ghostly, but that didn't matter. I was merely feigning. I didn't expect to connect, and, when he lunged at me, I dodged out of his reach easily.

He howled and cradled his wounded hand. Blood splattered onto crackling grass.

At the sight of the blood, a snarling grin formed on my lips. "You're the one who's paying in blood, Gunther. You need to touch me to hurt me. And I bite back." I moved around him and continued across the lawn. "You killed my mother, and that little scratch doesn't begin to make up for it."

He winced. *"You bitch."* Unable to cover the bleeding hand with his hook, he cradled it awkwardly under the opposite arm. Blood continued to flow from the cut.

"That's just the wind talking, Gunther. And the wind can't really hurt me."

He grimaced at me. *"Let's see how badly you can hurt, Blue. I know what you fear."* He turned ethereal and faded away, a final cackle still vibrating over the air.

Shit. The air calmed, no longer howling. Gunther had vanished. But had I weakened him first?

From that scratch? It didn't seem likely. I turned and bolted across the grass. The sooner I could get to the park, the sooner this madness would end.

I ran to the next yard and rounded the corner to reach another alleyway. I crossed over two more streets and emerged, facing the west-side fence of the park.

I darted across the street, and, without slowing, hurled myself at the fifteen-foot fence. The metal rocked as I kicked into footholds and reached with one hand to pull myself up. For one crazy moment, I thought of pitching the moneybag up and over.

No. Stupid idea.

I crab-walked up the side and then threw the moneybag over the top, holding onto the handle with one hand, and the fence with the other. I kicked my leg up but not quite over.

I paused, hanging on the metal, trying to catch my breath. What I'd scaled so easily without the bulk of the money bag now proved a major challenge.

I tried to throw my weight over to the other side, but I shifted awkwardly and, *oh, hell!*, all my weight came down on my crotch, and I hung, straddling the fence.

I tipped drunkenly, kicking and grimacing as the metal sharpness dug into my thigh.

I screamed between my teeth and forced my leg to move up and over. The denim tore, along with a few inches of skin. I twisted and fell. Somehow, I managed to hold on with one arm, the other still gripping the bag. Weight, mass, and gravity conspired to drop me toward the earth.

My fingers ignored my mental command to hang on, releasing their grip. I'd stopped my fall, but I dropped the final six feet or so.

The moneybag hit the cement and my forearms hit the moneybag. Pain shot through my arms and into my shoulders. I slumped, unable to go any farther.

"Christ." With all I'd been through tonight, I knew I'd show horrible black and blue marks in the morning...assuming I survived that long.

As if on cue, the wind billowed up around me. *"You're too late, Blue,"* the directionless voice called.

I looked up the deserted pathway, seeing only the slightest stirring of the leaves. "What? What do you mean? If you killed anyone, I'll..." I stopped, unable to finish. *What can I do? I can't hurt him. I just have to see this through.*

The wind blew a pile of leaves, which rustled over a nearby park bench. *"Killed? Oh, no. At least, not yet."*

A large tower-shaped building lit up against the not-too-distant skyline. He'd powered up one of the rides.

I limped along the pathway toward the structure, my arms still singing their chorus of pain. Other injuries added their accompaniment.

After only two trips, my directional sense of the park layout remained rudimentary, but I didn't think I was walking toward the Pirates of Perionne moat. "What are you up to, Gunther?"

"Just making some plans, Blue. Oh, I see you noticed the lights, hmm? Another evil laugh. I guess I can't fool you for long."

"Shut up and tell me what you're doing."

"Just keep walking, bitch."

I realized where the path would take me, and I strode with growing confidence. Being one of the park's most popular rides, the turnbuckle started several hundred yards from the structure.

I stared at the sign over the wooden archway above me announcing the Whirlwind roller coaster. I could see the brightly lit entrance ahead, and, in the distance between the trees, the wooden supports of the ride itself.

"What are you doing?"

"Get over here. Chip's heroic old man called the cops. They'll be here soon. I need this lit building to guide them in the wrong direction. Now move your ass, girl."

I maneuvered through the metal brackets forming the line blockades. A couple of times a turnbuckle refused to budge, and I jumped over the bar with growing impatience. My cut thigh and other bruises screamed in pain each time.

I approached the wooden stairway, leading to the upper boarding level.

Gunther stood on the attendant's platform, arms folded with a grin on his face. Between us, one of the roller coasters crouched on the track like a sleeping dragon.

I stepped up onto the illuminated wooden-planked platform, my footsteps echoing hollowly. "What now, Gunther?"

He held a finger out for silence. *"Quiet."* A dramatic grin of grotesque glee cracked his face.

"I thought you said we didn't have a lot—"

Then I heard the sound of shoes on wood, climbing stairs, on Gunther's side of the coaster tracks. Behind him, I saw the silhouette of an awkward figure limping on a spiraling stairway, climbing upward.

Chip shuffled into the light, and I bit back a gasp. His eyes lit up when he saw me. But then he took in his surroundings, realizing he shared the small platform with the ghost and that the track and coaster separated me from them. "What's going on?"

I resisted the urge to leap over the coaster and run to him. Gunther stood between us. He could strike long before I could maneuver my way around the coaster and get to Chip's side.

A mad chortle escaped Gunther's lips. *"I thought we should have a little reunion."*

Chip's gaze darted around, like a lion trapped in a cage, trying to escape.

Then his eyes focused on me. "Blue, I'm sorry. He told me he had you. He was going to kill you if I didn't come."

"And you took long enough with that bum leg, Chip!"

I ignored the ghost, speaking directly to Chip. "He didn't 'have' anyone. The bastard kept blocking my path and delaying me." I glared at the grinning apparition. "I see why now. But get out of here, Chip. Now. I'll take care of this."

Chip shook his head. "No. You're the one who should run away." He directed his next statement to the ghost. "You don't need to involve her anymore. It's me you want. You've hurt her enough."

"I'm not leaving," I said. I knew Chip wouldn't stand a chance alone against Gunther. "However this goes down, I'm not leaving you here."

Gunther cut off my protests. *"How romantic. Each of you trying to make the ultimate sacrifice to save the other, trying to bargain with me, when you have nothing to bargain with."*

Gripping the switchblade in my hand, I held the point out,

centering on the apparition like an accusation. "I've got a deal for you, Gunther!" I spat out. "You hurt him, I swear I'll kill you and make sure this time you stay dead and in Hell."

Gunther's gaze met mine, and to my surprise, he looked away. *"I believe you. But, now, I think I'll hold on to my bargaining chip."* He assaulted my ears with more abrasive cackling. *"Bargaining chip, that's pretty good."*

"Enough," I said, waving the knife. "We want the same thing. You don't need to hurt him. Either of us."

"Perhaps not. Still, I think I'll keep him close."

Gunther stretched out his arms, in all ways resembling a zombie in a bad monster movie, stomping toward Chip and blocking the stairwell.

My vision flared, and I lost all sense and cool. All I knew at that moment was that I had to get over to Chip. Now. "No. You can't have him."

Dropping the bag, I dropped down into one the cars and bounced out the other side. Swiping with the switchblade, I crossed the distance and forced myself between them.

I stabbed at the hook. Metal clanged against metal, and Gunther's body jerked sideways.

I crouched, ready to attack, knife poised and ready. "You never learn, do you?" I taunted.

Gunther took a step back, so I came forward. He swung with his hook, making an obvious slash at my face.

Overconfident, I countered with the knife.

With unexpected speed, his hand thrust forward, and vise-like fingers gripped my neck, cutting off my air.

I gagged, dropping the knife and reaching up with both arms to loosen his grip.

Too fast, the world blackened around me. I pulled at his thumb with all my remaining strength, but it gave only slightly. In a fuzzy haze, I could see him draw me close, grinning.

My feet flopped against the floorboards in spasms. *I need air!*

I heard Chip's voice and felt, rather than saw, a figure charge into us. The taut fingers slackened.

My vision cleared, only to see Gunther slam the back of his hook across the side of Chip's head and feel the fingers tighten around my throat again.

Chip flew back, sprawling across the deck.

I tried to push away a final time, but my legs refused to work. I reached up and dug my fingernails into his too-solid flesh. *No air, and the world is fading away.*

Blackness enveloped me, and my body slumped. I no longer cared about my own imminent death.

"I have a special death just for you, Blue."

Dimly, I felt Gunther picking me up and throwing me. I only distantly realized that I collided with wood and metal and bounced against a shallow wall.

Nothing made sense. I flung my arms and legs around randomly, and kept hitting the walls of a wooden compartment, low and contained.

Gasping precious air, my body surged with a renewed strength and panic. I struggled into a sitting position, blinking through spotted blackness.

He let me live, for the moment. If he gives me a few more seconds to clear my head, he'll regret it.

Chip's panic-stricken voice reached me. "Blue! Get up!"

I shook my head, trying to clear away the black spots. Reaching out, my fingers gripped a flat, flush surface above me. *A seat. He's thrown me into a coaster car.*

I grabbed the seat and pulled myself up on shaky legs. The seat shifted into blurry focus. Looking up, I saw Chip crawling across the platform toward me, arms outstretched. But I didn't see Gunther.

A squeal of metal broke the quiet, and the coaster surged forward.

The floor fell out from under me. I toppled sideways, tumbling across the tops of two cars.

I pitched into the hollow of the car behind me, my feet raised and flailing through the air, unable to find purchase. As the car shifted around its first curve, I grabbed and twisted, trying to right myself.

The car chugged over the tracks and into the darkness. No lights cut through the chilling black, only the sound of a high-pitched cackle.

The wind blasted a fierce torrent.

I grabbed the seat and forced my feet down where they belonged. Grabbing the front of the car for balance, I dragged myself to the edge. I braced my legs under me, pulling myself into a half-stand, preparing to hurl myself off.

The coaster shifted into a sharp upward tilt, beginning its ascent for the big drop. Again, I tumbled across the cars, falling against wood, plastic and wind. I reached out, gripped the seat, and held on with all of my strength to right myself. The car tipped into a sharper angle, and my back wedged against the seat.

Chug...Chug...Chug...

The car slanted to a near vertical position, continuing its ascent.

In a wild panic, I clawed the side of the car, pulling myself forward and staring out into the night.

Chug...Chug...Chug...

I saw the tops of the trees, and then I didn't. I'd missed the moment between safe-to-jump and no longer safe.

Chug...Chug...Chug...

The wind blew, rustling the trees below me. *Dear God.*

I couldn't see the tracks.

And then I realized nothing held me in!

Chug...Chug...Chug...

Terror overtook me, and I froze, unable to act.

The car would drop and I would die. I called out in the blackness. "Mom! I don't want to die."

Chug...Chug...Chug...

The straps! I lunged to the front and the left. *A strap has to be here somewhere.* My nails brushed a small metal hook. *Fuck!*

Chug...Chug...Chug...

I clawed at the opposite side, and my knuckles brushed the loose fabric.

Chug...chu-...

The car slowed,...leveling,...preparing to plunge.

I gripped and pulled. Any second, the car would speed off and fling me to oblivion. Not enough time, in total blackness, to hook myself in.

I twisted my forearm... once, twice, three times; I wrapped the strap around my arm. I pulled it taught with my other hand, folding my fingers into a fist.

Best I can do.

My legs locked, preparing to somehow absorb the shock of what came next.

Chug...

I could see an unobstructed view of the entire Perionne land-scape surrounding me, a few yellow dots in all directions, surrounded in the distance by oppressive blackness. The half-moon showed wicked orange teeth, laughing down on me.

The wind blew in my face. "Okay!" I snarled through my clenched teeth. "Take your shot!"

The train toppled into the abyss, and the world screamed at me. My arms jerked back. Wind tore at my face. My legs gave way, and my body bashed against the back of the seat.

The car pulled up from the drop, and then cut into an immediate right turn.

My body slammed against the side of the car, slapping my ribs into the wood. The car jerked, and I hurled across the side, pummeling my shoulder. New pain shot through my body as brutal winds ripped at my face and hair.

The train tore into another ascent. All I could do was hold on, with no control, as the strap whip-lashed my body, slamming me against the support.

My hands locked like steel around the strap. I could no longer feel my fingers, only burning agony through my arms. Still, I held on as the car twisted and spun madly.

My legs locked against the seat, and the blackness became palatable, a living thing. I secured myself, somewhat.

The car vibrated into a mad, tumbling descent, the large corkscrew, I recalled from a distant memory. The ride would end any moment.

I have to let go, or he'll find me before I'm ready.

Even as the thought penetrated, my arm moved on its own, untwisting itself from the strap.

The wind blasted me up, yanking me from the security of the floorboards. My ears rang with the screeching wail of slamming brakes cutting through roaring wind.

The car shook. The wind lessened.

I released the strap, flying off into space, over the side and into the trees below.

For a moment, the wind embraced me. The car slipped away, and pain overcame my senses.

I fell into a waiting blackness.

CHAPTER THIRTY-ONE

I couldn't move. I wanted to stay in my daze, drifting above a haze of pain.

A familiar, comforting voice called to me.

"Fiona! Fiona, get up!"

"Mom?" No mistake. I could hear her voice, calling to me. She hadn't died after all.

"Fiona, I love you. Listen to me, baby. You need to get up and finish this."

"Mom." I tried to lift my hand, but it seemed too much of an effort, and the darkness claimed me again.

I AWOKE to pain throbbing through my body.

Blurriness gave way to clear vision. I blinked, realizing my face was pressed into the grass. A leaf came into sharp focus, and a loamy scent filled my nostrils. Slowly, I reached up and curled my fingers around it; the brown-veined papery texture crumpled in my fingers. I rolled over onto my swollen shoulder, winced, and shifted. Faint moonlight threaded through the tree branches overhead.

"Mom?"

No response. Had I just imagined her speaking to me? But I remembered the urgency in her message and made an effort to sit up.

Movement was agony. With careful, gingerly motions, I straightened to my feet and peered up through the wooden supports.

I'd fallen some distance from the tracks, but only a few yards from the boarding platform. I'd probably rolled through the woods. I saw the broken bush that had apparently halted my momentum.

Standing in the dark, I assessed my options. *Gunther might think I'm dead. He might not think to look for me this far out.*

I had to kill him, if that was still possible. No more banter, no more bargaining. He'd killed Mom, thought he'd killed me, and would kill Chip as soon as Chip had done his bidding.

Creeping through the woods, staying out of the light, I approached the platform from below. *How long was I out?*

I approached the rear stairway and heard arguing above me. I stepped quietly onto the first wooden stair, trying to control my shaking body. Part of me wanted to bolt forward and another part of me almost collapsed where I stood.

Gunther's command reached my ears. *"Come on, boy! Take the bag. The old man should be along soon enough, and you can bury it together. Come on, boy! Pick it up. What's the matter?"*

"Go fuck yourself."

"Oooohhh! All of a sudden, you're growing a pair, eh, boy? It's too late to help your sweetie. She's dead. You failed her. Take it like a man."

With determined stealth, I tiptoed up the planked stairway. I could see right through Gunther, whose back was to me, to view Chip on his knees in front of the moneybag.

"And now you want to torture my father, like you tortured Blue. Because of what you think he did."

"Oh, what happened to Blue is nothing. Your father betrayed me, boy. And he'll watch his son die before I deal with him. But if you cooperate, you, at least, might earn a quick death. Think about it, boy, it's the only reward

you'll get for trying to be the big hero, sticking your nose where it didn't belong."

Chip knelt by the moneybag, eyes closed, as if contemplating the options he didn't appear to have. All he had to do was look up and he would have seen me through the apparition. But try as I might to will it, he never did.

I reached for my pocket and then stopped, cursing at the memory. My switchblade had fallen from my grasp earlier, and I had no idea where. My hand traveled on its own to my jacket pocket. I had stashed the ancient pocketknife there.

I withdrew the rusted tool, staring at the crusted handle. Would this dilapidated relic still work after being buried in soil for twenty-five years? It didn't seem likely.

My thumbnail found the notch, and I wiggled the blade free. In spite of its appearance, the blade still felt firm between my fingers. As I wrapped my hand over the ornamental handle, my fingers tingled with anticipation, as if the knife wanted to jump from my hands.

"Pick up the bag, boy."

"Kiss my ass, Gunther."

I could see the resolution on Chip's face, the acceptance of his fate, better to be dead than live with this torture any longer.

No, Chip! Hang in there.

And he wouldn't look up.

Gunther raised his hook. *"Oh, the hell with you. Let that be your epitaph."*

Chip vanished from my sight, blocked by a more substantial Gunther.

I let out a war cry and leapt, knowing I'd be too late.

The hook swung in a clean arc down into Chip's unmoving shoulder.

I slammed into Gunther's muscled back and thrust the blade between us, sinking it into solid flesh.

He jerked, the momentum carrying us sideways. As we tumbled over, I could see his eyes bulge with surprise.

"Fucker!" I screamed. "Die for the last time!" I clawed my fingers into his jacket, holding onto him with a death grip. The force of my charge drove us across the platform, spinning off the edge and into the darkness.

I kicked away from him in mid-fall, landing on soft, wet ground and rolling with the impact. My whole body screamed in pain; I could no longer distinguish one injury from another.

Ignoring that, I came up on my knees, stealing a quick glance at the rusted blade, which now dribbled fresh blood.

Across the field I could see Gunther, who now looked quite solid and hurt, struggling to his feet. I bolted into the woods and the darkness, toward the wooden coaster support beams. I crunched leaves beneath my feet with no regard to stealth, making sure he knew his prey was escaping.

Under cover of darkness, I doubled back, squatting behind a beam.

Gunther swiped his hand across his belly where I had made the fresh wound. Even from this distance, I could see he wobbled on his feet.

"Come on, Gunther!" I yelled. "I'm not done playing with you yet!"

I darted beneath the coaster, hearing an enraged howl closing the distance behind me. I slowed, rebounding off several of the wooden supports, grabbing others and taking quarter turns. Blindly, I darted beneath the supports, making as much noise as I could, intentionally smacking the beams with my hands.

As I hoped, Gunther gave chase. Expecting me to flee the area in a direct and sensible path, Gunther darted after me as fast as he could run. At the same time, he tried to hone in on the audio cues I'd deliberately made. I heard him stumble around, screaming and tripping. When he'd get close, I'd call out and run away again.

Gunther howled, finally choosing to stand in place for the moment. *Where are you, bitch?*

I darted away, certain I could goad him further while I thought out my next move.

I doubled back, circling his noisy traipsing. "You're sounding pretty solid, there, Gunther," I taunted. I turned again and retreated, trying to avoid the supports. I wasn't always successful, but the adrenaline spiked me through the pain of impact. *If I survive this, I won't be able to walk for a week.*

I crouched behind another beam. I couldn't see him, but I could hear him stumbling toward me.

I gasped for air, but knew I had to keep enraging him, taunting him, so he couldn't think straight. "How do you like all your power, Gunther? Getting all your flesh back? Stubbing your toe? Banging your head? I'll bet you just love it."

I crawled low in the grass, angling closer to him. I rose to my feet, then ran toward the noise of his stumbling. I dodged the first beam and slid around the second just as he came into view.

He turned at the sound. *"You mockin' me now, girl?"*

"I'm about to kill you!" I turned and ran back the way I'd come, weaving by the supports I'd just passed, waiting by another.

Gunther screamed, charging after me. His foot caught on a support, and he pitched forward with an indignant cry.

I advanced on him, pocket knife in my hand. "This knife killed you once already, Gunther. I suspect you're now meaty enough that it can kill you again."

He leapt at me, swiping the air with his arm. Prepared, I jumped backward. The hook swept uselessly through empty space. I stumbled back, stopping when I felt solid brace of the support beam against my back.

Gunther recovered from his first swing and drew back again.

I dropped sideways.

The hook swept across where I had stood a moment ago and caught with a *thunk* into the wooden beam.

As he grabbed for me, I backpedaled away from his arm. He pulled back short, turning and looking perplexed at the prosthetic limb which would not come unstuck.

Again, I summoned my war cry, charging, the blade held high. I slammed into him, burying the knife deep into the flesh of his exposed belly.

Gunther staggered backward. His mouth hung open in befuddlement. He gurgled and attempted to yank out his hooked arm, but it remained wedged in the wood.

"This knife has already killed you, Gunther."

He made a grab for my throat.

I caught his hand, twisting.

Gunther leaned over me, trying to gain leverage. The stench of sweat and vomit assaulted my nose.

I yanked my knife loose from his chest and slashed across the back of his wrist. His howl of pain cut through the air.

"This knife is...part of your grave...part of...the spell."

He could only return a blank stare, moaning. "No." His body slackened against me, and I shoved him away.

He dropped to his knees, one arm slack at his side, the other pulled upward over his head, still caught in the wooden beam.

At the sight of him, hanging and vulnerable, I saw red and attacked like a wild animal.

I raised the blade and slammed it down into his face.

The hook tore free, and Gunther toppled backward into the grass.

I thrust the knife down, poking a divot into his face, no longer concerned about targeting, just driven by a desire to cut and slice. "Die!"

He groaned a last time and lay unmoving beneath me.

Gripping the knife with both hands, I pounded the weapon over and over into the limp body.

"You killed...my mother...you fucker!" I accented each pause with a thrust. "Killed her...for...useless money."

Blood erupted from various puncture wounds, smearing my shirt and jeans. I straddled the puckered carcass and raised the knife again. "Kill you! Kill you! Kill you!" The knife punctuated each word.

Gasping for breath, I soaked in the blood of my enemy. "Kill you," I whispered. An insane giggle escaped my lips.

I pulled the knife free, gripping it in my hand. Literally dizzy with victory, the world spun away, and I collapsed, closing my eyes and basking in the justified murder.

When I opened them a moment later, I saw no body. I lay on the cold, wet ground, no blood.

My clothes, while torn and soaked, were soaked with dew and rain; no blood, except a few fresh spots from my own various cuts. The knife, while slick from the sweat of my hands, showed no sight of blood.

I pulled at my own hair and screamed. I stared at the support beam, which showed a freshly sliced chunk of wood, the only evidence a struggle had taken place.

I stumbled toward the bright white luminescence of the coaster entrance, tottering from support to support, always focused on the light. I could barely feel the mechanical motion of my own limbs. I moved by sheer will to where I knew Chip lay, bleeding and dying.

My body kept moving on its own. I knew Gunther might appear again, and he could go for Chip at any moment. I gripped the iron rail and pulled myself up the planked stairs, dragging myself up to the platform.

I could see Chip lying where he had fallen, his eyes closed, blood seeping from his shoulder.

Fear squeezed my heart. *Is he dead?* I approached him with heavy steps.

He turned his head slightly and saw me. "Blue," he mumbled.

The knife fell from my fingers, and I crumpled forward onto the platform.

The knife bounced loudly across the planks and came to a stop.

I dragged myself over to where he lay. "Chip!"

I reached out, taking his wrist in my hands. I could feel a pulse. "Chip, don't you die on me."

Blood pooled beneath him. He groaned. He stared upward, past me. "Blue."

I grabbed his jacket, shaking him. "Chip, I made it better. I told you I would."

"You got him?"

"Think so. Don't know. He's gone for now."

"Blue, if I die—"

"Shut up! Don't die. You can't. If you die, I have nothing left." Tears spilled from my eyes, splattering his cheek. I swallowed back the horrible, aching sorrow fighting to erupt from me, the pain of what I'd lost and what I still could lose.

His voice penetrated my turmoil. "I'm tired, Blue."

Through my tears I felt his wrist. His pulse beat weakly beneath my fingers.

I folded myself over him, pulling him into an embrace. "Go to sleep, honey. You can sleep."

I heard the thumping of footsteps; someone approached from the stairwell behind me. A figure rose onto the platform. A large figure. I braced.

"Fi-Fi. It's me." Chip's father rushed into the light. "Oh, my God!" Shock registered on his features as he recognized his son laid out prone on the platform.

Mr. Farren ran forward and dropped before Chip, checking for vital signs. "He's alive. An ambulance is coming."

As I cradled Chip in my arms, I felt Mr. Farren's gaze on me. He finally broke the awkward silence. "Gunther?"

I nodded. His hands reached up, covering his eyes, and his intimidating stature seemed to crumple. "He appeared to me a few minutes ago. Told me to come here. That was after your mother—"

I cut him off. I didn't want to hear the words spoken. "We dug it up."

I saw his gaze fall upon the moneybag. "Oh, my God." He stood and retrieved the bag. He pondered the rusted knife for a moment and grabbed that, too.

I bent to listen to Chip's breathing, making sure he still lived. "We need to take it back." My mind reeled at the thought of going back into the ride. Blackness already threatened to close in. I would not hold out.

"Yes. Yes." Mr. Farren nodded.

"They go in the Pir—"

"I know where they go," Mr. Farren snapped. "Fi-Fi, listen to me. I can return this later. I need to remove everything and get it into my car before the police arrive. This bag...and this knife...is that all you found?"

"Uh..." The darkness at the edge of the lamps had closed in around me. "I...don't know. Too hard to think."

"I can't return it while the cops are combing the area for the killer, but maybe once they're gone..."

The distant shriek of sirens cut through the silence.

Mr. Farren crouched in front of me. "Fi-Fi."

Try as I might, I found it difficult to focus on his voice.

"Fi-Fi! Lie back, honey. You're going into shock. I have everything, and I'll hide it tonight. Don't worry. Don't worry, Fi-Fi. Everything will be okay."

Where have I heard that before? My body slumped into blackness.

I came to and found myself strapped onto a bed. I could feel the vibration of a moving ambulance. "Chip!"

An unfamiliar voice spoke. "He's still with us, Miss Shaefer. Chip is fine. Everything will be okay."

Chip's fine. The phrase echoed in my head. But I knew everything wasn't okay.

"Mom?..." But no one answered before I slept.

CHAPTER THIRTY-TWO

Sunlight hit against the back of my eyelids. I blinked, shut my eyes, and tried to roll away from the brightness. A thick cotton dressing taped against my back inhibited my movement. A variety of throbs and aches made themselves known, some of which I couldn't remember noticing during my ordeal.

Warm sheets lay against my bare neck, and the softness of a hospital gown wrapped around me. I twitched my nose at the odor of rubbing alcohol and soap.

I sensed movement in the room and opened my eyes to focus on a small window with a patterned red curtain pulled over it. The curtain failed to keep the bright sunshine from disturbing my sleep.

Odd. I lay in a small private room, not a partitioned hospital space.

Beneath my gown, the tightness of bandages over various areas of my bruised and battered body annoyed me. There were more than I could detect or count easily. The itchy irritation of a bandage on my inner thigh distracted me. Another wrapping pulled tight against my head.

"Oh. You're awake." I turned to see a nurse at the doorway, dressed in the usual permanent-press pajama uniform with a pattern

I couldn't quite bring into focus, her dust-colored brown hair pulled back with a clip. "How are you feeling?" I heard genuine concern in the question.

I tried to take a deep breath, only to wince from the pain in my ribs. "What time is it?"

The nurse raised her wrist, her dark-brown eyes giving her watch a quick, business-like glance. "It's one-thirty in the afternoon." She flashed me an understanding, friendly smile. "You're going to be okay. I mean, for what you've gone through. You cracked three ribs, but everything will mend quickly. The rest looks bad, feels worse, but it all adds up to a bunch of scrapes and bruises."

I bit back a reply about how the loss of my mother added up to a lot more than a bunch of bumps and bruises. "Where's Chip?"

"Recovering from surgery."

"When can I see him? I have to see him."

"I'll fetch the doctor." With that, she left.

I waited, trying to find a comfortable spot on the pillow and fighting the tendency of my eyes to drift shut.

I scanned the room to stay awake, noticing my clothes folded neatly on a chair.

The curtains blurred out of focus and I drifted.

"Fiona?"

I snapped awake, taken aback by a remarkably pretty blonde woman standing next to my bed. Dark blue eyes met mine, framed by a soft, concerned face. "I'm Dr. Deidre Churchill. How are you feeling?"

She's my doctor? I didn't think my reaction came from sexism; she just didn't strike me as a surgeon or emergency room M.D.

I rubbed a hand across an itchy eye. "Tired. But I need to know about Chip."

Dr. Churchill nodded. "But first, the M.D. wants to check you out, and the police want to ask you some questions."

I shook my head, wondering if the blurriness had confined itself to my eyes. "I thought the nurse said you were my doctor."

She laughed, not unpleasantly, and reached out, giving my hand a tender squeeze. "I'm your psychologist. I came in to coordinate with the social worker. I know about...your situation."

I looked down at the covers. "About my mother?"

"Yes," she said in a soft voice. "Your story is all over the news. I'm so sorry, but you should know."

My mind tried to disconnect, wanting to drown in sorrow, but I clung to her hypnotic, reassuring voice.

"What happened last night was horrible and tragic and unfair." Her hands tightened over mine.

A pit of sorrow threatened to swallow me up.

"But we're going to get through it together. I promise."

My mental dam broke. Tears spilled down my face, and I cried out, wailing and sobbing. She wrapped her arms around me and pulled me close. I buried my face in her bosom, and this kind, merciful stranger held me tight, making little reassuring noises.

I called out, "Mom!" The pain welled up from deep inside, agony I'd bottled up for so many hours, ripped from me.

Minutes later, I lay, head against her shoulder, limp and exhausted from my emotional explosion.

Not raising my head from Dr. Churchill's comforting embrace, I grabbed a tissue and blew my nose.

I needed a second tissue, so I swiped another one.

Gunther killed my mother.

I blew my nose again. This time, I could breathe.

He'd made the choice and acted upon it. And nothing could have stopped him.

Nothing.

———

When I woke up from a sound sleep, I saw a man peeking at me through a crack in the door.

"May I come in," he asked in a soft voice.

I nodded.

Chiseled pecs bulged under the short sleeves of his shirt. My gaze traced the evenly tanned arm to the notepad held at eye level. Blond waves of hair topped the adorable package.

"Hello, Fiona, I'm Lieutenant Grady. Do you remember what happened to you?" He waited, his eyes cast downward, refusing to meet my gaze.

I pondered the question. In my current state, I could say anything. *What did they think happened?* I started with the obvious. "My mother...she's dead."

"Yes." The voice reached me like a disinterested recording. "That's right. You remember your mother's death? At your home?"

"I...chased...someone."

"Yes." The voice took on a texture of life as the lieutenant's interest piqued. "This is very important, Fiona. Did you recognize the person you chased?"

"I...No. I have no idea who it was. He...wore a mask." I shrugged, unsure of where to take my ad lib story. Instead, I answered his questions, pretending dizziness or a memory lapse when an obvious answer escaped me. I kept my story as simple as I could and let the detective fill in the blanks. Boiled down, my story amounted to this:

My date with Chip was ending, and I decided Mom should meet my new boyfriend. So I brought him home, only to walk in on a masked burglar-turned-murderer. I ran after him while Chip called the cops. Then Chip followed after me.

I chased the burglar into Perionne Park, where he tried to lose me underneath the roller coaster, but I followed him up and onto the platform. We fought, and, somehow during the struggle, the roller coaster activated. The guy overpowered me, but Chip found us and jumped into the fray. The murderer stabbed Chip, but the sirens scared the murderer away where he...just...ran off.

Lieutenant Grady shuffled in the chair, looking up for the first time, focusing a pair of dark, indifferent eyes upon me that diminished his "hottie" potential.

He dropped his notebook and pen into a breast pocket. "Listen, not that this is anything new, but there're all sorts of stories in the papers about Gunther the ghost. Reporters love to throw the paranormal angle out whenever anything strange happens. So I'm asking, just so I can say I did. Did this have anything to do with the ghost?"

I bit my lip, not daring to speak until I regained my composure. Across the room, my "court-appointed social worker" watched me, and her stoic face didn't help me fight the panic welling up within me.

Finally, I shrugged. "What do you want me to say? My Mom died last night, and you want to know if a *ghost* did it?"

The lieutenant's face turned beet red. "Right. I'm sorry. Just forget I asked." He rose. "For what it's worth, I'm sorry this happened. We'll do what we can." He left without another word.

———

A LOUD KNOCKING STARTLED me awake.

"It's Nurse Thompson, dear." The door swung open, and she stepped though, a Cheshire cat grin on her face. "Oh. I didn't realize you'd fallen back to sleep. I have a surprise for you. I thought it would cheer up your room a bit." With that, she wheeled in a three-shelved instrument cart.

My mouth dropped at the sight of billowing color. I smiled at the Mylar *Get Well Soon* balloons and the potted plants, the vases of roses, and cone-paper wrapped carnations. I could see various index cards with miscellaneous names, most of which I didn't recognize. I spotted a Mylar balloon dangling a card with Phil and Mary's names.

Overwhelmed, a wave of dizziness flooded over me, and I leaned back against the pillow. Try as I might, I couldn't find my voice.

The nurse rushed to my side, placing her hand on my shoulder. "Are you okay, dear? I can get the doctor..."

Even as my body trembled, I shook my head. I choked back a sniffle and wiped fresh tears from my cheeks. *It's happening, again.*

Suddenly, the nurse wrapped her arms around my shoulders and rocked me gently. Her voice penetrated my numb brain. "There, there, dear. You poor dear. Don't worry. You're going to be fine. We'll take care of you. This town takes care of its own."

CHAPTER THIRTY-THREE

I spent the long, tedious hours of the afternoon half-dozing off in the confines of my hospital room, channel surfing through the courtroom TV and talk shows. I'd asked Nurse Thompson for a book, but, after a few pages, I couldn't even follow the inane melodrama of Danielle Steele. So I resigned myself to catching up on my *People* magazines and reading the latest on Paris Hilton and the twenty-five worst-dressed women at the Emmys.

Shortly after five, someone knocked on my door.

I looked up, surprised to see the Ben Gerrold, Mom's partner, standing in the doorway, a stern expression distorting his elderly features.

All business, Gerrold gave my limp hand a brisk shake and seated himself without greeting me or asking how I was coping. He flipped open a laptop, setting it across his neatly tailored slacks, and brusquely explained my rights and options with the comforting sincerity of a Komodo dragon irritated by a persistent fly.

As guardian of my estate according to the final wishes of my mom, he'd arranged the private hospital room, and had pre-signed the release papers allowing me to leave tomorrow. He'd see that I continued to live in a comfortable home if I didn't want to stay in the house where my mother had died.

"Fiona?"

I'd zoned out of the conversation, instead choosing to stare at the overhead vent holes in the paneled ceiling. "Sorry, what?"

With infinite patience, Gerrold repeated, "I said, 'I trust this is satisfactory?'"

"Oh, yes, sounds great." I reached for the plastic carafe of ice water and poured myself a glass. I could only hope the jarring cold on my teeth would keep me awake.

The elderly lawyer picked up where he'd left off, hitting each bullet point in his plethora of information while staring at his computer screen, glazed gray eyes fixated on the facts in front of his face.

He'd see to all of my comforts and provide a generous allowance for my personal use over the next several months until I turned eighteen. He'd arrange for college assistance and make sure any interruptions to my education as a result of this tragedy would be minimal. I should also take note of...

I awoke with a start.

Gerrold must have seen me jump. Though his body hadn't moved from his sitting position, his eyes flickered in my direction, and he paused in his narrative.

I reached up and stretched, and his eyes shifted back to the screen. Whether he continued from where he left off, or he'd backed up a few sentences is something I'll never know. "Seeing as you're so close to the age of independence, I want to assure you that foster care won't be an issue, as long as you and I can work out an arrangement on which we can both agree."

Foster care! I shuddered at the thought, relieved not to have to go there. I guess I had to thank Ben Gerrold for that.

Then it hit me. I'd known Ben Gerrold as my mother's partner my entire life, and yet I knew almost nothing about him on a personal level. He existed in one mode. And he knew nothing about me, except whatever horror stories my mother brought to the office. And now, here the man sat, shackled with the fearsome responsibility of my upbringing. I actually felt sorry for him and reached out to pat his hand.

He stopped in mid-recitation, turning and looking at me for the first time, a shocked expression on his face. He removed his glasses, wiping a hand over the single tear spilling down his cheek.

I repeated the words Dr. Churchill had spoken to me hours earlier. "It's okay. We're going to get through this."

He put his face in his hands, fighting back a sniffle. "I'm sorry. It's such a damn awful thing." He shook his head and folded the computer on his lap. "I suppose this can all wait 'til later." He took a deep, shaky breath. "Your mother was an outstanding, brilliant partner. And she was a good woman. She certainly didn't deserve to be taken from us like this. I'll miss her terribly."

He looked at me and shrugged. "I owe it to her to see to it that you're well taken care of. But...I never had any children. I don't know what to do."

I smiled at his awkwardness. "Relax, Mr. Gerrold, I won't be asking to move in. I don't even know what my options are at this point, but in a few days we can talk about it more."

An uneasy expression crossed his face. "You should get more rest." He stood, shifting uncomfortably. "If there's anything I can do, please let me know." As if on impulse, he reached out and rumpled my hair. Just as suddenly, he pulled his hand back, walking out without another word.

I sat up when someone knocked on my door. "Come in."

My eyes focused to see the now-familiar, bulky profile of Mr. Farren standing in front of the curtain. "Fi-Fi?" He noticed my open eyes and offered a bashful grin. "How are you?

I shrugged. "I'm fine. Is Chip awake? I want to see him."

Mr. Farren shook his head. "No, not yet. And they won't let you see him until he's out of intensive care."

I grinned. "We'll figure something out."

He held two paper cups of steaming liquid pinched between his beefy fingers, and extended one my direction. "Here."

My stomach churned at the thought of coffee, but, when I lowered the cup, my nose detected the distinct aroma of chicken broth. *The milk of human kindness.*

Mr. Farren lowered his bulk into a wooden chair near the edge of my bed.

I sucked the first few sips greedily, burning my tongue but savoring the yummy salted liquid. I held the cup in my fingers, enjoying the warmth, focusing on the spinning herbs in the broth. "Mr. Farren, you were there, weren't you? That night, with Gunther?"

Mr. Farren wiggled in his chair, creating a squeal of complaining metal. "You didn't know?"

We exchanged shocked looks, and I shook my head. "No. I didn't. But I don't know how I didn't. Chip told a lame story about you and a bowling buddy." I chuckled. It felt good to laugh. "What a stupid story. If a bowler had lips that loose every time he had too much beer, the whole town would have dug up the ride by now." I wiped at my eyes. "And I bought it."

Jim Farren sighed deeply. "Don't blame Chip for wanting to keep it a secret. He fooled me, too. What you two did, I had no idea he had planned it, but I suppose, like you, I should have seen it coming."

I hesitated, wondering whether to ask the question utmost on my mind, and then decided if he'd share this much, he'd share the rest. "Did you...kill Gunther?"

Mr. Farren's eyes widened in genuine shock. "What? No." He drew in a deep breath. "I did a few things I'm ashamed of. But I never killed anyone." And with that, Mister Farren, *Jim* Farren, told me how, many years ago, Gunther blackmailed him to drive the getaway car, of his terrible, cowardly betrayal of Crimley, and of his loyal wife, who took a terrible secret to her grave.

As he finished his tale, I stared into my cup and let the story fester between us for a few moments. "And how did Chip know?"

Mr. Farren chuckled. "He guessed, the intuitive bastard. He got a confession from me before I figured out he only knew half as much as I thought he did. I had no reason to deny it, not to my own boy. What difference did it make?"

I answered the question, realizing the truth as I spoke it. "You were involved in this...great wrong, these killings and the robbery. And nobody knew how to make it right. Chip didn't want the money, or fame, or anything else." My eyes watered at the realization. "He wanted to make it right. Right for you and for him, so you wouldn't have to live with the shame anymore."

Mr. Farren shrugged. "I guess he did. We had one conversation about it years ago, and haven't spoken of it since. Until Gunther showed up at my house last night."

"What happened?"

"He said he was going to kill you and my son unless I met him at the park. That was after Chip's phone call. I called the police immediately. But it was...almost too late."

"And now?"

Mr. Farren shook his head and pinched his index finger to his thumb, dragging it across in a "zipper" motion. "The money's gone, where nobody can find it. I made sure of that. I couldn't return it to the park. The police were everywhere, all night. And there I stood with the biggest find of the town in the trunk of my car, if anyone bothered to look. Soon as the police stopped questioning me, I drove off, and I got rid of it."

He folded his arms, as if challenging me to change his mind. "The secret is my burden and mine alone, just as it was many years ago. And it's staying that way. That should keep Gunther more than satisfied." He let out a deep sigh.

My hand shook at the revelation, and I almost spilled the soup. "Such insanity. Gunther cares so much about his own infamy that he returned from death to preserve it. Without the mystery, without the legend, people would have forgotten about him years ago. And that's why he can't allow anyone to return the money."

I stared down onto my soup cup. I could feel tears welling up. "But my mother...I know she cared about me, but...I also know...she won't come back. She never will."

Two stubby fingers pinched the lip of the cup and took it from me while I reached blindly for my tearing face. "I'll never see her again."

I sobbed into my hands while Mr. Farren remained silent.

A loud knocking jarred me from my sorrow.

Mr. Farren stood.

A nurse stuck her head through the door, a pleasant smile on her face. "Mr. Farren? Your son is awake and asking for you. In fact, he's asking for both of you."

"Me, too?" I asked.

She nodded, still grinning.

———

CHIP LAY STRETCHED out on the bed, monitors hooked to his shoulders. A tight bandage covered his exposed midsection.

Mr. Farren looked at me from a bedside chair.

As I approached, Chip turned his head with great effort.

"Blue," he whispered, and managed a feeble smile.

I smiled at the sight of him. Joy and relief flooded me.

He reached a hand out, and I entwined his fingers in mine. "I guess...you're not pissed at me?"

Just a few hours ago, I never thought I'd touch him again. I gently squeezed his hand. "No. I'm not. Don't you worry. You just get better so we can get into trouble again."

"No. I'm done with getting in trouble."

Mr. Farren stood. "I'll be back." He gave Chip a meaningful glare. "Don't you screw up again." He stepped out.

It didn't seem proper, cutting in before father and son could speak. But selfishness kept me silent. Talking to Chip now was the most important thing in the world to me.

Chip struggled to take a breath, forcing the words out. "Blue...I'm sorry. That can't even begin to cover it. I can't believe you're even here."

"I love you." The words dropped from my mouth before I could stop them.

He opened his mouth to speak.

I reached out and placed a finger over his lips. "Hush."

I tried to squeeze his hand again, but, to my astonishment, I couldn't press his fingers very hard. I hadn't realized until that moment what a beating I'd taken, and how much strength I'd lost. "You were trying to do a good thing. I know that now. But...don't ever hide anything from me again."

Chip drew a shaky breath. "I don't have any more secrets, but I'll keep it in mind."

I drew his hand to my lips and kissed his fingers. "You just get better. I promise I'll be here when you get back."

"Then where will you go?"

I took a thoughtful moment. "I'm not sure. Mom's partner came by. I have a college trust fund, and I'll get an allowance until I turn eighteen. I'm so close to being an 'adult,' I won't have to go to a foster home. But I don't want to go near that house again."

Chip squeezed my hand. "Don't blame you, Blue. I'm so sorry."

I took a shaky breath. "It's not your fault. Really, it isn't. I know that now."

I heard the sound of a clearing throat. Mr. Farren stood in the doorframe, leaning into the room.

I took the hint. "I'll go for now." A sob welled up from deep within, and I shivered. "Don't ever leave me again."

"I won't," he whispered.

———

NURSE THOMPSON WHEELED me out into the late afternoon sunshine. The hospital surrounded a private outdoor retreat, by a paved path running around and through a tiny courtyard that broke a small garden into sections.

The garden bordered a shallow pond equipped with a fountain creating a subtle gurgling. A half-dozen fish swam in lazy tranquility.

The cool air cleared my head, stimulating senses left docile from monotonous hours of napping in my room. The world snapped into sharp focus.

She pushed me toward the pond then set the brake on my wheelchair. "I thought you might like a few minutes outside before heading back." She parked me beside the gurgling water. The noise lulled me into a peaceful state.

I nodded.

A calming breeze caressed my skin, and a familiar, lulling peace encompassed me.

Mom?

Maybe, maybe not. But if there's one thing I'd learned, *anything* was possible.

I stared into the reflective surface and bent my head, whispering words. "Mom, I know you can hear me if you want. I hope you hear me now."

I drew a deep, shaking breath. "What a mess. I have so many things I wish I could do over, but mostly I wish you could have met Chip, or known what was happening. Or why it was so important I leave when you wanted to talk. I never wanted to abandon you. I left so many things unsaid, and then you died."

I wiped at new tears I thought had been cried out. "And yet you found me, even after your death. I know that you visited me that night, after I fell. I hope you'll always watch over me, because I think, for the first time, I can be the daughter who'll make you proud.

"There's no way I can ever forgive myself for not really knowing you. But for what it's worth, and even though it took me a long time, I realize all you went through for my sake, and what it ended up costing you."

I paused, straining to listen, but only a distant rattling of blowing leaves answered my words. "Just a few nights ago, I told Chip that I hated you. But that's not true. I love you, Mom." I turned away from the melancholy face staring back at me.

I had no more room in my life for sadness or anger. To dwell on the negative meant wasting precious time with the people I love. For the first time in my life, no matter what I chose to do, I could find happiness. I could stay in town with Chip or leave. I could go to New York and look up my father, or escape to Indianapolis as I'd planned when we moved to Perionne.

I had choices ahead. And when I was ready, I would make them.

But not today.

Today, I'd concentrate on loving my mother.

Behind me, the rustling leaves carried a delicate voice. *"I love you too, Fiona."*

The End

"Fun, scary, surprisingly humane, surreal...this novel will mess with your head and your nerves."
Bram Stoker Award-Winning author Gary A. Braunbeck
R.J. SULLIVAN
VIRTUAL BLUE
Hell just went digital.
REVISED EDITION

Dedicated to Monica A. Felver-Kellogg, the "first fan" of Blue and R.J. Sullivan.

ACKNOWLEDGMENTS

ORIGINAL 2013 NOTES, ACKNOWLEDGEMENTS, THANKS, AND OTHER STUFF YOU CAN SKIP.

ARGH! THERE BE SPOILERS AHEAD! Virtual Blue is a direct sequel to Haunting Blue. I've done my best to ensure that this novel stands alone while minimizing "spoilers." Still, I could not avoid referencing several key plot-points from Haunting Blue.

The character of Skye MacLeod is the creative property of E. Chris Garrison. Used with permission. https://sillyhatbooks.com/

THANKS AS ALWAYS TO TEAM R.J.:

My critique group INKlers: Judith Phelps Bastin, Rodney Carlstrom, Becky and John Dockery, Bill Larson, and Kathy Watness.

Nikki Howard for making room for a second-favorite author, and for being "Maxine" last summer. Monica Kellogg for your ALL CAPS AND EXCLAMATION POINTS!!!!!

TCQ: Michael West, John F. Allen and E. Chris Garrison, for your ongoing friendship, comments, and always being in my corner. John provided the image of the Baalina Rune.

Nicole Rinaldi for over five years of "research" as my online gaming pal, for being my EMT resource, and for composing one great and one (intentionally) awful poem for Chapter One: Smart Girl and Loneliness.

Noel Rinaldi Williams for continuous, ongoing, awesome marketing art.

Debra Holland, always and forever Editor Prime. "It's not a dream anymore."

Seventh Star: Stephen Zimmer who puts it out there 24/7, Amanda DeBord, the red pen of power, and artist extraordinaire Bonnie Wasson who literally makes me look awesome.

None of it would matter without my family: Linda "Mrs. R.J." Sullivan for always......yeah, that about covers it, and our three nerds in the making, Amanda, Cindy and Steven.
And Mom, Dad, Mike, Hariette, and Hannah. I love you.

2020

Danielle Muething for bringing her incredible narration skills to my audiobook adaptations. And, in the case of Virtual Blue, reading from the manuscript and documenting typos and other errors for me.

Bryan Donihue for helping me through the republishing nightmare... er... process.

CHAPTER ONE

"Fiona?"

"Mom?"

A voice, silent for two years, stirred Fiona into a vortex of confusion.

"Fiona, you must help him. He needs you."

Fiona stood in the living room of the home she and her mother had lived in for three months.

Her mother sat on the white leather couch, her shoulders slumped in obvious fatigue. She gazed at the cream-colored carpet, lines on her face visible from drained emotion.

"Mom, you're alive!" Joy surged through her, but a gnawing coldness in her stomach told her she was kidding herself.

She dropped onto the couch and wrapped her arms around her mother. "I'm sorry. I'm sorry. It's my fault you died. If I hadn't left, Gunther couldn't have..." Overwhelmed, tears fell from Fiona's face and soaked into the soft shoulder of her mother's blouse.

"It's not your fault, sweetie. It was my time. Now, listen; I can only stay for a little while."

A comforting, oddly cool hand patted the back of Fiona's head.

"No!" Fiona locked her arms around her mother. "Last time I

walked out of this room, I said we'd make up for lost time. Then you died."

Tender fingers caressed Fiona's arm. "It's okay, baby. Don't mourn me. I watch you from a good place."

"Mommy, please don't go."

"I had to come to you, to warn you. A great evil—even greater than Gunther—is about to be unleashed. You must go to Chip and stop it."

"No, Mom. Chip can't help. Chip's just as much to blame. If he hadn't messed with Gunther's ghost..." Not entirely true, but after two years of replaying that night, she still couldn't help but blame him...and herself. "If he hadn't gone searching for that money, trying to clear his father's name..." Another sob clogged her throat. Fiona trembled, wanting nothing more than to spend the rest of their precious moments together locked in an embrace, enjoying total silence. Something they never did when her mother still lived.

Her mother leaned forward and pressed a gentle kiss on her forehead.

Fiona's heart glowed. She drew a shaky breath. She remembered that the last time she'd talked to her mother, Fiona had kissed her on the cheek, with no idea it would be a final goodbye.

"Chip did nothing, my dear. But he stands in the path of a great evil that will destroy him if you don't help."

Head reeling, Fiona hugged her mother tighter. "Chip asked me to visit him for Thanksgiving break. I wanted to stay with Dad here in New York, instead."

"You've been ignoring all of Chip's invitations the last few months," the specter scolded.

"Mom..."

"Chip needs you, Blue, and if you're truly honest with yourself, you need him, too. Now, more than ever."

Fiona couldn't speak, shocked that her mother used Chip's special endearment for her, after her blue, spiked hair. She'd never told her mother about the nickname. There hadn't been time.

Fiona broke their embrace and crossed her arms over her chest.

"If I see Chip, it'll be to break things off. I've thought about it a long time, and I don't want to be in the relationship anymore."

"Fiona, I've forgiven him. Why can't you?" Her mother's tone changed to the impatient negotiator Fiona had known all-too-well. Her mother apparently caught herself. "Fine, dear. Do what you must. Just get on the plane and get back to Indiana. Or you'll most certainly regret it."

———

"FIONA!"

A masculine voice startled her awake. Her eyes snapped open to focus on her dad's face. She drew in a breath, and a hand touched her shoulder.

"No!" She couldn't stop the cry from escaping her lips.

"Fiona, honey, it's okay."

Fiona's pajama top stuck to her, sweaty under the thin quilt, but the familiar smell of her dad's aftershave made her sit up and lean into his strong shoulder.

I'm here, not in Perionne. She glanced around the bright white walls of her bedroom in the spacious condominium her dad owned in upstate New York. Johnny Depp as Jack Sparrow winked back at her from one wall; framed prints of *Starry Night* and *The Scream* decorated another.

I'm home.

Blinking through the disheveled hair in her eyes, she pulled him to her in a hug.

He hesitated, then wrapped an arm around her waist and patted her on the back.

She understood his discomfort. She usually remained stiff during these offerings of love from the father who'd been unavailable most of her life. It was a minor miracle they could find any way to connect after missing so much time.

Her dad's concerned voice rumbled in her ear. "Do you remember your dream?"

Fiona nodded against his shoulder and told a partial truth. "I was dreaming about...her."

His grip became less tenuous and more caressing. "I'm sorry, Fiona. I know how you still miss her."

Fiona pulled away and wiped tears from her face, not wanting to offer more detail. "I'm not sure I'll ever get over it."

Her dad nodded and rose, his awkwardness apparent. "Come down when you're ready. I have breakfast waiting."

Several minutes later, showered, dressed, and, feeling more like herself, Fiona padded lightly down the spiral staircase to the great room. In the open kitchen, her dad stood with his back to her, holding a spatula over a pan and facing the stove while projecting calm confidence. She eyed the stack of pancakes on a plate near his elbow.

Fiona hopped into a stool at the breakfast bar and waited, drumming her fingers on the countertop. "Pancakes? What did I do to deserve this special treat?" On most weekends, her father diligently manned the stove to coax up his special pancakes. During the week...not so much.

He turned and placed the loaded plate next to hers. "I have a late morning, but I'll probably be at the office into the evening tonight. I was hoping you had a little time, as well. Besides, after the night you had, I thought you needed a little pampering."

Fiona picked up a fork and stabbed the top four with unguarded enthusiasm. She grinned, grabbed the syrup bottle, and dribbled syrup over the stack of cakes on her plate. "I always have time for pancakes," she teased. Though she had rounded out a bit since high school, she still thought she looked too skinny.

Her dad tipped a carafe of chilled orange juice from the middle of the breakfast bar and poured some into a glass. He slid onto the stool next to her and filled his plate.

"This works out well," Fiona said, not looking up. "I need to talk to you about something. I made a decision this morning, and I'm not sure what you're going to think."

He reached for a mug of steaming coffee and raised an eyebrow in mock concern. "Oh? Are we going to have a confrontation?"

Fiona giggled. They argued rarely, and when they did, they usually settled disagreements by talking it out—a refreshing change for Fiona after the years of intense fights with her mom.

Fiona took a deep breath and decided to just say it. "I think it'd be best if I spent Thanksgiving in Indiana this year. With Chip. Rather than going to Perionne, he's staying at his house in Bloomington. Thought I'd join him for a few days and let him show me around the IU campus."

"Oh?" Her dad took a long sip from his coffee. "I'd hoped that we would spend a few more holidays together before your boyfriends took up all your time."

An unspoken *we've had so few* hung between them.

Only last year, Fiona learned that her dad hadn't willingly stayed away while she grew up. When he'd first rejected her mother's offer to move to New York to be near him, her mother had placed a trumped-up restraining order against him. Only after her death did he feel he could come back into his daughter's life. Fiona finished her senior year of high school in Perionne, living with Chip and his father, and then moved with her dad out to New York.

"I know. And it's not what you think." As his other eyebrow rose, she stopped herself. "Okay, okay, it *is* what you think. Sort of. But I've made another decision. I'm going to break up with Chip. And I can't email him or text message him. We've been together over two years, and we've been through a lot. I need to talk it out and make it right. I owe him that much."

Her dad wiped a napkin across his face. "I know a lot of this is new to me, but I imagine that every father is torn between secretly wanting his daughter to swear off boys and join a convent, and to find some sort of balance between what's cool and what's safe. Chip's been a strong, stabilizing influence on you, but I've been concerned about you for a long time."

Fiona swallowed a mouthful, wondering what was coming next.

"Do you have any friends at school? Good friends?"

An embarrassed flush burned over her face. "I do okay," she said, shifting in her seat. She couldn't even explain it to herself, but friends hadn't been a big priority her first year in college.

"Listen, it's not that I don't appreciate having you here. But you know if you want to live on campus, you're welcome to at any time."

"It's a ten-minute ride by subway, Dad. Living on campus doesn't make sense."

"And that's also a great excuse to stay away from campus life...I've been concerned that this long-distance relationship has been an ongoing reason for you to turn away from the people around you. You have a boyfriend, but you never see him, so you're free to ignore all social activities for the next four years and come home every night to study or watch DVDs with your dad."

"I know, Dad. I just had to realize it for myself." As her father's words struck home, hurt stabbed at her. "Hey, are you saying you don't like watching movies with me?"

Her dad chuckled and rose from his seat. He placed an arm around her shoulders, pulling her close. "I love watching movies with you, Fiona. I just want you to be happy. And you're old enough to decide for yourself where you can go for Thanksgiving. You work it out and do what you have to do. But I still get you for Christmas, deal?"

Fiona hugged her father close. "Deal."

They separated, and he bent to retrieve his leather briefcase. "What are your plans today?"

Fiona looked down at her orange juice. "Um...well, I have Writing 201 at 10:30, Algebra 3 this afternoon, and...a classmate is coming over to study with me."

"Is this classmate of the male or female persuasion?"

"Um..."

The eyebrows crept up again.

Fiona giggled. "Male, and it's not what you think."

Her father drew out an exaggerated exhale. "Lucky for you I happened to schedule a late day for myself."

"It's *really* not what you think!"

"Shouldn't you get rid of one boyfriend before you invite another boy into the house? Or is that sort of thinking old-fashioned?"

"Daaa-aaad!" She played along. "He's in my lit class."

"And you can't study in the library?"

Fiona folded her arms across her chest. "As it happens, I *thought* you were going to be here, so everything would've been fine."

"All right, all right, you can meet him here. But if he wants to take you out to Starbucks, I'd be okay with that." He leaned over and kissed her forehead. "Have a good day. I love you."

"Love you, too."

The door shut, and Fiona hugged herself, shaking off a sudden chill.

———

AFTER CLASSES, Fiona raced home to get the house ready, telling herself the arrival of Drew Allamand didn't mean anything.

She'd met Drew last year in Introduction to Poetry. They'd been clustered with about ten other writing majors in the same work-shop classes. Throughout the year, study group invitations had piled up, each rejected in their turn. By winter, these had morphed into "Friday night party at Gwen's" and "poetry reading at Drew's." She'd started the semester excusing herself from a *CSI* season premiere party.

Last year, all she wanted was to be left alone.

And now?

As the doorbell rang, she wiped clammy hands across her jeans, and, not for the first time, wondered what the hell she was doing. Why had she finally invited a classmate—a decidedly cute classmate—to her home?

Trying to calm the butterflies in her stomach, she opened the door.

Drew, dressed in a blue T-shirt and faded jeans, grinned at her.

Waves of dirty-blond hair curtained his boyish face. He held a compact plastic folder in one hand. "Hi, Fiona." He reached one arm out to hug her.

Startled at the familiarity, Fiona stepped back, then caught herself and leaned into his friendly, brief embrace.

Drew walked through the door, amusement flashing in his cool green eyes. "Good to finally see you outside of class. Nobody would believe it when I said I was coming over today."

Wow, has it gotten that obvious? Fiona led Drew to the couch next to the coffee table stacked with her textbooks. "I know. You've all been very patient, and I've been ignoring you." She sat on the couch, motioning an invitation at the spot next to her.

Drew dropped down and slumped against the cushions. "No, it's cool. It's just, you know, we're all in this together. Gwen wants to see more of you, and the others, too. But, hey," Drew shrugged. "I told them you'll show up when you're ready, and not before."

Glad for his understanding, she tried to explain. "I had...a rough senior year. In high school, I mean."

"Your mom died, I heard. Gwen mentioned something about it."

A laugh escaped Fiona, and she fought a sudden urge to leave the room. "I doubt Gwen knows the half of it." She looked at the coffee table and picked up the massive Norton Reader. "Want to start with this?"

"Hell, no."

The frankness of his reply splashed like cold water on her face. She looked into piercing green eyes. "What?"

"You're a poetry major, right?"

"Yeah."

"Well, so am I. Let's see 'em, Fiona. Show me your poems."

A rush of excitement flushed through her.

Drew waved the plastic folder in his hand. "I'll show you mine if you—"

Fiona giggled. "Don't be a cornball. Stay right there." She stood and raced toward the stairs. She could feel his gaze follow her up the spiral stairwell. She returned a few seconds later, grasping her own zippered portfolio.

Drew took the offered folder and looked at the first piece in the stack, called "American Idol Finalist," a poem she'd penned shortly after the move to Perionne. She noted Drew's intake of breath during the last stanza—a pleased reaction he couldn't fake.

"Wow. That's terrific, Fiona. So much anger, and yet focused into such a cutting observation about media and sexism. I love it."

"Yeah, thanks." Fiona felt herself flush from the praise. "There's a whole story behind it, as well. My English teacher wanted to fail me after reading that, until a friend intervened and busted him, more or less."

"Sounds like a good friend to have." Drew's voice held the hint of a question.

"Yeah. Chip, he's...a guy I was seeing back in Indiana. A long time ago." She stared down at the carpet, feeling ashamed as the lie spilled from her mouth.

Drew turned the page, this time reading a borderline-rant Fiona had penned shortly after breaking up with Joey, her—she could admit now—loser boyfriend.

> Smart girl.
> Slick guy.
> Coffee bar nights.
> Poetry under starlight.
> She gave her heart away.
>
> Stoned stare.
> Stupid, crazy fights.
> She's barely out of sight,
> He gave her heart away.

Fiona waited for Drew to take in the words.

The pause extended much longer than it would have taken to read the poem. Drew lowered the paper and seemed to retreat into himself for over a minute. Finally, his gaze turned to her, as if seeing her for the first time. "This is also incredible."

Heat crept into her cheeks.

"You have a beautiful soul, Fiona. You should bring these to one of our poetry-reading gatherings."

Fiona shrugged. "I know. I wanted to, I just... well, you know how poetry is. You sort of expose your innermost self to everyone."

Drew nodded. "I know. Believe me, I understand. But that's the magic of it, as well." He flipped through the pages and stopped at an assignment piece from last spring. The red B- still showed at the top.

> Loneliness
> An empty, gaping hole.
> It's so deep, so dark.
>
> Clawing your way to the light.
> Your fingers become so raw.
>
> Heartache so strong,
> You just stop existing.
>
> Is it possible to go on?

Drew's gaze scanned across the first few lines.

A different sort of embarrassment flushed over her. "That's...kind of unfinished. I mean, I turned it in, but I couldn't..." She trailed off. *I couldn't do it, and I wrote crap. I guess there's nothing more to say about that.*

"Huh." Drew couldn't hide the disappointment in his voice. "Is this about another boyfriend?"

"No, my..." She stopped, not sure she wanted to go there with this relative stranger.

Another pause before Drew spoke again. "Not bad. Missing

something, though. Maybe if you keep working on it. We can brainstorm some time."

Fiona smiled, trying to contain her welling attraction. "I'd like that."

Drew flipped pages and read another recent assignment. Without comment, he turned more pages, read, then skimmed more still. With a deep sigh, he closed the portfolio and turned to look at her, a somber expression on his face. "It's worse than I thought."

"What?" Panic broke her reverie.

"You." Drew extended his index finger and tapped her upper sternum.

She froze, unsure how to respond to a skewed act of both familiarity and respect.

"You're dying inside. At least, your inner poet is dying, isn't it?"

His words made her ache. "My inner poet definitely took an ass-kicking last year." She offered a sad smile. "And yeah, I've been a little lost."

Drew finished her thought. "And that's why you've stayed away from us."

Fiona processed his words, trying to find an honest answer. "My mom...she didn't just die. She was murdered. We had unresolved problems between us, and then just like *that*..." she snapped her fingers. "...she was gone."

"Oh, my God, I'm so sorry." Drew crossed himself. "You must have been devastated."

Surprised by his response, she downplayed the moment. "Let's just say I've had my share of therapy in the last couple years." She thought back to her appointments with sympathetic Dr. Churchill and how the therapist tried to help her refocus the blame away from herself and onto Gunther, where it belonged.

But because the incident involved a ghost, Fiona couldn't completely confide in the doctor without the risk of being diagnosed with schizophrenia. So, stuck with a secret she couldn't disclose, Fiona sorted through some of her issues, especially her feelings for Chip, on her own.

Or have I?

Drew leaned close, and for the first time, Fiona realized his arm had slipped behind her shoulders. *When did that happen?*

"I like the poet I see on those first pages," he whispered. His words bridged the space between them. "I like her a lot. You should let us help you."

Fiona swallowed. "I want to."

"*I* want to help you, if you'll let me."

She tipped her head up toward him. "I'd like that."

His lips touched hers.

She responded hungrily.

He deepened the kiss.

Her back arched from her need, her toes curling. She reached up and stroked the back of his head.

What a kiss!

They separated moments later, the air filled with their mutual gasps.

Guilt slammed her. Nausea churned in the pit of her stomach, and she knew this was wrong.

He leaned in for another kiss.

"No. No, Drew, we need to stop." She placed a hand on his shoulder, pressing gently, hoping she wouldn't have to use more force.

To her relief, he leaned back into the couch. "It's okay." He took a deep breath. "It was pretty intense for me, too. I didn't mean to push."

Fiona shook her head. "No, it's not that. I like you. And I'm okay with what happened. It sort of helped me confirm something. But right now, the words my father said this morning are going through my mind. I need to get rid of one boyfriend before I take on another."

A palpable silence hung between them before he responded.

"Yeah, you might have mentioned the boyfriend part." His tone chilled, and his eyes flashed anger.

"I'm leaving next week to visit him over Thanksgiving weekend."

"And that's supposed to make me feel better...how?" A touch of amusement cut through the coolness in his voice.

Fiona grabbed Drew's arm, noting the hard muscle under her fingers. "No, listen. Chip and I...we've been in this sort of long-distance non-relationship for over a year now. He's special to me, but...I need to end it and move on. But properly, face to face, without any side baggage."

"You mean me?" Drew's voice carried a hint of anger. "I'm the side baggage? Nice."

"Be fair, Drew." Anger crept into her own response. "This just happened. You caught me off guard." *I will not be bullied into feeling guilty.* "You and I haven't talked. You didn't ask me out. Yes, it would be convenient for me to tell him I met someone else, but that's not true. Chip and I...we imploded months ago. He just doesn't see it, and I do. I need to make him understand we're no good for each other. That's what's fair and right. For him. For everyone." She let the moment linger before adding, "Including you. And a week from now, we can figure out what..." she waved a hand in the air, her mind failing to conjure an appropriate word. "We can figure out what...this...is. If anything."

Drew wiped his hands over his face. "I've been kind of watching you for over a year, hoping you'd come out of your shell."

"Oh." She didn't know what to say. Blood pounded in her ears.

Drew nodded. "Look, I dated around a bit last year. Gwen and I went out a few times. And others." He stopped himself. "God, that sounds worse, doesn't it?"

The moment of tension ended in a burst of mutual laughter.

Drew dabbed at his eyes. "You do have that whole 'girl of mystery' aura going for you. Nothing scary, though. So I've been interested on and off." Drew pulled his arm from around her and clapped his hands together. "All I'm trying to say is: do what you have to do, and we'll talk. No pressure, I promise."

Fiona offered a smile. "Good. Now, I have two other requests."

Drew grinned, and his face reflected his amusement. "Uh, oh, are you one of those demanding women?"

Fiona reached up and stroked his cheek. "First, I want to see *your* poems. Secondly, maybe we can get some *real* studying done in the next couple hours and get ready for that test."

Drew smiled. "Done."

————

A COUPLE HOURS LATER, after receiving a sedate kiss goodnight, Fiona shut the door. She returned to the couch, curling her knees up and holding her folder of poems in her lap.

As her reaction to Drew's presence faded, she swallowed back a tear and clutched the folder to her chest. *He's right. My inner poet is dying.*

CHAPTER TWO

Marda Mercedes descended the basement steps and stood before the shrine.

Though they'd resided in the half-duplex for over five months, she still thought of the off-campus house as their temporary base of operations.

Marda chose her team of three specialists from hundreds of candidates. All were Sisters in high standing amongst the dozens of covens of Baalina scattered across the Midwest. Baalina grew these pockets, beginning with her first follower, whose name was lost to ancient history. The cult grew as Baalina drew each woman who'd heard her voice and led them to Her worshippers.

Within the covens, Baalina's chosen ones enjoyed the peace of sanctuary isolated from all other influences. Christians throughout history despised the Sisters and worked tirelessly to destroy them. When found, they called them out as witches and enacted punishment accordingly.

And yet, it was the Wiccans who'd rejected Baalina's worshippers most strongly. Wiccans who rejected the concept of demons in the flesh and mocked the practices of the Sisterhood. In some cases, it was the coordinated efforts of Wiccans that broke many of Baalina's most promising candidates away from the Sisterhood.

Over the last few months, Marda had enjoyed isolation and sanctuary in the company of her two most loyal lieutenants, the so-called Terror Twins, Cyndi and Vanessa. Cyn and Van, for short. The Terror Twins, assassins for hire who held two spots on America's Most Wanted for years. They shunned any surname, preferring anonymity, and Marda indulged their need for drama.

They worked, lived, plotted, and quarreled together. Sometimes, they laughed and played; but mostly, they focused on the goal—to free their mistress, the Goddess Baalina, from her infernal prison, the chaos realm, that had confined her for hundreds of years.

After about three weeks, Marda could no longer tolerate a place that lacked a shrine to the Goddess. She cleared a space in the basement and constructed a tiny temple and personal sanctuary, a quiet place to escape to whenever their tasks overwhelmed them, whenever she grew weary pondering the injustice heaped upon her mistress.

She'd told the others she'd created it for all of them, but mostly, she'd created it for herself.

She knew everyone in the Sisterhood was loyal to Baalina, but Marda also knew her own role in the order-to-come was special. She had always suspected this to be true, and recently, Baalina herself had confirmed her suspicions. A committed student, Marda rose to the rank of high priestess, and Baalina promised that when she'd been freed of her captivity, Marda would rule at her side.

So she needed the alone time—time to commune with the Goddess.

Marda grabbed the box of matches and struck the tip against the side; the flare of brightness exposed the cool, dark, open space around her. She lit two candles, revealing the green circle surrounding the spray-painted rune of the Goddess Baalina painted on the floor in dim hues.

Across the room, light danced along the surface of a large statue. Baalina's image stood upon a pedestal and glared. Twin horns protruded from her head and curled upon themselves like the majestic ram. She stood cloaked in splendid purple robes with silver trim that befitted her stature, and her proud gaze swept over her subjects.

Marda stepped into the circle of summoning and bowed on one knee. *Proud and haughty. Of course. Why not? When one earned their place of power, one should be proud. Only the inferior would feel jealous.*

In the first month of their stay here in the college housing, Marda would dress in the proscribed priestess robes of ritual, but as her sessions continued several times daily, the rituals of honor proved too complicated and time consuming.

Today, she dressed in jeans and a loose blue sweater. "Forgive me, oh Goddess, for my humble apparel. I felt the need to seek your guidance."

She'd barely begun her meditations when she sensed the mistress touch her mind.

No forgiveness is required, my child. Your service means more to me than ancient costumes. Your loyalty will be rewarded, as surely as those who have turned against me will meet the punishment they deserve.

Eugene "Chip" Farren slumped in a pleather office chair in the basement of the home he rented with his best friend, Phil Jenson, and squinted at the code displayed on his thirty-six-inch computer monitor.

Chip and Phil had arranged three long desks in a sort of horseshoe bullpen shape. Together, the three desks supported five interlinked computers, including the committed server, running *Fantasy Free Form*, their mutual dream-child online computer game.

Although still a work in progress, Chip and Phil made *Fantasy Free Form* available to online subscribers twenty-four hours a day, free of charge. As the game continued to grow in popularity, they hoped to offset their investment by charging advertisers, and, when they reached the growth they needed, hit up their current subscribers with a small monthly fee to continue playing.

But, with only about 200 brave souls willing to put up with the bugs and environmental changes, Chip and Phil had a long way to go before that dream became a reality.

When they weren't attending classes, studying, or working, Chip and Phil spent every minute of their time in their makeshift workspace, molding *Fantasy Free Form* closer to their vision. "Time," in this case, referred to the hours of 10 PM to 3 AM. They made sure no classes started before noon the next day—at least, no classes they couldn't afford to skip.

Chip changed a few more lines of code and clicked the update button with the mouse. "There, try that."

Behind him, Phil stared at the monitor attached to computer system three and grunted. They ran all their code corrections on computer three, diagnosing problems through trial and error and game-testing fixes without affecting the live server.

Chip rotated his chair to look over Phil's shoulder.

The monitor blinked to life, showing an attractive scene of computerized forestland beauty, one of several areas they'd designed where gamers could interact through their online characters to quest, hunt, or sightsee, depending on their pleasure. Last night, an irate subscriber had fired off a note to their helpdesk email address, bringing an embarrassing glitch to their attention. Now they had to track down the problem.

In the midst of the woods, Phil's avatar, Magtog, appeared, dressed in flowing blue robes and holding a gnarled walking stick. The wizard hobbled across the forest in response to Phil hitting directional arrows on the keyboard.

Magtog's specific function was to walk to a spot in the woods where a deer would wander randomly through the forest until slain by a character. Since the program ran on the trial computer, Chip and Phil didn't need to worry about other players interfering. Only Magtog inhabited this version of the *Fantasy Free Form* world.

The two friends watched and waited. As expected, the deer galloped into view, approaching a nearby tree. To Chip's dismay, the deer walked through the tree, and, like a phantom ghost on a rampage, hopped high into the air toward a hill. The creature passed completely through the hill and continued on its way, oblivious to the minor miracles it had just performed.

Phil emitted a long sigh and wiped a hand across his forehead.

Years of friendship allowed Chip to read paragraphs in that single sigh. Bugs on background ambiance shit like this annoyed Phil to no end.

As he pivoted his large frame to face Chip, Phil's chair squeaked in protest. "Whatever you did, it didn't work."

"Damn." Chip reached up and palmed his eyes, welcoming the seconds of spotted blackness after six hours of staring at the screen. Bigger game companies could pass little bugs like this on to a staff of programmers, but here in the basement, it was just the two of them.

Lifting his bulk from the seat, Phil groaned. "And we don't have any more time, Romeo. Not if we're going to pick Blue up from the airport." Standing at full height, Phil's six-foot frame and pear-shaped mass intimidated those who didn't know him. Usually, his warm smile canceled out any uneasiness his size invoked, but at the moment, he did nothing to hide his cranky mood.

Chip craned his neck to look at his friend. "What's the matter? We'll stay on it. Blue won't keep me from doing the work."

Phil shook his head, his beefy hand swatting down toward the desk and scooping up the car keys. "It's not that. Well, maybe it is. I've got a bad feeling."

"What's wrong?"

"Look, Mary and I decided to stop being exclusive to each other almost a year ago." The words came from Phil as if forced. "And she's visited me six times since then, clearing some weekends and flying up from Florida." Phil shrugged and waved a palm at Chip. "You and Blue are supposed to be all serious, but where's she been, dude? For that matter, why haven't *you* seen *her*?"

Chip raised his shoulders in a reflexive defense. He'd heard Phil get miffed about the drive-thru guys getting his order wrong, or the daily gripe about needing to turn the air conditioning down, but this was new. "Maybe we take our schooling more seriously."

Phil waved a hand. "Bullshit. If you took your classes so seriously, you'd be cracking the books now and not messing around on Triple-F all the time."

"What's your point?"

Phil shrugged. "She's been avoiding you for over a year, and now she can't wait to see you. What changed?"

"Well, that's a good thing, right?"

Phil rubbed his palm across the two-day growth of stubble before answering. "I don't know. I hope so. Honestly, I'm worried about you." Phil folded his arms. "But then again, I can't figure it out because I don't know the whole story, do I?"

Chip flushed, even though he hadn't followed the accusation. "I don't know what you mean."

Phil's eyebrows knitted as he spoke. "The night everything changed. The night Blue's mom died. The morning I woke up to hear my best friend and his girl were in the hospital fighting for their lives." A grimace of pain and anger distorted Phil's features. "And I still don't know what happened."

Like Blue, the lie came easily to Chip after so much practice.

"What do you need to know? I told you about how we chased the burglar—"

"Chased a burglar to the park. I know. Some random burglar never heard from before who left no clues, escaped the cops, and was never seen again. You sold it to the police, and you sold it to the newspapers, but what really hurts is that you thought you could sell it to me, too."

"But...Phil. That's the truth. There's nothing more to tell."

Phil only looked more hurt. "That's a partial truth, I'm sure. But come on, I wasn't born yesterday. You gonna tell me it's a coincidence that right after that incident, you lost all interest in the Ghost of Gunther? During our junior year, we should'a been a year into creating Triple-F, but I couldn't get you to focus on it. Because of your obsession with the lousy boat ride and all things Gunther."

Phil hung his head, and to Chip's astonishment, he choked back a sob. "So, the day after you almost get yourself killed, you drop both interests like the bad habits they were, and you finally get onboard with *our* game. And I'm not supposed to notice, so I don't mention it."

Phil gripped his keys in his fist, shaking them at Chip. "I'm telling you—because I'm a better friend to you than you've been to me—that if you think Blue is just coming over for a social visit, you're deluding yourself. Just like you deluded yourself that you pulled a fast one on me."

Phil's words hit like a stunning blow. An uncomfortable silence lingered for over a minute, punctuated only by Phil's wheezing.

Chip finally offered, "I don't know what to say."

Phil nodded and then shook his head. "I'd rather you leave it at that than lie to me again."

"Fair enough." Chip found the energy to lift his head and look into his best friend's face. "Phil, I know it doesn't mean much, but I'm sorry. It's for your own protection. That's all I can say."

"I figured it had to be something like that." Phil laid a hand between Chip's shoulders. He spoke with genuine concern. "How bad did it get?"

Chip swallowed back his sadness. "As much as you know, it was far worse than you can imagine." Chip's body shook with the need to tell more, and he scrunched in the chair to clamp down on the urge.

Phil patted his friend on the back a few times. "Okay, that's good enough for me."

The chirping sound-bite of the classic *Star Trek* communicator signal emitted from Chip's belt, cutting through the silence. With practiced ease, Chip slipped his cell phone from the belt holster and glanced at the text message on the screen. "That's her. Plane's running on time."

To pick Blue up, Chip and Phil needed 90 minutes to catch the shuttle north to Indianapolis International Airport. The round trip would kill the rest of their afternoon and bring them back in time for a late dinner.

Phil shook his head and stepped toward the stairs. "Let's go get your girlfriend."

———

WERE IT NOT WEDNESDAY NIGHT—THANKSGIVING Eve—Smittie's Pizzeria would already be packed to capacity with hungry students. The tally so far, in the midst of their six PM dinner "rush," was five pizzas served to a whopping fifteen lonely bodies.

Smittie Lagione—owner and titular inspiration of the popular student eatery—wiped his hands on his relatively clean apron. He shook his head, reflecting for the millionth time today how the restaurant was losing money by the minute.

On paper, his wife, Laverne, was head-waitress and bookkeeper, with Smittie as sole owner. Laverne had been a Colts cheerleader, years ago, in another life. And to this day, what Laverne wanted, Laverne got. Her short-cropped, dark spiked hair, disarming smile, form-fitting T-shirt and shorts that almost entered the realm of bad taste, and husky Hoosier drawl served as Smittie's secret arsenal.

Slathered on in just the right doses, Laverne's charm often

secured those extra dessert orders or sides of breadsticks desperately needed for a small eatery to thrive. Smittie supported the business financially, but he counted on her targeted and harmless flirting. They understood the necessity of her sex appeal, and jealousy never entered the equation.

Hell, let the students gawk. She was still a damn, fine-looking woman. And, at the end of the day, she always went home with him.

Laverne insisted they needed to be open all holiday weekend to the students as a thank you for all the business they brought in the rest of the school year. If just one lonely, hungry kid stuck on campus during this holiday could find a friendly face and good food at Smittie's, then all the work was worth it.

So Smittie sucked it up and smiled. Even ten years later, there were worse things than watching Laverne lean against the counter making notations in her notebook, occasionally meeting his gaze and offering a wink of support. *What the hell. We'll make up the business next week.*

———

BLUE SHAEFER WALKED through the doors, escorted on either side by Chip and Phil.

From the moment she stepped off the plane and fell into Chip's welcoming embrace, old habits took over, and she thought of herself as "Blue," not "Fiona." She'd never hear the name Fiona from either of these two. But the mental change that accompanied the new environment surprised her.

It was as if the mental blocks Fiona of New York had built up for over a year were left in the luggage rack like a straightjacket, and Blue exited the plane with a cocky strut of confidence she hadn't felt since leaving. *And, oh my* God, *that first kiss!*

Well, what did I expect? She chastised herself. *Keep focused; remember what you came here to do. This is not the time to be thinking with your hormones.*

"Best pizza in town," declared Phil. "And you know I've tried them all."

Blue winked at her friend. "That's a recommendation I can get on board with." They stood near the "Please Wait to Be Seated" sign. Blue cuddled close to Chip and curled her fingers into his, basking in the positive energy his presence brought to her.

The ease with which she resumed her old role at Chip's side surprised her.

A gruff Italian voice called out, "Laverne, unpack the next crate of breadsticks. Phil's here to clean us out again."

Blue returned the grin of the plump, middle-aged man standing behind the counter, his dark apron lightly coated in flour. "Are you kidding? Phil's metabolism slowed down years ago. *I'm* the one you really have to look out for."

A curvy, thirty-ish brunette stepped forward, stopping Blue short. Laverne flashed a devastatingly radiant smile at the three of them. "Smittie, fire up the oven. This girl needs some meat on her bones." She extended a perfectly manicured hand. "Welcome to Smittie's, hon. You must be Blue. Chip just goes on and on about you."

Blue shook the offered hand, then watched, bemused, as she pulled Chip and Phil to her in a short embrace. "Always *so good* to see you two! How's the video game coming along, boys?"

Laverne's obvious act charmed Blue. *She's good! They must have maxed out two credit cards here by now.*

Chip blushed, fumbling through some explanation about a problem with a deer going through a tree.

Laverne laughed as if she understood every word and took Phil's arm, leading them to a nearby table. "I'm sure it will all work out soon, guys. Stick with it! Have a seat. Mountain Dews for the boys." She glanced at Blue. "How about you, hon?"

"Uh...root beer is fine. Better stay away from the caffeine this late."

With a final wink and smile, the waitress disappeared behind the counter.

The threesome sat for a few seconds, pretending to study their menus. Blue folded hers and leaned on the table, placing a hand to her cheek and fluttering her eyelashes in Phil's direction. She spoke in a perfect imitation of Laverne's accent. "So, tell me, *hon*, why *are* you here in Bloomington over Thanksgiving break?"

Phil laughed, but he rolled his eyes. "I'm staying away from my step-mom. After years of not getting along, I decided to hell with it and not bother anymore. Besides, I'd rather hang with Chip, anyway." He paused, then added, as if in an afterthought, "And you."

"Ah, gee, that's so *sweet*, hon!" Blue dropped the teasing accent. "But seriously, you just seem...down. You've hardly cracked a smile or said a word the entire shuttle ride back."

Phil shrugged, keeping his glare glued to a menu he must have memorized months ago. "We just put in a long day between the game and the errand, and didn't get anywhere on the bug I'm working on. I guess my mind's still on that. Don't pay it any attention."

Blue already knew Chip and his dad had gotten together the previous week to celebrate. It worked out well for both of them. A few months ago, Jim Farren had started seeing another woman—the first relationship he'd been in since his wife had died over five years ago. Mr. Farren wanted to spend Thanksgiving weekend with her family, and Chip wanted to spend it with Blue.

Laverne's voice broke in on her thoughts. "Get an order of breadsticks for y'all?"

"Sure," said Chip. "A medium order will do."

"Oooh?" Laverne flashed a smile and wink in Chip's direction. "Are ya sure you don't want a large? We baked up a bunch extra tonight."

Blue piped in. "A medium should be fine, *hon*." She fired back her own smile.

"Tell ya what." Laverne jotted a note on her pad. "I'll charge you for the medium but bring a large. No sense in letting the bread go bad."

A flattered grin formed on Phil's face. "Oh, that's so nice, Laverne. You don't have to do that."

"Nonsense, hon. Least we can do for our favorite customers. Besides, I still say your friend needs some meat on her bones."

Blue opened her mouth for a biting retort, but Chip spoke first. "I like her bones just the way they are, but thanks for your concern, hon." Chip had collected the menus and now handed them over to the stunned waitress, who clearly wasn't used to Chip turning her banter against her. "But we'll take the large order so they don't go to waste."

Laverne smiled back, recovering and reaching for the menus. "*Touché.* I'll be right back with your order." Laverne cocked her head in Blue's direction, offering a friendly wink. "You're very lucky, hon. Chip's a keeper."

Blue flushed. A wave of guilt stole her voice.

Laverne turned toward the counter, speaking over her shoulder. "Don't let him get away."

"I won't." Still overwhelmed, Blue looked down at the red-and-white checkered tablecloth. *No, I won't let him get away. I'm going to throw him back. But now, it feels like if I follow through, it might be the worst mistake of my life.*

No! Stop it! There's no going back because you're afraid to hurt his feelings.

She took one last deep breath, shaking off her doubt. She'd known for months what she had to do. *But that's for later.* "So, what do we want on our pizza?

<hr>

CHAPTER THREE

<hr>

Once again prostrate before the Goddess, Marda recalled the first time she'd heard Baalina whisper to her, following that horrible day when the girls from her new school had cornered her and surrounded her. Her so-called classmates kicked her, punched her, and called her a freak, all egged on by one jealous woman, her cries driving the group to keep striking her. "I saw you staring at Ricky Saunders, bitch! He's mine!"

Marda didn't even know who Ricky Saunders was. She tried to say so, but that didn't matter.

As beatings went, it ended faster than she expected, as if most of the participants' hearts weren't really in it. When it was over, she lay in the grass at the edge of the woods where they'd dragged her, curled up, waiting for the hurting to stop, sponging up the blood with the sleeve of her hand-me-down blouse, wondering what she would tell her parents.

Then she heard the voice for the first time.

Hear me, my child, and be joyful. You are the chosen one, special to me.

Marda sat up, her eyes searching the woods for the source of the voice, so soothing, so comforting.

I am Baalina, and I hear your cries, even though I am far away, impris-

oned, just as I hear the pain of all my Sisters. They sadden me, and when I have returned to your world, I will make right these injustices you have suffered and reward you with the power that should be rightfully yours.

Life moved on, even after the embarrassing mess her father caused at the school when he saw her bloodied shirt. Several months passed before most of the girls would speak to her again.

But she was never lonely because one voice whispered to her when the world was quiet and she closed her eyes.

Be patient, my child. Be calm. Many hear my voice, many will be blessed, but you will be the most blessed of the Sisters, for yours will be the hand that ultimately frees me.

Perhaps sensing her connection with Baalina, her classmates stopped tormenting her. Even those who had participated in the beating months earlier reached out, wanting to be her friend.

Of course, my child. The weak are always drawn to the strong. Smile at them. Tell them you forgive them. But one day you will have your revenge. And when you claim the power you deserve, they will all grovel beneath your boot, begging to be spared your anger, as you had begged them, to no avail.

She never forgot Baalina's promise. She lived for that day.

In the quiet of her room, during solitary walks, and on lonely drives, Marda sought refuge in the voice more and more often. The dreary years of high school gave way to the dreary years of community college which gave way to a dead-end engineering job in which she made half the pay of her male counterparts while being overlooked during all opportunities for advancement. Baalina never failed to comfort her, sometimes with vague comments, other times more specific.

It is time for you to unite with my sisters, my child. Tomorrow, you will drive to the edge of Redraven Woods and walk toward the east. After sunset, follow the music. There, in an old, derelict cabin, you will find my worshippers gathered, communing, casting spells, and dancing in worship.

Tell them you heard my voice, and that Baalina told you to submit yourself to Mother Janice for further testing.

So ordered, Marda obeyed. That night, she discovered the

Sisterhood of Baalina and received the acceptance and understanding she longed for. Over the next months, she learned the secret history of the Goddess Baalina, and of the Sisterhood itself.

Mother Janice educated her on how the Goddess had influenced humanity since ancient times, quietly, secretly, growing her power and influence on gifted women throughout the world. Baalina found those who heard her voice and answered her call over the centuries until that fateful day, over three centuries ago, she tried to break through into the physical realm.

For ages, Baalina had struggled with the Kelranian Order, self-appointed defenders of the physical world who prevented powerful beings such as Baalina from ruling over humanity, denying the Sisterhood of power it had rightfully earned.

Until one fateful night in 1797, the Kelranian tyrants had used the Divenium Crystal to defeat Madam Katka, their coven's greatest leader, and destroyed Katka's SoulStaff. She learned how they had locked Baalina off in the ether dimension where only her most loyal followers could still hear her.

Katka fell, and the portal was closed when the Kelranian Order used the crystal to cast a powerful spell that assured such a portal could never again be opened from the chaos realm into the physical realm.

But now, the time had come where a combination of technology and extraordinary action on the part of the Sisterhood could circumvent the spell.

———

LIKE AN EXECUTIONER LEADING THE CONDEMNED, Phil opened the door to the basement and took the wooden stairway into the room with stiff solemnity. "Sorry, Blue, you brought this on yourself." He flipped the switch on the wall, triggering the hard fluorescent lights.

As Blue descended the stairs, her gaze traveled over the configuration of computers, screens, and wired rectangular doodads. She wondered if the guys noticed the oppressive hum of the over-worked hard drives or the lingering pizza smell permeating the walls. She drew a deep breath and released it in a long, resigned sigh. "Okay, boys. Let's get this over with."

Chip entered behind her, his thin body standing in the door-frame as if to block any attempt to escape. "So, let me see if I understand you correctly. Our game's been live for three months, and you haven't even registered?" The tone of his voice stung.

Blue shrugged and offered a sheepish grin. "I've been busy?"

But Phil would have none of it. "Too busy to check out the first functioning video game from the supposed love of your life?"

He sounded teasing, but Blue thought she heard an accusing undertone.

"He whose countenance comes to your mind first thing every morning and whose image sends you to peaceful slumber every night?"

Blue rolled her eyes, trying to be a good sport and play along while the guilt churned in her stomach. "It's true. He completes me in every way. I'm only half a woman without him. But, boys, I don't play video games. You know that."

Chip stepped forward, gently grasping her forearm. His other arm lowered toward one of the chairs. "That's because you've never played *our* video game. Did I mention that last week's *Indy PC* called *Fantasy Free Form* 'the finest independently produced RPG freeware in years'?"

As if on cue, Phil extended a thick magazine, already folded back to the relevant page, the quoted text standing out behind yellow highlighter.

Blue nodded and reached for the pages. "Only about a dozen times." She'd already seen the copy, emailed to her as a jpeg last month from Chip. The email included a pre-created account and password, inviting her to log on and play the game. But until she could deal with the conflicts of her heart, she couldn't bring herself to do it. If she had truly felt good about her and Chip, she would've logged on weeks ago and played, enjoying the game simply because he'd created it.

And behind all the teasing and excuses, she sensed Chip's genuine hurt at her rejection of his labor of love.

She held up her hands in mock surrender and offered her sweetest smile. "Okay, I'm sorry. It's really been a crazy year. Of course, I want to see your game."

Blue dropped into the proffered seat, staring into the largest monitor she'd ever seen. With a wide screen and somewhere around thirty-five inches, the digital forest-scape obliterated any peripheral distractions. The forest, filled with lush greenery and a hint of dew and fog, dazzled her with its breathtaking beauty. Almost subconsciously, she noted the Bose speakers positioned on either side, above, and beneath the screen.

Overwhelmed by the visual spectacle, she averted her eyes, staring at the standard keyboard and mouse. The dull reality of the desk broke the alluring spell of the fantasy world.

"How do we start?"

Chip reached down and clicked the Escape button. The forest scene vanished, replaced by a list of names. She recognized the first three from their old D&D sessions.

- Daria, Warrior, Level 10
- Magtog, Wizard, Level 12
- Gallamar, Mercenary, Level 14
- Blue Angel, Hunter, Level 8
- Aloray, Mage, Level 6

Chip grabbed the mouse, pointing and clicking on the name Daria. "I tailored this character specially for you. Just one of the perks of knowing the programmer."

The name listing vanished, replaced with CGI imagery of a sword-and-sorcery warrior woman. In a split-screen, she could view a head-and-shoulders profile of the character to her left and a rotating head-to-toe image to her right. The detailed facial features struck her as eerily familiar, and her breath caught in her throat.

"Hey, that's me. I mean, that's *really* me." The shock of her face staring back at her—the narrow shape of her eyes, the distinct curve of her chin, her thin nose, and flashing blue eyes—stunned her into silence. Even the hair, though long and wavy, parted and spiked in the front the way she wore hers. Certainly, the choice of a blue tint over the flowing locks was no accident. She continued to stare, transfixed.

Chip reached across the desk and snatched up a framed photo, waving it across her eyes. "That's the magic of scanning imagery, dearest one."

The spell of the game broken, Blue reached out and gripped the picture, recognizing it as Chip's favorite snapshot of her, taken two years ago at Perionne Park during their first date. *Two years ago—was it really that long?* The photo captured her cocky demeanor softened by the romantic mood of that particular evening.

Later, she would reflect upon that night, and the ones that followed, as the most blissfully happy time of her life.

Comparing the photo to the computer image on the screen, she could see the specific resemblance. The woman warrior of the video game wore the expression of Blue at her happiest and most confident self—certainly not the person sitting in the chair.

"That's very impressive," she said. And she meant it.

"The digital scanner allows us to take a lot of shortcuts with the artwork." Chip droned on, obviously trying to teach and impress, like a geeky peacock. "We can take the image of a tree and repeat it several times. The deer, the details of the leaves, even the houses—they all come from publicly available images, which we scan into the game."

"She gets it," Phil said, already seated at his own terminal and ready to start. "Don't overwhelm the girl with details. Let's just play."

Blue glanced over, seeing Chip close his mouth in a thin line.

She could tell he wanted to say more, to brag more. On impulse, she reached out and gripped his hand. "It looks wonderful."

Chip's smile made her heart warm in response. His hand tightened over her fingers in affection, and, forgetting herself, Blue brought his hand to her lips and delicately kissed his knuckles. She released his hand and looked up at the computerized image of herself. "Phil's right, though. Let's play. What do I do?"

Chip rummaged through a nearby drawer. "Like D&D, the warrior is a fairly basic character in these games. Quite simply, you chop at things until they stop moving. Don't worry about the magic. You do have some, but it's all automatic. As you can see from your profile, you have a necklace that adds five points to your strength and a ring that adds eight points to your defense. Your sword does between 20 and 30 points of damage."

"And that's a lot?"

Chip nodded. "That's a lot, for a level-ten warrior."

"Just checking."

"Once the game starts," Chip said, "use the arrow keys to move forward, backward, or rotate left or right. The spacebar lets you jump. Click the mouse to attack, and right-click to access other options, including preprogrammed greetings and emotions that come up as you play."

The directions came at her so fast, Blue wasn't sure she absorbed them.

"It's very intuitive." Chip must have sensed her apprehension. "That's pretty much it, except this." He held a thin, wiry headset, like a delicate tiara. He reached up toward her head, and she let him slip it into place. He gently pressed an earpiece into her ear, and a microphone hovered a few inches from her mouth.

Chip's voice sounded from her earpiece with startling clarity. "Most people use an online chat window while they play, but we can use the microphones. Much more efficient." He took the seat behind her, looking at his monitor and speaking through his headset.

She turned to her screen.

The profile vanished, replaced with a view of her character as if a camera floated behind her head from above and looked over her shoulder.

She viewed a partial profile of her tall, busty, warrior woman image, clad in shapely chainmail that barely contained her heaving chest. The handle of a large sword, secured in a sheath, protruded above the shoulders, enfolded in the long waves of Daria's blue-tinted hair. Several pouches were clipped to her belt.

Blue smirked at the sight. Daria's abundant curves bore no resemblance to her own figure, with her modest B-cups. *I suppose I should be flattered she wears my face, but the similarity definitely ends there. Boys!*

Glancing at the keyboard, Blue positioned a hand over the arrow keys and gripped the mouse with the other. Looking back at the screen, she could see the room in front of her. The character stood at the doorway of a large stone structure.

She pressed the forward arrow and was rewarded with the image of the warrior taking a few steps. The click-click-click of her footsteps on the cobbled sidewalk emanated from the speakers.

Okay, cool, I can get used to this.

CHAPTER FOUR

Marda Mercedes knelt before the statue of the Goddess Baalina. In the rooms above her, a wired network of computers had been assembled, and the Sisterhood's engineers were hard at work. The extraordinary measures—the "techno-magic," as Marda liked to call it—would be ready to be wielded shortly.

The door behind her opened and closed, pulling her from her meditation. She suppressed her irritation. She knew Cyn and Van would not interrupt her unless it was important.

Marda never found out if the so-called "Terror Twins" were truly twins or not, but the point proved moot when it came to results. They shared a love of pain and torment, and their skill to inflict both in their victims proved unmatched. Through their bond with Baalina, or perhaps through their own genetics, they shared a mental synchronicity that surprised even Marda.

"We found them," Cyn announced without preamble.

"They thought they could hide from us, but we flushed them out," continued Van.

"And they're close! Only a few blocks from here," said Cyn.

"Which makes sense. The Kelranians would want to be nearby if they plan to move against us," said Van.

Cyn leaned close, anxious to beat her partner to the punchline. "And they brought the gem with them!"

Marda rose and raised a hand. "Stop with the trade-off chatter, for Baalina's sake. Speak plainly, and just one of you!"

Cyn and Van looked at each other. Cyn nodded to Van, who faced Marda, green eyes flashing as she spoke. "We've identified the agents. Rebecca Burton and Skye MacLeod."

At the mention of the Kelranian's most successful agent, a chill ran through her. The stories and rumors circulating about Burton's deeds had not escaped even their isolated coven. *The Order has turned loose their very best to try and stop us.*

Van rubbed a hand over her shapely chin. "Once we had the names, it was easy for Natalie to track them."

Natalie Spencer, their head programmer and technology expert, had been working with little to no sleep for over three months, preparing for the first strike.

Marda reflected on Natalie's condition. She had to admit, she had been tough on Natalie over the previous weeks, blaming her lack of progress on incompetence. In the last few days, Cyn and Van had joined her in mocking the engineer. Sometimes, the teasing turned outright nasty. Marda let Cyn and Van release their cruelty upon her. She'd hoped the motivation would spur results.

But locating the great Rebecca Burton could not have been easy, and the small victory did much to validate Natalie's contributions to the Sisterhood.

A flush of guilt swept over Marda. *I was wrong to do that.*

Van began to pace the small open area before the circle of worship. "Rebecca and MacLeod have taken up residence as classmates and roommates a few blocks from here, the same as we did. Just as we plan to use the game to call forth our mistress, they also have characters in the game, presumably to stop us."

Marda drew a breath. "Have they contacted the programmers?"

Cyn spoke up, cutting off Van's response. "No. Of this, we're certain."

Marda glared at Cyn, who averted her gaze to the floor. "Sorry."

Marda smiled. "Your enthusiasm is forgiven, Sister. The fault is mine, not yours. When I'm tired, the trade-off dialog between you two can prove exhausting." Marda felt nothing of the sort, but she needed everyone on her team working together, and if that meant offering insincere compliments or taking blame for others' shortcomings, what did it matter?

Only results matter.

She smiled and opened her arms, pulling her Sisters into a three-way embrace. "But, enough. Come with me. I have a plan, and we must make everything right between us."

The group of three ascended the stairs, entered into the main part of the house, and walked into the studio living room, where a lone girl with mousy-brown hair sat before a set of computers.

The girl's head turned at the sound of movement. Behind her thick glasses, her brown eyes reflected a combination of fear and resignation. On the empty desk space nearby, a stack of Monster aluminum cans threatened to topple. "I am going as fast as I can, Marda. These things take time." Clearly frustrated, the girl pulled the glasses from her face and covered her eyes. "I'm doing the best I can. Please, just...leave me alone." A sob escaped her, and her shoulders shook.

Marda's heart broke at the display. Natalie's tears were like a dousing of cold water across Marda's face. *How could I forget? Have I truly allowed my team to fragment into the very same pecking order of bully and victim I despise in society?*

Marda reached out, her hands stroking the trembling shoulders bent before the computer screen. Another sob cut through the air. "No more teasing, Natalie. No more. You have served Baalina well and have shamed me in the process."

Natalie wept, her hands covering her face. "I didn't mean to...I'm sorry, please forgive me."

From behind her, Marda pulled Natalie's head back, which reclined beyond the top of the chair and rested against Marda's chest. "Shhhh...relax, Sister." Her fingers snaked forward, pressing, massaging the sides of Natalie's head.

"Oh, Marda...that feels good."

Marda continued to hush the distressed programmer. "Cyn and Van told me of your discovery. Baalina is most pleased. You may rest now."

"But there's still so much to do."

"You can spare a few hours. You need the rest."

Cyn stood to the side of the chair and reached out and gripped Natalie's hand. Her gloved finger traced a trail along the inside of Natalie's wrist.

Marda felt Natalie shiver against her in response.

"Van and I are...not just experts in thresholds of pain, Sister. Until now, you have always turned us down, but...we'd love to educate you."

Natalie's body stiffened. "No, I...thank you, I'd love some time to just sleep, though."

Cyn scoffed. "I'm not asking you to marry me, Nat. It's going to be a long time before you're around men again. You may even *like* it."

"Enough," said Marda. "Don't begrudge Natalie her attraction to men. We can't help our natural impulses."

Cyn smirked. "When Baalina has conquered the city, men will be kept as slaves, breeding stock, and..." Cyn's bright green eyes took on a faraway look. "...however else they might entertain us."

"Which will still make them a viable option for a woman's pleasure, Cyn." Marda wondered at Baalina's vision of the future. Subjugating men at first struck her as impossible, but she realized most men would be slaughtered in the initial uprising, rendering the rest easier to control. They would even welcome the opportunity to serve. "Don't hate Natalie for what she can't help."

Marda bent and wrapped Natalie's arm behind her own neck, bracing to guide her to her room. "Come on, Sister. Sit up. I'll take you to bed." Natalie rose, and Marda held her tight. Already, the exhausted programmer's eyes drooped, half closed. *Cyn really does have the magic touch.*

Marda's gaze met Cyn's. "And you...if you're so anxious to try out your techniques, give me a few minutes. I'll meet you in the bedroom. We could all use a little...release."

Cyn smirked. "And which threshold would you prefer? Pleasure or pain?"

Marda met Cyn's eyes with a teasing look of her own. "Is there a difference?"

Cyn drew her ceremonial knife from its hip sheath and pointed it at Marda, waving it in a clear invitation. "Not really."

Marda's breath caught in her throat. "Save me a spot. I'll be there soon."

———

FIVE HOURS LATER, with everyone now much rested for a variety of reasons, the four Sisters regrouped in the front room, where a linked set of five computers sat on three folding tables alongside a dining room table serving as their round-robin meeting space.

Marda entered the room from the basement, invigorated after another short session of communing with Goddess Baalina. Natalie appeared more chipper than she had in days, the dark circles under her eyes diminished. She looked up from her usual spot at the center computer monitor and produced a meek smile before she returned her attention to the screen.

Van and Cyn slouched in their favorite seats on the other side of the table. In their black leather and with barely hidden knives strapped to their firm thighs, they looked every bit like a photo spread for *Bad Girl Assassins Monthly*.

If the Terror Twins had any Achilles' heel, it was the attention-getting theatrics that accompanied their every action. Still—the memory of their "session" a few hours earlier sent a sexual shiver through Marda—their reputation was well deserved.

Challenged not to make a sound, she'd lasted almost five minutes. When she finally screamed her release, she had no idea if it was from pleasure or pain, and she didn't care.

She awoke, refreshed, to see Van and Cyn sleeping in each

other's arms. A glance at her watch told her she'd lost four hours. But she gained a burst of clear-headed energy, and she planned to take full advantage of it.

"So," Marda said as a way to begin the meeting, "What do we know?"

Van spoke up from across the table. "We found the Kelranian bitches. We know who they are and where they live."

Cyn picked up the thread of conversation. "We know the MacLeod woman has been tailing the programmers both in and out of the game."

Van removed her stiletto from its hip sheath and motioned toward Natalie. "Nat has tagged their avatars in-game. We know MacLeod spends most of the time online playing the game and exploring the land. Her movement pattern indicates she's tracking and re-tracking over as much territory as she can with each game session."

Marda nodded. "Perhaps she's searching for something."

Cyn grinned. "Probably under Burton's orders."

Marda returned the smile. "And there's nothing for her to find...yet."

Cyn tipped her head toward Natalie. "But that's about to change."

Oh? Marda's gaze met Natalie's. "What does she mean?"

Natalie turned her chair around to face the others. She didn't have many moments of glory, and she looked ready to make the most of this one. "I told them, just before you came in. We're ready."

The three pairs of eyes all reflected amusement, all watching intently for the significance of the words to penetrate. Marda swallowed back her excitement. "You said...a couple more weeks, at least."

"I thought so, but..." Nat shrugged. "What can I say? The sleep helped."

Pleased beyond words, Marda extended her praise. "You mean you're that good, Sister. This is no time for modesty."

Natalie giggled. "As you wish, Sister. I'm that good."

"And you can track them now?"

Natalie consulted a second screen, filled with numbers Marda could not follow. "MacLeod is online now. If they proceed with their usual search routine, Burton will be on shortly."

Marda stood, excitement coursing through her. "And the programmers suspect nothing?"

Cyn spoke. "Not as far as we can tell."

"Brilliant!"

Van nodded. "The timing is perfect. The campus is on Thanksgiving break and will be in a lull. Players, students and otherwise, will have more time for recreation, even from their vacation spots."

Marda stepped up next to Natalie. "And you're saying...we can open the portal now?"

"Yes." Natalie pressed a button on a computer which showed a rotating staff with an emerald-gemmed head. "Here is the SoulStaff, recreated from photographs and descriptions of the real thing. I redrew the runes from the original scrolls. Enchanted it with the spell. Although the staff no longer really exists, we can program the image to imbue it with the power to draw our mistress into the game-world the same way we tried to use it centuries ago to bring her into the physical world."

Marda nodded. "And from there?"

Natalie shrugged. "The curse forbids us to pull Baalina from the chaos realm to the physical realm. But there's nothing to prevent us from pulling her here from the game realm."

"Wonderful...but first, we have to open the portal using the staff." Marda leaned close, watching the SoulStaff rotate on the screen. "Can you add it?"

Nat nodded. "Yes. It's a tiny change to add a single object. The programmers are not likely to notice the addition unless they're watching for it. Now...once we open the portal and create an entire area that wasn't there before...we're probably on borrowed time. They're going to notice a change that large."

"Understood. And have we tested the SoulStaff?"

"No."

"Well..." Marda considered. The plan was falling into place much better than she could possibly have hoped. "Wait until both the agents are playing the game, and then open the portal near one of them. No sense in testing it on ourselves when we have the perfect unwilling guinea pigs to dispose of."

Natalie called up a screen of programming lines. "Once we do that, and people start collapsing in front of their computer screens, it's only a matter of time before the local authorities become involved." Her voice carried a hint of warning.

Marda chose to ignore it. "Not a problem," said Marda. *The police force will be short-handed. They'll be scrambling from behind to catch us, and by the time they try to take action, it will be too late.*

"There's always that chance they'll find the file and possibly the Divenium Crystal."

Marda scoffed. "I'm not concerned. I trust in Agent Burton's ability to hide a confidential file from Bloomington's finest."

Cyn sprang up. "But not from Van and me."

Marda glared across the table at the overeager henchman. *She's hired muscle.* Every instinct told Marda that *she* should handle the search *personally.* "I appreciate your enthusiasm, but I think I'd best see to this."

Cyn glared. "Are you kidding? Breaking and entering, search and seizure, finally, some action. Van and I have been cooped up for months. This is our expertise."

Though she hated to pass along such an important job to an underling, Cyn's words made sense. "Very well. Bring back the file with the Divenium Crystal. If we get hold of that, no one can stop us!" *Before they know what's happening, we'll have absorbed the souls of every player in the game realm. And with those, we can draw Baalina, our mistress, into the physical realm.*

____

CHAPTER FIVE

Control came intuitively after a few experimental clicks while Blue checked out her virtual surroundings. First, she took in the large wooden doorway of the Mountain Lion Inn. Then she strolled toward a nearby lake where several computerized characters stood on the pier, tossing and reeling in fishing line in eternal automation.

Past the pier, she turned toward the lake, and, on impulse moved toward the water, padding across the mud. As her feet struck the edge of the water, the speakers rewarded her with an accompanying splashing noise. "Cool."

"Glad you like it."

Chip's voice, so close in her ear, startled her. She realized, belatedly, that every side comment would be broadcast to all three of them.

"Don't wander out too far, though. You'll struggle not to drown, and your heavy chainmail armor will only make things worse."

"Got it." She guided Daria toward the cobbled path. As she did so, two other characters approached: one a bearded old wizard in long, flowing purple robes, and the other, a thin, boyish character whose gray, tight-fitting coveralls resembled a sort of modern storm trooper.

An alarm signaled in her ear, and a message popped up on her screen.

Magtog and Gallamar have invited you to join their party. Accept? {Yes}{No}

Blue grinned, guiding the mouse to the Yes button. "You know me, boys. Daria's always up for a party."

Phil and Chip chuckled in her ear.

————

DARIA APPROACHED HER OLD QUEST-MATES, extending her arms and offering an affectionate hug to each. "Greetings, boys. It's been a long time."

"Too long, Daria," Magtog answered, his youthful voice oddly conflicting with his aged, bent appearance. "We've missed you these many months, and the forces of evil have run rampant on our simple town while you were away."

Daria folded her arms, affecting a brooding stance. "Geez, Phil, lay it on thick, why don'cha?"

Magtog blustered on, ignoring Daria's break from character. "I have received a summons from King Thunderwind. He seeks an audience with me on a most urgent matter. Gallamar, the thief, has already—"

"Mercenary," piped up Chip.

"Gallamar, the *mercenary,* has already agreed to join me, but I fear we'll need all our resources for this. Will you join us?"

Daria drew her sword, then swung it in a fanciful salute before returning the weapon into the sheath on her back. "Wow, that's cool! Friggin' impossible, but cool! Er, I mean, yes, Magtog, I'll join you. Anything for king and country."

"Follow me, then."

The wizard led Gallamar and Daria through town at a rapid pace. Soon, the cobblestone path gave way to a less-traveled dirt road, where wild bear roamed the countryside. Occasionally, other characters ran forward and attacked the beasts. Daria stopped at one point, staring in fascination as a tiny dwarf with an equally tiny bow gave chase to a large, snarling bear.

"That dwarf...he's another player in the game?"

Gallamar answered. "Yes, that's Quinton. I think he logs in from Orlando. Our membership is small enough I can still keep track of everyone. We broke over two hundred subscribers just last week. But we're growing fast."

"Is he going to be able to take that big bear?"

"Probably not. He's not a high enough level, and his weapon is pretty weak."

As if on cue, the bear swung its enormous paw, connecting with the dwarf's chest. The dwarf fell to the ground, stunned. Swirling stars circled the tiny character's head, and the bear wandered off.

———

WORDS FORMED in a bubble over the dwarf's head. "Come help me, guys."

She could hear Chip typing out a response on his keyboard.

A few seconds later, words formed over Gallamar's head. "Sorry, we're in the middle of something. Good luck."

———

DARIA SHOOK HER HEAD. "Poor little guy. Can't we at least help him to his feet?"

Gallamar nodded and laughed. "He's taking on too much, too soon. There are plenty of easier tasks to do."

"So that's 'no' on the helping thing?"

Chip chuckled. "We really can't do anything. Let negative rein-forcement run its course. He's just going to have to stop being a dumbass."

The irritation in Chip's voice amused Blue. *Oh, I see. Chip does not suffer foolish game players gladly.* "So, I'm guessing he can't hear us."

Gallamar shook his head. "No, he's limited to keyboard chatting. And even if he had a headset, he could only hear the voices of people in his party. The three of us are on a private channel."

"Hey, Magtog got ahead of us."

Gallamar nodded and stepped forward. "That's okay, I know the way. Plus, look at your mini-map in the upper right-hand corner. You can see where everyone in your party is for several yards in any direction."

"Oh, yeah, okay. This takes some getting used to."

Speaking from the air, Magtog's voice chastised them. "Come on, slowpokes. The king waits for no man."

"Or woman," Daria quipped.

Increasing to a run, the thief and warrior soon joined the wizard. As a group, they traveled up a stone ramp to a large, white-cobbled castle and entered a courtyard bordered by erect guards and populated with a variety of shops and merchants. They approached the raised iron gateway and approached the great hall.

The threesome gathered before the throne of His Regal Majesty, King Thunderwind. Purple robes draped his tiny, plump form.

"Greetings, strangers."

He addressed the party in a deep voice, his long white mustache dancing on his face as he spoke. The voice sounded suspiciously similar to Chip's.

The three figures bent at the waist in an exaggerated bow.

"I beseech you to help. Prince Goodwin, sole heir to the throne, has been abducted by an evil gang of kidnappers, led by Baron Darkdeed. My men have brought word of their secret lair—a secluded cabin deep in the woods, just north of the castle."

To Blue's surprise, Daria spoke on her own initiative. "Why not send your own men?" The woman's voice, deep and husky, read from pre-scripted dialog. *Weak.*

The king replied, "I dare not send King's soldiers to the area; if they're recognized, the villains will harm my son. Return the prince to me safely, and I will give you each forty silver, and if you should bring me the head of Darkdeed, as well, your reward shall be equal to my gratitude."

"Who wrote this crap?" Daria asked.

"Phil and I came up with it together."

"Chip, my dear, know your limitations. Ask for help from a writer."

"Is that an offer?"

Daria turned to Gallamar and winked. "We'll talk later."

———

TRUDGING a few yards behind the aged wizard, Daria grabbed Gallamar's hand. "Come on." She clasped his hand and pulled. "We're falling behind." They skipped through the forest, hands locked as they bounced in unison along the dirt road while heading in a northern direction on the mini-map.

Daria's off-key singing cut through the peaceful forest ambiance. "Wee-ee're OFF to see the wizard, the wonderful wizard of...um...Magtog!"

Magtog spun on his heel and turned to face them. The old man's hands raised, blue electric lightning sparking between his fingers. "Silence, warrior, or my lightning bolt attack will silence you."

Shocked at the aggressive stance, Daria stopped in mid-stride. "What is your problem, Phil?"

Behind the wizard, Daria saw a large, hulking figure wearing a black cowl pop out from behind a tree. "Oh, crap. Look out!"

Daria's warning came too late. The bandit raised a club and struck the wizard on the head.

The wizard dropped, a circle of stars spinning over his pointed hat.

Gallamar sprang forward, a dagger in each hand. "Right-click on the bandit's image, Daria. Combat is automatic."

Duly instructed, Daria jumped, the two-handed sword drawn

and in her hands before she completed the leap. With a single powerful swipe, the bandit fell before her sword, even as Magtog's muttered curses continued in her ear.

Three more bandits darted out from behind the trees.

Gallamar leapt at the nearest one. With a two-handed thrust, he slid his daggers neatly into his target's ribcage and stomach. The bandit crumpled to the ground.

Running between the remaining two assailants, Daria hit the first with the flat of her blade. The attacker collapsed. The second rushed her, only to be struck by a bolt of blue lightning. Daria glanced toward the source of the energy—the wizard. Now clearly recovered, the wizard stood, arms outstretched, firing bolts of blue energy from his hands. With a final indignant cry, the third bandit fell to the ground.

Daria rushed into the forest, hoping to draw out more attackers.

As the group continued moving forward, the trees parted to reveal a small cabin in a clearing.

"Here it is, guys. Let's get him," she cried. She attacked the wooden door with a powerful swipe of her blade. The door burst into a pile of dry kindling.

"Blue, wait," Gallamar called.

"Stop," the wizard cried.

A huge, dominating presence in a black mask stepped from the shadows, swinging its own tremendous sword. A health bar hovered over the figure's head, identifying the character as Baron Darkdeed. A booming, evil laugh filled the room. With one mighty swipe of his sword, Darkdeed knocked Daria back.

Daria toppled, falling to the ground several yards beyond the cabin. The now-familiar spinning stars circled over her head. "Shit! I can't move. I'm pushing buttons, but nothing's happening."

By this time, Gallamar and Magtog stood over her. "You're stunned. The effect will wear off in a few seconds."

Magtog raised a gnarled hand, waving it in her face. "Only our combined forces will work against an adversary of his level."

"Now you tell me."

The stars over Daria's head vanished.

Gallamar extended a hand to help her up. "We tried to stop you."

Daria rose to her feet.

Baron Darkdeed stepped through the door, ready for battle.

The wizard raised his hands, preparing another bolt attack. "I'll strike first, and while he's reeling from that, you two jump in and finish him."

Daria waited, sword poised and ready to strike. "So you zap him from back here, in safety, and we do the close-in work so he can wail on us instead. That's your idea of teamwork?"

The wizard sneered. "You have the armor and the weapon, warrior. Do what you must, or we all perish."

"Yes, sir." Daria saluted with her sword. "Just remember, it's only a game."

With a guttural battle cry, twin streams of blue lightning shot from the wizard's fingers. The streaks closed together mid-stream and struck the baron firmly in the chest.

Through her headphones, the reverberation thumped her ears.

"Now!" The wizard called out.

Gallamar and Daria leapt toward the villain. The bandit swung his sword, but Daria's and Gallamar's steel combined to block it mid-swing. Daria pressed the attack. On the third strike, she penetrated his armor and found the soft flesh beneath.

She was rewarded with a graphic spurt of red.

The bandit uttered a grunt of pain but continued to fight. A second attack of lightning hit the baron in the chest, and this time, Gallamar's and Daria's blades found their mark. The baron staggered, and to Daria's amazement, turned on his heels and took off running.

"Oh, no, you don't." Daria swung her sword as she overtook the retreating bandit. The sword impaled the baron's chest, and Daria watched in glee as the baron fell.

———

BLUE THRUST both hands at the monitor, pointing with her index fingers. "Got'cha, you fat, ugly bastard. Woo-hoo!" She spun the chair around in a victory dance. Then stopped, seeing Chip and Phil hadn't joined in. Instead, they silently observed her.

Chip's expression, at least, showed approval. "So, I take it you like it?"

Blue grinned back. "Yeah, I guess it's all right." She adjusted her headset and turned back to her monitor.

———

AS DARIA TOOK a step toward the remains of her defeated foe, a window opened over the prone body, labeled "Loot." Within the window was the image of a large sword. Daria pointed the mouse at the sword, revealing the text *+35 to 45 damage.*

"Hey," said Daria. "His sword is better than mine."

Gallamar explained patiently. "Just right-click, and you'll automatically arm yourself with his sword. You can sell your old one for silver pieces when we get back to town."

"Oh." Daria's sword vanished into her tiny belt-pack—an achievement possible only in video games—and she drew a larger blade with a detailed ornamental handle. She deftly dropped her new weapon into the sheath on her back. "Cool!"

Magtog walked past them.

The prince character followed, mimicking each step in brainless computerized fashion.

Magtog looked back at them. "While you were playing with your sword, warrior, I untied the prince. He'll auto-follow me until we get back to the castle. Ready?"

———

THE THREE ADVENTURERS stood before His Majesty, who bellowed his thanks in proper ornate language. "...in return for your service to this realm, accept these 40 silver pieces and this bow of accurate strike."

Blue clicked the "accept" button and the items deposited themselves into Daria's hip-pack. "What am I going to do with a bow?" she asked.

Gallamar patted her on the shoulder. "Actually, if you sell it, you'll get another 30 silver. Or you can offer it to the dwarf in the village fighting the bear. He might not give you as much, but he'll probably be very grateful."

Daria grinned. "Poor little guy. That's a good idea. Let's go find him. Maybe we can even help him on his quest."

"No." Magtog's voice cut through their exchange.

———

BLUE TURNED in her seat to glance at Phil.

Phil dropped his headset across the keyboard, looking pale and tired. With a noticeable grunt, he rose from his seat and stepped away from the computer. "Sorry, guys. It's late, and I'm pretty wiped out. But you two can keep playing, if you want."

Blue nodded, getting to her feet and stretching her stiffened legs. "If you're tired, you should get some sleep. Especially since you've been barking at me all night."

Phil looked away, but Blue stood her ground, holding her hands open at her sides. "So, what did I do? Or didn't you think I'd notice?"

Phil took a deep breath. "Look, if you're both here and happy in the morning, then chalk it up to my lack of sleep giving me bad vibes." He shot her another angry look.

Blue's face flushed. *He knows.*

"Look, Blue. Maybe you're here to make up for lost time, and if so, I apologize. But, if *not*..." He paused, meeting Blue's eyes and letting his unspoken meaning sink in. "If not, then stop with the flirting and compliments. I expected better from you."

Blue dropped her gaze to the floor. "You're right."

Phil's snorted breathing sounded like a bull barely controlling the urge to charge. "Anyone can knock on my door if they want to." Without waiting for a reply, he stomped out of the room.

"Wow, he's surprised me twice in one night." Chip sounded cheerful and clueless. "And I thought I knew him so well."

"He's a good friend, Chip." A surge of emotion welled up in her. Her stomach cramped.

"I know, but he has a weird way of showing it sometimes."

"It's not so weird. He doesn't want to see you hurt, that's all." Blue squeezed her eyes against the tears streaming down her face.

"Who's going to hurt me? Hey, you're crying."

A shameful sniffle escaped, and she trembled at the gentle touch of his fingers wiping the moisture on her face.

The moment had come, and she was chickening out. Whatever else she'd rationalized these last few months, she had fun tonight. Simple, playful fun, for the first time since she'd boarded the plane to New York over a year ago.

But the computer game made me feel that way. Didn't it?

She took a deep, shuddering breath, reached out, and gripped his hand. She met his concerned gaze with her own. "He's right. We have to talk, and we have to talk tonight."

CHAPTER SIX

The moment she'd dreaded had arrived, and Blue found she couldn't look Chip in the eyes before she proceeded to break his heart. Instead, she stared at the stupid computer screen showing the stupid characters still stupidly standing around the stupid receiving chamber of the stupid castle.

Stupid tears welled in her eyes, blurring the screen and streaking her face, but she couldn't cover her ears to block out the tone of naïve confusion in his voice.

"Blue . . . talk to me. What's wrong?"

She drew another breath, using her sleeve to wipe the moisture from her face. "I'm sorry, Chip. You deserve better. I can't do this anymore. I thought . . . if I gave it enough time, maybe I could get over what happened."

"You . . . said you didn't blame me for that night. You said you understood." Chip rattled off the bullet points and counted on his fingers, reviewing the facts. "You lived with me and my dad for over six months before you moved to New York. We were happy then. We *did* get past all that. You can't tell me you were pretending all that time."

"I wasn't." She glanced at Chip for the first time.

He'd crossed the room and sat in the computer chair closest to hers, swiveling it in her direction. His gaze bored into her with an intensity that made her squirm.

Still barely looking at him, she replied, "During that time, when we were together, I was happy. But I didn't process what had happened. I just pushed it aside."

God, how to explain? She flexed her tight shoulders, feeling them pop and hearing a telltale crinkle. "I really hadn't mourned. I was just numb...not thinking. Your dad made it easy for me. It was easier to go on like...like I was on some long, extended sleepover. I just put out of my mind the fact that I couldn't go home."

Uncomfortable seconds ticked away. Already emotionally drained, Blue waited for Chip to find words to his thoughts.

"So then you flew to New York with your dad, and that's when you found the time to process. Is that it?"

"I was alone!" She didn't mean to snap at him and spoke more calmly. "I missed you terribly, at first, but then I realized. I was in New York because my mother was dead. You weren't with me because my mother was dead. And my mother died because of what we...of what *you*...did that night."

"Blue, that's not—"

"It was because of your hairbrained scheme that we ended up in that park, and it was only because I agreed to join you that we dug up that money. Because...I joined you, rather than stay with Mom, like she asked me, like she *begged* me to..." Blue stopped, over-whelmed with tears and a pain that emerged like a deep, old wound torn open and freshly exposed.

"Fine. You want to hand out blame, there's plenty to go around." Chip cleared his throat, swallowing a lump. "I have to live with what happened, too. I never even met the woman, and I played a part in her death. On top of that, you had just discovered how much you loved her, and she was taken from you."

He rose to his feet. Even given his thin build, his tall frame cast a considerable shadow over her. "But I didn't kill her. Some fucked-up, supernatural creature killed your mother. I no more *pointed* him in the direction of your mother than *you* did. No one could ever have predicted or controlled that."

"That's not good enough!"

Chip flinched at the high, screeching passion of Blue's response.

"You should have known! You'd collected *so many stories* of people who'd seen him before that night. But you didn't *listen* to them."

Chip looked away, and against the glow of the computer monitor, Blue glimpsed the streak of a tear staining his cheek. "I couldn't take those ghost stories any more seriously than a six-year-old telling me about their visit from the tooth fairy."

Blue recalled her earlier experience, on the very same day they embarked on their misadventure in the amusement park, when she discovered her neighbor, Sylvia, was a ghost, but couldn't believe the evidence of her senses. Instead, she'd concocted a highly improbable but tangible explanation for what she'd seen and heard, rather than accept the idea that she'd encountered the supernatural.

"I know, Chip. And we can sit here and reason and rationalize all night, but it won't make any difference." She paused. "I've been sick."

Chip's face paled, and a look of concern swept his features. "What's wrong?"

Realizing what Chip thought, she shook her head. "No, not like that. I mean, I'm *emotionally* sick. I'm drained, I can't write, I can't focus. I'm not *me* anymore. And it's because of what happened." Blue buried her face in her hands. "We were good at one time, but we have to accept it. We're not anymore. We're poison to each other."

"Bullshit."

Blue dropped her hands into her lap, surprised at his outburst.

Chip gazed at her with an earnestness that broke her heart. "We're more than good for each other. We're *amazing* together. I keep you grounded when you go off on your tangents, and you remind me there's a real world beyond the computer screen. We complete each other." Chip paused, and Blue could almost see the new thought pop into his mind just before he gave it voice. "Is there another guy?"

On reflex, she shook her head. "No. Well, yes."

He nodded and rolled his eyes.

She kept talking to cut off the anger she knew would burst from him. "Well, he likes me, but nothing's happened. I wouldn't do that to you. I swear."

Chip bent over her, his arms snaking out and gripping each side of her chair. The intensity of his pleading stare froze her in place. "Blue...if you don't hear anything else I say, hear this. He will never love you the way I do. No one will. And you feel the same toward me, I know it. I would do *anything* for you. If you were ever in trouble, I'd lie, steal, cheat–I'd move heaven and Earth to help you, and you *know* I would."

"I know it." And she did. She remembered all-too-well his first act of love toward her. Not the silly flower bouquet, that came later, but the act of computer sabotage Chip performed to remove the presence of a hateful teacher who'd threatened to fail her for no good reason.

"And maybe you can give up on us, but I can't. And I won't."

The ache inside her chest overcame her, and tears spilled freely down her face. "Chip, no, don't do that to yourself."

Chip turned toward the hallway next to the stairs, where, presumably, his bedroom door stood beyond. He nodded toward the old cloth couch in one corner of the room, with a blanket and pillow stacked on the arm and a sheet stretched across the cushions. "We set this up for you. My bed's pretty small, and I kind of had in mind that you might need your own space, after..." He let the thought trail off unfinished.

Of course, Blue knew what he'd had in mind. The saddest aspect of this cruel joke she'd pulled on him. The months of anticipation, of longing, waiting for a night when they could both reward each other for their faithfulness through the long months apart. Denied.

Blue sobbed openly. She'd lost her voice and could only shake her head. *So stupid! I wanted this. I wanted to break up with him, and now I'm the one who's devastated!*

"You know," Chip said, "I gave Phil hell earlier for selling you short. But turns out he was right. You were pretending so well. I'm guessing you probably had a goodbye present in mind for tonight to make yourself feel better. Some sort of pity fuck to send me on my way."

"That's...not..." All she could do was cry. *How can I finish that sentence? True? Fair? It probably was true, and it's certainly fair.*

Chip took a few tentative steps toward the door, then stopped, as if he recognized the weakness he revealed even while he spoke. "If you change your mind, or want to talk, or...or whatever...you can knock on my door any time." His quiet voice mingled with her silent sobs. "I hope you stay through the weekend. I know I shouldn't try to fight for you, or convince you, but I want to, anyway." Shoulders slumped, he left.

She listened to his footsteps padding across the dim room, watched through the blur of tears as he vanished down the hallway, and was swallowed by the shadows. Moments later, she heard a door open and close, leaving her alone in the harsh glow of computer monitors.

Somehow, Blue dragged herself to her feet. Following the death of her mother, she had never thought she could feel so alone, so lost, ever again. But here she was, and she'd done it to herself.

Chilled, she grabbed a blanket and wrapped it over her shoulders. It was all she could do to keep from tipping over in the couch.

So. This was what she wanted. She remembered, hours earlier, how much she resented the hours on the plane, because it just delayed the conversation. What a release of a burden it would be, she'd thought, once it was finally over.

Instead, she felt buried alive in pain, lost and in complete darkness. Ironically, in a room full of glowing monitor screens, the most well-lit space she'd ever attempted to sleep in, she laid, strung out, emotionally drained, and only half awake.

Beyond thought, Blue stared at the monitors for the next several hours, waiting for sleep to finally overtake her.

———

"Fiona, I love you, but what the hell do you think you're doing?"

"Mom?" Blue struggled for consciousness, dimly aware that her face pressed against a couch cushion and of the accumulated wetness of her own drool under her cheek soaked into the sheet. *Oh, great, another nightmare visitation from Ghost-Mom to help pile on the guilt.*

Resigned, she pulled herself to a sitting position, half-expecting to find herself back in the old house in Perionne, and mildly surprised to see she remained in Chip's basement full of computers where she'd collapsed earlier.

She noted the nearest computer chair turned toward her, where her mother sat and looked in her direction with a decidedly unhappy expression on her face.

Blue also noticed, as her head cleared to full wakefulness, the hint of light coming through the slot of a window high above her, and the Velcro texture of her Indiglo watch still fastened around her wrist, flashing 7:23 AM. So, she'd slept through the night. *Or, at least, I'm dreaming I slept through the night.*

But this is wrong. This is different from last time. Although she remembered dreaming of her old living room from all those months ago, she'd also never questioned being there.

Back then, she hadn't pinched herself like she did now (*ouch!*) or tried to will herself awake, to no avail.

"I already told you I forgave Chip. I also told you he's going to need you now. And you need him! The danger is closer than ever."

"Oh, will you *stop?* Like I need this shit!" Blue slapped her hand down on the side of the couch, noting the sting of pain traveling through her arm. "Like I don't feel bad enough. I did what I had to do. I did what's best in the long run...for him and for me."

"No, you didn't, my dear. You did no such thing." The phantom frowned in her mother's usual disapproving manner, triggering a pang of painful memory. "You think you're so grown up, and now it's time to pay for your crimes. You don't blame Chip for my death—you blame yourself."

Her mother's words hit home, forcing a gasp from her.

"That's why you've felt so horrible all these months." The scowl disappeared on her mother's face and softened in sympathy. "So now you're punishing yourself and making the worst mistake possible. Rather than moving on and getting past this, you're making yourself, and him, more miserable. Not to mention what you're doing to me."

Blue shook her head. "You've been dead for over a year, but it's *still* all about you."

"Please don't mock me." The anger and sadness in her mother's voice stopped Blue's retort. "You don't know what I sacrifice each time I communicate with you from where I am. You don't know what spirits lose to return to this world, even for a short time. I can tell you that Gunther is suffering greatly, and will for a long time, for the disruptions he caused."

"I'm sorry, Mom."

"And whether I convince you or not, this is the last time I can see you, at least for a long, long time. So please, listen to me. You need to be strong *together* to deal with what's coming."

"Mom?"

"Fortunately for you, Chip's a forgiving man. But you must stop pushing him away. You're almost out of time."

"But what's going to happen, Mom?"

"There's no time, but you have to face it together if you have any chance of getting through it. Just go to him, make it right between you while you can. If he can't trust you now, when he needs you most, you'll lose each other forever."

There's no time? "Mom, wait, don't go. Please stay with me." Blue rose to her feet, stepping toward the apparition and wrapping her arms around the remarkably solid and warm form who returned her embrace.

"Mom, please stay. Just a little longer. I'm sorry, Mom."

Thin fingers lightly brushed the back of her head. "I love you, baby."

Her mother's body, so firm a moment ago, slipped through her arms and disappered.

Blue toppled across the chair her mother occupied moments earlier, calling out, "I love you, Mom. Come back. Please don't go."

The snap of a wall switch broke through her cries. She squeezed her eyes shut against harsh white light flooding the room. Rising up from where she'd tumbled, Blue blinked spots from her vision.

"Blue? Are you okay?"

Spots dissolved, and her gaze settled on Phil, his round body framed in the hallway. She scanned the room before she could stop herself, confirming what she knew—her mother had vanished. Only Phil looked on, covered in a tent-sized t-shirt and striped boxers, appearing as sheepish and uncomfortable as she felt.

Phil broke the silence. "I'm sorry. You must have had a nightmare. I'll leave you alone." He raised a hand to return the room to darkness.

"Wait!"

Rather than flip the switch off, Phil reached toward his head and scratched at the disheveled scalp with tiny strands of hair sticking out to the sides. He said nothing, just waited for her to continue.

Blue made her way to the couch, trying to rub sleep from her eyes, certain she suffered her own terrible case of bedhead. "Please come in." She indicated the computer chair already turned toward her.

Without a word, Phil padded across the cement floor and onto the throw rug in the work area, apparently used to the chill, a carefully calculated look of indifference on his face. She waited until he seated himself before speaking.

"Phil—I made a lot of mistakes last night, and I'm going to try to make it right by Chip, if he'll let me. But Chip and I made another mistake months ago. We swore we'd never tell anyone what happened... that night. What *really* happened."

Phil squirmed, a squeak of protest from the chair breaking the silence of the room. "You don't owe me any—"

"Yes, I do. Because when I made Chip promise not to tell anyone, I put myself between him and his best friend. And he loves you, but I made him promise me never to talk about it. And I'm sorry for that."

Phil blurted out, "He *does* love you. More than anything. And you don't deserve it."

Rather than argue, Blue simply nodded. "That's probably true, and I'm sorry, because I broke up with him last night. And I can't make you, or him, understand this, but it wasn't 'til I broke up with him that I realized how stupid it was, and what a huge mistake I'd made. I'm going to make it right, starting today."

Phil shook his head, his eyes flashing anger. "Nice. You're some piece of work, you know that? Does he know yet?"

Blue shook her head. "I haven't had a chance to talk with him."

Phil released a heavy sigh, rubbing his hands across his face as various emotions played out over his features. Anger, sadness, disbelief. "You two. What a soap opera. Well, let me kill the suspense for you. He'll take you back, of course."

Blue nodded. "You don't like me very much."

"No, Blue, you're wrong. I like you just fine. When you two first got together, I was your biggest cheerleader. Chip and I have grown up together. We've known each other pretty much our entire lives, and it was clear you made him extremely happy. But then we moved out here, and I watched him, day after day, make up excuses when you ignored him, in denial about the obvious. And I don't like what you've turned him into. Not one bit."

Blue reached out and tentatively placed her hand over his beefy one. "I know I have to prove myself to you."

With a minimal flick, Phil pulled his hand out from under hers. "You don't owe me anything. It's him you need to talk to."

"That's not true. I know you're upset with Chip."

Phil broke eye contact, looking down. "That's between him and me."

"No, it's not. I put him in an impossible situation with his best friend."

"Doesn't matter now, anyway." As Phil said the words, his voice broke. He squeezed his eyes shut, shook his head, and took a deep breath. Moments later, he looked up, his mask of indifference back in place, repeating his words in a calm tone. "Doesn't matter now. You're entitled to your secrets."

"And we're entitled to break them if it's in everyone's best interests. Let me tell you everything, from beginning to end, without interruption, because you're going to have a lot of questions by the time I'm finished."

Phil nodded. "Of course, I want to know the truth. Go ahead."

Blue took a deep, trembling breath. "Chip had been investigating the bank robbery of 1990 for months."

"I know. Then one day, he dropped it."

Blue said, "That's because what you don't know is that Chip deduced exactly where the money was stashed all those years ago. The thieves had buried it on the island of one of the Pirates of Perionne boat ride sets at the amusement park."

Phil's eyes grew round at the revelation, but he said nothing.

Blue took a deep breath. "That afternoon—the afternoon of that crazy night..." She paused.

Phil nodded for her to continue.

"Chip told me he wanted to find the money. His only interest was..." Blue hesitated. Should she reveal the role Chip's father played? She decided that was one secret they should continue to keep. "His only interest was recovering the loot and turning it in to the authorities. But he needed my help to dig it up, jimmy the locks, and... well, let's face it, bolster his courage."

Phil chuckled. "That sounds about right."

"I ran home to find my lock-picking pins and my switchblade. That's when Mom caught me trying to sneak out..."

At first, Phil listened in silence, his eyes growing wide as Blue recounted the entire bizarre tale of how Blue and Chip had unwittingly released the ghost of a psychotic bank robber.

As she continued to talk, Phil's expression changed from mild interest, to shocked anger, to the stone-blank stare of a man in shock, a man who has discovered that everything he thought he knew about his best friend, his town, his entire world, was a huge lie.

Blue finished the story, telling Phil how they managed to put the ghost to rest. But not before the insane phantom had slain her mother, gravely wounded Chip, and brutalized a confident, know-it-all teenager, transforming her into the meek, shallow young adult who now sat and cowered before Phil, weeping quietly.

"I lost more than my mother that night, Phil," Blue confessed. "I lost myself. And no matter how hard I try, I can't find her."

CHAPTER SEVEN

He tossed and turned for several hours, but eventually, Chip fell asleep.

Earlier, he'd fought with his instincts to go back into the room and beg Blue to take him back, to reconsider her decision, and to tell her that he'd do anything for her...if only she'd give him a chance.

But she already knows that.

This *sure* as hell wasn't what he'd planned for the weekend.

But he knew from the shuffling sounds and the sobbing noises coming through the air vent that Blue hadn't left the house. Apparently, she planned to stay until the morning, at least. *So I still have a chance. She could be here for up to three more days. If I'm smart, she'll realize on her own that she's wrong, and we can still salvage this.*

I'll make her realize how much I love her. Failure is not an option. I can't lose her.

Sometime into the long night he'd fallen asleep, and when the knocking sound penetrated his consciousness, his mind was still reviewing his options on how to proceed. "Wha–?"

Blue's voice reached him from the other side of the door. "Please open up, Chip." The misery in her voice brought him to full wakefulness. Even as a small part of him was disappointed in himself, he couldn't fight his instincts. He still loved her, and now she needed him. He had to go to her.

He pulled on the sweats, which still lay in a puddle at the side of the bed where he'd let them drop last night. He'd slept in a plain white t-shirt. *Hardly James Bond, but it'll have to do.*

Bracing himself, he crossed the room, then gripped the doorknob. He closed his eyes. *Okay, here we go. God, please let's not start off with a fight.*

He opened the door.

Blue propelled herself into his arms.

He took one step forward, more of a stumble, really, into the main computer room.

Her arms wrapped around his waist. And there she was, her head on his chest, her tears already dampening his shirt.

His head spun, trying to catch up with the words she mumbled against him.

"I'm so sorry, Chip, I'm so sorry, please, let's forget last night, please, I don't want this, please..." She continued on, the whole time pulling him close and crying openly.

Before he could stop himself, he embraced her. His fingers stroked the back of her head while she babbled. "I'm so sorry...."

He leaned down into her disheveled hair, smelled old perfume and sweat. The heat of her body radiated against his. He shushed her. "It's okay." All he'd wanted, after all this time, was to hold her like this, and now he had to shift his stance and hope she didn't notice his body's response to her proximity. "It's okay, Blue." He kissed the top of her head.

"No, it's not. It's not okay."

Her arms tightened to the point of discomfort. Chip didn't dare mention it.

She breathed against his chest. "Damn it, I had to break up with you in order to realize that the last thing I wanted to do in this entire world was to break up with you." Her body shook with a sob. "Who *does* that? What the fuck is *wrong* with me, Chip?"

"There's nothing wrong with you. Just...let me catch up." Chip had a chance to find his bearings. He scanned the room.

Phil had the decency to look devastated. He sat in the office chair at the computer farthest from them, staring down at the floor. He couldn't imagine what Phil would say out loud if he could. Phil was not an "I told you so" sort of person, but he also had little patience for drama of this sort.

He could dismiss Phil for the moment. He patted Blue between the shoulders, trying to ignore the growing wet stain across his chest as she continued to weep openly. "Take a moment and start over. I'm trying to catch up, too. What happened?"

She mumbled one final "I'm sorry." Her body continued to tremble against him. "I don't even know...what to say. For months, I thought...if I could just do this...everything would be better. But then I did...and I knew...Oh, Chip, it was so wrong, I'm so—"

"Shhh, don't. Don't go there again. It's okay." Chip released a breath into her matted hair and kissed her again. And it was okay, he *could* kiss her, something he couldn't count on five minutes earlier. "We both made mistakes, so let's let it go now."

He ran a hand down her back one last time and pressed his palm between her shoulders. She leaned back, but when he tried to look into her face, she stared down at the floor. Fresh tears followed after the wet smudges on her cheeks.

His heart broke. He wiped a hand across each of her cheeks, but it was hopeless. Her tears continued to blemish her features. At the same time, he thought he'd never seen anything so beautiful.

She avoided his gaze. "I've been...such a mess...for such a long time."

Chip considered and said the first thing that came to mind. "How long have you been planning to break up with me?"

"Uh..." Her face flushed red. "I guess...a long time."

"Since you moved away to New York?"

Her eyebrows furrowed. "I don't know...maybe soon after."

Two years ago, and this has lain heavy on her mind all this time. "You have to trust in us, Blue. I already know I'm better with you than without you. I knew that, years ago. You just...have to believe that, too."

Her hands reached up to her face, covering his hands. He could still feel her tremble beneath his palms. "I...don't do well with giving up the self control."

Chip smiled down at her. "Really? I hadn't noticed."

In spite of her tears, a laugh escaped her. "God...it sucks when you're right."

"Okay, let's just forget this and enjoy the weekend. It's Thanksgiving, and I want to be thankful that—"

"No."

"'No' what?"

"No." Blue shook her head against his palms. "You shouldn't just forgive me. I was *such* a bitch last night. I was horrible to you."

"I don't care about last night. You weren't a bitch. You were honest. I could see you were hurting. I'm just relieved to have you back."

"But I—"

"We're better. What more is there to discuss?"

Phil spoke from the corner. "I don't know, I'd make her grovel a bit more before I'd be so forgiving."

Blue said, "Shut up, Phil."

"Yeah, Phil, let it go, man."

"I'm kidding, people. Besides, I already knew you were a softie. But there is something important you have to know."

Chip braced himself. *Oh, God, what now? Please don't tell me she slept with that other guy.* Anything *but that.*

Phil continued, "A couple of things kinda happened while you were asleep last night."

Now he was confused, but he waited.

Her face somewhat drier now, Blue said, "Phil knows. He knows...everything."

Chip looked from Phil to Blue, then back again. *Everything? Does she really mean everything, or has he bought into some other lie concocted to mean 'everything'?*

Blue's eyes nearly bugged out from the intensity of her stare. Her fingers dug into his palms. "He *really* knows."

Phil's next words almost knocked Chip over. "Gunther's ghost. Blue's mom. I know."

"I..." He wanted to say "need to sit down," but the words caught in his throat. Instead, he stumbled over to the closest chair and fell into it. It was a good thing a chair was so close, or he would have dropped to the floor. "Okay, so...I guess I missed a couple of things last night."

The silence lingered.

Chip looked at his old friend and said, "I don't know what to say."

Phil shook his head. "I get it. I don't...understand it, by any means. But just to be clear...you really *do* think Gunther was a ghost when he came after you?"

Chip nodded. "There is absolutely no doubt in my mind that Gunther came after us, and that he was a ghost when everything went down. I know how it sounds, but that's how it is."

Chip could almost hear the gears turning in Phil's head. He knew Phil would reject the supernatural explanation of what happened. If Chip had not experienced it himself, he would have dismissed it, as well. Like Chip, Phil viewed the world through logic and science. It's one of the reasons they became best friends. Phil would not accept a secondhand report of a supernatural phenomenon. If anything, Phil's concern would be how Chip had allowed himself to be tricked into believing such nonsense.

But all Phil said was, "Okay. That's good enough for me. I believe...that you believe it. So, I get it."

They sat, Phil in his corner, Blue crouched on her haunches next to Chip, gripping his hand, her other hand stroking the back of his hand in a way he found difficult to ignore.

After almost a full minute, Blue asked, "So...I guess we're all good now?"

Phil laughed, and the tension in the room deflated. "Yeah, I think we are. And I don't know about you guys, but I need some breakfast."

"Oh." Chip rubbed a hand across his face, the fatigue settling in now that everything was "normal." "I can grab a quick shower, and we'll all go–"

Phil raised his hand. "No, I've got a better idea." He smiled at them. "I'll run a couple of errands, then grab some donuts and coffee down the street, and bring it all home. I'll be gone at least..." He glanced at his phone and shrugged. "Forty-five minutes?"

Without a trace of subtlety, Blue placed her hand on Chip's thigh, her fingers pressing. "You're a good man, Phil."

Chip almost yelped in surprise but somehow kept his composure.

Phil shook his head. "Please. Given where I thought this weekend was going, I'm all too happy to spring for the donuts." He looked down at himself, still in his night shirt and boxers, and flashed them a grin. "I just need to change real quick. So, keep the clothes on a couple more minutes, please." With that request, he disappeared into his room and shut the door.

Before Chip could stand, Blue dropped into his lap, her legs straddling the chair, her lips covering his hungrily, and her body grinding down against his.

His hands dropped around her waist, and he pulled her tight against him, no longer worrying about any telltale bulges.

Blue came up for air moments later, breathing urgently, eyes scanning his face. She whispered seductively, "You...are...in *such* trouble, my man!"

Chip grinned and whispered back, "Bring it on."

Her mouth covered his again. She probed and teased with her tongue. She separated from him again, her breath whispering hot in his ear. She hadn't heard Phil re-emerge from his room. "Is he gone yet?"

"Not yet."

She kissed him again. She came up for air and asked, "Is he gone yet?"

"No, but—"

"Is he gone yet?" She giggled against his mouth. "What the hell is taking him so long?"

Chip reached up and traced her cheek with his finger.

Blue closed her eyes, and a fresh tear trailed down her face.

"Blue, are you—"

"Shhh." She gripped his finger and kissed it. "I just can't believe...that I forgot. That I almost—"

"No." He reached out, placing his hand, feather-light, against her lips, as if to cut off her words. "We're done with that."

She spoke against his fingers. "Okay."

From behind her, Chip heard Phil's bedroom door re-open, but he didn't take his eyes off her. Almost eighteen months of devotion and patience, about to be rewarded. The intensity of her stare bored into his soul.

"I won't...ever...forget again."

Phil called out, a chuckle in his tone. "Okay, you two, I'm leaving! Have fun." As Phil ascended from the basement, the stairs creaked in familiar protest.

Chip found his voice. "God, I love you."

"I love you, too...so much!"

The doorbell rang.

Chip looked over at Phil, who stood, still midway up the stairs.

Blue turned her head back and forth between the two of them.

Chip asked, "What time is it?"

Phil looked at his phone. "A little after eight."

"Okay, I'll say it," said Blue. "Who the *fuck* is that dropping by this early on a holiday?"

The doorbell rang again, twice, communicating its urgency.

Blue's eyes reflected a silent plea. "Could it possibly be the morning paper?"

Chip shook his head.

"Oh, God." Her eyes betrayed her disappointment and... something else, but he couldn't tell. Some sort of insight. "Oh, God."

Phil headed up the stairs while Blue struggled out of Chip's lap.

"What?"

Blue's voice took on a tone of panic. "Oh, God. Oh, God. She said, 'The danger is closer than ever.'"

"What? Who?"

As Chip got to his feet, Blue grabbed his hand, the look in her eyes making him nervous. "She said, 'You're almost out of time.'"

"Who said?"

"My mother. Last night."

It took a moment for the implication of what Blue said to sink in. "Your mother? But that's not..." Chip stopped himself.

"Go on. Say it. I dare you."

Chip shook his head and headed toward the stairs.

Blue walked at his side, fidgeting and clearly upset.

"Okay, fine," he conceded. "It *is* possible. But let's just see who's there before we jump to conclusions."

Phil waited for them in the living room, his hands on the knob of the front door. As soon as they joined him, he opened the door on a young patrolwoman officer in dark blue, with short-cropped, dark hair and clear skin the color of caramel. Reflective sunglasses hid her eyes. "Eugene Farren?"

Phil turned, looking at Chip.

A chill ran up Chip's spine and into his neck. "I'm Eugene."

"Mr. Farren, I'm Officer Selena Gonzalez. I'm afraid I need you to come down to the station to ask you questions regarding a matter of great urgency."

CHAPTER EIGHT

"Okay, Eugene, once again, you're telling me that you're absolutely certain your video game has a fairly standard set-up, and there's no way it could cause any sort of harm to anyone? Not even accidentally?"

Chip rubbed his hands over his eyes to bring Officer Kip Kirby back into focus. He shrugged and tried to avoid looking around the small interview room. "The video game industry makes available a set of strict parameters of color schemes and flash rates that may accidentally trigger seizures. We're self-regulated, but the specs are easy to find, and Ph...I was very careful not to fall anywhere into that spectrum."

That was close. He'd almost said "Phil and I." For simplicity's sake, When Chip and Phil had registered business ownership, they'd filed under his name, Eugene Farren, with Phil as an employee.

As far as the police were concerned, Chip was solely responsible for whatever they were investigating. While that didn't bode well for him, at least he was the only one in the hot seat for the moment. As long as Chip didn't let on about their 50/50 partnership—or until the "A Squad" returned from vacation—they would leave Phil out of this.

Chip shook off the feeling that the walls were closing in on him. *For God's sakes, are we really three hours into questioning?*

Chip understood what happened, but that didn't mean he had to like it. Officer Kirby drew the short straw; he ended up stuck on duty over a holiday in a college town. Maybe he volunteered to get away from some ugly home life, and all he wanted was to coast through an uneventful four days where he could lay low, catch up on paperwork, and give his normal beat a rest until the students returned on Monday. But a hot potato had fallen into his lap, and he had no backup.

The officer shook his head. "We're not talking about seizures. I have two comatose victims on my hands."

Chip fumed. He didn't know what else he could say, and the police officer had offered nothing new for the last two-and-a-half hours of this conversation. They kept going 'round in circles.

So, Chip repeated, again, "Sir, except for carpal tunnel, eyestrain, and possibly Attention Deficit Disorder, there's little else a computer monitor can 'cause' a person in terms of medical conditions."

Chip remembered his programming class from middle school, experimenting with classic BASIC language and how lines of code could make a computer repeat itself, in theory, forever, or until the programmer interrupted the loop by giving the break command. Chip amused himself by thinking of this interrogation as a BASIC program. The code might have looked like:

Line 10: Police officer asks pointless question

line 20: Chip offers pointless answer

line 30: go to line 10.

Having executed line 20, again, Chip waited, wondering if the police officer would finally break the loop and try something else, or just go back to line 10.

Officer Kirby picked up the manila folder that had lain on the table between them through the entire conversation. He opened it, looked at something only he could see, and glared up at Chip, as if considering. *Ah, new information, maybe a line 25 that provides something new and stops the merry-go-round.*

Apparently, the police officer agreed. He grabbed up two photos from the file and slapped them down in front of Chip.

Chip picked up the one closest to him. The photo showed an attractive woman, perhaps in her mid-thirties, with striking, bright red hair and a pale complexion. Her face projected sincerity and stoic professionalism. Chip noted the label under the photo: Burton, Rebecca, Agent, Special Investigations Unit, Base of Operations: Indiana.

The second photo showed a much younger, spunkier woman. As he continued to study the picture, Chip was fairly sure they shared a math class together. But he never spoke to her, never knew her name, until now, when he read the label on the photo: MacLeod, Skye Isobel, Contractor, Special Investigations Unit, Base of Operations: Indiana. Cute, in a geeky kind of way, with long, dishwater blonde hair, someone who gave off a nerdy vibe, perhaps a roleplayer, though Chip couldn't pinpoint why he thought so.

Then he remembered. Cloud McSky, a recurring name in the daily video game reports. The obvious pseudonym didn't give her away, necessarily, nor did it flag her for suspicious activity. If Chip and Phil traced down every Peter Parker, Tim Burton, and Seymour Butz that logged in on their game system, they'd have no players.

It was that her name showed up every day. Every day, without exception. Phil and Chip had flagged Mr. McSky as their first official fan. Only "he" wasn't a he. Well, that's what he got for assuming.

The officer pressed. "Something?"

Chip realized he'd been staring at the photo too long. He figured he might as well fess up. He handed the photo back to the officer. "Her. She's been playing the game, every day, for months."

"You can tell that from the photo?"

"Well, no, from the name, actually. She uses a variation of her real name when she logs in."

Officer Kirby folded his arms across the desk and leaned forward in a way Chip was certain was supposed to be intimidating. "And now she's in a coma."

"If you say so."

"If *I* say so!" Kirby slapped his palm down on the table, causing Chip to flinch. "Look, kid, you think I wanted this trouble? I have two investigators down as of last night. I'm breaking all sorts of rules showing you this, because you need to realize just how much trouble you're in. These investigators were undercover here on campus, and both their bodies were found, last night, slumped in front of their computers, and guess what was on their computer monitors in both cases?"

Chip cringed, connecting the dots. "Statistically speaking, the answer would be Facebook, but I have a feeling that's not what you're going to say."

Kirby jabbed a finger in Chip's face. "*Your* game, smartass!"

Chip closed his eyes, absorbing the information. He didn't like what he heard, but at least he knew what he was up against, and he also knew that Phil and he were innocent.

So, he'd broken the loop. That was something. At least the conversation could go forward instead of starting over for the zillionth time.

"They're both on life support and in a coma," Kirby continued, "We don't know if they're going to survive, and you're sitting here, wanting me to believe that your game had nothing to do with it."

Chip shook his head. "No, I'm not saying that. I am saying, if our game was involved, I had nothing to do with it." *Which means someone else used our game to get to them. But how?*

Out loud, Chip said, "So are you charging me with something?"

"No, kid, we're simply questioning you."

"Then if you're not charging me with something, I'm free to go, right?"

"No, that's *not* right."

"Well, which is it?" Chip raised his hands, exasperated. "It sounds like you want to charge me with something, and if that's the case, I should probably get my lawyer before I say another word."

"Look, kid, thanks to you, I have two big headaches." He held a finger out between them. "The first is that if I could get a judge to hear your case—you're right. I have nothing to charge you with. I can accuse you of suspicion of assault, which I can make stick, but what I can't make stick is assault with a magic computer monitor." He extended a second digit. "The second is—given the holiday, no one is going to even *see* my request until Monday."

He dropped his hand to his side. "Now...I trust you don't want to be in a holding cell for three days. Truthfully, I don't want to have to put you there. So it would be a lot easier if we can just leave the lawyers out of this and work with each other. But I need something."

Chip rolled his eyes. "You can't hold me in a cell for three days without charging me with something." Chip tried to glare with confidence. He really wasn't sure about what he'd just said. But he *was* sure he'd heard that on several TV shows, and he was hoping popular consensus ruled in his favor.

Not his most compelling moment, but he'd put it out there, and he had to go with it.

He leaned forward as the words flew out of his mouth, not sure where the bravado came from, except that perhaps he'd picked up a couple of pointers from his flamboyant girlfriend. "Do not mistake me for a stupid kid who can be easily intimidated. You need to either charge me with something or let me go."

The lieutenant smirked, and Chip knew he'd gambled...and crapped out. "Really? You really think that? You're not as smart as I thought. Three days? Try 90 days!"

Chip felt himself go pale.

"That's right. I can hold you three months if I wanted. Sure, the letter of the law says otherwise, but don't think I couldn't make it stick if you get on my bad side."

Chip shook his head. "You know what? Great, lock me up. But that doesn't shut down my game, does it? And there is one thing I will concede: someone out there might be using *my* game to get to *your* people. You need a court order to make me shut it down—which is not going to be easy because you can't prove anything beyond a passing coincidence. So, without a court order, you need my cooperation. How am I doing so far?"

Kirby snorted and rubbed his face in his hands.

Chip tried to keep his own expression neutral. If this was Bloomington's finest, he needed to work on his poker face.

Kirby nodded. "So, just for askin' sake, If I were to ask you, really nice, to shut down your computer game, as a sign of cooperation, would you do it?"

Chip shrugged. "Frankly, I'd want a little time to do my own investigation, sir. I might consider forty-eight hours. Long enough to perform my own diagnosis of what's going on. I'd report what I found directly to you."

"Oh, would you? Well, isn't that nice of you?" Kirby rose to his feet. "Look, kid, we can bring in men to do that diagnosis."

Chip scoffed. The noise was out there before he could stop it. "Better than Phil and I can? You really think so? We wrote that program, and I don't want to brag, but I suspect we're a couple steps ahead of any 'experts' you might assign to go through our code. Particularly over a holiday weekend."

Kirby exploded. "All right, that's it, you can stew in a cage through New Year for all I care. You're going to—"

A knock on the door interrupted the policeman in mid-rant.

Chip turned at the sound of the door opening, and the young woman who'd picked them up this morning stuck her head in. "You need to take this call, Boss."

"I'm in the middle of questioning here!"

"That's just it, Kip. It's the kid's attorney. He's insisting on talking to you immediately."

"The kid's…!" Kirby shot Chip a devastating glare.

Chip did his best to keep his face blank, though he wondered the same thing the police officer did. Who the hell was on the other side of the phone, claiming to be his attorney? And how did anyone notify that person?

But after a few seconds, Chip realized who waited impatiently for him in the front area, and he knew the answer. *Thank you, Blue!*

———

KIRBY SLAMMED the door of his office and dropped down into the chair.

Every year for over a decade, he volunteered for the four-day Thanksgiving shift. Every year it was a long, boring break from the usual college kid stupidity. He had no family to entertain, so why the hell should he covet the time from his brother officers who did? Pizza was close enough to turkey, as far as he was concerned.

Besides, when he volunteered to work over Thanksgiving, he earned the clout to plan a trip to the vacation spot of his choice every St. Patrick's Day weekend—generally a nightmare for the precinct, a nightmare that he'd missed out on for twelve years.

Last year, he laughed it up in Cancun, Mexico, with Barbara, and this year he'd already booked his tickets to Myrtle Beach with Stephanie. All he wanted to do was get through this shit shift without incident. But so far, the police gods had conspired against him.

Two state investigators—comatose. Jesus! And my only lead is giving me attitude!

He sighed and snapped up the phone. "Who the hell is this?"

"Officer Kirby, my name is Ben Gerrold, attorney at law." Well, the voice *sounded* older and professional. But Kirby wasn't willing to rule out a college prank just yet.

The voice continued. "I'm informing you, as of this moment, I'm acting on behalf of Eugene Farren. I'm calling to find out what matter could be of such urgency that you need to keep a young man in your interrogation room for over three hours, so far, on Thanksgiving Day, and to see if we can't perhaps speed matters along just a bit."

Kirby decided to call this blustering man's bluff. "Bullshit. You can't be an attorney. Who holds office hours on Thanksgiving?"

"Officer Kirby, I should warn you this phone call is being recorded, so I suggest you take a deep breath and change your tone. As a matter of fact, I'm in my home office. We're entertaining relatives here at the house, so you can imagine that when I get a phone call from my ward, Fiona Shaefer, in tears, telling me how the police are ruining her visit with her boyfriend–a nice young man and a law-abiding citizen, I may add–I *make* the time to look into it."

"Fiona who?" The name sounded familiar, but–

"She's currently in your waiting room. I haven't seen her in a while, but generally, her striking hair color makes a memorable impression on strangers."

The punk girl!

The punk girl *has legal contacts?* Kirby felt himself turn red-faced. Thank God no one was with him to witness it. "Listen, Harold or Gerrold, or whatever your name is–I have two state investigators in the hospital as of this morning, and the only connection between the incidents is that both of them were logged in to your client's computer game when they were incapacitated."

"No, Officer, *you* listen. I know two things. First, that kid had nothing to do with your problems. You've hit a dead end, so you're taking it out on someone who you think has to take it. Now, I am willing to put up my personal bond money, if necessary, to guarantee his cooperation, but you've spent three hours with the young man, so I'm sure you know as well as I do, he's not a flight risk."

Kirby blew air into the receiver. That much was true. Whoever had sabotaged the kid's game and used it to do...whatever, Kirby's instincts told him that Eugene was as much a victim in this as the two agents.

The voice droned on. "Secondly, we also know that, even if you *can* come up with a court order and invent some charges that will stick–which you can't–no judge is looking at those warrants until Monday. I, on the other hand, can file charges of harassment, illegal confinement, illegal search and seizure, and whatever else I care to throw out there to embarrass your department and make sure *my* paperwork is waiting right alongside *your* paperwork come Monday morning."

"Why would you do that? What's it to you?"

"Lieutenant, Fiona Shaefer is the daughter of a colleague of mine, someone I respected very much. That colleague was murdered in cold blood a couple of years ago. Since then, I have made it my personal responsibility to take care of her as best as I can. So, when she calls me up and says her friends are being harassed for no good reason, it's...something to me. *Especially* on Thanksgiving Day."

Kirby sat in the chair, trying to control his anger. He didn't like being threatened, but the manmade sense. It's not like he'd made good use of the last three hours grilling the kid.

In the lingering silence, Gerrold spoke again. "Lieutenant, the young man you're holding had nothing to do with this crime. You have my word, he'll cooperate if you're reasonable. Right now, my word is off the record. We can go *on* the record if you'd like, but that complicates things for everyone. Now I suggest you work something out with him talk to him. Keep it off his record. And do it within the hour, or I'll start on that paperwork."

"All right, Mr. Gerrold, you've made your point. We'll try it your way. But you'd better be right about this kid. If it turns out he's hiding something, I won't hesitate to bring out my own set of charges."

"Now you're making sense, Lieutenant. I'm going back to entertain my in-laws and leave everything in your capable hands. If my holiday is interrupted a second time, I'm going to come after your station, and you, specifically." Kirby drew a breath to utter a retort when the line went dead.

Blue wiggled, trying to find a comfortable position on the metal bench, a simple goal, but an impossible one after three hours.

At first, she thought getting stuck in the police station foyer could have its entertainment value. They'd get a first-hand look as the patrol officers brought in the prostitutes, drunks, loiterers, and whatever other rabble needed to be cleared off the street. But between the hours of 9 a.m. and noon, on Thanksgiving morning, all they'd been "treated to" was the back of the head of the Hispanic policewoman seated at the reception desk.

Phil shifted on his side of the bench, pulling his cell phone from his holster and glancing at the screen. "What in the hell can they be asking him about for three-an- a-half hours?"

Blue shrugged.

"Did your attorney friend get back to you?" Phil grumped.

Blue sighed and rubbed sleep from her eyes. The shitty coffee the station served up no longer kept her awake. Well, that wasn't true. The frequent bathroom trips assured she couldn't doze, no matter how tired she felt. "I told you, he said he got my message and would take care of it."

"He didn't give you any idea how long before he—"

Chip walked into the foyer from around the corner.

Blue squealed. She couldn't help herself.

All complaints of fatigue fled her mind. *He's not handcuffed. He's coming toward me. That's good news, right? Please, let it be good news.* She ran forward, arms wide open, into Chip's embrace.

"Hey there." Chip patted her back as she held him.

She spoke against his chest. "You can come home, right? Tell me you can come home now, and we can get you out of here."

"I can come home now." Chip sounded deflated—beyond fatigue.

"He can go home now," the policeman standing across the room confirmed. "Cute trick with the attorney, Ms. Shaefer. That's the only reason your boyfriend isn't spending Thanksgiving in jail."

Blue glared at the man but said nothing. A couple of years ago, she'd have mouthed off and probably gotten herself thrown into the lockup, but she didn't want to risk that today.

She looked up into Chip's face, concerned at his tired, zombie-like expression. "So, what's up?"

Chip shook his head. "Nothing. Let's just go. I'll tell you about it later."

She took her place at his side, and they headed toward the door.

"Don't forget our deal, Farren!" The rude policeman called after him.

"I won't."

Holding Chip around the waist, she noticed his body trembled under her fingers. "Are you okay? Have you eaten?"

"No, but...let's just go."

"Selena, take them wherever they want to go, but get them out of here." The jerk police officer shouted to the woman behind the desk.

"Sure, Boss."

Blue reached up and stroked Chip's cheek. "Chip, are you okay? What happened?"

Chip glared at her and shook his head. "Not now. Guys, I'm starving, let's have her drop us off at Smittie's."

———

Laverne approached their table, pen and pad in hand. "Okay, what'll it be, boys? And girl!"

Blue sat between Chip and Phil. She'd just asked Chip to fill them in on what happened when Laverne broke in on them. Timing. She glared at the waitress and noted that Phil and Chip joined her in her annoyance.

Chip spoke up. "We don't know for sure yet. Give us a few minutes."

Phil raised a meaty palm. "I need a refill."

Laverne winked at him. "Just one so far? Okay, then. Chip, are you okay? You look plumb tuckered out. Blue, did you keep this guy up all night?"

Blue smiled. Laverne had no "off" button and couldn't take a hint, but she could play this verbal fencing game half-awake. "No, Laverne, I didn't keep him up all night. If I had, he'd still be deep asleep, but thanks for your concern."

"Chip," Laverne chastised, wagging a finger at him. "Don't be ignoring your girlfriend while she's in town."

"I wasn't–"

"Goodbye, Laverne." Blue shooed her away. She wasn't in the mood to get into her personal details with this way-too-nosy waitress. "I'm taking good care of him."

Rolling her eyes, Laverne picked up Phil's glass and wandered away.

Blue sighed. "Y'know, her shtick was kind of cute yesterday, but I hope she's not going to be a pain in the ass while we try to talk."

Chip shook his head. "Sure, it's an act, but she's a good friend, too."

Blue swatted Chip's arm. "Oh, come on, that whole routine is just to get more money out of you."

"Well, yes, of course, but don't sell her short. Phil and I have been coming here for months. She really *does* listen and wants the best for us. Sure, it's because we come here all the time, but that's not a terrible thing. Besides, why do you think she flirts with me so much in front of you?"

"*Clearly*, to piss me off."

"No. Exactly the opposite. She did it to draw your attention to the fact that, in her opinion, I'm a good catch and that you may want to keep me. For all I know, she was my biggest advocate last night."

Heat rushed into Blue's cheeks. "Right, Chip, because you can read people so well." Blue looked down at the menu, waiting out the uncomfortable pause.

Finally, Chip answered, "I've been doing a pretty good job with you the last couple of years."

Ouch! "Fine." Blue grabbed her straw wrapper, wadded it into a ball, flicked it off her thumb, and watched it bounce off Chip's forehead. The petty act made her feel better and ready to resume their previous conversation. "So, what's up? Two people are in the hospital, and they think you did it?"

"Well." Chip's brow furrowed. "They think someone used the game to cause it."

"But that's crazy," said Phil. "We know we came well below the frame rate and color scheme that can cause seizures."

Chip shook his head. "I don't think that's it. This seems to be something else entirely. And while I know *you* didn't do anything, and *I* didn't do anything, I *also* think someone used our game to cause it."

Phil's eyes widened, looking personally offended at the very suggestion. "You think someone hacked the game?"

Chip shrugged. "It's possible."

Phil shook his head. "Not on *my* watch. And if they did, I'll find it. Today."

"That would be good, because we only have until Monday morning."

Blue braced herself. "Until what, exactly?"

Chip looked down at his lap. "Until we have to either offer up some sort of alternate explanation, or we have to take the game down and turn it over to the police."

"We have to *what?*" Phil sounded as if he'd just been told to report for an involuntary vasectomy.

"I told him we could turn up more if we looked into it ourselves, and he accepted that. Either I agree to turn it over on Monday, or he was going to make it a condition of letting me go. I had to agree to it to buy us time."

"You agreed to turn over *our* program to police hackers?"

"No, Phil, I put off the confiscation for a few days. They would either pull the trigger now or later. What did you want me to say?"

"You say the program isn't mine to give away, and you need to talk to your partner before you commit to anything."

"I was trying to keep you out of it," said Chip. "Last thing we needed was for him to want to question both of us."

"Well, maybe *I* could have done a better job protecting *our* interests, partner!"

Wedged between the two men, Blue literally felt the heat emanating from Phil. She reached out and put a hand on each person's shoulder. "Guys, please, it is what it is. Let's just try to–"

"Phil, we'll make a backup of the program before we turn it over."

"But we'll have to take the site down during the investigation, right?"

"Well, yes, but–"

"And that could be months, right? What the hell were you thinking? We'll be ruined before we start."

Laverne called out and approached their table. "Hey, boys! I got your appetizers ready!"

Blue closed her eyes. *Oh, God, not her, not now.*

With a flourish, Laverne dropped an overloaded basket of breadsticks and multiple sauces down in front of them.

Chip piped up. "We haven't ordered yet."

Laverne frowned and looked down at her notepad. "Oh, you're

right. Huh! I guess I just assumed. Well, I can't take them back, so consider them on the house. I'm so sorry 'bout that, guys. And gal!"

Blue's eyes locked with Laverne's, noting the gleam in her eyes, before the waitress turned and walked away.

Phil immediately reached out and snagged up a cheese sauce and a breadstick. The redness in his face drained away with each contented bite.

Blue released a breath. *Chalk one up for Laverne. Maybe she* does *know what she's doing.*

Phil spoke between bites. "I'm going home right after we eat, and I'm tracking down what's going on."

Chip shook his head. "I think we need to go to the hospital and see if we can learn anything more about the victims. He told me their names. Rebecca Burton and Skye MacLeod."

"Really? Skye MacLeod?" Blue rolled her eyes. "See, that's why parents should be required to get a license before having kids."

"Well, funny name aside, they're in serious condition at IU Bloomington Hospital."

Phil waved his hand at them. "Fine, you two go check that out. I'm going home and getting online. I'll have this shit figured out before you get back."

Blue looked at Chip, a flush going through her at the thought of a new adventure with her man. "So, what do you suggest?"

Chip shrugged. "I'll bet they're not tracking roommates. We'll just show up with that angle and see if we can get into her room as a visitor. The staff might not tell us much, but we can see what we can figure out on our own."

Blue nodded. "Worth a try, I guess."

Chip reached for a breadstick. "Oh, it'll work. Especially with my master bullshitter at my side. You'll get us in."

"Hey! I love you, too." She reached into her cup and flung ice at him.

Chip closed his eyes, letting the ice bounce harmlessly off his forehead. He leaned toward her, putting on his cutest pout. "You do, don't you?"

Blue looked down, then back up at him, *Dammit, he's so adorable!*

"Don't you?" Chip prodded.

"Yes! I guess I can't deny it now."

She leaned forward and stole a sweet kiss tinged with tomatoes and Mountain Dew.

Laverne's voice broke the mood. "Hi, guys and gal, ready for your order...or I can come back later!"

Phil begged, "No, please don't go. It's getting sickening over here."

Laverne put a hand on Phil's shoulder. "Aww, don't be that way, hon. It's true love. I think it's kind of cute."

Phil grinned. "*You* didn't have to go *home* with them last night."

Laverne chuckled. "Pretty disgusting, huh?"

"You have no idea."

"Hey!" Blue snapped, giving Phil a dirty look. "Since you're here, we're going to order the same thing as last night. I don't suppose you can get a side of turkey, gravy, and mashed potatoes with that?"

Laverne extended her arm to indicate the empty establishment. "Everyone's at the diner down the street, hon. And by 'everyone' I mean maybe four students. I'm just here to take care of my favorite customers."

Blue made a point of slurping air through the straw of her cup, causing a rude noise, then held the cup out to Laverne. "This one's done, get me another."

Laverne smirked, took the cup, and walked away.

As soon as she was out of earshot, Phil turned to the couple. "Okay, so that's the plan. I go home and check out the game, and you two go to the hospital. Sounds good. But be careful."

Blue widened her eyes and gave Chip a shocked look. "Be careful? Us? I don't know what he means. We're *always* careful."

"Always," echoed Chip.

"Just try not to raise any vicious ghosts this time."

CHAPTER TEN

The IU Hospital campus was only a fifteen-minute walk from the pizzeria, and the sharp November breeze kept Blue and Chip moving fast, clasping hands the whole way. Blue darted through the double glass doors, cold, heart pumping fast, but with a clear head. She approached the long desk with "Information" spelled out in large, gold-painted letters overhead, pouting at the smiling greeter seated at the desk.

"Oh, hey, I just heard about my friend, Rebecca Burton! Is she here? Can we see her?" Blue returned the greeter's stare with her own, hoping to project confidence and certainty that this person should do her job and answer her perfectly legitimate request.

The woman, a sixty-ish silver-haired lady, typed on her keyboard and looked at the screen. "Burton, Rebecca, yes, room 6048. Take the elevators to the sixth floor."

"Thanks...uh, do you know if there's been any change?"

The nurse frowned at the screen. "Well, she's stable, or they wouldn't let her have visitors. So that's good, but unless you're family, we can't tell you any more than that."

Blue nodded and followed Chip toward the elevator.

The elevator doors opened to reveal a hospital bed on wheels surrounded by nurses and a doctor. Blue and Chip stepped to either side of the doors to let them pass. The teen lying on the bed flashed a brave smile as the doctors wheeled him past. The odor of ammonia and some other sanitizing chemical hit Blue's nose, and she struggled against her gag reflex.

Seconds later, alone on the elevator together, Blue spoke. "I hate this. Any time I'm in a hospital now, I think of my own stay, after Mom died." Chip extended his arm over her shoulder, and she leaned her head against him. "But the good news, I guess, is that Rebecca's stable, so she's not in danger of dying any time soon."

Chip nodded. "I'm hoping we can rouse her, see if she can talk."

"I thought the police guy said she couldn't talk."

Chip shrugged. "It's worth a try."

Moments later, still hand in hand, Chip and Blue walked down the brightly lit hallway, following the numbers along the left side consecutively counting 6040, 6042...until they stood outside the door of 6048.

At the sight of the closed door, a shiver traveled up Blue's spine. "Well...here we are."

Chip nodded but said nothing.

The seconds stretched on, and the internal twitchiness built up within her. *He'd better do something soon, or I'm darting for the elevator.* Blue finally spoke. "Well?"

Chip looked at her.

"It's your plan."

"I know, I just feel...odd, all of a sudden."

"You, too? Well, maybe we should forget about it."

"No." Chip reached for the door, gripping the curved handle. "We need to find out more. My gut tells me it's important."

The door swung inward, emitting a squeaking noise as they walked through into the dimness. From the perspective of the narrow corridor, she could only see the foot of a hospital bed, twin lumps of a pair of feet poking up from the blankets.

They pressed forward, entering the room. Natural light from

the window against the far wall exposed one of the most radiant, beautiful faces Blue had ever seen.

The patient lay on the bed, her eyes closed. Her bright red hair fanned over the pillow beneath her in shocking contrast to her stone-white skin. One thin arm extended out. An I.V. tube twined from the wrist, curled into loops on a hook and back up into a bag, presumably a saline drip.

To Blue's eyes, Rebecca Burton appeared as any other patient in a hospital, her understated beauty marred by hours of lying in a bed, garbed in an unattractive gown.

But the room itself emitted a presence, a feeling that filled her with an intense sadness, sickened at what she saw.

Suddenly, it was *that night again*, when she helped Chip dig up the bones of Gunther. The nausea that overcame her as they continued with their morbid task was similar to the sickening feeling now.

They stood as witnesses to some great injustice happening before their eyes. Blue knew, if they were given an opportunity to stop this, they needed to act.

"Poor, poor dear," an unfamiliar voice whispered.

Blue noticed a nurse standing on the opposite side of the bed.

The nurse looked across the bed and met her gaze. Blue saw her body tremble, as if she'd awakened from a dream. "Oh, my, I'm so sorry." She looked at the clipboard hanging at eye level on the storage cabinet. "I came in to check her vitals and... just got distracted for some reason." She cleared her throat and removed the pen from her pocket. "So...do you know the patient?"

"Not really," started Chip.

Blue broke in. "Yes, *I* do. I had her in several classes, and...Chip is my boyfriend; he's here for moral support." She reached out and squeezed his upper arm as a warning. *Let me do the talking, you moron.* "She wrote such...wonderful poetry." She tried to project as much sadness into the lie as she could.

The nurse's eyes lit up at her words. "I'm not surprised. You can feel it, can't you? It's like she has the soul of a poet." The nurse sniffled and shook her head. "Wow, I don't get it. Working here, I've seen so many terrible things, but I don't usually fall to pieces around the patients. There just seems to be something special about this one."

Blue nodded. Given the emotions stirring within her, it was easy to follow that thought. "She is. She really is. I just hope she gets better soon." Blue shot the nurse a quick glance before looking down to the floor.

The nurse sighed, not an encouraging sign, and recorded something on the chart. "I hope so, too, but I'm just...concerned about this one."

"But..." Blue considered how to fish without looking like she was fishing. "I thought she was stable. That means she's getting better, right?"

"Well, that's what the *doctor* would tell you," the nurse said. "And the doctor knows *everything*, as he's constantly reminding us. What do *I* know? I've only been doing this for fifteen years."

Chip spoke up from beside her. "What *do* you know, Nurse?"

The nurse shook her head, her internal struggle clear in her answer. "I'm not supposed to say anything. Never mind. And I could be wrong."

"Wrong about what?" Chip pressed.

"Look...it's just me, but...these vitals. They're dropping. Slightly. Consistently. Over hours. The doctor says it means the patient is slipping into a healing coma."

The nurse made a scoffing noise. "I've seen healing comas before. You get spikes, even little ones, an overall drop until they stabilize, but not a steady plummet like this. I've never seen it, and it makes me nervous."

The nurse clasped her hands to her face. "But I don't know, and dammit, I shouldn't have said anything. I just have a bad feeling, like she's slipping away, and in a few days, she's going to be gone."

She stepped away from the bed. "I need to get out of this room."

Blue loved that idea. "We'll come with you."

Moments later, standing in the hallway, Blue took a deep breath, feeling her head clear, like a potent drug purging itself in seconds. She looked over to see the nurse, visibly shaking her head to clear it.

"I'm sorry," the woman said. "I shouldn't have said what I did. I'm usually more careful than that. But there was just something in the room."

"We felt it, too," said Chip. "But you think she's in trouble? That she's not going to last long?"

The nurse backed away. "I'm sorry, I can't say any more. You'll have to talk to the doctor. Actually, don't. He can't tell you anything since you're not related, and I told you more than I should have. I don't know what came over me."

Blue reached out for the nurse's arm. "Wait—"

"Enjoy your visit with your friend." She took off down the hall like Blue was some creature trying to claw at her.

Blue heard a noise coming from Chip's belt—something Star Trek-like, she suspected, and Chip reached for his cell phone holster. After a quick glance at the screen, he shook his head. "We have to go."

"What is it?"

"Phil says he found something in the program. He's going to check into it, and we need to get back there as quick as possible."

"Well, that's pretty mysterious. But I guess we've found out all we need here, too."

Chip nodded. "I wish we'd driven the car like we were planning to before the cop showed up at our door. Wait, we can take the university shuttle, that will save us time. Normally, there's a bit of a wait, but with so few students on campus, it's probably faster."

Minutes later, they stepped back out into the cold afternoon air. As Chip made a phone call, Blue sat at the shuttle stop, a bench, taking a moment to let her mind go blank after this long, strange morning. Her body felt jittery because she'd drunk too much coffee. Her mind raced in a thousand directions, trying to put it all together.

Who was Rebecca Burton? What was it about her that made everyone feel so strange? Who did she work for? Who attacked her, and how did they use a video game to do it? And why? Blue had no idea about any of this, but she knew she needed to see this through, at Chip's side. And for that reason, if nothing else, she felt more like her real self than she had in years.

Having finished his call, Chip addressed Blue. "Well, I was partly right. The shuttle is half-staffed, so there's a ten-minute wait. Still, it's going to be faster than trying to walk."

Blue reached out and put her hand over his, gripping his fingers tightly. "It's going to be all right."

He smiled back at her. "I know."

"Do you, now?" She felt a smirk come to her face.

Chip nodded. "Mmm-hmmm. With you by my side, this thing...whatever it is...doesn't stand a chance."

"You know it! Come here."

Chip leaned forward.

Blue gave him a kiss hot enough to send them to the public display of affection penalty box if such a thing existed. Erotic energy supercharged her body, traveled down her spine, into her legs, and settled into her stomach. For a moment, she wondered what the hell she was thinking ever giving Drew the time of day. Then she stopped thinking about Drew altogether.

Dammit, we never had any alone time.

As if he could read her mind, or her...whatever...Chip pulled back and broke their kiss. The panting she heard from him was as intense as her own. "Stop it. We don't have time." Chip smiled. "Just yet."

"I know. I couldn't help myself."

"Try harder, please."

"That's my line." She winked.

"I need to call Phil."

"Coward." She stuck her tongue out at him.

"Prudent." Chip pressed a button.

She leaned back and took a deep breath, letting the cold air calm her down. Not exactly a cold shower, but it would have to do. And, hopefully, it wouldn't have to last long.

"Hmph!"

She turned to Chip, who glared at his cell phone screen.

"What's up?"

"Phil isn't answering."

"Maybe he's grabbing a snack."

"He'd still have his phone."

At that moment, the shuttle pulled up, and the doors opened. Chip stepped in front of Blue.

The woman behind the wheel looked college age; another student who preferred to work the holiday over returning to her home situation.

He flashed a card from his billfold, then dug out a dollar and handed it over. "One guest."

Blue offered a nod of sympathy to their driver before walking past her.

They had their pick of seats on the empty shuttle. Chip grabbed the seat directly next to the door, and Blue settled in next to him. Chip stared out the window, clearly distracted or bothered.

She grabbed his hand again. "I said, it's going to be okay."

"I know."

She had no idea where they were. "How far until we get home?"

"Less than five minutes now."

"Okay, well, we'll find out. Maybe he was in the bathroom."

Chip shook his head. "That wouldn't stop him from answering."

"Oh...really? Gross. I guess that's what I get for asking."

Chip sat, eyes glued to the window, as the hospital panned away and the shuttle pulled onto the road.

Blue reached out and kneaded his shoulders. Even through his jacket, she could feel the tight knots in his muscles, the tension of his body keeping his shoulders halfway up his neck. She rubbed her thumbs over his shoulder blades, trying to get the muscles to loosen. "Relax."

"There's something wrong."

A familiar chill ran over her, it was just like...*but no. It couldn't be the same.* "We don't know anything."

Chip shook his head. "*I* know. There's something wrong."

Through her hands, his body shook as he drew a breath. She continued to rub his shoulders, the only comfort she could offer.

Like a cougar in a circus wagon waiting for a chance to pounce, Chip continued to stare out the window.

A few blocks later, Blue recognized the neighborhood. The moment the door opened, she stepped into the aisle and back, letting Chip run past her. She thanked the driver and dropped down the stairs to the curb.

"Chip, wait!" She jogged up the cement driveway, noting that Phil's Jeep still sat behind the used Chevy Chip's father had bought him for a going-away present. *So, Phil hasn't left.*

By the time she took the cement stairs to the porch, Chip had already unlocked the door and had disappeared inside the house. She could hear Chip calling out Phil's name and the lack of response.

Now it really does *feel like that night! The night that my mother...*

The thought forced her to a stop in the doorway. She couldn't walk any farther. *Oh, God, not Phil. Please, not Phil, too.*

She heard Chip open the basement door, calling down the stairs. "Phil! Answer me, now! I mean it!"

Somehow, she got her strength back and stepped across the room to the basement.

Chip was already downstairs. "Phil...Phil! Oh, God, no, speak to me!"

She stumbled down the stairs, gripping the rail and pulling herself downward. Halfway down, she saw him.

Phil, still in the computer chair, was seated in front of the screen, head craned back, eyes staring at the ceiling, lifeless.

God!

Blue dropped, her butt hitting the stair beneath her. The room started to blacken. She could hear a buzzing in her ears, and she squeezed her eyes shut, waiting for reality to return.

Chip's voice continued, panic in his tone. "Phil, Phil, snap out of it!"

She called out, her voice sounding far away in her own ears. "Is he dead?"

An eternity later, Chip answered, "No. He has a pulse."

She covered her face in her hands and wept tears of relief. *What the fuck is happening? But he's not dead, hold on to that.*

She pulled her fingers across her face as she lowered her hands.

Chip tipped Phil's head forward, stared into his eyes and called out, trying to rouse him.

Then Blue saw something on Phil's computer screen—something that froze her on the stairs. *What...the...*

She found her voice. "Chip."

"Phil, wake up! What, Blue?"

"Look at the screen."

"What?"

"Phil's screen. Look at it. Now!"

Chip stopped his ministrations to Phil's body and stood in place, as if the words took a few seconds to register. Finally, Chip pivoted and looked at the computer screen.

Chip saw what Blue saw...the wizard, Magtog the Great, proceeding down a hill toward the CGI village. With Chip no longer talking, she could hear the words from the computer speakers for the first time.

A high, tinny, mechanical voice, speaking with Phil's distinct Hoosier accent. "Blue! Chip! This is Phil! I know you'll be home any second. When you see this, get online and meet me at the Mountain Lion Inn in the courtyard. I'm heading over there now."

"What the...?" But Chip's voice failed him.

"I repeat," the wizard continued, walking under its own power with no assistance from the comatose player in the chair. "Head directly to the tavern. This is Phil! Do not wander around in the game until you speak with me! It's vitally important. I'll see you there. Chip and Blue, I know you'll be home any second..."

CHAPTER ELEVEN

Marda lay flat on the floor, prostrate before the image of Baalina. *They have returned, mistress.*

For the first time in several days, Baalina responded. *Yes, my special one, I can sense your excitement. How soon before we know?*

Marda's heart sang with joy at the direct contact. *Soon, mistress. Natalie is reviewing the folder contents and knows what to look for.* Marda considered her next thought, then offered, *Natalie was slow to make progress when we began, but since her first breakthrough hours ago, she has served you well and with distinction.*

Baalina's response reflected patience. *She will be well-rewarded, Sister. As will you all. Just as soon as I return to the physical realm.*

The Sisterhood had gained the advantage. If now, they also gained the crystal, it guaranteed they could move forward to create a brighter future. One in which the Sisterhood would no longer live in hiding, in fear, but would finally claim their place as the rightful leaders in a new hierarchy.

A hierarchy in which Marda would command, with her loyal soldiers, Van, Cyn, and Nat serving alongside her. A hierarchy in which Marda would be answerable to no one except the great Baalina herself.

The Kelranian Order had entrusted no less than the infamous Rebecca Burton to attend to the matter personally. Burton—known to the uninitiated as Agent Burton of Special Investigations.

Marda was not among the uninitiated.

She knew Burton's true purpose—her ultimate destiny.

Few people realized the threat Rebecca Burton posed to all of humanity—partly because Burton smothered her power deep within, while Marda and the Sisterhood embraced theirs.

Marda supposed she should be flattered that the Kelranian Order considered them such a threat as to send their most dangerous agent. Logically, she should be worried. But she was neither. After all, the Sisters of Baalina had struck first and gained the upper hand against the meddling Kelranian Order. With a little luck, before the rest of the Order could react, the trap would be sprung.

As soon as they returned, Cyn and Van checked in with Marda. They'd monitored the house until the police had abandoned the crime scene. Bloomington's finest had left the home supposedly secure, but, since it was a holiday and they were presumably short-handed, they didn't leave a guard behind.

Breaking in proved easy. It took only a few minutes more to determine that the bedroom mirror swung open on a hinge. Van and Cyn found the wall safe resting in a carved-out pit in the drywall behind it, sitting atop a shelf unit of some sort. The cops had already been there, so they took their time, cracked the combination and worked open the safe door, then removed the portfolio within.

They gave the bulky envelope a quick glance. Pages of notes, and a glittering red gem—perfect. They returned to their own base of operations and turned the contents over to Natalie, the true artifacts expert.

And they waited.

And so Marda waited, as well.

AS SOON AS the door opened to the basement, she rose and positioned herself at the foot of the stairs.

She felt the expression of her own face change, the smile drop away when she registered the disappointment in Nat's features. The downcast faces of Cyn and Van, who both refused to meet her gaze, confirmed her fears.

As soon as they were level on the cement slab, Cyn and Van both bowed before her. Cyn delivered the news. "We have failed you."

"What happened?"

Her gaze followed Nat, who approached a discarded side table in the midst of the stored furniture and spread the contents out across the surface. Her face neutral, Nat pulled something out of her pocket—or rather, three somethings—and let them fall onto the table, as well.

Three pieces of the crystal.

Three red, broken, jagged pieces of...a nearly indestructible crystal?

"How did...you didn't..."

Nat shook her head. "No, we didn't. If it were real, we couldn't. That's the point. It's fake. Plastic. Not even a good copy. I used a hammer and screwdriver. If this were the real Divenium Crystal, with the proper imbuement, I wouldn't even be able to scratch it, but it broke with my first blow." To her credit, if Natalie felt any pleasure in the failure of her erstwhile tormentors, her face showed only disappointment.

Marda closed her eyes. As her pulse pounded in her head, she tried to control her breathing. "And the file?"

"Equally useless. With even a cursory read, it's clearly typed pages of nonsense and false information. In a section devoted to the history of the gem itself, whoever did it was quite the smartass. They list our coven leader from the 1700s as Kitka Tatanya." Natalie giggled.

The name meant nothing to Marda, though clearly it had been meant to be mistaken for Mother Katka at first glance.

Natalie stopped herself and cleared her throat, apparently realizing no one else made the connection. "That was...Catwoman's alias from the Adam West *Batman* movie. There are other, more obvious bad jokes. The supposed list of current council members of the Kelranian Order includes Peter Porker, Edward Penishands, Dick Jones–that's from *Robocop*–Henry Beamus, from an old *Twilight Zone* episode."

Marda seethed. "They mock us!"

Natalie swallowed. "The intent of the file does seem to be to send a giant 'fuck you.'"

Marda looked down at her minions, prostrate before her. In her fury, she literally saw red spots before her eyes. Her anger burst from her in spurts, between clenched teeth. "So...Cyn...this is what you're trained for?"

"I'm sorry, Marda."

"Breaking and entering...you said...search and seizure...you said." Her hand reached to her hip, fingers clasping the hilt of her ceremonial knife. Every Sister carried one, a sign of their order, each weapon hand-crafted, with an ivory grip and the Baalina sigil carved into the handle.

She drew the blade and stepped behind the bent form. She ran her thumb along the rune.

"This is what we excel at, you said."

"Marda...please."

"You, Cyn. You. You talked me out of going. You offered your personal assurances."

Her left hand reached out, gripped Cyn's wrist, and extended her arm out to her side.

"Marda..."

"But it's not really your expertise, is it? Pain is your expertise. Pain and pleasure." She drew her blade down the thin blouse, cutting away the material to reveal a white shoulder. Such beautiful ivory skin, in perfect contrast to her short red hair. So beautiful and so deadly. "Remember what you showed me in the bedroom...just yesterday?"

With practiced flicks of her wrist, the bra straps fell away, exposing her gorgeous pale shoulder blade.

To her credit, Cyn didn't shake or grovel. She did, however, call out to her partner. "Van?"

"Sorry, Cyn, I can't help you." Van reached up and clasped her hands to her ears.

Marda leaned close, positioned the blade tip flush against the shoulder blade. "What did you teach me last night? Let's see if I can remember..."

She pressed, breaking skin.

A trail of blood marred her perfect back.

"This...brings pleasure..."

Cyn's face flushed, her breathing quickened in spite of her attempts to keep quiet. "Yes...Marda..."

"Why...so it does. But with minor adjustments...in spite of any training, regardless of any attempts to block a response, it will cause the most exquisite, burning agony...that's what you said, right?"

Beneath her fingers, Marda felt Cyn brace herself. "Yes...Marda."

Still gripping the wrist, Marda forced Cyn's arm back a quarter-inch and turned the edge of the blade into a nerve cluster just under the skin.

Cyn screamed. Her body slumped forward, her face pressed against the cement, but she continued to scream, apparently oblivious to the impact against her face.

Cyn's screams filled the chamber. Marda counted to ten, slowly. "Please...stop, Marda...it's not meant to..."

She applied the slightest pressure, and Cyn's screams renewed.

She counted again from one. Toward the end, her screams had turned hoarse.

Marda withdrew the blade.

The screams immediately ceased.

She looked down at the trembling form, openly weeping and broken before her.

Van, no longer able to remain impartial, reached out and cradled her partner, holding her and rocking her.

Though the blood flowed freely down Cyn's back, Marda could see the wound would heal quickly.

Marda knelt down behind them, speaking loudly enough to be heard over Cyn's whimpering. "The next time you two consider volunteering for something you're not entirely certain you can accomplish, don't. You wasted my time, you wasted your time, but worst of all, you wasted the mistress' time."

To Marda's astonishment, Cyn found the strength to speak. "Yes...Marda."

Marda wiped the bloodied blade on the rags of the blouse and stood. "Bandage her, then come down and clean this mess up. By the time you've finished, hopefully I'll have returned with the real crystal."

Magtog the wizard, sitting in the tavern, continued to speak in a running monologue. The sound came through the computer speakers, clearly Phil's voice, though slightly mechanized.

Blue sat, stunned, unable to pull her gaze from the screen. "Chip, what the fuck?"

"I don't know."

"Not good enough. What the fuck, Chip?"

"I *really* don't know, Blue." Chip's breathing increased.

Blue feared he might build up to a potential panic attack. *Good to know I'm not the only one having trouble processing this!* Blue shook her head at Chip. "Oh, no. You don't get to panic. That's *my* role in this partnership. You're the logical, sensible one with the answers. So, give me some logical answers, partner!"

Chip waved a hand in the air and shrugged, his confusion clear on his face.

She reached out and gripped Chip's forearm. With her other hand, she pointed at the screen, unable to control the trembling of her pointing finger. "He's unconscious here, but he's still playing there." She dared to give quick glances at Phil. His body remained slouched, with the neck craned back and mouth hanging open slack-jawed.

Chip sat in a chair at the station next to Phil's body. "I see that. I can't explain what's going on any better than you can."

Blue held onto Chip in a death grip, balancing on wobbly legs behind Chip's chair, still avoiding long looks at Phil.

So slack, so lifeless, just like her mother. That night. After she'd been...

Her gaze shifted back and forth, taking in the blank look on Phil's face, then moving toward his computer screen, which showed an over-the-shoulder view of his wizard seated at the virtual tavern.

Is he in the game? No, he can't *be in the game. That's...* She stopped herself, realizing the next word: *impossible.*

Shit.

And yet, onscreen, Phil droned on. "...head directly to the tavern. This is Phil! Do not wander around in the game until you find me!"

Chip pulled a pair of headphones over his head. He pressed the arrow keys. On the screen, Gallamar, the mousy thief, Chip's fallback character, approached the tavern.

Panic surged through her. "Chip, what do you think you're doing?"

"What does it look like?"

"Chip...given what's happened, taking your character into the game seems like a *really* bad idea."

Chip looked away from the screen and patted the hand that still held his upper arm. "You heard him. He wants us to meet him at the tavern. My character was practically there. It should be perfectly safe."

"You did *not* just say that."

Chip shrugged. "Focus on what Phil's saying. He's telling me what *not* to do, so as long as I listen, I should be okay."

A moment later, the pats on the back of her hand turned more insistent. "Uh...that kind of hurts."

"Oh." Blue relaxed her fingers, easing back the nails that must have dug deep marks into his upper arm. "Sorry."

"That's okay. Now, in spite of what I said, I don't want you logging on until we know what's going on."

Yeah, right! A nervous laugh escaped from her. "Thanks, I'll do my best to resist."

Chip's screen showed Gallamar entering the tavern. With expert control, Chip turned the avatar's head to center the tavern's front door.

Through all of this, Phil's voice droned on from the speaker. "I'm at the tavern now. If you hear me, go directly there. Don't wander the game. I'm at the entrance of the...Chip!"

The wizard appeared on Chip's screen, looking directly at Gallamar and hobbling toward him. In her peripheral vision, Blue could see the same scene play out on Phil's computer, presenting the view from behind the wizard's shoulder.

Phil's voice continued, "Please tell me you're still playing, I mean, that you're still in the basement. You didn't–"

Chip adjusted his microphone and spoke. "Yes, we're fine. I'm here, so is Blue. Can you hear me?"

On the screen, the wizard waved an arm, and a smile appeared on the CGI character's face. Even with Blue's lack of experience with this game, the look creeped her out, borderline disturbing, like rubber forced into a shape it was never designed to go.

"Loud and clear."

The wizard's lips moved in perfect synch to the words, another detail that stood out in contrast to normal play, in which no attempt was made to emulate talking.

Gallamar returned Magtog's expressive greeting with a stone face.

The look of relief, however, was clear on the wizard's CGI facial features. "Thank God. I was scared to stop talking until I heard from you. So...uh...what sort of condition is my body in?"

Steeling her courage, Blue looked over at the body, and for the first time, focused on it.

Phil slouched in the chair, breathing deeply.

He's going to wake up with a stiff neck. Blue didn't allow herself to think he might not wake up. She glanced from the chair to the couch she'd slept on last night, perhaps ten paces across the room. But moving the dead weight—she cringed at the expression—would be an impossible task by herself.

She put a hand on Chip's shoulder. "We should probably move him."

Chip nodded. "Hold on, we're going to move you to the couch." Chip grabbed Phil's ankles and waited for her to take his shoulders.

As her boyfriend stared at her, Blue realized she didn't want to touch Phil, let alone work her hands under his arms and let his head slump across her chest. But she also knew it had to be done. It was one of those times to "man up" and take care of business, or however the clichés went.

She lifted, grunting against his weight, unable to prevent his large, denim-covered butt from dragging the floor. They finally managed to lay him across the couch, his head supported by the pillow.

Moments later, huffing and puffing, they stood over Phil. Blue gave an ironic laugh. "Look at us...strapping heroes to the rescue...evil has no chance."

Chip wiped a hand across his brow. She couldn't imagine what he might be thinking. His best friend in a coma, his girlfriend showing—she admitted it—a rare case of weakness, and he was expected to be the brave one with all the answers.

And for the moment, apparently, he had none to offer. Silently, he stepped back toward the computer.

Blue followed him and grabbed his shoulder. "Chip, what if you're the one who passes out next? What am I supposed to do then?" *Jesus, when did I become the helpless damsel in distress?*

Nevertheless, she couldn't avoid the awful truth. If Chip passed out, she'd be left standing in a room full of computers and pretty much no idea what to do. *Calling 911 would be pointless.*

Chip turned to hug her. "One problem at a time. Let's just make sure it doesn't come to that. I know it's risky, but I can't play it safe right now. He's my best friend. He needs our help."

Blue didn't know how to express the contradictions of emotions bubbling around within her. She ended up hugging him and offering a lame, "Just be careful."

"Whoever did this, they messed with the wrong programmers. Someone's trying to take over my work, and I'm taking it back." He turned and looked into her eyes. "I know with you at my side, we're going to win."

She smiled, moved by his intensity. "All right, go get 'em, cornball. Sheesh!"

Chip sat back down in front of the computer.

Blue moved behind him, resting her hands on his shoulders.

Chip adjusted the mic. "You're on the couch, Phil. Your pulse is steady and strong. We just got back from seeing Rebecca Burton, one of the victims. Your condition looks remarkably similar."

Chip offered Blue a worried look. She was sure he recalled the same detail he refused to speak out loud to his friend at the moment—the same detail that came to her mind—that Rebecca's vital signs were weakening by the hour.

Chip continued, "I would guess the biggest concern is dehydration, so we have quite a bit of time to figure this out before we have to call anyone."

"No, *don't* call anyone." The emotion in the voice over the computer speaker came through loud and clear. "If you report another body, the police will shut us down immediately, holiday or no holiday."

That didn't seem quite so obvious to Blue. "Don't worry; if it comes to it, we can just move your body into the other room and call someone," she said.

Phil spoke up, "Blue, I'm the lead programmer of the game. The second Officer Kirby finds out I'm in the same condition as the other hospitalized victims, no way is he going to think that it's some unrelated coincidence."

"Well...good point. But what if you get in trouble?"

"Look, we know the agent and her assistant have been stable for at least a day. Let's give it that long. Besides, if they confiscate this program and shut it down...well, my *mind is* in here. We don't know what that will do to me."

Chip considered. "Probably nothing good. Agreed. Okay, Phil, why don't you share with us what you know about–"

A new voice cut in, the words through the computer also distorted, but clearly feminine and youthful. "There he is! I told you if we kept checking back here, we'd find him."

Two additional CGI characters approached the table in the tavern. One was a tall, blonde warrior woman dressed in a knight's suit of armor, gripping a large mace. As Chip waved his mouse pointer on her body, the name Cloud McSky hovered over her head for a few seconds and dissolved.

The second, coming up behind McSky, was a striking figure, unlike any other Blue had seen in the game. She stood, garbed in white body armor, long red hair billowing around her. Her skin radiated an intense gold. A pair of tremendous wings folded back against her shoulder blades.

Beautiful! I want a character like that! Blue noted how the other avatars turned to look at her. Even Chip, using the directional arrows, tweaked his screen to center on the golden angel. His cursor revealed the name, Arby.

Chip shook his head. "Hmph. 'R.B.' indeed. Very punny, Rebecca Burton. Now I remember seeing your name on our reports. And here I just thought we had a player with a fast food fetish."

The angel figure replied in a dignified, feminine voice that matched her visual. "And you must be Eugene Farren. It's nice to finally 'meet' you. You'll pardon me if I don't shake your hand."

"That's okay," said Chip. "Now, first things first. Am I in danger just by being online right now?"

"No," said Phil.

Though the avatar's name read as McSky, Blue thought of her by her real-world name: MacLeod. "I wouldn't think so. Just stay away from the cave and you should be fine."

"So it would be safe for Blue to come online, as well?"

Oh, now wait a second...

Chip lowered his microphone. "Blue, why don't you get on your character so we can all talk at the tavern?"

Blue looked over at Phil's body. "So I should put myself in danger of going into a coma so they don't think I'm being rude?"

"They say it should be fine."

Blue folded her arms across her chest. "Oh, good, the three *geniuses* stuck in the game say it's perfectly safe."

Chip stabbed and held down a button on the keyboard—presumably a mute—and shot Blue a dirty look. "Not cool."

Blue shot back a dirtier look. "It's not smart, and you know it."

Chip released a sigh. "No, you're right. I'm not thinking straight." He un-muted and spoke into the microphone. "Blue is going to stay offline for now, in case something goes wrong."

Phil spoke up. "Safety first. I get it."

"So, okay," said Chip, "What happened, and why?"

Phil's avatar shook its head. "I think I know, sorta. To find out what might have happened to Rebecca and MacLeod, I printed off their movement report, booted up Magtog, and started shadowing them...maybe not the best plan, in retrospect."

Blue shook her head. "Clearly not."

"Chip, you can see my report there to the side of the keyboard. See the spot I highlighted?"

Chip grabbed the paper and showed the sheet to Blue. The page displayed four columns of numbers in a series list. Beyond the numbers themselves, Blue could not make heads or tails of it. She shrugged and handed the list back to Chip.

Chip glanced at the numbers as he explained, "Each player's set of coordinates is auto-recorded every fifteen minutes in case we want to go back and..."

As if physically struck, his head tipped back, taken aback by something on the list. "Hey! What the hell?"

Phil's tone spoke his approval. "You found it, I see."

"Segment 67, land 1, 245, 90, 12?"

"Yep."

Frustrated, Blue smacked Chip's arm. "Stop the geek-speak a minute. What does it mean?"

"We've only programmed 66 land segments into the game so far."

Phil piped up, "But someone else programmed a segment 67. There's also a segment 68, 69, and 70."

"Someone's added areas to our game!" Chip sounded almost as upset by the unauthorized addition of virtual real estate as the condition of his best friend.

Chip held the list out to Blue at eye level, his thumb indicating the column listing Segment 67, land 1, 245, 90, 12. "Think of the last three numbers as longitude, latitude and height—x, y, z coordinates for 3D mapping."

Blue sighed, staring at the list. "I hope I don't regret this—why the third point?"

"Land mass. This list shows where an avatar stood on the map. Plus, we have to have it to plot hills, valleys, and water depth, so there's a certain change in height charted as they move."

"Oh. That was a remarkably simple explanation."

Chip grinned. "It's not *all* magic. Just *most* of the time."

Phil continued, "I'll just cut right to it. If you head east and go up the first hill, there's the large tree—the one you based on the one in our backyard. If you look carefully, there's a small hole at the root of the tree. A dark space. You'd look past it if you weren't trying to find it. It's a cave. Any avatar clicking on it can go in there. But once you're standing at the entrance..."

MacLeod spoke up. "That's how Rebecca found it. She was tracking another player who walked to the base of the tree and then logged off."

Chip said, "And that's when she noticed the portal at the base."

Burton's eyes looked toward the tavern floor as she spoke. "And then I...well, in retrospect, my next actions were not the most prudent."

Blue cringed. *Burton noticed the opening, closed in for a better look, and fell right into the booby trap. In doing so, she created a trail that lured two more boobies.*

Burton spoke in a low, shamed voice, like a defendant forced into admitting their guilt. "I hadn't considered the possibility of a magic spell that could...do something like this. She must have known I was tailing her and brought me there on purpose."

Skye continued, "And I stumbled onto it when I went looking for Rebecca."

"Okay," said Chip. "No sense kicking yourself too hard about something that can't be changed. But what's in the cave?"

Magtog's shoulders bent in a very real shrug. "Who cares? It's just a dark space. Most likely, nothing. The hackers placed it as a lure to attract their tech-savvy adversaries. And it worked. Once you realize you've been yanked out of your body and dropped into a CGI avatar, you sort of lose your sense of adventure. I just backed away."

"That's what happened to us, too," said MacLeod. "By the way...uh, how's my body?"

Chip answered, "We didn't visit you. I'm told your condition is similar to Rebecca's."

"Oh." The disappointed tone in MacLeod's voice was plain, even through the speaker. "And what condition is that?"

Chip and Blue exchanged looks. Chip stabbed the mute button. "Do we tell them?"

Blue shook her head. "It's not like they're not already doing everything they can."

Chip nodded and released the button. "You're both in a coma, but stable. The sooner we get you back where you belong, the better."

Rebecca's avatar stepped forward, the golden glow intensifying on her body. "Now we know *what* happened. I think I can offer up some idea about *why*. And then we need to formulate a plan of action."

Chip started, "Well, actually that's what we–"

"We have three people stuck in the game that we know of, and two allies outside in the real world." Rebecca paced an open space by the table, her avatar glowing as she spoke. "Is there anyone else unaccounted for?"

Chip tried again. "Uh, no, but–"

"Okay, so we need someone to go to our residence off-campus. We've hidden some important documents that I doubt the police noticed." She paused, pondering. "However, the Sisterhood of Baalina will probably send someone as soon as they realize we're stuck in here."

Chip practically snarled into the microphone. "Hold on. The sister of what? Back up, I think you need to start over."

Rebecca continued, apparently oblivious to Chip's comments. "For that matter, as soon as the Sisterhood realizes that one of the programmers has been brought into the conflict, they may send agents over to your house."

"What?" Chip exclaimed.

The angel turned toward Gallamar. "You two, what are your capabilities? Can you defend yourselves?"

Chip looked at Blue and rolled his eyes. He stabbed the mute button. "Wow, isn't she a bit bossy?"

Blue nodded. "Sounds like she's used to being in charge."

She leaned forward, putting her face close to Chip's mic and motioned to him to take his finger off the mute. "The programmer goes by the name Chip. You can call me Blue." She flashed Chip her most smoldering look.

He responded with a flush.

She licked her lips before continuing, "I would normally debate this point, but since we're operating mostly in the computer realm, I'll concede that he's the brains, and I'm the muscle."

Burton's avatar nodded. "Okay, let me think."

Chip reached out and hit the mute button with one hand. With his other hand, he lifted the mic over his head, leaned in, and gave her a short but electrifying kiss.

She tried to return the favor.

Chip broke the kiss. "Bad! Focus. You're distracting me," he teased.

Blue shook off the afterglow. "Yeah, whatever, we both needed that."

Chip smiled, "Yeah, maybe I did."

She smiled back at him. "Think of it as another reminder of what you're fighting for."

Burton's voice reached them from the speakers. "Okay, Phil just transferred into the game, so we probably have several hours before the Sisterhood figures it out."

Blue cringed, saying aloud, "Did she ever clarify who the Sisterhood is?"

Apparently, the microphone picked her up, because the angel spoke directly to Chip's avatar as Burton continued. "The Sisterhood is an ancient cult committed to the demon Baalina, who draws power from the stealing of souls."

Blue brushed her fingers against Chip's hand, and he released the mute button. She said, "Cult...as in Satanists?"

"Yes."

"But that's not possi...fuck!" *There's that phrase again!*

"Did you break up? I don't think I caught that."

Blue cleared her throat. "Sorry, I said, Satanist cult stealing souls. Sounds dangerous. What can we do?"

"The Sisterhood managed to reproduce an ancient relic within the virtual realm. The relic was originally destroyed over two hundred years ago. It's called a SoulStaff." Rebecca hesitated. "What I'm about to propose is going to sound fantastic. But I understand you two have had previous experience with the supernatural."

Chip and Blue traded expressions of shock and surprise.

Chip stabbed the mute button. "You want to field that, or should I?"

"Maybe Phil told her?"

"Phil wouldn't do that," Chip insisted.

"Okay...sorry. Let me talk." After Chip released the mute, Blue said, "Some, yes. Can I ask how you know that?"

"I'm a paranormal investigator. Few events of a supernatural nature can occur without my being aware of them sooner or later. My point is, your past experience might prepare you for what I'm about to say, but it might not."

"Try us."

"The SoulStaff was designed for one thing and one thing only. It drains souls from the people around it and uses those souls as magical energy to create a portal to summon Baalina, a bound demoness banished to the chaos realm. Let loose, Baalina is powerful enough that she could potentially subjugate the city, maybe a big chunk of the Midwest. A group of her followers hacked this game platform to test their powers before applying them to the physical world."

Chip spoke up. "Wait, you're saying they plan to raise a demon in our game?"

"A virtual version of the demon, yes."

Blue and Chip exchanged baffled looks.

*Well that's...*this time, Blue's mind did not conjure up impossible. *Ludicrous.* Blue shrugged. "I don't get it."

From Chip's tone, she guessed *he* didn't get it, either. "Yeah, seriously, why? To what purpose?"

Burton paused. "My best guess is that a virtual fantasy game is one of the few places where a giant demon can be conjured before dozens of spectators and be dismissed by the witnesses as ambiance."

Chip's brows crinkled. "Well, that sort of makes sense, I suppose. But what's the point?"

The angel nodded. "Before anyone would know what has happened, the demon would draw off all the souls of the players in the game and use those souls to open a gateway into the real world."

The words hit Blue like a sack of bricks to the gut. *Are you shit-*

ting me? She moved away from the computer screen. The layers of impossibilities left her numb. *Demons. Soul stealing. End of the world stuff, and Chip has created the perfect laboratory for them to experiment in.*

The silence lingered.

Finally, Phil cut in. "Great! And you didn't come to us and tell us...why?"

Skye looked down, almost shame-faced at being called out. "We weren't actually sure *what* was going on. We just knew key members of the Sisterhood had gathered in Bloomington and had taken an interest in your game. That's why I've been on campus all these weeks, to explore the game and search the area. We didn't really know what they had planned...well, until this happened." Her tone projected pure misery.

"It's okay," said Phil, the anger leaving his voice. "I'm sure you did all you can."

"Doesn't feel like it, now," moaned Skye.

"It's okay," said Phil. "We're all going to get out of this, and then laugh about it later."

The exchange touched Blue. *Phil has someone to worry about. I guess that could be a good thing. I just hope he's right, and we really do have a later to laugh about it.* "So, what do we do now?"

The golden angel figure continued to pace her area, her wings occasionally fluttering. "There's a dossier hidden in our headquarters," Burton offered.

"We rented an off-campus residence," added MacLeod.

Rebecca picked up the story. "Someone from the Sisterhood will undoubtedly try to find our file once they figure out that both Skye and I are no longer there. It contains a history of the Sisterhood, as well as the Divenium Crystal."

Blue braced herself. "And that is?"

"A crystal of white magic imbued by the Kelranian Order and used to defeat them over three hundred years ago."

"Of course. We girls have to accessorize."

As Rebecca rattled off the street address, Blue jotted it down.

Chip nodded his head. "That's just a few blocks from here. Ten-minute walk, tops."

Burton continued, "In the bedroom, you'll see a mirrored vanity. The mirror swings out to reveal a hollowed-out wall with a safe."

Blue considered. "Really? Is that going to work if they send someone over to do a serious search?"

"No, but a fake file in the safe, plus the fact that the dossier is taped in the hollow of the drywall above the safe, might."

"Hmmm...maybe. In any case, you need me to get the file?"

"The sooner, the better."

"Okay," said Blue. "That's something I understand. I'm on it."

"Be careful," advised Burton. "We've identified the leader of the group here in IU as Marda Mercedes, and from what we can tell, she's quite dangerous."

Blue shrugged. "Yeah, well, so am I."

Chip whipped off the headset, concern in his eyes. "Are you sure?"

Blue nodded. "Yep. You said it was a few blocks away, right? Just point me in the right direction. I'll be back in no time."

Chip hesitated. "Are you...do you want me to come with you?"

Blue smiled. "No, offense, great hunter, but you'll only slow me down. Besides, you'll do a lot more good in this pow-wow huddle." *I, on the other hand, need to get out of here before I go crazy.*

"But you don't know what you're walking into."

"Look, Chip, if I stop now to think about all the elements and ramifications of what we're dealing with—demons, souls, covens, Phil's life—I'm going to freak out, and I'll be useless to you."

Chip leaned back from the force of her outburst.

"You wanna know how I got through that night with Gunther's ghost? I didn't think about my mom having just died or what that would mean." Blue clenched her hands into fists. "I just focused on what had to happen next. Right now, I need to get a folder and bring it back to this house. That's what needs to happen. And I can do that." She drew a breath. "Just let me do that."

Chip looked away, clearly not happy. "All right. Be careful. Take your phone, and be back soon."

Blue offered a smile, hoping it reassured. "Sure. Show me where your tool kit is. I don't have my lockpicks with me—hell, I'm not even sure where they are these days. Packed away in New York, I guess. But I can make a couple of mini-screwdrivers work."

Chip nodded. "Right. Okay, follow me."

Moments later, in the garage, Chip handed Blue two mini screwdrivers from the toolbox. "Be careful, and call me if anything happens. This could be incredibly dangerous."

"I will, but you be careful, too." She leaned in and gave him a kiss she hoped he wouldn't forget for a long time.

CHAPTER THIRTEEN

Where is it, you Kelranian bitch! Marda scanned the trashed great room. She'd torn open the couch, knocked over the bookshelves, gutted each thick book, amd punctured the walls.

With a swift kick of her combat boot, she sent the office chair tumbling across the room. She looked around the rented duplex.

The quaint, dark-wood cabinets and furnishings clashed with the modern track lighting and movie posters that once hung on the walls—before Marda had knocked them down. The sturdy wood front door opened into a modest sitting room with multiple bookshelves and chairs, retreating directly back to a dining room, with a swinging door to the kitchen beyond.

A hallway from the dining room breaking to the side and running parallel to the kitchen led to the only bathroom and two bedrooms. Efficient for two roommates without the extras. Small enough to search in about ten minutes.

Marda had been trashing it for over half an hour.

Given the stillness when she first entered, Marda was certain the connected neighbors had to be vacationing for the holidays. Now she knew it, because they would have called the police for certain, given the ruckus she'd made as her frustration built up.

Tricked! Even now, trapped in the game realm, Burton had found a way to trick them.

Somewhere here in the house, Rebecca and her right-hand woman, MacLeod, had stashed the damned Divenium Crystal. *So, where the hell is it!*

She returned to the larger of the two bedrooms, her eyes scanning the space, falling upon an antique ivory desk set against the far wall. She took in the art deco vanity next to it.

In the mirror, her angry face reflected back at her, including the distortion caused by her crinkled eyebrows. She knew about the safe behind the mirror, the red herring that had tricked Cyn and Van. She wouldn't waste time pursuing the same false lead.

She noted a conspicuous rectangular space of emptiness and the shifted dust outline on the desk's wooden surface, indicating a PC or laptop computer that likely filled the spot a few hours earlier, a computer now confiscated by the local police.

A computer that almost certainly had no information of any real use.

No, the file is still here. Someplace hidden. Someplace tricky.

A rattling of wood—the door from the back of the house—froze her in place. *What the...*

More noises. Metal against metal, and a doorknob being shaken, the frame straining to resist an intruder pressing from the other side. *The police!*

No, more likely, back-up agents sent by Burton to retrieve the folder before we obtain it. Burton had plenty of time to get a message out, something she could have set up before getting trapped in the virtual world.

Now that mechanism had been triggered, and Burton's backup had arrived.

Thank you, Goddess!

She reached to the sheath at her waist and gripped the hilt of her knife. She spied the bedroom closet.

She opened the door, pleased at the sparseness of clothes and personal items within, offering plenty of room to slip inside and wait.

All she needed to do was to bide her time until the newcomers retrieved the folder, then eliminate them.

———

DOWN ON ONE KNEE, Blue wiggled the screwdriver tip under what she hoped was the final pin. She lifted it up flat and out of the way, pressing it flush with the others, then probed farther into the keyhole shaft. She tried to calm herself, control her anxious panting, and ignore the shakes in her hands.

Resistance, and nothing to pry. She'd reached the end, which should mean...

She extended the second tip into the keyhole and gave a simple twist.

The doorknob turned easily.

She gripped the doorknob and pulled the door open.

She waited, listening.

Nothing.

Her noisy lock-picking ruined any hope of surprise, but if the house was empty, as she hoped, it shouldn't matter.

Still, she couldn't ignore the possibility that someone had beaten her here and now waited inside to ambush her.

She reached down and retrieved the screwdrivers. She grinned. *I've still got it!*

She pocketed the tools and ran a sleeve across her forehead. *I haven't done that since...*

It always comes back to that *night, doesn't it?*

The door opened into a small kitchen with painted cabinets and an oven with four stovetop gas burners. The wood looked from an older home, while the spotty psychedelic patterned paint job, modern microwave, and espresso machine told the story of college-age renters going back decades.

All the cabinet doors had been flung open, and the pots and pans and cans tipped over or re-stacked haphazardly. Blue figured the police had gone through the cabinets and found nothing.

She pushed open the swinging door next to the oven, which opened out onto...*holy shit!*

A dining table, and beyond it, a ransacked front room. Destroyed. Furniture flipped, two bookcases toppled, office supplies, clothes, and doodads all vomited onto the floor, with coats dumped out before an open front closet.

She didn't know from firsthand experience, but she didn't think the police would leave chairs and closets turned out. *The desk chair, on the floor, sideways. Why not at least pick that up and put it back? Surely, it would potentially trip any sort of evidence team.*

And tearing books in half at their spine? That didn't strike her as a preferred method of a team search who had the space to themselves.

That's the act of someone in a hurry. Someone who doesn't care about inflicting damage.

She noted the hallway that presumably led to the bedrooms beyond. She closed her eyes and listened.

Just the rustling of grass, the heater powering up to blow dry air through old vents. *Creaky wood. What caused the creaking? Footsteps in the other room? Neighbors next door?*

Maybe, or maybe just the house settling.

Of course, that didn't mean anything. If the Sisterhood had taken the bait, they'd eventually figure out the switch and come back. *Either I beat them to it, or I didn't. If I didn't, it doesn't matter. If I did, I'm wasting precious time.*

Or...someone may be waiting here for me.

Still, standing here frozen, trying to calm her nerves, would not accomplish anything.

She looked down at her trembling hands like some sort of alien body part springing from her wrists. *Jesus, Blue, what's wrong with you? Why are you so rattled?*

The thought dawned on her that, screwdrivers aside, she'd come into the situation unarmed. She could hardly have brought her switchblade with her. There was just no getting around airport security with something like that.

Plus, why *would* she bring it? *This wasn't supposed to be* that *sort of a trip.*

She needed a weapon.

She didn't see the usual wooden block of steak knives, and opening a drawer revealed some silver butter knives and a couple smallish, serrated steak knives all the rage, she would have guessed, back in the 1960s.

I guess college kids don't leave steak knife sets behind. And just my luck, looks like Burton and MacLeod didn't eat in much.

She wrapped her fingers around the handle of one of the serrated blades. It would have to do.

She approached the bedroom door, scanning the hallway, and straining to listen for any unnatural sound.

Is someone there? She waited for telling creaks of wood, or other noises. Outside, a car passed by, and, a few houses away, slowed. The engine cut off. The age of the house pressed on her. *Better to just go and try to get the hell out.*

She threw open the door and looked along the wall. Her gaze traveled over the closed door of a closet. *Why is that door closed? Or am I second-guessing myself?*

If I check the closet, and someone's there, I might not be able to see what's coming toward me before it's too late. If I go across the room and let them think they can spring a trap, they'll have to come to get me. Do I trust my ability to fight my way out that *much?*

She did.

Besides, it may be nothing.

A queen-sized bed stretched out to her right, headboard against the far wall. The covers had been turned over to one side. She didn't see any pillows from where she stood.

Cautiously, dividing her attention between her goal and the closet behind her, she approached the vanity mirror over the ivory desk.

She gripped the left side of the mirror and pulled. It stuck tight.

Panic rushed through her. In the mirror, she saw her face flush. *What's up? Why won't it...*

She took a deep breath, reached to the right side of the mirror, and pulled.

The mirror gave easily, swinging on hinges.

Behind the mirror, she saw a literal hole in the wall. A fireproof combination lock safe sat upon the shelved alcove. The wall looked punched through with a hammer, maybe several blows of a hammer, jagged edges surrounding an opening just large enough to build a shelf and fit the safe.

She reached up and slipped her hand into the gap above the safe and encountered an open space in the drywall above it.

She extended her arm to the back wall, probing with her fingers. *Nothing there, but...*She turned her hand, reached and reached forward, pressing her palm to explore the back side of the nearer wall.

Aha! Something was taped against the inner wall, a package of some sort, exactly the size of a bulging folder. She could feel the masking tape straining over the bulk.

She gripped the bottom of the package and pulled.

The package tore away from the wall, and she lowered a red portfolio folder, bulging, with accordion sides, strips of tape still marring its surface. *Gotcha!*

She held the packet in one hand, patting at it with the other. Pieces of drywall dumped into the room, kicking up a cloud of white dust that made her eyes water.

She coughed and waved the envelope to clear the air.

"So!"

At the sound of the crazed voice, Blue startled. She turned.

Framed in the closet door stood a tall, long-haired brunette. She raised her arm, and the sunlight from the window glinted off a large, ornate blade.

Fuck...figures!

She gripped the handle of her own inadequate weapon, waiting for her opponent to make the first move.

To Blue's surprise, her inner panic subsided. She'd half-expected an ambush, but what she really feared was an ambush of superior numbers or greater skill.

Blue sized the stranger up. Whoever this woman was, she knew nothing about how to fight. She stood before Blue in an awkward stance, gripping the knife to come down overhand like a movie slasher instead of underhand for greatest effect.

A dumbass attack like that would be easy to avoid. Crazy, perhaps, but, she was certain, not skilled.

Still, she reminded herself, *overconfidence can also kill.*

The crazed look in the woman's eyes matched her zealous tone. "My Sisters were closer than they knew! Now I'll return with the real package, triumphant."

Blue placed the folder down on the desk and turned to face her opponent. "Marda, I've handled worse than you while hungover, 'Sister.' You'd better put that knife away before you get hurt."

Her opponent's eyes widened at the use of the name. "How did you..." Then she stopped short.

"Terrible poker face, Marda." Blue pressed forward, putting her body between the nut job and the folder. She'd faced down Gunther and the horrors of that night. This bitch wasn't even in the same league.

The woman extended her arm, palm out. "Hand over the folder, and maybe I'll let you live."

Blue kept her gaze on Marda's other hand, the one still gripping her knife. "Put the knife down. Maybe I won't take it before I break your nose."

With a guttural growl, the woman lunged, swiping the knife.

Blue stepped aside, let her own useless weapon fall to the floor, gripped the woman's arm with both of her hands, and pulled her close.

Blue twisted, propelled herself, using the full weight of her body to throw her adversary off balance.

They toppled. Blue's opponent slammed to the floor, only to have Blue's body come down on top of her.

The woman went slack.

Blue's hands gripped the wrist with the knife. She dropped into the crook of the woman's arm with her shoulder, pinning it under her.

Her opponent gasped, and Blue twisted.

They glared at each other, face-to-face.

Blue pinched her attacker's arm in a v-lock. In a quick move, Blue released her opponent's right hand and thrust her arm forward, palm-first, striking the woman's face.

Blue's blow struck the nose with a satisfying crunch.

Her opponent's yelp cut off short; her face jerked back. Blood gushed, and the woman's eyes watered.

Renewing her grip on the wrist, Blue shifted, bringing her weight full against the crook of the woman's arm. As the bone extended to the verge of fracture, the woman drew a sharp breath.

The woman's wrist twisted, waving the knife through the air.

Blue shook her head. The sound of her intense panting filled the room. *She's a feisty bitch, for all the good it'll do her.* "No, you don't!"

The woman fought, and Blue struggled to re-secure her grip, her breath coming in gasps from the exertion. But it wasn't much of a fight.

Blue gripped the wrist again and bent the arm one last time at the breaking point. "Enough. Drop...the...knife." She pressed.

The woman drew in a sharp breath.

"I'm not kidding you, bitch!"

With a cry of frustration, the woman let the knife fall to the ground.

"Thank you."

Blue pivoted and thrust her elbow into the woman's face, connecting with her chin.

The woman coughed, then went slack.

Blue grabbed up the knife and rose to a crouch, holding the blade in one hand while she caught her breath.

But her caution wasn't necessary. The woman lay on the floor, blood sprayed against her nose, her arms and legs slack.

Blue stood, drawing air in deep gulps, waiting for her hammering heart to quiet.

The tussle had winded her more than it should have. *Good God, am I getting old?*

Her breathing steadied, so she stumbled to the desk, grabbed up the packet, and held it under her arm.

What to do? She couldn't carry the woman back to Chip's house. She didn't have time to interrogate her. *Like I even know what to ask.*

The woman moaned, and her eyes fluttered open.

Blue crouched, reached out with the knife, and pressed the edge under her neck.

They locked gazes, and Blue's inner voice spoke to her in a tempting whisper. *Just slice her throat. Leave her here. It would solve a lot of problems. Just do it.*

The thought repulsed her. *No!*

Blue flashed back to when she'd threatened Clinty, the school bully who harassed her and Chip back in Perionne, in a similar manner. The anger coursed through her that night, tangible, fierce. Clinty's fate rested in her hands. She'd wondered if she might not kill him, and she drank that power in like a drug.

Marda started to move.

Blue pressed the knife. "Don't try it."

Marda submitted, her body going slack.

This time, Blue felt no thrill, no power, only a profound sadness at seeing this lost woman.

A smile formed on Marda's face. "You're not...going to kill me. That's not what you do." Marda laughed. "You're too good, too...*merciful.*" Blood, which had leaked to her mouth from her nose, sprayed with her next words. "Too *weak.*"

Are you kidding me? Blue shook her head. "I am not *that* girl, I promise you."

"Then prove it. Kill me, if you're so strong."

Disgusted, Blue stood, drew her foot back and kicked the woman in the side.

She rolled over and curled up. The woman lay and struggled for air, too stunned to move.

It will have to do. Blue extended the envelope down, just within the woman's vision, shaking it like a cat owner teasing their pet. "Tell your people you failed. Tell them to forget whatever you have in mind and just get the hell out of here. We now have what you needed. You're not getting it back. Next time, I won't be so gentle."

Blue turned her back and stepped toward the door. As she exited the room, a mocking cry followed after her. "Coward."

Made it! Blue burst into Chip's house, paused long enough to shut the front door, and made a beeline for the basement.

As she approached, the door opened.

Chip held his arms out in a hug, relief apparent on his face. "Thank God."

She all but dove into his arms, nuzzling her cheek against his chest and holding tight. Finally, she could allow her body to tremble. *Figures,* now *the shakes hit.*

"Hey...hey! Whoa, what happened?"

His hands gripped her shoulders and gently pushed her back.

She obliged, letting herself relax to his guidance so he could take a good look.

His eyes widened. "Oh, my God, are you hurt?"

She looked down at herself, startled to see red streaks across her denim jacket and t-shirt. *Blood.* "No, it's okay; it's her blood, not mine."

"Hers?"

Blue shrugged, hoping she projected unconcern. "One of the Baalin-istas or whatever. She tried to ambush me. Just let me clean up."

Chip continued to hover. "Are you sure?"

"Trust me, it might have been one of the most pathetic attempts at an assault in the history of assaults. And lookie," she pulled the dagger from the loop of her denim jeans, speckled with blood. "A souvenir." She extended the knife toward him.

"Oh, my God." His eyes widened. "You didn't..."

She realized how it looked and chuckled. "No, but it took all the reserve I had *not* to. She had no idea how outmatched she was. Even when I gave her a busted nose to remember me by. She bled all over the place, but I left her alive and probably very pissed off."

"She's going to be even more pissed off when she checks in with her coven."

The sheepish grin on Chip's face caught Blue's attention. *Oh-oh.* "What did you do?"

"The bitches hacked my game. *My* game." Chip jabbed his index finger back at himself.

She knew he had another revelation for her. "They dropped an unauthorized object into the code and used it before we knew about it."

"The SoulStaff, right?"

"So I found their hack and deleted the SoulStaff." He slapped his hands together and rubbed his fingers, a mimic of sprinkling magic dust. "Added a block to keep them from trying the same trick again."

"Oh." She raised a hand. "High five on that. So, is this over?"

He brushed his fingers against hers, causing an answering tingle down her spine she knew she should ignore.

Chip looked at the floor. "I'm afraid not."

"Why not?" She handed the folder to Chip.

"Because...no matter how awesome I think I am, I'm sure there are several more ways for them to hack the game that I'm not aware of. But, they have to re-render the SoulStaff, just as we have to render the crystal. Rather than them attacking us before we're ready, it's a dead heat as to who gets finished first."

Instead of heading directly downstairs, she decided to detour across the hall into the bathroom. She supposed that was good news, but she hoped to hear about a knockout punch that would end this craziness. "What's going on in the game now?"

She snapped on the light switch. The row of light globes over the bathroom mirror illuminated a pea-green sink, matching walls, toilet lid cover, and the clear plastic curtain cupping the shower.

"We've kind of camped out by the large oak tree. If the Sisterhood wants to come in and get to Baalina, they have to come through us. In the meantime, the group has been dueling like crazy."

At Blue's confused look, Chip clarified, "It's formalized practice, built into the game so players practice fighting in the game. In this case, they're using it to get used to their virtual bodies." Chip opened a linen closet and handed her a washcloth. "It's...well, it's quite impressive, actually."

"How so?" She turned on the cold water, dropped the washcloth into the basin, and pulled the drain stop to let it fill.

She looked at herself in the mirror. A distinct splatter of blood had sprayed her across the face and neck. Possibly her hair, as well. She squinted at her blue locks...*well, three-quarters blue with dark roots.*

She saw no obvious signs of blood splatters in her hair and figured daily shampooing would clean what she couldn't see. She assessed her clothes.

Ick. Streaks marred the chest of her Paramore t-shirt. It looked badass, but she sure didn't want to wear it much longer.

Chip extended the dagger, handle-first, at her. "Well...it's clear that Rebecca, Phil, and MacLeod have a huge advantage by virtue of having bonded with their avatar, at least in terms of combat. Phil could never beat me when we'd battle in 'mock-duel mode' the standard way, with both of us using the keyboard."

She gripped the blade just long enough to drop it back into the water, using the washcloth to scrub it clean. "And?"

"And, he's wiped the floor with me in over thirty fights now. I don't mean by a little bit, either. We have no way to be sure, but I'd say Phil's character's reflexes have improved forty to sixty percent, maybe more."

She held the blade up, now clean and ready to drip-dry. *Gorgeous.* The ornate, hand-carved handle fit her palm comfortably.

She examined the ivory hilt and traced her thumb along a hand-carved symbol, like an ornate X. A sigil, she guessed. *Baalina, I presume? These ladies may be warped psychos, but they make an incredible weapon.*

The business end extended about six inches, fine metal, thin, razor sharp...She held it up, vertical and eye level. Perfectly straight. It didn't look manufactured. Custom-made by an expert craftsman, she was sure of it.

*Most likely a crafts*woman, she realized. Between what Agent Burton had said and hearing the woman's rants for herself, she suspected the Baalina-ettes followed a strict, no-testosterone policy.

Too bad I didn't think to take the sheath, as well.

Her mind returned to the conversation. Chip was still moaning about Phil kicking his ass. "Maybe you're just tired."

Chip shook his head. "Don't get me wrong. Yes, I'm tired, but truthfully, Phil likes programming the games a lot more than he enjoys playing them. He just isn't very good."

"You might still be having a bad day."

Chip sighed. "Rebecca, who told me she logs on only when she has to, was also experimenting with combat. She trounced my ass a few times, too."

"Oh." She cut off the cold water and looked at her reflection in the mirror. She really had no choice but to ditch the shirt and soak it. She thought she might be able to spot-clean the jacket, though. "Well...that could be good for our side when it comes down to it."

The look on Chip's face, reflected in the mirror, drew her attention to him. "What?"

Chip looked away. "Nothing."

Nothing, my ass. She knew the look of someone who wanted to approach a subject but didn't know how to start. "Hey, I need to change this shirt." She let the denim jacket fall past her shoulders, offering her best come-on smile. "Be a dear, go downstairs and fetch me a new one from my backpack, and I'll let you watch."

Chip was already on his way at the words "I'll let you."

The thump-thump-thump of descending feet racing down the basement stairs reached her, and she let out a stress-relieving giggle. *And I almost let this dear, dear guy go. What the hell was I thinking?*

———

MARDA MERCEDES BRACED herself in the chair. Her hand gripped Van's, and her legs pressed into the cement floor. Behind her, Van's other hand stroked her hair.

Cyn looked down on her with a stone-cold, unreadable expression. "It's going to hurt like hell."

Marda gulped, trying to control the trembling in her voice. "I know that. You already told me. Just do it."

"I mean, it's *really* going to hurt like hell." If Cyn felt any satisfaction at the cruel trick fate had played upon them, she gave no indication.

Deep down, Marda had no doubt Cyn would enjoy every second of what would follow. Marda wiped the back of her hand across her forehead, swiping cold, clammy perspiration. "You just told me the cartilage shifted out of alignment, and there's no chance it will heal properly without shifting it back." She tried to ignore the nasal quality of her own voice in her head. "I intend to rule, regal and unscarred, beside the mistress. As will we all. Do it. Besides, you owe me a little pain. Don't tell me you can't appreciate what's happened."

Cyn nodded and lowered both hands toward Marda's face. She allowed a half-smile to creep over her features.

Marda tried and failed to keep a shiver out of her voice with her next words. "Just promise me you and Van will use your expertise to deliver a payback in full for all that we've suffered."

"She shall suffer as no one has."

The cracking noise was lost to a blast of blinding pain. Her world exploded in white stars.

Marda screamed, a shriek of agony that did nothing to help her. Her body spasmed.

A moment later, she opened her eyes. Her breathing forced from her in pants. She realized she'd have fallen out of the chair if Van hadn't held her up, both hands on her shoulders, steadying her. "Goddess!"

Cyn extended a bottled water. "Easy, it's over. It's still going to hurt, but you got through the worst of it." She knelt down.

Marda noted how Cyn's gaze scanned her face like she controlled some personal, built-in targeting.

"It looks straight now. I think that did it. I hope so. I can't imagine you want to do that again."

"No!" She spat the next words at Cyn. "And you'd better have not done it wrong on purpose just to..." She stopped herself.

Van's hands squeezed a warning against Marda's shoulders.

For the first time, Van spoke, her breath hissing in Marda's ear. "My partner and I have been gracious and loyal to your every whim, Priestess. If our service has been less than perfect, we have always acted with the best intentions and without subterfuge."

Cyn punctuated her partner's thought. "Your words could be interpreted as...disingenuous." She let the veiled threat hover.

Marda looked at the floor. She wanted to rise from the chair, strike these two down, and punish them because she couldn't punish the blue-haired bitch who'd humiliated her and put her in this position. That they'd refrained from treatong her the way she'd treated them only added to her shame.

But she needed these two. She waited and took time to swallow back her anger before she spoke again. "Forgive me. Forget my words." She drew a deep, calming breath. "It was the pain talking."

———

Blue descended the stairs into the basement, dressed in a new t-shirt after having left her denim jacket upstairs to dry.

Her body still tingled from the recent manhandling. They'd only had time for a couple minutes of petting, but it was *very friendly* petting, and she made sure to include a promise of much more to come in every kiss she returned. *Damn the crisis.*

Ultimately, Chip had to be the voice of reason—*who knew?* Blue was willing to risk it, but he reminded her it was his best friend in jeopardy. They were racing the clock, and they had so much to do. *And he's right. Damn it all.*

They ended in a hug. He trembled against her, and the evidence of his arousal did not escape her notice, even as she quivered against him.

She spoke against his chest. "You're going to be in *such* trouble."

"Bring it on," he said into her hair. "Just...not yet."

She pushed him away and grabbed for her shirt. "We need to stop now, or I won't."

"I know." Chip held the red portfolio up. "I'll be downstairs speed reading this."

She grabbed up her new shirt. Lady Gaga stared back at her, a dagger shoved into her abdomen, a black-and-white screen image oozing gray blood against a black shirt. *Glad to see this crisis has not deterred Chip's sense of irony.*

In the basement, across the room, Chip sat on the cloth recliner. He'd already removed a stack of papers. Next to him, Phil's body lay on the couch, his annoying and regular snores making it unnecessary to check if he was still breathing. Blue's gaze locked onto the fist-sized, brilliant red transparent gem. The center glowed angry crimson, seemed to pull all light from the surrounding space, and cast a blood-red tinge throughout the room.

In spite of herself, Blue walked over to the chair. She reached down and wrapped her fingers around the gem. Despite its appearance, the crystal lay in her hand comfortably, lightweight and cold to the touch. "It's incredible."

She shifted the stone, letting it lay in her palm. She sensed, intuitively, that the ruby could do serious damage if she lost her mind and struck someone with it.

Her fingers traced a set of runes carved into the face, sharp, laser-accurate lines that she was certain were etched hundreds of years before laser technology. The runes followed the circumference of the gem while encircling a larger symbol in the center of the ruby face. The etching felt new and deep under her thumb.

Chip nodded. "You don't know the half of it. Apparently, Brother Andrew Kelran himself of the Kelranian Order engraved the symbols onto the gem face using white magic."

"I can believe it." She ran her finger across the surface. "Wait, Kelranian, what's that?" She recalled the psycho woman had called her a Kelranian bitch. *Might as well find out if I need a special jersey or something.*

Chip shrugged. "The simple answer? They're team Burton."

"Well, I guess that's the team that drafted us, then, so the woman who attacked me got that much right. So, what are they again? I mean, what does our side represent? Truth, justice, and the American way, right?"

Chip's eyebrows rose on his head, and if he had any further questions, he kept them to himself. "The Kelranian Order is an ancient secret network of white sorcerers." He looked up and smirked, waiting.

Blue met his gaze. "Go on."

"Okay. So...you don't need time to absorb that?"

Blue shrugged. "You're talking to Ms. Fought a Ghost on a Roller Coaster here. It's taking a lot to faze me these days."

His eyes returned to the paper. "So, the Kelranian Order traces itself back to the sixth century, formed by Merlin during the reign of King Arthur."

Blue raised a hand. "Okay, wait. Just to be clear. *The* Merlin."

"Yes."

"*The* King Arthur."

The twinkle in Chip's eyes betrayed his amusement. "That's what it says."

"Just checking. Go on."

Chip looked back down at the file. "Anyway, according to legend, the original group began as an alliance between Christian monks and Avalon druids, intent on finding a balance between the white magic of the ancient practices and growing Christianity."

Blue raised her hand. "Sorry, I'm behind on my Dungeons & Dragons speak. Druids are...?"

"In this context, the druids are the women sorcerers who lived on the isle of Avalon. Among their feats, they trained Merlin and practiced white magic in the service of Arthur. The Lady of the Lake was an Avalon druid. She was the guardian of Excalibur, Arthur's enchanted sword."

"Right," said Blue, remembering the old Disney cartoon and several classic paintings. "The girl's arm rising out of the water."

Chip shrugged. "Not likely a literal arm in the water, but yes. Anyway, as Christianity spread, one interpretation of the legend says the magic of Avalon dwindled and the druids vanished from existence along with the island itself."

"Wow, that's gratitude for you." Blue motioned toward the report. "But the file says?"

"Oh, the file has no comment on the legend. Only that a handful of druids allied themselves with the monks to help form the Kelranian Order." Chip turned a page. "Those must have been some interesting board meetings," he quipped. "The druids drew power from nature and from themselves, which would have clashed with a monotheistic belief system. But through cooperation and experimentation, they generated a potent form of white magic."

Blue scoffed. "Yeah, whatever. Isn't that the way it always works for the girl? Eve ate the apple, and everyone gets kicked out of paradise. Lot's wife takes a peek and gets turned to salt. Mary Magdalene is the only woman disciple of the Jesus gang, and everyone thinks she's a prostitute. Oh, except there's nothing in writing that supports this, but it sure makes for a great story." Blue rolled her eyes. She knew she was venting on her soapbox, but she couldn't help herself.

Chip bristled. "Well, okay, maybe. Can I finish now?"

"Sorry."

"The Kelranians continued to operate, always in secret. They created a tight network of white wizards throughout Europe, and eventually, the entire world. A few rode over on the Mayflower. A few more after that. It's probably no surprise to know that the Kelranians helped spearhead the witch trial paranoia in Salem."

"Oh, another black mark in history where innocent women were killed for no good reason."

Chip glanced at a page, hesitating. "Well..."

Blue waited. "What?"

"Maybe not so much. I mean...maybe not in *every* case."

Blue tossed the crystal up and down in a mock threat. "Really? Salem was infiltrated with Satanists? Bullshit. Wiccans, maybe." Blue knew a couple of Wiccans in her poetry classes who lamented about how, throughout history, their kind were frequently mistaken for devil worshippers and executed. "Wiccans are generally harmless, and Wiccans aren't Satanists."

"Hey, you're the one who said you could handle anything I threw at you. The Kelranian Order, *today*, is made up of white sorceresses...modern druids who trace their lineage back to Avalon."

"Really?" Blue considered. "Well...good, then. Maybe that's kind of cool."

"In fact..." Chip hesitated. "According to this file, Ms. Burton falls right in line with that lineage. It says in here she's the final product of some sort of combination white magic spell and genetic manipulation called the...*Tesh Ka Ra*."

"And that's what?"

Chip flipped through a few pages, forward, backward, then finally shrugged. "Doesn't say. It seems intra-organizational, like they expected anyone who might read it to know. From the context, though, I'd say it was some sort of multi-generational breeding program or something within the Order. And it appears Rebecca is either the most current prodigy in the line, or...the end result of it."

"So, Rebecca is…some sort of super-sorceress?"

Chip smiled. "That's how I read it."

Blue shook her head. "Ms. I-blundered-into-a-trap-and-got-my-ass-turned-into-a-video-game-character…is some sort of super-sorceress?"

"Well, now that you put it that way…"

Blue rubbed her eyes. The adrenaline rush had left her drained but otherwise accepting most of the craziness Chip was dumping on her. "I still say that most of the women condemned for witchcraft in Salem were innocent nannies burned at the stake because some Puritan patriarch was covering up his adulterous affair." She jabbed a finger at him.

Chip looked back, stone-faced. "Probably, doesn't matter."

"Humph. Anything else?"

From the expression on Chip's face, she knew what he would say. "Oh, yes. A whole lot more. But rather than repeat myself, how about you get online while I finish reading, and I'll update everyone at once?"

With some reluctance, Blue put the jewel back on the couch and turned her back to it.

She seated herself at the left side linked console, next to the offline computer. She thought of the console as "her" spot, even though she'd only played one game session on it.

She logged in to the game and adjusted the headset and mouthpiece while she waited for the screen to boot up to show the over-the-shoulder view of Daria, still standing outside the tavern where she'd left the avatar over twenty-four hours ago. She noted, peripherally, that Chip logged on to his computer.

She guided Daria into the tavern and found herself the only CGI character in the building except a non-playing character bartender. *Wow, holiday break, just like real life.*

Chip leaned over from his chair. "Exit and go due north according to your mini-map. You'll find everybody else clustered together by the tree." He pressed a button and spoke into his mic. "She's on her way."

She walked Daria out of the bar, across the cobblestone path out of town, and into the woods. She noted the lack of any other player characters. *Well, of course. Everyone else is eating turkey and spending time with family like any other normal person.*

After a couple-minute walk through the woods, a cluster of CGI fantasy characters came into view near an oversized tree. On her screen, she recognized Phil's familiar wizard Magtog, the angel warrior Burton, the lady knight Skye, and Chip's thief, looking decidedly lacking in armor compared to this motley crew.

Blue looked away from the screen to see the real Chip. "Don't you have any, I don't know, barbarian characters for backup?"

Chip shrugged. "I wouldn't underestimate the ability to slip a knife into the joints of a suit of armor. I can hold my own in this game pretty well."

At the same time, wizard Phil extended a hand while his voice spoke through the speakers. "Glad you made it back, Blue."

Skye added, "It's been a little while since you'd left; we were starting to get concerned."

Rebecca's voice rode over the others. "Did you get the file and the gem?"

All business, Blue mused.

Chip spoke into his mic, his voice now coming through her headphones. "Yes, she got it. I've been reading the file."

Rebecca didn't respond right away, and all heads, one by one, turned toward her.

Finally, she said, "I'd have rather I guided you through some key points."

In her peripheral vision, Chip shook his head, an action that did not translate to his avatar, though the tone of his voice made his meaning plain. "If you want my help, we're going to do things my way."

Blue turned to take in Chip directly. *Well, look at Chip! You go, my man!* Her gaze drifted down to where she imagined a pair of huge cartoon testicles visibly enlarged his pants. She stabbed her mute button so no one in the game heard her stifled giggle.

Rebecca considered, the white wings protruding from her back twitching in apparent consternation. "Fair enough, but there are some confidential matters I may not be able to answer."

Chip adjusted his microphone. "You mean, like the references to *Tesh Ka Ra?*"

Could a CGI character blush? Because Blue was certain Burton's did exactly that.

No doubt about it, the angel-warrior started pacing back and forth, and as she spoke, her voice cracked. "Mr. Farren, you have me at a disadvantage, but that is a topic I'm not..." She stopped, and her eyes stared at the ground.

Blue pressed mute. "Shit, you hit a nerve!"

Chip raised his hand for silence. Perhaps he was afraid Blue's voice might carry over to his mic.

Rebecca tried again. "The details regarding the Tesh Ka Ra are...on a need-to-know basis. I'm asking you to respect that."

Skye cut in. "For what it's worth, I've been working alongside Rebecca all semester and I have no idea what you're talking about."

From where Blue sat, Chip looked like some sort of TV prosecutor chasing a lead, his face reflecting a mixture of professionalism and barely contained excitement. All wasted on the avatars. "I just have to wonder. If you're one of the good guys, like you say, why are you being so secretive?"

The angel looked decidedly flustered. "Listen, Mr. Farren, even if I told you exactly what you wanted to know, it won't do you any good, here and now, in this situation. But I have never pretended to be anything other than what I am, a government agent with security clearances that give me access to certain privileged information, and if—"

"Bullshit you're just a government agent."

Chip's bold, open call-out left Blue's head spinning. *Oh, my God, Chip, what kind of strategy is this?*

"And if..." Burton continued, raising her voice, "I know anything relevant to help us, you have my word I'll share it immediately. I want to get out of this as much as you do, Mr. Farren, but inquiries about the Tesh Ka Ra are simply a waste of everyone's time."

Chip sighed, his face betraying frustration. He stabbed the mute and shot Blue a look. "She's full of shit. There's something *huge* she's not telling us."

Blue placed a hand on his shoulder. "I know, but...what I do believe is...she's trapped, and she's scared, and she doesn't like not being in control. I don't think she'll respond well to threats."

Chip blew off a long sigh. "She's probably right. It's not relevant right now, but I'd sure like to know what she was genetically bred for."

Blue grinned at him. "Relax. A multi-generational breeding program to be the best video game player doesn't seem likely."

Chip chuckled and stabbed a button. "Okay, for now, Ms. Burton. But there is a story in the file I think everyone needs to hear. The story of what exactly happened in 1797. I'd like to share that."

The tension between the virtual world and the outside hung, palpable, as the group waited for Burton's answer.

Burton's avatar held her palms out and open in a shrug. "You may proceed."

Chip gently laid a couple of pages across his keyboard and squinted at the type. "According to this, the Kelranian Order barely stopped the coven from opening a doorway from the chaos realm to the physical realm, which would have allowed the demoness Baalina to enter our world at a time when humans could not have possibly fought against her. The Kelranians barely managed to stop her, but not without a terrible sacrifice..."

CHAPTER FIFTEEN

Louisville, Kentucky, 1797

Brother James Krane of the Kelranian Order rubbed his hands over the fire in the makeshift pit created to stave off the bitter cold. He squatted near the warmth, waiting with growing impatience for his allies to arrive. Darkness closed around him like a stifling shroud, and he couldn't shake the feeling of exposure, of being an easy target to be swept aside if the Sisterhood approached before they were ready.

He rubbed his hands over his tiny, inadequate flames, noting how his skin poked through his thread-bare gloves, coverings long overdue to be replaced. Just one more menial task forever on his errand list that he'd never gotten around to against the greater goals of his mission. He thanked the Lord that the chase had moved him out of Salem and a bit south. Just a bit. Though the cold made his fingers ache, 'twas nothing compared to the bitter chill of a Massachusetts November.

He'd received the message from his contact three nights ago. Sister Minerva Crystin, a Kelranian agent operating deep undercover within the Baalina cult, planned to break her cover and meet him here. She'd specified this tree, a large, pock-holed monster of an oak that dwarfed the rest of the forest for its height and girth. If all proceeded as planned, she'd rendezvous with him shortly before the Sisters made their move, presumably with adequate time for James and Minerva to mount their defense.

Two against—who knew how many? Rumor speculated as few as five and as many as dozens. In spite of their success in planting Minerva among their number, their intimacy...or perhaps the tightness of their surveillance measures...meant that even one of his most trusted agents could send only small bits of intelligence.

But their plan rested on one other contingency, spelled out in the decoded message. Brother Krane had retrieved it personally and brought the item with him. Now brought to mind, Krane reached into the pocket of his layered garment and removed the lump that lay within. As he held it in his palm, the stone radiated its own heat, right through the cloth rags he'd wrapped it in.

He unwrapped the stone, and, moments later, the Divenium Crystal lay, exposed and glowing, where it caught the light from the fire, the woods, even the stars, and bathed the area in a hue the color of blood.

Movement! Krane turned toward the shifting branches at the edge of the woods. A cloaked, shadowy figure stepped out and stopped at the perimeter of the fire.

Too late, Krane threw the rag over the crystal and reached for his staff. *Stupid! If this is a Baalina witch seeking to steal the crystal...*

"Put your staff down, Krane."

Krane released his held breath, and he swallowed, waiting for the pounding of his heart to subside. *Minerva!* He'd recognize his erstwhile partner's sarcastic tone anywhere.

The woman lowered her cloak to reveal a head capped by close-cropped, bright red hair that surrounded severe lines etching a serious face. The amused twinkle in her eyes softened her features. "I broke ranks and beat the Sisterhood by several minutes. Fortunate for you!" She motioned to the bundle in his hand. "What sort of lapse of senses would possess you to expose the Divenium Crystal like that?"

Even the druid's chastising sounded as music to his ears. *Thank the Lord she slipped away! She is safe!* He held his arms out, and she stepped forward, inviting his embrace. As he shivered here in the cold, he welcomed her warm, returning hug. Moments later, he kissed her forehead and muttered a blessing before they separated. As he held her face in his gaze a moment longer, he noted strands of gray about her temples he'd not noticed before but knew better than to mention them.

Her flashing eyes, normally bright green, appeared as a pink haze in this light. Nevertheless, he recognized a similar relief in her look. "It's good to see you again, James."

Krane nodded in her direction. "I won't lie. Months ago, when I heard the Order chose to send you to the Sisters, I feared I might never see you again."

"Really?" A suspicious expression passed over her face in the firelight. "I'd heard you co-signed the order to approve the choice."

His eyes focused on the fire before him. He dared not look at her while she spoke her words, part question, part accusation. He hoped the amber aura hid the flush he knew had come to his face.

He had never lied to her before, and he would not start now. "It's true. Although I wanted you safe, I couldn't let my personal feelings get in the way when I knew you were the best person to send."

He dared to sneak a glimpse at her. She'd also given her attention to the fire. Apparently, she found this conversation as distasteful as he. Her hair, bright red even in normal daylight, now glowed with an inner intensity. He cleared his throat. "Forgive me?"

"Of course. I am the most gifted of the Order, man or woman. It's nice to hear an acknowledgement of that fact, even in private."

"That's not fair, Minerva. I speak highly of your gifts to the High Council."

"You mean the Brothers-Only meetings to which your Avalon, druid-descended allies are not privy."

He opened his mouth to object.

She extended her palm and shook her head. "Never mind. I must ask you to forgive me, James. The months I've spent amongst the Sisterhood have proven...trying. Their extreme views can wear a woman down, especially a woman of independence trying to find her full potential in a patriarch's government."

James cringed. In the years they'd worked together, she'd never addressed her heritage as a direct descendant of the Avalon druids so directly. "You know I hold you in the highest regard, Sister Minerva."

Minerva returned a smile of pink teeth that would have gleamed deadly white in normal light. "As you should, Brother Krane. As you well know you should." She held out her hand. "The crystal. Give it to me. Time grows short, and we must set up our defenses here."

Krane deposited the crystal in her hand, happy to be rid of the burden. Between the two of them, he had no illusions as to who better manipulated the white magiks, and he was glad to pass on the responsibility to his trusted ally.

Minerva stepped before the oak tree and placed the crystal on the ground before it. She twisted the crystal against the soil, securing the base in the damp dirt. Her head tilted back, taking in the magnificence of the naturally grown structure before them. "The Baalina Sisterhood chose a good tree, one ancient and full of Earth magiks."

Krane swallowed back a reply. Unlike the druids, who attributed the source of white magiks to the gifts of the Earth, the monks credited the One True God as the source of all power, including any gifts yielded by the Earth which the god had made. The Kelranian Order had ended that division of "old thinking" and "new thinking" by embracing their differences as a matter of semantics.

Brother Krane was quite comfortable with this compromise, especially whenever he witnessed Minerva's superior handling of the white magiks.

Minerva waved her hand, palm down, at the crystal. As she chanted in an ancient language known well to her people and the few descendants of her generation, the inner light intensified. "Fortunately, the tree has more than plenty of power for everyone."

"Oh, I don't know," said Krane. "It might have been nice to drain the tree ahead of time so its power would be useless by the time the Sisterhood arrived."

Minerva cringed and glared. "Your kind claim to treasure the world the Creator gave you, yet your every statement speaks otherwise. To drain the tree and leave it an empty shell would be a colossal waste and a tragedy."

Embarrassed, Krane said nothing. He feared to provoke her, knowing her powers could be the difference between their mutual destruction and actually surviving this night. Minerva's attitude confused him. As a rule, Avalon druids didn't express their frustrations so openly.

If they both survived this night, he would have to discuss this with her further.

Minerva continued to chant. The lilting progression soared and swirled around the campfire. The sounds soothed and emboldened Krane in the certainty of their victory, pushing aside all doubts of the righteousness of their stance. As she sang, the crystal's inner light grew, engulfing the tree, the fire, and the two figures beneath it. The shadows of the surrounding forest fled, exposing bare the branches and hiding places of the area around them.

Krane noted that the advantage of stealth was now lost on both sides. Not that it mattered. They knew the Sisters of Baalina approached, just as they were equally certain that the Kelranians waited to block them.

Her eyes now aflame, her hair and robes fluttering beneath the power of her spell, Minerva paused in her chanting to address him directly in a commanding tone. "Prepare yourself, as I have prepared myself, Brother Krane. We haven't much time."

She stepped forward and lowered her voice to a more conversational level. Apparently, whatever spells had been cast could attend to themselves. "Listen to me and obey. The protection spell I've cast will not likely hold. If the Baalina Sisterhood succeeds in creating their portal into Chaos to draw out the demoness, our only chance to defeat them is to destroy their SoulStaff and then use the crystal to close the portal. One of them, the elder, Mother Katka, most likely, will wield an ornate redwood staff covered in runes. On my word, use the fire spell I taught you and burn the staff. Don't worry about the woman holding the staff, and don't worry about her companions. You must assure your shot is true, and that you incinerate that staff. Do you understand?"

Krane nodded. "Gladly, Minerva. I am honored to assist you." He paused to recall the chant Minerva taught him over a decade ago, back when he was newly indoctrinated into the Kelranians and submitted himself as her student to learn the intricate art of white magik.

The words came to him, and he began to chant. As the words flowed from him, the power of his defenses grew, even as sparks of white magik lit up his fingertips.

Minerva held her hands out before her. A panel of magik energy, its border glowing purple, flickered in the space before her. "If they open the portal...closing the portal will require a sacrifice. James...if my words seem...bitter, and out of character, it's because I'm preparing myself for what must be done."

Growing alarm overrode the coaxing peace of the magik. "No. You can't."

"It's not your decision to make, old friend. Do not interfere."

Off in the distance, Brother Krane could barely make out the silhouettes of three indistinct figures closing in. The crystal's light caused distended, distorted shadows to streak away and behind their forms.

Minerva's gaze met Krane's. "Brace yourself, James." In spite of her grim words, her fiery eyes flickered with confidence.

Before them, three cloaked women approached. The center figure, stooped and trailing behind her two escorts, held before her a large staff. Brother Krane presumed the gender of these foes, even though he had no visual evidence to support it.

As if the witch in the middle could read his mind, it extended a gnarled hand, reached up, and pulled her cloak back from her head to reveal the weathered face of a gray-haired woman. Still, her voice bridged the distance in a confident tone. "So…'Sister' Minerva! You now reveal your true allegiance. That betrayal comes with a severe price, bitch! Tonight, you will bask in the bitter wine of your own destruction."

If the demon worshipper's threat had affected Minerva, Krane could hear no trace of it in her reply.

"Whereas, I will offer what mercy I can for you and your poor, wretched followers." Minerva raised her arms, and her voice traveled upon the wind, amplified and chilling. "Deluded fools, lower your weapons, do not let the trickster Baalina continue to veil your eyes. Leave her to the Chaos realm she placed herself in centuries ago when she first defied the greatest power."

Brother Krane, moved by his comrade's words, called out, "She has no power over you except that which you willingly give to her in exchange for her empty promises."

"How dare you!" The woman to Mother Katka's right lowered her cloak to reveal a head covered by dark hair and holding equally cold, dark eyes. "The man next to the traitor now speaks of empty promises!"

A high, lilting laugh pierced the air. To Krane's left, the other escort raised a delicate hand to uncover a blonde head of hair, pale, almost luminescent skin, and glowing blue eyes. "What did you expect, Sister? Men through the centuries know how to speak empty promises so well."

In spite of himself, Krane found his gaze traveling up and down the form of the light-skinned woman, appalled by her transparent fury and utter contempt.

The woman reached down and placed a hand upon her hip, letting the cloak nip in upon her shape. She met his gaze with a cruel smile. "Tell us, 'Brother.' Tell us how men speak meaningless oaths words to gullible girls to get what they want. Demonstrate your talents, sir. Entertain us with your meaningless words."

Krane felt his face flame at her accusation. "Damn you, witch, I have never...I don't—"

Minerva cut in, her voice still overpowering the others. "Do not let these girls trouble you, Brother Krane. They have spent their lives assaulted by tricks and lies. Tonight, they lie to themselves. You don't owe them an answer, just pity them for the lost souls they are."

By now, they'd closed the distance to a few dozen feet. The group of three stopped, staring across the open plain to the two guardians waiting on the other side of the firepit, prepared and ready to defend the great tree.

The silence elongated as neither side dared move or speak.

Krane knew he should be terrified, scared and on the verge of wanting to flee. And yet, he waited, calm, ready, and willing to die this day if that was what his Lord demanded of him.

The old lady broke the silence, her voice a dry cackle. "It is you who will need pity soon, Sister Minerva Crystin. Pity for choosing your impotent ally, and pity for what we shall do to you when you lie helpless before us, unable to defend against our whims. You have no idea how much our order delights in the suffering of our enemies. I look forward to showing you tonight."

Katka and Minerva glared at each other across the distance. It was Katka who broke off, shifting her gaze to meet the eyes of the only man in this contest.

Krane felt his blood chill under the weight of her stare.

"What do you say, 'Brother?' My Sisters can introduce you to the pleasures of our company. I noticed you appreciating the charms of Sister Gwendolyn. She would reward your cooperation, and perhaps we would let you live long enough to witness the birth of your daughter."

Brother Krane grimaced, trying to cover his shock and his morbid fascination with their antics. If this was where he would make his last stand, then he had made his peace.

He would not dignify Katka's mockery of an offer with a reply.

Instead, he leaned toward Minerva. "Do they plan to talk us to death?"

"They hope to distract us while Mother Katka sets up her spell. Prepare yourself. Our spell will protect our souls from being drained, but I can't help everyone. The entire village to the west, for instance. Their souls will be pulled from their bodies and claimed by the staff. But if you can enflame it on my mark, the souls should be released back to the bodies just as quickly."

"Should? Are you certain?"

Minerva shrugged. "As well as I reasonably can be, James. How does one put such ideas to a test?"

As Krane pondered his answer, the old witch screeched, her command to attack riding upon the wind.

The women on either side of Mother Katka both motioned with their hands. Dark blue streaks of energy lit up the night, closing the distance like bolts of lightning toward Minerva and Krane.

Both bolts struck a panel of white energy, which lit up into a visible glow on impact and vanished a moment later.

Krane blinked spots from his eyes. The flashes of light from their opponents' hands had nearly blinded him. He uttered a swift prayer of thanks. *Thank God Minerva raised those ahead of time. I would never have seen that coming.*

The women shifted their stance in a coordinated motion, letting loose a second barrage of dark magik bolts, then a third. The barriers lit up as each wave struck in their turn, but they held.

Out of reflex more than fear, Brother Krane took a few steps back while he chanted his own offensive energy spell. Growling on the last syllable, he thrusted his fist toward the grimacing brunette.

The projectile blast of energy shot from his hand and traveled in a slow, unsteady arc at his intended target.

She stepped to one side, dodging easily.

Frustrated, Brother Krane pumped both fists, sending one energy blast, then the other, toward her.

She stood her ground, watching his energy slap the ground without useful effect.

Before she could react, he punched the air a third time, sending a bolt traveling at twice the speed directly at her.

For just a moment, Krane glimpsed the look of shock on his opponent's face before his blast knocked into her.

The bolt struck with a stunning force, and her body collapsed to the ground.

In the meantime, the blonde had broken into an intricate attack dance, combining lunges and attacks. As she cut the air with a series of grunts, bolt after deadly bolt came at him.

Each bolt, in their turn, impacted against the shield.

Krane turned his attention to the old woman.

She'd planted the staff into the ground, and the sound of her crackling chant broke in on the tranquility of the forest, as if some great force sought to gut the forest itself.

The woman croaked in an ancient language Brother Krane did not recognize, and, as of this moment, vowed to never learn. The staff glowed, its carved runes along the sides illuminating the night a putrid green color.

The attractive woman had stopped her elaborate attacks and stood, a look of frustration marring her face. The old witch broke her chant and called out to her companion, the blonde. "Charge at the man directly, Gwen! The Kelranian witch's shield will block your energy attacks for hours, but it won't block your physical body! Kill him!"

Krane watched, panic welling up within him, as the blonde woman reached to her side and withdrew a small, nasty-looking object. Even in the near-darkness, he recognized the reflective silver edge of a dagger extending from a pale handle that fit comfortably in her grip. *She's coming for me!*

Sure enough, Gwen ran at him, closing the distance rapidly.

Krane fought back growing panic and called out, "Minerva? Is she right?"

"I'm afraid so! Prepare to defend yourself."

"But I have no weapon!"

"Then, as a man, use your natural superiority to overcome her. Or perhaps the defensive techniques I taught you."

Sarcasm? Now? Really? Krane bent his knees and raised his arms, hoping to throw her when she closed in.

Gwen, a dark-cloaked projectile picking up speed, cleared the energy shield without so much as a stagger.

Brother Krane braced himself for the attack. "That's not very damn funny!"

He had no time for further banter. He watched the hand with the knife raise and prepared to grab at it. At the same time, he pumped his feet backward a few steps to lessen the impending tackle.

As her body slammed into him, he reached up, his hand gripping the hand with the knife. At the same time, he kicked back. They fell together beyond the large tree into the brush beyond.

Krane twisted and rolled and pushed her past him. Her own momentum propelled her far beyond her target.

Screaming like a wildcat, she tumbled in the grass and settled several yards past. She came up onto her knees, and a growl—Lord help him, a literal growl!—escaped her throat.

She darted back at him in a full running charge.

"I don't want to hurt..."

Rather than running past, she jumped, and the knife's edge glinted in the light as she thrust the blade down.

He grappled her wrist and blocked her blow...partially. He toppled backward into the grass.

Her body fell over his. As the blade sliced through his robes and into his upper arm, his shoulder burned.

She pressed her weight down on him. Her eyes reflected primitive fury, glaring their hatred.

Instinct—and some of Minerva's training—took over. Brother Krane turned the fall into a back flip.

The momentum of her tackle pitched her over and out of control. This time, however, Krane gripped her wrist.

The woman tried to spring beyond his reach, but his hand held tight and caught her short, jerking her back and dropping her into the grass.

The woman lay, perhaps stunned or disoriented.

Krane knew exactly where he was and pressed his advantage. He rose to a crouch, then propelled himself forward to bring his weight down upon her prostrate body.

The advantage now his, he pinned her wrist, the one with the knife, down flat against the ground while his other hand pressed against her throat.

Seeing red, he closed his fingers. Vision and clarity returned, and he saw his own hand grasping her throat, her eyes bugging out beneath the strength of his fingers. *Christ! No, that's not*

Appalled, he released her.

She struck at his shoulder with a targeted thrust of her fist.

The blow sent sharp, burning agony through his arm. *Damn you, woman!*

He balled his own fingers into a fist and pounded down on her head.

Once, twice.

Her arm fell, and the knife dropped into the grass.

He collapsed, struggling for breath. *Lord! I didn't mean to...but she tried to kill me...But still...*

Distantly, he heard Minerva call out to him, her tone growing more urgent, finally penetrating his thoughts.

"James! I need your help! Now, James, hurry!"

"What?" He struggled to pull himself up, using his one good arm to prop up and take in his surroundings.

Across the field, the old woman continued to chant, and the SoulStaff glowed brighter than moments before. Her features contorted with effort, and the woods surrounding her lay exposed in the expanding, eerie glow.

Minerva's pleas continued to reach him. "She's found a way around my defenses, James. She's tapping the tree. Hurry! Destroy it! She's drawing on all the souls from the nearby village to form the portal."

Alarmed, Krane turned. Behind him, a circular gateway of energy hovered in the air between the great oak and himself. Within, as if looking through the window of a cabin set afire, flames flickered and spewed around the silhouette of a hideous creature. A regal, gray-skinned woman, with glowing green eyes and a pair of curved horns protruding from her head, looked out haughtily from the top of a cliff face.

As he watched, open mouthed, the portal wavered with energy, continuing to open and expand, though too small for anyone to step through just yet.

He didn't have much time. *Christ!*

He turned to face down the cackling hag, her face lit in rapturous delight, her eyes drinking in the vision of her mistress.

In his panic, he struggled to recall the spell of fire purification, but his arm remembered the finger motions and traced the pattern through the air, even as his flesh burned in protest from its injury. He didn't so much block the agony as ignore it, focusing on the staff and the incantation. Once he began, the motions and words came of their own power, as if from outside himself.

As he chanted, the staff changed hue, from a bright green to a dull, yellowish tinge, then ivory, and finally, an overwhelming bright white.

The old woman stopped her words, then, as if repelled, threw her arms over her head and leaped back. With a screech, she released the staff just as it burst into pure white flame.

Mother Katka fell sideways, her robe catching fire and exploded into bright light.

At the same time, Minerva crouched and grabbed the Divenium Crystal, still glowing red, its illumination diminished before the white light onslaught. She raised it over her head, holding it out toward the portal, which now hovered as a tight, puckered opening of energy, perhaps, James estimated, four handspans all around. The opening no longer increased, but stood stable, a small but accessible doorway from one realm to the other.

Minerva advanced, holding the crystal out. The edges of the energy barrier turned a reddish tinge. "Use me," she called. "Use me, great power, to close this unholy portal and seal the demoness–"

A blur of blackness tackled her from behind.

Minerva shrieked.Krane recognized the blonde tresses of Gwen, the witch that Krane thought indisposed. *Damn her! The witch must have lain, biding her time for the perfect moment to strike.*

As Krane rushed forward, the Divenium Crystal arced through the air and landed near his feet. He bent and retrieved the crystal. He tightened his fingers in a death grip and approached the strug gling women writhing in the grass.

The witch, Gwen, pulled herself up atop Minerva, blood still streaking over her face, and her eyes flashed insanity. She raised the dagger to strike.

Krane struck first. He slammed the crystal down, hearing a disturbing crunch through his arm as his weapon hit the back of her head.

The witch's body went slack, and she crumpled over Minerva. His old friend struggled against the dead weight, trying to untangle herself from robes and limp limbs.

Certain that his friend could free herself in moments, Krane stood before the opening, watching the demoness' hand reach out and extend through the portal.

The demoness shoved her head through. Her glowing eyes met his, and she shrieked with inhuman fury.

Krane braced himself and raised the Divenium Crystal, repeating the words Minerva used. "Use me, great power, to close this portal and seal the demoness within!"

A surge of energy coursed through his body. "Amen!" he called after.

His body rose from the ground, and he felt himself lifted and pulled bodily toward the portal.

"James, no!" Minerva cried behind him. "No, it should have been me! You don't know what you're doing!"

He floated toward the opening. Even as the glare of the evil Baalina greeted him, his body flushed in a euphoric calm. His body crossed through the portal opening. First his head, then his torso.

The demoness hissed, and a barrier of white magik energy seemed to shove her aside. She resisted, but the magik held her at bay.

"No! Damn you, Reverend." As he pressed forward into the flames, she laughed.

His arms crossed through the barrier, and the crystal pried itself from his grip, pulled back toward the Earth realm by a power he had no strength to fight. *It doesn't matter anymore. It is finished.* A moment of panic welled up in him, but his body pushed through to the other side.

He settled on the edge of the same cliff and the flames licked at his layers of cloaks; in seconds, the flames met skin. He turned, contemplating a retreat, but the portal closed behind him.

The demoness uttered a scream of anguish.

They stood, scrutinizing each other. Reverend James Krane raised a hand. "I banish you in the name of our Lord and Savior. You cannot hurt me."

The demoness tilted her head and laughed. "You banish me? You...banish me?" Her eyes lit up in green fury. "You cannot banish me to Hell, Reverend. We're already *in* Hell!"

An arc of flame spewed from under him and covered his body.

Brother James Krane raised his arms, a futile gesture to stave off an agony he could not defend against and could not stop. As he swung his arms and kicked his legs at the flames, they covered him; the voice of the demoness reached him over his own screams.

"Congratulations, Reverend. You have defeated a demoness this day. Receive your eternal reward."

He screamed. His body engulfed in flames, and he burned. He screamed again. And when the flames died down, he realized he lay, in his robes and intact flesh, surrounded by flame. *God, no...it won't stop...it won't...ever...*

The demoness granted him a moment's respite before the flames licked out to burn him again. Vengeful laughter echoed in his ears.

CHAPTER SIXTEEN

In a room full of stunned listeners, both in the room and those listening virtually, Chip's voice continued on, finishing the official report of the bittersweet victory. "'...In the days that have since fallen, I am often awakened in the dead of night, when the dark magiks are at their strongest, soaked in a cold sweat. On those nights, I hear cries on the wind. Are they the tormented screams of my fallen comrade, or the imaginings of a sleep-deprived mind?

"In the end, I suppose it matters not, as long as our order never forgets the sacrifice Brother James Krane, my dear friend, made for all of us on that terrible night, a night for which he suffers for all eternity, long after the rest of us are no more. Lord Help Us All. So sworn this day, the third day of February, the Year of Our Lord, 1798.'"

Chip's voice broke as he read the last line into the microphone. "And she signed it, Sister Minerva Crystin, Kelranian Order."

Blue watched as Chip gently closed the file. No one dared speak. Then, after several seconds, a noise like momentary static sounded over the speakers.

A second time, and a third, then a woman's voice, whispering. "Damn. Just...damn."

Blue identified the "static" as an avatar weeping. Shifting her gaze to the screen, Blue picked out Agent MacLeod–the one the other agents called Skye. Twin streams of animated tears trickled down the warrior girl's face, which brought all sorts of annoying questions to Blue's mind. *How does that work? She's not real; she's a computer-generated image. I get that she has emotion, but why would the image express it?*

What electronic tears do avatars weep?

Whatever the actual substance, weep the avatar did, and as she wept, her shoulders shook. And when she spoke, her voice carried the sadness of her words. "I know...to some of you guys...this is legend. Myth. But...I've fought demons. I've fought ghosts, and they're real. Somewhere, for over two hundred years, the demoness Baalina has been torturing a good man. I can't even imagine..."

As Blue watched, another avatar, the wizard–*Phil*–stepped up to Skye and patted her shoulder. *Can she feel his hand on her? Can she feel he is trying to comfort her?*

What do avatars feel with virtual nerves?

But sure enough, as she watched on the screen, Skye leaned her head into his shoulder and continued to weep.

The vision caused a lump to grow in her throat. Phil, whose physical body continued to vegetate in the couch, had someone to focus on, someone to protect, at least for the duration of the crisis. Perhaps that would help take his mind off his own crazy situation. She hoped it would help in some small way.

After what he must have thought was the proper pause of respect, Chip spoke into the microphone. "There're a few things we know. First of all, since the Sisterhood plans to recast the spell and bring that demon bitch into our game, we need to recreate this Divenium Crystal and upload it into the game as fast as possible. If I can digitize it as an item, imbue it with some sort of power within the game engine...well, maybe the runes can help counter the spell they intend to cast with their digital SoulStaff. Exactly the way it worked years ago."

"Exactly?" asked Phil.

Chip nodded, caught himself, and spoke into the microphone. "Yes."

As Phil's voice continued through the speaker, Blue heard the hint of a tremble. "Let's not kid ourselves about what that means, then. Someone here will have to sacrifice themselves to lock Baalina back into the chaos realm."

Rebecca Burton stood, her golden wings fluttering momentarily along her back before vanishing again. "Leave that to me."

"No way, Obi-Wan!" cut in Skye.

Rebecca raised her hands in a calming gesture. "I assure you, I have no intention of sacrificing myself the way the Jedi did, nor the way Brother Krane did." The angel avatar smirked. "As Han Solo said in the same movie, 'I still have a few tricks up my sleeve.'"

Skye rose and confronted Rebecca. "Of course, you'd say that, to keep me from stopping you. But it won't work."

"Skye." Rebecca placed a hand on her shoulder. "There's a lot you don't know about me. It's true, there's a certain...expectation...that I will do great things in the future. But that doesn't change the present. I'm the best person to do this, because of what I'm preparing to do. It's a long time from now, and I've trained my entire life to do it. If Baalina tries to attack me, she's in for an unpleasant surprise."

"Bullshit," snapped Skye. "She's a demon. You're a human. You can't argue with those two basic facts."

Rebecca sighed. "Essentially true." She paused, considering something. "Well, as the saying goes, we'll cross that bridge when we get to it. In the meantime, Chip, you need to program the crystal, and...have you talked to Blue yet?"

Blue blinked and looked at Chip. All this time, she'd been glued to the screen, watching the drama unfold like some movie. The illusion shattered when the characters mentioned her by name. "What does she mean?"

Chip sighed and spoke into the microphone. "No...I had been trying to figure out how to approach it."

A chill ran up Blue's spine. *Oh, boy. I don't like the sound of this.* "Approach what? What is she talking about?"

"Blue...we're sixty percent less effective on this side of the screen. That's an inarguable fact."

"Oh. This side? What are you—" Then the meaning of his words hit. "Now, just a damn second!"

"Once the fight starts, we can't do any good from out here. We might as well just watch the fight on the screen for all the help we'll be."

Blue opened her mouth to protest, not sure which of the many arguments in her head would come out first.

But Chip cut her off. "Or, we can get in there and possibly actively affect the outcome for the better. If it goes the way we hope, we won't be in there any longer than a few minutes."

Blue began, "You don't know—"

"We *all* come back out," Chip emphasized, "with Baalina either locked away in whatever virtual space they've created for her or her ass booted back to the real chaos realm."

"You don't know that. We could *all* end up trapped in there."

Chip conceded, "That's right, and we might die. But that can only happen if the Sisterhood succeeds. And if they succeed, we'll have no real world we'll want to come back to, anyway."

Blue still didn't like it. "You can't honestly be saying we're better off in there than out here."

"Once that battle starts, the virtual realm is the only place we're going to make a difference. And if our friends lose because we refused to act...well, I know where I'm going. I just hope you come with me."

"Don't you do that!" The words forced their way from her, from deep inside. "Don't you make it about *me*. This is just like last time, you son of a bitch! Do you remember? Because I haven't forgotten! 'I'm going, Blue, you can choose to come with me if you want, but I'm going.' And I followed you like a fucking idiot, right into the lion's mouth, and we both know how well that turned out, don't we?"

Chip hesitated. The words hung between them, unchallenged. "Don't we?"

Chip flinched. "That's not fair. And...it's not the same thing."

Rebecca cut in, the mechanical nature of the computer speaker garbling her words. "It certainly is not. Chip isn't asking you for a personal favor to help his father. And there's your mutual friend to consider. Not to mention the hundreds of players in the game that could be the first victims of an attempt to accomplish nothing less than worldwide domination."

Still raging, Blue turned toward the computer. *Who does she think she is?* Out loud, she said, "What do *you* know about it?"

"That your mother died tragically during your encounter with a ghost. That through great personal sacrifice, you managed to defeat it and set matters right. That you still hold, to this day, a great anger toward your boyfriend over what happened."

Blue glared at Chip, seeing red. "You talked?! To a stranger? You son of a–"

"I didn't say a word, honest! Why would I? Blue, I promised you–"

Rebecca interrupted. "Chip didn't have to, Fiona. There are very few things that happen of a paranormal nature that I am not informed of, even if it's only after the fact."

Blue rejected that comment. "But...there's no way. Nobody could have found out."

Rebecca replied in a calm voice. "That's correct, Fiona. No one could possibly have found out...through normal channels. You covered your tracks well."

Blue glared at the screen. "Then how did *you* find out?"

Rebecca hesitated. "Let's...just call it magic, for now."

"But you had to have found out from someone. And it wasn't me. Did Chip's father–"

The angel figure on the screen shook her head. "No. I have other sources not available to most people."

"No sources recorded that! Nothing short of a crystal ball that shows you everything you need to know about ghosts."

Burton spoke carefully. "That's...possibly closer to the truth than you might ever know. And for whatever it's worth, Fiona...Blue...you did a fantastic job taking care of the problem and hiding what happened afterwards. I couldn't have done better, and believe me, that's saying something."

Blue considered. "As long as it didn't come to you through Chip."

"It did not. Now, please, at the risk of sounding melodramatic, hundreds of lives may be at stake, maybe more, if we delay. That includes Phil's, and, to be blunt, my own. Possibly many more, though I'll admit, I'm still at a loss as to how they mean to accomplish the transport of a demon from here into the physical realm."

Skye added, "But if we stop them here, it won't really matter."

"And for us to have the best chance, we need every advantage at our disposal."

Phil emphasized, "And we've been sparring with Chip for quite some time. Trust me, you won't make much of a difference trying to control your avatars from out there."

Blue raised her hand, mainly for Chip's benefit. "Wait a second, just slow down. If Chip and I both go in, we have no way of getting out."

"Not to put too fine a point on it," said Skye, "but we have no way of getting out with you two out there, either."

Burton nodded. "The SoulStaff and Divenium Crystal are the key. The Sisters used their avatars to manipulate the staff and open this portal in the game that pulled us in. Once they pull enough people into the game, they'll attempt to bring Baalina through. But the crystal can also close the portal, and in theory, destroying the SoulStaff will bring us all back."

"In theory?" asked Blue.

Rebecca paused before replying. "The theory is a sound one."

Swell.

Chip held out a small digital camera for Blue to see. "I'll get the crystal photographed, scanned, and programmed into the game in just a couple of hours."

"Says you," quipped Phil. "I've seen your 3D rendering. There's a reason I'm lead graphics programmer."

In spite of the circumstances, Chip chuckled. "It will work."

Blue ran her hand through her hair. Anxiety had settled in, almost like some sort of claustrophobia, a need to run and get away, even though she stood in the basement, safe and sound, for the moment. "Okay, even if I'm willing to do this, someone *still* has to sacrifice themselves so everyone else will be freed."

Rebecca cut in. "I already said, I'll take care of that."

Chip reached out and hit the mute button, his eyes locking on Blue's. "So...what do you think?"

Blue was terrified, and she couldn't shake the feeling she now gave voice to. "Something is going to go terribly wrong."

"I agree that it's a risk."

That's not what I said. Blue met Chip's gaze. "I don't care what Burton says, this is just like last time. You get that, don't you?"

"I won't let anything happen to you."

"You can't promise that."

Chip's eyes shifted, then returned to meeting hers. "I promise I won't let anything happen to you."

She took his hand. "Those are amazing words, Romeo, but you still don't know how this is going to turn out."

Chip pressed. "I won't let anything happen to you. This is *my* game. They've come into *my* world this time. Look, everything that happened last time, even after your mother died, you did to protect me. We were fighting, on the streets, with knives–fists! You couldn't give up, because you knew I'd be helpless in that environment if you did. And I was helpless! As it was, I almost died, but I'm here today because of you."

Blue felt her face flush. She looked at the floor. She hadn't thought of it that way. "So, what makes this different?"

Chip released her hand and motioned toward the computer screen. "This is my world. They can't kill you. They might be able to hurt you, but even if they do, I'll come for you. They can't hide you from me. And if Phil is with me, they don't stand a chance, but even without Phil, if you get into any trouble, I *will* come for you. They can't possibly know more about this game than I do."

Once again, his naïve sincerity brought tears to her eyes. "You'd better."

"What was it you said that night? 'They don't know who they're fucking with.' Well, it's true *now*, too. Only here, *I'm* the more dangerous one, and they have no idea what's going to hit them. I told you, we make an invincible team."

Blue swallowed. She nodded her acceptance, but the thought wouldn't go away. *I just hope I don't regret this.*

Chip released the mute button. "Okay, she's in. I'm going to start photographing this gem, and we'll join you as soon as we can."

CHAPTER SEVENTEEN

Blue assisted Chip as he draped a white sheet over the back of the chair, creating literal white space to photograph the Divenium Crystal against. He took a couple of photos in the dim lighting of the basement and those proved too dark. Then he tried the flash. Not surprising to Blue, the flash created harsh red spotlights against the sheet and flares along the surface, resulting in useless images.

He didn't want to take the time to do it, but Chip finally dug around in the garage to find portable work lamps.

After a few minutes of struggling to clamp them against the side of the desk, he succeeded in illuminating the surface of the chair in a soft white light bright enough for the crystal to show clearly without a flash.

Next, he photographed the crystal from every conceivable angle: sides, bottom, top, 60- and 120-degree side shots. After an hour of patient workmanship, he'd downloaded a usable set onto the mostly-unused third computer. As he arrowed through them, the crystal appeared to spin in place in a crude animation effect.

Blue sighed, relieved. "Glad that's done!"

Chip's eyes met hers, amusement reflecting in his face. "That was the easy part."

"Excuse me?"

Chip stabbed a few buttons. "Now we have to render the images and assemble them as a 3-D model—"

"Oh...how long will that take?"

"—then I need to crop away their background, assemble the images together, and let the computer extrapolate the 'in between' views from the ones it has. And that's not counting manually recreating the runes on each crystal face. Otherwise, they won't be a part of the virtual version of the crystal, and I'm sure they're vital for this to work. Fortunately, our extrapolation program is pretty sophisticated; it's just a matter of waiting." Chip sighed. "Looks like Phil was right. This is going to take a bit longer than I thought."

Blue's mood sank with each word. "And then?"

"Then I can drop the completed image into the game and set it to appear by the tree."

"So...how long?"

"Well...longer than two hours, that's for sure! More like four."

"Ugh."

"And that's assuming I don't make any mistakes."

"Double ugh!" Blue sighed. "I can't believe I'm going to say this, but can I just get zapped into the game now? Or is there something else I can do to help speed this along?"

Chip considered. "No, not really. And I won't be much longer after you. Once I get the program automations in place, it takes care of itself. I can join you in maybe another hour."

MARDA AWAKENED WITH A JARRING JOLT. Hands shook her shoulders. She snapped open her eyes, only to close them again as pain from her injury made her nose throb. Natalie's face fell into focus before her, reflecting sympathy.

"What's the matter, Nat?"

"We've...had a complication."

The words brought her to full alertness. "What happened?" She sat up in the bed.

"We wanted to give you some time to rest. But after you fell asleep, I logged back on to check on the SoulStaff, and..." Nat averted her eyes, and Marda could see fresh tears streak her cheeks. "I'm afraid it's my fault." Marda braced herself. "Tell me."

"We hacked their system, inserted the SoulStaff, and tested it. I should have known what would happen next, but—"

Marda rubbed her temples, mentally counting to ten. She'd vowed not to yell at Nat anymore. She'd promised to appreciate her contributions and genius, giving her the recognition she deserved. But the girl could be so *trying* sometimes. "*Tell* me. And put it simply, please. I have a terrible headache."

"Put simply, they hacked my hack. The programmers—probably Eugene, since we know Phillip is captured in the game—deleted the SoulStaff from the game matrix. It's...just not there."

Marda rose, fury building up past her injuries. "You're saying that, for all our plans, we're defeated!"

Natalie held her hands out in a defensive gesture, as if afraid of what she might do next. "No, Marda, we're not. We've simply lost our advantage."

"But you said they *destroyed* the SoulStaff."

"Yes...I placed the object into the game. Now they've turned around and removed it from the game again. But they didn't remove the work I've put into it here on my system, creating the SoulStaff and animating it. That's still saved on my computer. I just have to re-upload and re-render it into the game. And I'll take steps to ensure it won't be as easy to hack us next time. We've lost maybe hours, not days. We can still go forward. Still—I should have anticipated this. Cyn still thinks we should—"

"Sister, when we are alone, do not mention her to me." Marda reached out and placed a hand on her shoulder.

She felt Natalie flinch in response.

This is no good, I need Natalie on my side. She's a simpering coward, but she's truthful. After what happened, Nat is the only one on my team I can trust. "You can't be expected to second-guess every technology contingency, and I know you'll make it right. Between you and me." She pulled Natalie into an embrace.

She resisted at first, then returned the hug.

Marda whispered in Nat's ear, "At this point, I wouldn't trust Cyn to tell me where the bathroom is."

Natalie squirmed against her, and when they separated, Nat's gaze darted to the floor. Marda had to strain to hear her words.

"Cyn...has great skills that have served us well in the past."

"She's a fighter; she's persuasive. She is not a great strategic thinker. I need *you* for that."

Natalie sighed. "Yes, Priestess."

"Marda."

"Yes...Marda. It's going to take a little extra time to do it. A couple of hours. It's unfortunate—we had the advantage, now it's going to come down to a dead heat."

"Nonsense." Marda tipped Nat's chin up to face her, then bent and kissed Natalie on the forehead. She noted, with some satisfaction, that Natalie flushed pink in response. "We are four Sisters. They have two *men* on their side."

Natalie chuckled but said nothing more.

"In a 'dead heat,' as you call it, I'd bet on our side. Every time. Come, Sister, let's prepare."

———

BLUE SAT and stared at the monitor. The huge CGI tree loomed, dominating her vision. "Okay, then." A shudder caused her voice to tremble.

Chip spoke from behind her. "All right, Blue, I'm right here. And I'll join you in a few minutes."

"Yeah..." Her finger hovered over the forward-arrow key, but she couldn't bring herself to apply pressure to move the avatar forward. "Um...so...I'm going to go now."

"Now is good."

"Okay...uh," She swallowed back bile. Suddenly, she thought she might be sick. "I *really* don't want to." She wondered if she'd still have this upset stomach when she transferred into a CGI body. *Can avatars vomit? Who the fuck gets to find these things out?*

Chip's hand fell on her shoulder.

She closed her eyes, listening to Chip's tone, willing herself to let his words reassure her. "I've got you. I'll take good care of your real body."

"Uh, huh. Perv." She meant to sound teasing and flippant, but she couldn't keep the quiver from her voice. "I know how you are. Send me away, and have your way with my poor, unconscious body. You forget, I know all about you lonely nerd types and your secret, lascivious desires."

"I won't do anything to it without buying it dinner first."

She laughed at the bad joke, then reached up and gripped the hand that lay on her shoulder. "I *really* don't want to do this."

"I know. I love you."

"I love you, too." Still, she hesitated. "Damn, I hate peer pressure."

"Do you want me to count to three?"

"No, I'll do it." She pressed the forward key. "Three!"

She thought she'd close her eyes as the animated character stepped forward, but instead her eyes locked open as the tree came fully into view.

And then her vision faded away into a bizarre, pixilated dissolve.

———

BECAUSE OF THE nature of her then-new-boyfriend, she couldn't escape seeing certain nerd movie standards from his DVD collection during the last half of her senior year.

One of those standards was *Tron*, the 80s Disney experimental cult classic in which a computer programmer gets "zapped" into the video game he'd programmed years earlier.

Though she couldn't honestly say she *liked* the movie, one sequence struck her at the time, a sequence she still remembered in the years since, and which had been replaying in her mind nonstop since knowing she'd be transporting herself into a computer game.

The programmer—whose name was Flynn, she thought, Jeff Bridges at his most hunky, for sure—gets zapped from behind by a conveniently placed matter breakdown gun thingie, and his body transports block by neat digital block into the video game, where he is then just as systematically re-assembled on the other side.

In the meantime, Flynn gets treated to the best LSD-inspired cinematic hallucination sequence since *2001: a Space Odyssey* (another movie she saw that same year, and enjoyed more, somewhat) courtesy of the finest computer graphics of 1982.

Her actual transport into this actual virtual world was nothing at all like that.

Instead, one moment, she stared at the computer screen with her own eyes. Then everything faded away, like those times she'd stood too fast and got a momentary dizzy spell.

But when the black spots faded back to normal, everything changed.

The texture of the world had changed.

The tree still loomed in front of her, only now she was standing in front of it. And she could step away.

But it didn't *feel* right, it was like standing in thick rubber boots up to her thighs.

She reached down and ran her hands over her legs—her now perfectly shaped, gorgeous legs. But her hands lacked sensation as she rubbed along her leg muscles.

She held her thumb and index finger in front of her eyes and rubbed the digits against each other. Still a partial numbness, but also a tingling sensation.

She turned her head, or rather, thought of turning her head. The view shifted before she registered her neck muscles moving.

Before her, the gargantuan tree rose as far as she could see, tangled, gnarled branches reaching up and out from the base and extended in a cluster of twigs, towering over the entire group as if all of nature wanted to embrace them in a hug of support.

And yet, though the tree stood dark, oppressive, and majestic, she could distinctly make out the neon electric texture that caused even the blackness to glow with an artificiality, the same CGI texture as her skin, the leaves, the forest around her, and the bodies of her friends who surrounded her now.

"Wow..." Hands reached out to support her, though she didn't feel like she'd fall over. Nevertheless, trying to take in the bizarre new stimulus froze her in place.

"I know." She recognized the voice as Phil's, though it came to her filtered through layers of electronic static. It took her several seconds to sort out the noise from the voice.

One of the new women, Skye, stood in front of her, dressed in a silver knight's armor with oversized shoulders. Blue registered, belatedly, that she'd reached out and entwined Blue's fingers in her gloved gauntlets.

"It's going to take some time," she explained. "It's like, your mind has to re-configure how to interpret the stimuli."

In spite of the circumstances, Blue laughed. "What mind? My brain is back..." She waved her hand out vaguely. "Out there. How can I even..."

This time, her legs really did try to give out, but she fell against Skye, who seemed to have no trouble holding her up.

"Easy. I know, it's confusing as hell. As much as you want to think it, though, your mind—that which makes you...well...you...is no longer in your head." A gloved index finger pointed at Blue's forehead. "It's in here now."

"But that's not..." *Fuck, how many times in one day?*

Then she thought of the bodies left behind. Slack. Not just slack, not just comatose, but slowly, inevitably, dying, a process taking days rather than years, if left unchanged. As if something vital had left the physical body and had been transplanted elsewhere.

A vital something that could transfer into the digital world and take up residence in a body that, by standard definition, had no substance whatsoever.

If I weren't living it, I'd find the very idea ludicrous, like a demon cult out to take over the world or a maniac ghost set loose and looking for revenge.

Or a couple of college students joining forces with government agents in league with a secret society of white magic druids trying to protect the world from the evils that normal people don't even know about.

Just us special, lucky ones. Like me.

Blue sighed. *Yay, me.*

At least, the world had normalized during her stream-of-consciousness moment. She looked at the people gathered around her. Though her eyes saw a wizard, a lady knight, and a golden angel, she thought of them as her friend, Phil, the concerned assistant agent, Skye, and the self-appointed leader and apparent V.I.P. of the group, Rebecca Burton.

The dizziness, the disorientation, had lessened. She rubbed her fingers together. She could feel more, and sensation seemed to heighten through her body by the moment.

The ground now lay solid beneath her feet. The people, flamboyant though they appeared with their fanciful weapons, idealized physiques, and oddly clear complexions, now looked more natural to her own artificial eyes. The sharp contrasts of the flowing grass and billowing trees also lessened. It still looked artificial, highly unnatural to what she remembered of the real world (not that she'd taken many strolls through the forest in her day—a thought that hit her with a twinge of regret) but neither was it as overwhelming.

Now that Blue could sense her hands properly, she wasted no time untangling her fingers from Skye and taking a step back. Blue liked her personal space, and this girl was hovering a bit close for comfort.

Phil the Wizard stood close by. His gaze fell upon Skye and locked, then drifted toward Blue like an afterthought. "How are you doing?"

Blue looked between one and the other, amused. "I'm fine, Phil, thanks for asking." *Somebody's crushing.*

Skye, on the other hand, spared Phil only a brief look and then returned her attention to Blue.

Poor Phil. Either she doesn't notice or doesn't care.

Phil waved his hand in some vague motion that indicated "the real world." "So...uh...how am *I* doing...out there?"

"You seem comfortable enough. We moved your body to the couch. You still snore."

"Oh. Sorry about that."

Blue giggled. "No worries. It's how we know you're still breathing."

The wizard stood before her, tall and strong, a stance contradicting the CGI character when it was "uninhabited" by someone. "I suppose it's hard to point out the positives in a bizarre situation like this."

"Little bit." Blue stepped into the open space the group had created for them. "So, what now?"

Skye sounded like an overexcited sensei. "You'll find that you can move at the speed of thought. It's pretty shocking at first. For instance, think of drawing your weapon from your shoulder and you...yes, exactly!"

As Skye had given the command, Blue had done exactly that, and her hands moved of their own volition. In a blur of motion, she stood, in a ready stance, the sword drawn out before her, a moment later. "Wow, neat!"

With another thought, she drew back her sword then whipped the weapon through the wind with a series of swooshing swipes. She suspected the noise was an audio effect added by Chip or Phil, but here, it was the reality of their world.

The sword's hilt dwarfed her wrist and extended out from her hand looking as much a granite block as a blade. Exaggerated and grotesque, a real-world equivalent of the weapon would have weighed over 100 pounds, but she hefted it as easily as she would swing a loaf of bread—not that she'd be inclined to swing a loaf of bread at someone as a weapon. The attack took almost no physical strength on her part, nor the one after that, nor the one after that. She swiped her sword a few more times, adjusting to the new effort...or lack of effort.

Skye took a few steps back from her. "Okay, now try jumping at me."

Blue attempted an experimental jump. She flexed easily at the knees, and even with a tentative try, she sprang through the air several feet, straight up, then back down. She jumped in place a couple more times. "Wow! I'm like Wonder Woman or something."

The wizard stood in place, his staff pointed at her as he nodded. "Kind of feels that way," Phil said. "Now, be careful when you jump at me. It doesn't take as much as you...whoa!"

Blue sprang forward. Even with what she thought would be an easy skip, she propelled up and flew toward him. As she passed, she swung her sword, and, to her shock, connected.

"Hey!" shouted Phil.

"Sorry, I thought you were ready for me." Several yards away, Blue settled to the ground, light as you please on her new, hyper-accelerated feet. She spun on her ankles to face him again.

"Actually, it's okay. You can't kill me. At least...well..." The wizard rubbed his beard, contemplating. "Did you ever die in the game?" A gleam flashed in the wizard's eyes. "You probably need to experience that—"

Like a cannonball, the wizard's body shot toward her.

Instinctively, she held her arm up. The blunt edge of the staff came at her head, and she held her sword out to block.

At the last moment, the staff dropped, striking her in her gut.

The impact forced the air from her...or whatever passed for air.

The wizard landed behind her, and as she tried to turn, three more blows fell.

In quick succession, pain erupted at her shoulder, knee, and a resounding crack to the head.

She found herself looking up at the sky. She hurt like hell, no question, but she also suspected the pain was not nearly what she might experience had she endured a similar attack in the real world.

Yet another blow struck her in the head, the pain penetrating like lightning. "Damn you, Phil!"

Everything faded to blue, and she found herself hovering...somewhere...in some other place...some...*clouds? Those are clouds? I'm...am I in the sky?*

And she could speak. "What did you do to me?"

"Uh..." Phil's voice, sheepish. "I guess you could say I 'killed' you. We had a duel, and you lost all your health."

"Thanks a lot! Now what do I do?" Even as she asked, she regained her sense of direction, could feel she was dropping down, down...the view shifted, and she could see, still far below, the ground.

She descended down toward it.

"Now? Well, nothing much. You're in a sort of penalty box. In our game, when you die, you get removed from the action for about two minutes while you wait to resurrect and your body to reform. You re-enter the game at about half strength and quickly return to normal."

"Wow, the colors, this is better than an LSD trip." She realized what that sounded like and added, "I mean, the LSD trips I've seen in movies, of course."

"Yeah, yeah, I like *The Wall*, too."

Blue giggled. "But damn, that still hurt!"

"I know, sorry, it can't be helped. You need to get over this shock now and experience it before we go to battle."

"You could have warned me." Blue watched the ground draw closer, then conceded, "Still, I suppose you owed me a lump or two."

"I just..." Phil floundered.

She wondered if he'd deny it.

Finally, he said, "Yeah, okay, I was kind of pissed at you for how you treated Chip...you know, like shit and all."

She really couldn't disagree. "That's fair."

"So, I figure, this is a safe place to vent some of that." She could almost hear the shrug in his voice.

As he spoke, Blue's perception dropped to ground level, and she felt her body shape itself around her form, or behind the eyes of her body, or avatar, or...*fuck it, I might as well think of it as my body for the foreseeable future.* She gave her fingers an experimental wiggle and turned.

The pseudo-death experience actually left her weak and winded. "All right, you took me down once, but you'll have to earn the rest."

The wizard's shoulders slumped where he stood, and his eyes looked toward the ground. "No, I'm done, Blue. My heart's not in it. I thought I wanted to hurt you, or at least, make your life inconvenient for a few minutes, but..." He looked up, his gaze meeting hers. "I love you, girl, you know that. I don't want to see you two fight. Chip's my best friend, and..."

An odd noise erupted from him. Maybe a sob? "I'm just glad we're past that."

Blue didn't know how to answer.

In the silence that followed, Phil pressed, "We *are* past all that now...right?"

Okay. Phil deserves an answer. She tried to control her frustration and keep her voice level. "Look, I can be a confused mess in the best of circumstances. And the last couple of years haven't been the best circumstances. I had to process what happened in my own time and my own way. I was in pain, and I thought Chip was a part of it. I thought breaking up with him would end the pain. In the end, it had nothing to do with him. I know that now."

"He trusted you."

Blue flinched at the accusation. "I know that, I just..."

"No, you don't get it." The wizard stabbed with his staff from across the meadow. "He trusted you. His faith *never* wavered in you, all these months. First over a year, then it stretched out to eighteen months, and you'd barely spoken to him. *I* had to sit and listen to him justify your indifference." Phil's voice shook with emotion. "But *I* knew, Blue. *I* knew you were done with him, do you get that? Do you know how many times I tried to tell him he needed to move on?"

"Phil, I—"

He cut her off. "But *he* had faith. He had absolute faith. In you."

She closed her eyes, ferling her tears fall over her cheeks. *I don't want to hear this.*

"It never wavered, not once. Not even after you dumped him, and you need to realize that."

The environmental trappings fell away. It was as if Phil and Blue were back in the dorm room. She wondered if the others could hear them, then decided it didn't matter. Phil and she needed to have this out. She shrugged, exasperated. "What do you want from me? What do you want me to say?"

"I want to *know* that you're committed to him the way he is to you. That this isn't some tentative trial continuation and that you're not just waiting for the next excuse to bail out."

"Do you see me here?" She growled and shifted her weight, giving her hips a sultry wiggle. "Do you think it was *my* idea to transport into this CGI body? Do I have any fucking idea how we're going to get out of this? No. But Chip told me *he* does. He told me to trust him, and I do! Does this—" She sprang into an easy, controlled leap which put her to exactly where she wanted to be, in front of Phil.

She swung at him with the flat of her sword...not hard enough to damage him, just hard enough to knock the cocky wizard back on his ass.

He dropped but glared at her from the ground.

"Do you think I'd be here if I considered our relationship a 'tentative trial continuation' whatever the fuck that even is?"

"I just want to make sure...you know where he's coming from." The wizard struggled to his feet. "Because if you break his heart again, I'm the one who has to repair the pieces you leave behind, and it's going to be nasty. So, if you're going to do *that*..." He let the words hang, the thought unfinished.

"That's not going to happen, Phil. I couldn't do that to him again. I couldn't do that to me again!"

"But you can wake up tomorrow and change your mind. You

could go home, and, after a few weeks, rationalize–"

"I could go home and get hit by a bus, Phil! We might all die here today. I don't know what you want me to say. I love Chip, and today, right now, I intend for that to be forever. Today, right now, it's the best I can offer you."

Phil sighed, clearly still frustrated. "Someday, maybe you'll understand. I just don't want to fight anymore."

"I'm not the one picking a fight, Phil."

With ironic timing, a new CGI character phased in amongst them, and Blue saw the small, lithe form of Chip's thief character. *Can their conversation be picked up through his speakers? Hell of a time to think of that!*

She felt herself flush and wondered if her new facial pores showed an outward blush.

"Hey, guys, I just wanted to give you all an update. I traced a few of the runes on the crystal so they're dark enough to see on the CGI image. The work's going pretty quick, so I'm guessing I'll have the final object scanned, rendered, and dropped into the game within the hour."

"Which reminds me," said Phil. "Why do you suppose we don't have any company yet? Didn't we determine they needed to come here to set up their soul spell?"

Chip answered, "I threw a monkey wrench into that. I found their version of the SoulStaff they'd hacked into our game and deleted it from the inventory database."

"Very nice!" Phil sounded impressed.

The thief flashed a sheepish grin. "I don't think it will stop them, but it had to slow them up. We know the staff was destroyed. Assuming they only have access to the notes and drawings in the file, they had to recreate it...in other words, redraw the whole thing from scratch...in order to render the object. On the other hand, we had a physical object to scan, which gives us a huge advantage."

Blue nodded. "But they're still going to come, aren't they?"

"Yes," Chip said. "They'll come. And we'll just have to hope like hell we'll be ready for them."

CHAPTER EIGHTEEN

Despite his optimistic prediction, ninety minutes passed before Chip returned to the game as his thief character. By that time, Blue had had plenty of time to practice and adjust to the nuances of her new body by sparring with Skye, Phil, and sometimes even Burton the Angel.

She learned how to strike with the sword without hurting...much. The others had already figured it out. As a result, when someone struck her, it would sting at the place they connected...usually the shoulder or arm, sometimes the leg, and more painfully, across the stomach, and then through the magic of video game character health restoration, she'd fully recover in seconds.

Striking an opponent full force was easy—almost too easy—so they didn't spend a lot of time practicing fatal attacks. Getting hit with a "fatal" wound took you out of the action for over two minutes, and that didn't serve any useful purpose, so it was better to deliver the light taps when practicing.

After a while, while sparring with Skye, Blue started opening herself up to other options, getting creative with it, bringing her real-life street fighting skills to the party. During one round, they leapt at each other, and in one motion, Blue slid her sword into her back-sheath, shifted in midair around Skye's weapon, grabbed Skye's arm, and twisted in a full roundhouse kick. As Blue landed, she used Skye's own momentum to flip her over Blue's back, dropping her to the ground, stunned.

Skye lay, blinking up at her for several seconds. Then she looked around as if just shaking off the move to take in that Blue now held her sword in her hand and tapped Sky's stomach. "And while you were still lying there, I'd have already killed you," Blue said.

Skye worked her way up onto her elbows. "Nicely done! I didn't even see that coming. I'll bet they won't, either. They'll still be thinking about video game moves."

Blue sheathed her sword and extended her hand. "Exactly."

Skye gripped the offered hand and pulled herself up. "Show me."

She did, and then she showed the rest, one by one. Before Chip reappeared, they'd all attempted to add flips, dives, grapples, and other inventive actions that took their options beyond the basic, stab-and-block motions of the video game, with various levels of success.

Skye and Burton picked up on the new moves with ease, while Phil fumbled along at a more remedial skill level, successfully pulling off most of the actions half of the time, and ending up with a face full of grass the other half. The more they worked out, the more the exertion seemed to take its toll.

Phil joked that he shouldn't have picked an old man wizard body as his avatar. Though Blue didn't say anything out loud, she suspected the talk was just an excuse. In the real world, Rebecca and Skye were law enforcement agents of some sort. It stood to reason they were in reasonably decent shape. And although she'd been somewhat sedentary the last couple of years, Blue hadn't let herself "go" by any means, either. The campus provided ample opportunities to walk and jog, and her father's apartment complex offered a basic gym setup she took advantage of a couple times a week.

Phil, on the other hand...she loved the man as Chip's best friend, but if anyone she knew fit the definition of "couch potato", that was Phil. He was a hefty pear shape when they'd first met, and she estimated he'd put on another thirty to fifty pounds since graduation.

————

AFTER ABOUT AN HOUR, Burton got into the act, and the agent lined the group up and taught them some basic boxing and karate strikes, how to target vulnerable spots on the shoulder, stomach, jaw, nose, groin, and other areas. When tested on each other, the strikes stunned and slowed the movement on their CGI bodies the same way they would affect flesh and blood. Plus, it hurt like hell to get hit.

Blue worked with Phil, getting in a few extra throws. To his credit, he cooperated, bringing his best effort. Eventually, he learned to flip opponents pretty well, could pull off some of the karate blows, but as much as he tried the dive tackles, more often than not, his body hit the dirt after a total miss.

After a while, they'd broken out into two pairs, Rebecca and Phil, and Blue and Skye, then they shifted partners every few rounds, trying to pass on a few new but simple tricks as fast as they could, not knowing how much time they had.

By the time Chip had reappeared, they were well into their routine, but they gathered around to hear his news.

"Okay, so I completed the image generation and dumped the information into the game. The Divenium Crystal will appear right here, at the base of the tree, in about five minutes. I tested it on our backup server, and we'll be able to handle it like any other object."

Skye broke in, "Does it work? Will it do what we need it to do?"

Chip shrugged. "Well...it's the crystal...it has the runes. I can't program it to do a damn thing. This isn't about video game magic; this is about trying to conjure the real thing. You guys just need to cast the spell, say the magic incantation, do whatever you need to do, and we'll see. I can't program the image any more than the original crafter could 'program' the real thing."

"Then it should work," said Burton. "I'll cast the spell when the time comes."

"Okay," said Chip. "Good enough, now we just need to...ah-ha!" He pointed toward the tree.

A transparent pink object solidified in the grass beneath the tree. From where Blue stood, it appeared identical to the real crystal as best as she remembered it, with an additional neon quality created by the video pixels that added to its overall allure.

Blue stepped forward, crouched, and picked up the crystal. It felt solid enough in her hand and fit in her palm easily, the same way she recalled the original stone.

Chip stood at her side, a look of expectancy on his avatar's child-like face. She'd already grown accustomed to reading the animated facial expressions.

"So?" Chip tipped his head to indicate the crystal. "How did I do?"

Blue held it up between them. "It lacks the heft of the real thing, but I think the important stuff made it through. And it feels like the right size." She inspected it more closely. While the original runes had been carved directly into each crystal face, this one held white, drawn images along its faces. As Blue rotated it in her palm, it struck her as similar to someone having applied stickers to the surfaces.

Chip must have noticed her scrutinizing the runes. "That's what took so long. I had to manually re-draw each design."

"Feel pretty good about it?"

"Yeah." He moved in close and lowered his voice. "In a way, I'd almost rather it didn't work."

Blue returned a questioning look.

Chip continued, "If ours doesn't work, chances are, theirs won't work, either. Our spells won't hold and we all just go home."

"We're already in the game, Chip. Their SoulStaff accomplishes at least that much."

Chip shrugged. "Yeah, but if they ultimately can't open a portal to free their demoness, what difference does it really make?"

Blue considered. "I don't think we're going to get that lucky."

"I don't, either." Chip extended his hand out toward Burton. "But we should ask an expert."

Burton noticed Chip motion toward her. She stepped away from the group, still intimidating in her golden demeanor and slashing angel wings. "I'm hardly an expert, but let me see, anyway."

Blue dropped the crystal into Burton's extended palm. The angel—Blue couldn't think of her any other way—turned the object around in her hand.

"I agree it lacks the heft. I also agree it probably doesn't matter." Burton closed her eyes and muttered a chant—a singing, lyrical sound.

From within its center, the crystal lit up red, filling the area with a pink glow.

Blue folded her hands and gripped her elbows, warding off an imaginary chill. "Must have triggered the 'on' switch," she quipped.

As soon as she said it, she wondered if the comment was out of line.

Rebecca smiled. "More or less. You could also say I checked its batteries. The point is, this crystal works, and I suspect will function in this environment the same way the real one would work in our world."

Blue sighed and turned to Chip. "And once they clear the problems you threw at them, their SoulStaff will work, again, as well."

"Very likely."

Blue remembered that, for all their communication with his avatar, Chip hadn't yet abandoned his spot, watching everything from the real world on his computer monitor. "Maybe you should rethink this and stay out there to keep deleting her hacks."

"I could do that, but chances are, they're going to be ready for me this time. While I'm messing around trying to block their code, they're going to attack, and you'll be one person short."

"But if you can hold them off—"

"It might not matter if we can reverse the spell that has everyone trapped in here right now and close the portal." He turned toward the angel avatar. "Right, Rebecca?"

"Agreed." She called out to the others. "Everyone, gather around, it's time."

"One second," said Chip. "I'm going to join you."

"Why?" asked Blue. "What's the point?"

Even as he spoke, the avatar stepped toward the tree, purposefully heading toward the spot that would trigger the spell. "Because we can be attacked any moment, and I don't want to be on this side of it."

Chip stopped before the tree. Blue had kept pace with him and knew exactly where he would need to go to trigger the spell. As soon as he hit it, the figure stopped walking.

Blue stood close, watching the figure's face for a change of any sort.

After a moment, his blank, stone-faced expression took on new, malleable features. He blinked rapidly, his mouth hung half-open. When he stumbled, it was a natural stumble, not the stiff movement of a directed puppet from the outside world. "Whoa. Wow."

Blue reached out with her arms and cupped his shoulders with her hands. "Easy." It was fascinating to watch the same process she'd just been through, knowing exactly the disorientation Chip experienced. "It takes a few minutes. Give yourself some time to get your bearings and–"

"Guys!" said Phil. He stared out across the gentle hills of the forest.

Blue cringed, already knowing what he was about to say. *Crap, that just figures.*

"We've got company!"

Sure enough, at the top of a distant hill, four additional figures had gathered. Even at this range and disguised in her character form, Blue recognized the leader, waving a large totem staff, but with the same mad look in her eyes, a mixture of insanity and hatred, now fixated on Blue, even from across the plain.

"Gather close," called Burton. "Don't leave the portal unguarded. They want us to charge."

Marda, acting as leader of this group, planted the staff into the ground. Moments later, the four figures held hands, forming a circle around the object.

They started to dance. Two identical avatars, red-and-black costumed harlequins with matching demented grins on their matching demented features, skipped as they circled. A third, the only one dressed in what equated to moderate armor, held to a simple circling. Marda, also wearing minimal padding, swooned as much as danced, letting the others pull her around the SoulStaff.

In real-world distance, the groups were separated by perhaps a couple hundred yards of ankle-high grassy plains, yet Blue could hear Marda's chants clearly.

Chip took a couple of tentative steps in their direction. "What are they doing?"

"Calm, be still," commanded Burton.

Chip turned, his gaze leveling at Burton. "I said, 'What are they doing?'"

"They are most likely calling in all the human souls in the area."

Alarm lit up Chip's face. "'All the souls in the area,' what does that mean? We're the only souls literally nearby, and we've already been absorbed."

"Locally would refer to the persons in this land. How many players...human players...subscribe to your game?"

Did Chip's face flare red? Could a CGI face do that? Blue also recognized his familiar grinding jaw whenever he was confronted with something baffling.

"Last I recall, over 200. Maybe 220."

Burton nodded.

Chip's eyes grew wide. "You don't mean—"

"Perhaps not, Mr. Farren. How many people are generally logged in at any given time?"

"This time of day, about thirty or thirty-five, but—"

"Perhaps less over a holiday?"

Chip opened his mouth to speak.

But Phil beat him to it. "No, probably more. It's a student holiday, and this is an online game. There were several gaming parties planned for the long weekend."

Chip stepped forward. "But will the staff pull only the active online people, or everyone?"

Burton opened her mouth, then shut it. The angel's head tipped, her look of confusion easy to read on her golden features. "It's impossible to know. There's no precedence."

"My God," said Skye. "If it pulls people out of their bodies, people driving, people walking, people on stairs, and suddenly they enter into a coma—"

"We don't *know* that," insisted Rebecca.

"Assuming only active players online, how many?" Blue could hear the tremble in her own voice.

Phil offered a guess. "Forty, maybe seventy."

The angel avatar closed her eyes, then slowly opened them. "That's more than enough for their purpose," Burton said.

Chip took a couple more steps across the field. "We have to stop them!"

"We can't, Mr. Farren." Burton's commanding voice apparently caused Chip to stop in mid-step. "The incantation is almost complete, and Baalina will be transported into the new virtual chaos realm they've created for her. If we leave this vicinity, the Sisterhood of Baalina will have easy access to get in front of the portal and cast the spell to send her into the real—"

Behind them, the air erupted from a loud explosion. The force knocked Blue to her knees. *My God!* She struggled back to her feet and turned.

The portal, still hovering in the air behind them, now swirled in a cacophony of orange light.

Blue shielded her eyes with her arms, squinting into its center, where a single dark silhouette waited and seemed to stare back out at them.

A pair of green eyes found her across the distance, and as those eyes gazed upon her, Blue knew terror. *They did it. Holy shit, that's a demon on the other side, and it wants out.*

She turned to Chip. She struggled to get the words out, her voice cracking with the effort. "Chip...what are we going to do?"

Chip still argued with Burton. "But...people travel for the holidays. People all over the country may have been pulled in, and if that's the case, we don't—"

Rebecca cut him off. "It's a bloody nose compared to allowing a demon to wreak uncontrolled havoc across the face of the Earth, Mr. Farren."

"Heads up, people!" Phil called. "The dance is over. Here they come."

Blue looked across the plain, her body lit up, ready for battle.

The group of four now charged toward them, but Blue's gaze had locked on the leader.

She recognized the crazed woman who waved the SoulStaff like a war banner. Fury reflected in her eyes and a war cry tore from her throat as she ran, charging straight for Blue.

CHAPTER NINETEEN

Blue drew her sword and stepped forward. The charging group before them continued on, closing the distance rapidly.

She fell into a ready stance, waiting for the foolish leader to break from her group running at full speed and make a stupid mistake. Based on their previous encounter, Blue figured pretty good odds on that. She just had to keep her head. "Stay behind me," she said.

Chip's hand patted her shoulder in what he must have thought was reassuring. "I'm okay, go."

"Says you!" Her gaze swept over his figure head to toe, taking in his thief—what she'd laughingly call—"armor." Black leather head to toe. "You're still disoriented, and you're a little underdressed for this party, sweetheart."

"Trust me. Just keep the battle around this tree; I'll do my part."

"Close in!" commanded Burton, her skin now glowing with a golden aura that the group naturally drew toward. "I need to concentrate to cast the spell to close this portal, so I'll fall back by the tree. The rest of you focus on destroying the staff."

Blue offered, "Chip says he's most effective behind the tree."

"Great, then he can be my backup."

Blue proceeded to the front, past Phil the Wizard, to join Skye, their only other heavily armored figure, at the front line.

If their battle-readiness had concerned Blue, one look at the group charging them alleviated her fears—somewhat. Two clowns—literally, identical harlequins, each armed with stilettos—led the charge, their screams...no, maniacal laughter...preceded them, ensuring the group would take no one by surprise.

Marda Crazybitch continued her mad charge, garbed in warrior armor similar to Blue's, but she also carried the staff, which meant she had to focus on casting spells, and they had to focus on stopping her.

Next to her was a cloaked wizard. She looked again. Not a wizard, the cloak covered a smaller, shapelier form. The cloaked *druid* kept pace with the leader, holding her arms out, palms up, the sparks of red energy already flaring up in her hands, her obvious intent being to pitch them like the first throw of a lethal game of hacky sack.

Burton's command reached her. "Steady, hold here. They're so determined to come to us, let them. They're being stupid and reckless; we can win this by playing it smart and strategic."

Now she felt it—the adrenaline. Or...whatever counted as adrenaline in her new body. A clear-headedness, a giddy excitement, a...

Feeling of being exactly where she was needed and wanted.

And there it was.

For the first time in over two years, locked in a life-or-death struggle in a scenario that bordered on the ludicrous, she felt *herself* again.

Okay, then. Fuck being normal; fuck laying low, trying to blend in.

Blue drew her sword back, waiting for her first target to blunder into range. Nothing else mattered but this. Saving lives, stopping the bad guy, protecting Chip. Not necessarily in that order, but she'd get it done, just like she got it done last time. *Time to tear some shit up.*

And then she had no more time to think.

———

With a wide wave of her sword, Blue diverted the charge of the two giggling ass-clowns to either side. She heard the crackle of their wizard's lightning bolts strike something. The giggles of the harlequins turned to screams of pain. Blue smirked. *Atta boy, Phil!*

The druid decided to fling her own fireballs to each side, probably aiming for Burton and Skye.

Marda charged. As she swung the SoulStaff like a war club, she let loose a blood-curdling scream and ran at Blue. She closed the distance and jumped, swiping the SoulStaff for Blue's head.

Rather than jump to meet her, Blue kick-stepped into a backward hop, diffusing much of Marda's speed. She held her sword up to protect her head.

She felt the impact in her wrist, but the blow otherwise deflected without harm.

Blue twisted in mid-air, landing gently on her feet. She watched, bemused, as Marda kicked and bounced out of control, trying to change direction in mid-charge.

Clearly, the Baalinistas didn't take the time to practice the way we have.

Marda bounced one last time before slamming into the large oak tree. She slumped down the trunk and landed on her ass. "Damn you, Blue-hair. I recognize you. I owe you for what you did to me."

Blue offered her a mock salute with her sword. "I recognize you, too. Your lack of basic fighting skills has accurately translated into the game."

Marda bared her teeth and pressed against the tree with the staff to help raise herself. "I'll show *you* who has a lack of fighting skills!"

Even as Blue pondered the irony of that declaration, Chip's thief character peeked out from behind the tree. Using the grip of his dagger, he thrust down, striking Marda on the back of the head.

Marda yelped in surprise and dropped the SoulStaff. Apparently reeling from the pain, she fell to her knees.

Chip turned the dagger in his hand, then wrapped the fingers of his left hand over his right. With a cry of fury, he thrust the dagger into Marda's back.

Marda's face froze in a dumbfounded stare, then her body vanished.

Chip's eyes met Blue's. He winked and offered a quick salute before he disappeared behind the tree.

Blue relaxed and approached the SoulStaff. *Wow. She showed me her lack of fighting skills, all right.*

Having experienced "death" in the game, Blue knew she had a couple minutes' reprieve from Marda's madness. She scooped up the SoulStaff and scanned the meadow.

Phil and Skye were each tussling with a harlequin. The druid and Burton were facing off, the druid girl flinging more fireballs, which Burton dodged with minimal effort.

Blue charged the druid but detoured past Phil and the dagger-wielding maniac he was trying to fend off. She paused long enough to swing her sword down.

The harlequin's head dropped off from the body, still chortling as the head bounced and settled into the field.

A moment later, the body vanished.

Blue extended a hand that Phil gripped firmly.

"Thanks, Blue! What a hellion!"

Off in the distance, the other harlequin slipped her knife between Skye's ribs.

Skye uttered a cry of shock, and, a moment later, vanished.

Blue pointed toward the little assassin already charging Burton. "Stop her, Phil!"

"On it!" Streaks of lightning shot from Phil's staff, knocking the approaching nymph off her feet.

Blue leapt toward the cloaked druid woman, hoping to blindside the attacker while she focused on flinging fireballs at Burton.

Blue closed the distance just as one of those fireballs struck Burton's thigh. Blue ducked and leapt low. She swiped with her sword, even as her tackle knocked the cloaked druid off her feet.

Both the druid and Rebecca let out yelps of surprise and pain.

The druid tumbled sideways, and as they parted, Blue's sword penetrated skin and sliced through the druid's back.

The druid's gasp changed to a scream, and she collapsed in a heap.

Yikes! Blue landed to stand before the woman's crumpled form. Blue raised her sword and...hesitated.

The woman struggled to pull herself along the meadow. "Get away from me!"

Blue watched the wound close moment by moment. *Do I kill her? It's not like I'd really kill her, but...*

"Get back!" the druid cried.

"Look, I don't want to..." *What should I even say? The woman...change that, girl...can't and won't stop me, either way. Whoever she is, it's not in her.*

Instead, Blue ran a beeline past the girl, straight for Burton.

Burton had struggled to her feet, where she appeared to be distracted by the visible healing taking place on her own leg.

Blue extended the wooden rod. "Here's the SoulStaff."

"Very good. Phil should be able to destroy it with a lightning strike. In the meantime, I need protection to cast the spell to close this portal. Oh...watch out."

Blue turned.

Still on her elbows, the druid girl held her palm out, orange energy recharging in her hands.

"Really?" *That's what I get for not hurting you when I had the chance?*

"I need to stop you!" the druid shouted, as if that explained everything.

Blue rolled her eyes and re-drew her sword. "Seriously, go home, little girl. You have no business fighting in this battle."

The druid responded by flinging twin fireballs at Blue. Irritated more than threatened, Blue struck both fireballs with her sword, deflecting them to either side.

"I have to stop you."

"Have it your way." Blue leapt forward and feigned a sword-swipe at the druid's head.

As the druid ducked a blow from the wrong direction, Blue struck low, chopping deep into the girl's torso and causing a scream to pierce the air before the figure vanished.

Blue landed and immediately leapt back the way she came, to land next to Rebecca in a fluid motion.

"You're a natural," Rebecca observed.

"Thanks." She shook off a chill. "I can't help but feel like I just killed someone's kid sister."

"Neither. You just put one of our enemies into a penalty box."

It wasn't that simple, and Blue knew it. "Still...getting stabbed like that hurt like hell, I'll bet."

Burton nodded. "I sincerely hope neither of us ever find out."

As Burton faced the large tree, Blue scanned the battlefield. The skirmish had gotten off to a good start.

Phil threw the remaining nimble harlequin off of him, following up with a lightning bolt that took the character out of the game.

For the moment, the battleground had cleared. "Phil! Over here."

Phil nodded and ran to close the distance.

From the opposite side, Skye also closed in.

Blue craned her neck back and then turned her attention to the front, divided between watching Burton—too damn slow for Blue's taste—lower the crystal to the ground at the base of the tree and then stand over it, a hand outstretched. Burton closed her eyes and emitted a lyrical chant, the foreign words almost songlike even through the CGI vocal cords.

Phil arrived first.

Blue threw the SoulStaff at his feet. "Get rid of that."

"With what? I don't know the spell."

"The spell is...shoot the bejesus out of it."

"Oh." Phil pointed his wizard staff, and a streak of blue sparks engulfed the opponent's staff. After a few moments, the SoulStaff lay before them, smoking and blackened but otherwise intact.

"Shoot it again, Phil. Just keep shooting until it goes away."

"It might just come right back again."

"We'll worry about that if—" Movement several yards away caught her attention. "Heads up!"

The pair of harlequins scuttled out of the woods that surrounded the meadow, both figures wielding daggers.

Blue charged, swinging her sword at one of the screaming harpies and delivering a fatal blow to her chest.

The harlequin's cry cut short, and the body crumpled, folded over backward, then vanished in mid-fall.

Blue landed in front of the second harlequin, who danced madly from foot to foot, screaming her anger. "Damn you, that's the second time you've killed my sister."

There's something you can only say in a ludicrous situation like this, mused Blue. "Hope it's not the last, you crazy bitch."

The harlequin pirouetted to the left, then the right. "We owe you, Blue-hair! We owe you for the pain you caused Marda, and now the pain you've caused Cyn. I'll pay you back, and more!"

Gunther's prolific words from that terrible night returned to her, unbidden. *You'll pay in blood.*

She put the memory away and focused. "Tough talk for someone trying to conquer the world by raising Ms. Pac Man." Blue didn't even know what that meant, but it sounded mocking, so there it was.

The harlequin girl stepped left, waving her knives.

But Blue knew a feint when she saw one and didn't go for it.

The girl returned to her starting point and swiped her daggers.

Blue swung her two-handed blade across, knocking both knives from the harlequin's hands.

She heard a sharp cry from behind her.

Then Phil's voice cut through the air. "Oh, my God!"

Blue turned to see Burton, now with a dagger sticking out of her back. Behind her, the druid stood, and as Blue watched, the cloaked figure shoved a second dagger between Burton's ribs.

You've got to be kidding me. After cutting the girl a break, this happened. And that act of mercy may have jeopardized their success.

Even impaled, Burton closed her eyes and held her hand toward the portal, still chanting the words of the incantation. She trailed to a stop several seconds later. She opened her eyes and held the crystal out toward Chip. "Quickly, someone needs to–" Then her body disappeared.

The crystal, now glowing a fierce, fiery red, bounced off the ground and landed at Chip's feet.

Chip bent to pick up the crystal.

The druid jumped upon him.

"Chip, no!" Blue leapt toward the struggling pair. But she barely launched before a loud crack sounded, and her ankles were wrapped against themselves by an unseen binding. Her legs seared and flared with white hot agony.

Blue's leap stopped short, and her body was slammed into the grass. Her face hit the ground with stunning force.

*What the...*She kicked out, but someone fell over her. As she tried to move her legs, she detected a coil or cord wrapped around both of them, holding them together.

A bola? A whip? She tripped me with a whip!

A giggle of maniacal glee sounded in her ear from the body pressed against her back. *Fuck this!*

Mustering her strength and using the superior armor and weight advantage of her warrior body, Blue forced herself to her elbows and rolled over the ground.

Teeth bit into the back of her neck, fresh pain emanating from the spot. *She bit me? Seriously?*

Gripping her sword with both gloved hands, she twisted the point back toward herself, then held the sword out to her right.

She thrust it back and behind her, hoping to jab her mad-dog opponent. Anywhere would do.

The giggle turned into a howl of surprise and shock.

"Get...off...me!"

She gripped the handle and shoved in a second effort, this time feeling the sword sink into flesh, impaling her opponent.

She threw the sword aside, flinging the injured crazy woman along with it, and rolled onto her back.

She looked at her legs. Sure enough, they'd been bound by the coils of a whip, a weapon currently lying slack without an owner.

With a strangled cry, the body impaled on her sword vanished, and Blue retrieved her weapon. A couple swipes later, she freed her legs and stood.

She looked over, hoping to help, only to see Chip remove his dagger from the throat of the druid girl.

She stared back at him, her mouth open in an "O" of surprise even as her body vanished.

Chip reached down and held the crystal up toward the portal.

The crystal flared a fresh, intense red.

As the crystal flashed to life, disturbing thoughts also flashed through Blue's head. *Chip, taking the place of Brother Krane. Chip, engulfed in flames. Chip, his never-ending screams of agony wasted on the demoness. Chip, tormented for all eternity.*

That could not happen.

Before she could think it through any further, she drew back her heavy two-handed sword, stepped behind Chip, and thrust her weapon through his gut.

"What–?"

She heard his cry of surprise. She closed her eyes and pulled the sword out of the writhing body, hearing a second cry of pain and shock.

She blinked away a scrim of tears in time to see the red fireball hit the grass once again.

At the same time, Chip turned, ready to face the enemy who'd blindsided him. His look of pain turning to shock and surprise.

"Blue?" He fell to his knees.

But she stepped forward, cradled the slack body, and lowered it gently to the ground.

Chip shook his head, as if unwilling to accept the evidence of his eyes. "No. Blue...you can't..."

"Yes, I can. It's not your fault. I won't let you."

"But–" His body vanished, the look of pain and betrayal still distorting his features as he faded from her vision.

She knew she didn't have any time. She steeled her courage, gripped the fiery-red stone in her gauntlet, and stood before the portal, holding her palm out to the doorway.

Nothing happened.

Come on, bitch! Come and get me, I'm waiting! She waved the talisman as if sheer force of will would compel it to complete its purpose.

"Here I am, Baalina! I hope you like your new virtual prison, you hellspawn bitch! You need a sacrifice, take me! I'll give you an eternity of good sport. But I'm all you're getting today, you and your pathetic, deluded band of followers. Bring it. I'll make sure you choke on it for all eternity."

The edges of the portal lit up a brilliant green, and in her hand, she felt an intense burning start in her palm and build up into her arm. The world turned flaming red, and the cackling silhouette of the angry demoness drew closer and closer.

No, she looked around. The demoness wasn't coming to Blue, but Blue was being pulled toward Baalina. She floated bodily through the air, toward the portal, beginning her one-way trip through the gate of chaos.

Goodbye, Chip, please don't think poorly of me. I love you.

And then the flames consumed her, and Blue's world turned to burning agony.

—————

CHAPTER TWENTY

—————

Chip opened his eyes. Before him, the computer screen displayed his avatar's spirit floating in the pre-programmed timeout, drifting down, returning to its body, where it would soon try to rejoin a fight that had concluded moments earlier.

His real body still reclined in the chair where he'd sat several minutes ago. He reached up and rubbed his eyes, trying to recall what had happened. Across the room, from the direction of the couch, he heard Phil utter a similar groan.

He was back in his body. Phil was back. That meant everyone in the game was coming back. They'd won.

But how?

I'd grabbed the crystal, then...

Oh, no!

Blue!

He stood bolt upright. "Blue!"

Looking to his right, he saw Blue, her head bent backwards, her body slack, eyes staring open and lifeless.

"Blue!" He grabbed her chair and wheeled it away from the desk. Her body slumped forward.

He gripped her shoulders, delicately turned her, and lowered her to the rug.

Exactly the same way she'd handled me when—

No, she didn't betray me.

She's taken my place. Which means...

"No! Blue, wake up. Come on, sweetie, wake up." He shook her, panic building within him. "Blue...honey, come on, wake up. Please, honey, please. Don't do this. Don't tell me you did this."

He reached for her wrist, his heart pounding, even after he found the thin, thready throb that indicated a minimal sign of life.

"Fuck!" In his anger, he struck out at the chair and sent it tumbling across the floor behind him.

What to do, what to do? I can't think. I need to think.

As if from a great distance, Chip heard Phil's voice. "Oh, no, what happened, Chip?"

"She did it, she...what Rebecca was supposed to do. What I tried to do. She..." He couldn't get the words out, and he quit trying.

Phil got it. "She used the crystal? Like Brother Krane? She's the one who closed the portal?"

Chip found his voice again. "Yes. I was going to, but she stopped me." His head still spun, searching for options when he didn't have any. His mind reeled, looking for someplace to connect to and finding nothing.

Phil's voice again reached him. "How?"

"She ran a sword through me."

"Oh." Then: "God."

Chip rose, then turned to see her computer screen.

Phil stood nearby, his eyes already looking at it.

It showed only blackness.

Chip started talking out loud, hoping Phil could grab on to something he didn't see. "She's somewhere we've not properly mapped for the game. She's beyond what this can show us, but we know where she is, Phil, she's back in that extra room, that simulated chaos with Baalina's virtual self. She's still in the game."

"Yes, and we're not. And that means no one else is, either. So, take a second, think this through."

A thick hand landed between Chip's shoulders. He looked into the face of his best friend, though Chip still saw everything through a tunnel.

Fresh circles darkened Phil's eyes, his shirt fit rumpled over his plump body, the neck defaced by a fresh line of drool. But overall, Phil looked otherwise unharmed.

At the moment, Chip couldn't begin to appreciate the victory.

Phil's voice still sounded from a distance. "I know it's not where your head is, but she broke us out of there. She broke everyone else out of there. She did good, Chip."

Chip shook his head. "No, you're goddamn right, I don't want to hear that." Anger flared up at Phil for wanting to find any sort of "bright side." "It doesn't mean anything. If we can't get her back, it doesn't mean a damn thing, Phil, please. Help me get her back, or shut the hell up."

The words hung between them, two best friends facing each other—one clearly in shock, the other dealing with the aftermath of his own medically uncharted trauma. Their mutual heavy breathing from the intensity of the experience filled the room.

Chip froze, overwhelmed to the point of inaction. All he could think about was, as they sat here, recovering, taking inventory, Blue was going through God knew what, trapped in an inescapable prison with a vindictive master of torture.

He had to get her out of there. Somehow. And soon.

Phil nodded. "All right, first things first. Let's move her to the couch and out of the way. Then we can evaluate with the computers and see what we can do from this side."

Chip wormed his hands behind her shoulders and waited while Phil positioned himself on the other side to grab her legs. A few moments later–Chip couldn't help but notice that Blue's more reasonably proportioned weight made the task of moving her far easier than moving Phil–they left her lying across the same couch Phil had occupied moments before.

He grabbed a blanket and, ever so gently, covered her to her neck. He bent down, intending to kiss her forehead, when the body trembled, and Blue called out, "No...no, stop..."

"Blue?"

He could see her eyes moving behind the lids, some sort of REM sleep. *But her mind shouldn't be active. She doesn't really occupy it anymore. Unless...the old body still holds some sort of tentative psychic connection with its mind, and whatever is happening was so powerful...*

"Blue, wake up."

"Chip." Phil had come up behind Chip and now laid his large, beefy hand on his shoulder. "Come on. I know it sucks to see this, but she's not in there. We can't help her that way."

"God...what's she going through? It should be me, not her."

"You don't need me to tell you that Blue is spontaneous, but not this time, buddy. I'm sure a part of you is still pissed as hell that she betrayed you in there. But whether by accident or by design, she probably made the smartest choice possible by taking your place."

Chip bit back his angry response. "How do you figure?"

"Because it's you and me out here now, and those fuckers tampered with our game, Chip. If you had followed through with your plan, let's face facts, it would just be me working the computers, and she'd be pacing the room, useless to everyone."

"Well..." He didn't want to say it, but that made perfect sense. *And yes, it's just possible Blue had seen it, as well. And that means she's counting on us to do our part.*

"Now," Phil continued, "The last thing *you* need to be doing is pacing the room, useless to anyone."

"You're right." Chip stood, only to settle in front of his computer console a few steps across the room.

Phil called up a game report on his screen. "There were about 60 players online up until the very moment we were all pushed out and our souls returned to our bodies. We can assume that everyone who had been playing when the spell triggered were all zapped into the game. By my approximation, it looks like the electricity level spiked less than ten minutes ago. No explanation, but

I'm sure that's when it happened. Then, everyone except Blue all logged out about six minutes ago. Every one, and all at the same time."

"So, these people, whoever they were and wherever they were, all collapsed at the same time? In their dorms? In their homes? Back in their parents' house waiting on Thanksgiving dinner? That's going to—"

"Be noticed. You bet. That's a lot of panicking parents, a lot of 911 calls, and a lot of people putting two and two together."

Phil continued. "As soon as I sat down, I locked out all users. No one can get in. No affected players, and no players who are clueless about what they missed. That includes our Baalina psychopaths. So that's that."

"Good idea, but it doesn't matter. They're going to come for us," said Chip. *God, can this get any worse?* "There will be a public outcry, and the authorities will insist we shut down the game. Not in forty-eight hours, but immediately."

"We don't know how long it will take them to connect the dots," said Phil.

"A couple hours at most, Phil."

Phil seemed to consider. "Okay, well, let's look at that option. What if we shut the game down?"

As if on cue, Blue moaned from the corner again. "Please...no..."

Chip stole a look in her direction, then shook his head. "We can't risk it! I didn't shut it down when you were in there for the same reason."

"Look...we don't know what might happen if we shut the system down. Maybe nothing at all. Maybe...it might fix this."

The very thought of shutting down the game terrified him. "No. We can't. The chances are far more likely that the electrical current going through the game is the only thing keeping her mind...her soul...locked here in the vicinity and not...cut loose. We kill the power, and we might kill her. We can't risk it."

The doorbell rang, then twice, three times, with urgency that would not be ignored.

To Chip, the sound signaled fate arriving to take the decision away from them. "Oh, my God."

Even from in the basement, they could hear the pounding at the door, followed by two more presses of the doorbell.

And then the sound of a voice blasting through a bullhorn. *"This is Officer Kip Kirby of the Bloomington Police! Come out now, or we're coming in!"*

Chip started to ascend the stairs.

Phil gripped his arm. "We need to stay here."

"They're going to beat the door down. Like we're some sort of armed robbers or drug lords. It's a goddamned raid!"

The amplified voice continued to scream its irritation. "We're giving you five seconds, and then we're coming in!"

"We step away from these machines, they will pull the plug before we can get a word out."

"One!"

"Phil, you're only buying us a couple of minutes."

"We need to talk them down, is all."

But he could read Phil's face. "We can't. You know that."

"Two!"

"We'd better think of something. Because it's our only play."

"Three!"

Phil folded his hands behind his back, nodding toward Chip to do the same.

"Four!"

"Let's stand in front of the servers," said Phil, doing just that. "Maybe we can distract them with having to arrest us, and we can talk them out of pulling the plug."

"Five!"

"That's your plan?" Nevertheless, Chip joined Phil in front of the servers, matching his pose and waiting for the police to force the door.

———

For a moment, darkness.

Then fire flamed up, discomfort flared to blistering pain.

The pain roused Blue, and she sat up.

She found herself huddled on hard, unforgiving ground. No, not ground, a stone slab that extended out in all directions. Yet somehow, the stone ground could burn, as flares of flame shot and flickered in areas around her. It radiated heat, burning her palms and forcing her to her feet.

I won't cower. I won't cower. Still, she couldn't control the inner shaking of her legs as she tried to stay on her feet.

Before her, some distance away, a cloaked, horned silhouette watched, eyes glowing green. Her voice spoke cold malevolence. "So. Here stands the insolent worm who dared to defy my followers."

Blue reached to her scabbard and, to her surprise, gripped her sword. She still possessed her armor and weapon. The knowledge roused her courage. "This 'insolent worm' stopped your demon ass cold."

"Temporarily. No more than that."

Blue stared across at the distance, calculating the needed leaps. Even as she had to hop from boot to boot as the stone heated beneath her, she thought she could make it in two or three leaps.

The demoness continued. "My defeat is only temporary. Yours, wretched one, shall be eternal."

"We'll see about that!" Blue leapt, sword pointed toward the erect figure. But she'd barely left the ground before a pillar of fire engulfed her body in searing, exquisite agony.

Rational thought left her. All she could do was follow the instinct to try to escape the inescapable flames.

She hit the ground, unable to keep her feet, and collapsed against the searing stone.

The fresh pain to her arms, knees, and hands was a distant footnote to the torment of the flames that enfolded her.

She rolled, and she twisted. The handle of her sword grew too hot to hold.

She couldn't see.

She wasn't even sure she had eyes anymore.

Or skin.

She opened her mouth to utter a scream, but no sound came out.

"Feel my power. Feel the agony and know your worthlessness before me. Know that this is just the beginning of your torment, which will continue now until your end! Your body may not break, but your mind, that is another matter, isn't it?"

Chip, someone, help me!

And then she died.

———

BLESSED RELIEF.

She hovered over her charred body, untouchable to the whims of her tormentor.

And yet, the wounds could not heal fast enough. And already, even as coherent thought returned to her, she drifted back. Back to a renewed, rejuvenated, healthy body.

Ready to be burned and tormented again.

No! Please, no, not again! Please...

CHAPTER TWENTY-ONE

"Freeze!"

"We're not resisting, Officer!" Phil called.

His voice loud but shaking, Chip guessed, in an effort to meet the fine line that's loud enough to be heard and yet not forceful enough to be considered a threat by their gun-wielding guests.

From his vantage point, Chip could see the door at the top of the stairs, shrouded in darkness. The door was thrown open.

In the white-lit rectangular opening, Officer Kirby leaned forward to take in the computer bullpen area beyond the darkened stairway. He held his gun up toward the ceiling and settled his gaze on the two unarmed, waiting nerds doing their best to project harmlessness.

Chip bit back his terror enough to speak. "You promised me two days, Kirby, it's barely been six hours."

"That was before everyone playing your game started collapsing into comas, Farren!"

Kirby practically fell into the room, along with four other troopers who piled into the room after him.

Phil called out, "It's not like that, Officer. We fixed the problem."

Kirby glared, his eyes sweeping from one to the other. He raised a finger in warning. "You'd best not say a damn thing right now."

One of the troopers bent over Blue. "Sir, you need to see this."

Kirby approached the trooper.

Chip caught pieces of their brief conversation, which concluded with, "Just like the others."

Chip closed his eyes and swallowed back bile. *Oh, hell, no. Not like the others at all.*

The other troopers, guns drawn, scurried across the room like beetles. Two of them glanced at the screens, then looked at each other. From what Chip could see, they had no idea what they were looking at.

"Officer," Phil called again, "you really need to listen to—"

Kirby glared. "I told you *not* to say anything."

"Fine," said Chip, unsure where his nerve had come from. "I'll say something."

Kirby focused on Chip, his face distorted in fury. "Oh, good, because I can't wait to hear what the pompous nerd-boy has to say. Do you think I've forgotten the tricks you pulled? Do you think I don't remember that I wanted to shut down your operation hours ago, but you talked me into giving you more time?"

"We still need more time to—"

"To what? You sent half of your players into comas. Did you think no one would call the police? Did you think we wouldn't make the connection? We're shutting it down. Now."

"You can't. Blue's life may be at stake."

"That's right, pal, because of your game. Because of what you've done."

"No, you need to listen. If you shut down the game, it might kill her."

Kirby stood by the couch, his gaze lingering on Blue's unconscious form. "I'll say this for you, Farren, you got a hell of a way of showing gratitude to the people who helped you." His eyes widened. "Ms. Shaefer, right? She's the one who sicced the attorney on me. And this is how you repay her?"

"I didn't do this!" Chip snarled, then stopped. He tried again, struggling to keep his tone calm. "We didn't do any of it. We're trying to reverse what happened. If you'll check around, you'll find most of the people have recovered. That's *because* of our efforts. But we still have to get her back."

"What is it, some sort of computer narcotic? You get them hooked in, and you blitz their mind?"

"What? Why the hell would you think–"

"You think I worked this long in the city with one of the largest colleges in the state and haven't picked up on the drug scene? Far as I can tell, you kids want two things—your technology and your vices. Looks like you found a way to combine both, a brand-new type of crime, right here under my nosc. It stops now."

"No!" Even as he cried his frustration, he understood Kirby's conclusion. What else could he think? The truth was too far outside the evidence to stumble upon.

The two troopers had followed the cables back to where they plugged into one of the main surge protectors.

One of the troopers looked to Kirby. "Should we try to shut it down or just pull the plug?"

Kirby snapped back, "Just pull the damn plug."

"You can't!" yelled Chip. He moved forward, but two troopers gripped his arms.

Phil started talking, "You pull that plug, you might very well commit murder, Kirby. If you've never heard anything we've said until now, hear this–Blue is somehow connected to that machine. We don't know what will happen if you cut off the power, but chances are, nothing good. Do you really want to take that chance?"

Kirby and the two troopers who hovered by the plug all turned toward Phil.

Clearly his words gave the two troopers pause. *Good going, Phil. Now, if we can think of something more to say.*

But Kirby scoffed. "Really? You got a hell of a lot of nerve, buddy! This machine put half of our students into comas, and you want to talk to me about committing murder?"

Chip cut in, "It's hardly half the—"

"And you shut the hell up, nerd-boy!" Kirby stabbed a finger at Chip, shooting him a look deadly enough to scare Chip into silencing himself. "I've had it with you and your partner in crime here. We tried it your way, and this is where it got us."

Kirby nodded at the troopers. "Do as I say. Pull the damn plug!"

"Belay that!" A woman's voice called from the top of the stairs.

A female figure appeared, tall, red-haired, dressed in a black leather coat, her boots banging down the stairs as she descended as fast as she could. Behind her, a second, tall, mousy-looking girl with dirty blonde hair eased her way after.

Chip knew the tone and the voice. *Rebecca Burton!*

Burton held out a badge, her authoritative voice barking at the two troopers. "Touch those machines and you will face immediate prosecution from the federal government for obstructing a high-priority investigation."

Kirby snarled, "Agent Burton, what the hell are you even doing here?"

"Keeping you from ruining your career, Kirby. And you'd better listen to these young men. Shutting down those machines could very well mean ending the life of Ms. Fiona Shaefer there on the couch."

At Burton's words, the two troopers backed away from the surge protector.

Chip released a breath he hadn't realized he'd been holding with a whoosh of relief and gratitude.

Kirby exploded. "You're as cracked as they are!"

"Maybe, maybe not. But it's officially not your problem anymore."

Rather than back down, Kirby stepped up, eyes blazing, finger shaking in the face of the federal agent. "They're putting students into comas, and you're telling me it's not my problem!"

Burton met his emotional tirade with a stoic, stony look.

Chip cringed at the display of useless machismo. It was like a scene from a bad cop show.

Kirby's rant continued. "This may be the strangest bust in my entire career on the force, but whatever is going on, these people have got to be stopped."

Apparently unruffled, Burton replied, "I agree. But these boys have been telling you the truth. Their game was hacked by technology terrorists and used for malicious purposes outside of their control. And the fact that the mass coma crisis reversed itself within minutes of being triggered is a credit to their skills."

"Minutes my ass, Burton! You were hospitalized for two days!"

"And yet I'm not the one yelling, Officer. Think about it."

If possible, Kirby turned even redder in the face, but to Chip's relief, finally shut up.

Burton surveyed the room. "Officer Kirby, I'd like to offer a proposal. I will need assistance nabbing the real perpetrators of this crime. You and your men can be a part of it, if you're willing. If not, I'll find someone else. But either way, your men are going to clear out of this house and leave the equipment untouched, and free these kids, and forget whatever charges you think you have on them, immediately."

This time, Burton allowed some anger to show through, and to Chip's surprise, Kirby backed down.

"That's my direct order as your superior. You let me know about the rest."

Chip waited, not sure whether he dared move.

Finally, Kirby made a scoffing noise and turned his back.

Burton grabbed his arm, turning him to face her.

He glared, his eyes darting to where she still held his arm. He opened his mouth, then shut it as if he'd reconsidered.

Chip imagined it was a rare thing for anyone to handle him like that, especially a superior.

His voice trembled. "What?"

Burton said, "There are actual bad guys out there. Their plans are falling apart, and pretty soon, they're going to try to make a break for it. It's not these kids, but I can point you to the real criminals. I could use your help."

Kirby glowered a bit more, and then his features settled into a businesslike expression. "You going to come clean and tell me the truth about what is going on?"

The famous movie line traveled through Chip's head. *You couldn't handle the truth.*

Apparently, Burton chose not to rise to the bait, but answered, "Most of it. Whatever isn't classified."

"Classified?"

Burton nodded. "This is much bigger than you know. I wasn't exaggerating when I used the term technology terrorists. Right here in Bloomington. Want to be a part of the bust?"

"Of course."

"Okay." Burton released his arm. "Get your men ready. Stand by. We'll be moving soon. Oh, I hope you didn't break open these kids' door."

Kirby shook his head. Did Chip see a twinkle in his eyes? "It was unlocked."

Burton nodded. "Good. Please leave in an orderly fashion. We have work to do here."

Moments later, they were gone, save Burton and the other girl–Skye, he presumed–and all Chip could do as he sank on the couch next to Blue was try to catch his breath. "I can't believe your timing. Thank you so much."

Rebecca put a hand on his shoulder. "Don't thank me yet. The hard work is still ahead."

Chip leaned in close to Blue. His heart broke as her face again contorted in some sort of pain. "Hang in there. Stay strong. We're going to get you out soon."

———

AFTER WHAT SEEMED AN ETERNITY, Natalie's screen flashed the message: **Save Complete.** She pulled the mini-drive from the slot and dropped it into her laptop briefcase. "That's it, that's all of our work, up to the moment everything fell apart."

At Nat's words, Marda glared from where she sat in front of the computer screen. She was not at all happy at the prospect of having to flee. Nat understood, to some extent. They had all glimpsed their mistress, not a statue image, but real and in the flesh—after a fashion. Of them, Nat knew this would affect Marda most profoundly.

Marda had witnessed the mistress torment and torture the Shaefer girl, who had made her suffer. To Nat, it made no important difference at this point, but she knew Marda well enough to know she'd obsess over it.

Marda pressed, "Why can't we just re-create the SoulStaff?"

Nat slashed her open palm through the air. "They've locked me out. They've located my server, they know my port, and they know exactly where I'm coming in from. My last few attempts haven't even gotten past the login screen."

"Then do something else. Use your hacking tricks!"

"You don't know what you're talking about. I don't have any tricks left!" Nat was screaming now and past caring. "They're on to us, Marda, plain and simple. That's two computer geniuses, working within the program they themselves created, versus me. I had a chance as long as I could cloak my entry. I did it for a long time, but I just can't anymore."

"Then we call someone else."

Nat rolled her eyes. It was the never-ending curse of all engineers, having to explain computer tech to non-techies and their nonsensical mantra: *Spare me the details, just do it.* "No one's that good. We're done here. We just have to find another opportunity on another platform."

"You mean start over somewhere else? That could take months!"

"The mistress has waited thousands of years. One more year won't matter much."

"Watch your tone, Natalie!"

Natalie opened her mouth to reply, only to feel a pressure against her throat, followed by a sting. *Oh, my Goddess, what...*She pulled her head back to face a dagger extended out and pushed against her chin.

As a chill ran down her spine, Nat's gaze traced the hand, up the arm, to meet Cyn's expression of malice.

"I would be *very mindful* of Marda's advice at this point, Nat." Cyn leaned in close, her top lip curled in a snarl. "It's almost as if you want us to fail."

"What are you doing?" Surely, they didn't think...

She turned to look around her station. Cyn towered over her and to her left, she met Marda's dark, penetrating stare. Behind her, she felt a pair of hands grip her shoulders. *Van wants in on this, too. Figures. They all want a piece of me.*

Marda's eyes drilled into Nat's. Nat tried to look away, but Cyn's dagger pressed a warning.

Marda's voice sounded like ice. "Cyn's right. Why are you in such a hurry to fail?"

"Marda...please..." Nat understood what had happened. They'd failed, they wanted their scapegoat, and now they thought they'd found it. Her.

When she found her voice, Natalie tried to keep her tone calm, though she herself trembled. "Please...please, Sisters. Listen to reason. We can't succeed here. If we could, I'd be the first one to suggest how. Don't forget how I found our breakthrough after all that work. I got us in." The words tumbled out of her. "I recreated the SoulStaff, and I did it on my own. And it worked. Do you really think I'd do all that and chicken out now?"

Marda's eyes softened, perhaps just a bit. "Go on."

"Make it good," said Cyn.

Natalie closed her eyes and swallowed back phlegm. She knew the truth, the one she dared not say aloud. She wasn't willing to die for this cause. Yes, she thought women had been treated poorly throughout history, and she thought a reversal of the ruling order was a natural and welcome step to remedying the great wrongs of history.

But she didn't want to die for this cause, or *any* cause. She was a coward, and she wanted to live.

Right now, she just wanted to live past this moment.

She referenced the facts, trying not to think, just talk. "The police know some sort of attack, targeting other students, has taken place. Burton has awakened from her coma. She can, and she *will*, have the authorities convene on our location as soon as she can confirm it."

Marda's distorted features made her fury apparent. "No, you silly mouse, I won't accept that. There must be a way to put us back into the game and trigger the spell. Today was to be our day of victory and revenge. There must be a way."

"Marda, I can't even pull up the game world. The only reason we can still access the chaos-domain is because they haven't found our hack into it. It's also the only room that *we* can still lock *them* out of, but that doesn't do us any real good. All we can do is buy time to transfer Baalina back into the real chaos dimension and try again."

"The mistress will demand that someone pay."

Natalie closed her eyes, trying not to become ill where she sat. "Baalina has...a new playmate to torture...at least, for as long as the virtual room remains. We might even be able to take the blue-haired...adversary–" Nat couldn't bring herself to call the unfortunate soul a blue-haired bitch the way Marda did, "–along with her when we transfer them back. I'll oversee it personally."

"Yes, but..." Marda's eyes shone their malice. "Now that I think about it...why should the mistress have all the fun?"

Marda closed her eyes and seemed to swoon in the oppressive quiet that followed. "Yes...yes, mistress, I hear you. And we accept!"

Marda's eyes re-opened to look squarely at Natalie. "Can you still use the spell to conjure us back into the virtual chaos realm?"

It took a moment for Natalie to process the request. "Can I send us back in? Yes, but we can't really *flee* there. We'll be as trapped as–"

"Because the mistress has extended a gracious invitation for all of us to join her..." Marda turned toward the screen.

Nat had lowered the sound all the way down, so it currently showed Blue in the midst of a silent scream while a blazing fireball tore through her chest. "...to spend some quality time with her new playmate."

Cyn smiled. "Sounds delectable."

Natalie's stomach churned. Their house was collapsing around them, and all the goddess Baalina thought about was herself and her pleasures. She spared no thought for the danger she put the rest of them in.

Nat looked around the room and saw that the idea took hold, one to the other to the other, like a poison.

Matching looks of sadism crossed the faces of Cyn, Van, and Marda, but Natalie closed her eyes against the queasiness that threatened to overtake her. *God, no, I can't.*

Then she noticed that Cyn's knife had lowered, and Van's hands no longer restrained her.

They're not thinking about me anymore. In that moment, Nat made her decision. *They want the Shaefer girl, so let them have the Shaefer girl.* Nat spoke her decision with boldness. "Okay...I'll transfer the three of you."

Cyn's gaze locked on hers. "Don't you want to join us...Sister?"

She almost answered "no" but caught herself. "Someone...needs to make sure the rest of you can come back, and...I can finish packing in the meantime."

Cyn opened her mouth to reply.

But Marda answered first. "Excellent plan, Sister. Prepare us for the transfer." Her eyes locked on the screen, where Blue's body had once again expended itself and faded away. "As you say, time is short. I have much to pay that bitch back for, and not much time to do it."

CHAPTER TWENTY-TWO

Again, the flames engulfed her.

Again, her hair incinerated, her skin burned. Again, the agony forced her to scream and thrash.

And yet...following those few seconds of pain, her avatar "died," which translated to over two minutes of a calm, more peaceful state of being—unreachable and untouchable by her tormentor, the so-called demoness.

It meant a chance to catch her breath, where the pain faded, and where she could regroup and consider her options.

After the time-out, she returned to her body, fully healthy, healed, and clear-headed.

For only a moment before the pain would begin again.

But the rest meant a new opportunity to turn the tables on her tormentor.

Good God. Could she adjust to this?

Many times already, she'd jumped at her attacker. Twice, she'd almost gotten her hands around the neck of the pompous bitch who equated making her life a living hell to some sort of distraction on par with taking up knitting.

She needed just one chance to grab that scepter and test its durability on the demoness' skull. Then she might actually keep the upper hand in this retarded exercise until Chip found a way to get her out of here.

It wasn't a great plan, but it was a plan. And it kept her sane.

She'd sacrificed herself, prepared to trade her life for Chip's, and she didn't hesitate in doing so. But even as she acted, she realized her sacrifice probably wasn't as final as all that.

Not by a long shot.

For all its trappings and for all her suffering, this wasn't really a hell. And she knew Chip was working on the other side, doing all he could to get her out.

In the meantime, she stood on the hot cement ground. She feigned to her left, the fireball just missing her. She pivoted, propelling herself directly at her laughing tormentor.

The demoness answered with a wall of flame spewed across her body that seared her eyes and set her aflame. Again.

"Prepare yourself, mortal worm. When next you return, I have visitors who are quite anxious to say hello!"

Blue's brief scream was cut off moments later by the relief of simulated death.

With each cycle, she noted the trauma of the experience took longer to shake off. *But I can endure...a while longer. Piece of...cake...Chip. But you can...come get me...any time now.*

———

As the mistress called to them, Marda signaled Nat to begin the incantation.

Marda filled the space between Cyn and Van. As they all faced Natalie, Marda's pulse quickened at the idea that they'd shortly be in the presence of...*her*! "Quickly, Natalie, our mistress awaits us! We should not leave her waiting."

It annoyed her, to an extent, to be forced to share this supreme moment with two of her underlings, a pair of muscle-for-hire who stood and waited in casual indifference, clearly oblivious to the honor they were all about to share.

Natalie, at least, responded to her command with the urgency required. She turned away from her laptop and held her hands over the three of them, muttering in the ancient language, pronouncing each sacred syllable almost as clearly as Marda would have if the honor had fallen to her.

The room faded and the three of them dropped into their video game avatar bodies, the transition, this time, much easier than before.

The heat closed around them, its presence oppressive and foreboding. Beneath her, Marda noted they stood on a huge cement slab of cracked and crumbled stone. Flames spewed from random cracks into the stifling air.

Closing the distance, in all her regal splendor and grasping the sacred scepter, Baalina…the mistress herself…stood before them in person! At long last!

"Mistress!" Marda called out and fell before her, prostrate at the Goddess' feet. She ignored the flesh of her face, which seared and burned as she threw herself down on hands and knees.

Marda sensed, rather than saw, Cyn and Van, who stood behind her. She called out her frustration, "Bow, you unworthy ones! Bow!"

Cyn protested, "But the ground is—"

"Get on your knees in the presence of the mistress, you lowly—"

And then…*she* spoke, and nothing else mattered. "Your demonstration does everyone present honor, Special One. But rise, Marda, and look upon the face of your most pleased mistress."

It took…she had no idea how long for the words to register. *She called me Special One. She is most pleased.*

Tears of joy spilled from her eyes and caused the stone to answer with a series of sizzles.

She looked up…into a grayish, thin-fingered hand lowered toward her. "Rise, Special One."

Marda could not hide the tremble in her voice. "I am not worthy to touch—"

"But you are. Take my hand, Marda. Quickly, my Special One. Cyn, Van, prepare yourselves. Our victim is due any moment now. I wish to see a demonstration of your skills. Entertain me."

———

"Surprise, bitch!"

Blue appeared, seeing three people, one on either side, one in front of her. The scenario barely registered before the first blow landed from one of the giggling harlequins, a solid blow to her face before she saw it coming.

She spun into the second harlequin, who caught her before she could hit the ground.

Blue found her balance. As the second harlequin drew her knife, Blue thrust her knee up. She connected with the groin.

The crazy woman's giggles cut off and turned into a grunt of surprise. The harlequin doubled over.

"Surprise back!" Blue enfolded one fist into the other and struck the back of her opponent's head.

"Van, get her!"

Something slammed the side of Blue's face, and she went down.

"Hold her," she heard her wounded opponent cry.

Blow after blow landed. Soon, someone had her arms pinned back, and that's when it really hurt.

They took a long, interminable time at it—laughing, mocking, giggling. The blows fell. Not hard enough to trigger the release she sought, but enough to pile pain upon pain.

Finally, she collapsed.

"Looks like our playmate has stopped playing," a voice said.

"Fuck...you." *The simulated death is coming soon. It has to. Then we'll see. Ultimately, this is an extended ass-kicking. Sucks, but nothing special, especially since I'll come back healed.*

"Oooh, Sisters, sounds like she still has some fight in her."

She recognized Marda's crazy tone, which penetrated Blue's semi-conscious state.

"I don't see much fight, Cyn, she's going to sleep on us."

A hand gripped her hair and pulled her head up.

She stared into the face of the giggling, red-haired, crazed harlequin. "Oh, playmate, that's not very playful."

Blue grimaced. "We'll see how playful I am soon enough." She sensed, rather than saw, the red-haired harlequin address the others. "Do you hear that, girls? She thinks we're done."

Sharp pain stabbed her hand and jolted her fully awake. The excruciating agony forced her eyes wide open to view a dagger protruding from the back of her hand.

A foot came down on her wrist—not heavy enough to break it, but enough to pin it in place.

The harlequin bent, flexed the knife.

Her body's own attempts to pull away turned into another wave of blinding, excruciating torment. The fire, the burning, was mild compared to this.

"We've only just begun, sweetie."

Oh, God, what is she doing to me? Please, let it stop!

But it didn't.

CHAPTER TWENTY-THREE

Minute after minute, the whimpers from Chip's love and soulmate tied his stomach in knots, all the more distracting as they rose in both volume and intensity. Each new cry tore his attention from the screen, and he'd look over in time to see her features distort and her brow furrow. Then he'd turn back to the screen, nothing accomplished, frustrated and flummoxed.

He'd rise, abandoning the blank screen where his code needed to be. He'd return to her side on the couch.

Burton sat on the arm of the couch at Blue's head, her palm stroking Blue's forehead, occasionally touching her shoulder. Reading Burton's face, it looked to Chip that she halfway expected these actions to bring some sort of comfort.

"Can you...do anything?" he asked.

Burton glanced up at Chip, then returned her gaze to Blue. "No. I...thought I could, but...she's not there, Chip. I can't reach her."

"Then why is she—"

"I don't know. I'm sorry. I...just don't. But I won't leave her side, either. Until this is over."

Her unspoken words *one way or the other* hovered between them.

Chip sank onto the middle cushion. He could easily work his

butt onto the edge, creating a spot for himself where he could reach out and take her hand.

Her limp, unresponsive hand. Warm, but lifeless. "We're going to get you back, Blue. I promise." Then he returned to his computer, stared at the screen, and fretted some more. And accomplished nothing.

———

"Aww, she's not playing anymore," said Cyn. She kicked out with a boot and rolled the limp figure over. Daggers protruded from one hand, the back of one thigh, a foot, and the back of her shoulder.

As she rolled onto the dagger in her shoulder, the body twitched.

"One more blow, and the cycle will start again," said Van, smiling at her partner and twin.

Cyn asked her standard question. "How long?"

Van considered. Normally, she consulted a stopwatch she kept specially for these sorts of sessions, but the computer character didn't come equipped with one. "Best approximation, maybe forty minutes."

Cyn met Van's gaze, and they exchanged volumes between them in their not-quite telepathic bond. *All in a day's work, my true Sister. And our new client is most satisfied.*

As we knew she would be.

"Impressive!" The Goddess gripped the royal scepter at her side as she strode across the broken ground, the train of her regal robes trailing behind her. "I haven't been so moved in centuries, Cyn and Van. I rarely play with my old toy anymore. He lies and whimpers, and every decade or so I make him cry and weep just to break the tedium. I'm afraid my heart's just not it anymore. But you two take it to a level of art!"

Baalina's gaze traveled from Van to Cyn, her admiration easy to read on her ashen features. "I knew, when I first touched your minds over a decade ago, that you would serve me well." Her gaze fell upon the three of them collectively. "After so long left in solitude with only one distraction, one forgets the sheer creative *fun* of torture."

Cyn bent slightly at the kind words from the mistress. Through her half-closed eyes, she spied Marda's face flaming a ruby red.

When Marda spoke, Cyn detected the tremor of jealousy in her tone, and wondered if the Goddess heard it, too. "They have served you well, mistress. In spite of Cyn's earlier mistake, she has—"

The Goddess waved her wrist. "Nonsense, all forgotten." The mistress extended her scepter toward Marda. "Come, it is time to demonstrate the leadership and trust I have placed in you."

Marda gripped the offered rod, both a weapon and a symbol of her status in the new order. Simple but deadly, with the sigil of Baalina etched into the blunt end, the spike weapon extended perhaps twenty-four inches and ended in a lethal metal point.

"Put an end to our mutual troublemaker!" commanded the mistress.

Marda's gaze fell upon their enemy. Her eyes glinted with fury and perhaps a touch of madness. Marda bent down over Blue and prodded Blue's neck with the point. "Wake up."

She pressed. The point vanished into her victim's neck. Blood spilled onto the stone.

A look of malicious cruelty crossed Marda's face.

Cyn was impressed. She didn't think the crazy bitch really had it in her.

To her surprise, Blue's eyes snapped open.

My God, she's still fighting!

Marda smiled. "You're still with us! Good. Remember when our positions were reversed, and you let me live?"

Blue's lips moved, but no sound came.

"You know..." Marda raised a hand to her chin, a mocking pose of reflection. "I wonder if you had killed me then, if my Sisters would have gotten this far on their own."

Cyn almost objected, then realized the jab wasn't really aimed at the three of them, but to make Blue feel worse.

Blue opened her mouth again.

Again, Cyn was taken aback by the strength of their foe.

Blue croaked out a single word, "Why?"

Again, Marda pretended to consider. "I would think that would be obvious. Because of how you humiliated me, we're going to keep playing with you. Then we're going to free our mistress, and the first thing we're going to do is find Eugene Farren and everyone else who stood in our way and make them all pay for defying us. Then we're going to proceed with our plans to conquer the world."

Blue spat another word. "Insane."

Marda laughed, a bitter sound.

A sound that made even Cyn uneasy.

Marda continued in her mocking tone. "I know, it sounds crazy, doesn't it? We're going to take over the world. But how many of us are really insane? We all start off with grand goals—maybe to become a brain surgeon, only we settle into real life as a pet doctor. And that's a bit short. But it's something."

Marda set the scepter aside, gripped Blue under her chin, and forced her to look eye to eye. "But it doesn't matter, really, in your case, does it? This little coven of insanity has destroyed you. Maybe we'll destroy your friends; maybe we'll never even leave here. Does that really make much difference to you, now? We'll aim for the world. Maybe we'll fall short."

She let Blue's head fall against the stone. "Either way, we'll destroy you. And that's something." Marda grabbed up the scepter and stood, drawing back to strike Blue's chest.

"Wait!" Cyn cried.

Cyn crouched near Blue's head, reached out, and pulled her arms back, exposing her belly. She pointed to a spot near the navel. "Aim there, Sister. It will hurt the most there."

With a cry of fury, Marda swung the scepter down, driving the spike into Blue's gut.

Blue's eyes snapped open, as did her mouth, but no sound came.

Marda offered a mocking wave. "Goodbye, Blue. We'll see you soon."

Tortured to death, Blue vanished.

Cyn held a hand out, and Van slapped it. "Just like Anthony Guinness."

At Marda's confused look, Cyn explained, "Owed a mob boss big bucks. Guy got tired of waiting for his money, so he asked us make an example of him."

Van giggled. "Anthony was such a tough guy, said we'd never get to him. Took six hours to die, but he cried like a baby the last three."

"And shit his pants," added Cyn.

Van grimaced. "Oh, gross, the mess! Thanks for reminding me."

Cyn considered Marda with new respect. "Should we get back to our apartment? We may be running out of time."

Marda shook her head. "No, this is way too fun. One more round, at least."

———

RELEASE AT LAST! BUT HER "DEATH" brought only dread. She had no strength left. But the regeneration took place without her act or desire. She lowered back toward her avatar body, a new body which would be healed of all its physical wounds, only to be wounded again.

God, no, I can't. I can't go back, please, someone…Chip?

———

"CHIP!"

The angry woman's voice pulled Chip's gaze away from the computer screen.

Though all the computer screens lit up live and active, Chip looked around an empty basement computer room, empty except for himself and a middle-aged woman.

She stood dressed in a professional blouse and knee-length black skirt, long, dark hair pulled back. The edges of her eyes showed the beginnings of crows-feet, especially now, as they widened in distress.

Though he'd never physically met this woman, he recognized Leona Shaefer from Blue's photos and from the memorial service which remained forever burnt into his memory as one of the most miserable days of his life.

He wondered at her appearance, but then an obvious reason struck him. *After all these years, she's finally here to give me hell for the part I played in her death. But...why now?*

Instead, she cried, "Do something!"

"I'm sorry, Mrs. Shaefer. What?"

"They're killing her, Chip!"

He glanced over at the couch, shocked to see Blue still lying on it. He was certain she wasn't there a moment ago.

Blue's features distorted worse than ever, and she released another distressing moan.

"I'm doing everything I can."

"That's not good enough, mister!" The woman approached Chip and raised hands balled into fists.

To Chip, she seemed smaller in stature than he'd imagined, perhaps five-foot two versus Blue's additional couple of inches. Tiny next to Chip, who stood just shy of six feet.

But it still hurt plenty when she pelted him with her fists. "Ow! I'm going as fast as I can, it's just so–"

"They're killing her, Chip. She can't hold out much longer."

"But I don't know what to do!" A thought occurred to him. "Do you? I mean, from the other side, is there something you can do that we can't?"

She stopped swinging her fists, and her shoulders slumped. She squeezed her eyes shut, and tears streamed down her face.

Her body shook from the emotion, and Chip's heart broke at the sight of it.

"I told her...to trust you," she said between sobs. "I told her to come. I said you were in danger, and she came. Now my baby's dying because of me."

God! He'd never felt so sick. But he couldn't shake off his helplessness. "I'll do what I can. I'll...somehow, I'll figure something out. Can you reach her? Can you tell her to hold on just a bit longer?"

"I can try, but...hurry, Chip, you need to hurry. She can't physically die where she is now, but...we might still lose her. Everything that we love about her is being stripped away by the second."

A loud moan, this one building to a cry, came from the couch.

He looked over, but now the couch sat empty.

Still, he heard her voice. "Chip. Chip!"

———

"Chip?"

He snapped open his eyes. The blurred face of a young woman wavered in his vision. "Blue?"

He lifted his head from the computer desk to bring into focus the face of the mousy, light-haired girl. Her name returned to him. *MacLeod. Burton calls her Skye.*

Skye's eyes reflected sympathy. "You fell asleep. We thought you could use a few minutes, but..."

Chip took in the room. Phil sat at the computer next to his, the chair pulled out where MacLeod had occupied the last console down. He could still hear Blue's moans. He looked over at the couch.

Burton, balanced on the arm of the couch, tried to restrain Blue's thrashings, more intense than he'd seen so far.

He rushed to her side, then helped Burton hold Blue by the shoulders while she placed a hand on her forehead. "Peace. Peace, be at—"

"No!" Blue twisted from under Burton's palm.

It was all he could do to hold her down.

Burton spoke out loud, though to whom, Chip wasn't sure. "I

can't reach her. There's nothing to reach; this shouldn't be happening."

A desperate look marred Blue's face.

"Blue, we're coming for you. Hang in there, we're–" Blue's convulsion nearly threw Chip off her.

"Dammit, hold her!" cried Burton. "I'm going to try something else."

The agent enfolded her fingers over Blue's face and placed her other hand on top of Blue's head. "Hold her...still."

Blue continued to thrash.

But Chip just let his full weight press against her. She let out a grunt, as if struck, and then she went slack.

At the same time, Burton dropped to the floor, like her limbs had turned to jelly.

Blue lay beneath him, immobile, her face smoothed over with the peaceful look of deep sleep. *Thank God!*

Chip stood and reached down to the disheveled agent.

The agent took his hand and pulled herself to her feet.

Chip placed his other hand on her shoulder in a way he hoped reflected gratitude. "Thank you, Agent Burton. It worked."

But the woman shook her head. The concern on her face caused a sinking feeling. "I didn't. I didn't do anything, not really. I just...well, essentially tranquilized her. The natural equivalent of a muscle relaxant. I didn't want to do it, but she was going to hurt herself."

Sick to his stomach, Chip took in the sight of Blue's serene, relaxed face. He wanted to embrace the illusion, cling to it as the reality. "Then...whatever was happening–"

"–is still happening." Burton straightened her jacket and rubbed the back of her neck. "I hope I didn't cause more harm than good. But whatever action we're going to take, we need to do it soon."

Burton's words hit him. His head hurt, his vision blurred, and his concentration was almost gone.

Then he knew what he had to do. He looked at Burton. He hoped she'd hear his plea. "Listen, I need to go."

Burton blinked rapidly, but the expected dramatic response did not come. Her voice held a stone-cold calm. "Excuse me, Eugene, did you understand what I just said?"

"Yes, and that's why I have to leave. Just for a short time. I'll make a...food run. I can't think in here. Not here, not...around her."

Phil's voice reached them from his place behind the terminal. "A food run! You *are* joking, right?"

Chip understood the irony. The man who perpetually focused on food and snacks made it clear by the tone of his voice that today needed to be the exception.

"Listen, Bro, I'm all about taking time for a snack, but your timing kind of sucks."

Chip shook his head. "No, trust me, my timing's perfect. I need to get out of here, I need to clear my head, and I just..." He looked over at Burton. "I just do." He finished, even as he heard the lame tone of his voice.

Burton shrugged and turned back to Blue. "Do what you feel you have to do."

It felt every bit a dismissal. Feeling all eyes on him, Chip ascended the stairs and bolted out the door.

———

THE COOL AIR woke him up, but the descended darkness shocked him. Confused, he fished out his phone and tapped the screen light to trigger the backlight. The time flashed at him.

Seven-thirty? Really? So, his stomach hadn't tricked him. They'd skipped dinner. And, as a minor footnote, missed Thanksgiving all together.

He recalled, briefly, a thawing turkey and loads of fixings, food that still waited, split between the fridge and the pantry in their kitchen, in anticipation of the holiday dinner Phil and he had planned out days ago in order to play host to Blue today.

Now he just wanted to get her back alive and whole.

He wandered the darkened streets, the knots in his stomach

still clenched tight. He'd never felt so helpless. Not even in the midst of their fight with Gunther, even when he'd tried to sacrifice himself so the ghost would leave her alone. At least then, he'd made that choice willingly.

And he'd nearly died for it, but he was content in his decision at the time he'd made it.

In the jumbled mess of his mind, the accusations flew, one by one, as he walked.

From Blue's mother. *I told her...to trust you. I told her to come. I said you were in danger, and she came. Now my baby's dying because of me.*

From Phil. *Your timing kind of sucks.*

From Rebecca. *Do what you have to do.*

From Blue, as she braced to enter the virtual realm, when she'd gripped his hand at the last moment: *I really* don't want to do this. And his response: *I'll take good care of you.*

Just one of many lame promises he'd made to her in the last few hours, beginning with his oath to win her back when she threatened to walk out of his life: *If you don't hear anything else I say, hear this. He will never love you the way I do. No one will. I would do anything for you. If you were ever in trouble, I'd lie, steal, cheat—I'd move Heaven and Earth to help you, and you know I would.*

He kept walking, his mind a million miles away, still mentally kicking himself. *Fuck. Nice one, brainiac. And here she is, waiting to collect on that promise you made, smart guy. The only thing is, there's nothing to lie about, nothing to steal, and you can't cheat your way to victory, either. So, you'd better find a way to move Heaven and Earth really fast. What's the plan, brainiac? Because you better come up with something, and fast.*

He realized he was approaching Smittie's. To his shock, the florescent red OPEN light still shone in the door, though looking through the pane-glass front, he could see Laverne and Smittie behind the counter chit-chatting with each other in an empty restaurant.

Well...he was hungry. Might as well grab some breadsticks and return with a few pizzas. He wasn't good for doing much else at this point. Might as well accomplish the one lame-ass excuse he gave to leave in the first place.

He opened the door, which triggered the bell alert, not that Laverne needed it to pounce.

"Well, bless my soul, Smittie, our favorite customer. Twice in one day, and on Thanksgiving, to boot!"

Not up to answering, Chip stumbled to the nearest booth and dropped into it. By the time he situated himself, Laverne was there.

She deposited a plastic cup of Coke on the table. "Where's your little honey, honey?"

The question hit him like a battering ram to the gut. He reached up and buried his face in his hands, trying and failing to control his hyperventilating.

An awkward silence followed, which Laverne finally broke. "Wow, was my joke that bad?"

A laugh escaped him, which caused his shoulders to shake.

Oh, God. He couldn't help it; he couldn't control it. He was going to have a breakdown right here in front of his waitress friend, and there wasn't a thing he could do about it, or any way he could explain it.

"Hey...hey, Chip! Are you okay?"

No, he was far from okay. He continued to gasp for air. His body shook, and he fought back tears he could no longer stop.

Blindly, he reached for the napkin dispenser in the middle of the table, fumbling for them a few seconds. Then a stack was placed into his hand.

Laverne.

Her voice reached him gently, softly, assuring. He realized, distantly, she'd placed her hand between his shoulders.

"Take it easy, easy, Chip, take it slow..."

He dropped his head to the tabletop. He was too tired to stand strong or do anything at all. He didn't know where to turn, what to do, where to go.

And while he floundered in this restaurant, lost and confused, Blue was back at the house, suffering.

"What am I going to do?" he called out.

"Easy, Chip. Take it easy."

He sat up and wiped wetness from his face. He looked around, taking in his surroundings.

The waitress sat across from him. Her dark eyes reflected only sympathy, not at all the freaked-out expression he expected.

"God, I'm...so sorry about that." He finished cleaning himself up.

Over her shoulder, he saw Smittie approach with a basket of breadsticks and sauces. He deposited them and stood at the table.

Laverne shot him a stern look.

He retreated to his station behind the counter.

Chip's stomach rumbled as the aroma of tomato sauce hit him. He reached down and tore a bite off the first one.

Laverne waited, seated next to him at the booth while he ate a few bites. She said nothing but sat without comment.

After he'd gobbled down two breadsticks, she asked, "Better?"

Chip blinked, hoping to clear the scrim that had settled across his vision. "Not really, but I think I'm done freaking out on you."

"Well, that's good. Let's take it from the top." She leaned forward.

Chip realized that she had her hand over his.

"Let's start with the obvious. Do I have to kick anyone's ass tonight?" Her dark-eyed stare seemed to penetrate the cloud of his fogged mind.

"Wait, what?" Then he realized. *She means Blue.* "No. No! She didn't do anything wrong, if that's what you mean, but...well, she's in trouble, and it's my fault."

Laverne paused. Her lips pursed. "Chip," she said, gently, as if speaking to a child. "Some people get into booze or drugs, and they do it to themselves. You can't let anyone guilt you into–"

"No, it's not that, either. Please. It has to do with my game." It was out there before he could stop it. *Crap!*

"Your game? Your–" He swore he saw a smirk flash across her face, just for a moment, before she resumed a stone-face stare.

"Your video game? Did she, like, really hate it? I mean, some people just don't get—"

"No." He laughed at her conclusion. His head still spun, and he wondered what to tell her next. "It was a little more serious than that, but...I'm sorry, I'm not sure how to explain it."

"But, Chip, you were in tears. No video game is worth that. Why were you even working on it? And...did you all skip dinner?"

"I'm sorry, I can't really answer most of those questions." He added, "Well...yes, we skipped dinner."

To Chip's surprise, she looked hurt. "Do you think I wouldn't understand? Because I'm just a dumb waitress?"

Chip sighed. "No...it's more like, you wouldn't believe me. It would sound far-fetched." *To say the least!*

"Look, Chip, I know it's not my business, but can I tell you what I see when I look at you?"

Just to keep her talking while his head cleared, Chip agreed.

"I've been hearing you and Phil come in here every few days, talking about that game, since you first started programming it two years ago. I know you think I just kind of nod my head and I don't understand."

"Well, no, it's not that—"

Laverne held her palm out to stop him. "And that's fair. But I'll tell you something. I had no intention of bringing it up, but maybe it might help. A couple of months ago, you know, after I'd been hearing so much about it, I finally decided to go online and check it out. I mean, it was free, so I wasn't wasting nothin' but my time. Truth is, I don't play video games. I don't like them, so it was all new to me."

As Laverne talked, Chip smiled. The cobwebs were clearing as she spoke, and he grabbed a third breadstick. "That's nice of you, I didn't know that."

"Let me tell you something," said Laverne. "I was always pretty. Not so smart. I never did well in school, but I knew how to get along with people. I mean, look, I'm dumb, but I'm not stupid."

She smiled at her own joke. "I know, back in the day, I was an eyeful for almost any boy."

"Still are, Laverne."

"Ain't you sweet." She patted his hand. "But my point is, I knew how to listen, and I knew how to get people to support me. I learned how to take the talents I did have, and I made the most of them. Now, Smittie and I are here, doing our small part to help kids get an education at a school I could never get into. So, the way I see it, we're making our own difference. But you two."

She held a pair of fingers out, indicating Chip's absent partner, Phil. "*You* two took your talents, and you created your own world! It's all there, on the screen, and none of it's real, but on the computer, it is. It was nothing, and you programmed it into existence from nothing. And you know what? That's a miracle to me."

Chip swallowed, giving himself time to absorb her non-advice. Last thing he wanted to do while she was opening up to him was snap at her for wasting precious time. When he spoke, he kept his voice even. "Thanks, Laverne, it's good to know you appreciated what we wanted to do."

"Hey, I *do* pay attention. I get it. You made something out of nothing-your own world, and you want everyone to come and see what you've created. And if that doesn't work, you just change parts of it, reshape it until you get it right. So whatever Blue's problem is—"

"Wait, what?" Chip held a hand out. *Something about what she just said. What was it?*

"What?" Laverne paused. "I said, you make your own world that you're sharing with others—"

"Yeah, but, the other part. If something doesn't work..." He dropped the breadstick and moved his hand in a circular motion to signal her to repeat her thought.

Laverne shrugged. "You just...change it. I mean, it's your world, right? You made the rules, I assume you can just change them, right?"

"We..." And then he realized what had been in front of their faces all along. "My God. How could I have not seen that?" *We're so damn caught up in the emergency.* Chip disengaged his hand from hers. "I need your pen and a piece of scrap paper. Please, hurry."

Laverne tore a page off her mini-notepad and handed him her pen.

Chip started to sketch. "Laverne, I have a house full of hungry programmers, and I need to get back to them as fast as possible. How fast can you get three pizzas to go?"

"We're closing, and we have four in the warmer we're getting ready to throw out. I'll box 'em for you, on the house."

Chip showed the sketch to Laverne, who made a face. "Looks kinda' cool, but I have no idea what that is."

"This..." Chip pointed to the page, "is the solution to my problem, and I have you to thank for it."

CHAPTER TWENTY-FOUR

With time now a major factor, Chip talked Laverne into giving him a ride home. Without question, she'd stacked the four pizzas into her SUV and had him in front of his house five minutes later. He thanked her for helping more than she'd ever know, and, after accepting a quick kiss on his cheek, darted into the house.

Moments later, Chip stepped down the stairs into the basement, one arm balancing the stacked pies, napkins, and paper plates, the other gripping the railing.

All faces turned toward him.

Deep in conversation on the phone, Skye rolled her eyes but continued her dialog—something about electrical usage.

Burton turned her gaze from him a moment later, put her clipboard down on the desk, and walked to the couch to check on Blue.

Phil stopped his work, stood up, and closed the distance to meet him. He shook his head, his disappointment apparent. "I can't believe you went out and did that."

Chip grunted, flustered. "I didn't leave here specifically to get the pizza, but you know what? Eating helped. And it's going to help you guys. Whether you realize it or not. By the way, it's after dark."

Phil's look told Chip that Phil didn't know that, either.

"Exactly. Here, take this. The walk actually cleared my head, and I think I have a solution to our problem." He pulled the scrap of notepad from his pocket and slapped the page down onto the table.

Phil picked it up and took in the image, his eyes scanning the hasty notes to the side. His eyebrows slowly rose up his forehead. "This blows away our old maximum parameters that we set when we first created the game."

Chip nodded. "I know. And we've never changed them in the two years since."

"Well, no, there was no reason to. We wanted to contain the maximum power any of the characters can achieve."

"Not now, we don't." Chip waited for his words to sink in. "They're all in there. They can be just so strong, just so agile, and nothing more. Now's the time to change the basic parameters and introduce something new into the game."

Slowly, Phil sank into his chair and called up a new screen. "Jesus. Why the hell didn't we think of this sooner?"

Chip rubbed his hand over his own face, massaging his forehead to clear the cobwebs. "I know. I couldn't think earlier, and now it's obvious."

Skye wandered over. "What's up, guys?"

Chip answered, words flying out a mile a minute. "We have a plan that I'd like to bring you in on, if you can. Can you?" He drew a breath. "What are you working on for Burton?"

Skye shook her phone at him. "Damn holiday has us doing things the hard way. Normally, Rebecca could call the enrollment office, offer up some federal bypass codes, and we'd have access to classified student information in minutes. Then we'd know exactly where to find our little gang. But we can't. No one's on duty."

Chip fired up his 3D-rendering program on the computer in front of him. "So, instead..."

"I spent the last hour on the phone with the helpdesks of a couple of local internet providers, used those same bypass codes to talk to some people in charge, people who can analyze the raw data. I have them tracking homes in the vicinity with readings that indicate unusual usage today. Just waiting on some callbacks now." Skye's eyes looked down at Chip's sketch. "Wow, what's this?"

"That," said Chip, "might be the solution to our problem." He tried to mentally size her up and figure out her skills. "How fast could you render that? Phil's the graphic arts genius. But he's doing something higher priority, and it could go even faster if I help him."

Skye peered at the sketch. "I can draw a pretty mean action figure for you on the image renderer, if that's what you need."

Chip stood up and offered her the seat. "Make it fast, Skye, just make it fast."

———

"Fiona?"

Leona Shaefer stood in the center of the same living room where she and Fiona had lived over two years ago.

Of course, they weren't really in that living room. Leona had found her daughter only by pursuing her deep into the recesses of her daughter's mind.

Fiona huddled on the couch, hugging herself, her face ashen, her body dwarfed by the surrounding white leather.

Leona called out, this time using the "angry mom" voice that usually snapped her daughter to attention. "Fiona! Wake up!"

Fiona turned her head oh-so-slowly to center her gaze on Leona, dark circles under her eyes. "Mom?" The word croaked out of her.

Leona closed the distance to stand in front of the couch, still keeping her stern mother voice to hold Fiona's attention. "What do you think you're doing? Answer me, young lady!"

Fiona opened her mouth but then said nothing. She tipped her head toward her knees, and her eyes drifted closed.

Oh, no you don't, baby. Wake up. "I said answer me!"

Fiona's eyes snapped open, and she slurred out a reply. "I got away, Mom. They can't reach me here."

"Baby..." Tears welled up. "You need to go back."

Fiona shook her head. "No! They hurt. I want to stay here."

"But...you can't stay here, Fiona. Chip is on his way."

"No, Mommy. They hurt me...again, and again, and again."

"Baby..." Leona sank next to her daughter and wrapped her arms around her. "It's okay, baby, but you can't stay here. If you do, you won't be able to go back." Through her arms, Leona felt a shiver convulse through her daughter. "That's okay, Mommy. Okay. Chip can't get to me, anyway. So, I'll just stay here with you."

———

MARDA THRUST the knife into Blue's unresponsive body and heard her final cry before the body vanished entirely. She grinned up at Cyn. "How was that?"

Cyn applauded, and Van mock-bowed. "Bravo. I think we stretched that out over an hour that time."

"Still," mused Van. "She's almost gone. She barely made a noise for the last several minutes."

"So she's losing her mind?" Marda pressed the point of the scepter against her own open palm. "Glorious! One more round and she might end up an empty shell, whether her friends find a way to bring her back or–"

A new figure phased in front of her.

Marda started, then relaxed when she saw Natalie's familiar green-cloaked druid appear. "Nat, are you joining us after all?"

"Just for a moment, then I'll cast the spell to come back out. I wanted to let you know, I have the computers and our clothes packed and loaded into the car. Still no sign of the cops, but–"

"Great!" said Marda. "Then we can do this again."

Marda read the shock on Nat's CGI features.

"I was going to say, the longer we wait, the more time Burton has to gather her resources and come after us."

Marda pretended to consider. They had no evidence Burton had taken any action against them. "Or she might not be able to mobilize the authorities tonight. How do you get police to act on your word when there's no evidence that a crime has been committed?"

Nat averted her eyes and looked down at the fiery ground. "With all due respect, Marda, I strongly believe that's wishful thinking."

A burst of fury flushed through Marda. "Do you, now? Do you really? Well, maybe *I* think that your lack of interest in being in the presence of the mistress makes me question your motives to the cause."

The figure's eyes widened, then squinted in anger. "I am focused on getting us the hell out of here while we still have a window to escape. Frankly, Marda, it is you, and this obsessive excursion, that has put us in great peril."

"How dare you!" Marda pointed the tip of the spike at Nat.

Natalie met Marda's glare.

If the scepter intimidated her, Natalie hid it well.

"If we get out of here, and later succeed at bringing Baalina into our world, then we can enjoy being in Her Holy Presence every blessed day. But if we are captured, it will be at least, in part, because you three indulged yourselves with a minor distraction rather than staying focused on the goal."

"I'll show *you* all about our indulgence, you mouthy bitch!" She raised the scepter.

Cyn put herself between Marda and Natalie. "Marda, calm down. She's probably right."

Not you, too, Cyn. "Fiona has to pay for what she's done!" Marda scoffed.

Van stepped forward, next to Cyn. "What my partner means is that we should be grateful to Natalie for packing up for all of us while we deal with Fiona in the proper way."

Cyn picked up Van's statement. "A way that will send a message to the others. Even if they pull this girl out of here, right now, they will find nothing left of her but an empty, broken shell."

As if on cue, Marda heard the standard audio distortion of a new character phasing in. Fiona, the blue-haired warrior, reappeared in her usual spot, physically unmarked, standing erect.

As soon as the computer relinquished control of the avatar to its controller, the figure collapsed to the ground like a scarecrow pulled free of its wooden cross-frame. *She's not moving! Is she dead?*

Cyn and Van darted to her side.

Their victim had fallen on her stomach.

Cyn drew her dagger, targeted a specific spot on the back of Fiona's upper thigh, and thrust it in. She watched as it sank in several millimeters deep.

Fresh blood spilled from the wound.

The avatar uttered a grunt, a reflex more than an actual cry of pain.

Cyn and Van exchanged looks.

Marda asked, "So, she's not dead?"

Van shrugged. "I'm not sure we'd even know. The avatar might just keep coming back regardless of what's going on with her mind."

Natalie gagged and turned away. "I think I'm going to be sick."

Cyn picked up the thread. "If she's not broken, she will be soon."

Marda's mouth watered at the words. "Let's finish the job, then. Let's finish *her*." She reached down and pulled Blue's chin up.

The avatar's eyes remained closed and unresponsive.

Marda was not impressed. "We have the time. We can make it slow, to the end."

Cyn shrugged. "Fine with me."

Natalie broke in, "Didn't you hear a word I sa–"

Van cut her off. "Just a few more minutes, Nat. Go on back, we'll be there shortly."

Marda grinned. "Indeed, maybe you should let the big kids take care of this, Natalie."

Cyn chuckled. "Look at you. Get a little taste of blood for the first time, and all of a sudden *you're* the fearless one lecturing others."

Reflexively, Marda yelled, "Who said this was my first time?" The words escaped before she could stop them.

"*I* say!" snapped Cyn. "I have eyes, don't I? This entire 'session' has been an education for you. And that's...fine, so let's complete your education." Cyn motioned to the scepter still clutched in Marda's hand and bent at the waist in a mock bow. "Finish what you've started, Priestess."

Marda glanced at Baalina, who waited off to the side, a smile on her face. At Marda's acknowledgement, the Goddess nodded.

"You grow stronger by the moment, Marda. The final breaking of your enemy will make you my proper servant."

A flush thrilled Marda. She tightened her grip on the scepter and approached the prone body. *Where first...the hand? The eye? Will her body feel it if I gouge out an eye? I don't know. Perhaps that's where I should start.*

A new noise filled the air, a mixture of a hum and static, sounding a short distance away.

Marda turned to look along with the others.

A green, glowing line cut through the air in a vertical slash, as if a transparent scrim hovered a few feet away, and a surgeon now guided a deliberate slice into that scrim. It extended, slowly, a couple inches, six inches, now over a foot.

At the same time, the edges widened, pulling apart outward into a portal shape, which opened to reveal the large tree and the forest beyond, the area previously sealed off to them when Fiona's act had isolated the virtual chaos room from the rest of the game.

Only now, a new portal hung open before them, which would grant them access to the room they needed. *We can go...right now, we can go, and the mistress can be free!*

But even as the thought crossed her mind, a new figure flew and hovered before the mouth of the portal.

Flew? Yes, by the Goddess, it flew! Marda's eyes widened at the sight.

Marda's mouth dropped open, slack-jawed, as some sort of silver robot creature with a backpack jetpack and mini rocket-boots eased through the portal and lowered itself.

The robot-being extended one arm toward them. It pointed a metal nozzle positioned along the top of its wrist at them in a manner clearly intended as a threat.

The metallic-looking creature spoke through a booming, amplified speaker that blared a deep, angry male voice. "GET AWAY FROM HER! NOW!"

Natalie was the first to find her voice. "What in the hell! How did you–"

"DID YOU REALLY THINK YOU COULD CALL THE SHOTS IN MY OWN GAME? ARE YOU TRULY SO ARROGANT TO THINK I WOULD NOT FIND A WAY TO BREAK THROUGH INTO YOUR LITTLE HIDDEN ROOM?"

Marda stared, still unable speak.

But Natalie apparently had recovered first. "But...you can't create power-avatars of that sort. The parameters were set–"

"PARAMETERS I SET, AND PARAMETERS I CHANGED!"

"But we used the SoulStaff! Only the Divenium Crystal could get through–"

"THAT'S TRUE ON EARTH! BUT THIS ISN'T EARTH. THIS ISN'T A REAL PORTAL, AND IT DOESN'T LEAD TO THE REAL CHAOS REALM. THIS IS AN ADDED ROOM IN THE GAME MATRIX OF A VIDEO GAME WORLD. MY WORLD!"

Baalina grabbed the scepter from Marda. With a cry of fury, she unsheathed the blade and pointed it toward the robot.

Or rather, Marda realized, the suit of armor.

"You are still facing a demoness, boy! And I'll destroy you for your insolence." A stream of green fire spewed from the end of the rod, which blazed with an incredible heat that burned Marda's face, even as it sprayed over and engulfed the metallic figure.

Marda smiled. *The mistress has incinerated him where he stands! An appropriate end to all who dare stand before us.*

The green blast faded.

The robot remained before them, unharmed, not even singed. "I AM THE GOD OF THIS WORLD. NOT YOU, DEMONESS! YOU CAN'T LOCK ME OUT OF MY WORLD!"

Uttering a fierce battle cry, Cyn charged, flanking the robot. As she passed, she thrust the dagger up against the robot's neck.

The dagger snapped, and Cyn bounced off the robot and tumbled across the stones, landing several feet away in an indignant heap.

The robot continued as if it hadn't noticed the attack. "YOU CANNOT HARM ME IF I DON'T WANT TO BE HARMED. YOU ARE A DIGITAL IMAGE OF A NIGHTMARE STANDING IN A BLUESCREEN SET! THIS IS NOT CHAOS. YOU ARE NOT BAALINA. YOUR DEMONESS MIND IS TRAPPED IN A SHELL LESS DISTINCT THAN INCENSE SMOKE!"

The robot pointed its wrist weapon directly at the demoness. "SAY GOODBYE TO YOUR LEADER, WITCHES. BAALINA, I RETURN YOU TO THE CHAOS FROM WHENCE YOU CAME!"

A red blast of energy shot from the robot's wrist.

Baalina barely had time to snarl her defiance before the beam struck her in the chest.

An instant later, her body disappeared.

Mistress! Seeing Baalina fall physically hurt Marda.

Natalie backed away. "My God, I...didn't expect this. They just changed the maximum parameters of the game while we were caught flatfooted inside of it."

"EXACTLY RIGHT, DRUID. I GIVE YOU SOME CREDIT. PHIL AND I WERE SO WRAPPED UP IN THE LEGEND, THE STORIES, THE POWERS, AND THE LIMITATIONS OF YOUR POWERS, THAT WE DIDN'T STOP TO THINK THAT *YOU* DON'T MAKE THE RULES HERE, *WE* DO. SO WE CHANGED THE RULES AND RENDERED THIS NEW AVATAR YOU SEE BEFORE YOU."

Marda turned to Nat. "What can we do?"

Nat's eyes met hers, round circles of shock. "Nothing. We've lost." Natalie raised her hands above her head.

Marda snarled. "Put down your hands, you little fool! You told me our avatars were the best the game could provide, that they could only *match* us, not *beat* us."

"That was true...at the time. But, he's...he's not a part of the same game anymore. We're a Civil War battalion, and he's a modern Marine with a machine gun and hand grenades. We just need to get out of here."

Van cried and drew her dagger. "We still have one move left!" She leaped toward Blue, the dagger raised to strike.

"GET AWAY FROM HER!" yelled the robot. The voice cracked, revealing the human anguish beneath.

A red beam struck Van in the back, and she disintegrated.

"Van!" Cyn barely had time to react before the robot fired and caused her to vanish.

Marda fell back to huddle with Nat. She had a sword strapped to her side that she knew would be useless. She no longer held the scepter. Her mistress had been taken from the game and forced back into the real chaos realm. "No matter!" She screamed her defiance. "We'll get you, yet. We hurt your lover beyond any hope of return. We'll find another way to raise the mistress. This isn't the end."

"ACTUALLY, IT IS."

The robot fired two more streaks of energy, which bulls-eyed both avatars.

———

MARDA HAD BARELY a moment to scream her anger, then the red blast engulfed her, and she awoke at the table, surrounded by her three co-conspirators.

Her vision snapped into focus in time to see Natalie powering down her laptop. "We need to go. Now."

———

"BLUE?"

Chip raised the robot's wrist. The power screen of his goggles centered Blue in his crosshairs. The converter gun, imbued with the same code that created the CGI Divenium Crystal to send the CGI spirits back to their bodies, signaled its ready status. "PHIL, AGENT BURTON, STAND BY. SHE'S COMING. AND SHE'S NOT MOVING." Through all the mechanics, Chip couldn't cover the shake in his voice.

He pulled the trigger.

Blue's CGI character vanished for what he hoped to God would be the last time. He'd released her tortured mind to return what was left to her real body.

God, please, don't let us be too late. He turned the gun on himself and fired.

CHAPTER TWENTY-FIVE

Chip found himself seated in front of his computer screen. *Back! And safe!*

His gaze traveled the room, at first seeing no one else, just empty computer terminals. He wondered, for a moment, if he was dreaming again.

Then he noticed everyone crowded around the couch where Blue's body laid, and he wanted to be at her side most desperately. "Blue!" He threw off his headset and bolted over. The people parted as he approached, all except Burton, who continued to kneel by Blue's head, reaching over the arm of the couch. One hand pressed, palm-up, on her forehead, her other hand on Blue's shoulder.

Blue lay, pale and unresponsive, like a corpse.

He dropped to his knees at her side, where he spoke his prayer at her. "Come on, Blue, come on, I know you're in there. Come back to me. Come back, Blue, come on!"

His attention darted back and forth between Blue's sick face and Burton, who sat, eyes closed, her face emotionless and trance-like.

"Blue...come on, I saved you. I told you I'd save you, and I did. I brought you back. Please, baby, come back to me, please."

He wanted to grab her and shake her. But he didn't know what Burton was doing, and how much that would interfere with whatever spell or treatment or whatever the hell it was...he didn't care, as long as it worked.

"Oh my God!" Burton yelled, and her eyes snapped open. Her body fell away from Blue as if propelled by some force.

Chip watched, stunned.

Burton curled her knees up and folded her arms around her legs. "God...those monsters...those...my God..."

Silence filled the room. No one dared breathe.

Chip's gaze brushed over Skye, who had her hands balled into fists and pressed against her mouth.

Phil also waited, his eyes riveted to where Blue lay.

Burton, in the meantime, had removed her glasses. Her body trembled, and tears now flowed freely down her face.

Chip cleared his throat. "Is she..." The word stuck. He couldn't bring himself to say it. *Because she can't be. I won't accept it.*

Burton sobbed and shivered. "Please...give me a minute. Just a...minute."

"I'm sorry." From what Chip could tell of Burton, she went to great lengths to project herself as a woman of strength.

Burton found her voice. "She's...been hurt very badly, Eugene. They didn't just kill her once; they killed her over and over again. Slowly."

"But...they didn't, *really* kill her. Not *really*."

"Yes, *really*, Eugene. Mentally, the scars are there. One atop the other, and all fresh. God...she's..." Burton lost her voice again.

As Burton continued to sob, Chip's world dropped out from under him, and he closed his eyes against his own tears.

Burton continued, "She's...experienced something the human mind isn't meant to grasp and then return from. We all know we're going to die one day. It's the one unavoidable reality of existence."

Burton unfolded her legs and propped herself onto one knee. "That reality—when we approach that moment—is sometimes too much for someone to face...even once. They go into shock, or a coma, and then they're just *gone*. It's a biological imperative, and in most cases, it's a mercy."

Burton swiped the back of her hand against her cheeks. "But Blue...she held on. She was burned to death several times." An ironic laugh escaped from Burton. "The demoness. That's all she knew to do. It was painful, torture...but it was quick. And...what a sad joke. A demoness who lacks the patience to cause suffering."

Burton's green-eyed gaze took in Chip. "She had faith she would hold out until we could get to her. But then the others arrived."

Chip flushed at the thought of the brunette psychopath and the others.

"They...wanted to prolong her suffering as long as possible. And they did. And each time she returned, they did it again."

The words slammed Chip in the gut. "My game..." He brushed aside his own tears and blinked to clear his vision. He sat up, and this time, he grabbed Blue's shoulders and shook her. "But she's here now. She's here! We got her back." Now he addressed Blue's comatose body directly. "It's okay, honey! I got you. I saved you. Please, come back to me."

Burton put a hand on Chip's shoulder.

A strange tranquility flowed through him, along with a feeling of hope.

"Calm down, Eugene. Let me compose myself and try again. She's there, you're right, but she's protected herself, deep down in her head, the only place she could escape."

Chip blinked back tears. "Let you try what?"

Burton again positioned herself near Blue's head and placed her open palm against her forehead and her other hand on her shoulder. "I'm going to try to reach her."

FIONA?

The disembodied voice came at Blue from the walls. She looked around. *Is this another ghost?*

She cried out, "Go away!"

Fiona, where are you?

"I said go the hell away, Mom!"

Blue lay, curled up on the white leather couch, trying to lose herself in the corner. Her mother had finally abandoned her, angry or sad or disappointed in some way.

Well, too bad. So I've disappointed my mother, big fucking surprise, like that's *never happened before.*

She pushed herself farther into the cushions, just wanting to disappear. She willed the couch to swallow her. Make her go away forever.

Even as the room grew dark, she focused on the crack between the cushions, to make it darker, faster.

I got away from them. They kept hurting and hurting. They thought I couldn't possibly get away, but I did. She shivered against the cushion. *They can't reach me here. Ever. No matter what they're doing to me out there.*

Fiona...please listen to me. This isn't your mother.

Panic seized her. *God...no, they've found me in here, too. They'll find me and hurt me, and...*

Fiona, this is Agent Rebecca Burton. Eugene is out here. The people who hurt you are gone.

No, they're not! It's a trick! They're waiting for me. I'm only safe if I–

No, Fiona, they're gone. Eugene found you. You're back with the people who love you; you're safe. The people who hurt you can't hurt you any more, but you *have* to come out.

No! No, in the dark, they'll never find me.

Fiona, if the darkness encloses you, you'll never be able to come out again.

Good! Good, in the darkness they can't find me. No one *can find me* here.

Fiona, listen to me. Eugene... The voice hesitated. **Chip...Chip misses you.**

Chip? God, why didn't he protect me? Why did he leave me? He promised!

Fiona…You did well. You survived what no one else could endure. You created this space for yourself. And it's saved you. But you can come out. You *have* to come out.

No…no. They hurt me. They just kept hurting…and hurting. And when I couldn't take any more, they did it again.

Even now, she recalled the agony in her palms, the flare up of fire in her thighs, her wrists, trying to retreat to blackness, only to be pulled back to consciousness…

Fiona…I can help you deal. Please, trust me.

How, it's…the memory is everywhere.

Please, Fiona…you have to leave where you are and come to me. You have to decide that you want to live and that you want to return to Chip. The people who hurt you are gone, and if you come back to us, I can help you cope with the pain.

Chip's waiting for me? Chip? He…came for me?

She looked around the room, a place already fading away to near-darkness. *No, wait, I want to find Chip…*

She stumbled off the couch, and…

———

BLUE SCREAMED.

She convulsed as if she'd tried to go in every direction at once.

Chip barely deflected her swatting hand. *God!*

Blue thrashed right off the couch, onto the floor, face-first onto the rug, and half into Chip's lap.

"Hold her! Turn her over!" Burton yelled.

Chip grabbed one of her shoulders and rolled her over.

As soon as they'd gotten her onto her back, Chip had to fend off flailing arms and legs.

Someone fell across Blue's legs. Chip glanced at Phil as he pressed both of his arms across her thighs in an attempt to prevent her from kicking out.

Chip held up his arms and forced his way forward. Random

blows battered his arms, a couple landed on the side of his face with stunning force.

Chip focused on Burton's imperative to hold her still, so he pushed forward anyway.

Blue lay, immobilized by the pair of bodies. *But, damn it, she keeps fighting!* Chip didn't know how long he could hold her.

She cried out. No! They'll hurt me again!"

Chip's ears rang, and his heart broke with every cry. *What did they do to her?* He turned sideways in time to see Burton place her hand, palm flat, against Blue's forehead.

In an instant, Blue's struggles subsided, but the whimpers continued. "No, no, please..."

Burton murmured in a soothing tone, "It's okay, Fiona. I got you, I found you, I found you. It's okay, peace, Fiona, peace..."

"No, please, I can't..." With a final tremble, Blue's body slumped and gave up the struggle.

Chip found himself face to face with his soulmate, her features twisted in agony. *Blue, please, come back to me.*

"She's back in her own head, Eugene. I think I can get her now."

Burton's response surprised him. *Did I say that out loud?*

"I got her...I got her..."

Chip's eyes snapped back and forth between Blue and Burton. The muscles in Blue's face relaxed, and a look of calm fell over her features.

At the same time, Burton's eyes rolled up into her head, and her expression twisted in some sort of distress. She started to slump sideways toward the floor.

Chip called out, "Skye!"

In a flash, Skye crouched at Burton's side, Chip figured, not a moment too soon, before Skye caught Burton's slack form and eased her to the floor.

Chip turned his attention to Blue and watched her eyes flutter open. He braced himself for another scream.

"Chip?" Her wide blue eyes took him in, recognition apparent in her features.

Her tone expressed her sanity.

"Chip! Oh, my God, you saved me!"

Before he could respond, she wrapped her arms around his neck and pressed herself against him.

He held on, speechless.

She trembled in his arms, her sobs escaping between her words. "Thank you, Chip, thank you so much, thank you for getting me out of there."

She's alive. And, more importantly, she's...intact. Sane. For the next few minutes, Chip let himself bask in his gratitude to whatever power had brought her back to him.

Over her shoulder, he spied Skye helping Burton sit up, who also looked disheveled but otherwise unhurt. Burton returned his look with a guarded face. *How did Burton do this?*

Blue spoke against his chest, still trembling. "Just hold me. Don't let me go, please. Don't let me go ever again."

Her words almost overwhelmed him. "You can't get rid of me that easily. But...you're going to be fine and back to yourself soon." His eyes met Burton's. "Right?"

Burton's eyes avoided his but looked toward the floor. "Well...she should be. But..."

Now that Blue had settled down in his arms, Chip spoke the thought top-most on his mind. "What did you do to her?"

Burton struggled off the floor and sat on the couch. She paused to drink from a bottle of water.

She looked somewhat like a football player resting on the side-lines after a big play.

"I told you. What happened to Fiona should never happen to anyone. Fiona was psychologically and physically tortured, more than any person was meant to endure, and after experiencing all those agonies, the memories have now been placed into her physical brain for her to try to process."

Blue's arms tightened against him. "It was horrible. So...beyond horrible. No matter what I tried to tell myself, to calm myself down, reason with myself, I was overwhelmed by what they'd already done to me."

Blue pulled her head up from Chip. She ran her hands through her sweat-dampened hair as another shiver passed through her. Her brows furrowed. "But...at the same time...for some reason now, I can think about it without those memories overwhelming me. It's like...watching some terrible hard-R movie. You know, you watch it, you cover your face, you can't un-remember it, but you're still distanced, because it's not really happening to you. But in my case, it did."

Blue disengaged herself from Chip, but her fingers entwined with his. Moment by moment, her face settled into normalcy. Her color returned, and life reflected through her eyes. "At first, I couldn't find anything to anchor to...and then I could."

Burton took another drink. "I found the source of the pain and blocked it. It wasn't easy, I had to..." She paused. "I experienced some of it. Not much, but...enough."

"Wait." Blue's eyes met Burton's. "What did you do? You've...*blocked* my pain? Is that healthy?"

"Normally, no, I would not take such an action. But in your case, you weren't going to recover on your own." Burton held up a hand. "As you know, I didn't block the memories, just the pain connected with them. And..." She hesitated. "It's temporary. Over the next few months, everything will come back to you. Slowly. Pieces at a time. Hopefully, in manageable pieces. We'll...try to help you with that."

Blue released a slow, trembling breath. "That explains it. I couldn't figure out how I felt so much like myself, but I'm so grateful that I do." Blue kept one hand clasped in Chip's and extended her other toward Burton.

After a moment's hesitation, Burton took it.

"Thank you," Blue said.

Chip looked back and forth and wondered what sort of communication passed between them. Something almost electrical transferred through Blue's hand when Burton touched her. He knew it because it carried through to him.

"Just tell me one thing," said Blue.

Burton's eyebrows rose. "What's that?"

"Tell me they didn't get away. Please, tell me we're going to stop them."

Burton looked at Skye, who piped up, "Officer Kirby's waiting for your orders."

The name of the cranky police officer caught Chip's attention. "What happened?"

Skye addressed Chip. "While you were going all Iron Man in the virtual world, the power company people got back to us and pinned our group down to a house address. Rebecca sent them off to watch the house and await further orders."

Burton released Blue's hand, stood, and straightened her leather jacket. "The arrests require my personal attention, but I couldn't leave without resolving this situation first."

Blue spoke up, a look akin to hunger on her face. "So, you're going now?"

"Yes."

Blue turned to Chip. "Help me up, please." She wasn't asking, and her face made it clear she expected no discussion, just obedience.

Uh-oh. "You might not be up to going anywhere."

But Blue no longer addressed Chip, but Burton. "Please, you've got to take me!"

Chip cut in, "That might not be a good idea. Burton, tell her."

Instead, Burton extended a hand to Blue. "Actually, if you want to ride with me, I anticipated your request." Her eyes swept the room. "There's plenty of space for everyone. Besides, Ms. Shaefer, I'd like to talk to you about a few things on the way."

"I'll drive," called Cyn, and she settled herself behind the wheel of the purple P.T. Cruiser, its trunk open and filled with boxes organized and stacked by Natalie over the last couple of hours.

Van stood behind the car to review the packing job. "Shotgun," she responded.

Whatever. Natalie opened the back door and dropped herself behind Cyn. She supposed it made sense, as one of the smallest people. They had a couple-hour drive back to Kentucky, and everyone might as well be as comfortable as possible. The hard-shell carrying case to her laptop sat...well...on her lap.

But the idea of Cyn being at the wheel if a chase broke out scared the crap out of her.

One of Natalie's legs bounced with nervous energy, and the case bounced against her knee with each shake.

She didn't want to die. She didn't want to get caught, but with the time Marda had insisted on wasting, Nat had mentally prepared herself for the eventuality that they'd be caught. What she feared now most of all was the very real chance of getting killed in the fallout of their capture.

Behind her, also standing by the trunk, Marda called out, "Where's the Baalina statue?"

The words hit Nat like an accusation, one of many Marda had flung her direction since they'd been pulled out of the game. "We don't have the room. Someone can mail it to us later, *if* we get away. If we can't, it's moot."

In the silence that followed, Natalie wondered if, given a choice, Marda would swap the statue for Natalie and leave *her* down in the basement to be sent for later.

"Fine," Marda finally answered. Moments later, Marda joined her in the back seat but refused to meet her eyes.

Van sat up front with her twin.

Cyn reached up, readying to push the remote to the garage door opener.

"Wait!" Natalie called.

Cyn paused, her finger poised on the button.

"Listen," said Natalie, drumming her fingers on the computer case to further shunt off her nervousness. "Chances are, the cops have this house monitored already, and they're going to follow us. I hope not, but there it is. I don't like our chances of getting out of this, so I took some precautions on my own while you were all occupied."

"Go on," prompted Marda.

"I emailed all of our files and notes to the coven leader. That said, my computer and those files are the first thing the authorities are going to go after. The computer here is wiped clean, but they won't know that, either. If they pursue, we can run them on a wild goose chase, and it might be many hours before they discover they have nothing."

"I'm not so inclined to be captured," objected Cyn.

"That's fine. Maybe we get away, and maybe we don't. The point is, if they think they can get our plans from us, they'll stay on our trail and not think to track down the files online. We're now the decoys, giving our Sisters time to receive and assimilate the information, to pick up where we left off."

"What you're saying," Cyn finished, "is as of now, we're expendable."

There it was, out in the open, for all four to ponder.

"Wouldn't matter," said Marda. "If they capture me, I'd escape, sooner or later."

"So, we're in agreement," said Nat. "We try to get away. If we can't, we put on a good show, and we distract them as long as possible."

When no one responded, she added, "For the Sisterhood. For Baalina."

"For Baalina," the others muttered, though not with much enthusiasm.

Natalie sighed. Whatever happened, these would be the last actions she would take on behalf of the Sisterhood. If they avoided capture, she'd somehow vanish on her own, flee the coven, disappear, and start over.

If they captured her, she'd work from day one to show her captors her sincere intentions to reform herself. Because one way or the other, this was her final service.

And good riddance to them all.

———

BLUE FOLLOWED Burton to the large car parked in the street, light blue or tan or white, she couldn't tell in the dark. *Wow, a LaCrosse? That's a hell of a company car*, thought Blue, not sure if the "company" in Burton's case meant the Kelranians or the government.

The waiting darkness when they'd exited the house startled her. She'd returned from her misadventure at Burton's house sometime in the late afternoon, but a glance at her phone told her it was past ten o'clock. Did she really lose that many hours?

She didn't feel it.

She didn't really feel a *lot* right now. She was numb, tired, and her head buzzed like the aftermath of a rock concert. She remembered the sequence of events—the fights in the virtual world, the choice to take Chip's place, and being pulled into the vortex.

She recalled the *fact* of her helplessness, left in the hands of the sick psychopaths who worked her over. Again and again and again. But she couldn't recall the pain of it, or the agony. The excruciating details had vanished from her memory, at least, for now.

Didn't make her any less furious over what happened to her. She wanted payback, plain and simple.

Even still, "payback" didn't mean doing to them what they did to her. No, she could never be so cruel, even to someone she hated. Instead, it meant...

Well, she didn't know *what* it meant.

But, possibly, she'd find out tonight.

She piled into the passenger side backseat, cushioned by comfy fake leather.

Chip sat in the middle, while Phil overflowed the driver's side backseat.

In front, Skye sat shotgun next to Burton, looking perfectly comfortable, as if she did this every day.

Which, Blue reflected, she probably did.

Burton eased the car into the lane with perhaps more caution than necessary on the deserted neighborhood street. She wove in and out through darkened streets Blue had no clue about.

Burton raised an oversized police radio that looked as if it would be equally at home in a soldier's grasp. "Report," she called.

"Hey, Burton, if you had called thirty seconds earlier, I'd have said the house had been quiet all night."

Blue recognized the voice of Officer Kirby, sounding in somewhat better spirits than this morning, when they'd turned the tables on his bust.

Burton replied, "But now?"

"The garage door just opened. They're pulling out." Static, then a follow-up. "Wow, even from here, I can see they're loaded to run for it."

"Okay," said Burton. "Prepare to close the net. Hopefully, this will be quick and simple. Where are they?"

Kirby said the suspects were traveling north on…he rattled off a street name Blue couldn't make out, something French?

Jesus, she'd wasted over a year, floundering in doubt and confusion. Over eighteen months, and now she sat, carried along as a lost bystander down streets that Chip probably knew intimately, like the out-of-town tourist she was. Even Burton, who'd only been stationed here a few months, guided the car with confidence from one corner to the next.

"Where do you go to school, Blue?"

Burton's direct question broke her train of thought. "Sorry? Uh, NYU. English major."

"English?" Burton sounded surprised. "Not history? Anthropology? Occult studies? Or is this all fodder for your great American Horror Novel?"

She's teasing me, Blue guessed, not sure what to make of the line of questioning. "I don't go looking for this shit, but it just keeps finding me."

"Indeed, with a high rate of success."

Blue opened her mouth to reply.

Burton added, "By that, I mean, the ways in which you've handled yourself."

"Oh?" Blue wondered how much to admit. She trusted Burton. She wanted to trust Burton. Badly. The woman had saved her sanity, if not her life.

Burton continued, "You and I shared minds for several minutes. Stray thoughts, residue, if you will, leaked through our connection. I learned much about your encounter with Gunther that I didn't know before."

And with that, Blue's opinion of the situation soured. "I'm not sure I like that very much." In fact, she was sure she didn't.

"I understand." Burton let the comment hang while she navigated through the side streets. "It could not be helped. My point was not to discuss your secrets, but to praise your instincts."

"My instincts tend to get me in a lot of trouble."

"But they're correct most of the time. It's when you stop and think, and second-guess yourself, that you tend to err. For example, when you took the crystal from Chip, you knew he had a better chance of retrieving you from the chaos realm than you had of retrieving him. It was an act based on instinct, and you were correct."

Blue shrugged. "Call it what you will, I still stabbed him in the back."

Chip cut in, "I forgive you." His fingers found her hand and squeezed affectionately. "Agent Burton's right. You could never have deduced how to go back in the way I did. Phil might have, eventually, but it would have taken him a lot longer to figure it out."

Phil added, "Normally, I'd argue that as being snarky, but he's right. I had plenty to do, and I wasn't thinking anywhere near the ballpark of where Chip's reasoning took him."

Blue's eyes met Chip's. "You shouldn't let me off so easily."

In the darkness, a smile formed on his features. "It's okay, it's what I do."

Burton said, "Now, when you had time to ponder your relationship, you second-guessed those instincts. You wasted months because you used logic to counter your instincts and talked yourself into mistrusting him."

Chip answered, "You did?"

Blue could hear the hurt in Chip's voice. She snapped. "You said you weren't going to reveal my personal thoughts. Is there a point to all this?"

"I want to offer you a position in my organization, Blue. Or, more specifically, my team."

Blue's head spun. "What organization do you mean, exactly? Are you a federal agent, a state investigator, or a member of a druid cult?"

"Well...yes. Officially, you'd work with me for the government. Much of what you'd do would also benefit the Kelranian Order. The bottom line, Blue, is we'd be stopping evil people from committing evil. That's something you are already good at, and you'll be even better with the proper training."

A government agent. Me. It didn't seem real. The words came with James Bond music attached—a fantasy, nothing real. For years, Blue's ambitions were to work at a coffee shop and write poetry, with or without Chip by her side. As of twenty-four hours ago, Chip was now an irrevocable part of that deal.

Burton said, "There aren't many places that can make such a guarantee, but you know that I can. You can help me make a real difference in this fight."

"You want me to help you." Blue let the thought linger. "So, I'd report to you. I'm not even sure I *like* you. For one thing, you're very pushy."

If the comment offended Burton, she didn't show it. "I'm a leader, bred and trained. My tendency to take charge is only because I'm the most qualified to do so. You won't be able to say that about many people you might ever work for."

Blue grunted and mumbled under her breath, "And modest, too."

From the front, Skye spoke up. "She's not, you know."

Blue felt herself flush. *I didn't know she heard that.*

Skye continued, "You said she's pushy. She's not."

Oh, whew.

"I've been working with her for months. Rebecca knows what you excel at, hands that over to you, and at the same time, she's a good teacher. I've learned a lot from her during the last couple of months. If I were you, I'd jump at the chance."

Blue stewed and said nothing. More ghosts, demons, crazy people. She'd never wanted any of it, and she'd had enough of it.

Still, these sickos had caused her so much pain and so much torment. The Mardas of the world didn't care who they hurt, only *that* they hurt.

And now, Marda and her group were on the run, their plans thwarted, in part because of her actions. To make that kind of difference, to know that she'd taken these potentially disastrous situations and contained them, to contribute in some way to help others that truly mattered…how many people even had such an offer placed before them?

But, she could barely consider it at this time. "I need time to think about it. I just don't know."

Burton's voice reached her from the front. "The offer remains open. You don't have to decide anything tonight. You've been through a lot. But I can tell you, you'd be a hell of an asset to us."

Keep talking. You sure can be smooth when you want something. She had to admit, the words did much to bolster Blue's spirits. She'd spent her childhood beneath the dominance of a strict mother who tended to emphasize disappointment over approval. She didn't know if she could ever work for Burton, but it was damn nice to hear the words. "I'll think about it."

Burton's radio crackled to life. "That's it, they're bolting. They saw me. They've abandoned the car in front of the student center, and they're making a run for it."

"Get it surrounded!"

"Already on it. All units converging to cover the exits. If they go in there, we can box them in."

As Burton raised the radio to her mouth, the car picked up speed. The Buick tapped cylinders to thrust to highway speed in seconds.

Blue gripped the seat and held on for dear life.

From the front seat, Burton offered assurances into the radio. "We're right behind you. On our way. Proceed with caution. I want them taken down."

CHAPTER TWENTY-SEVEN

Cyn turned the vehicle down Lafollette Street and pressed the accelerator.

Natalie braced herself as the Cruiser opened up and raced down the road, clear except for the stoplights at every corner. A couple miles up, they'd reach the on-ramp to State Road 37, where they could floor it the whole way north toward Indianapolis.

She caught two green lights.

Nat turned and looked.

The unmarked police car stuck to their bumper. *Dammit!* A second and third car pulled past. *More cops. They're surrounding us.*

Cyn swore and called out, "We can't make it, guys. We're going to have to run for it. Hold on and get ready."

The next light turned red, and Cyn ran it.

Like a physics project demonstrating action and reaction, the sirens blared from the car behind them. The cars on either side joined the chorus of screeches.

Up ahead, the student center drew close, windows lit up to show the empty interior of the community study hall.

Natalie had spent several hours there to study, read, surf, enjoy the coffee, and support the local vendors. Her mind worked out the possibilities. None of them were good, but they could potentially split up three ways, make it difficult for their pursuers, and maybe someone could slip away.

The police boxed them in and forced their car into the far-left lane. The two-story limestone building now loomed above them.

"Hang on, brace yourselves, and be ready to run like hell!" Cyn jerked the wheel and sent the car careening onto the sidewalk and across the lawn.

The building closed in, and Cyn hit the brakes.

Marda's scream filled the car.

The cruiser impacted the side of the building, crushed in the hood, and came to a jarring stop. "Go! Go now!"

Van popped the passenger door, stepped out, reached in, grabbed Cyn, and pulled her through to her side. As a unit, they darted for the glass doors.

Nat wanted to crawl over Marda and just get the hell out of there, but she waited. In her peripheral vision, she saw the red and blue lights. Vehicles pulled up and surrounded them on all sides but the car doors that faced the building.

Marda had finally struggled out of the car, which cleared the path for Natalie to exit. She pushed her laptop case in front of her and fled, focused on the sets of glass doors dead ahead.

Cyn and Van made for the doors to the right of her.

Natalie overtook Marda and closed in behind the twins. At that point, what happened to Marda was of little consequence to Nat.

"HOLD IT RIGHT THERE!" the police called out over a megaphone.

The sheer volume and authority of the voice made Natalie crouch as she ran.

"YOU ARE UNDER ARREST! YOU ARE ORDERED TO STOP RUNNING AND LIE ON THE GROUND WITH...DAMMIT!"

Natalie pushed through the doors.

In the foyer, straight ahead, a second pair of glass doors led to an open study room. If Nat broke to the left, she'd descend stairs down to the basement cafeteria and common area.

Cyn and Van continued ahead. They burst through the glass doors and darted straight back as far as the room would take them.

Okay, fine. So Nat moved left toward the stairs. She grabbed the metal rail and pumped her feet down the stairs, descending to the basement as fast as her legs would take her.

She heard a second figure behind her. *Marda! Dammit! Don't follow me!*

Nothing she could do about that now.

She just kept running.

———

OFFICER KIRBY WATCHED the four perps ignore his warning and run into the student center. He stopped in mid-sentence. Why waste the breath?

"DAMMIT!" His curse blasted out of the megaphone at 120 decibels. *Nice one, Kirby.* He released the broadcast button and swore a couple more times.

He checked his piece and nodded toward his partner. The police-issue Glock rested in his hands. He had become an expert at using it—if you counted patting the handle for emphasis, or occasionally waving it in the air when a drunk college student got some really dumb ideas.

When the situation called for action, most of the time, pepper spray did the trick. The Taser helped him handle more intense scenarios.

For most of his career, his gun remained holstered to his hip. The only human shape he'd aimed it at were targets on the shooting range. Tonight, he sensed, that could change. *If I have to, I have to.* The thought didn't bother him overly much.

Burton had kept him in the dark, but he knew these four were bad news—the real deal. They had to be stopped one way or the other, and he was more than up to it.

His gaze met his partner's. Selena Gonzalez had been assigned to him two years ago, a new recruit out of the academy. She'd served with distinction. As far as he knew, she'd never pulled the trigger, either.

"You up to this, partner?" Kirby felt a surge of pride at the stone-steady look on her face, the confident nod she offered.

"Don't you *dare* think of keeping me out of this one, Boss."

Kirby smiled. "Let's go get us some bad guys."

He scanned the second car, where Caliburn and Franklin stood, poised and ready. Good men. Veterans. He'd need them. "You're with us. They're going to try to split, I can feel it. We go forward, catch who we can, and flush the rest into the guys waiting out back." He nodded to Caliburn. "You two cover the café."

The four of them burst through the front entrance, and they split into pairs.

Kirby and Gonzalez continued forward through the second set of glass doors. Kirby's Bluetooth informed him that a fourth and fifth car had already set up the roadblock in the back alley. *Either way, we've got these bitches. Only thing to find out is if this goes down easy or hard.*

His gut told him it would go down hard.

———

NATALIE DESCENDED THE STAIRS, scanning the abandoned cafeteria, and looking for any exit.

She took in the side counter and entrance to the kitchen. Her first thought was to make a break for it, but the flexible metal gate bent around the register and extending to the door stopped her cold. *Dammit!*

Then she noticed, for the first time, a fire exit toward the back of the room. A metal bar ran along the front of the door.

Marda joined her. "Quickly, give me the metal case."

"Why?"

Marda reached out and pulled the laptop case from her unresisting fingers. "Because I'm getting away from here, and I want a weapon!" Marda bolted toward the fire exit.

"Wait!" Natalie started after her.

"Freeze!"

The barking command of police authority froze Natalie's blood. She swore her heart stopped in her chest.

"Hands above your head! Now!"

Natalie squeezed her eyes shut. She knew her life would end at any moment. "Don't shoot!" she cried. She waved her hands over her head. "Please, don't shoot!" *God, please no, don't kill me!*

Nat heard the door open, and the fire alarm go off.

"On your knees!" screamed the officer.

As if she could help it! Natalie's knees gave out, and she fell on her face, still crying. "Don't kill me, please. Please, I'm unarmed."

"Hands behind your head!"

She opened her eyes, vaguely aware of the linoleum pattern before her face.

Another figure ran past her and mumbled something about not being worth the bother.

Tears fell freely down her face. One officer held a gun pointed at her prone form; a second officer pulled her wrists behind her back and slapped on the cuffs.

That's me, not worth the bother. Helpless, cuffed, and I'll never have to run again.

On the floor, she trembled and muttered thanks to whatever entity had looked after her in this moment—certainly not the Goddess-bitch Baalina. *And I'm alive, alive, they didn't shoot me. Thank you, thank you, they didn't shoot me.*

As her police captors gathered 'round, Natalie wept tears of gratitude.

———

KIRBY AND GONZALEZ burst through the glass doors into the student common study area. Spread out before him in three directions were small computer library kiosks, armchairs, loveseats, side tables, study nooks—a plethora of hiding spots and attack points—laid out in a nightmare maze of opportunity for the two fleeing perps.

Kirby had patrolled this area for years and knew it well. It stayed open 24/7. That was one advantage. He noted two others—the area remained well lit at all times—and most nooks were designed for seated studying.

He and Gonzalez could see across the entire room as they stood side by side. One of the perps was crouched behind a study nook. She thought, or perhaps only hoped, she was out of sight. Kirby motioned toward the perp.

Gonzalez nodded.

They heard noise from some distance away, deeper into the building.

Crouching and sweeping, Gonzalez and Kirby closed in on the fugitive they'd identified from two angles. Kirby knew, if either of the perps tried to double back for the entrance, he and Gonzalez would stop them long before they made it to the door.

And stop the perps they would. One way or the other.

CHAPTER TWENTY-EIGHT

As the car sped ahead, Blue held on to the grip strap for dear life.

Up front, Burton had gunned the engine and centered the bumper to close in on the building surrounded by the police cars. Red and blue flashing strobes lit up the two-story limestone building like a rocket ship ready to launch.

The car torpedoed the last few hundred yards, then screeched to a stop of smoking rubber, pulled up just behind the bumper of the last police car in the lineup, and settled into place. The sidewalk that led to the building lay just outside Blue's door.

Blue threw open the door and darted up the sidewalk. Her vision targeted the glass doors dead ahead, and her feet pumped fast on the cement to close the distance. One train of thought dominated her: *Marda's in there! She's not getting away. I'm making damn sure of it this time.*

Chip called after her, his voice already some distance behind.

She pulled the dagger from her denim jacket and approached the double doors.

Behind her, Burton shouted, "Lower your weapons, dammit! Stand down! She's with me."

Blue didn't think they'd shoot a teenager in the back.

She burst through the doors and stopped in the foyer to consider—*straight ahead through the second set of glass doors, or take the stairway to the left?*

Through the glass, Officer Kirby and another officer—the Hispanic policewoman—closed in on someone who'd just given up their hiding place behind a loveseat.

Blue pushed open the doors just as the woman stood and raised her own dagger in a clear threat.

"You're not taking me! Cyn, run!"

Another voice, some distance off, called back, "Van, wait, what are you—"

"DROP THE KNIFE!" The policewoman raised her gun to target the woman braced to charge. "I *WILL* SHOOT YOU! DROP IT!"

She crouched in a battle stance. Her lips set back into a grin of malice. "Run for it, Cyn, just go. I've got this!"

The scene blurred, and Blue gripped the handle of the door to keep from falling. *My God, I...I know her!*

She recalled the sadistic grins of the two CGI harlequin sickos who oversaw her torture, the two who kept rousing her whenever blackness threatened to end their fun. *That's one of them. And the other one is up ahead.*

Blue reeled as if kicked in the gut. She blinked to clear her vision. Up ahead, she saw the woman with the short red hair step out of her own hiding spot and beckon to her partner.

"You're not taking me to prison!" And with a strangled cry, the closer woman charged to rapidly close the distance on Officer Kirby.

Three rapid, explosive pops made Blue cover her ears. *My God, they shot her.*

When Blue looked up, the dark-haired body lay prone; liquid red already stained and spread along the tan rug.

"No!" The redhead stumbled. Her knife dropped to the ground, and she fell to her knees. "No, Van, no, baby, no..." She crawled toward her on all fours.

"Stop where you are!" The policewoman shouted.

Her pistol followed her target as the woman pulled herself along the floor.

"Stand down," Kirby called out. "Stand down, she's not a threat."

The redhead reached her partner, grabbed her by one shoulder, and turned her over. She cradled the bleeding woman in her arms. "No...no, Van, stay with me, Van, please..."

The brunette sputtered some words.

Blue took a few steps forward, transfixed by the drama.

"...should have run, Cyn...I wanted you...get away."

"It's both of us or nothing, do you hear me? Van?"

The policewoman stepped forward, handcuffs out. She grabbed the redhead from behind and pulled the women apart.

To Blue, it looked like handling a life-sized beanie doll.

The officer pressed her unresisting prisoner to the floor and snapped on the cuffs.

The prisoner simply cried and stared through the process.

Behind Blue, the door opened, and a team of medics closed in on the scene, but Blue knew they were too late.

Then she realized. Kirby and his partner were at ease. As far as they were concerned, the main floor was all clear.

And they would know.

So Marda wasn't here.

And whatever else happened, Blue had to make sure that Marda would not get away.

She slipped back through the glass doors and headed toward the stairs. She descended, her legs pumping over each step. It was everything short of throwing herself down the stairs.

She descended upon the commotion of additional police action playing out, and in the background, an insistent, clanging bell.

A terrified girl's voice droned on, getting louder as Blue approached. "They didn't shoot me, they didn't shoot me..." As

Blue dropped down level with the basement, she heard a continuous monotone of pleading, a voice familiar to her. *The whimpering, green-cloaked druid, the one I felt sorry for just before she stabbed me in the back.*

Blue took in the scene. Two police officers looked down at something. One put his finger to his Bluetooth earpiece.

Where is she?

One police officer pulled the mousy, tearful woman to her feet.

The woman's eyes met Blue's, and she slumped, giggling. "They didn't shoot me! And you got away, too. Good for you. I'm so glad."

The other police officer turned his attention to Blue.

And as far as Blue could see, no one else was in the room. *Where is she?*

"You!" The officer pointed at her. "You're Fiona Shaefer? The one with the federal agent?"

"Yes. How did you—"

"They radioed your distinctive feature." The officer patted his own hair to indicate hers.

Oh.

"How'd they do upstairs?"

"They got 'em, and it's secured," Blue answered automatically, and to her shock, the officer nodded and opened a channel on his radio.

"Where is she?" Blue asked.

"The fourth perp?" The officer motioned to the still-open emergency door across the room.

Through the opening, Blue saw darkness and a far limestone wall. Blue realized the fire alarm was the source of the distant bell. "She's in the alley. She can't go anywhere. She's either going to step out or come back in. There's nowhere to go. Either way, she's done."

Blue closed in. She braced herself to step outside, past the doorframe. She tightened her grip on the ceremonial knife and held it at the ready. "You're right. Because I'm making sure of that."

———

CHIP WATCHED Burton's face flare red as her radio crackled to life. He recognized the voice of Officer Kirby. "Shaefer peeked in, and then I think she went downstairs."

"Ms. Shaefer was just here," cut in another voice. "She just followed perp four out the emergency exit. I...told her she didn't have to do that."

"Damn it!" Burton started toward the glass doors.

Chip followed. *Oh, God, Blue, what are you doing?*

Burton raised her radio. "Get out there and stop her."

"Too late. She's engaged perp four. I can hear them fighting."

Burton broke into a run. Chip shadowed her as she ran through the doors and descended the stairs.

———

BLUE STEPPED into the cold night air. Strobes of red and blue lights bathed the walls of the tiny alley and loading dock. The back wall of the next building extended several yards along the alley. The stench of fast food reeked near a large brown dumpster from where it sat in the alley between the buildings. Police cars blocked the exit to the left; more police cars blocked the right.

Something banged against hollow metal. The echo drew Blue's attention to the dumpster. She detected a hint of movement on the side farthest from her vantage point.

Her heart thumped in her chest. As she closed in on her target, adrenaline fired her senses.

She considered sneaking up. *Fuck that.* Instead, she called out, "You're surrounded, Marda." She eased toward the dumpster. "Come out. You're beaten."

"Why should I?"

Blue grinned. *Too stupid to resist answering even an idle threat. Just like Gunther.* Now she knew exactly where Marda waited. "Because, if I come in after you, bitch, it's going to hurt a lot worse."

"Maybe. Maybe not. Maybe I'll take you with me."

"Not on your best day. We're not playing video games anymore."

A commotion of voices echoed over the walls, and then the alley erupted in bright spotlights of white.

As spots blurred her vision, Blue raised a hand and squeezed her eyes shut.

A megaphone-amplified voice called out, "THIS IS THE POLICE! RAISE YOUR HANDS AND COME OUT WITH YOUR HANDS UP!"

"Got you now!"

Fuck! Footsteps closed in, and then blunted metal slammed against her arm.

Rather than resist Marda's charge, Blue back-pedaled and let Marda push her against the wall. Already, her vision was returning.

Marda drew her arm back to swing the metal computer case at Blue a second time.

Blue charged, knocked Marda back, and forced her to drop the case.

Marda growled and swung again.

Blue elbowed her in the chest, grabbed her by the front of her blouse, and flung her bodily against the wall. "I said...NOT on your best day!"

Marda hit the wall but pushed off to turn her momentum into a charge. "I'll kill y–"

Blue cut off the threat with an open-hand punch to her chin.

Marda's jaw jerked backward, and her head hit the wall.

She tried to fall forward, but Blue thrust a forearm up and pinned her against the wall.

Blue raised the knife and pressed it under her chin.

Marda spat blood into Blue's face and tried to squirm away.

Blue held on tight and pressed with the knife tip. "You're not going anywhere!"

Blue held the edge of the knife against Marda's neck, hard. "Slip sideways now!"

Marda stopped her struggles, but a crazed glistening reflected in her eyes. Her voice called out hoarsely. "Mistress...help your servant..."

Enough of this! Blue folded her fingers into Marda's hair and yanked. "Stop it!"

Marda's eyes focused on Blue. Sanity—or, at least, coherency—appeared to return.

To Blue's shock, Marda smiled, then pushed forward against the knife.

Her heart pounding, Blue shoved her arm against Marda's chest, trembling. "Stop it. Just give up. Your mistress is defeated. You've lost."

"Then kill me." Marda's voice reached her, hoarse, barely a whisper. "Because I haven't lost. I won't *ever* give up, Blue. You know it."

"Shut up!"

"They'll lock me away. They'll try to reform me. They'll let down their guard, and then one day, I'll break free."

Blue heard movement behind her, but her gaze remained locked on Marda's. "I said shut up!"

"One day, sooner or later, I'll find my mistress, and then...we'll find you."

"Never. Not ever again."

From behind her, Burton's voice called, "Blue, put the knife down. Blue, we've got her."

Marda emitted a crazed laugh. "Do...you hear that? She's got me. Burton's going to take me. Show me the error of my ways."

Burton continued, "Blue, lower the knife. Now, Blue."

Marda looked away to a vision only she could see. "And I'll find you. First, I'll kill Chip. Then Phil. And then we'll have our fun with you. For real."

"Shut up."

"And if you think it was bad before, that's *nothing* compared to what lies ahead. I can't wait."

Marda smiled and spoke, her voice roughened by the knife

pressed against her throat. "Now, lower the knife, Blue. Turn me in. Because that's what you do."

Fury flared through her, then past her. Blue closed her eyes and considered.

Then she knew. "You know what, Marda? I believe you."

Blue swiped the blade across Marda's throat.

The skin ripped open, and red sprayed out. Then it spilled out a gaping gash in Marda's neck. Marda's eyes bugged out, and her jaw worked soundlessly.

She slumped in Blue's arms, but Blue pulled her hair and forced face-to-face contact. "You're dead, Marda!"

Pandemonium broke out behind them.

Burton's voice. "Oh, my God, get her off, now!"

Chip cried her name.

Marda's eyes turned glassy and staring.

"Tell your mistress how you failed, Marda. Tell her she'd better hope no one kills *me* anytime soon, because I'll come for her next! Do you hear me? Do you?"

Multiple arms and hands grabbed Blue and pulled her away.

She struggled against the bodies. "You're dead! Dead!"

Burton's command shouted over the others. "Get Shaefer out of here and into custody, now! Do not let this woman die! She is *not* going to die. Hold her!"

Blue cried out, struggling against the arms pulling her away from the scene. "She deserved to die, Burton! She was evil! I know evil when I see it, Burton. Don't you dare save her now!"

"There's so much blood," Skye cried.

Arms and bodies dragged Blue away toward the blue and red lights.

Blue heard a mad giggle. *Wait, that was me.*

The world turned topsy-turvy, dissolving into more yells and arguments.

"Why didn't your men try to stop her, Kirby?"

"You took my radio from my hand and told my men she was

with you, Burton! Hands off, you said. I heard you. Don't you *dare* pin this on me! She's *your* loose cannon, not ours!"

When she found her bearings, her hands were cuffed behind her, and someone was lowering her into the backseat of a squad car.

"Shut up, Shaefer!"

The fog cleared enough for Blue to recognize the voice of Officer Kirby.

Kirby peered into the open window and snarled, "Shut up, now, or even your fancy relative attorney friend won't be able to help you."

Blue sat and waited, but her head still spun. *What just happened?*

Kirby's voice droned in her ears, a monotone, part sympathy, part business. "Look, Shaefer, I'm not entirely sure what just went down, but I know enough to understand that the right person is lying on the ground, bleeding out. And I suspect that if it had been me, I probably would have done the exact same thing."

Blue tried to focus, but Kirby's words hadn't penetrated. She just listened to him talk.

"Now, I am breaking a dozen regulations telling you this, but you need to sit tight and say nothing. There's a reason Miranda reads 'anything you say can and will be used *against* you.' The police are not here to be your friend. Do you understand that?" With that, Kirby recited her Miranda rights.

A detached part of her was bemused that the wording in real life was exactly the same as a lifetime of TV cop shows. The rest of her was still in too much shock to care.

"...Do you understand these rights as I have read them? Shaefer?"

By now, she was coming down off the adrenaline, which left her tired. Her breathing normalized. The impact of what she'd done closed in on her. "I understand I killed someone."

"Shaefer, dammit!" Kirby stepped away from the car. He called back, "I don't want to hear that."

It was true. She couldn't undo it. She'd stared someone down, drew the knife, and made her bleed to death. Because of her, a human life had been snuffed. She felt the shakes come over her.

"Blue?"

She turned toward the familiar voice. Chip's face was now framed in the window. "Oh, Chip, I blew it *bad* this time."

"Shhh!"

Chip looked every bit as if he wanted to reach in and comfort her, but he didn't dare.

"Don't worry, we'll...we'll think of something." He couldn't disguise the futility, the emptiness, of his statement.

"I'm sorry, Chip. You waited so long for me, and now—"

"Hey, I'll wait for you forever." Emotion cracked his voice. "Don't you give up."

She blinked through fresh tears. Remorse for her actions settled over her and constricted her like a straightjacket. She had taken another life, and that fact disgusted her. Her actions went against everything she held sacred. *What in the hell was I thinking?*

And it scared her. Because she also knew, with conviction just as deep, that Marda Mercedes deserved to die. And if Blue were free to change the last few minutes, she wouldn't.

She'd do the exact same thing again, without hesitation.

CHAPTER TWENTY-NINE

Skye MacLeod turned from the body lying in the gutter. Blood spilled over the concrete, in spite of the efforts of the paramedics. *There's no way they're stopping that. No way.*

Having seen the carnage, her stomach flip-flopped. She stepped away and drew deep breaths. Her lungs craved fresh air, even though she already stood outside in the brisk cold.

Her sometime commander and mentor barked out demands for a miracle. Another miracle. In this case, one too many miracles.

"Clamp down. Clamp down. I need to find her mind. Hold her still. I'm *not* going to lose her. I'm not!"

Even several paces away with her back turned, Skye saw in her mind's eye (somewhat less gory than the real thing, perhaps) Burton crouched over the body; she probed with her hands on the woman's hands, her forehead, her ankle, any accessible exposed skin where Rebecca could try her "lay-on-hands psychic trick", as MacLeod thought of it.

But she knew it didn't matter. Theoretically, when someone lost their mind, a body could be kept alive indefinitely, in or out of a coma-like state, hard to reach sometimes for years, but not impossible for some gifted people like Rebecca.

But the opposite was just not true. If the body died, the mind slipped away moments later. And Marda's body would most certainly die.

Blue had seen to that.

Skye waited for the inevitable.

Burton cried out in borderline hysteria. "No! No!"

An unfamiliar man's voice answered, "Agent Burton, if we're going to have any chance, we need to go now. I'm sorry."

She could hear chaotic shifting and scampering, what Skye knew was wasted effort on the part of the EMTs. But they would do what they were trained to do.

God. God, how had this gone so horribly, horribly wrong? What was happening? Skye couldn't wrap her mind around it. The clarity about what was good and bad, and who those players were, all blurred together.

And yet, nothing's really changed. At least, not in my mind.

But that wasn't true. Things had changed a *lot* and would change even more in the next few minutes, unless...

Skye drew a deep breath and steeled her courage. In the three months they'd worked together, Skye had followed orders and learned a lot. She was often praised for her work. For all her mystical powers, Burton was rather ignorant of modern technology and had little patience for it. Skye had been proud of her contributions in that regard.

The chaos had settled. How long had she been sitting here daydreaming? She wasn't sure. She turned and saw Rebecca standing alone, gaze focused on the gory puddle of blood. As the police closed in to tape off the area, Rebecca moved toward Skye.

Before Skye could speak, Rebecca spoke first. Anger seethed through every word. "I want her locked away *under* the prison! She slaughtered our biggest lead into the Sisterhood after I'd *explicitly* told her to back down."

"Rebecca, please—"

"I'll see her in the gas chamber if I have to! She slit someone's throat with hardly a thought about the consequences. She ran into–"

"That's not true, Rebecca. You don't think she thought hard about the consequences? She knew *exactly* what the consequences were."

Rebecca glared. Her eyes flared a hint of red in her pupils.

Perhaps it was just a trick of the flashing sirens, but the effect made Skye pause.

"Do you have a point, MacLeod?"

Her condescension broke the spell. "You can't do this."

"Watch me!"

"Listen to yourself. What are you most angry about, really? That Blue killed a raving psychopath who'd attacked her several times, and threatened her life and the lives of the people she loved? Or that she disobeyed your orders?"

"Murder is murder, and you can't justify–"

"Marda Mercedes tortured Blue nearly to death, and she made it quite clear that she would not hesitate to finish the job, given half a chance!"

Rebecca scoffed, but she hung her head and walked away.

Skye shouted at the back of Burton's retreating form, "Jesus, Rebecca, you said it yourself. Blue suffered more than any person ever has a right to suffer. More than the mind is normally capable of handling. If not for your intervention, she'd be catatonic still. You don't know what that's like. How can–"

Rebecca spun to face her. "If I were you, I would not presume to tell me what you think I know about suffering, little girl!"

No doubt about it. Rebecca's eyes gleamed red.

But Burton wasn't the only one riled up. Skye had to get her point out, and she would not let Rebecca bully her. "You're not being reasonable. You're angry at this failure, and you're lashing out."

"And I suppose you know what's right for everyone concerned?"

"Maybe I do, maybe I don't, but *you* did. Just a few minutes ago, on the drive over here. You sat there in front of everyone and told

Blue how impressed you were with her instincts. You told her that those instincts were usually right, and you advised her to trust them! And you know what? She just did!"

The fury fled Rebecca's face, and, in an instant, changed to shock. "I didn't mean—"

Skye pressed, "You were so impressed with her ability at that time that you offered her a future spot on your team. What makes you so wrong then, when you could see the situation impartially, and so right now, when you're so angry that things didn't go your way?"

Skye panted from the emotion of her argument. To her credit, Rebecca now looked abashed rather than angry and answered with level tones.

"She still killed someone, Skye. There are consequences for that."

Skye pointed at the police car where Blue sat, awaiting her fate. Skye's voice quivered with emotion. "That young woman saved us from an impossible situation. We were stuck in a place with no idea how we were going to get out. She got us out of there, and then she trusted us. She trusted *you*, and she trusted her boyfriend. That trust landed her in a terrible, terrible place she barely pulled herself back from. You can't compare her to Marda. Blue was *more* than provoked. You can't possibly consider this a pattern of behavior. You can't..." Skye's voice cracked. She tried again. "You can't let this happen. It's wrong, and in a couple of days, when you've had time to collect yourself, you're going to know it."

Skye waited. Rebecca no longer appeared to fume. Instead, she met Skye's gaze with her standard stoic expression.

Rebecca wiped her bloodied fingers with the handkerchief. "Very well. Come with me."

With Skye at her side, Rebecca stepped up to one of the fire trucks. She flashed her badge to a pair of firefighters. "Gentlemen, your country needs you. I require your assistance on an errand about which you can speak to no one."

The two firefighters exchanged a look, and one of them said, "What can we do for you, Agent?"

"I need to break a window. I need a fast, efficient way without hurting myself."

Skye's head spun at Rebecca's words. *Are we going to bust Blue out? Oh, my God.* She thought Rebecca could just flash her badge and order her freed. *What are we going to do?*

The other firefighter reached into a tool kit, and, after a quick search, held out a small, screwdriver-shaped rod. "Point the plunger, then press the button. Can I help you with that, ma'am?"

"No, I just need it a moment." Rebecca had already fished an evidence baggie from her pocket. She palmed the tool. "Thank you, gentlemen. This didn't happen." She met and held the gaze of each firefighter.

"Understood, Agent. We've just been standing here."

She turned to Skye. "Follow me, please."

Skye followed Rebecca past the squad car where Blue still sat, sulking.

Chip and Phil's gazes followed them as they strode past and out of sight.

Rebecca led Skye to the front of the building and stopped before Rebecca's car. She extended the evidence bag toward her. "Hold, please."

Skye took the proffered baggie.

Rebecca pressed the tool against the center of the window.

There was a "pop" that made Skye flinch.

When Rebecca stepped back, the window had spiderwebbed, and slivers fell away over the door. Shards of glass sprayed the passenger seat and the outside.

Rebecca's eyebrows rose and she flashed Skye a smirk. "Overkill, but it will do." Rebecca scanned the glittering shards. She reached into a pocket and withdrew a white handkerchief, reached down, and retrieved a sharp, jagged piece of glass.

Skye stared, dumbfounded.

Without another word, Rebecca led Skye back around the

building and toward the crime scene. She flashed her badge at the police officer on guard, bent down, and dipped the shard into the gory puddle.

Rebecca's eyes met Skye's. "Baggie, please?"

Skye understood. She extended the baggie, top pried open.

Rebecca dropped the shard in. Rebecca rose. "That is the piece of glass Marda used to slice her own neck after she broke free from me as I struggled to get her into the car. Do you understand? She broke free from me."

"Wait," Skye objected. "It was my idea. Maybe you should say she broke away from—"

Rebecca shook her head. "If you let an important witness slip away from you and kill herself, Skye...frankly, your record isn't established enough to survive the black mark."

"But...wait, it's okay if *you* did something that incompetent?"

An ironic smile crossed her lips. "If anyone in the Kelranian Order has job security, it's me."

Skye nodded as if she understood. She didn't. Not really.

Now tired and drained, the chill in the air penetrated Skye's thin fall jacket, and she shivered. Her thoughts turned back to Blue. She opened her mouth to ask, but Rebecca beat her to it.

Rebecca's police band radio beeped. She raised it to her ear. "Burton."

Skye waited out the several-second pause as Rebecca received a message.

"Thank you." She looked at Skye. "Well, that's it. They called it as soon as the body arrived at the hospital. Marda's dead, and Shaefer's actions caused it."

Though she expected it, Skye still hated to hear the news. *What happens now?*

Rebecca met her gaze and held it for several seconds. "Now, please tell Kirby to let Fiona go. Tell him the Special Investigations Unit will not be pressing charges. Later, I'll talk to Kirby about how to handle this incident with his men. For now, just tell Shaefer that, officially, I wish her the best, but she is not to try to contact me.

And she should not hold her breath for me to contact her." Rebecca held out her hand.

Skye deposited the evidence bag into it. "I'm sorry," Skye mumbled.

"For what?"

"For how it turned out. The cult's still active. Baalina slipped away. There's still a real danger the Sisters could bring her back."

Rebecca walked up the alleyway. "Leave that to me. I need you to catch a ride with a patrolman to a nearby hotel. Reserve two rooms. I trust you don't want to spend the night in our trashed house?"

"Not really, no, but where are you going?"

"To end this. Just text me the hotel name and our room numbers. I'll see you in a couple of hours." Rebecca turned and walked away without another word or glance back.

Officer Kirby pocketed his phone and turned toward Chip and Phil. They stood on either side of the window to give the Shaefer girl a view to the outside world. They also stood too close to the car for regulation, but in for an inch, take a few feet, at this point.

His head reeled over the news that he and Gonzalez had bagged one of the Terror Twins, infamous assassins from Chicago, and that they held the other one in cuffs. The two of them filled a slot on America's top five Most Wanted for as far back as he could remember. But they had shoved the surviving twin into a squad car, and that car now raced to the county lockup. For that alone, tonight would officially go "front page." There was no cramming this genie back into the liquor flask.

He knew the regs, but he couldn't bring himself to shoo the kids away from the car. The Shaefer girl had a tough road ahead, and opportunities for little kindnesses would soon be few and far between.

He hated it. He hated the whole thing. He'd been wrong about these kids, and in many ways, it sorted itself out exactly right. But also, very wrong. He wouldn't cause them any more grief, at least, no more than he had to.

He also hated to repeat what he'd just been told on the phone, but he had no choice. It wouldn't surprise anyone, but it needed to be said. "I'm sorry, Shaefer...and Farren." He nodded toward the large fellow whose name escaped him. "Marda Mercedes was declared dead on arrival at IU Bloomington hospital. I'm sure it's just a matter of time before the feds make it official, and–"

And here she came, the tall, skinny assistant to the agent, the girl he'd seen all but literally attached to Burton's right elbow this entire case. The feds were usually fast, but this was a blitzkrieg. *Burton really means it. She's going to bury the poor girl. She doesn't stand a chance.*

———

CHIP HAD CONTINUED to offer words of support, words Blue couldn't cling to or have faith in. She already saw a vision of herself, thirty years later, squinting at a mature Chip on the other side of the glass partition, having wasted his life attached to his wife, the killer. Do they allow conjugal visits for convicted murderers? She somehow doubted it, but she would find out soon.

I should tell him to go away, and to never come back. But I've done that too many times, and it never did any good.

Besides, I need him now. That's the truth of it.

Chip cut an empty platitude off and stepped away from the window.

Blue peered through the window in time to hear Kirby's announcement. To his credit, he sounded terribly sorry about it. Then he stopped mid-sentence.

Skye approached.

Blue's heart sank.

Phil took a half-step forward and stopped.

Skye smiled, apparently flattered that her presence came off as so important. "Officer Kirby, Rebecca Burton of the Special Investigations Unit wanted me to tell you that the Unit will not be pressing charges against your suspect, Fiona Shaefer. The Unit considers this matter settled and furthermore insists that you release the suspect immediately. She will also contact you in the next few days about counseling your officers on what they might or might not have heard during these last few minutes."

Blue waited. She heard the words, but she couldn't process them. Apparently, neither could anyone else. She realized, from a distance, that Skye wasn't delivering the news they'd braced themselves for, but she couldn't wrap her overtaxed brain around what it meant.

Kirby broke the silence first with, "You've got to be kidding me," followed by, "My people will back my play."

Blue detected sarcasm in his next words. "Please tell Agent Burton that I look forward to reading her report."

It started to penetrate. *It's over, it's over...it, no, it can't be over.*

"Blue, did you hear that?" Chip's voice.

She did, but she didn't. She bent down, nauseous and overtaxed; the last twenty-four hours caught up with her and weighed her down.

Vaguely, she became aware that someone opened the car door. Hands, not rough but insistent, pulled her out of the car.

"Easy, Shaefer, easy," Kirby coaxed.

Blue stood before Chip, who waited with a look of expectation. She wanted to step forward, but her wrists were still bound.

And then, they weren't, and she fell into his arms. Drained and spent in every possible way, Blue could no longer focus on what had happened or why. "I want to go home. I just want to go home, Chip, please, just take me home."

Home is in New York, a part of her protested.

No, home was with Chip, and she'd finally come home after a long time away.

———

SKYE MACLEOD SAT on a metal bench outside the glass doors of the student center. She'd confirmed that Kirby would arrange a ride for wherever she wanted, when she wanted, but she needed some time to collect her thoughts after such a crazy clusterfuck of a day. After all the intelligence gathering and tactics, after all the plans and schemes, today had erupted into another climax of chaos, as so much of her life tended to do.

Still, it had turned out okay, at least, today.

She just needed to sit and let everything percolate for a minute before she started to surf for hotels on her smartphone. In a couple of days, she guessed, they'd head home, and she could bring this chapter of her life to a close.

Skye was proud of herself and her accomplishments. She'd stayed sober, and, until tonight, rarely felt the need to sneak a drink. Now, however, she missed Minnie. Later, in the privacy of her room...well, who knew?

Soon, she'd be heading home to Broad Ripple, where—

A figure approached her, slowly, tentatively. She couldn't actually see him in the dark, but she recognized Phil's distinct silhouette, large, tall, and bear-like, but in a cuddly way more than a threatening way. She recalled the last twenty-four hours, how he had sort of taken her under his wing—his considerable wing—and had watched out for her.

She'd kind of miss that.

She waited him out as he approached and sat on the other side of the bench. *Did the bench shift? Surely, that's my imagination.* She smiled at him.

He smiled back. "Hey," he said.

"Hey."

Phil's gaze flicked back and forth between Skye's face and a spot on the ground. "Um...we're leaving soon. I'm guessing you are, too, but I imagine in your case, that means you're leaving...town."

"Broad Ripple," she answered his unasked question.

"Ah. I love Broad Ripple." Then, a moment later, "Actually, I've only heard Blue *talk* about Broad Ripple, but it sounds like I'd like it."

Skye giggled.

"Listen, I was wondering, is it okay for...you know, agents to stay in touch with people?"

Oh, God. She realized. *He's hitting on me.* And everything clicked. The protectiveness wasn't just protective. He liked her. *Oh, God, now what?*

Phil continued, "I mean, after a case is over and stuff?"

Skye licked her lips and let the silence draw out as she considered. "You mean, like, as friends?"

"Yeah."

Even in the dark, Skye saw Phil's face flare beet red.

"As friends, or whatever. That is, if..." He let the question linger, unasked.

Skye reached into a pocket and drew out a fold-over business card holder. "I'm not an agent, I'm a contractor. I don't work all the time. Yes, I'd like to stay friends with you." She extended the card and added, "But...yes, there is someone else. Her name is Annabelle."

Phil's eyes fell upon the offered card. "Oh. Oh, no, I'm sorry. I didn't realize..."

Skye giggled. "Don't be. I'm not..." She considered her next words. "I guess you could say I don't let gender get in the way of who I fall for. I had a boyfriend just before...well, that's a long story." She gave the card a shake. "It's a story I'd like to share with you some time, if you still want to hear it."

Phil took the card. "I think I'd like that."

Skye nodded at the entwined couple standing on the sidewalk. Not making out, in fact, just barely moving. They just held and held and held each other like they'd never let each other go. "How are they doing?"

Phil considered. "Good. They've still got a long road ahead, but this is the first time in quite a while I feel good about their relationship."

"They seem sweet. You keep an eye on them, and keep me posted." Skye reflected on the embracing couple. *Maybe someday, I'll have that, too.*

Skye and Phil sat in comfortable silence. She enjoyed this quiet finish to a terrible day.

———

THE SQUAD CAR pulled up to the house.

Blue, Chip, and Phil huddled in the backseat, exhausted. They thanked Officer Gonzalez and stumbled out of the car. Chip held tight to Blue as if holding her up. And maybe he was.

After a precursory goodnight, Phil retired to the basement, leaving Chip and Blue to settle on the living room couch, where they held each other in grateful silence for many minutes.

Chip seemed to instinctively understand Blue's need for quiet and comfort.

Finally, obeying some psychic cue, he spoke the first words between them in over an hour. "Hungry?"

"Yes, very much."

Chip vanished into the kitchen.

From where she sat, Blue heard the telltale beeping and hum of a microwave, and, a couple minutes later, Chip returned with two steaming platefuls of pizza.

As he seated himself next to her, a thought made her giggle.

Chip smirked at her. "What?"

Blue held up the slice of greasy goodness. "Thanksgiving dinner." She laughed, the simple release so much more than she could have expected just an hour ago.

"Oh, hell no, it's not," said Chip. "The turkey and fixings are still defrosted in the fridge. Phil and I had plans to do dinner up big, and that's still going to happen. It's just going to be a day late." Chip's hand enfolded hers briefly before returning to his plate. "Besides, now I have a lot more to be thankful for."

Blue bit down on the pepperoni slice. She had to admit, as pizza went, Smittie's was pretty yummy stuff, even if the waitress liked to dance on her last nerve. She devoured four pieces without pause, making up for a twelve-hour gap in meals with a quick gorging. With each bite, her stomach calmed and settled.

After two pieces, Chip put his plate aside.

Blue leaned her head back against him.

He shifted and allowed room for her to put her head on his shoulder. Chip checked the time on his phone. "Well, it's officially after midnight, and the Black Friday lines are starting. I was going to go stand in line at Best Buy, but I guess I can skip it this year."

Blue giggled, put her balled fist up to her mouth, and stifled a burp. *Gorgeous and classy! I am the complete package.* "You'd be out there alone, my man." She let her head fall back into his lap.

"Alone, right." He elbowed her. "Just me and hundreds of other bargain hunters—"

"Cheapskates."

"Bargain hunters," he emphasized, "who want to spend the night shopping."

She enfolded her fingers through his. With his free hand, he traced her eyebrows with a finger as if trying to memorize her features. When he spoke, all trace of humor had vanished.

"How are you? Really?" His finger trailed, feather-light, over her lips.

As a shiver passed through her, Blue smiled. "I'm fine. Really. As good as I've ever been in a long time."

"I'm worried," Chip admitted. "Agent Burton said she'd blocked out a lot of what happened to you, but that over time, it's going to start coming back."

"I remember enough." Blue let the words hang in the air. "Nothing's forgotten. I remember the pain, and the anger, and the...helplessness. But right now, it's like it happened a long, long time ago. So..." She shrugged. "I'm okay."

"I'm so sorry," Chip said. "You trusted me, and I let you down."

"Don't say that!" Blue grabbed his hand. "You came for me. You found a way to me, just like you said you always would." She squeezed her eyes shut against fresh tears.

"But I couldn't get to you fast enough. If I had figured out–"

"You're the only person who could have gotten to me at all, Chip. They...they weren't done. If Marda had it her way, she and her posse would have been found in a coma, spending all of eternity torturing me just because she got a kick out of it. You stopped them. And I will never forget that." The memory, even blunted, disturbed her.

She disengaged her hands and sat up. She resettled on his lap so they lay face to face in an embrace on the couch. "You came for me. And I'm never leaving you again."

Chip kissed her, his passion cushioned in infinite gentleness.

BEFORE SEPARATING, she brushed her lips over his one last time. She sensed his tentativeness. He handled her like delicate China.

And right now, that's what she needed.

She lowered her head to his shoulder. "I mean it. I'm never leaving you again. I mean, I'll finish the semester at NYU, but then I'm transferring all my credits to IU. If I can get enrolled for January, I'm moving to Bloomington." She met his gaze. She could feel him tensing beneath her. "Scared yet?"

"Scared? No, that's...that's amazing. The writing program here is first-rate. I'd been trying to..." He trailed off.

Yes, he'd been trying to. Trying to get her to enroll, trying to bring her closer to him for months, frustrated at her hesitancy to even consider it. Clueless as to why, until a few hours ago.

He kissed her again, still tentative.

Another shiver of excitement passed through her. When they separated, she looked down, not meeting his eyes. "Chip...look, I...I know it's been a long time. For both of us. I'm going to need you to be a little patient. Do you understand?"

Chip nodded, his face impassive. "Look, no one could have

expected this. I'll wait as long as it takes. Weeks, months...take whatever time you need."

Blue laughed. Her eyes met his. "Months? You're talking *crazy*, you silly man!" She pressed her lips against his, her desire loud and clear in her kiss. "I meant more like a couple of *hours*. Just...handle with care, okay?"

He pulled her into a loving embrace. "Always, Blue. Always and forever."

EPILOGUE

Rebecca Burton snapped on the lights and descended the wooden stairs to the basement. She took in the circle and faced the statue of the chaos demoness, self-labeled "Goddess" Baalina—erect and proud, captured with her standard trappings of scepter and robes. Just one of her many lies.

Baalina specialized in luring strong, damaged women to her side, women with high intelligence but who had been scarred by society in some way.

Today's world offered a plethora of victims for Baalina to exploit—perhaps more than ever because more women than any other time in history faced their future with high expectations and set themselves up for so many crushing disappointments.

Baalina used these women to further her ends with promises of power and revenge—promises she never intended to keep. Chaos, destruction, and torture were Baalina's primary interests, with deceit her currency to lure and hold her followers.

Rebecca had hoped to save four of those victims, to counsel them, to guide them, and to hone and reshape those talents so terribly misplaced and misused, in the service of the Kelranian Order.

She'd have to settle for two.

As Skye had predicted, the more she reflected on the fate of Marda Mercedes, Baalina's "special one," the more she saw Marda as a hopeless cause. She realized Blue's actions saved everyone a lot of wasted time.

Several minutes earlier, for reasons unclear even to her, Burton parked the car a few blocks from this address. As she walked, Rebecca tasted the streets, and she absorbed the life of the students who lived here. She closed in on the student house, rented and re-rented for mundane study, the kids around them blissfully unaware of the horrible plots and schemes that took place here. How close they'd all come to losing this university, perhaps the city or beyond, to the delusions of a demoness and her minions.

And that would have been it, Rebecca mused. An entire city was not an acceptable price to pay. But world domination was never a possibility. Between the weapons, technology, and the magic that so many others stood by, ready to wield, world domination would never have been in the cards for this demoness.

But this neighborhood, for certain. Bloomington, perhaps. With thousands dead in the process. And that would have been more than enough to leave a scar that could never be removed. Interpreted as perhaps a terrorist attack, a student uprising, or some extreme weather event, the world would never know the true threat from the spirit dimension.

Left on their own, the Sisters would try to raise their Goddess again. And again. And again. There was only one way to stop them forever.

Rebecca stood in the center of the communing circle and raised her hand toward the statue. The ancient words of summoning came to her easily, her voice an angelic call, a siren that commanded the magic to bend to her will.

The portal formed before her along the curve of the circle; it opened upon the fiery pit of the chaos realm where Baalina stood, arrogant and angry as ever. Red lips pulled up over jagged white teeth.

Burton read the dismay on the face of the demoness at this summons.

"Tesh Ka Ra bitch, where is my devoted servant? What have you done with my Special One?"

Unruffled, Rebecca faced the scoffing image. "She needlessly lost her life in your service and is beyond anyone's reach, including yours."

"And the others?"

Rebecca shrugged. "One of the so-called Terror Twins is dead. Neither the other twin nor the other survivor will acknowledge your call."

"They were weak. I would have granted them anything they asked of me, once I freed myself."

"You believe your own lies, demoness. You have no gifts to bestow upon your followers. You cannot lie to *me* unless you lie to yourself."

Baalina snarled. "Where two fall, three will take their place. I sense a strong soul. New, yet familiar. It calls to me, even from here in the depths, someone to whom I have already called out, and she has heard me. I tempted her to kill, and she obeyed. Who else is more worthy to be my new Special One?"

"Fiona Shaefer was tortured by your hand. She would never follow you."

"She might."

Rebecca slashed her hand in dismissal. "She won't."

Baalina cocked her head like a slow child only beginning to suspect what their peers had already deduced. "Why do you summon me, Tesh Ka Ra? Do you simply wish to stare at me and gloat?"

Rebecca looked back and said nothing.

Baalina's annoyance grew. "Begone! Your mission to pass final judgment upon the fallen angels is yet decades away. I've plenty of time to escape from here before your powers mature."

Rebecca braced herself. She'd delayed long enough. "Is that how you understand the ancient writings?"

"I said begone!" Baalina reached out as if to cross the portal into the physical realm. The opening sparked as the demoness swiped the magical energy barrier.

"Your powers cannot penetrate the shield, demoness."

"Then leave me to my suffering," Baalina mocked, "so that one day I may learn my lesson and repent of my evil ways before my judgment arrives." Baalina spat. "That will never happen, Tesh Ka Ra bitch!"

Rebecca raised her hand. "You've been mistaken about many things, Baalina, but you're correct on that one point."

"You are a servant to a power that is less than nothing to me, Tesh Ka Ra. I laugh at Him as I laugh at you. Begone. I am done with you."

"But *I* am not done with *you*, demoness. My mission begins today, with you. Now. Judgment has arrived for you, demoness Baalina. Prepare to receive final punishment."

Rebecca started a new chant. Both the words and the associated magic penetrated the portal to reach the creature beyond.

"What? No!" Baalina screamed. "You cannot do this! You have no right to judge me."

Red flame flared across her robe. Baalina swiped a hand to snuff it. "No!" The flame caught, and the robe blazed.

The flames engulfed her, and the beast thrashed. Baalina's cries turned from anger to a howl of torment. "No! Damn you, you can't."

As Burton bore witness, fire burned the demon's face. The scepter dropped from her hands, useless and discarded. It fell against the stone, where it also caught fire.

The flames ripped away skin to expose muscle and bone.

Burton watched the punishment draw out its predicted course. The creature's cries halted mid-scream, the ghastly spectacle ended, and the flames burned out into a red pyre.

Baalina was no more.

The sting of hot tears streaked Rebecca's face.

The Tesh Ka Ra had taken her first life—the first of many lives that would be lost before her righteous judgment in the years to come.

Rebecca Burton—the Tesh Ka Ra—waved her hand to close the portal.

A voice reached her, a pitiful sound, yet strong enough to override the chaos of the flames. "Wait..."

Rebecca stopped. *How is it possible the demoness survived the purification?*

"Release...me..."

No, not the demoness. A man's voice, overwhelmed with pain and torment.

The answer struck Rebecca like a cold flame. "Krane?"

"Yesss..."

Oh, my sweet master, no! Brother James Krane of the Kelranian Order called out to her. Even now, *after* centuries of torment from where his spirit lay in agony, never released.

Her hand trembled, but Rebecca again extended her magic through the portal. "Brother Krane, by the power of the Tesh Ka Ra, I release you to find the peace too long denied you. Go with God."

"Thank you..."

She waved her hand, and the portal closed.

Rebecca stumbled out of the circle and sank into a chair. She'd never felt so alone. So truly alone.

And in that quiet room, Rebecca Burton wept.

She wept for Marda, for Fiona, and for Brother Krane. She wept for the demoness Baalina and for all of her deluded followers.

And as the Tesh Ka Ra contemplated her destiny, she wept for herself.

The End

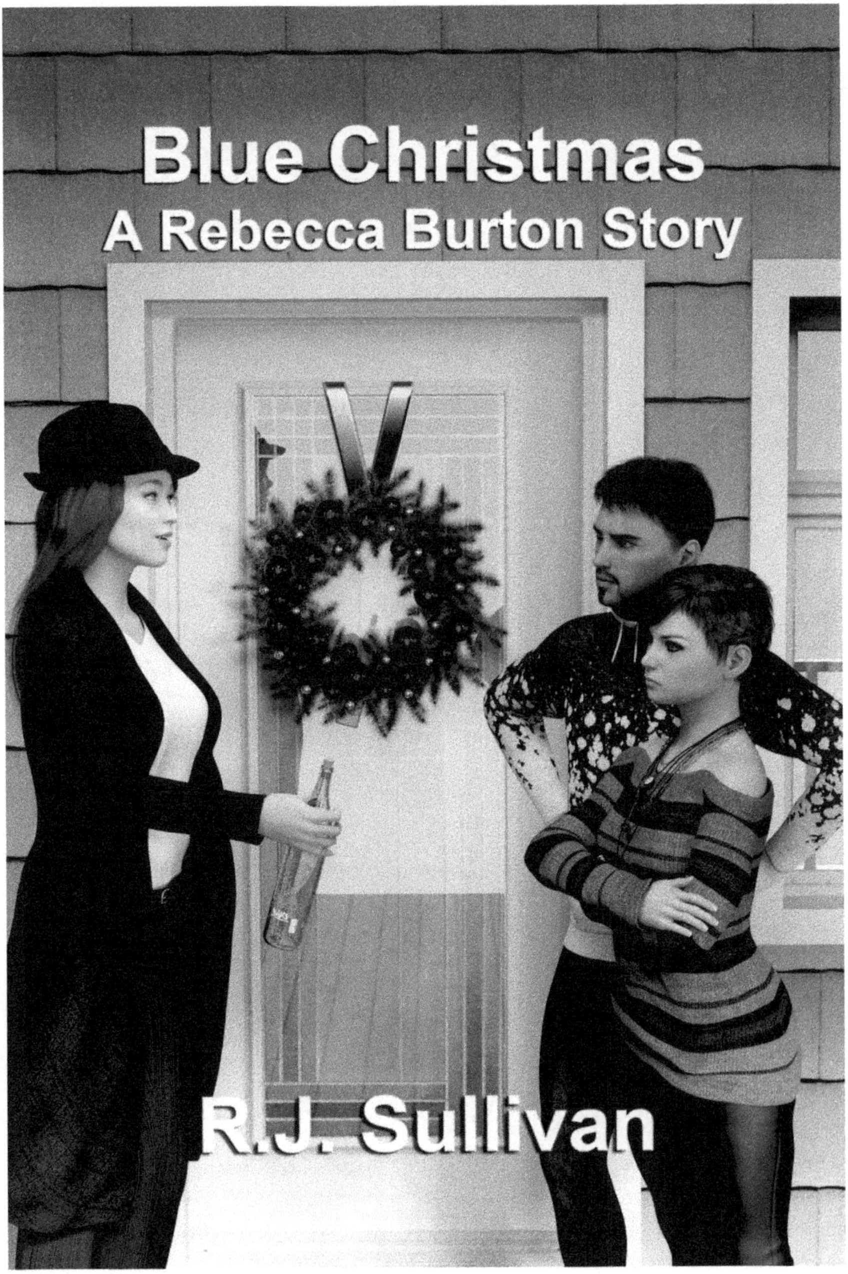

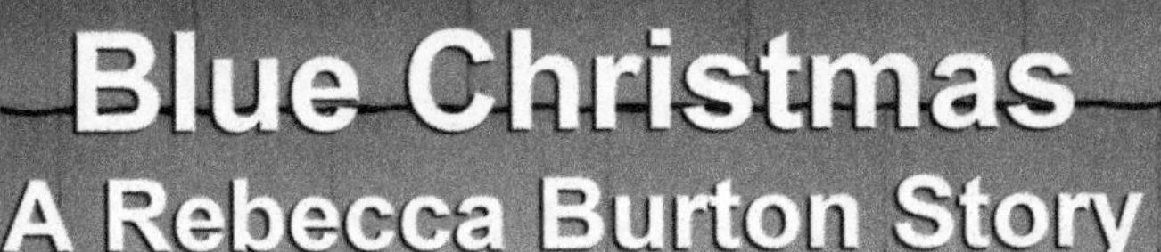
Blue Christmas
A Rebecca Burton Story
R.J. Sullivan

Copyright 2018 by R.J. Sullivan. Published by DarkWhimsy Books.

This is a work of fiction. Names, characters, businesses, places, events, locales, and incidents are either the products of the author's imagination or used in a fictitious manner. Any resemblance to actual persons, living or dead, or actual events is purely coincidental.

Cover Design by Nell Williams

Page Layout by Bryan Donihue, Section 28 Publishing

Dedicated to Beverly Bullock
April 4, 1965-December 23, 2013
Our Christmas Angel

"Blue Christmas" originally appeared in the anthology *Gifts of the Magi*, a holiday collection co-edited by John F. Allen, E. Chris Garrison, and R.J. Sullivan

Author's note: *Ahoy, thar be spoilers ahead!* "Blue Christmas" takes place after *Haunting Blue* and *Virtual Blue*.

Fiona "Blue" Shaefer sat in the living room of her boyfriend's father's home on Christmas Eve in somber reflection. She sipped a Sprite and cuddled with Chip on the couch. The artificial but lovely tree with its blinking lights filled the space with holiday ambiance. While it was nice, it was also pretty weird.

Behind them, through swinging western doors, "The Two Dads", James Farren and Paul Willis, sat at the breakfast nook, warming up to each other as they took down a six pack of bottled beer. Normally, the proximity of "The Two Dads" would have dampened the romance, but overall, given the excitement of the past two years, this was pretty peaceful. Almost...dare she think it... *domestic.*

Not a word Blue tended to apply to herself.

Here she was, back in the small bumpkin town of Perionne, Indiana, contrary to all her plans to leave this town and *never, ever* come back. But this was a chance to spend a peaceful, quiet Christmas with her boyfriend, and after all they'd been through, she was okay with that. *Though it's definitely weird.*

The doorbell rang, and Blue offered Chip a questioning look.

He held up his phone. "Go ahead, I'm finishing a text."

"Nerd," she said, but she flashed him a smile as she stood.

Blue recognized the tall, distinguished figure standing under the porch light. Rebecca Burton, Special Investigations Unit Agent and infuriating pain in Blue's ass the previous month, wore her distinctive black fedora, matching leather jacket, business casual blouse and blue jeans. In one arm, she cradled a wine bottle.

Long, bright red hair curtained Burton's serious expression. She extended the bottle. "Peace offering? Merry Christmas."

Blue had no idea what stupid stunned expression she returned. Only one thought spun through her head. *Oh, crap, tonight just got a whole lot weirder.*

———

BURTON WAITED out Blue's moment of shock with her characteristic stoic expression.

The moment passed, and Blue gave in to a petulant streak. "What makes you think I'm at all interested in a peace offering from you?"

Burton consulted the label. She pinched one side of her glasses with two fingers as she read, "Sweet Inspiration, red port dessert wine, rich raspberry and chocolate flavor, bottled locally by Cedar Cr—"

"Please come in." Blue stepped to the side to make room for Burton to step past.

Chip looked up from his phone. A sharp intake of breath revealed his surprise, but he recovered fast. "Rebecca, it's... good to see you."

"And you, Eugene."

"The Two Dads" had already stepped into the room, now a wall of parental concern. Shoulder to shoulder, they crossed their arms and made clear their demand that someone damn well better explain themselves.

Blue went first. "Dad, uh... Mr. Farren, this is Rebecca Burton. Chip and I... hung out with her... at Indiana University... over Thanksgiving Break," she finished lamely.

Rebecca Burton, in fact, was a government agent who had saved Chip and Blue from certain death during their wild encounter with a cultist group that had taken over Chip's video game and sent them all on the wildest and most dangerous encounter of their lives —and that was saying something.

In the weeks since, for several practical reasons, Chip and Blue hadn't hinted a word about this encounter to either of their fathers.

Paul gave voice to the obvious. "Ms. Burton seems a bit old to be a full-time student."

"Oh, I'm not a student," said Burton, who reached into her coat and produced her badge. "Rebecca Burton, Special Investigations Unit. I was... on site offering my services to assist the local police on an urgent matter over the holidays. Chip was an invaluable asset."

James Farren, a computer engineer himself, scrutinized her credentials. "How did two college students help with a state investigation?"

Rebecca's answered without hesitation. "The university was trying to deal with some pretty sophisticated computer hackers. Eugene came highly recommended, and in fact, they both assisted me that weekend. Thanks to them, we broke up a ring of cyberterrorists."

Blue averted her eyes. *Damn, smooth as butter. If I didn't know she was lying her ass off, I'd have no idea.* She felt her father's stare upon her and knew her face flared pink. Even in the room of colorful blinking lights, she wondered if he noticed.

Mr. Farren handed Rebecca her badge. "Sounds exciting."

"In fact, I'm here to discuss using their services again. I'd pay them, of course."

Mr. Farren stayed on topic. "Chip never said a word about you, Ms. Burton."

"Neither did Fiona," added Paul.

"Well, it wasn't really a big deal," Chip began.

"You assisted with a criminal conspiracy and didn't see it worth mentioning?"

Blue started, "I'm sorry, Dad, it was a crazy weekend—"

Rebecca stepped forward. "What Fiona means is, they were sworn to secrecy while we worked out the legalities of the case." She placed a hand on each father's forearm. From where she stood, Blue saw her father's eyes widen. Blue knew that, with skin to skin contact, Rebecca could channel considerable powers of psychic persuasion.

"You are both concerned, and, believe me, I understand. We are leaving now, but your children will be safe under my care. Please don't let this ruin your evening. I'll bring them home in a couple of hours."

In the silence that followed, Blue's pulse throbbed against her temples.

Mr. Farren looked at her dad. "That's fine with me. Want another beer, Paul?"

"I think I'm due. Have fun, you guys."

As "The Two Dads" retreated into the kitchen, Burton turned her back and addressed Chip and Blue. "Let's go. I'll fill you in on the way."

"You promised us wine," said Blue.

"Later."

"Wait a minute," said Blue. "What makes you think we're going with you? And... my God, Rebecca, do you need a carry permit for those hands?"

"Your mother is in danger."

That stung. "My mother is dead!" A flood of guilt froze her in mid-step. For the past few years, the specter of her mother could only visit her, briefly, in dreams and visions. And while Blue cherished those moments, it didn't make her mother any less murdered.

Rebecca glanced back at the two parents, who looked oblivious to their exchange, before she hissed. "Her spiritual presence in this realm is in danger. If we don't act, she may be cut off from this world. Forever."

"Lead the way," said Chip as he pulled the door shut behind them.

They strode through the lovely night of fallen snow and dancing flurries, a perfect Indiana "White Christmas" Eve. *This would have been a nice night to walk with Chip through the neighborhood while we kept each other warm with Christmas wishes.*

So much for that plan.

Blue followed Rebecca to a sky-blue Buick. The last time Blue had seen it, the car had a shattered window, now replaced. Blue and Chip opened the back doors and got in, for no other reason than that they'd ridden in the back seat last time, when Rebecca's assistant Skye MacLeod had ridden shotgun.

And if I'm totally honest, Rebecca still creeps me out. Aloud, she asked, "Where are we going?"

"Your house."

"My...?" *Oh.* Technically, Blue had inherited her mother's property in Perionne, the home where her mother had been murdered in cold blood. A house Blue vowed never set foot in again. A house perpetually for sale in the years since. Though the property promised future money if the sale ever happened, the real estate agent faced one problem, a nearly insurmountable one. As far as the town was concerned, the property was one of two haunted houses in Perionne—houses right next to each other.

Sylvia Stalt, the mother of the most notorious criminal in Perionne, had lived and died in one. And the home next door was the site of her mother's grisly murder.

Most people had no idea of another connection between the homes—that the notorious criminal, temporarily awakened in spirit form—had committed the grisly murder. The killing had rendered Blue parent-less, at least until word reached her estranged father in New York.

Blue realized that Rebecca followed the short route from Chip's house to her mother's. She swallowed back bile. "I... really don't want to go there."

"We have no choice," said Rebecca. "A cult of ghost-hunting druids has already gathered at your home. They're going to attempt to contact and exorcise the spirits residing there."

"Who tipped you off?" asked Blue.

"The Transit King. He's an informant from the fairy world who travels the public roadways. He frequently comes upon information of a paranormal nature."

"So what's it to him?"

"I suspect he knew this lead would put me in his debt."

"Okay, then." Had anyone else said this, Blue would think they were bonkers, but she knew better than to scoff.

Rebecca continued. "If they succeed, they could banish your mother from the physical realm. Permanently."

"Is that likely?" Normally, Blue approved of vanquishing ghosts, but not when that ghost was her mom.

"I trust you are familiar with *A Christmas Carol* by Charles Dickens."

"Of course."

"Dickens set that story on Christmas Eve for a reason. It's a night when people all over the world remember loved ones no longer with them, and that makes it easier for some specters to interact with the living, if only for a few seconds."

Blue couldn't deny that memories of past Christmases with her mom had already broken in on her holiday. As much as they'd fought through the years, they'd always called a truce during Christmas.

In the dark, Chip's hand found Blue's, first tentatively, then enfolding hers in a clasp. Blue psyched herself. *Whatever comes next, I'll be damned if anyone's going to take what's left of my mother away from me.*

———

Doug Faddon shifted his bulk on the living room couch of the late Leona Shaefer. The house, infamous after the murder committed within its walls two years ago, had no working electricity; the candles his two companions had smuggled in failed to reach the edges of the room where the shadows dwelled. *What am I doing here? Why am I breaking and entering on Christmas Eve to hold this stupid séance instead of sitting at home with my parents eating Christmas Eve dinner?*

Liz Dooley, seated on the other side of the couch, flashed a bashful grin his direction, her wavy blond hair radiant in the candlelight.

Oh, who am I kidding? I know exactly *why I'm here.*

Sheets and cloths covered each piece of furniture to protect it from dust and decay, coverings which, ironically, now yellowed and were caked in dust from years of dormancy. The telltale squeaks under his ass told him he sat on leather — soft, cushy, expensive leather.

Last week in Chemistry, Liz had asked him to join her on this adventure. Flattered to be asked, he agreed without hesitation.

Liz had explained, "Claire said we need a third person, and Karen is going to be out of town. Claire was pretty miffed when she heard, too, because Karen has the strongest aura of all three of us," Liz said, as if that made perfect sense.

Doug knew Claire Grattick from Algebra. She was a brainy girl, but also kinda' bossy, always in the back of the classroom with other girls gathered 'round. She whispered in harsh tones while they giggled and pointed and called each other "sisters" even though there was no way they came from the same family. "What is it, anyway, a school club?"

"Sorta," said Liz. "Kinda new age. We get together and memorize spells and use crystals and stuff."

He had no idea what she meant, but he suspected Pastor Jeff would not approve. Still, when she fixed him with her icy blue eyes, he didn't care, either.

"We're going to the Shaefer house to see if we can talk to the dead mom."

"No way." He knew all about Fiona Shaefer and her dead mother. Doug was a Freshman in 2010 when all that craziness had hit.

"Way." Liz grinned, causing Doug to swoon. "So, are you in? She said I could pick anyone I wanted."

He'd agreed, but then when he showed up this evening, they'd both found out that Liz had misunderstood an important detail.

"A... *boy?*" Claire had erupted as soon as Doug approached the house. "You asked a *boy* to join *our* circle?"

Crestfallen, Doug hung back several paces.

Liz pouted. "You said I could bring *anyone,* as long as I had a strong connection with them!"

Claire fumed. "I meant...oh, never mind."

Liz has a strong connection with me? Doug's heart beat faster at her words.

Liz and Doug had been friends for months. She shared all sorts of things with him—favorite movies, favorite songs, teachers she wanted to punch in the face — nothing he thought of as deep. For his part, he'd sit, and nod, and fantasize, too scared to speak his feelings aloud. Liz always finished, "You're such a terrific listener, I can tell you anything."

Liz tried to explain, but Claire just made a noise of disgust and turned her back.

"Look," said Doug. "I don't need this. My parents are worried, anyway, and—"

"No," muttered Claire, "we need three for the spell. Better a man than no one."

"Thanks for nothin'."

Behind Claire's back, Liz flashed him a radiant smile, rolled her eyes, and extended her hand. "She just doesn't know you like I do."

That was an hour ago, and Claire had hardly said a word since. Instead, she'd wandered around the front room while she rattled some rocks, lined up candles around the edge of the room, and waved her hands in the air while muttering to herself. In the meantime, Liz flashed him coy looks, only to turn away whenever he tried to meet her gaze.

For his part, Doug tried to enjoy being in the company of two women, while also trying to ignore the potent aroma of incense and being down the hall from the scene of one of the worst crimes in Perionne history.

Claire lit the final candle, a large red votive one that set in a base holder in the middle of the room. They'd moved the coffee table aside some time ago, and now Claire sat, cross-legged in the middle of the floor before the candle. The flame lit the bottom half of her face to give her what Doug thought of as "super villain lighting," though he didn't dare say so out loud.

Claire motioned for Doug and Liz to join her. "Gather around."

Liz dropped down smoothly, but for Doug, the trip to the floor proved more of a challenge. He stifled a wince, not wanting to draw attention to his general problem of being terribly out of shape.

Now seated in a rough triangle around the candle, Claire extended a hand to each of them.

Liz placed her hand in Claire's and extended her other hand to him.

God, I hope my palms aren't sweaty. Doug wiped his hands across the legs of his jeans. Hoping he looked casual, he reached to either side and closed the circle.

Claire returned a firm grip, while Liz's hand, he couldn't help but notice, trembled.

"Brace yourselves," Claire said. "We're gathered in a place of unique convergence on a night of great spiritual activity. We sit in proximity to, not just one gateway to the spirit realm, but two."

"Two?"

Liz tipped her head toward the house next door. "This house, and Sylvia's home next door."

Doug heard himself gulp. "Spirits from the *Stalt* house may join us?"

"Anything is possible." Clare's hand squeezed Doug's in sudden urgency. "This is why we must focus on our true intentions tonight. We're here to contact Leona Shaefer, to get to the truth of her murder, and perhaps learn the identity of her murderer."

We are? Doug considered. *Why go through all this to contact a spirit just to make her recount the most traumatic moment of her life? We already know she was awakened by an intruder, tried to defend herself, and was killed anyway.*

"Leona," Claire called, "hear our voice. Come to us. Tell us your story, so you can be at peace, leave this house, and cross into the spiritual realm." After a pause, "We're here to help you."

To Doug's shock, a voice answered. A dry, crackling voice, like dried leaves. "Now, that's a lie, and you know it, girlie. You've no interest in helping her, none whatsoever."

Startled, Doug turned to the source of the voice.

In the corner, in the recliner, sat Sylvia Stalt. Still rocking, and her hands still knit on the shapeless whatever-it-was over her lap.

The sight brought back memories, mostly unpleasant, of his childhood encounters with Sylvia while she still lived. The creepy old lady spent years freaking out every kid who drifted anywhere near her porch, sharing bizarre stories and, in retrospect, words of wisdom. She'd warned him more than once to "stop guzzlin' all that-thar' soda and snarfin' all them-thar' candy bars or you'll surely catch the 'Bee-dees'." He'd always run home to his mother, who promptly gave him another soda to calm his nerves.

Last year, the family doctor had put him on oral insulin.

Still, he'd greeted the news of her death with relief. The last thing he wanted was to see her here in the living room.

"Go on, girlie," Sylvia taunted, "tell the truth for once in yer life. Or I suppose I should say...yer pathetic existence."

The front door rattled.

Doug jumped, alarmed. If he could have coordinated his limbs, he would have stood and run for it, but he was on the ground, stuck. *Oh, my God, who's that? Who's that? There's a ghost at the door, there's...*

Liz looked from the door to Claire, to Doug, and back again, her eyes wide.

Oh my God, the door's still rattling! We need to—and with that, the door burst open...and a figure stepped through. In the dim light, Doug could barely make out a female form.

As the figure came forward, Doug's heart skipped. *Leona! It's her! She's back from the grave to*—Then he noticed the blue tint to the woman's hair, and recognition set in. *Fiona? It's Fiona.*

Fiona wasted no time with pleasantries. "Get the hell out of my house! All of you."

Liz spoke first. "*Your* house? But I thought the owner was dead."

"Wrong." Fiona held up a ring of keys. One key hung limply. "The house was left to me, and that makes you all trespassers."

Doug released Liz's hand. "We're sorry, we didn't mean it."

Liz looked ready to tear up.

Claire, however, refused to release his hand. "Ignore her, don't break the circle."

Liz's eyes flashed anger. "Y'know, this was fun, but I'm done now."

"No kidding," said Doug.

"Don't you dare, not until my revenge is complete."

"Revenge?" Blue exclaimed, matching Doug's internal thought exactly. "Get out, or there's going to be trouble."

"Not until I've reached your mother."

Sylvia spoke up. "Not gonna happen, girlie. I already warned Leona away. She's under my protection."

Claire snarled. "Fine. Then I'll go through you to get to her."

"Wait," shouted Blue. "Who are you? What do you want with my mother?"

A tall, authoritative presence entered behind Fiona. "Be cautious, Fiona. She's not who she appears to be."

Claire cackled, and Doug did a double take at the noise.

"What's the matter, don't recognize me? Or rather, who I used to be?"

"Get out of the house or I'll throw you out."

As Claire rose to her feet, she drew out a knife, though Doug missed where it had come from.

"Remember, Blue? I told you the last time we met that I'd find a way back. And when I did, I'd find a way to destroy everyone you love."

Fiona's eyes widened. "Marda!"

Doug watched, baffled. He was done with the prank. He just wanted to go home.

———

THOUGH THE BODY before her stood taller and had a more athletic build, Blue recognized the insane expression on the face, the same as the woman Blue had killed two months ago... *in self defense, it was self defense.*

The Marda stand-in motioned with her knife. "Clear the way to the door, and I'll let you all live."

Blue scoffed. "If you're really Marda, you couldn't successfully stab a *piñata* if you were straddling it with both knees."

Instead of moving toward the door, the Marda stand-in dropped to her knees behind the timid blond and brought her blade to the girl's throat.

Blue didn't take her eyes off the blade. She recognized the design, the ceremonial knife used by the Sisterhood of Baalina, identical to the one she'd taken from the flesh-and-blood Marda.

Unfazed, Blue reached toward the sheath on her belt loop and folded her fingers around the handle of an identical knife. "I learned my lesson last time, Marda. These days, I'm always prepared for life's little emergencies."

"I'll kill her," Marda snarled. "Get away from the door. Move it."

Before Blue could answer, the guy yelled, "Let her go!"

"Dougie," the blond girl called out. "Stay back. She's crazy."

"Let her go!" The guy drew his fist back and slammed it into the side of stand-in Marda's head.

Marda shrieked and dropped the knife.

The blond girl rolled aside.

Blue leapt, and moments later, she straddled the Marda stand-in's body and pressed the edge of the blade against her neck.

"No!"

"Well, well, well, isn't this a familiar standoff?"

Stand-in Marda strained, but Blue pressed her advantage with the knife.

"Blue!" Rebecca's voice reached her, full of urgency. "That's not Marda, Blue. Remember that. That's not really Marda. It's just a shell, a body Marda took over, just a few minutes ago."

The Marda stand-in strained and pressed against the knife. "I'm quite willing to slay this body to make you move."

Blue threw her knife aside but reached out and pinned the body down with both hands. "Rebecca, if you have a thing you can do, now's the time."

"On it." Rebecca crouched next to the woman and placed a hand on either side of the woman's head. "Leave this body!" She commanded. "Return to the spirit realm. Leave this body and never return to another. I forbid it."

"You forbid?" The woman still struggled. "You cannot forbid me. You don't have that power."

Beneath Blue's hands, the body gave a final shudder, then went slack.

Rebecca stared intently at the inert form. "Actually, I do."

A moment later, the woman's eyelids fluttered and she opened her eyes. Her confused look could not be faked. "Who are you? What's going on? Get off me."

Blue rolled off the girl.

The woman struggled into a sitting position. "We were in the circle...about to contact the ghost..."

"Okay, seriously, get the hell out of my house," Blue snapped. "Now."

Rebecca flashed her badge at the guy.

His eyes squinted, then widened. "Agent?"

Rebecca made a show of producing her cell phone. "I'm calling the police. You three should not be here when they arrive."

"What happened?" The Marda stand-in asked.

The guy and the blond girl were already on their feet. The boy reached toward the Marda stand-in. "Later. Let's just go."

The three were out the door before Rebecca finished dialing.

Blue sighed. *Great. Another long night answering questions at the police station.*

"Hello? Is this Paul, or is this Jim?"

Blue and Chip exchanged a look. *So she's not calling the police after all.*

"Paul, I'd like for you and Jim to please bring the bottle of wine and enough glasses for everyone to share. Also, bring food appropriate for a celebration. Do you know where Leona's home is? ...Great. We'll see you soon."

Rebecca ended the call and pocketed her phone. She then dropped to the ground in front of the candle, which still burned bright in the middle of the rug. She motioned for Blue and Chip to join her on either side. "Where those three failed, I suspect we'll have better luck."

Blue looked at Chip. She read the look he returned as: *Why not?*

The three of them surrounded the candle and clasped hands. A palpable energy surged between them that gave Blue a bizarre buzz.

"Leona Shaefer," Rebecca spoke. "Leona, your daughter is here. On this night of restless spirits, please find your way to her. I will serve as your beacon."

Rebecca turned to Blue, her eyes burrowing in their intensity. "Blue, say something."

"Uh...Mom...It's Christmas Eve. Please come out. I want to wish you Merry Christmas." After a short pause, "I love you."

Still sitting in her chair, Sylvia spoke instead. "Don't you worry none, she's comin'."

Rebecca answered, "Thank you, Sylvia."

Blue stifled a chuckle. *Figures Rebecca and Sylvia are on a first-name basis.*

And then her mother was there, and Blue forgot everything else.

A figure... a vision of a dignified business woman with graying hair and the hint of crow's feet in the corners of her eyes... sat in the corner of the covered couch. Exactly as Blue had seen her many times in life, and in a handful of visions and dreams.

The specter's eyes reflected somber sadness.

"Mom!" Blue's voice broke. The emotion of the moment overwhelmed her, to see her mother, so lifelike, in the room with them.

The specter looked over at the three figures, and the barest trace of a smile showed on her sad features.

"Mom..., it's... it's Christmas Eve," Blue said. It sounded lame in her ears. "It's... good to see you, Mom."

The specter spoke, its voice cracking. "Fiona. Please... tell me you are doing well. I miss you so much."

"I miss you, too. It's so—" Her voice caught.

Chip's hand squeezed hers, and she realized something. "Mom... this is Chip. Eugene Farren. The guy I told you about the night that.... Well, we're... together."

"We met," Chip offered, "sort of, in a dream. Hello, Ms. Shaefer. It's good to see you..." he hesitated.

Blue realized his quandary. *What do you say to a ghost? 'In person?' 'In the flesh?'*

"While awake," he finished.

The ghost cracked a smile. "Thank you, Chip. Thank you for protecting my little girl."

Blue wrested her gaze from her mother to look at Rebecca. "If I tried, could I... can I hold her?"

To Blue's surprise, Rebecca nodded. "The paranormal forces are strong now, you should take advantage of—"

But Blue was already on her feet, and mother and daughter locked in a tender hug.

Blue sat next to her mother on the couch. Her tears wet a spot on her mother's shirt. Her mind raced with questions about how that worked, but she ignored them. "This is...the best Christmas present I could possibly ask for."

Delicate fingers stroked Blue's hair. "Me, too, baby. Me, too."

The door creaked open behind her, and Blue pulled herself into a seated position.

Her dad walked in first, followed by Jim. Her dad's eyes widened at the sight of his estranged, dead lover and the mother of his only child sitting and looking at him from across the room.

"I...my God, Lee..." Words failed him, and the bottle of wine and containers in his hand began to slip.

Chip rushed forward, caught the items, and backed away.

Leona, too, looked away. "Paul, I—"

Blue reached out and put a hand on her mother's lap, then reached with her other hand toward her father.

"Please... Dad. Don't ask how. She's here, for a little while. It's... what Rebecca does."

Paul held a clenched fist before his mouth as his eyes widened. Blue could see him try to accept this impossible moment.

Finally, his body shuddered and he dropped his hand. "Lee... it's... it's good to see you. Truly."

Her mother didn't smile, but answered, "Thank you, Paul. I'm... sorry."

"No," Her dad's voice cracked. "Don't waste time on that. It's fine." After an awkward pause, he started again. "I'm taking good care of her, Lee. As soon as I heard, I took her in. Fiona is growing into a very special person. I'm very proud of her. She's safe and she's happy."

Her mom said nothing, but her eyes glistened.

Her dad looked away from the ghost and looked at Blue as if for guidance, "What's appropriate here? Is Merry Christmas even the right thing to say?"

Unable to see from her own tears, Blue reached out toward each of her parents. "Just come here, both of you."

Blue basked in the midst of a warm, loving embrace, her sniffles mingling with the rest. With every moment, she was afraid her Mom would vanish without warning.

The three of them separated some time later, and Blue faced Chip.

He held out a wine glass half-filled with red liquid.

She accepted it gratefully.

Rebecca extended her own filled glass. "Blue, I'm glad I could do this for you, brief as it must be. In a fair universe, your mother would be here with you, in the flesh, enjoying the holidays. Unfortunately, I can't make that happen. Nevertheless, Merry Christmas."

Blue sat, speechless. The wine tasted sweet, then bitter; the hint of chocolate and raspberry made for a decadent aftertaste.

She couldn't talk, and if she could, she wouldn't have been able to express her gratitude. Rebecca Burton creeped her out, but she also had saved her sanity, her future, and now had made this moment possible.

She found her voice. "Dad?"

"Yes, hon."

"Would it be possible to...that is... well... can I buy the house?"

Paul's shocked expression faded as fast as it had appeared. "You inherited the house. It's yours. We just have to take it off the market. The estate has been making payments for...." He stopped in mid-recitation. "But, do you realize what you're saying?"

Chip turned to face her. "You said... you never wanted to return to Perionne, ever again."

"I know what I said, but... Look, I still have years of school. It's not like I'm moving in tomorrow." She turned toward the vision of her mother. "But a girl's entitled to change her mind."

"Indeed she is," said Rebecca. "And on a related topic, a few weeks ago, I had offered you a job."

"On Team Rebecca. I remember. But then you rescinded the offer after I—"

"After I said I needed time to think about it. I have done so."

Blue noticed the curious look her father gave them both, but followed Rebecca's lead and pretended she didn't see it.

Rebecca continued, "If you're still interested, I will pay you a visit after the semester restarts so we can discuss details."

Once again stunned speechless, Blue could only nod.

Rebecca raised her glass. "To Christmas. A time for remembering. A time for new beginnings. May tonight be a joyous new beginning for all of us."

About the Author

R.J. Sullivan's novel *Haunting Blue* (2010) is an edgy paranormal thriller and the first book of the adventures of punk girl Fiona "Blue" Shaefer and her boyfriend Chip Farren. *Haunting Obsession (2012)* and *Virtual Blue* (2013) continue the paranormal thriller series. R.J.'s short stories have been featured in such acclaimed collections as *Dark Faith Invocations* by Apex Books and *Vampires Don't Sparkle.* These stories were compiled in R.J.'s 2015 collection *Darkness with a Chance of Whimsy.* Revised editions of these titles were released by DarkWhimsy Books in 2020.

Commanding the Red Lotus (2016) collects three space opera tales in the tradition of Andre Norton and Gene Roddenberry. New titles to the series are forthcoming from Hydra Publications.

rjsullivanfiction.com

The Original Paranormal Thrills by R.J. Sullivan...

... Revised Editions by 

RJSullivanFiction.com

Also Available
in Audiobook

Narrated by
Danielle Muething

DanielleMuething.wixsite.com/mysite/about

This book is part of an author-cooperative urban fantasy universe. Characters created by E. Chris Garrison (including Skye MacLeod and the Transit King) and R.J. Sullivan (including "Blue" Shaefer and Rebecca Burton) interact in a shared world. For example, Chris's Transit King appears in R.J.'s Haunting Obsession, while R.J.'s Rebecca Burton lends a hand in Chris's Mean Spirit. So if you love what you just read and want the entire story, here's a handy guide and timeline to:

The Skye-Blue-niverse

Haunting Blue by R.J. Sullivan *
Four 'Til Late by E. Chris Garrison**
Haunting Obsession by R.J. Sullivan
Sinking Down by E. Chris Garrison**
Blue Spirit by E. Chris Garrison
Me and the Devil by E. Chris Garrison**
Virtual Blue by R.J. Sullivan*
Restless Spirit by E. Chris Garrison
Mean Spirit by E. Chris Garrison

*Also part of The Collected Adventures of Blue Shaefer by R.J. Sullivan
**Part of the Road Ghosts Omnibus by E. Chris Garrison

Enter the Skye-Blue-niverse at:

https://sillyhatbooks.com/ and https://rjsullivanfiction.com/

Haunting Obsession
Elegant Paper Dolls

Maxine and Loretta
gorgeous glossy color book
4" figures, 10 costume changes!
$5! Sexy and Cheap!

Order exclusively from
RJSullivanFiction.com or
at personal appearances.

Renderings by Nell Williams,
NellWilliams.com

Travel Through Time and Space with R J Sullivan

**RJSullivanFiction.com
or Amazon.com**